Dead Over Heels

'Infectious prose, engaging characters, crafty plotting; recommended' *Library Journal*

'Harris' love of life, mysteries, most things southern and the inevitable and saving humour found in everyday life and not-so-everyday events colours another welcome adventure in this delightful mystery series' *Mostly Murder*

A Fool and His Honey

'Live-wire action, small-town antics, unexpected plot ramifications and a humorous tone make for fine reading' *Library Journal*

'Readers who like mysteries starring strong, witty southern women will like this one too, but they had better be prepared for a surprise' *Booklist*

Last Scene Alive

'Harris' style is well suited to the material, frothy and fast-paced with a wealth of witty descriptions' *Publishers Weekly*

'Ms Harris skilfully captures small-town life, giving the story added realism' *Romantic Times*

Poppy Done To Death

'The mystery delights and confounds with each added layer. Harris' attention to detail and lively prose are thoroughly engaging' *Romantic Times*

'Roe is a genuine steel magnolia . . . entertaining fare' *Booklist*

Also by Charlaine Harris from Gollancz:

SOOKIE STACKHOUSE

Dead Until Dark

Living Dead in Dallas

Club Dead

Dead to the World

Dead as a Doornail

Definitely Dead

All Together Dead

From Dead to Worse

Dead and Gone

A Touch of Dead

Dead in the Family

True Blood Omnibus

True Blood Omnibus II

HARPER CONNELLY

Grave Sight

Grave Surprise

An Ice Cold Grave

Grave Secret

The First Aurora Teagarden Omnibus

The Second Aurora Teagarden Omnibus

The Lily Bard Mysteries Omnibus

Wolfsbane and Mistletoe (co-edited with Toni L. P. Kelner)

The Second Aurora Teagarden Omnibus

Dead Over Heels
A Fool and his Honey
Last Scene Alive
Poppy Done to Death

Charlaine Harris

GOLLANCZ
LONDON

First published in Great Britain in 2011 by Gollancz
An imprint of the Orion Publishing Group
Orion House, 5 Upper St Martin's Lane,
London WC2H 9EA
An Hachette UK Company

A CIP catalogue record for this book
is available from the British Library

ISBN 978 0 575 09649 3 (Cased)
ISBN 978 0 575 09650 9 (Export Trade Paperback)

1 3 5 7 9 10 8 6 4 2

Typeset at The Spartan Press Ltd,
Lymington, Hants

Printed in Great Britain by Clays Ltd,
St Ives plc

The Orion Publishing Group's policy is to use papers that are natural, renewable and recyclable products and made from wood grown in sustainable forests. The logging and manufacturing processes are expected to conform to the environmental regulations of the country of origin.

www.charlaineharris.com
www.orionbooks.co.uk

Dead Over Heels

For my agent, Joshua Bilmes

Chapter One

My bodyguard was mowing the yard wearing her pink bikini when the man fell from the sky.

I was occupied with adjusting the angle of the back of my folding 'lounger', which I'd erected with some difficulty on the patio.

I had some warning, since I'd been aware of the buzzing of the plane for several seconds while I struggled to get the back of the lounger to settle somewhere between totally prone and rigidly upright. But Angel had one of those little tape players strapped to her waist (the plastic belt looked strange with the bikini) and the headphones and the drone of the lawn mower made her oblivious to the unusual persistence of the noise.

Circling low, I thought with some annoyance. I figured an aviator had spotted Angel and was making the most of his lucky day. Meantime, the ice in my coffee was melting and my book was lying on the little lawn table unread, while I wrestled with the stupid chair. Finally succeeding in locking the back of the lounger into a position approximating comfort, I looked up just in time to see something large falling from the little plane, something that rotated horribly, head over heels.

My gut recognized disaster seconds before my civilized self (which was pretty much just saying 'Huh?') and propelled me off the patio and across the yard to knock Angel, all five feet eleven of her, away from the handle of the mower and under the shelter of an oak tree.

A sickening thud followed immediately.

In the ensuing silence, I could hear the plane buzzing away.

'What the *hell* was that?' Angel gasped. Her headphones had been knocked off, so she'd heard the impact. I was half on top of her; it must have looked as if a Chihuahua was frolicking with a Great Dane. I turned my head to look, dreading what I would see.

Luckily, he'd landed face down.

Even so, I was nearly sick on our newly mown grass, and Angel quite definitely was.

'I don't know why you had to knock me down,' Angel said in a voice distinctly different from her flat south Florida drawl. 'He probably missed me by, oh, thirteen inches.'

We were pushing ourselves to our feet, moving carefully.

'I didn't want to have to buy a new lawn mower,' I said through clenched teeth. A side chamber in my mind was feeling grateful that our lawn mower was one of those that stop moving when the handle is released.

Angel was right about it being a man, judging from the clothes and the haircut. He was wearing a purple-and-white check shirt and brown pants, but the fashion police were not going to be bothering him anymore. A very little blood stained the shirt as I looked. He'd landed spread-eagled; one leg stuck out at a very unalive angle. And then there was the way his neck was turned . . . I looked away hastily and took some long, deep breaths.

'He must be three inches into the ground,' Angel observed, still in that shaky voice.

She seemed preoccupied with measurements today.

Paralyzed by the suddenness and totality of the disaster, we stood together in the shade of the oak, looking at the body lying in the sun. Neither of us approached it. There was a stain spreading through the grass and dirt in the head area.

'And of course, the guys aren't here today,' I said bitterly, apropos of nothing. 'They're never home when you need them.' Angel looked at me, her jaw dropping. Then she began hooting with laughter.

I was unaware I'd said anything amusing, and I was at my most librarian-ish when I added, 'Really, Angel, we've got to stop standing around talking, and do something about this.'

'You're absolutely right,' Angel said. 'Let's put some tulip bulbs in potting soil on top of him. They'll come up great next year.'

'It's way too late to put in tulips,' I told her. Then, catching myself, feeling the day had already spun out of hand, I said, 'We've got to call the sheriff.'

'Oh, all right.' Angel stuck out her lip at me like a six-year-old whose fun had been spoiled, and laughed all the way into the house.

I hadn't seen Angel Youngblood laugh that much in the two years she'd been my bodyguard.

She was serious enough an hour later, when Padgett Lanier was sitting on my patio with a glass of iced coffee. Lanier was perhaps the most powerful man in our county. He'd been in office in one capacity or another for twenty years. If anyone knew where all the bodies were buried in Lawrenceton, Georgia, it was this man. With a heavy body, scanty blond hair, and invisible eyelashes, Lanier wasn't the most attractive man in my backyard, but he had a strong presence.

The 'most attractive man' prize had to go to my husband of two years, Martin Bartell, vice president of manufacturing at Pan-Am Agra, Lawrenceton's largest employer. Martin is a Vietnam vet, and at forty-seven he's fifteen years older than I. He pumps iron and plays various one-on-one competitive sports regularly, so his physique is impressive, and Martin has that devastating combination of white hair and black eyebrows. His eyes are light, light brown.

Angel's husband Shelby, who was lounging against the kitchen door, is swarthy and graying, with a Fu Manchu mustache and pockmarked cheeks. He is soft-spoken, polite, and an expert in the martial arts, as is Angel. Shelby and Martin are longtime friends.

Right now, Angel and I were the only women in sight. There were three deputies, the coroner, a local doctor, the sheriff, and our husbands. There were two men in the ambulance crew waiting to take 'the deceased' to – wherever they took things like that.

Lanier gave me a thorough head-to-toe evaluation, and I realized I was wearing shorts, a halter top, and dried sweat, and that my long and wayward hair was sloppily gathered into a band on top of my head. 'You musta been enjoying the sun, Miss Roe,' he said genially. 'A little early in the spring for it, ain't it?'

Now my friends call me Roe, but I'd never counted Lanier among them. I realized it was Lanier's way of handling a problem. I'd kept my own name when I'd married Martin, a decision on my part that I don't yet understand, since my laughable name had been the bane of my life. When you introduce yourself as 'Aurora Teagarden' you're going to get a snigger, if not a guffaw.

Padgett didn't know whether to call me Miss Teagarden, Mrs Teagarden, or Mrs Bartell, or Ms Teagarden-Bartell, and 'Miss Roe' was his compromise gesture.

My husband was watching the activity by the mower, standing with the relaxed attitude of a guy who comes home every day to find a man embedded in his lawn. That is to say, Martin was trying to look relaxed, but his gaze was following every move the lawmen made, and he was very busy thinking. I could tell because his mouth was an absolutely straight line, and his arms were crossed across his chest, the fingers twiddling: his Thinking Stance. The slightly taller Shelby lounged over to stand beside Martin, his hands stuck in his jeans pockets to show how relaxed *he* was. With the synchronicity born of long association, the two men turned and looked at each other, some silent comment about the fallen dead man passing between them.

I hadn't responded to Lanier, and he was waiting for me to say something.

'Well, we were taking turns mowing the lawn,' I answered. 'And that's always hot work. I did the front, so Angel took the back.' If I mow the front, I count it as my exercise for the day, and I don't have to pop in that stupid videotape and dance in front of the TV. We live a mile out of town, in the middle of fields, and we have a very large front yard, and a big back one.

Martin, listening, shook his head absently, as he always did when my distaste for (most) strenuous physical activity crossed his mind. But he was still looking at the man embedded in our backyard.

'Do you think he'll be recognizable when he's turned over?' he asked the sheriff suddenly.

'No telling,' Lanier said. 'We've never had one dropped from a plane before. Now I wonder, do you suppose that body landed here on purpose?'

He had our full attention now, and he knew it. I felt a jolt of dismay.

'Would you like some more ice coffee?' I asked. (I know it's 'iced', but that's not what we say.)

He glanced at his glass. 'No, ma'am, I reckon I'm fine right now. Did that plane circle around before the man fell?'

I nodded. Lanier's gaze moved to Angel, where it dwelled wonderingly. She was something to see.

'Mrs Youngblood, you said you didn't see it?'

'No, Sheriff. I had the lawn mower running and I was listening to a tape.' Angel, who'd pulled a white T-shirt on over her bikini, was getting plenty of surreptitious attention from the deputies and the ambulance men. It ran off her like water off a duck's back. Angel is not pretty, but she is tall, very muscular and lean, and golden as a cheetah. Her legs are maybe a mile long.

'Miss Roe, you actually saw him fall?'

'Yes. But I didn't see him come out of the plane. When I looked up, he was already in the air.'

'You reckon he was already dead?'

I hadn't considered that. 'Yes,' I said slowly. 'Yes, I think he was. Because he was . . .' I had to take a deep breath. 'He was all floppy.'

Martin moved behind me and put his hands on my shoulders.

Padgett Lanier shook his glass a little to hear the ice cubes tinkle against the sides. 'I wonder, when we turn the deceased over, if you all would mind taking a look at him.' He held up a placatory hand before we could respond. 'I know, I know, it's an awful thing to ask anyone, especially these ladies, but we do need to know if you have seen this man anytime or anywhere, before today.'

I had never wanted to do anything less. My husband's hands gripped my shoulders bracingly.

'Sheriff! We're ready when you are!' called the taller of the deputies, as he pulled on an extra pair of plastic gloves. Lanier heaved himself out of his chair and strode over to the body.

This was a process I did not want to watch, and I covered my face with my hands. I heard some sounds I definitely didn't want to match to an image.

'You needn't bother, ladies,' called Lanier. His voice was very unsteady. I wondered if I ought to tell him where the bathroom was. 'You needn't bother,' he said again, in a lower voice. But the people in our yard were so quiet, it was easy to hear. 'I recognize him myself . . . I think.'

I dropped my hands in amazement, caught a glimpse of what was being lifted from the lawn, and put them back up hurriedly.

'Who is it?' Martin called, close to my ear.

'Detective Sergeant Jack Burns, City of Lawrenceton Police Department.'

Padgett Lanier, no doubt about it, had a certain sense of ceremony.

After some dreadful minutes, the envelope of broken bones and jellied organs that was Jack Burns's body was maneuvered into a bag and then into the ambulance. Lanier, obviously shaken but still maintaining his official face, ambled over to the patio. I was feeling very shaky, and Angel was an interesting shade of green. I thought she might be sick again. Martin and Shelby looked even grimmer than they had before.

'How long has it been since you saw Jack Burns?' Lanier asked me. 'Seems to me as though you and he never got along too well, am I right?'

'I never had any quarrel with Mr Burns,' I said steadily. That was the truth. Jack Burns's dislike of me had not had its basis in any one incident, but in cumulative distrust. 'And I haven't seen him in – maybe years.' Which had been fine with me; I'd feared Jack, with his blind zeal for his own brand of justice. It's bad to have a policeman as an enemy.

'And you, Mrs Youngblood?'

'We did have a run-in a couple of weeks ago,' Angel said

calmly, though her color betrayed her. I tried not to show any surprise.

'And just what was that about—?'

'He ticketed my car downtown, for some completely bullshit city ordinance he'd looked up in the books.'

'Now why would he do that?'

Angel put her hands on her hips, and her arm muscles rippled. 'I came out of the bank and found him putting a ticket on my car and we had a little talk, kind of sharp.'

'Anyone around during this little talk?'

'Sure,' Angel said wearily. 'It was downtown on a Friday morning. I saw that man that works at the library with Roe – Perry Allison – and I saw that pretty round woman who works at Marcus Hatfield, the one with the dark hair who has the little girl.'

'Carey Osland,' Lanier decided.

'Right, if you say so.' Angel seemed indifferent to the question of the woman's name.

Martin looked at me, his eyebrows arched: Did you know about this? I shook my head almost imperceptibly.

'Why do you think, Mrs Youngblood, that a detective sergeant would give a parking ticket?'

'Because he thought it was Roe's car,' Angel said bluntly. 'We both have blue Chevettes. Mine's the same age, I got it used. Though mine's a slightly different shade of blue, we basically have the same car.'

'Did you have a conversation with Jack Burns?'

'Not what you would call a conversation,' Angel said dryly. 'He looked kind of taken aback when he saw it was my car, but then it was like he figured if I lived out here in Roe's garage apartment, giving me a ticket was almost as good as giving her one. And he was right, I probably *was* seven inches from the curb instead of six. But I wasn't in a good mood.'

This had been a real speech for Angel, who did not tend to be chatty. But Padgett Lanier wanted more.

'So you had words?' he prodded her.

Angel sighed. 'I asked him why he was giving me a ticket and he told me I was parked too far from the curb, and he asked me how Roe was doing, had she found any more bodies lately, and I told him he was giving me a bullshit ticket, and he said he was sure there was some ordinance still on the books about public bad language, and did I want to see if I could karate-chop my way out of a jail cell.'

Lanier stared at her, fascinated. 'And what did you say?'

'Nothing.'

'You didn't respond?'

'No point to it. He'd decided he was going to give me the ticket.'

Lanier seemed nonplused. He eyed Angel a moment or two longer, then asked Martin if he'd seen Jack Burns lately.

'The last time I saw Jack Burns was two years ago, about the time I met my wife,' Martin said calmly. His fingers dug into the tight muscles of my neck and I tilted my head back.

'And you, Mr Youngblood?'

'Hadn't ever met him.'

'You weren't mad about your wife getting a ticket?'

'If you park seven inches from the curb, you gotta take what's coming to you.'

Padgett Lanier's pale face had a tendency to flush easily. We watched now with some trepidation as he turned a tomato red. The sheriff dismissed us curtly, and turned his attention to the search his men were making in our yard. I wanted to beg them not to trample my poor little just-plowed garden, but I decided that would be unfeeling.

With the passage of a couple of hours, supper had become just possible. I called the Youngbloods' apartment to ask Shelby and Angel if they wanted to share our meal, but Angel said she'd rather lie down than eat, and Shelby didn't want to leave her.

Martin and I had pork chops, fried green tomatoes (a rare indulgence), Waldorf salad, and I'd made some biscuits. But we were just picking at the food. Martin had been quiet throughout the meal, which was unusual. Normally, we talked to each other at the table, before we went about our separate pursuits in the evening. (Sometimes they were mutual pursuits, but that usually came later. About bedtime.)

Our house felt very quiet after the onslaught of county and city police. We hadn't had that many people around since the last year's Christmas party.

'Roe, I'm worried about this,' Martin said finally. His pale brown eyes focused on me; Martin looks into the eyes of the people he's talking to. That can be intimidating, or exciting.

'I know. I am, too, of course.'

'Not just Jack Burns being killed, but him being dumped here.'

'Of course,' I said again, not understanding what Martin was getting at.

'As Sheriff Lanier pointed out, people know that you and he didn't get along.'

'But I was absolutely, provably on the ground when he landed. So I couldn't have done it,' I said dismissively. 'Besides which, I can't fly a plane.'

'There's something wrong about it.' Martin was having some problem formulating his thoughts, unusual for him. He's used to expressing himself quickly and decisively in front of a lot of people.

I didn't want to say 'Of course,' again, but that was what I was thinking.

'How long has it been since you talked to him?' Martin asked.

'The sheriff asked me that this afternoon. The best I can recall, I haven't seen Jack to speak to since . . . two and a half years ago at the Anderton house. Same as you.' The day Martin and I had met. He smiled at me now, warmly but briefly, to show me he, too, remembered that day very well.

'Did you think Angel reacted normally today?' Martin said suddenly.

'No, I don't think so at all,' I said, glad he'd said it instead of me. 'I don't know what's wrong with her. Angel's not one to flinch away from anything unpleasant, and she has the strongest stomach of anyone I know. For some reason, this just threw her for a loop.' And I remembered Jack Burns rotating in the air, and was sorry I'd used that expression. I put my napkin by my plate and pushed the plate away.

'Something's up with her,' Martin said. 'I could tell Shelby was worried, too. And I could swear he'd never heard this story about the ticket.'

'Would you mind doing the dishes tonight?'

'No.' Martin seemed glad to shake off whatever dark thoughts he'd been having. 'Are you going out? Is it Friends of the Library night, or some church meeting?'

'No,' I said. 'I've got to go pay my condolences to Bess Burns.'

'Roe, do you think that's wise?'

'I've always liked her, even if I didn't like him. I've gotten to know her at Friends meetings.'

Since I'd resumed working at the library on a part-time basis, I'd met everyone who worked there as a volunteer. And Bess Burns, since she'd retired from teaching, was one of our best workers.

Martin continued to look at me in a troubled way, but he nodded. 'I don't mind doing the dishes,' he said. 'Have you fed that cat yet?'

'I'll do it before I go,' I promised. Martin and Madeleine, the fat old cat I inherited from a friend, have a touchy relationship at best. Madeleine's favorite perch is the hood of Martin's Mercedes-Benz, and Martin is very proud of that car. We even got doors installed on the garage and we check to be sure they're closed every night, but we have to search for Madeleine before we do.

I went up the stairs in a hurry, mentally selecting my visit-to-the-widow outfit. Not black, I wasn't a member of the family . . . navy. My new navy blue dress with the white trim. I'd just bought it at Short 'N Sweet in Atlanta – a petite shop, I'm four eleven – and I glanced at the label, gloating over the smaller size I'd been buying lately, before I pulled it over my head.

Living with a health- and exercise-conscious man like Martin, and having the athletic Angel as a companion, had had a happy result as far as my figure was concerned. I'd even gone to the beauty shop my mother patronizes, Clip Casa, and gotten Benita to streak my hair. It took hours, since it's thick, tightly wavy, and halfway down my back. But the result was worth it. Overall, what with being happy with Martin and secure financially, I looked and felt better than I had at any time in my life.

After wiggling into pantyhose – a process I wouldn't let Martin watch – I slid my feet into pumps and pulled my frivolous streaky hair back with a barrette. I fed Madeleine hastily, grabbed my food offering from the refrigerator, and backed out my old Chevette, a car Martin detests almost as much as he detests Madeleine's paw prints.

Though we live a mile out of town, I can almost see the back of my mother's house from my own backyard, and the Burns home was only one street south of hers. But it was a street that made a lot of difference; Mother's home on Plantation was a roomy two-storey with a large lot, and Bess and Jack owned a fairly modest three-bedroom ranch.

There were two cars parked in front of the Burns home, one of them a familiar blue Lincoln Continental. It would have taken Mother five minutes to walk, but she would never willingly arrive anywhere flushed with exertion. Mother was actually coming toward me with a bowl in her hand as I got out of my old car, clutching my own dish.

'What you got there?' I asked.

'A cold pasta salad. It's all I had in the house to make.'

My mother, Aida Brattle Teagarden Queensland, is a slim, husky-voiced Lauren Bacall look-alike. She is also a very successful Realtor, and a few short years ago she married John Queensland, a retired businessman. Since then, she's become a stepgrandmother a couple of times. Once the shock wore off, she's enjoyed it.

I peered through the plastic wrap. 'Looks good.'

'Thanks. I see you brought your Waldorf salad. Well, are you going to ring the doorbell?'

I did so, and the door swung open after the correct interval. The Burns's neighbor to the right, Marva Clerrick, had on her formal smile. It changed into a less strained one when she recognized us.

'Am I glad to see you!' she exclaimed in a violent whisper. 'The strangest people are here talking to Bess! I have no idea what's going on!'

Marva, an athletic extrovert and the wife of my sometime boss, Sam Clerrick, was one of the most popular teachers at Lawrenceton High School and a good friend of the recently retired Bess Burns. Marva had been aptly named by parents who must have had some premonition that Marva would be able to cook, teach English during the week and Sunday School at Western Hill Baptist Church, bring up two very good girls, and cope with the moody Sam. In the summer, her off-season, Marva taught swimming at the local pool and led rug-hooking classes at Peachtree Leisure Apartments.

For Marva to be confounded by a situation, it must be strange indeed. Of course, we were agog.

'What's going on?' I asked in a stage whisper.

'There are two men here I've never seen before in this town,' Marva hissed back. 'And to fall out of a plane! How could that happen by accident? What was Jack doing up in a plane?'

'I hate to bring this up, but I think Jack was already dead when he came out of the plane,' I said hesitantly. No one had asked me not to tell, and if Mother found out from another source she'd never forgive me.

'Already dead?' my mother said. She and Marva stared at me with twin expressions of distaste, fascination, and horror.

'He sure looked like it,' I said, involuntarily seeing the body turning in the air. 'Of course, someone else was flying the plane.'

'Oh, girl, you don't mean you *saw* it?' Marva asked breathlessly.

I nodded, surprised at this failure of the rumor mill.

'I heard it was that young woman that lives in your apartment out there, the gal with all the muscles,' Marva said indignantly.

'Oh, we were both out in the backyard.'

'Did you see the airplane, too?' Mother asked.

I shrugged. 'It was just a little ole plane, red and white. I didn't notice any of the numbers on it.' It would be hard to find someone who knew less about airplanes than I did.

'I can't believe it, in our little town,' Marva said, forgetting to whisper. 'Maybe it was somebody Jack had sent to prison?'

Mother and I shrugged simultaneously, and shook our heads to back the shrug up.

'Well, see what you make of this situation here, and let me know,' Marva said. 'I've been minding the door for an hour now, but I have to go home soon, I've got bread coming out of the oven and I don't know if Sissy will remember to get it out of the loaf pan after ten minutes' sitting.'

'Where is Bess?' my mother asked directly, tired of all this hissing by the front door.

'Straight through,' Marva said, nodding her head at the door at the rear of the foyer. 'The kids haven't gotten here yet, but she's talked to both of them on the phone. They have long drives.' I remembered the Burns children, Jack Junior and Romney, went to different colleges in different states.

'We'll put our bowls in the refrigerator before we talk to her,' Mother told Marva firmly.

Bess's kitchen looked just like mine usually did, basically clean but messy around the edges, with bills sticking out of a letter caddy on the wall and an open box of teabags by a pitcher. Another neighbor was working out her helpful impulses by wiping the counter, and we smiled and nodded at each other in a subdued way.

I opened the refrigerator to put in my offering. It was half-full of similar dishes, plastic-wrapped food that people had brought to Bess Burns in her time of trouble, to help feed her surely incoming family. By noon tomorrow, there would be no available shelf space.

Somehow reassured by the correctness of the refrigerator, Mother and I made our way to the den at the back of the house.

Bess was sitting on the couch with two big men flanking her. I'd never seen either man before. They wore suits, and ties, and grim expressions, and as the slim red-haired widow blotted her face with a white handkerchief, they offered her no comfort.

'We're so sorry,' Mother said, in a perfectly calibrated tone of sympathy calculated not to start the tears again.

'Thank you,' Bess said. Bess's voice was almost expressionless from exhaustion and shock. The lines across her forehead and from nose to mouth looked deeper, and traces of red lipstick stood out garishly on her pale face. 'I appreciate you coming, and Aurora, too,' Bess said with great effort.

I bent awkwardly across the coffee table to give her a hug. Bess, who had only retired at the end of the previous school year, was still wearing her schoolteacher clothes, one of those relaxed cotton knit pants sets with the loose tunic. Hers was blue with a giant red apple on the front. It seemed ludicrously cheerful.

'Do they know why, yet—?' my mother said, as if she had a perfect right to ask.

Bess actually, opened her mouth to answer, when the blond man to her right held up a hand to silence her. He stared up at us from behind tortoise-shell-framed glasses.

'It's still under investigation,' he said heavily.

Mother and I glanced at each other.

Mother was not to be bested on her own territory. 'I am Aida Queensland, a neighbor,' she said pointedly. 'I don't believe I've met you?'

'I'm John Dryden from Atlanta,' he said, which was an answer that told us nothing.

I didn't like people being rude to my mother.

'You would be Mr Pope, then,' I said to the other man, who was darker and younger.

'Pope?' He stared at me curiously. 'No. I'm Don O'Riley. From Atlanta.'

Though Mother was trying to give me a censorious face, she was really stifling a smile.

'Bess, why don't you come with us out to the kitchen?' I said. 'Show us what we should put out for you and your friends to eat.' They clearly weren't friends, and whoever they were, they were upsetting Bess even more than she already was. 'It's so late, and I'm sure you haven't had a thing.'

'No, I haven't eaten,' she said, looking as though she liked being talked to directly. Before her two 'friends' could stop her, she stood up and circled the coffee table to go to the kitchen with us.

The neighbor who'd been there had left, leaving behind spotless counters and a feeling of goodwill. Bess stood and stared as though she didn't recognize her own appliances.

'Were they bothering you?' Mother asked.

'They have to, it's their job,' Bess said, with the weary endurance of a law enforcement wife. 'I shouldn't say anything about this, but Jack knew the identity of a – person – here in town who's been hidden . . . well, I better not say any more. They wonder if it might be related to his being killed.'

'Ah,' said Mother with great significance, which was more than I could think of to say. She turned to fiddle with a dish of spaghetti she'd gotten from the refrigerator, and I saw her eyes close as if she was wondering how in the hell she'd gotten into this kitchen hearing this fascinating but bizarre revelation.

'You saw him fall, Roe,' Bess said directly to me. The air of exhaustion was gone, and in its place was a dreadful intensity. 'Was he dead when he fell, or did he die from the impact?'

'I think he was dead when he came out of the plane,' I said, trying not to cry in the face of her pain, since she was keeping her own tears in check. 'I don't think he felt a thing, or ever knew he was falling.'

'Thank you,' she said quietly.

'Mrs Burns, here you are,' said the blond Mr Dryden sharply, though he could have had little doubt about Bess's location. He was tucking his glasses into his breast pocket. Without them, his face looked even more alert. 'You have a phone call you need to take in the living room. Ladies, thanks for coming to see Mrs Burns in her time of grief.'

None of us had heard the phone ring.

'We'll just set your meal out, and then we'll leave,' Mother said firmly. 'Bess, if you need us, we'll be *right here*.'

'Thanks so much,' John Dryden said – dryly. And damned if he didn't stay in the kitchen, watching us get out paper plates (since we couldn't feature Dryden and O'Riley helping with the dishes) and heat up spaghetti in the built-in microwave. We prepared three plates of spaghetti, Waldorf salad, and green bean casserole, and set the table as best we could, what with having to search for the forks and napkins and glasses.

'Mr Dryden,' said my mother, as he escorted us to the front door without our having caught another glimpse of Bess, 'can you tell us when the funeral will be, and the name of the funeral home? I need to arrange for some flowers.'

'I don't believe we're certain at this time about any of that,' Dryden said cautiously. 'There has to be an autopsy.'

So Dryden was a stranger to Bess Burns, if not to Jack. Any Lawrenceton native would know the Burns's burials would be from Jasper Funeral Home, since Jerry Saylor of Saylor's Funeral Home had divorced Bess Burns's sister. From the way Mother and I looked at each other, Dryden knew he'd said something significant; you could see him trying to figure it out, abandoning the attempt.

'I suppose the funeral date will be in the obituary in tomorrow's paper?' my mother persisted.

He looked blank.

'I'm sure it will be,' he said.

We didn't believe him for a minute.

'Jack Junior and Romney had better get home quick,' my mother said darkly as she slid her elegant legs into her car.

I drove home slowly, more questions in my mind than I'd had when I'd set out.

Chapter Two

'I think Dryden and Pope – I mean, O'Riley – were some kind of federal agents,' I told Martin as he pulled on his maroon pajama bottoms that night. He just uses the bottoms, except on very cold nights, and we don't get too many of those in Lawrenceton. I've never figured out what to do with the tops. Sometimes *I* wear them. 'FBI or CIA or federal marshals.'

'As long as they weren't interested in me,' Martin said.

'You're out of all that now. Jack's death couldn't have anything to do with you, no matter who's investigating it.'

Discovering Martin's secret life had been the most terrible blow I'd ever sustained. Martin was born to be a buccaneer. For a while his love of danger had been satisfied by a brief stint working for a shadowy CIA-funded company following the war. After he'd begun working for Pan-Am Agra, he'd been approached again, and had resumed his clandestine activities. Only his complete withdrawal from the gun smuggling he'd been facilitating on his legitimate business trips to Central America had made our marriage workable.

I had just about recovered from the fact that he hadn't told me anything about it before we married; but it had taken a while. For a couple of months, separation had been a real possibility.

I didn't like remembering that time. Angel and Shelby dated from those days also, but I'd managed to regard them as friends and employees rather than bodyguards, for the most part. Martin had made some enemies along the way in his clandestine trade, and he was out of town a lot; installing Shelby and Angel had seemed like a wise precaution to him. Though Shelby had at first worked at Pan-Am Agra as cover for his real job – guarding me – it looked as if he actually had a career there now. He'd risen to crew leader and another promotion was looming on the horizon. That seemed the oddest by-product of the whole thing.

As I was sitting in our king-size bed with my crossword puzzle book on a lap desk resting on my knees, the thought occurred to me that, like Martin, Jack Burns was a tough man with a few enemies.

Jack, who must have been in his early fifties, had spent most of his working career on the Lawrenceton police force, though I remembered he'd tried the Atlanta police for a four-year stint. Jack had hated Atlanta ever after, and more than just about any other resident of Lawrenceton, he had resented our town's ever-nearing inclusion in the sprawling Atlanta metroplex. Jack had hated change, and loved justice, which couldn't come pure enough to suit him. He'd had an almost total disregard for his personal appearance, beyond getting his hair cut and shaving every morning; he'd always looked as though he'd reached in his closet blindfolded and pulled on whatever came out, pieces that often seemed totally unrelated to each other.

'I wonder how he came to be in the plane,' I murmured, putting aside the lap desk and book. 'Seems like to me he took flying lessons at one time. I think I remember Bess saying he thought it might come in handy on the job.'

Martin was brushing his teeth, but he heard me. He appeared in the bathroom door to make gestures. He'd tell me in a minute.

I heard gargling noises, and Martin emerged blotting his mouth with a towel, which he tossed back in the bathroom as an afterthought. It landed sort of in the vicinity of the towel rack.

He's not good about hanging up towels.

'While you were out tonight,' he said, 'Sally called.'

I raised my eyebrows interrogatively. Sally Allison was the kingpin reporter for the *Lawrenceton Sentinel*.

'She wanted you to know, for some reason, that Jack Burns had rented the plane himself, from the Starry Night Airport ten miles away on the interstate.'

'He rented it *himself*?'

Martin nodded.

Good friend that Sally was, she knew I'd be intrigued by that little fact. I clipped my pencil to the puzzle book and tried to imagine how someone had gotten Jack into the plane and then killed him and thrown him out; could one person do that? Could little planes be set on autopilot? Wouldn't someone be at the airfield to monitor arrivals and departures?

'From the very little Burns's wife said to you, he knew the identity of someone here in Lawrenceton who'd been hidden by the Federal Witness Protection Program,' Martin said.

'So why would the – I don't know, what do you call 'em, protectee? Why would he kill Jack?'

Martin raised his eyebrows at me. I'd missed something very obvious.

'I imagine whoever killed Jack Burns wanted the new name of the hidden person.'

Naturally. I should have seen that before. 'But if these were the people this witness had testified against, wouldn't they know what he looked like?'

'Maybe he's had plastic surgery,' Martin said. 'Or maybe these people only suspect they know who betrayed them.' But his interest in the subject had ebbed. Once he'd decided we were safe, not implicated, he'd begun losing interest in Jack Burns's death, except as it upset or concerned me.

'But why in our backyard, Martin? You were worried about that earlier,' I challenged him. 'Let's hear a good reason.' I took off my glasses (I was wearing my blue-framed ones that day) and crossed my arms under my breasts. They were more or less covered in ivory lace, the top of a concoction Martin had given me for his birthday.

'Do you think our yard was picked on purpose?' Martin asked.

'Yes . . . maybe. I didn't want to make a song and dance about it when Padgett Lanier was here, but the plane circled to get the drop right. The body could have been dumped in any of the fields around here and lain for days with no one the wiser and no way to trace the plane. They risked Angel and me seeing the plane, to dump Jack *here*.' I pointed down, as if our bed had been the target.

'It was a threat against the protectee, as you call him,' Martin said calmly. He seemed to feel better about the implications of Jack Burns ending up in our yard now. 'Saying, "Here is the body of the man who knew you, we're coming to get you soon".'

'Could be. But why here?'

'They wanted the body found as soon as possible, to get their message across. They saw a nice big yard with two women in it who were sure to call the police right away.'

Not for the first time, I realized how much I'd come to rely on Martin's decisiveness and authority. If he said this was nothing for me to worry about, I was fairly willing to accept it. And I also recognized something I should have spotted earlier; my husband was furious. Protective Martin did not like his wife frightened by falling bodies, especially when he'd decided the body had fallen near her by design. Martin was as full of pressure as a preemptive volcano.

It was too bad we didn't have a home racquetball court. That was Martin's favorite method of letting off steam.

He had another one, however.

'Martin, I was really scared today.'

Instantly he moved to his side of the bed and slid in, and his arms went around me. I nestled my head in the hollow of his neck. He held me carefully, delicately. I know a man's protection is illusory, but illusions can be awfully comforting sometimes. I raised my face to his and kissed him. When I was sure we were both thinking the same thing, I switched off my bedside lamp, turned back to him, and gave his neck a tiny nip.

We were much more relaxed when we went to sleep.

Sally Allison's story in the *Lawrenceton Sentinel* the next day said nothing about two big men from Atlanta. Martin left it folded open on the table by a clean coffee cup, waiting for me; he'd had to go in early for a breakfast meeting with his division heads.

> Jack Burns, longtime member of the Lawrenceton police force, was killed sometime early Monday afternoon. His body, thrown

from a low-flying airplane, landed on the property of Aurora Teagarden and Martin Bartell, about a mile out of town on Mason Road, at approximately 2 P.M. yesterday.

Burns, a native of Lawrenceton, was not known to have any enemies. His wife, former teacher Bess Linton Burns, expressed bafflement at the motive for her husband's death. 'I can only think it must have been someone he arrested, someone out for revenge,' she said.

'The means of his death are not known now,' stated Sheriff Padgett Lanier. 'Only the autopsy can tell us that.'

Lanier went on to say the sheriff's department is investigating how someone else could have entered the Piper plane, rented by Burns from Starry Night Airport yesterday, and overcome Burns. The plane was found returned yesterday, and no one at the tiny airport can identify the pilot.

See Obituaries, Page 6.

I could imagine Sally's frustration at being given so little to work with. When she'd called me the night before to offer me the tidbit about Jack Burns himself having rented the plane that took him to his final landing place, perhaps she'd been in search of some additional detail to pad out the story. Accompanying it was the usual grim shot of the two medics loading the covered stretcher into the ambulance. You could tell the covered bundle was sort of flat – I gulped and pushed the memory away.

I glanced at the clock. It was a relief to have to look at it again, to have something to plan my days around. I'd resumed working part-time at the library in Lawrenceton four weeks ago when Sam Clerrick had called me out of the blue to tell me his oldest librarian had suddenly turned to him to say, 'I can't shelve one more book. I can't tell one more child to be quiet. I can't deal with this new aide. I can't tell one more patron where the Georgia collection is.'

Left in a bind, Sam had called me since I'd worked for him before. I'd agreed instantly to take the job; and Sam had agreed to see how my working part-time would do, at least while he scouted around to see if anyone wanted to work full-time. So I was working nine to one for five days a week, with one of the days changing every week, since the library was open on Saturdays from nine to one. No one wanted Saturday every week, including me. The aide took over in the afternoons, sometimes in conjunction with a volunteer.

I was ready to go in early. Might as well get the inevitable inquisition from my co-workers over with.

It was a beautiful spring Tuesday, with lots of sun and a brisk cool breeze. Angel was sitting on the steps leading up to the Youngbloods' garage apartment, looking muddy, the result of pallor under her chronic tan.

'What's the matter?' I couldn't remember Angel ever being ill.

'I don't know,' she said. 'The past few days I've just felt awful. I don't want to get up out of bed, I don't want to run.'

'Do you have a temperature?'

'No,' she said listlessly. 'At least, I don't think so. We've never had a thermometer.'

I tried to imagine that. 'Did you try to run today?'

'Yeah. I got about half a mile and had to come back.' She was still in her running clothes, sweating profusely.

'Look, let me take you in to the doctor. I've got an hour before I really have to be at work,' I said impulsively. I hated to think of Angel driving to the doctor by herself; she was so obviously ill.

'I've never been to a doctor except to get stitched up in an emergency room,' Angel said.

'Let me go call him,' I said, when I'd recovered from my shock. 'You go take a shower and pull on some slacks.'

Angel nodded wearily and pulled herself up by the railing. She was trudging the stairs as I went inside to call the doctor and the library. 'I promise I'll work the hours today,' I told Sam. 'I just have to take a friend to the doctor. She hasn't got anyone else.'

'There are disadvantages to having an employee who doesn't really need the job,' Sam said distantly. 'Is this going to be happening much?'

'No,' I said, a little offended, though I knew he was in the right. 'I'll be in on time tomorrow. It's just today that I'll be a little late.'

When I got out to my old blue car, Angel was sitting on the passenger's side in white slacks and a yellow tank top, though it seemed cool for a tank top to me. I remembered how profusely she'd been sweating after her short run. She was leaning her head against the glass of the window.

Angel's indisposition was worrying me more and more. I'd never seen her anything less than 100 percent physically, and I'd always envied her Superwoman physique – though not enough to work out every day so I'd have one like it. Angel was silent and listless during the short ride into town.

Dr Zelman's waiting room was not as full as I'd feared. There were two elderly couples; probably only one out of each pair needed to see the doctor. And oddly enough, there was blond Mr Dryden, who was arguing with Dr Zelman's receptionist, Trinity.

'Would you please inform the doctor that I'm here on official business?' Dryden was saying in an exasperated voice.

'I did,' Trinity said coldly.

I could have given Mr Dryden some good advice right about then, had he been in the market for it. 'Never alienate the receptionist' is the first rule of all those who have a limited pool of doctors to draw from.

'Does he realize that I need to get back to Atlanta very soon?'

'He does indeed realize that.' Trinity's face under its fluff of brown-and-gray permed hair was getting grimmer and grimmer.

'You're sure you told him?'

'I tell Dr Zelman everything. I'm his wife.'

Dryden resumed his seat in a chastened manner. It seemed the only two adjacent seats in the waiting room were the ones next to him. After we'd filled out the necessary 'new patient' and insurance forms, Angel and I settled in, with me next to Dryden. I wriggled in my seat, resigned to discomfort. My feet can never quite touch the floor in standard chairs. So I often have to sit with my knees primly together, toes braced on the floor. I was wearing khakis that morning, and a sky-blue blouse with a button-down collar. My hair, loose today since I'd been in a hurry to get Angel to the doctor, kept getting wrapped around the buttons. Since Angel obviously didn't feel like talking, once I'd disentangled myself I opened a paperback (I always keep one in my purse) and was soon deep in the happenings of Jesus Creek, Tennessee.

'Aren't your glasses a different color today?' inquired a male voice.

I glanced up. Dryden was staring at me. 'I have several pairs,' I told him. I had on my white-rimmed ones today, to celebrate spring.

His blond brows rose slightly above his heavy tortoiseshell rims. 'Expensive,' he said. 'You must have married an optometrist.'

'No,' I said. 'I'm rich.'

That kept him quiet for a while, but not long enough.

'Are you the same Aurora Teagarden into whose yard the body fell yesterday?' he asked, when the silence seemed to stretch.

No, I'm a different one. There are several of us in Lawrenceton. 'Yes.'

'And you didn't say anything at the Burns house last night?'

'What was I supposed to say?' I asked, bewildered. ' "Gee, Mrs Burns, I saw your husband's body. It looked as though someone had run over it with a meat tenderizer"? Actually, she did ask me if he was dead before he hit the ground and I told her I thought he was.'

'I see.'

About damn time.

'However,' he continued, 'we need to interview you about the incident.'

I noted the terminology. 'Then you'll have to do it this afternoon. I have to go to work after I take my friend home. And I have to get my husband off to Chicago.' I added this last out of sheer perversity, since Martin, experienced traveler that he was, always packed for himself and drove himself to the airport in a company car, not wanting his Mercedes to be the target of thieves or vandals in the long-term parking lot. The only thing I had to do with Martin's trips was to miss him.

I'd been missing him a lot lately.

Dryden suggested four o'clock at my house, I agreed, and I returned pointedly to my book. But Dryden had his talking shoes on.

'So, your husband is the plant manager at Pan-Am Agra?'

'His job just got upgraded to vice president in charge of manufacturing.' I turned a page.

'Have you been married long?'

By golly, I was on the verge of being rude. Really.

'Two years,' I said briefly.

Then, thank goodness, Trinity called Angel's name.

'Please come in with me, Roe,' my bodyguard said quietly.

Considerably surprised, but pleased to be escaping Dryden, I tucked my book in my purse and rose to my feet. Dr Zelman's new nurse took over from Trinity, leading us to a cramped examining room with rose-and-blue walls and a table that would barely hold Angel. Something about the nurse seemed familiar. As she talked to Angel about her aches and pains, efficiently taking Angel's blood pressure and checking her temperature, I realized the woman in white was Linda Ehrhardt, whose bridesmaid I'd been in the long, long ago. She'd been Linda Pocock for years now. As she turned away from Angel, she recognized me too.

After the usual exclamations and hugs, Linda said, 'I guess you heard I got divorced and moved back home.'

'I'm sorry. But it'll be nice to see you again.'

'Yes, that'll be fun. Of course I brought my children, and they're in school here now.'

'I'm sorry, I've forgotten. Was that two girls?'

'Yes, Carol and Macey.' Linda extracted the thermometer from Angel's mouth and glanced at the reading. She wrote it down on Angel's chart without a change of expression.

'Mrs Youngblood, you'll need to disrobe for your examination,' Linda said rather loudly, as though Angel's habitual silence meant she was short on wits rather than words. 'There's the cubicle in the corner, just put on one of those gowns.'

Angel glared at Linda after she'd looked at the cubicle, and I had to admit I couldn't see Angel's changing in that tiny area as a possibility. But she managed, grumbling to herself. So I wouldn't be just sitting there listening to her, I brushed my hair with the help of the mirror over the sink, carefully drawing the brush all the way through the mass of streaky brown waves, trying not to break off my ends by pulling the brush out too soon. I gave up when it was flying around my head, wild with electricity. By that time Angel had managed to reensconce herself on the table with the obligatory sheet across her lap, though she was clearly unhappy with the whole situation and not a little afraid.

Dr Zelman burst in just as Angel was about to say something. He never just came into a room, and he never just left; he made entrances and exits. He almost never closed the door completely, something his nurse or his patient's friends had to do. (I crept behind him to do it now.) Now in his early fifties, 'Pinky' (Pincus) Zelman had worked in Lawrenceton for twenty years, after a short-lived practice in Augusta that had left him inexplicably longing for something more rural.

'Mrs Youngblood!' he cried happily. 'You're so healthy you've never been to see me before, in two years here, I see! Good for you! What can I do for you today?' Dr Zelman caught sight of me trying to be unobtrusively solicitous, and patted me on the shoulder so heavily I almost went down. 'Little Ms Teagarden! Prettier than ever!' I smiled uneasily as he turned back to Angel.

Angel stoically recited her symptoms: occasional exhaustion, occasional queasiness, lack of energy. I winced when I thought of asking Angel to help me mow the yard the day before. Now quiet and intent, Dr Zelman began examining her from head to toe, including a pelvic, which Angel clearly hadn't expected (I hadn't either) and which she barely endured.

'Well, Mrs Youngblood,' Dr Zelman said thoughtfully, rooting for his pencil in his graying hair (it was stuck behind his ear), 'it's really too bad your husband didn't come with you today, because we have a lot to talk about.'

Angel and I both blanched. I reached out and grabbed her hand.

'Because, of course, Mrs Youngblood, as I'm sure you guessed, you *are* pregnant.'

Angel and I gasped simultaneously.

'I'm sure you knew, right? You must have missed two periods. You're at least ten weeks along, maybe more. Of course, with your wonderful physique, you're not showing.'

'I'm not regular at all,' Angel said in a stunned way. 'I really didn't notice, and it didn't occur to me to wonder, because my husband . . . has had a vasectomy.'

I sat down abruptly. Fortunately, there was a chair underneath.

For once, Dr Zelman looked nonplused. 'Has he had a recheck done recently?' he asked.

'Recheck? He got snipped! Why should he have a recheck?' For once, Angel's voice rose.

'It's wise, Mrs Youngblood, wise indeed, to have that recheck. Sometimes the severed tubes grow back. I'm sorry I gave you the news so blithely, since it seems you and your husband had not planned to have any children. But a baby's on the way, Mrs Youngblood. Well on the way. You're in such excellent condition and so slim that the baby may not show at all for another month or so, especially since this must be your first pregnancy.'

Angel was shaking her head from side to side, disbelievingly.

'If your husband wants to talk to me,' Dr Zelman said gently, 'I can explain to him how this happened.'

'I'm pretty sure he's going to think he knows already,' Angel said dismally. 'But I would never in this world. . .' She shook her head, finishing the rest of her sentence in her head.

I had to help Angel dress, she was so deeply shocked. I tried not to burble, since she was upset, but I was so excited by proxy that it was hard.

A baby.

'How can I work?' Angel said, but not as if she was really concerned.

'Pooh, as a bodyguard? I don't need a bodyguard anymore, now that Martin's out of – that mess,' I said soothingly. 'If you still want to help me out around the place, we'll work something out. Maybe I could keep the baby for you? Some?'

She heard the yearning in my voice.

'This should be happening to you,' she said with a faint smile on her thin lips.

'Oh, Martin's worried about his age,' I said, and thought right away of kicking myself: Shelby Youngblood was Martin's age, forty-seven, and Angel was twenty-eight to my thirty-two and a half. 'Anyway,' I said bracingly, 'you tell him to call Dr Zelman, okay? He may get kind of upset, having had a vasectomy and all.'

'Oh, I just bet he will,' she said grimly.

Angel walked out to the car in a state of stunned silence. I made sure she was in the car and then I ran back in to get my purse, which I'd left in the examining room. You could tell I was excited and upset, since normally I'd be as likely to leave my arm as my purse. I explained to Trinity Zelman, who waved me on back, and Linda was waiting at the door to the examining room with the purse in hand.

'Knew you'd come back for it,' she said. 'Give me a call, now!' She hurried down the hall to the little lab, and I turned to go out, passing the first examining room on one side and Dr Zelman's office on the other on my way to the waiting room. Dr Zelman's office door was typically ajar, and I heard Mr Dryden's pleasant accentless voice inside. He'd finally gotten his five minutes with the doctor.

'I see that the widow has urged me to talk with you about her husband's condition,' Dr Zelman was saying without much enthusiasm. 'So I'll answer your questions.'

I walked slower.

'In your opinion, was Jack Burns an alcoholic?' Dryden asked directly.

'Yes,' said Dr Zelman. 'Just this past two or three years, he came to me on several occasions with drink-related injuries. He'd hit his head when he fell, one time. Another time, his car had hit a tree. There were a couple more things like that.'

'Did it seem to you, from what you knew of Jack Burns, that his judgment was impaired?'

'Yes, he . . .' and then I had no excuse to loiter, though I dearly wanted to, because Trinity came out of the reception area and started to go to the doctor's office with some files.

I had more to think about than I could cram in my brain. I'd dropped Angel off at home, promising to take her prescription for maternity vitamins to the pharmacy on my way home from work. Angel clearly wanted some time to herself, and I could understand why. Telling your forty-seven-year-old vasectomied husband that he's about to be a dad was not an enviable proposition. I wanted to talk the situation over with Martin, but of course I couldn't tell him Angel was expecting until she told her own husband. So probably it was just as well I had to go to work.

The Lawrenceton Public Library is a large two-storey block with a low addition to the rear of the building for offices. This brand-new addition, achieved mostly by a bequest from an anonymous patron, a few other donations, and matching community improvement funds, is easily the nicest part of the library, and it's a pity I get to spend so little time in it. It consists of a large employee break room with a row of bright lockers for personal possessions, a microwave, refrigerator, table and chairs, and a stove; Sam Clerrick's office (with space outside for a secretary, though now he only has a volunteer part-time); and a 'community interest' room, where various clubs can meet free of charge if they are careful to schedule it well ahead of time. And there's a nice employee bathroom.

The rest of the library, where I get to spend my working hours, is a plain old creaky public building, with indoor-outdoor carpeting that resembles woven dead grass with trampled-in mustard, the usual row upon row of gray metal shelves, a two-storey entrance and nice staircase up to the second floor, which has a gallery running all the way around with various Dewey Decimal categories lining it, and lots of table-and-chair sets for kids doing homework or genealogists doing research. There's an area set aside by clever use of shelving and extra bulletin boards, and it's designated as the Children's Room.

Whatever its drawbacks, overall there is that wonderful smell of books, and the relaxing, intelligent feeling of being surrounded by generation after generation of thought.

I've got libraries in my blood.

Of course, there are a few things I have to put up with to work in this wonderful place, and one of them was bearing down on me. Lillian Schmidt, buttons bulging and girdle creaking, had her eyebrows up in that 'Hah! I caught you!' look.

'Late today, aren't we?' Lillian fired as her opening shot.

'Yes, I'm afraid so. I had to take a friend to the doctor.'

'Wonder what would happen if all of us did that? Guess the library just wouldn't open!'

I took a deep breath.

'I'm late enough as it is,' I said with a smile. 'Excuse me, Lillian, but I can't stand here and chat.' I pulled out the little key to my locker, used it, and stuck my purse inside, pocketing the key in my khaki slacks. I was due to tell a story in two minutes.

The librarian I was replacing, at least temporarily, was the children's librarian.

Perhaps ten preschoolers were already seated in an expectant semicircle when I plopped down in the big chair in the middle.

'Good morning!' I said with enough glee to raise a hot-air balloon.

'Good morning,' the children chorused back politely. This was the First Church of God the Creator day-care group, with a couple of other loose kids thrown in, story-time regulars. The moms and the daycare providers sat in a little group over in one corner, their expression one of relief that someone else was shouldering the burden, at least for a few minutes.

'This morning, I'm going to tell you about Alexander's bad day,' I said, casting a covert glance at the book the volunteer for the morning, my friend Lizanne Sewell, had left by the chair: *Alexander and the No-Good, Awful, Very Bad Day.* Most of the kids turned hopeful faces in my direction, though a few were looking anywhere but at me.

'I'll bet some of you have had bad days at one time or another, am I right? What happened on your bad day, Irene?' This to a little girl with a wonderful, large easy-to-read name tag. Irene pushed her shaggy black bangs out of her eyes and squashed the slack in her T-shirt in one grubby fist.

'On my bad day my dad left my mom and me and went to live in Memphis,' Irene said.

I closed my eyes.

It was only ten o'clock in the morning.

'Well, Irene, that *was* a bad day,' I said, nodding soberly to show I was giving due weight to her problem. 'Has anyone else ever had a bad day?' I looked around the circle, hoping no one could top Irene's.

'I knocked over my cereal bowl one day,' offered a little boy the color of ground coffee. I tried not to look relieved. His mother was not so guarded.

'That was a bad day, too,' I acknowledged. 'Now, let me tell you about Alexander's bad day . . . and if you sit still, you can see the pictures in the book as I tell the story.'

Over to one side, Lizanne was shaking her head gently from side to side, her lips pursed to hold in a giggle. Not daring to glance again in her direction, I began the book, one of my favorites.

The rest of the story time went by without a hitch, and most of the children seemed to enjoy it, which was not always the case. Only one had to go to the bathroom, and only two whispered to each other, which was quite good. Irene was one of the day-care children, so her mother wasn't there to upbraid me for traumatizing Irene with my probing interrogation.

'It would be better for Irene if he didn't come back,' one of the day-care workers murmured in my ear as they gathered up their flock to return to the church. 'He drank like a fish.' I thought briefly of Jack Burns driving his car into a tree, then forced myself back to the present.

I realized the woman was trying to make me feel better, and I smiled and thanked her. 'Come back soon, kids!' I chirped, being perky all over the place.

The little ones all smiled and waved, even the ones who hadn't listened to a word I said.

Lizanne was ready to help me change the bulletin board, and in fact she'd made most of the items to go on it. With construction paper and some contact sheets, we'd created butterflies, hummingbirds, fish, books, baseballs, and other signs of warm weather. Maybe we were being unduly optimistic about the books, but the summer reading program had always been one of the library's best features, and Sam was counting on me to start plugging it early.

After we'd commented on the way story time had gone, Lizanne and I began to work together companionably, referring to our sketch of the finished product from time to time, handing each other push pins or border and so on. From time to time Lizanne would stop and press a hand to her protuberant stomach; the baby was moving a lot, since she was in her sixth month. Every time, Lizanne would smile her beautiful slow smile.

'Has Bubba made plans for what to do if the baby comes while the legislature's in session?' I asked.

'At least ten plans,' Lizanne said. 'But maybe it'll come before he reconvenes.'

Bubba Sewell, Lizanne's husband, was a state representative and a local lawyer. Bubba was ambitious and intelligent, and, I think, basically an honest person. Lizanne was beautiful and slow-moving and somehow almost always managed things so that they pleased her. I could hardly wait to see what the baby's character would be.

Lizanne left to eat lunch with her mother-in-law, to whose opinions on the baby's upbringing she was blandly indifferent, and I helped some preschool children pick out books. One mother of a nine-year-old boy with a stomach bug came in to get some books and videos to keep him amused, and I collected a few natural history books with plenty of gross pictures of frogs and snakes.

My stomach was growling inelegantly at one o'clock when the library aide came to the children's room to take my place. The aide was a heavy woman with pecan-colored skin named Beverly Rillington, who couldn't be more than twenty-one. Whether it was because of race, age, or income level, Beverly and I were having a hard time geeing and hawing together. She and the previous children's librarian had also had personality conflicts, Sam Clerrick had warned me. But Beverly, hired under a job-training program, was efficient and reliable, and Sam had no intention of letting her go.

'How's it going today?' Beverly asked. She looked down at me as though she didn't really want to know.

In an attempt to break the ice, I told Beverly about the morning story hour and the disconcerting answer I'd gotten from Irene.

Beverly looked at me as though I should have known in advance I'd hear more than I bargained for. If Beverly made me anxious, terrified I might step on her many sensitive toes, I clearly waved a red flag in her face just by being who and what I was. Beverly never volunteered anything about her home life and did not respond to references to mine. Making contact with her was one of my projects for the year.

('I'm damned if I know why,' Martin had said simply, when I'd told him.)

As I told Beverly good-bye and prepared to go home to see my husband off and be interviewed by Mr Dryden, I found myself wondering why, too.

But the answer came to me easily enough, in a string of reasons. Beverly was naturally good with kids, any kids, a knack God had left out of my genetic makeup. Beverly was never late and always completed her work, i's dotted and t's crossed. And, oh happy day, Lillian Schmidt was so terrified of Beverly that she avoided the children's area like the plague when Beverly was at work. I owed my aide thanks on many levels, and I was determined to put up with a certain gruffness of manner for those reasons, if no others.

Chapter Three

I'd forgotten Martin had decided to drive to the airport directly from work. He'd leave his Mercedes at the plant and pick it up when he came in three days from now. The higher-ups of Pan-Am Agra had scheduled one of those events that made Martin's blood curdle: a seminar on sexual harassment, recognition and avoidance thereof. All the plant managers were flying in to Chicago to attend, and since Martin had no particular friends among them and hated meetings he wasn't chairing, his most positive attitude was grim acceptance.

When he called me to say he was leaving for the airport, he reminded me over and over about setting the house security system every night. 'How's Angel?' he asked, just when he was about to hang up. 'Shelby said she hadn't been feeling well.'

'Um. We'll talk about it when you get back. She's going to be fine.'

'Roe, tell me. Is she well enough to help you if you have an emergency?'

I was the only librarian in Lawrenceton, quite possibly in all of Georgia – perhaps even America – to have her own bodyguard. I thought of Angel, stunned and scared, in the doctor's office that morning, and I thought of calling her for help. 'Sure, she's okay,' I said reassuringly. 'Oh, by the way, I saw one of the – well, I don't know exactly who Dryden and O'Riley work for . . . they never said – well, I ran into him this morning, and he says he has to come out here to talk to me this afternoon.'

I'd almost said I'd met him at the doctor's, when I'd taken Angel; and then Martin would have asked what the doctor had said, and I didn't want to lie about it.

'Why does he have to talk to you?' Martin asked.

'To tell you the truth, I'm not sure.'

'Roe, have Angel in the house with you when he's there.'

'Martin, she's not well.'

'Promise.'

Now Martin almost never pulled that string, and it was one we both honored.

'Okay. If she's not actually throwing up, I'll have her here.'

'Good,' he said. 'Now, what can I bring you from Chicago?'

I thought of the big stores, the endless possibilities. I didn't like that many choices myself.

'Surprise me,' I said with a smile he could hear in my voice.

We said some personal good-byes, and then he went back to his work world, which I could hardly imagine.

I piffled around the house for a while, cleaning the downstairs bathroom and sweeping the front porch, the patio, and the steps that led up from the covered walkway running between the garage and the side kitchen door. Finally, I called Angel.

She said dutifully that she'd be over before four o'clock, and I apologized for disturbing her on such a day. 'Martin made me promise,' I explained.

'It's my job,' Angel said. 'Besides, I don't want to just sit here and wait for Shelby to come home.'

The doorbell rang.

'There's a florist's van in the driveway,' Angel said. She must have been on her portable phone, looking out the front window of the garage apartment. 'I'm coming down.'

She hung up unceremoniously, and I went to the front door and turned off the security system. I heard Angel unlocking the side door leading into the kitchen as the doorbell rang a second time. By the time I shot back the dead bolt, she was standing behind me.

'Delivery to this address,' said the young black man in blue coveralls. *DeLane* was stitched on the left chest pocket. He had in his hands a huge arrangement of mixed spring flowers in a tall, clear glass vase. It was lovely: daffodils, baby's breath, irises, roses.

'Who's it for?' I asked.

DeLane looked very uncomfortable. 'It only says, "To the most beautiful". You ladies have to fight over it, I guess,' he added more cheerfully. He'd had a look at Angel, and I could tell he'd decided who would win.

'Who placed the order?' Angel asked sharply.

'We got it Call-a-Posy from Atlanta,' he said with a shrug. 'It seemed pretty strange to us, too, but the shop in Atlanta said it had been paid for. Probably someone'll call you ladies before long, tell you he sent it.'

'Thanks,' Angel said abruptly. She took the vase from his hands.

I said good-bye and shut the door.

Angel was holding the flowers, looking them over carefully. She put them on the low coffee table and peered at the stems through the clear glass; she gently poked the flowers apart with a long finger.

'I don't like things coming without a card, coming "to the most beautiful",' she said. 'That's creepy. Presents without names on them make me very suspicious.'

I wondered if Martin could have sent them, perhaps stopped in at a florist's on his way to the airport. I didn't think so. He knew there were two women at this address, he would have signed a card, it just didn't feel right. And the same thing held true for Shelby, who was much more likely to buy Angel a new running outfit or a punching bag than a huge bouquet of flowers. (For Christmas he'd gotten her a new holster for carrying a concealed gun.)

' "Mirror, mirror, on the wall, Who's the fairest one of all?" ' I quoted, trying to make light of the situation. 'You want to take them home, make Shelby jealous? Or maybe he sent them.'

Angel shook her head morosely. 'Having to answer questions about these flowers would just complicate things even more, and I know damn good and well Shelby didn't send them.'

Our formal dining room lay between the living room and the kitchen, so I went through the large open archway to put a plastic mat in the center of the dining room table. Angel came after me, still frowning, and put the vase on the mat, wiping her hands on her jeans right afterward as if rubbing off the feel of the vase. We both stood and gazed at the flowers some more, but since they didn't suddenly communicate who had sent them, or blow up, or do anything but sit there looking like flowers, this had limited appeal. I was on the verge of suggesting to Angel we go stare at the inside of the refrigerator when the doorbell rang again.

'Oh, gosh, it's four o'clock,' I said, glancing at my wristwatch. 'It must be Dryden and O'Riley.' I looked up at Angel. 'I should be safe with them.' I was smiling, but she was not.

'I said I'd stay.'

'Okay.' I went to the door, my heels making a little click on the polished wood floor, a sound that almost always improved my spirits. My house was now about sixty-three years old, and we'd restored it to wonderful condition. It was just an old family home, not even *my* old family home, but I loved it.

I hadn't reset the alarm system, so Dryden was admitted more rapidly than the florist's deliveryman.

I looked behind him, but O'Riley was nowhere in sight. I was conscious of feeling glad, as I stood aside to let him in, that Angel had decided to stay. At that moment, Dryden's gaze lighted on her, and his mouth yanked up at one corner, an enigmatic twitch I was unable to interpret. It could have been anything from deep admiration for such a fine specimen of womanhood to irritation that I'd asked someone else to sit in on our conversation.

'You're by yourself,' I said, since I've never been afraid to state the obvious.

'O'Riley's on another interview,' he said, pushing his tortoise-shell-rimmed glasses back on his nose. As if the gesture were contagious, like yawning in a meeting, I pushed mine back, too, and we stared at each other solemnly.

'Please have a seat,' I told him. 'This is Angel Youngblood. She was in the backyard when Jack Burns fell, too.'

'Thanks for saving us a trip out here,' Dryden said, and I still couldn't read his expression. He must have recognized Angel as the woman with me in Dr Zelman's office in the morning. He must have read all the police reports, and must have known already about Angel's presence during the free fall of Jack Burns. Yet he didn't seem interested.

I was getting more and more confused by John Dryden.

He finally sat on the couch, and Angel and I picked single chairs opposite him. He turned down my ritual offer of coffee or iced tea, though it was a warm day outside and his suit jacket must be hot.

I looked at Dryden closely for the first time. He was big, and square-shouldered, and husky, but not fat, not at all His eyes were blue behind the glasses, and if he had any gray hair, his light blond hair color concealed it. Of course it was cut very short, as I'd always been led to believe FBI agents wore their hair – if he was an FBI agent – and it lay on his head as smooth as polish. The only other man I knew with hair that blond was Detective Arthur Smith, once my significant other, now married and a father. Lately when I'd run across Arthur his eyes had been hungry. Suddenly I wondered if he'd sent the flowers.

I guess I got lost in conjecture, for a loud throat-clearing brought me back to the here and now with a jolt. Angel and Dryden were both waiting for me to say something.

I sighed. 'Excuse me, I wasn't paying attention. Could you repeat that?'

'Do you know how to fly an airplane?'

I laughed at the idea. 'No,' I said, since he obviously wanted an answer on the record. 'I don't think I've ever been in the cockpit of a plane.'

'What about you, Mrs Youngblood?'

'I had a few flying lessons in Florida,' she said calmly. I noticed Angel's long fingers were resting across her flat stomach. It was incredible to me that a child could be in such a small space, invisible and unknown to anyone around Angel. What an amazing thing to carry inside you; the other choices were so mundane or deathly, like a cold, or cancer, or appendicitis . . .

I had been drifting again.

'. . . you remember the name of your instructor?'

'Bunny Black. She was the owner of this little flying school,

Daredevil . . . but we had to move and I never had another chance to get my pilot's license.'

Dryden was jotting all this down, which was plain ridiculous, since Angel had been standing, both feet very much on the ground, while the plane had been absolutely up in the sky.

I said as much, politely.

He shrugged, and continued to scribble.

If he was this exasperating at home, his wife would take a meat cleaver to him one of these days. I leaned over slightly to check his left hand. No ring. Well, I wasn't surprised.

Suddenly he looked up from his notebook, his eyes unexpectedly sharp and blue. We stared at each other for what seemed like a very long moment.

I eased back against the chair with an uneasy feeling I'd just contacted Mars.

We continued trolling drearily over the horror of yesterday, with Angel and me unable to add a scintilla of information to what we'd already told the county people. I began to be sorry I couldn't suddenly recall some amazing fact to tell him. 'I just remembered! I had a camera in my hand and I think I clicked the button just as the pilot leaned out of the window of the plane!' I bet *that* would change the expression on Dryden's face . . .

Shoot, I'd done it again.

'About your relationship with Jack Burns, Ms Teagarden . . .' Dryden was saying, and I snapped to attention in a very big hurry.

I couldn't help glancing over at Angel. Her eyes narrowed, she was looking at Dryden carefully, as if deciding where her first blow would fall.

'I never had a relationship with Jack Burns,' I said flatly.

'So it's not true that he expressed hostility to you publicly on at least two occasions?'

'I didn't count,' I said flippantly, and was instantly sorry. 'Truly, Mr Dryden,' and I abruptly remembered police remarking in some article I'd read that suspects invariably were lying when they prefaced a statement with 'To tell the truth,' or 'Honestly'. 'To the best of my recollection, Mr Dryden, I hadn't spoken to Jack

Burns in over two years, so I don't think you can say that we had a relationship.' Jack Burns had just seen me in the vicinity of too many corpses to suit his strong police sense. He'd felt I just about had to be guilty of *something*.

But I didn't want to try to explain this. And I didn't feel I should have to.

'Mrs Youngblood, you live in the garage apartment over there?' Dryden pointed with his pencil to the garage, clearly visible out the south windows of the living room.

Angel nodded.

'You rent from Ms Teagarden here?'

'We live there rent-free in return for helping Roe and Martin.' Angel looked completely relaxed, completely blank. She just almost wasn't there at all.

'Helping?'

Angel raised her eyebrows very slightly. 'We help with the yardwork, I help Roe with her housework, we do all the things you need an extra person to do. Martin travels a lot, and it works out conveniently for Roe.'

I would like to see the day I asked Angel to help me with my housework. But a realistic answer – 'We're bodyguards' – would require a lot more explanation than either of us wanted to give.

'And this working relationship has existed for how long?'

'Oh, come on, what possible bearing can this have on Jack Burns being murdered?' I asked, suddenly sick and tired of the presence of Dryden in my house, the boredom of these interminable and uncomfortable questions. I could think of lots of things I needed to be doing and would rather be doing than this. And Angel's husband would be home in about ten minutes, and she should be preparing for a tense and critical evening.

I rose to my feet.

'Mr Dryden, I don't mean to be rude,' though I suppose I really did, 'but I assume you have better things to do than this. And I know I do. All we did was be absolutely random witnesses to this terrible thing.'

Dryden, his mouth flattened in anger – at least, I thought it was anger – was putting away his pencil and notebook.

'I hope it won't be necessary to disturb you again,' he said, quite calmly. He looked over my shoulder, through the archway to the dining room. 'Pretty flowers,' he said, still without inflection.

'Thanks for coming,' I said, with, I hoped, firm civility.

Angel looked down at me, shaking her head, when he'd left.

'What?' I asked indignantly.

'When you do that, it's just like being bitten by a dachshund,' she said, and drifted to the kitchen door. 'Don't forget to set the alarm after me,' she called over her shoulder. I watched her through the kitchen window, loping across the covered sidewalk to the garage, bounding up the wooden steps and unlocking her door. I obediently punched in the right numbers on the panel set in the wall, and I prayed for her and Shelby and the baby.

That evening I got another one of those annoying phone calls. I'd been getting quite a few lately, the wrong numbers that don't say anything when an unfamiliar voice answers the phone. The least the caller could do is say, 'Excuse me, wrong number,' or 'I'm sorry to bother you.' Finally I let it ring until the answering machine picked up. So of course, my next caller was Martin. I just let him assume I'd been too far from the phone to pick it up on the first three rings; no point in telling him about the hang-ups. He'd just worry, maybe call the Youngbloods and get them to worry, too.

I didn't tell him about the flowers, either.

I didn't tell him about Angel's pregnancy.

I did tell him about my interview with Dryden. When Martin realized Dryden had come alone, he did one of the things that made me love him; he didn't say one word about his foresight in insisting Angel be present. But I could hear the difference in his voice as we talked; there was the steel there, the hardness and the edge, that I seldom heard. Maybe that was how he was at work all day, and didn't bring it home; or maybe only danger brought it out, some perceived threat to him and those people or things he held dear.

And you couldn't accuse him of paranoia, of being too cautious; not with the things I heard on the news every day, not with the horrors he'd seen in Vietnam and Central America. It would be insane egocentrism for me to believe none of these horrors could happen to me.

From far away in Chicago, a city I'd never visited, Martin told me to use my common sense, and for God's sake to remember to set the security system.

Chapter Four

Madeleine had jumped on the bed in the middle of the night. She was there, curled in a large golden ball, when I woke up. Madeleine was an older cat now; she'd been at least six when I'd inherited her, and Jane Engle, her first owner, had now been dead for about three years. Madeleine still managed to catch the occasional mouse or bird, but she sometimes missed her jumps, and her facial fur seemed whiter to me. The vet gave her high marks on her annual checkups, and since everyone at his office would have loved to find an excuse to put Madeleine to sleep, I had to accept his verdict.

Now she purred in a rusty way as I scratched behind her ears. Martin hated Madeleine getting on the bed, so she only got to stay there when he was gone; I vacuumed or washed the bedspread before he came home. As my fingers tickled lower on her neck, they encountered something unfamiliar.

I sat up and really looked at Madeleine for the first time. In addition to her brown leather collar to which were attached her rabies disc and her name-and-address tag, something else had been tied around the cat's neck. It was a ribbon, a fresh-looking pink satin ribbon, tied in a precise, perky bow.

I tried to come up with a reasonable explanation for the bow. It was ludicrous that something as pretty as a pink bow could frighten me.

I looked at the clock. The Youngbloods would be up. I punched in their number on the bed-table phone.

'Yep,' said Shelby flatly.

'I'm sorry to call you this early in the morning. But unless you or Angel did this, and frankly I can't see how or why you would, someone caught Madeleine and got her to hold still while he tied a ribbon around her neck.'

'Run that by again.'

'A man or woman. Got hold of Madeleine the cat. And tied a pink ribbon. Around Madeleine's neck.'

'Why the hell would anyone do that? That cat would as soon dismember you as look at you.'

'Did Angel tell you about the flowers?'

'No.'

Then I remembered they'd had more important things to talk about the night before.

'Someone ordered flowers delivered to this address yesterday. The card was unsigned.' I told Shelby what the card had said. 'Either your wife or I have an unknown admirer. This is unsettling.'

'I'll be over there soon.'

'To do what? Look at the ribbon? What good would that do?'

Shelby was silent for a minute.

'I'll take the cat to the vet this morning,' he said. 'He needs to draw some blood to find out if she was drugged. And I do want a look at the ribbon. We need to keep it, in case we have to call the police.'

'Okay. I'll cut it off with scissors.'

'Then I'll come to get her in about ten minutes.'

Very casually, so as not to alert Madeleine, I got my fingernail scissors from my vanity table. I began scratching her gently behind the ears again, and she stretched her neck and purred. Then I scratched her forehead, so she'd shut her eyes. Gently, gently, I slid the thin blade of the scissors under the pink band, and just as gently I closed the blades together. Of course, the little snick of the scissors and the feeling of release brought Madeleine's head up with a snap and she bit the hell out of me. I'd expected it; Madeleine had never been a cat who'd known tolerance or temperance, and most often she was a sorry pet indeed.

After I'd sworn a little and put antiseptic on my wound, I wrapped my robe around me and retrieved the cat carrier from its storage in a downstairs closet. Right on time, Shelby knocked on the kitchen door.

I punched in the code to deactivate the alarm and let Shelby in.

Shelby, so tall and pockmarked and grim, can be intimidating. I had come to be at ease with Angel, but Shelby still made me a little anxious.

This morning was different.

'Roe, you got time to talk?' he asked quietly.

I glanced at the clock. I didn't have to be at the library for an hour.

'Sure,' I said. 'Want some coffee?'

He shook his head. 'Roe,' he said directly while I poured a cup of my own, 'have you ever seen anyone out here when I was gone?'

I set my coffee down with a thunk, walked over to Shelby Youngblood, and slapped the tar out of him. I was so mad I couldn't talk for a second.

'Don't you ever ever imply that your wife has been unfaithful to you!' I told him. 'If you had been there in that doctor's office yesterday and seen how upset she was, if you had seen how scared she was you wouldn't believe her, you would *never* say a stupid thing like that.'

And then I realized Shelby wasn't the only one saying and doing stupid things. I had just slapped someone who could snap my neck quicker than I could picture him doing it.

'So you believe what this doctor says?' Shelby asked in a controlled, reasonable voice.

'Sure I do. You know Angel. You and she are just like male and female halves of the same thing.'

'But that female half is pregnant and that male half had a vasectomy.'

'So go get tested,' I challenged him. 'Would you rather go' – and here I was stuck for a moment over how to put it – 'put a specimen in a jar at the doctor's, or would you rather believe your wife cheated on you?'

'Put that way . . .' he said, and to my amazement he hugged me.

It was then that I learned a lesson about the vagaries of chemistry. I loved Martin, and Shelby loved Angel. But for a moment, something crackled in my quiet morning kitchen, and I was very conscious that my breasts were not tucked in a bra. I looked up at Shelby and saw his eyes darken, before the current of electricity reversed and we flew apart.

If we didn't acknowledge it, it would be even worse.

'We'd better not do that again,' I said weakly, and found I needed to clear my throat. I turned away and took a swallow of coffee.

Shelby was silent. I peeked at him and saw he was still in the same spot, his arms still out a little. 'Shelby?' I said anxiously.

He jumped. 'Right,' he said, doing a little swallowing of his own. 'Martin would kill you and Angel would sure kill me, and we'd deserve it.'

I drew my cloak of niceness back around me. I had never wanted to be one of those people I'd secretly scorned, people who could not keep their promises.

'We'd better hurry,' I said briskly. 'I've got to get to work and you know how long it can take to catch Madeleine.'

The decoration of Madeleine proved to be a strange start to a strange day. Every staff member at the library had gotten out of bed on the wrong side, even Sam Clerrick. As Sam hopped all over Lillian Schmidt for speaking sharply to a patron the day before – we could hear his voice in his office as we put our things away in the lockers – I raised my eyebrows significantly at Perry Allison. He rolled his eyes in the direction of the office, in a what-are-you-gonna-do gesture.

Perry, the only child of Sally Allison, had worked at the library before, about three years ago. Overwhelming emotional problems and some substance abuse had put him in a hospital and then an outpatient home in Atlanta, where he'd flourished. After long thought and much negotiation, Sam had agreed to rehire Perry on a provisional basis.

Perry had terrified me before, but now I tended to think his time in the hospital and in the home had been time well spent. Perry, who was my age, seemed to be on an even keel and well in control of himself. Perry had dark hair, which he wore in a fashionable brush cut on top and rather longer on the sides and back. He had brown eyes, like his mother, and they were magnified by the aviator-style wire-rims he affected. Though he was weedy in build, Perry always looked good in the starched shirts and bright silk ties he regarded as his work uniform.

As we both shut our lockers and tried not to listen too obviously to Sam's high voice, I realized that I'd accepted Perry with few reservations. At first it'd been hard, working with someone I used to be frightened of; I'd been tense every day. Now, I almost took him for granted.

'Who'd Lillian offend?' I whispered.

'Cile Vernon. You didn't hear?'

I shook my head, pouring myself a cup of coffee from the staff pot. It had been Lillian's morning to make it, and whatever her other faults, she made good coffee.

'Cile wanted to check out one of Anne Rice's witch books, and Lillian told her she wouldn't like them, they were full of witchcraft and sex, and Cile said she was sixty-two, she ought to be able to read whatever the hell she wanted.'

'She did not!'

'Yep, she did. And then she marched into Sam's office and said for a librarian to comment on what a reader checked out was tantamount to censorship.'

'Sam waited all this time to talk to Lillian about it?'

'He had to go yesterday afternoon, after you got off work. He and Marva went to help Bess Burns pick out Jack's coffin.'

'The kids haven't gotten in yet?'

'They'd just gotten in, they were wiped out. I hear they're furious someone killed Jack, but not exactly devastated with grief that he's gone. I hear he'd been drinking a lot.'

I thought about the mooshy feelings I'd been having over Angel's pregnancy, and I realized I was seeing the flip side of the coin. Children and parents didn't always have close and loving relationships. Like marriages, the pairing of parents and offspring sometimes didn't work out.

As I went to my desk in the children's area, I reminded myself forcefully that bearing a healthy child didn't mean you lived happily ever after.

Then I saw my aide Beverly, remembered this was the morning we worked together, and felt my day take another downturn. Fixing a pleasant smile on my face, I sat at my desk.

Beverly was shelving books and muttering to herself. This was one of Beverly's most irritating habits, especially since I was almost sure she was saying unflattering things about me just low enough for me to miss. Despite my mental recital of her good qualities only the day before, I felt my heart sink at the prospect of trying to deal with the woman. That chip on her shoulder was the size of Stone Mountain, and everything you asked of her, everything you said or did, had to be filtered through Beverly's resentment.

Feeling the familiar twinges of guilt, I recited my comforting mantra to myself: I was as glad to see black library patrons as white, I thought black kids were as cute as white kids, I worked as well with black librarians as white. Except Beverly Rillington.

Still, there were days when Beverly would just do her work and I'd just do mine, and I'd hoped fervently this would be one of those days.

But it wasn't.

I could hear the book cart slamming into corners as she rolled it along from shelf to shelf. The muttering faded and grew stronger as she turned from the cart to the shelf, then back to the cart. I couldn't quite make it out, of course, but I had a stronger-than-ever feeling it had to do with my faults.

I sighed and unlocked the desk to get out my scheduling notebook. I had two telephone message slips waiting on the blotter, and they both contained requests for special storytelling times for a couple of daycare centers. WeeOnes had asked for the time I'd slotted for another group; I searched the appointment book and made a note of two different times it would be convenient for them to come. Kid Kare Korner wanted to come in the afternoon; that would be feasible only if I stayed late or if Beverly were willing to do the story hour.

I sighed again. Getting to be a habit.

It would almost be better to work late without getting paid for it than to ask Beverly to do a story time. She violently resented being asked to do it, but she was offended if you didn't ask. In a cowardly way, I put off making a decision, and began to work on the list of suggested books one of the kindergarten teachers had asked me to prepare. I'd gone over the list compiled by the previous children's librarian and taken a dislike to a few of the books she routinely recommended, so when a new list had become necessary I'd found myself combing the shelves. I had a pile on the table in front of me I'd been reading, and I picked up the top one to whittle down my stack still further.

'Some of us have to come in here and really *work*, not just sit at a damn desk,' the muttering resumed, suddenly quite clear.

I clenched my hands. I read another page. If the children's area had been a real room, instead of a corner of the ground floor, I would have shut the door and had a discussion with Beverly. As it was, I could just hope to ignore her until I could talk to her away from the patrons. There weren't many, but there were some; I saw Arthur Smith waiting impatiently at the checkout desk while Lillian put a pile of children's videos into a bag, and Sally had come in and was talking to Perry in a hushed tone by the water fountain. A youngish man I didn't know was browsing through the new books shelved close to the entrance, and it occurred to me that he'd been there an awfully long time.

To my surprise, Angel came in the double front doors, dressed quietly in blue jeans and a striped T-shirt. She was carrying a shopping bag from Marcus Hatfield and a gift-wrapped box. I didn't recall Angel ever coming all the way inside the library before, and she was looking around now curiously, her head turning smoothly from side to side like a large cat surveying a new territory.

She spied me and came toward me just as the volcano that was Beverly Rillington erupted.

'Does just one of us work here?' Beverly asked venomously, approaching me from the left side.

'What?' I could not believe I was hearing her correctly, and her stance was even more threatening. Beverly was too close, her hands clenched, leaning forward, aggression in every line of her body. Beverly had never been pleasant, but she was obviously under a stress so extreme she had lost all judgment.

I was afraid that if I stood up Beverly would actually hit me, so I stayed in my chair at the low desk with the open book in one hand. Angel, who was approaching Beverly from the side, had quietly put down the bag and box. I suddenly knew I couldn't bear it if Angel defended me here in the library, my own stomping ground.

'Beverly,' I said very quietly, aware that Perry and Sally had looked over curiously. Well, just about everyone was looking over. 'Beverly, you are mad at me, but let's not work it out here. We can go in the staff room or Sam's office.'

'All you have to do is do your damn job,' Beverly hissed. 'You're sitting on your butt doing nothing, I'm doing all the work.'

There's very little point carrying on a conversation with someone who is absolutely convinced you are wrong and bad. Instead of thinking of strategies I found myself speculating, not for the first time, on Beverly's mental health. But I had to defuse the situation somehow; Angel's face had gone blank and she was concentrating on Beverly as a target. If Beverly took one step closer to me, Angel would hit her. And then where would we be?

'Maybe you're right,' I said. 'Maybe you've been doing too much of the work and I haven't been pulling my share. Why don't we talk to Sam about it?'

'He'll just side with you,' Beverly said, but there wasn't quite as much repressed fury in her voice as before.

'I'll call him right now,' I said, and lifted the phone and punched in the correct numbers.

'Sam,' I said briskly when he picked up the receiver, 'Beverly and I are having some problems working together. Beverly feels she's carrying too heavy a load.'

'She does,' Sam said thoughtfully. I heard his chair creak as he leaned back. 'It has been more work for her, not having a full-time librarian in that section.'

'We'd better make an appointment to meet with you and discuss it,' I said very evenly. 'In *your office.*'

'Roe, do you have a situation out there?'

'As soon as possible,' I said, so calmly I could have been discussing spraying the roses for aphids.

'Right. I gotcha. Okay, then, one o'clock today when you get off.'

'That's fine. I'll tell her.'

'We're to meet in his office at one o'clock,' I told Beverly, putting the phone down very gently. To my relief, her posture was less aggressive. Sally had gone back to talking to her son, but Perry's eyes remained on us watchfully. Arthur was browsing through the new books, though he'd completed checking out the videos. A couple of other patrons who had tried to listen without showing overt attention, courteous Southerners that they were, went back to their activities with some relief.

Beverly turned to resume work, I thought, and spotted Angel. 'Whatchu lookin' at?' Beverly snarled, in an exaggerated street drawl. The two women stared at each other for a long minute. But even Beverly had to concede defeat against Angel, and with a 'Humph!' to show contempt and save face, Beverly returned to her book cart.

I bent back over the book on my desk and put my hands down in my lap to hide their shaking. Tears stung my eyes. Things happening in public were so much worse than things happening in private, and if anything had happened in the library . . . if it had come to blows between Angel and Beverly . . . in the *library!*

Oh, I just hated for people to see me cry. And of course there weren't any Kleenex in my desk drawer. A crying child had used the last one two days ago and I'd forgotten to restock. Hellfire and damnation.

A hand appeared under my nose, a white cotton handkerchief in it. The hand dropped the handkerchief on the desk, and I swooped it up gratefully and applied it to my dripping eyes and nose.

'Thanks, Arthur,' I said in the clogged voice that is one of the more attractive features of crying.

'Don't mention it,' he said. 'How'd you know it was me?'

'I remember your hands,' I said without thinking.

I looked up in horror when I realized what I'd said, and saw that Arthur's face was slowly flushing red, as it always had when he . . . well, when we had personal moments.

If today got any better, I'd just spend tomorrow locked in the attic of my house. It'd be a safer place.

Angel was standing at a discreet distance, her eyes on Beverly, who had gone back to shelving books. At the front desk, Lillian was now eyeing Arthur and me with avid curiosity. Sally was gone, and Perry was watering the large, ugly potted plant (I am not an indoor plant person) that flanked the double main doors.

Arthur slowly returned to his normal coloring, said 'Good-bye' in a rough voice, and left. The water in the plant overflowed into the large dish the pot sits in. Lillian bent down to get a book from below the counter to hand to the young man, and Angel handed me the gift-wrapped package.

It was as if someone had changed channels on a television. Suddenly, everything was back to normal. The Beverly incident might not have happened.

'It's for you, for taking me to the doctor yesterday. And I don't know what you said to Shelby, but suddenly he seems okay about this. Who's the bitch over there?'

'Thanks for the gift. Shelby loves you. Beverly Rillington.'

'What's her problem?'

'I'll tell you later,' I said quietly, hoping Beverly wasn't listening. 'Can I open my present now?' I tried to scrape up a smile that would pass for normal.

'Sure,' Angel said. 'Guess what I've got in my shopping bag.'

Angel was being a will-o'-the-wisp today. Generally, I'd found

Angel to be a very thorough, slow worker, unless you were in her professional field, martial arts and protection services. Then she was quick and lethal.

Now, this quick, lethal woman had bought me a golden brown silk blouse that I thought was perfectly lovely.

I told her so.

'It looked like something you would wear,' she said shyly. 'Is that the right size?'

'Yes,' I said happily. 'Thanks a lot, Angel. I hope you bought yourself something?'

Angel looked proudly embarrassed. From her Marcus Hatfield bag she pulled a maternity T-shirt in white and blue, a white maternity blouse, and a black jumper.

'Oh, they're pretty. Are pants going to be a problem?'

'Sure are,' she said, perching on the edge of my desk and refolding her purchases. 'I'm too tall for all the pants and about four fifths of the dresses I tried on. This jumper'll have to do.'

'You need a dress soon?' I asked. I'd never known Angel to wear a dress.

'Yes. The funeral,' she explained. 'Jack Burns. You know?' And she made a graphic tumbling motion with her long thin hand, culminating in a splat on the surface of my desk.

'When is it?'

'Within a week. They'll have the body back by then.'

'And you're going?'

'I feel like I ought to, somehow,' Angel said. 'I knew him, too. You know, besides the ticket thing.'

I tried not to stare. 'No. I didn't know that.'

'He had started coming to the Athletic Club in the evenings, getting on the treadmill. He knew I lived out by you.'

'He talked about me?'

'Yeah,' she said casually, slipping her hand through the plastic grips of the shopping bag. 'He had a bee in his bonnet about you, Roe. Well, see ya later.' And she strode out, golden and tall and lean, and for the first time since I'd met her, radiantly happy.

Chapter Five

When I came in to work the next morning, I was not feeling exactly cheerful. The discussion with Sam the day before had gone about as I'd expected it to go, Beverly stoutly denying she was difficult to work with, accusing me of many things, all but saying that had she had my education she would now have my job. That may have been true, but it was not the issue we were there to discuss. Even if I'd agreed with that assumption, it wouldn't have changed a thing.

After an upsetting forty-five minutes, during which nothing had been settled and Sam's hair had turned a little grayer right before my eyes, I'd gone to pick up Madeleine at the vet. They'd gotten the blood sample and sent it to a lab, Dr Jamerson had told me with determined cheerfulness, and he expected to get a reply from the lab in a few days, maybe a week. I'd loaded Madeleine in my car with the strong feeling that the vet and his staff wouldn't have minded a bit if the hypothetical drugger had used something stronger and more lethal, or perhaps tied that bow a little tighter.

Somehow I'd expected Dr Jamerson to have the answer ready right then – had Madeleine been drugged or had she not? – and not knowing had thrown me even further off course. As Madeleine yowled on the way home, I had found myself thinking of getting a dog, a medium-sized stupid one who was everyone's friend. A mutt with brown rough hair and a black muzzle . . . but Jane Engle, who'd left me Madeleine and a heck of a lot of money, had somehow astral-projected her strongly disapproving face right into my consciousness.

So I trudged into the library's back door feeling dispirited. At least Angel had been out running this morning as I was driving in to town. She'd grinned and waved at me. A smiling Angel – and one with a bulging abdomen – was something I would have to get used to. I smoothed my own oversized orange T-shirt over my stomach; I was wearing orange leggings, too, and there was a big gold sun on the front of my tee. I was hoping the children would think it a cheerful outfit. I'd pulled my hair back with an orange-and-gold barrette, and I was wearing my gold-framed glasses. Just a blaze of color, that was me.

'Who was that woman who came in to see you yesterday?' Perry asked, as I stowed my purse in my locker. He was using the microwave to make hot chocolate, which he drank regardless of the outside temperature; he had quite a sweet tooth, though by his leanness you wouldn't have guessed it.

Here I was, I thought wryly, glowing all over the place, and as usual, I was being asked about . . . my bodyguard.

'Angel Youngblood.'

'She's not local.'

'No. She's from Florida.'

'Married?'

Well, well, well. 'Very,' I said firmly. 'And a black belt in karate, as is her husband.'

Perry didn't seem dismayed by this news. 'She's just stunning,' he said. 'I could tell by the way she walks that she's an athlete. And her coloring is so unusual.'

'Yep, she's gold,' I answered, burrowing in my locker for a tube of breath mints. I'd had this conversation with many men (and some women) about Angel. 'I thought you were pretty tight with Jenny Tankersley?'

'Oh, we're dating,' Perry said casually, though his mother Sally had told me they were all but engaged.

Jenny wouldn't have been pleased to hear Perry dismiss her so cavalierly, from what I'd heard of her. She'd been married for a few years to a man who ran his own crop-dusting service, and when Jack Tankersley had made a fatal mistake regarding plane altitude one summer, Jenny had ended up selling the business and doing very well for herself. She'd stayed on as general dogsbody for the three pilots who'd bought it, doing every task from answering the phone to ordering supplies to making out the cheques, and occasionally she flew herself, as she had with her husband.

Perry seemed drawn to strong women.

'Your friend Angel must be the woman Paul was talking about last night,' Perry said, stirring his Swiss Miss with a plastic spoon. I was standing awkwardly, my weight on the foot closest to the door, waiting to terminate this conversation so I could get to my area, though I was dreading seeing Beverly. I had a kindergarten class coming in fifteen minutes, and I'd left a note requesting yesterday's volunteer to cut out twenty-two spring flowers, one for each child to write his or her name on, to stick to the ends of the bookshelves. Hopefully, each child would bring a parent into the library to see the flower, and the child and the parent would both check out books. I had to get out the yellow stickum, and I had to count the flowers . . .

'You had supper with your mom's ex?' I said with some surprise.

'Paul and I have always gotten along. He's been more like a father than an uncle to me. Especially since I've only seen Dad a few times in my whole life,' Perry added with understandable bitterness.

The fact that Sally's latest ex, Paul Allison, was the brother of Sally's first ex, Perry's father Steve, made the situation a little complicated emotionally. I was glad there wasn't a third Allison brother, and I was willing to bet Sally was too.

'Jenny's giving flying lessons now,' Perry said, determined to chat. 'I'm taking, and so is Paul, and your friend Arthur Smith . . .'

'That's great, Perry, and I want to hear more about it later,' I said insincerely. 'I've got to get to work now, I've got a group coming in.'

But even as I banished visions of the Lawrenceton police force on air patrol, focusing instead on visions of little kids who were going to want some individual recognition in about ten minutes, Sam came out of his office and strode over to us looking very worried. Sam is not very good with people; he is a great manager of things, but not a great personnel guy. He's become aware of that in the past few years, and whenever he has to say anything that is going to upset someone, he stews over it.

That's why I didn't expect anything awful; he was probably going to tell me the board had decided to hire a full-time children's librarian and my job was terminated. I had a moment to think of this before he put his hand on my arm and said, 'In view of our conference yesterday, I don't know how you're going to take this, but Beverly Rillington was so badly beaten last night they don't know if she'll live.'

'What? Why?' I asked.

'Sit down, Roe, you're white as a sheet,' Sam advised. He pulled out one of the chairs that had been tucked under the round table.

Perry sat down right by me, and I noticed he was on the pale side, too.

'Beverly's mother Selena was hit by a drunk driver a month ago,' Sam said. 'She's still in a coma at the hospital. Beverly goes to see her every night. When Beverly got out of her car at her house after visiting her mother, someone jumped on her from behind and hit her with a piece of pipe. More than once.'

'Oh my God,' I said. I shook my head. What a dreadful thing. 'Sam, did you know about her mother?' Beverly hadn't breathed a word to me, and I suddenly realized the pressure Beverly had been under. Had pride kept her silent?

'She didn't tell anyone here,' Sam said, shaking his head.

'It was in the paper,' Perry volunteered. 'The wreck, that is. But I didn't realize the injured woman was Beverly's mom.'

'So . . . is Beverly . . . how bad is it?' I asked.

'Severe head wounds,' Sam answered succinctly. 'Listen, I've got to tell the others, and send a flower arrangement to the hospital; don't you have a group coming in this morning, Roe?'

I glanced at my watch and shot out of the chair.

Five minutes later, I met the kindergarten class at the door with a shaky smile, and hoped they wouldn't notice my hands were trembling as I passed each of them a bright construction paper flower.

After they'd left, I had a little time to think between helping patrons. I wondered if someone had it in for Beverly's family. Had her mother's accident really been an accident? Or was the attack on Beverly totally unrelated, a kid on some kind of high taking the easiest money available?

A person would definitely have to be chemically altered to have the nerve to tackle Beverly, who was physically as well as mentally formidable. As I sat with my hands folded in my lap at my little desk, staring blankly at the shelves of books that walled me in, I wished Beverly and I hadn't had our fracas the day before – and when I thought twice about it, I wished even more it hadn't been witnessed by so many people.

Sure enough, when I was called to the phone, Arthur Smith was on the other end, at the police station. The Rillingtons' house was in the city limits, so the city police were handling the investigation into the attack on Beverly.

'Roe, I wonder if I could talk to you after you get off work, about that incident in the library yesterday,' Arthur said. He had always been blunt. Once upon a time, I'd found that directness very exciting.

'Okay,' I said with a detectable lack of enthusiasm.

'Could you come by the station this afternoon, say around two o'clock?'

'I guess so. Why the station?'

'It'll just be more convenient,' he said.

I liked this less and less. But it seemed paranoid to wonder if I needed a lawyer. Why was Arthur calling me, anyway? He was a robbery detective. Lynn Liggett Smith, his wife, was the only homicide detective on the Lawrenceton force, so other detectives were detailed to her sometimes, but why Arthur?

I began to wonder if I shouldn't call Martin out of his seminar in Chicago and ask his advice. Nah. I'd talk to him tonight. Then I wondered if I should call my mother, and it didn't seem like such a bad idea to tell her where I was going. Naturally, since Mother owns a prosperous realty business, the line was busy. So I figured I'd just stop by on my way to the police station.

Mother's office, established in an old house and redecorated in calm, elegant colors, always made me feel inadequate. I'd hoped once to get interested in real estate, had even started studying for my license, but at last I'd had to admit that my only interest in real estate was in buying my own. When terms like 'equity' and 'Fannie Mae' and 'assumable mortgage' began to be bandied about, my brain glazed over. But when I watched the controlled and purposeful bustle on good days at Select Realty, I felt a pang of regret.

Mother's terrifyingly perfect receptionist, Patty Cloud, had graduated to office manager and then to Realtor. Her understudy, Debbie Lincoln, now controlled the desk in the reception area. Debbie had done some evolving of her own, from a rather slow, silent girl with cornrowed hair and baby fat to a slim, streamlined, fashionable babe who'd become the office computer expert. In the process, Debbie had gained a lot of artifice, and shed some of her natural charm. She'd also acquired confidence and lost her diffidence around older people.

As I entered, she gave me an 'I see you but I'm in the middle of this' smile and waggle of magenta fingernails, the phone clamped between ear and shoulder, her fingers busy separating computer sheets, collating and stapling them.

'Uh-huh. Yes, Mrs Kaplan, she'll be there at three. No, ma'am, you don't need to do anything special. She'll just look over the house and tell you what she'd recommend you ask for it . . . no, ma'am, that doesn't obligate . . . no, ma'am, you can call in as many as you like, but we hope you'll list your house with us . . . right, three o'clock.' Debbie blew a breath out after she'd hung up.

'Difficult?' I asked.

'Girl, you know it,' Debbie said, shaking her head. 'I half hope that woman doesn't decide to list with us. Dealing with her is almost more trouble than it's worth. Your mom is showing a house now, so if you wanted to see her, you may have quite a wait.'

'Heck,' I said. I wondered whether I should leave a note. 'Debbie, do you know Beverly Rillington?' I asked out of the blue.

'Oh, isn't that terrible, what happened to her?' Debbie stapled the last batch of papers together and tossed the result into Eileen Norris's basket, which was half full of phone message slips already. Debbie followed my glance. 'Eileen can't get used to coming out here every time she comes back in the building,' Debbie said. 'So her stuff kind of piles up. I don't really know Beverly that well, she goes to a different church,' she added. 'But Beverly has always been a real tough individual, a real loner. She had a baby, you know, when she was just fourteen . . . and then, when that baby was about a year old, it choked on a marble or something and died. Beverly hasn't had it easy.'

I tried to imagine being pregnant at fourteen. I tried to imagine my baby dying.

I found I didn't want to imagine that.

'I guess I'll just leave Mother a note,' I told her, and started down the hall to Mother's office. It was the biggest one, of course, and Mother had decorated it in cool, elegant gray, with a slash of deep red here and there for eye relief. Her desk was absolutely orderly, though covered with the paperwork on various projects, and I knew the notepads would be in the top right drawer – and they were – and that all Mother's pencils would be sharp . . . and that I would snap off the point of the first one since it was so sharp and I pressed so hard. Having gone through that little ritual, all I had to do was compose a message to let her know I was going to be at the police station at a detective's request, without propelling her out the office door with her flags flying.

Maybe such a composition wasn't possible, I decided after sitting for several blank seconds with the (now blunt) pencil actually resting on the paper.

After a false start or two, I settled on: 'Mom, I'm going to the police station to tell them about working with Beverly Rillington at the library. She got hurt last night. Call me at home at four o'clock. Love, Roe.'

That should do it. I knew if I wasn't at home at four she'd storm the bastions and get me released.

The car by which I parked at the police station/small claims court/county sheriff's office/jail (known locally as 'Spacolec' for *S*perling *C*ounty *L*aw *E*nforcement *C*omplex) seemed very familiar, and after a second I recognized Angel's car, the one Jack Burns had ticketed. Then I recalled Angel telling me she was going to the funeral because they'd worked out together; the two stories seemed mutually exclusive.

I mulled it over for a minute as I trudged through the hot parking lot to the glass double doors leading into Spacolec.

It was still making no sense when I saw Arthur Smith waiting for me right in front of the wall-to-wall admissions desk. Arthur had changed little in the three years he'd been married to Lynn. Marriage had not put a gut on him or lined his face; fatherhood hadn't grayed his tightly curled hair, though it was such a pale blond that the gray, when it did appear, would be enviably hard to detect.

Perhaps he'd changed in the way he held himself, his basic attitude; he seemed tougher, angrier, more impatient, and that was so apparent that I wondered I hadn't noticed it before.

Arthur, who'd been chatting with the duty officer, turned at the hissing sound of the pneumatic doors; He looked at me, and his face changed.

I felt acutely uncomfortable. I was unused to being the object of unrequited desire. Now, Angel (whom I now saw coming toward me out of the set of swinging wooden doors to the left of the reception desk) must have encountered panting men from adolescence onward. I would have to ask her how it made her feel. Right now she looked washed out, and her stride did not have its usual assurance.

'Are you okay?' I asked anxiously.

She nodded, but not as if she meant it. 'I'm just going to go home and lie down,' she said. 'I don't think I've ever been this tired in my life. And I'm hungry. Really, really hungry.'

'Need help?'

'Nah. Shelby'll be home in an hour.' She hadn't spoken to Arthur directly, but her next words were aimed at him. 'If you're not home by then, I'll call Bubba.'

Bubba Sewell was my lawyer.

'See you later,' I said, and she was out the glass doors and into the parking lot. I watched her reach her car, unlock it, stretch her arms up and rotate her shoulders to relax, each movement economical and controlled despite her weariness.

'Come this way, Roe,' Arthur said, snapping me back to the unwelcome present. He was holding open the wooden doors, nodding at the woman in uniform on duty at the desk behind bullet-proof glass, gesturing me forward. As I went through the doors, he put his hand on my back to steer me, a controlling gesture I particularly dislike. I don't much care for being touched casually. I stiffened a little, but put up with it.

When I realized I was only tolerating his touching me because he had once been my lover, I stepped away a little quicker, leaving his hand behind, and his arm dropped to his side.

Arthur waved a hand at his own little cubicle to usher me in. He indicated the only other chair besides the one behind the desk, and murmured something about being back in a minute. Then he vanished, leaving me nothing to do but examine his 'office'. It was a bit like being at a car dealership where each salesman has to usher you into a little area partitioned off at neck level, and there present you with pages of scrawled figures. I could tell Arthur worked there; there was a picture of little Lorna, though none of Lynn. But there wasn't clutter, there wasn't even much office material on the desk: no Rolodex, no blotter, no stapler. There were stacked in and out trays, and a chipped Christmas coffee mug holding some pens and pencils. That was it. I'd exhausted the possibilities of Arthur's office.

Then I observed that though the partition walls were made of beige metal and padded with what looked like carpet, each panel contained a Plexiglas window. I could see down the row of similar cubicles. Lynn was two squares away, bent over some paperwork on her desk. She looked up as I was still gazing curiously in her direction. She gave me an unreadable stare and then looked down at her desk pointedly.

From being mildly uneasy at being here, I escalated instantly into very uncomfortable. Had I been brought here as some ploy in Lynn and Arthur's marital wars?

Arthur reappeared just as I was thinking of leaving. He was holding two unmatched mugs of coffee, one with cream and sugar and one black. He put the black in front of me. 'I remembered that was the way you like it,' he said.

I could read nothing in his tone. I thanked him and tried a sip. It was awful. I put it down carefully.

'Why am I here, Arthur?'

'Because you had a very public quarrel with Beverly Rillington yesterday. Because she was attacked and her purse stolen last night. When I heard Mrs Youngblood had been present during the quarrel, I called her in too. Faron Henske just finished questioning her.'

So that's why a robbery detective was handling the case. They were treating the attack on Beverly as a robbery gone berserk. 'Why couldn't you just ask me about it at my house, or over the phone, or at the library?'

'Because this was the best place,' he said, very male tough policeman.

I raised my eyebrows slightly. I pushed my gold glasses back up on my nose. 'Then ask your questions.'

So we went through the miserable scene at the library again: the rising rage of Beverly, the arrival of Angel, Angel's exchange with Beverly, the gradual defusing of the crisis.

'Did you think Beverly was physically threatening. you?' Arthur asked quietly. He was sitting back in his chair, his gaze locked on me in a way I'd once considered flattering and exciting.

'I had a second of worry.'

'Weren't you glad your bodyguard was there to handle it for you?'

I could feel my eyes fly open even wider, my shoulders stiffen.

Arthur looked pleased to get such a response. 'Did you think we wouldn't figure it out, Roe? Back when the Julius family turned up, we checked out your friends the Youngbloods. Shelby Youngblood and your husband have quite a history together, don't they?'

'Martin and Shelby have been friends since Vietnam.'

'Involved in some murky doings after that, weren't they?'

'What are you getting at, Arthur? You know Martin was out of town last night. Are you implying that one of the Youngbloods attacked Beverly Rillington because she gave me a few bad moments in the library?'

'There are telephones in Chicago.' Arthur had been leaning negligently back in his chair. Now he abandoned the relaxed pose and leaned forward, his hard eyes still fixed on me.

'So you're saying that my husband was so upset that I had a few words with Beverly – in front of many witnesses – that he told the Youngbloods to beat her up.'

'I didn't say that. But it seems pretty coincidental that after a decade of giving people grief, Beverly Rillington gets beaten within an inch of her life just after a quarrel with you and your bodyguard.' He gave the last two words a twist that was distinctly unpleasant. I began to think that Arthur had gone off the deep end of the pool without checking to see if there was any water.

'You're certainly not suggesting that I did it,' I said reasonably, though I felt anything but reasonable. 'I think Beverly has a few inches and pounds on me.'

'No,' Arthur said, never letting up on the stare. 'No, not you. But someone who cares for you.'

I started to say, 'What about someone who cares for Angel?' Because it seemed to me that Angel had been insulted publicly too, and if the theory that the incident in the library had sparked this attack held any water, Angel could be the inspiration for the beating far more feasibly than I. No one ever forgot Angel.

But expressing this would be tantamount to pointing the finger at Shelby, at least in Arthur's present state of mind.

'So. You're sure I didn't hurt Beverly. So – why am I sitting here being questioned if you are telling me you're sure I didn't do it?'

And without pausing to give him a chance to respond, I gathered up my purse and stalked out of Spacolec. My back was tense with expecting him to call me at any moment, but he didn't.

Like most of my grand gestures, this one was ruined by the situation I came upon out in the parking lot. Instead of sliding into my car and speeding away with a spray of gravel, I had to deal with two more angry people.

Angel was standing in front of her car, her face expressionless but her attitude tense. Beside her, talking into a radio, was Detective Paul Allison, who for once looked agitated. On the hood of Angel's car, giving the impression of a spilled bag of garbage, was a battered black imitation-leather purse, gap-mouthed and leaking the miscellany of a woman's life: comb, wallet, Kleenex, crumpled shopping lists, a tube of mints.

I recognized it. It was Beverly's purse, surely the purse that had been stolen from her during the attack the night before.

Chapter Six

'Is this your car?' Paul Allison said sharply, hanging up the radio in its place in his vehicle, a tan Ford, pulled in next to Angel's.

It took me a moment to realize that Paul was speaking to me.

'No,' I said. 'Mine's this one.' I pointed.

I'd known Paul, at least to speak to, for years, and he'd never changed; he was about five ten, slim, with light blue eyes and thin light hair, worn cut short on the sides and combed straight back. Paul was in his midforties. He had a sharp nose and a square jaw, thin lips and a pale complexion. If you were a civilian, you had to know Paul for a while for him even to register; he was that nondescript in appearance.

But from the time I'd dated Arthur, I knew Paul was unpopular among his fellow officers who saw Paul as being secretive, self-righteous, and charmless. Paul didn't drink or smoke, and barely had tolerance for those who did; he didn't hunt, or watch football, or even buy nudie magazines. His brief marriage to Sally had been his only one. Apparently, law enforcement was Paul's life, as it had been for his former boss, Jack Burns.

'I told you it was my car,' Angel said with barely maintained patience.

Since I was keeping a sharp eye on Paul, I could see rage roll over his face like a tidal wave. He was so angry I was surprised to see there wasn't a gun in his hand, that he wasn't ordering Angel down on the ground.

'Paul!' I said sharply.

He blinked and looked at me. I put myself right by Angel. His eyes went from Angel down to me, back up to Angel, with the strangest expression.

Being weighed and found wanting was never a pleasant

experience, even being found wanting by someone you didn't give a flip for. I sighed before I said, 'Could you explain why this purse is here?' It seemed safe to talk now; Paul's face had resumed its normal color and his eyes were focused and sane again.

'I was just about to ask this woman the same thing,' Paul said, in a much calmer voice.

'I'm Angel Youngblbod,' she said, in an equally cool way. 'I found this purse on the hood of my car when I came to get in after coming out of the Law Enforcement Complex, and then the convenience store.' She nodded her head toward the Shop-So-Kwik about thirty feet from the end of the Spacolec parking lot. She had a little bag in her right hand. She waved it.

Paul made a gesture, and in response, Angel opened the bag. Inside was a little package of Tostitos, a Diet Coke, and a giant cookie in its own cellophane wrapper. 'Hungry,' she said by way of explanation.

I had *never* seen Angel eat food like this; tasty junk, but junk.

'So the purse was exactly like this when you returned?' Paul asked. His voice resumed its normal flat, faintly sour tone.

'No, I opened it and poked in it to try to see who it belonged to,' Angel said with perfect logic. 'I looked around the parking lot first to see if I could spot a woman who might have put it here, but when I didn't see anyone, I looked inside. I was just about to open the snap on the wallet when you popped out of your car.'

Paul pulled a pencil out of his shirt pocket, turned the purse over on the hood of the car, and levered out the wallet. He stuck in the end of the pencil to work the snap, and unfolded the wallet with it. It fell open to a driver's license. The picture and the name were that of Beverly Rillington.

I wasn't surprised, since I'd been sure I recognized the purse. But Angel drew in a sharp breath, the equivalent of a scream for those of us who don't count on danger as a way of life.

'Maybe we'd better go in and talk,' Paul said, and I didn't think he was making a suggestion.

'No.' My mother would be arriving with troops if I didn't get home and call her, and there was no sense in making more of this than necessary.

'What?' Paul had a puzzled expression, as if he hadn't quite understood what I meant by 'No.'

'When I drove into the parking lot and stopped by Angel's car, the purse wasn't there. When Angel went by my car, the purse wasn't *there*. And what a senseless thing for either of us to do, put Beverly's purse out. We might as well go on and put the handcuffs on ourselves! Gee, here we are at the Law Enforcement Complex, let's put incriminating evidence on the hood of a car?'

Paul's thin mouth curved in a reluctant smile. It was the first time I'd had a glimpse of what Sally had seen in him.

'Okay, Roe. But if you didn't leave the purse on Mrs Youngblood's car, and Mrs Youngblood didn't, who did? Why?'

Angel looked down at me, and I knew our blank gazes were a match. But Angel could see when a thought reached my brain, and shook her head, a tiny gesture as firm as a hand clapped over my mouth.

'We're not detectives,' I said, looking at Paul. Angel unwrapped the cookie from the bag and started to eat it. Since her mouth was full, she had to shrug.

Though Paul fussed at us some more, he eventually hooked a pencil under the purse strap and carried it into Spacolec. Angel had finished the cookie and opened the Tostitos and the Coke.

'Someone has it in for you,' I observed.

'How do you figure that?' Angel asked around a Tostito.

'The flowers, sent to get you in trouble with your husband. The ribbon around the cat's neck, to let you know you weren't secure. The beating of Beverly Rillington after you had a standoff with her in the library. The placing of the purse on your car.'

'That's the oddest thing,' Angel said. She gave me a look full of significance. And I couldn't read it.

'Hell, it's all odd!' I said, puzzled. 'But you mean, because putting the purse out here was so open? Everything else could be done in the dark or long distance, so to speak.'

Angel looked away and finally nodded.

I had to restrain myself from asking her to explain all this Enigmatic she was giving me. We'd known each other for two years now, been neighbors for that time, and I thought we were as close friends as we could be, given the fact that she was my employee and we had very different characters. I did at least know Angel well enough to be sure that she would tell me what she was thinking when she was good and ready, and not a moment before.

By the look she was giving me, I could tell Angel thought I was being as dense as I thought she was being secretive. Mutually baffled and exasperated, we got in our respective cars and went home, Angel obeying the speed limit meticulously all the way. I followed behind her, driving automatically. My state of mind might best be described as confused.

I couldn't help but remember Arthur's long absence, his return with the coffee. Had Arthur Smith planted that purse on the hood of Angel's car while she was in the market? If he thought discrediting Angel and perhaps by extension her husband and mine would somehow induce me to think more kindly of him, Arthur was not just mistaken, but seriously deranged.

I trailed slowly into the house, just in time to hear the phone ring. I dashed down the hall, past the stairs, to the second door on the right leading to our study/library/television room.

'What now?' my mother asked in her cool voice. But I could hear the mixture of anxiety and exasperation underlying it, the two emotions that seemed to dominate in her dealings with me.

I glanced at the desk clock; of course, it was four on the dot.

'It's okay. I just got in from Spacolec.'

'I think it's outrageous, them asking you to come in to that place. They should have driven out to your home or talked to you in that new wing you gave the library.'

'Mother!' No one was supposed to know I'd given the kickoff donation for the new staff area. 'How'd you find out?'

'I have my ways,' she said calmly, without a trace of humor.

'Well, don't you ever tell anyone else,' I said hotly. If my gift became common knowledge, it would be pretty hard for me to keep working at the library; that wasn't logical, but it was true.

'Did that woman really get hurt badly, Aurora?' My mother was back on track, even if I wasn't.

'Sam told me that she might die.'

'What a terrible thing. And since you had an argument with her the same day, I know what you must be feeling.'

She did, too. It was a milder version of having a fight with your spouse, who subsequently drives off and has a car wreck. That had happened when Mother was still with my father, when I was twelve. He'd left soon after, neck brace and all.

We talked about Beverly Rillington for a little longer, and then my mother asked me which policeman I'd talked to today.

I'd been dreading that question. 'Arthur,' I told her reluctantly.

I swear, I could hear the phone line sizzle. My mother has never forgiven Arthur for dating me and then dumping me to marry Lynn Liggett, who was visibly pregnant at the wedding. (Well, it certainly hadn't been my favorite episode in the Life of Roe either, but I'd weathered it and eventually let it go.) God bless my mother, in some respects she was totally motherlike; anyone who made me suffer was in her black book forever.

'Roe, you stay away from that man,' she said, in her Absolute Last Word voice. 'He has separated from his wife. Last week Patty showed him a townhouse over where you used to live, and he was moving in by himself. You don't want to look as if you're paying him any attention whatsoever.'

'I hope they work it out and get back together,' I said fervently. My suspicion that Arthur had called me in to the station to wave me in Lynn's face was correct. I'd gotten over my initial rush of anger, and now felt simply appalled that Arthur would do something so low. I'd never seen that side of him, and I didn't want to believe it had always been there.

As I microwaved a low-fat dinner I'd gotten at the grocery for just such an evening, I realized I wasn't exactly looking forward to Martin's nightly call. It was going to be hard to explain some of the things that had happened to me today, and harder still (actually impossible) to explain them in a way that didn't make him angry at someone. And it would be futile anger, since he was too far away to act on it. Also, I didn't want the peculiar incident of the ribbon on Madeleine's neck to cause him concern.

But I don't like to lie, and I'm not good at it.

Luckily for me, it was late when he called. He'd gone out to dinner with some other executives, and they'd made an evening of it. Martin is not much of a drinker, since he despises people who lose their control; but I could tell he'd had up to his limit. So he was sleepy and sentimental over the phone, and it was easy to tell him that I'd give him a rundown on the day's happenings when he came home.

That night I tossed and turned, suffering an unusual episode of sleeplessness.

I couldn't track down the source of the anxiety that was keeping me awake.

The security system was on, so I knew no one could break in; but it was gusty and raining outside, and I could hear the wind moaning around the corner of the house. I would doze off, only to jerk awake with the feeling of having just missed something vital, something to which I should have been paying close attention.

Every time I woke up, I thought of something new to worry over, either Angel's pregnancy and its effect on her marriage, or the bizarre episodes of the ribbon and the purse, or the sight of Jack Burns falling, falling . . . and Angel and Shelby would need a bigger place, they could never live in that glorified one-room apartment with a baby . . .

I got up to go to the bathroom, I went downstairs to get a drink of water, I worked a crossword puzzle, I finished the book I'd started in Dr Zelman's office.

At four-thirty, I gave up. I wrapped myself in the dark blue robe Mother had given me for Christmas, slid into my slippers, and went downstairs, officially up for the day. The coffeepot's automatic timer hadn't had a chance to kick in; I switched it to On and heard the comforting hiss of the water starting through the brewing cycle.

Perhaps the paper had come? Morning coffee just didn't seem

right without a newspaper. It was awfully early; I realized I really had no idea how early the Atlanta paper and the Lawrenceton paper landed in our driveway.

Tying the belt of my robe more securely around me, I stepped out onto the front porch. The rain was still coming down lightly, giving the air a sharp cool edge. I reached inside the door for an umbrella and unwisely opened it before I pushed out the screen door. Of course it got wedged in the doorway and I had to do an inordinate amount of pushing, angling, and cursing to get it through.

Going outside at such a strange hour in the mild cool rain was a little adventure. I needed a flashlight, too, but the umbrella incident had made me so grumpy I refused to be sensible. There was a huge strong automatic light in our backyard, but not one in the front; outside the range of the porch light the driveway was in darkness. I followed the stepping-stones leading to the right so I could walk down the driveway. We'd had it paved the year before: at least I wasn't stumbling over gravel, but the asphalt was streaming with rain, and my slippers were getting soaked.

I went to the area where the Atlanta paper usually landed, and sure enough, there it was in a plastic sleeve. Feeling that virtue had been rewarded, I tucked it under my umbrella-holding arm and lifted the skirt of my bathrobe with the other. I turned to go back inside, happily confident that the coffee would be ready and that I had cinnamon rolls in the freezer I could pop into the microwave. The Lawrenceton paper would just have to wait until light.

I was concentrating on watching my feet as I transferred from the driveway to the stepping-stones, but something butted on the edge of my awareness. The light had been behind me as I left the house, but now that I was returning, I could see a few things I hadn't noticed before; and one of the things I could make out was a bush planted where no bush had been the day before.

I paused on the seventh stepping-stone from the front porch. I tilted my head and stared, trying to puzzle out what I was seeing. A large dark heap, right in front of the foundation plantings . . .

my slippers would get thoroughly soaked if I left the stepping-stones to investigate. I shifted my feet, peering with no better luck at the vague and immobile shape, and realized that my slippers were doomed.

I stepped gingerly onto the soggy grass, clutching the paper and umbrella.

Seconds later I'd dropped both.

The dark shape on my lawn was Shelby Youngblood. He was unconscious, lying on his side, wearing a dark raincoat with a hood. He was immobile because someone had hit him on the back of his head. When I pulled the hood away from his face, the hood was filled with blood.

I foolishly wasted seconds trying to arrange my umbrella to shelter the wound. Finally realizing I was acting like a woman with no sense, I tore into the house and hit 911 on the phone in the study. Once I'd explained to the calm voice on the other end what my problem was and where I was, I hung up and punched in Angel's number. For some reason, I feared she was hurt too. But she answered, in the groggy normal voice of someone wakened at four forty-five by the telephone ringing.

'Come outside, now,' I gabbled. 'Shelby's hurt, but I've already called the ambulance.' My eardrum echoed with the sound of her receiver crashing down. I slammed down my own telephone and ran back outside, my heart and lungs in a race to see which could work fastest. But I had pulled open the right-hand drawer on Martin's desk as I dialed Angel, and this time there was a flashlight in my hand.

I crouched by Shelby in the rain, which of course picked this moment to come down in torrents. Though anyone lit up by a flashlight in the dark is not going to look great, it seemed to me that Shelby was an especially bad color. I held the umbrella over him, wondering if there was anything I could do.

Well, I should see if he was still alive.

I slid my hand inside his raincoat, found that Shelby didn't have a shirt on, and lay my hand on his chest. It was moving in and out, how deeply I couldn't gauge; but Shelby was breathing, and at the moment that was all I cared about.

I'd been concentrating on him so hard that I didn't hear Angel coming. Suddenly she was crouching on the other side of her husband. She was barefoot and in a nightgown, with a shirt of Shelby's pulled over her. Her hair hung in a loose tangle around her narrow face.

'Is he breathing?' Her voice was sharp.

'Yes.'

'You called 911?'

'Yes.'

'How long ago?'

'Five minutes,' I guessed. 'They're on this side of town, they'll be here any minute.'

Sure enough, I saw the blinking red lights far down the road toward town. I tried to pray, but the rain was plastering my hair to my skull and dripping down my neck, and Shelby seemed so close to leaving us that all I could do was urge the ambulance forward mentally, hoping that the best team Lawrenceton had to offer was on duty this cool spring night.

I had a flash of sense as the young man and woman were loading Shelby into the back of the ambulance. I dashed into the house, opened the coat closet, and yanked out Martin's lined raincoat. Pounding down the porch steps, I yelled to Angel just as she was about to climb in the ambulance. I could see the flash of annoyance on her face, but she realized she needed more body coverage than she had, and she turned her back to me and held her arms a little out and down, and I slid the coat over her wet arms and nightgown as quickly as I could.

With a scream of the siren the ambulance was off, and I could finally go inside. Everything I had on was soaked through, and though the morning was not really cold, I was chilled to the bone. I stripped right inside the front door so I wouldn't get more water on my wooden floors than I absolutely had to – I could see the splotches left from my previous entrances and exits – and I sprinted upstairs to the shower to let the hot water wash the dirt and rain off. I dressed in record time, turning on the heat lamp in the bathroom to start my hair drying, and I plugged in my usual handheld dryer too; but with a mass of thick hair like mine, it took too long, and I drove to the hospital with damp hair that was curling and waving around my face like streamers of confetti.

I'd taken the time to use my emergency key to the Youngbloods' apartment to grab some clothes for Angel. It felt very strange to be poking through her things, dropping the basic garments into a plastic Wal-Mart bag. I included shoes, a toothbrush, and a hairbrush at the last second.

Angel was sitting in the emergency waiting room at the little Lawrenceton Hospital, her hands folded and her face blank. She didn't recognize me for a moment.

'What have they told you?' I asked.

'Ahhh . . . he's got a concussion, a bad one. He has to stay here for a few days.' Her voice was expressionless, numb.

'He's going to be all right?'

'We'll see when he wakes up.'

'Listen, then, Angel . . . are you hearing me?'

'Yes. I hear you.' She was a pathetic sight. She was as wet as I had been, and she had pulled on Martin's raincoat over her wet clothes, so she was warm enough for the moment; but the damp was sealed inside the coat. Her blond hair hung in rattails down her back, and her feet were bare and streaked with dirt and bits of grass. The passivity of her strong body was so upsetting I had to retreat into briskness.

'I brought some clothes and shoes, and your toothbrush, and your hairbrush. Is Shelby in a room yet?'

'No, he's still in emergency. They brought in a portable X-ray machine, and since I'm pregnant I had to leave. They didn't even want me to put on the heavy apron, they wanted me out.'

'Well. We're going to find out what room they're going to put him in, and you're going to go in there and take a shower, and by then the cafeteria here will be open, and we're going to go in there and eat.'

Angel blinked. She seemed a little more aware.

'That sounds okay,' she said hesitantly. 'But no one will be with him.'

'You don't need to watch him, they're doing it for you. He's going to be okay,' I said soothingly. 'Now, I'm going to find the admissions person, and see about getting all this started.'

The 'admissions person' was glad to see me, since she hadn't been able to get much out of Angel besides Shelby's name and his birthday. I gave the clerk Shelby's insurance program group number, the same as Martin's since they were both covered by Pan-Am Agra's group plan. I gave the clerk an address, next of kin, everything but Social Security number, and I promised her Angel would remember that after breakfast. By dint of being cheerful and persistent, I was able to get Shelby's future room number, and took Angel there, resisting the impulse to ask to see Shelby myself.

After fifteen minutes with Shelby's admissions hygiene kit, a hot shower, and clean clothes, Angel was a new woman, and after we talked our way into the employee cafeteria and she downed a plate of grits and sausage and toast, she was approaching normality.

It was while we were sitting there, Angel with another glass of orange juice and me with my third cup of coffee, that the deputy found us.

He was a young man I didn't know, dressed in a crisp uniform. He seemed concerned and wary, all at the same time. He introduced himself as Jimmy Henske.

'Do you have a relative on the town force?' I asked.

'Yes, ma'am, my uncle Faron. You know Uncle Faron?'

'Yes, I do.' He'd questioned Angel the day before, Arthur had told me. Faron was a good ole boy, with a heavy Southern drawl and an unreconstructed attitude about women on the force and black people having power and money. But Faron was also a courteous and anxious man who had no idea he was biased and would swear on a stack of family Bibles that he was fair to one and all.

Jimmy had the family coloring and build. The Henskes tended to be tall, thin, and reddish, with high-bridged noses and big hands and feet (including the women). Jimmy was trying to pay courteous attention to his conversation with me, but his eyes kept straying to Angel. I sighed, trying to keep it quiet.

'Now, Ms Teagarden, I understand you found Mr Youngblood in your yard?' He'd torn his gaze away from her to begin his questioning.

I told him what had happened, said I hadn't heard any noises in the night (though with the wind and rain it would have been surprising if I had), and explained that my husband was out of town. Jimmy Henske instantly came to attention; if he'd been a bird dog, he would've been pointing his nose. Clearly, he was wondering if Angel had bashed her husband because Shelby was sneaking over to see me. Or perhaps (and his gaze swung my way) I'd done it when he'd tried to make advances to me?

I did my best to disabuse him of those suspicions by telling him that while Martin was gone, Shelby sometimes patrolled the yard, and that I was sure he must have been doing so the night before because of the incident of Madeleine's ribbon.

It was lucky Shelby had taken Madeleine in to Dr Jamerson, I thought as I explained the incident to Deputy Henske, because it was confirmation that we suspected someone had been on my property.

Jimmy didn't know what to make of a prowler sneaking into the yard to tie a ribbon on Madeleine's neck, and to tell the truth, I didn't either; but I was glad to think the solution was his problem rather than mine.

After a confused-looking Jimmy Henske left for Spacolec, his little notebook full of indecipherable squiggles, a nurse came to tell us Shelby was in his room, and conscious.

Angel was on her feet faster than lightning, and I put our trays on the appropriate rack and followed at a slower pace. She needed time alone with Shelby, and I had to call Pan-Am Agra and tell Martin's production head that he would be short a crew leader that day, and for several days following. I took care of that little chore, wondered if I should pick up Shelby's paycheck, and snapped to when an orderly eyed me curiously. I was standing by the pay telephone in the hall, my hand still resting on the receiver, staring blankly at the coin input slot. Lack of sleep was catching up with me as the emergency-produced adrenaline ebbed.

A glance at my watch told me it was all of eight o'clock by then. It had already been a long day.

With a sinking heart, I realized I had to go in to work. With Beverly in the hospital, it was especially important for me to show up. I wondered how she was doing. Well, I was in the place to find out.

I went to the nurses' station and inquired about both Beverly and her mother, Selena. The nurse, a young woman I'd never seen before, told me briefly that both mother and daughter had died in the course of the night.

I sat in the waiting area for a while with a magazine on my lap, hoping no one would talk to me, feeling sick at heart.

When my mind finally began functioning again, I was almost sorry. My thoughts were all unpleasant ones. Could it really be a coincidence that Beverly Rillington, who had threatened Angel publicly, and Angel's husband Shelby had both been admitted to the hospital with head wounds in the same week?

Finally I roused myself to find Shelby's room, and knocked gently on the door. Angel stuck her head out.

'How is he?' I whispered.

'Come in.'

Shelby looked horrible. He was asleep, but Angel told me in a low voice that the doctor had said he must not sleep long at a stretch. He had to be woken up periodically. There was a good reason for this, but my overloaded system didn't absorb it.

'He didn't see whoever did it, Roe, he doesn't remember anything since he ate supper last night. He didn't remember putting on his clothes and his raincoat, or why he thought he ought to go outside . . .'

I stared at Shelby while Angel murmured on and on. She was chatty with relief now that she was reasonably sure Shelby was going to recover.

Shelby's face was stubbly with unshaven beard, a state I'd seen before, but the skin underneath the bristles was a distressing gray. The hair protruding from underneath the bandage was matted with blood and stringy from drying with rainwater on it. There was a huge dark bruise on his right arm, which Angel thought was a defense wound. Shelby had taken a blow on that arm defending his own head, but it hadn't worked a second time. One of his ribs was broken, too, Angel said . . . he'd been kicked when he was down.

I didn't have to look at Angel to know she would kill whoever had done this to Shelby if she could find him.

After a while, Angel ran down. She stood looking at Shelby as if her eyes could glue him to her, as if his life could not escape him if she were there to make sure it stayed.

I was thinking my own thoughts. Why hadn't Shelby heard the attack coming? He'd made his living as a bodyguard for years. He was tough and quick and ruthless. Had the sound of the rain and wind dulled Shelby's senses, so the approach of the trespasser was totally unexpected?

Or had he turned to see someone he knew, someone he did not think of as an enemy?

Chapter Seven

Normally, when Martin returned from a business trip I got to tell him about the kid who threw up on the Berenstain Bears book, or what the plumber had told me when he'd come to repair the hot water heater.

When he walked in the front door late that afternoon, I hardly knew where to begin. As it turned out, Martin had stopped at the Pan-Am Agra plant, so he already knew that Shelby was in the hospital. After his first anxious questions, he settled down to listen with that total concentration that made him such a good executive.

I think Martin was just as shocked by Angel's pregnancy as by Shelby being attacked in our front yard. And when I told him about the ribbon around Madeleine's neck and the deaths of Beverly and Selena Rillington, he had to get up and walk around the kitchen.

It was still raining, and I watched the drops hit the large window by the table where Martin and I usually ate, the window overlooking the side of the garage and the steps up to the apartment, as well as some lovely pink azaleas hidden now by the darkness. The drops might hit at random, but they ran down the glass with monotonous regularity. The rain increased my sense of being stockaded against the danger outside, besieged.

Martin strode through the dining room, out into the living room, back through the archway into the dining room. He circled the table and shot back into the kitchen again, stopping by the window to stare out into the blackness.

'Who sent the flowers?' he asked abruptly, and I glanced into the dining room to see that they were still in their vase on the table. A few blossoms were shriveling, and one or two bits of baby's breath had fallen to the polished surface of the old table.

The delivery of the flowers seemed so long ago I'd forgotten about it completely. Now, when I added it to my list of happenings, Martin gave me a sharp look, one that said effectively, 'All this you didn't tell me over the telephone?'

Martin often reminded me of the Roman officer in the New Testament, the one who told Jesus that when he said 'Go,' people went, and when he said 'Come,' people hopped to it. Now, he was apparently trying to decide what he could do about this situation, and he was angrily seeing that there was nothing he could do.

'Do you think the little hospital here is the best place for Shelby, can he get the best care available? I could have him moved to Atlanta by ambulance.' Martin looked almost happy at this prospect of action.

'I don't believe there's any need of that,' I said gently. 'Besides, the doctors here are very aware that the city hospitals have things the Lawrenceton Hospital doesn't have, and they would have sent him to the city without hesitation if they thought his situation warranted that. Plus, you know,' I said even more gently, 'that's Angel's call, not yours.'

Diverted back to Angel's pregnancy, Martin said what I'd been dreading he'd say.

'I like Angel just as much as you, but don't you think it's stretching belief to have her turn up pregnant when Shelby's had a vasectomy? She worked out with Jack Burns and she's going to his funeral, but she blasted him in public when he gave her a ticket. And she didn't react at all when they turned him over the other day. I don't want to believe anything bad about Angel, but doesn't that all add up?'

'You know, Shelby asked me if I'd seen anyone else out here when he was gone,' I said evenly.

'What'd you tell him?' Martin turned to me, hands thrust in his pockets to keep them still.

'I slapped the tar out of him.' I looked at Martin steadily, blocking my faintly guilty memory of Shelby's embrace from my mind, so he couldn't read it in my face.

Martin looked back at me, eyebrows up in surprise.

'And – what did he do?' Martin asked faintly.

'He believed that he is the father of Angel's child.'

Martin slowly took a deep breath, released it, smiled. 'Okay. So is he going to get rechecked?'

'He'll have to if they don't want any more children,' I said.

'I can't believe old Shelby is going to be a father,' Martin said absently, shaking his head.

I bit my lip and looked down so Martin wouldn't see the tears well into my eyes. He pulled his reading glasses (a recent necessity) out of his shirt pocket suddenly, and went to the wall phone to flip through the tiny Lawrenceton directory.

He punched in numbers and stood waiting, his face in its executive mode: mouth in straight hard line, sharp eyes, impatient stance. I thought it was pretty sexy, providing he dropped the look when he turned to me.

'The room number?' he asked me crisply. I gave it to him, propped my chin on my hand, and watched my husband as he talked to Angel, and then said a few words to Shelby.

'He's still groggy,' Martin informed me when he had hung up the phone. 'But better. Angel said they want to keep him one more day for observation, then he can come home, providing he stays away from work for a few days.' Martin clearly felt better since he'd done something, even if it was only punch numbers on a phone.

I glanced down at my watch, and saw to my surprise that it was nearly eleven o'clock. I'd been up almost the whole night the night before, and gone through a great deal of excitement and anxiety since then. Martin's homecoming had given me a jolt of energy, but suddenly I felt as if I'd run into a wall.

'I have to go up to bed,' I said, and heard the weariness in my voice.

'Of course, honey,' Martin said instantly. 'You haven't had any sleep.' He put his heavy arm around me and we started up the stairs. 'I'll give you your present in the morning,' he murmured.

'Okay.'

'You *are* tired.'

'Won't be this tired in the morning,' I mumbled, I hoped in a promising way. 'I am glad you're home.'

I pulled off the clothes I'd pulled on so hastily so many hours ago and gratefully slipped into a nightgown, realizing that I had no memory of work that day at all, though I'd gone in and (I supposed) functioned more or less normally. I brushed my teeth and washed my face because I am constitutionally unable to go to bed without that little routine, and I was vaguely aware of Martin unpacking as I sank into sleep.

Before I open my eyes in the morning, I try to remember what day it is. There's always that happy moment when it's finally Saturday, and I don't have to go anywhere I don't want to. I think that's one of the reasons I had wanted to go back to work; otherwise every day was Saturday, and that little happiness was gone.

I opened one eye and looked at my bedside clock. It read nine-twenty. Since that was clearly impossible, I closed the eye again and snuggled into my pillow. But the room certainly seemed light, and I could feel the emptiness of the other side of the bed. Reluctantly, I opened both eyes and wriggled closer to the clock. It was still nine-twenty.

I hadn't slept that late in years.

For ten minutes or so, I basked in the novelty of being still in bed at such a late hour. I was too awake to drift back to sleep. From the lack of movement downstairs, I thought Martin was gone. He often went in to work for a few hours on weekends, especially when he'd been out of town; or maybe he'd gone to the Athletic Club to play some racquetball. Going downstairs in a nightgown this late seemed faintly sleazy, so I took my shower first and pulled on my favorite Saturday jeans and a green T-shirt. To atone for my laziness, I carried down a hamper of dirty clothes and started a load of wash before I even poured my coffee. Martin had made a full pot and left it on for me, with a clean cup waiting invitingly beside the pot. He'd also left, squarely in the middle of the table by the window, a package wrapped in white paper and topped with a blue bow.

I drank my first cup of coffee and read the Lawrenceton paper to postpone the pleasure of opening the package. And the paper dampened my happiness some; the attack on Shelby had made the front page, which was not too surprising. But what was surprising was that the incident of the bow on the cat and the body of Jack Burns landing in the yard were included in the story, tying all the different incidents together in a way that left me disturbed.

I'd been sure Jack Burns had been killed because he knew the identity of a local who was being hidden in Lawrenceton under the Witness Protection Program. I couldn't see what that had to do with Angel's unknown admirer. Combining all these incidents, the story implied my house was radiating evil, as though it was an eminently suitable candidate for exorcism. I wasn't surprised to see a stranger's name on the byline: Sally wouldn't have written it that way.

I tried to regain my relaxed mood by reading the Garden Club meeting report, which was usually a hoot. It didn't fail me today. My old friend Mrs Lyndower (Neecy) Dawson had wreaked havoc by proposing that the war memorial outside the courthouse be surrounded by ivy instead of having its planting regularly switched by the club. Reading between the Garden Club correspondent's careful lines, one could surmise that the ensuing debate had created bad blood that might last as much as a year, by which time Neecy could have forgotten she'd made the proposal. Or have gone to her great reward in the Garden in the Sky, as the Garden Club membership might have put it.

A flash of white and orange outside caught my attention, and I saw that Madeleine, to whom I'd given scant attention the past two days, had finally been driven to desperate measures. She was stalking a sparrow foraging in the grass. One thing I admired about cats was their focus; I'd never had a pet as I was growing up, so observing Madeleine had been an education for me (one I sometimes felt I could have done without).

However, when Madeleine bothered to hunt, the process was impressive – the intensity of her concentration, the stealth of her approach, the narrowness of her vision. *Can birds see color?* I wondered.

Whether it was Madeleine's marmalade stripes or her bulk that attracted the bird's attention, this sparrow took off. Madeleine sat up and directed a baleful gaze after the bird, and began to clean her paws in a sulky way. I was recalled to my obligations, and fed her; she did her very best running when she heard me call her for food.

Then I had the pleasure of opening my package. It was heavy, and I wondered how Martin had managed to cope with it on the flight home. I slid off the ribbon and put it aside, and tore off the paper. The box was a plain brown one of thick cardboard, not one of the thin ones that clothes come in.

Not jewelry, not clothes . . . hmmmm.

Books. Seven books by some of my favorite mystery writers. Bookmarks from a Chicago bookstore protruded from each one, and I opened the top book, a Sharyn McCrumb, at the marked page.

Each one was signed. Not only signed, but personalized.

I examined each book happily, looking forward to hours of reading, and tried to think of a special place to keep my gift.

While I was still smiling, the phone rang.

There was silence on the other end of the line after I answered. It wasn't empty silence, like when the other person has realized he didn't mean to call your number after all and has hung up – this was heavy silence, breathing silence. My smile slid off my face and I could feel my scalp crawl.

'Hello?' I said again, hoping against hope someone would speak.

Someone did.

'Are you alone?' asked a man's voice. And the phone went dead.

I tried to slow my breathing, reminded myself that everyone

gets prank or obscene calls from time to time (such is humankind's determination to communicate, on whatever low plane) and I should not particularly be upset by this. But I felt so alone today; Martin wasn't here, and the garage apartment was empty, too.

The phone rang again, and I jumped. I stared at it, wondering whether to answer it or not. As it kept ringing, I crossed the hall to the study and waited for the answering machine to come on. Martin had recorded the message, and hearing his voice made me feel better. When the recording ended and the signal beep came, the voice leaving the message was also reassuring.

'Sally!' I stopped the recording and picked up the phone. 'What are you up to?'

'I wondered if you were free to take a little ride with me,' Sally said. 'I didn't know if that husband of yours was in town or not.'

'He's in town, but not at home right now, so I'm footloose,' I said, relieved at having a reason to leave the house without calling it retreating in fear. 'Where are you going to go?'

'I'm going to drive to that airport where Jack Burns was taking flying lessons, the one where he rented the plane before he took his *final* flying lesson, so to speak. I need an extra person – I have a plan – and since I haven't gotten to talk to you in a coon's age, I thought I'd combine the two goals.'

Put like that, how could I resist?

'Want me to drive in and meet you at the newspaper office?'

'That's where I am now. That'd be great.'

'Okay. Give me a few minutes, I'll be on my way.'

I called the hospital to ask Angel if she needed anything urgently, and she told me that Shelby was much better, but still didn't remember anything about the attack. She sounded a lot better herself. She'd run home the night before to change clothes, and she told me she might come home to take a nap in the afternoon if he continued to improve.

Then I called Martin. If he was at the plant, he wasn't answering his phone. I left a message at the Athletic Club with the intimidatingly streamlined girl who answered the phone, kept the sun-bed appointment schedule, and presided over the check-in book. She sounded quite pleased to have a reason to approach Martin.

I ran upstairs, looked myself over in the mirror, and decided that almost anything was good enough to run an errand with Sally. I brushed my hair quickly, securing it at the nape of my neck with a green band to match my T-shirt, and cleaned my Saturday glasses, huge ones with white-and-purple mottled frames.

Sally made a choking sound when she saw them. 'God Almighty, Roe, where'd you get those? You look like a clown.' She was shoveling papers and fast-food bags out of the passenger's seat of her car.

Talk about the honesty of friends.

'They're my Saturday glasses,' I said with dignity, locking my car and walking over to Sally's even older and more beat-up Toyota. The parking lot that served the newspaper staff was empty except for our cars and a Cadillac in the corner, which I recognized as the property of Macon Turner, owner and editor of the *Lawrenceton Sentinel.*

'Indicating that on Saturdays you are in a whoopee mood? Carefree and fun-loving?' Sally's voice was muffled as she bent back in. She'd opened a garbage bag and was swiftly sorting through the debris. Between the assorted paperwork, grocery bags, and cardboard cartons, I figured Sally had a whole tree in her front seat.

'Sorry about this,' she continued, as she emerged and carried the garbage bag over to the Dumpster. 'I have to do this under duress or not at all, and asking you to ride with me provided the duress.'

Sally was wearing slacks, which she seldom did on weekdays, but her bronze curls and careful makeup were unchanging. Sally hadn't altered much in the years we'd been on-again, off-again friends. She'd had a wonderful but brief episode of gourmet cooking, tried marriage the same way, and now was back to Chick-Kwik, burgers, and the single life, without gaining a pound or wrinkling a crease. The only thing that made Sally look her age (which I estimated to be fifty-one) was her son, Perry.

I watched while Sally went down a mental checklist, giving a tiny nod as she reviewed each point on a list only she could see. Then she slid behind the wheel and said, 'Coming?'

Soon we were flying down the interstate, for Sally believed the speed limit was just a guideline. This belief accounted for Sally's knowing every highway patrolman in the area by his first name. But today, we weren't stopped, and we arrived at the Starry Night Airport having exchanged only a modicum of gossip.

We had left the interstate just five minutes east of Lawrenceton and had taken a state highway north a couple of miles, passing the usual seven million pine trees. Sally turned onto a road that scarcely deserved the name. It had been paved at one time, but that had been long ago. This alleged road terminated at the romantically named Starry Night Airport.

It was evident that Starry Night was a marginal business. Rendered invisible from the highway by a strip of pines and a ridge, the little airport had been carved out of the woods a long time ago. There were two runways, and even to my ignorant eyes it was apparent they were suitable only for small planes. Very small planes. The parking lot was small and graveled, delineated by landscape timbers. A concrete sidewalk led to the office, a little building about half the size of the ground floor of my house. This green-painted cement-block building had windows running nearly all the way around. Though the windows were curtained, the curtains were all wide open.

If you didn't turn off the sidewalk to enter the office, you continued past to the hangars. There were two. From the office, only the first few feet of the interior of each hangar would be visible. While both hangars were in use – I thought I could detect at least three tiny planes in the first, and two larger ones in the second – I couldn't see any people at all. Nothing moved.

I surveyed the grounds again. 'Now, wait a minute,' I said. Sally, who hadn't moved at all, looked at me with a little smile.

'You're wondering how the murderer got Jack's body to the plane?' she said.

I nodded. It would be brazen to carry the body to the plane past the open windows of the office, no matter how deserted the place seemed to be.

'Look,' she said, pointing out her window at a narrow gravel road, just wide enough for one vehicle, leading out of the parking lot and running up the ridge that rose behind the hangars.

'What about tracks?' I asked.

'No rain here for three weeks before Jack's body was dropped,' she said. 'The ground on either side of the gravel was rock-hard, so if there were tracks, they wouldn't amount to much. Now that we've had rain, it would be a different story.'

Instead of hopping out and going to the office, as I expected, Sally turned to me and said, 'Now, here's the reason I brought you along.'

I felt a warning bell go off in the 'better sense' area of my brain.

'Let's hear it,' I said, the caution in my voice making Sally purse her lips in exasperation.

'Well, Dan Edgar, the kid who wrote the story on the attack on Shelby, was too lazy to get out of bed this morning to help me, and the other reporters are all gone or sick this weekend.'

'So naturally you thought of me.' I raised one eyebrow, but possibly this effective expression was invisible behind my big glasses.

'Yes,' said Sally without a trace of irony. 'Actually, I did. You're small, you're quick, and if your husband's out of pocket, you're bored.'

'Well,' I said blankly, for want of something better.

'Anyway, this won't take long. Do you want to be the sneaker or the diversion?'

'How much trouble can I get into?'

'Oh, hardly any. I'll take responsibility.'

I tried raising the eyebrow again.

'Oh, okay, maybe yelled-at trouble, not jail trouble.'

I opted for the sneaker. I figured I already had so much trouble, a little more wouldn't make any difference.

'Okay,' Sally said. 'Now, here's what you have to do. When I was out here doing the story on Jack Burns, of course I asked the owner, an older guy named Stanford Foley, how it was possible for Jack and someone else to get in a plane without him even seeing it. He said it just couldn't happen, that he was here the whole time. The police can't make heads or tails of that, and I can't either.'

'Your story said Jack had rented the plane himself.'

'Yes, I said that, but I was counting on Foley too much. It turns out, Jack had reserved that time and that plane, but I don't think Foley saw him at all. I think Jack was brought here dead – he certainly wasn't killed in the plane, the cops tell me – and loaded into that plane by his killer. Jack's car was parked at the police station and nothing was wrong with it, so he didn't come here on his own and he wasn't killed in his own car.'

'So, what do you want me to do?'

'While I go in there and talk to Foley, I want you to sneak in that hangar and get in a plane. Actually, the plane that you saw that day, the one that transported the body, may be back here. It's one Mr Foley keeps to rent out to whoever wants it. Jack had actually flown it several times.'

Getting in a plane didn't sound too hard.

'According to your theory, the killer had Jack's body in the car and drove close to the hangar,' I said, feeling sure there was more to come.

'Well, right. Actually, that's what I want you to do, get the body to the plane. Just to prove it can be done without Mr Foley knowing anything at all. I want you to drive my car to the back of the first hangar – that's the one the plane Jack reserved was in – and drag the bag in my trunk down to the hangar. I want you to load that bag in a plane and get in yourself. You don't know how to fly a plane, do you? It would be great if you could actually take off without him knowing.'

'You should have asked Perry, he's taking lessons,' I reminded her, and she grimaced as if she'd bitten a lemon.

'Perry wouldn't do it, he'd just think of something else he had to do urgently,' Sally said. 'I don't know if Perry's so much learning how to fly a plane as learning how to fly Jenny Tankersley.'

I wasn't going to touch *that* one.

'So, just get the bag out of the trunk, down the hill, and into the plane,' Sally prompted.

This sounded trickier and trickier. 'How heavy a bag?' I asked, stalling for time.

'Oh. Pretty heavy – after all, it's supposed to be a body.'

'What if someone comes?'

'We'll just – tell them what we're doing!'

Sally seemed to think that would take care of everything. I was far from sure that was the case.

'Okay,' I said, hearing the doubt dripping from my voice.

'Good,' Sally said happily, gathering her purse and notepad. 'I'll meet you back here. You have ten minutes, okay? And the object is not to let Foley see you. Or anybody else.'

Sally had made it sound like a kind of game, maybe a macabre version of hide-and-seek. But as soon as I began the experiment, it felt all too real. While Sally entered the office and hopefully began an intense conversation with Stanford Foley, I drove her old Toyota out of the parking lot and up the little graveled trail. The car lurched as I navigated it through the ruts, and my stomach began to match its motion.

I was up behind the first hangar in no time. I parked and got out, Sally's enormous bunch of keys hanging from my hand. No one ran out of the hangar or the office to demand an accounting of what I was doing. If I looked hard I could see Sally's head through one of the back windows of the office.

Time for phase two. I unlocked the trunk and stared at its contents with dismay. When Sally had said 'bag' I'd thought of a garbage bag filled with laundry or yard rakings. What Sally had wedged in her trunk was an actual punching bag that she'd appropriated from someone's garage. The chain it had dangled from was still attached to three rings on the top of the bag, coming together to link on one large ring.

'Son of a *bitch*,' I said from the bottom of my heart. That certainly didn't mean anything in the context of my predicament, but it really made me feel better. 'Okay,' I said, trying to bolster my courage and muscle power. 'Okay, here we go.' And muttering further encouraging things and heaving with all my might, I got the punching bag out of the trunk.

If the chains hadn't been attached, Sally's little experiment would have ended right then and there. The only other way I could get the bag, which I estimated to weigh seventy pounds, down the slope would be to roll it. That would work with the bag, though the trip downhill might be rather uncontrollable, but with Jack's body it would not have done at all.

So I grabbed the chains, for after all, Jack could have been grabbed under the arms, and I dragged the bag downhill, feeling toward the end that my arms were going to come out of their sockets. I was quite certain that Sally owed me in a major way.

Halfway down the hill I achieved some self-knowledge. I would never have done this if I'd been single, because of the embarrassment of possibly being seen and questioned. But now that I was married to Martin, I was not so concerned. He gave me the confidence to do what I wanted to do, though it might be incredibly stupid. Like pulling a punching bag down a hill behind a very obscure little airport in northeast Georgia.

Then my foot touched concrete, and I realized I'd made it to the hangar. There was an enormous door right in the middle of the wall and it was wide open. Mr Foley was not a man to worry about security, despite what had happened the week before. Before I tried to get the bag in, I reconnoitered. The hangar, which felt cavernous, was full of shadows. The plane closest to the back door was green, but there were two little red-and-white ones, both with a Piper logo, either of which might have been the plane that dumped Jack Burns so unceremoniously into my yard. Though the concrete floor certainly had stains on it, the hangar was surprisingly neat, a credit to Mr Foley. There were shelves on the side, a little room in the corner, and metal drums holding rags and things I couldn't identify.

Well, the floor being clear was the main thing. I pulled the bag, which I was beginning to hate with all my might, across the smooth floor to the nearest of the red-and-white Pipers. It was unlocked, to my astonishment. I peered into the tiny cabin, feeling a little curious even though I knew I was supposed to be hurrying. I'd never seen the inside of a plane so small.

I hadn't been able to figure out how one person could fly the plane and dump the body out at the same time, but now that I could see the cabin, it was obvious that it would be easy. The pilot could lean across the body, which would be propped into the passenger's seat, open the passenger door, and give a good push, and the thing would be accomplished. It gave me the willies when I put Jack's face on the passenger, pictured it actually taking place.

Suddenly the loneliness of the hangar felt threatening rather than reassuring. I wanted to get the hell out of there. What was a nice girl like me doing in a place like this? With a strength born of sheer exasperation, I hauled the bag to an upright position, squatted, embraced the bag, and lifted. I almost got it in the passenger's seat, but my height was the problem. Jack's assailant too must have had a terrible time unless he was at least a foot taller than me – lots of people were, of course.

I looked around desperately. There, some wooden pallets were stacked against the wall. I ran to get one, put the bag on it, stood on it myself, and with the extra height I managed to wrestle the bag into the plane. It was not sitting up neatly in the passenger's seat; it leaned awkwardly over into the pilot's side. But it was in the plane, as Sally had specified.

I returned the pallet, wiped the bag with a rag to remove my fingerprints (wondering all the while why I felt that was necessary), threw the rag back in the metal drum, and hightailed it out of the hangar.

I had to back down the track until I came to the point where it led down to the parking lot. There I was able to maneuver Sally's car to face downhill. Once I had her car back in its original position, I looked at my watch. Ten minutes, most of which had been absorbed by extricating the bag from the trunk, and hoisting the bag into the plane.

It felt like double that, I closed my eyes, scrunched down in the passenger's seat, and wondered if I could go to sleep. No, here came Sally accompanied by an older man who had a fine head of gray hair and an orange jumpsuit that looked quite good on him. An earphone set was around his neck, the little gray pads looking like buds on the ends of the metal arc. Wires led down to a tape player strapped to his waist, like the set Angel listened to so often while she did yard-work.

Sally was smiling and Stanford Foley was smiling, and I wondered if I was seeing the start of a Good Thing. The tall older man caught sight of me in the car, and said something to Sally, something on the order of 'Why didn't your friend come in?' because I could see the question on his face. Sally said something with a conspiratorial smile and he began laughing. I decided Sally's debt had just escalated.

She said a few more words, then traipsed down the sidewalk and slid into the car. Stanford Foley watched her with a happy face. I handed Sally the keys, and she started the motor under the watchful beam of her new swain.

When Sally had finished smiling and waving, and actually reversed the car, I asked in an acidic voice, 'When are you and Stanford going out?'

'Oh, Roe,' she said in a wounded way, 'can't I enjoy a man's company for just a little minute?'

'Not when I've been yanking my muscles all to pieces for you,' I said, and I meant it.

'So, tell me about it. How long did it take? I couldn't believe it when I looked out the window and the Toyota was back.' Sally could be tactful when she chose, and she could tell she'd better choose now.

I gave her as long an account of my ordeal as I could, since it had lasted only ten minutes.

'How'd you do with Mr Foley? Other than the obvious.'

'He's really a sweet guy. Did you know he lives in half of that little building? I think the line between being at home and off duty, and being at work and being alert, have kind of blurred for Stanford.'

'I saw he was wearing earphones.'

'That seems to be his main pleasure, listening to music on that Walkman set. He likes country and western.'

'He play it loud?'

'I got the feeling he does.'

'So did he even hear you park the car in the lot?'

'No.'

'Did he know I'd moved the car?'

'No.'

'Did he even look out in the lot and ask how you'd gotten out to the airport?'

'No. He was in the living quarters when I knocked on the door. He had the earphones on, and he was singing along with the tape. It took him forever to hear me. He never looked out the window the whole time I was there.'

'He could have missed the car or truck with Jack in it completely, then.'

Sally nodded, her attention focused on turning back onto the interstate.

'How does he know it was Jack who reserved the plane?' I asked.

'Jack called. He said to reserve the plane for ten o'clock on Monday morning. He asked if anyone else had reserved a plane for that morning, because he might have the Piper up for a while.'

'So Foley told him there were no more reservations.'

'Right.'

'How come Mr Foley's so sure it was Jack that called?'

Sally looked over at me sharply. 'Well, because that's who he said he . . . Oh.'

'Right. Who's to say it was Jack? Couldn't the killer have made the reservation? All he'd have to know is that Jack used this airport.'

'You mean it was planned in advance.'

'Why not?'

Neither of us spoke for a minute, viewing with distaste bordering on nausea the murderer plotting with such care, perhaps seeing Jack often in the time between the call and the fall.

'Well,' said Sally, shaking herself and pulling out to pass a pickup that was surely going over the speed limit, 'I'll have to think about that some more. Later. Hey, I hear your friend Angel is pregnant!'

'Yes, she found out a few days ago.'

'That's great! Shelby Youngblood's pretty old to be a first-time dad, isn't he?'

'He's the same age as Martin.'

'Then you and Martin better get on the stick, girl. I had Perry so young that when I see these women having them late now, it seems funny to me. I know your mother would like a grandkid of her own – her husband's got three now, doesn't he?'

'She enjoys John's grandchildren a lot.' I turned to look out of the window at the secondhand car dealers and fast-food places that were beginning to line the road from the interstate to Lawrenceton.

'So what about your own?'

I kept my face averted. 'Sally, I can't have children.'

Horrified silence.

'Roe, I'm so sorry.' We'd come to a stoplight. Sally patted my hand, and I restrained the impulse to slap hers.

'You've checked with specialists, I'm sure.' Still, there was the question in her voice.

'Yes. I don't ovulate and I have a malformed womb.'

Laying it on the line.

'Roe, I don't know what to say, except I'm sorry.'

'That's all anyone can do,' I said, trying to keep the tears out of my voice.

'How long have you known?'

'Couple of months.'

'How's Martin reacting?'

I took a deep breath, trying to stay composed. This was too new a sore to touch without considerable pain. 'Martin wasn't sure he wanted more anyway. You know he has a son, Barrett, who's an adult now. So starting over had limited appeal for him.'

Sally finally seemed to realize I didn't want to stay on the subject. 'Well, I'll take you out to lunch when we get back, as a thank-you. And then I have to take the bag back. How about Beef 'N More?'

She pulled in neatly beside my car in the *Sentinel* parking lot.

I sat there with my eyes shut tight, waiting for the storm to begin.

I could feel Sally shift in her seat to look at me. She said sharply, 'What?'

'Um. The bag is still in the plane, Sally.'

'*What?*'

'You never said anything about putting it *back* in the car, Sally,' I said defensively. But I could feel the corners of my mouth turn up, and I was suppressing a laugh.

'Don't you dare smile! That was Sam Edgar's punching bag! He gave me strict orders . . . you mean, it's still sitting in the airplane?' She couldn't quite believe me.

'Uh-huh.'

Unable to suppress it anymore, I began to laugh. After a second of staring at me with her mouth hanging open, Sally starting giggling, too.

'Which one is it in?' she gasped, wiping her eyes with the back of her hand.

'One of the little red-and-white ones.'

'Oh, dear. Oh no. How am I going to get it back? How am I going to explain it to Stanford?'

'Sally, my dear,' I said, sliding out of the Toyota, 'that is your problem. I guess our lunch is off now?'

Sally was shaking her head in exasperation, but still smiling a little, as I pulled out of the parking lot.

*

Martin was in the storage shed at the back of the garage when I got home. He had indeed been to the Athletic Club; he was still in his workout clothes.

Since he was soaked with sweat and smelled accordingly, maybe my hug was a little sketchy. 'I thought I'd finish mowing the yard,' he explained. 'You and Angel didn't get to finish last week, and the backyard looks . . . peculiar.'

It certainly did. I strolled across the covered walkway leading from our house to the garage, and looked at the yard for the first time since Jack Burns had made his reentrance into my life. Martin had already been at work; I could see he'd filled the depression in the sod. You could see the mowed trail in the grass where Angel had let go of the lawn mower when I tackled her.

I shuddered, and was glad to answer Martin's irritable call. He'd discovered the can of gas for the lawn mower was nearly empty, so I had to run back into town to get more. When I returned, I saw that Martin had gotten out the trimmer and started to clean up the edges of the yard and the tall grass around the stepping-stones in the front. The trimmer cord had gotten stuck and he was working over it with grim intensity.

'We are too used to having Shelby and Angel around,' Martin said, after struggling with the trimmer for several more silent, tense minutes. I'd been watching him work with, I hoped, an encouraging air, but I'd been contemplating retreating into the house on some pretext. I could tell Martin was very close to losing his temper, a rare and awful occurrence.

'I'll mow, if you want to keep working on that,' I said helpfully.

Martin told me in no uncertain terms that he never wanted to see the trimmer or touch it again as long as he lived.

I gathered that he would rather mow.

'Well, I'll fix lunch,' I offered, trying to think of something out of the ordinary that I could produce with speed.

'Only something light,' Martin said, pouring gas into the mower tank with the same concentration he did everything. 'Remember, we have the Pan-Am Agra banquet tonight.'

'Oh, right,' I said, trying not to sound as depressed as the thought made me feel.

The downside of being Martin's wife was having to attend so many *dinners*. We had to go to dinners in private homes given by plant officials, we had to go to annual dinners for the boards of this and that (naturally Martin was asked to sit on many boards), we had to go to charity fund-raising dinners . . . the list went on and on. And since Martin was a vice president of Pan-Am Agra, the highest-ranking local executive, I was expected to be the first lady, so to speak.

I am naturally polite and have decent table manners since my mother brought me up right. And I like to wear pretty clothes and get some attention, because I am a human being. But the constant feeling of being under observation, the anxiety that I might embarrass Martin, and above all the numbing sameness of these events, had dimmed my enthusiasm pretty quickly.

I trailed into the kitchen to make a fruit salad and checked my calendar. Yes, I'd written in the dinner and at the same time had made an appointment with Benita at the Clip Casa to have my hair put up, and I had to be there in twenty-two minutes.

I chopped fruit with vigor, left the kitchen in a mess, and yelled to Martin out the back door to let him know where I was going. Martin had left the garage door open since he'd been tinkering with the trimmer, and Madeleine, as always, had taken advantage of the situation to put paw prints on Martin's Mercedes. I told her again how stupid that was, wiped off the paw prints with a rag, ejected the cat from the garage, backed my car out, and pressed the automatic closer while Madeleine was still sulking on the stairs to the Youngbloods' apartment.

Benita was idly picking at her orange hair when I hurried in the door. I was four minutes late, and on a Saturday that was a sin. But I was contrite enough to talk her back into a good humor and she so seldom saw me that she had a great fund of family happenings to relate.

The beauty shop atmosphere was soothing, and my muscles, strained from their session with the punching bag, let me know they were glad to rest. The smell of the chemicals and the pastel decor, Benita's drawl, and the drone of the hair dryer made me feel sleepy and content. Benita decided my ends needed trimming, took care of that, and began the long process of putting my mass of hair up. All I needed to do was say 'Really?' or 'Oh yes,' from time to time. I flipped through a magazine, as always surprised and a little dismayed at what other females apparently found interesting – or at least the publishers thought they would – and planned what I'd wear that night. A few other women connected with the Pan-Am Agra plant came into Clip Casa to get beautified for the banquet, and I was polite to everyone, but I didn't feel like talking and didn't initiate any conversation.

By the time I left the beauty parlor it was late in the afternoon.

I cautiously surveyed the backyard and observed it had been mowed and trimmed. With considerable relief, I went in the kitchen door, and found the kitchen completely clean. I crossed the hall to the study, and found Martin wrapped in his golden brown terry robe, watching the news. He switched off the set and got up to give me a kiss and walk around me to view my hair. Benita had slicked it back, braided it, and wound the braid into a knot at the nape of my neck.

'You look great,' Martin murmured, closing in from behind to kiss my neck. I shivered pleasantly and we both looked at the clock on Martin's desk.

'Will you be careful of my hair?' I asked strictly.

'As careful as can be,' Martin said, not letting up on the neck work.

'Beat you up the stairs,' I said.

But gee, he caught me.

Chapter Eight

We had to get there early to meet and greet, but we found time to stop by the hospital. Shelby expected to be discharged the next day, and Martin promised to help, after he had a good look at Angel. She was obviously uncomfortable and exhausted after sleeping on the lumpy roll-away the hospital had provided. Shelby told us with more than a hint of exasperation that he'd urged her repeatedly to sleep at home.

Jimmy Henske had been by that day to question him again, but Shelby said he'd had to tell Jimmy that he still could not recall why he'd been roaming around the yard on a black rainy night, what he might have seen, who might have hit him.

Shelby's room was pleasantly cluttered with offerings from the men he worked with; paperbacks, sports magazines, a basket of fruit, and some get-well cards jostled each other for space on the broad windowsill.

As Martin and I made our unnecessarily complicated way out of the hospital (I wondered if the architect had just read a book on English mazes before he began on the hospital plans) and into the overcrowded parking lot, I noticed I was again experiencing the unease I'd had earlier, the chill of loss, as though the Youngbloods, bound to us by employment and friendship, were moving away from us for good.

I was in no party mood when we pulled into the parking lot of the community center. Martin cut off the motor and we sat looking at the concrete-and-glass building, the fresh-painted parking lot with its rudimentary trees in the medians. We heaved simultaneous sighs.

'We'll get through it,' Martin said bracingly.

'I know.' But I heard the complaint in my voice and said, 'At least we get to look marvelous for the evening! And I'm looking forward to seeing so many of the people I only get to see at Pan-Am Agra things.'

Martin hated being part of a receiving line, so we just happened to be close to the entrance; anyone who felt like it could shake Martin's hand or hug my neck, or give us both stiff bobs of the head. I resigned myself to being called 'Mrs Bartell' all evening, since the constant correction 'Ms Teagarden' would have been tedious.

For this annual occasion, Pan-Am Agra had rented the newly built community center, which boasted a huge room that could be adapted to many purposes. This evening it looked festive, with giant Easter eggs and streamers and balloons combating the general institutional atmosphere. A potted bare artificial tree stood in the middle of the room with large plastic eggs hanging from it, each containing a slip of paper describing a door prize. I'd already been informed I was the designated distributor, and I watched with resignation as the glass bowl by the entrance filled with more and more slips with names scrawled on them, as more and more Pan-Am Agra employees slapped on their hand-lettered name stickers and moved into the room.

This was supposed to be a dressy occasion; but as always, nowadays, there were people who came in blue jeans or stretch pants. My mother would have shuddered. I felt grateful I'd dressed down in a rather plain cocktail dress in cream and gold. I was wearing heels, which I hated with a passion, and every time my feet throbbed I told myself this was my sacrifice for Martin, a return for all the times he took it for granted I would go my own way and do whatever made me happiest.

I caught glimpses of my husband surrounded by men in suits who were laughing, holding glasses of nonalcoholic punch (Pan-Am Agra could not support drinking and driving), and from time to time glancing over to the tables where their wives were already seated. Martin was at ease, dealing with the conversation with good humor and a natural facility.

I wasn't faring as well. I was getting a bit tired of so many women telling me in so many words that I was lucky to have such a handsome husband. If Martin and I had been the same age, they wouldn't have commented; I couldn't quite work out why the age difference apparently gave them license to speak frankly. I was willing to bet none of the men were complimenting Martin on my big boobs.

Every now and then, I'd get to talk to someone I really liked, like Martin's secretary, Mrs Sands, a tall, thin forty-five with luridly dyed black hair and a broad sense of humor. Tonight, I could only view Mrs Sands with awe. She was decked out in a red-and-gold sequined sweater, red slacks, and gold sandals with three-inch heels that made her even loftier. My own modest heels looked sedate in comparison. Mrs Sands, Marnie to her friends (but not to me), gave me the dignified greeting one potentate accorded another of slightly greater stature. Though I was the sultan's wife, her manner implied, she was the Grand Vizier, the one who held true power.

Actually, she was right in many ways. I didn't mind giving her credit; Martin said she was a great secretary, gauging perfectly when to allow plant personnel to have access to him, when to leave him undisturbed, and how to locate him at any moment.

'Honey,' said Mrs Sands, 'I need to talk to you.' She glanced around; we were a little apart at the moment. I looked up at her, surprised and interested; usually we just exchanged compliments and small talk.

'Fire away,' I said.

'Now, I know Mr Bartell is a man who can handle any situation, that's one of the reasons I like working for him, but you're his wife and there's something building up out there I think you ought to know about.'

Mrs Sands cocked her head and her teased black hair leaned a little, like a loose helmet. She was deeply tanned and the wrinkles around her dark brown eyes looked as though they'd been incised with a chisel.

'Tell me,' I said invitingly.

'You know Bettina Anderson?'

'Yes. We had supper at Bettina and Bill's house one time. Oh, and she left a couple of messages on my answering machine I haven't had a chance to return,' I recalled guiltily. As a matter of fact, the dinner at the Andersons' had been the first one Martin and I had attended as a married couple; and it had been the first evening I'd realized that the future held many such unwanted but obligatory invitations.

Bill Anderson, the plant safety manager, had been wished on Martin by his superiors. The Andersons had been in Lawrenceton about three years. Bettina, a stout copper-haired woman of about forty, was the most self-effacing wife I'd ever encountered. 'I haven't seen either of the Andersons in a few months, I guess,' I said lamely, aware that Mrs Sands was waiting for me to say something more.

'Well, I think she's going through some kind of thing about Mr Bartell. I can't *believe* she's tried to call you!'

My mouth fell open.

'Bettina Anderson, who's married to Bill, head of the Safety Division,' I said, just a little question in my voice, because I simply couldn't believe my ears.

'That's right, I can't believe it either,' Mrs Sands said, responding to my tone and my statement at the same time.

I looked down at my shoes, off-white leather with a gold cap over the toes. I bit my lip to keep from giggling.

'Mr Bartell usually handles situations like this himself, he sure don't need help with that,' Mrs Sands continued, and I abruptly lost any tendency to laugh. I wondered how many other 'situations' Martin had handled without my knowledge. I could see how it would be hard for him to say casually, 'Fended off another admirer, honey.'

'But this time, this woman is acting so weird, and so's her husband,' Mrs Sands said, disgust in her stance. 'Weird' was one of the worst epithets Mrs Sands ever used, and she did not use it lightly.

'Weird in what way?' I asked, returning my gaze to my shoes. This conversation was embarrassing, but fascinating.

'Well, Bill shows up at times when he doesn't really need to see Mr Bartell.' My husband was the only 'Mister' at the Pan-Am Agra plant, to Mrs Sands. 'He just hangs around until Mr Bartell gets rid of him – you know how quick he can do that.'

I nodded. I did indeed.

'And Bettina?' I prompted.

'Honey, that woman calls on the phone, and she's come to the office! Course, I told her he was out of town.'

'Oh, dear,' I said inadequately.

'Now that you know, I feel better,' Mrs Sands told me. 'I'll be seeing you, Ms Teagarden.' Mrs Sands always gave me the correct name, but accompanied it by a sharp look. Keeping my name had cost me many points with Mrs Sands, but she was trying to forgive me, since I seemed like a proper wife for Mr Bartell. She gave my shoulder a squeeze and strode off to join a group of her cronies, who'd been glancing our way.

Before I had a chance to recover from this remarkable conversation, before I could even wiggle my eyebrows at Martin to indicate I wanted to talk to him, the Andersons came in the door. Bill was wearing a suit, of course, and Bettina was wearing a very pretty green dress. When she shyly eased in front of me, I was able to give her an honest compliment. Bettina smiled back uncertainly. I noticed her hands were twisting the strap of her purse.

I emitted some more social chitchat, which Bettina interrupted abruptly. 'Could we talk tonight? It won't take long. I'm sorry I have to talk to you here, but you didn't return my calls. Of course,' and she held up a hand to ward off my speaking, 'I understand, because you've had a lot of things to think about lately. But I have to talk to you tonight.' She had spoken in a low urgent voice, with a glance toward our husbands that certainly must have clued any onlooker that she was up to something surreptitious. Of course in such a throng some people were sure to be looking at us, and I tried to make my face as blank as possible.

'Sure, Bettina,' I said, as soothingly as I could without sounding patronizing. 'What about right now?'

'Oh no, people are looking, and it's just about time to sit down.' So she was having that watched feeling, too.

'This is awfully crowded,' I said. 'Why don't we have lunch Monday?' If I could get through this evening, I could surely endure a public lunch with Bettina Anderson.

'That's too late, I can't wait that long,' Bettina told me. There was an edge of desperation in her voice that I couldn't ignore.

'All right. When the dinner is breaking up, come to our table and we'll find a quiet place.'

And then I had to put on my social smile, because here came (to my dismay) Deena Somebody-who-worked-in-the-shipping-department. Deena had deemed skin-tight jeans appropriate for this occasion, and I had to admit she filled them beautifully, but I had doubts that she would be able to bend at her knee and hip joints to sit in one of the folding chairs. I would have been interested in a video of the process of Deena getting into those jeans. Deena shrieked, 'Hello, Roe!' as if she were a close friend of mine, and hauled her date out to show me she had one. To my amazement, the man she had in tow was quiet Paul Allison.

'Hi, Roe,' said Paul in his calm way. 'I'm sure you know Deena Cotton.' I must have been fascinated by Deena's bottom half for too long – she was eyeing me nervously.

'Deena, how's shipping these days?' I murmured, proving I recognized her and knew where she worked.

'Just fine, always busy. Thank goodness!' And Deena gave a high-pitched giggle that made me wonder just how far Paul was willing to go in reaction to Sally, who would never in her life have made a sound like that. He was willing to go pretty far, as it turned out, for he put his hand firmly on her butt while we talked, and she seemed pleased rather than annoyed. I tried to imagine getting out of clothes that tight in the heat of passion; just as I had decided Paul would have to stand at the end of the bed and pull on the legs as she held on to the headboard, I became aware that Deena had turned red and Paul was staring at me fixedly, waiting for me to speak.

'Hope you enjoy yourselves tonight,' I said briskly.

I looked down rather than show my irritation, pushed my wire-rims up with one finger to give myself an excuse for glancing away. 'Perry,' I said over Paul's shoulder, 'Good to see you.' To my surprise, Paul's former stepson had come in right behind him with a woman who must be the remarkable Jenny Tankersley. Paul and Deena were moving away, and I tried not to even glance at the rear view.

'Jenny's airstrip is where the Pan-Am Agra plane lands when the president flies down,' Perry was explaining. 'This is the second year Jenny's been invited to the banquet.'

I didn't remember her from the year before, but perhaps she just hadn't come up to meet me. I was sure I would have had no trouble recognizing her if I'd been introduced. Jenny, who was the same height as Perry, had gleaming beautiful white teeth, which she frequently bared in a predatory smile. Her hair was cut very short, with bangs, and it was a glossy brown that contrasted well with her heavy gold jewelry and orange dress. I had heard many stories about this woman, and I was interested in talking to her, but now was not the time to get to know her better.

I said a few polite words, to which Jenny responded instead of Perry, and then the younger couple drifted off to sit with Paul and Deena Cotton. I noted that Deena had somehow managed to sit, but she was bolt upright.

I assessed the incomings – down to a trickle – and the seated employees – a great majority – and knew it was time for the banquet to officially begin. Martin met my eye, with his usual good timing, and together we glanced around for seats, which would be simply the first two side-by-side we saw. At the annual banquet, Martin and I were supposed to be just part of the gang, with the result that some plant workers were in for a very tense evening sitting with the boss.

I spotted a table about fifteen yards away, and as Martin and I made our way there we passed a head of pale curly hair I thought I recognized. When I glanced back in amazement, I confirmed my suspicion; Arthur Smith was there with another woman, this one a very young twenty-something with her hair actually in a ponytail.

I looked straight into his eyes, which were focused on me, gave him some anger in the look, and turned my face to my husband.

Of course, Martin hadn't missed it. 'What the hell is he doing here?' he murmured through a genial smile. Martin and Arthur had always had a profound dislike of each other.

'He and Lynn have separated.'

'So he's out with a woman half his age?'

I wisely said nothing. I didn't think the woman was *that* young, but she was maybe fifteen years younger than Arthur, who was about thirty-four. I didn't think it was the right time to remind Martin he was fifteen years older than I.

'Are Lynn and Arthur going to get divorced?' Martin asked, sliding my chair out for me while nodding at the others seated at the table, who were displaying an interesting variety of reactions to the presence of the boss and his wife.

'I hope not, for the sake of the little girl,' I said. 'And it would be his second divorce.'

Then we had to drop our own conversation and tend to our social duties. Martin knew the name of every worker at our table, and met their spouses with great aplomb. I didn't have that gift, but I worked hard, and I hoped not obviously, at matching Martin's geniality and his easy conversation.

Every time I had to go to an affair like this one, my earnest prayer was that I would think at least once before I spoke, twice if possible. I didn't want to provide fodder for any amusing anecdotes.

I discussed school-system problems with a mother of three, sewing one's own clothes with another woman, and planting roses with another. I plowed steadily through the evening, eating little of the barbecued chicken and slaw, but doing my corporate duty. When the Employee Services man, who had to act as MC on these occasions, stood up to tell a few jokes and introduce Martin, I sighed a silent breath of relief.

Martin rose to the occasion with a few well-chosen words about the increased productivity at the plant, his goals for the year, and the pride he took in working with such a fine group of people. He went on about how he'd taken Georgia to his heart, turning this into a reference to his marriage to a true Georgia peach; and then he concluded neatly, pleasing those who had come with any tendency to be pleased.

I kept my face turned toward Martin and an indulgent smile pasted on my lips, but I was more interested in scanning the faces I knew in the crowd. Paul was looking at Martin, but as if he weren't really seeing him. It was obvious that his thoughts were far away. Perry was not paying any attention at all; if I was right, he and Jenny were up to something under the tablecloth. And Arthur was neglecting his young date to glare at Martin as though my husband were saying derogatory things about Arthur's ancestry. Marnie Sands was listening to make sure her boss did her proud, and the Andersons were whispering anxiously to each other.

Martin gave me my cue as name-drawer for the door prizes, all donated from local businesses that Pan-Am Agra patronized heavily. There were ten prizes to distribute this year, and I had to reach in the bowl, draw out a slip with a name scrawled on it, and search the crowd for whoever looked happy when I called the name. Then I unhooked the string attaching one of the giant eggs to the tree and handed it to the winner, who was supposed to open the egg on the spot so everyone could admire the donated largesse. It was kind of nice to be able to give people things that made them happy, especially at no expense to myself, and I enjoyed this part of the evening, though deciphering the scribbled signatures on the slips of paper could sometimes be a problem.

One of the recipients happened to be seated at Arthur's table, and as I called the man's name I noticed that Arthur was staring at me as if he hadn't eaten his dinner and I was a barbecued chicken breast.

I had the strongest yearning for a water gun.

At last, the evening dragged to an official end. The couples we'd been sitting with said ceremonious goodbyes, Martin excused himself to congratulate the Employee Services man on his organization of the event, and I was alone for the first time in what felt like years. I surreptitiously opened my compact below the table level to check my face for wear and tear, discovered a crumb of roll on my cheek that must have been there for an hour, and took care of that little problem. I spotted a clean napkin and polished my glasses, wondering how long the E.S. man would keep Martin talking, and if there were actually blisters on my feet. And then I was no longer alone.

True to her word, here was Bettina Anderson, who had fared even worse than I in terms of visible wear – she had a prominent grease stain on the skirt of her green dress. She was just as tense, just as wired up, as she had been earlier in the evening.

I felt sorry for her, and very wary.

'You have to help me, Aurora,' she said earnestly. Her heavy mouth had lost its lipstick and her nose needed powder. She clutched my arm, and I gritted my teeth to endure the contact.

'Tell me what's wrong,' I said evenly.

'Jack Burns died in your yard. Did he say anything before he died?'

Back to Jack Burns again. I tried not to see him falling. His funeral was tomorrow, and I dreaded the thought of it. 'No,' I said wearily. 'Bettina, I'm sure he was dead when he fell. He couldn't have said anything.' She looked unconvinced. Stung clean out of courtesy, I said, 'And besides, what business is it of yours?'

'I'm so scared,' she said. Now *that* I believed; I could feel her fear.

'He knew about us,' she said. For one horrifying moment I thought she meant Jack Burns had knowledge of an affair between Bettina and my husband.

Then I was back in my right mind and I put a couple of things together.

'Is your husband the one in the Federal Witness—?'

'Hush! Hush!'

I looked around. There was no one within ten feet.

'How'd you find out about that?'

'That was just the rumor . . .'

'Someone's talking, oh, God!'

'So John *is* the one?'

'Not John! Me!'

'What—?'

'I was the bookkeeper for one of the shell businesses run by Johnny Marconi.'

'Wow.' I gaped at this ordinary woman who had helped bring down a vicious man involved in peddling every kind of vice, a man who was a murderer many times over.

'So did they find out from Jack before he died who we were, where we were?' She stared at me as if she could will me to know the answer.

'I don't know,' I said, wishing I had a better reply to give her.

'Dryden can't find out, no one can find out, and we sit every night and wait for them to come.'

'Mr Dryden must have seen the autopsy reports,' I said. 'Did they show Jack was tortured before he fell?'

'No. But some things would have been obliterated by the fall,' she said. 'And they might have threatened him with a knife or something, without actually using it, before they killed him.'

I cast around to think of something comforting to tell this woman.

'They would have come by now if Jack had told them,' was the best I could come up with. I tried to picture Mafia hit men from Chicago traveling to Lawrenceton, Georgia – asking questions at the Shop-So-Kwik. My mind boggled.

'Did your husband work for Pan-Am Agra in Chicago?' I asked.

She stared at me for a moment. 'No, but he had a similar job at a similar company, and he was familiar with Pan-Am Agra's benefits, and he knew they had a plant down here and another in Arkansas. Either would have done, but it happened they needed a safety director here, so it was arranged. No one locally knew who we really were, except Jack Burns. Or so we thought.'

This was all as interesting as could be, but I became aware that her husband and my husband were waiting for us, making weary conversation. If Bill Anderson had wanted to have the same conversation with Martin that his wife was having with me, he showed no signs of it now. Martin saw me look at him, and wiggled his watch arm, his signal that he really wanted to leave.

'I wish I could tell you something either way,' I said honestly.

'Dryden doesn't think we've been compromised. But we're going on vacation, starting tomorrow, and the watch will be kept for anyone asking questions. We'll be back. I would hate to move, but we just may have to. You know,' she added as she rose to her feet, 'if you tell anyone about this, we may end up getting killed. I tried to talk to your husband, but I think he could tell we had secrets, because he wouldn't meet with me privately, and Bill couldn't make up his mind whether or not it was a good idea to talk to Martin. He figured that anything you knew, you would have told your husband, and he knows Martin better; and I'd just met you that one time, at our house. Now you know about us, and our lives are your property. But I had to ask if you knew anything, had seen anything. We have to know. We just have to.'

And without further ado she walked slowly away, a stout red-haired woman in fear for her life, whom I'd always known as the boring and self-effacing Bettina Anderson. She put her hand on her husband's arm, said something to him quietly, and Bill shook hands with Martin in leave-taking.

I wondered what her christened name was. I wondered how her husband felt about hiding with his wife. I wondered if they had grown children in Chicago, what those children had been told.

'What was that all about?' Martin asked. I'd been so preoccupied I hadn't noticed him approaching, and I jumped. 'They've been asking me weird questions for a week,' he continued, 'and wanting to meet with me privately without either one of them telling me why. After Bill was foisted on me by the Chicago guys, I smelled something strange about the Andersons, and I just don't want to be involved in whatever trouble they're in . . . after all my own problems with our government.' We exchanged a look; that was a time we didn't talk about anymore.

'I thought maybe she had a thing for you,' I confessed.

'I was worried about that, too,' he admitted. 'Though it didn't have that feel . . . but all the secrecy. So, are you going to tell me?'

'I don't know,' I said, dismay showing in my voice. 'I don't know if I can.' I couldn't think of anything I'd ever withheld from Martin in our two years together, but I couldn't dismiss Bettina's plea for secrecy either.

'Can I think about it?' I asked Martin.

'Sure. I often feel I know more about my employees' private lives than I want to know, anyway.' But I could tell by the set of his shoulders that he was piqued with me.

As we neared the exit (Martin good-byeing right and left to people who'd lingered to talk) we came face-to-face with Arthur Smith and his ponytailed date. Martin's hand gripped mine more tightly. 'Hello, Sue,' Martin said to the girl. 'How are you?'

'Fine, Mr Bartell,' she said self-consciously. 'Have you met Arthur Smith?'

The silence held on too long for even young Sue to ignore. 'So you guys have met,' she said nervously, finally aware there was something going on.

Martin and I gave Arthur identical stiff nods, and Martin said, 'Night, Sue. See you in Ag Products tomorrow.' Martin held open one of the glass doors for me, and I stepped out into the cool evening air. Martin appeared beside me again, and took my hand. I heard the door swoosh shut, and then open again for young Sue and Arthur.

We stepped into a knot of people who had been tempted by the beautiful evening to linger to chat on the sidewalk; Perry and Jenny Tankersley, Paul and Deena Cotton, Marnie Sands (who seemed to be groping for something in her purse). Bill and Bettina Anderson had been waylaid by one of Martin's division heads, a balding paunchy man named Jesse Prentiss, who was introducing his wife Verna.

Just at that moment all hell broke loose, all hell in the form of a swift and terrified gray cat that streaked across the circles of light and dark dappling the parking lot, a cat hotly pursued by a large and shaggy dog with a length of frayed rope flying from its collar.

There was a hoot of laughter here and there, an exclamation of alarm from those who couldn't immediately see what was causing the hoopla, and a few halfhearted attempts to call the dog or grab the length of rope. The scene drew the stragglers in the parking lot together in a loose knot. After a moment the animals were gone, continuing their chase into the modest residential area on the next street. The yelping of the dog was still clear.

My eyes, like everyone else's, had followed the cat, who'd bounded onto and then over a car parked in the shadows at the very far reaches of the community center lot. I listened with half my attention to the comments and jokes the incident had sparked in the little crowd, while trying to figure out if I had indeed seen a blond head in the car that the cat had cleared in her escape.

Sure enough, I caught a glimpse of blond again, and one of the sodium lights caught a gleam of glasses.

Well, well. To cap off a jarring evening, who did I spy lurking in the parking lot but Mr Dryden. Agent Dryden? Marshal Dryden? Even his protectee had only called him 'Dryden'.

Was he waiting to see if anyone followed the Andersons? Or was he watching us?

I was so engrossed in my thoughts in the seconds following the animals' exit from the parking lot that I was taken utterly by surprise by the sudden pressure on my back.

I heard a woman scream. My hand was ripped from its loose grip with Martin's.

To my bewilderment I found myself being pressed down to the ground by a warm weight that I could not support, though my feet shuffled for balance and my knees braced to push back. I heard another shriek, and thought *That wasn't me*, and a deep groan followed by a curse, all in the second that this inexorable, inexplicable weight drove me to the pavement. I threw my hands out in front of me to break my fall, but even my braced arms couldn't stop my cheek from hitting the sidewalk.

In the long, long minute before the weight was lifted, as I lay prone under the terrifying burden, I felt something wet on my face and opened my eyes to see blood dripping to the gleaming new sidewalk a half-inch from my nose.

After a frantic little inventory of pains, I was pretty sure it wasn't my blood.

Out of a cacophony of voices I discerned Paul Allison bellowing for calm, and I could hear one woman set up a steady howl for help – Bettina Anderson, I thought. 'Ready on three,' I heard Martin say, and the shuffle of feet all around me. 'One, two, three!' Martin said, and the weight on top of me was eased off. I had had the breath knocked out of me, and was frantically trying to take in air, with the usual result that I was foiling my own attempt.

I saw some knees hit the pavement beside me.

'Don't move,' Martin said tensely. 'Baby, is anything broken? Are you hurt?' Struggling for breath, I couldn't answer.

'Call 911!' exclaimed a male voice, Jesse Prentiss's, I thought. 'You! Perry Allison! There's a phone in the manager's office to the left of those glass doors!' Running feet, light; Perry pounding obediently into the community center.

Running feet, heavy. 'Who got hurt?' Dryden, breathing raggedly. So I'd been right; he'd been parked at the far reaches of the lot.

'Move back, people, police are on the way,' Paul Allison said loudly in his police official voice. 'I've already radioed from my car. Step back, everyone, unless you're an EMT.'

'I am,' Jenny Tankersley was saying as I felt Martin's hands running over my body.

'Then get over here,' Martin snapped, and Paul Allison said in a shocked voice, 'Has Roe been hurt?'

'She took a fall, she's okay,' Dryden said – rather cavalierly, I thought. 'But this man here is really bleeding.'

'There's blood on Roe,' Paul pointed out tensely.

And then I could breathe. Nothing had felt as good in weeks as that deep intake of air.

'I'm okay,' I croaked. 'Just help me up, Martin. I don't think it's my blood.'

I managed to push up with my arms to achieve a kneeling position, and then Martin lifted me up the rest of the way, frantically touching my head and neck to see where I'd been hurt.

We were a little apart from the activity now, which was centered on someone lying on the ground. The girl with the ponytail, Sue, was sobbing hysterically by one of the lampposts. 'He just fell down,' she said over and over, 'he just let go of my arm and fell down.'

'Not my blood,' I reassured Martin. This time he listened.

'Tell me how you're feeling,' he said.

'I bumped my cheek on the pavement,' I gasped. I took another deep breath and started again. 'I'm going to have sore hands and arms from trying to stop my fall, and my knees are scraped. Other than that, I'm fine. How'd I get knocked down?'

'Something happened to Arthur Smith,' Martin said slowly, his eyes never leaving my face. 'He was right behind you. Without any warning, he began to fall, and fell on you and took you down with him.'

'Did he have a heart attack?' No, the blood. 'Was he shot? How could he have been hurt?'

'Here comes the ambulance,' Martin said. 'Maybe we'll find out.'

Jenny Tankersley had been working on Arthur, ripping off his shirt to find the source of the bleeding, checking his pulse. The EMTs pelted out of the ambulance.

'He's been hurt on his shoulder somehow,' she told them, moving aside. No one was talking to Arthur himself, though I could see his eyes were open and he was taking in what was going on around him. He looked as dazed as I felt. But when his eyes focused on the first man out of the ambulance, Arthur seemed to collect himself. He said clearly, 'Murray, I was stabbed in the shoulder.'

A hush fell over the little crowds. Martin put his arm around me and I leaned on his chest. I had a moment of thankfulness that

Martin had been holding my hand when the attack on Arthur occurred, so it was out of the question that Martin could have been involved. Not that he would do anything like that, but other people, knowing of the dislike between them, might make something of Martin's proximity.

Then I realized what must have already occurred to everyone there. If Arthur had been stabbed instead of shot, it had to have been by one of the people in the small cluster on the sidewalk.

As the ambulance rolled off with Arthur in the back, the Prentisses offered Sue a ride home.

'I'm afraid we're all going to have to stay here for a while,' Paul said in his calm way, and to reinforce his words, two police cars flew into the parking lot, shortly to be followed by two more.

A police detective was down, and this made the second officer in a week who'd been attacked. Before the evening was over, I'd seen every member of the force come and go at the community center.

We were all searched, even me, which made no sense at all, as Martin pointed out several times.

'Martin, I don't mind,' I told him wearily, as I got up to go to the women's room with a female officer – thankfully, not Lynn Liggett Smith. 'I just want to get this over with and go home.'

So off I trudged, my little evening bag tucked under my arm, to submit my bag and my body to an examination.

No knife or any other pointed object was found on any person in the group.

It was as if a knife had fallen from the sky, stabbed Arthur in the shoulder, and been pulled back up by an invisible cord.

Chapter Nine

I woke in the morning to a warm bed, Martin still asleep beside me, and rain lashing around the house outside. I peeked at the clock on my bed table; only seven-thirty. Plenty of time to get ready for church at nine-thirty. I squirmed over to press against Martin.

He's a quick waker. As soon as I heard his breathing change he turned over and put an arm around me.

'Martin, about last night,' I said, my voice still heavy with sleep.

'Not right now,' he whispered, his hands beginning to travel.

'Ummmm,' was the next thing I said, and then I didn't say any more for a good few minutes.

In fact, I didn't say one coherent word until Martin was coming out of the shower I'd previously vacated. As I was tucking my beige-and-black silk blouse into my long beige skirt, I gave him an exaggerated leer. He held up a hand in protest, which caused the bath towel to droop interestingly.

'Don't even think of it,' he said. 'Remember my advanced age.'

I laughed, and began brushing my hair. 'I'm pretty sure I could overcome your feebleness,' I said. 'But I don't want to be late for church. Of course, there's all afternoon. . .'

'So you're not going to the funeral?'

'Oh, shoot.' I put my brush down and made a face into the mirror. 'I wish you hadn't reminded me. I guess I could think of an excuse, but I really ought to go. After all, he fell into our yard. I think that obliges me.'

'You Southerners have the strangest sense of obligation,' Martin observed.

He didn't often begin a sentence that way, so I forgave him.

'I know you have to go get Shelby, so you won't be thinking

about going to church,' I said carefully. 'Do you think you'll be home in time for the funeral? Do you even want to go?'

'I should go out to the plant for a while,' he said, pulling on his left sock, 'especially since I was gone for a couple of days this week.' I tried not to let my face fall. Martin felt he had to go in to work most weekends.

'I'll try not to stay long,' he continued.

I made a resigned face at my reflection and rummaged among the lipstick tubes in my dressing table drawer. But I wouldn't change the sheets; I still had a faint hope that later in the day it would prove to have been wasted effort. Actually, I'd settle for sitting in the same room while we read. Though our sex life was often wonderful, our 'together' time was minimal. I scanned the closet for my black pumps and slid my bare feet into them.

'No hose?' Martin said as he zipped up his blue jeans. He reached in a drawer to pull out a T-shirt. He seldom got to dress this casually.

'My knees have scabs from hitting the sidewalk last night, in case you didn't notice. And they're pretty sore.'

'Oh, honey, did I hurt you? Earlier?'

'If you did I didn't notice! But now that I'm up and around, I can tell I hit the pavement.' I flexed my leg and winced.

'Maybe while I'm at the hospital I'll check to see how Arthur Smith is,' Martin said, with a marked lack of enthusiasm.

'That would probably be good for appearances, anyway,' I said. 'Thank God you were holding my hand when he was stabbed . . . or whatever happened to him.'

Martin stood behind me and bent to kiss my neck at the spot that always makes me gasp. 'Some people that you dated, being around them doesn't bother me. But being around Arthur does, not because I think you have feelings for him but because he must still have some for you. He always gives me this look, "I had her first, I know all about the mole on her back", crap like that. And once Lynn and he have separated, what does he do? Puts himself right in your line of vision and looks at you as if he was a painter and you were the Mona Lisa.'

'And gets stabbed,' I said, to point out that Arthur's evening hadn't ended well, however much staring he'd done. I polished my black oblong-framed glasses, the ones I almost always wore to church, since they made me look serious. I peered into the mirror to check my makeup and decided I was entirely too pale. Maybe this year, for the first time since I was a teenager, I'd try to get a tan. If I went about it carefully, perhaps the sun wouldn't hurt my skin too badly. 'You know, Martin, I'd think I had it worked out if it wasn't for Arthur,' I said, pulling a Kleenex out of its box to blot my lipstick.

Martin, bent over to tie his Avias, said, 'What? You worked out what?'

'All this violence.'

'What's your theory?' Martin leaned his elbows on his knees to listen.

'I think it's because of Angel.'

Martin was astonished. 'How do you figure that?'

'Okay,' I said, holding up my fingers. 'Jack Burns's body was dropped in the yard while she was out mowing.'

Martin nodded cautiously.

'Then Beverly was rude to Angel in the library, and Beverly got attacked.'

I was busy folding fingers down and Martin was nodding.

'Then Beverly's purse was found on Angel's car.'

'What does that mean?'

'Whoever did it was saying to Angel, "Look what I did for you!" Like Jack's body falling in her yard. Just like Madeleine.'

Martin raised his eyebrows, as if to say 'Explicate'.

'I was watching Madeleine the other day as she was hunting, and I was thinking how yucky it was to have to clean her kills off the doormat. Then I realized that she brought them as an offering to me: like, "I'm a useful cat. See what I did"?'

Martin was looking a little dazed by my excursion into cat psychology.

'So, Jack was an *offering*. Like a dead mouse. "See what I did for you? He gave you a parking ticket, so here he is, delivered to your doorstep".'

'You think someone is in love with Angel and is showing her that by hurting people who upset her?' Martin raised his eyebrows, the picture of skepticism.

'It makes a perverted kind of sense,' I said stoutly. 'And poor Beverly's purse being put on the hood of Angel's car. To underline the fact that the attack was – in Angel's honor.'

'So, Shelby was hit on the head because he's her husband?'

'Right.'

'Why wasn't he killed?'

'Maybe because I turned on the downstairs light?'

Martin nodded slowly, not as if he was in love with my theory, but to indicate he was giving it consideration.

'But what about Arthur?' he asked. 'That won't wash, with Arthur. I don't think he and Angel have exchanged two words since she moved here.'

'That's where you're wrong,' I said smugly, having that instant figured out where Arthur might tie in. 'Remember, Arthur had called her in to the police station before he questioned me.'

'So this hypothetical admirer just decided he'd given Angel a hard time?'

'I guess. Actually, Faron Henske interviewed her, not Arthur.'

'Angel,' Martin said slowly, doubt in his voice. 'I don't know, Roe. Angel's not the stuff dreams are made of.'

'Not *your* dreams. But I've seen men just about hang their tongues out when she walks down the street,' I said. 'It's because she's so strong and sleek, I expect.'

'Hmmm. That's an interesting theory . . .'

He didn't believe it for a minute.

'And,' I added, having had a few more thoughts, 'the police won't think of it, I bet, because they're seeing this as attacks on two policemen. Beverly could've been mugged and Shelby could've heard a prowler.'

'Roe, the police could be right.'

'Well . . . maybe. But I think I am. I just can't understand,' I added, as I slid the beige-and-gold-enamel barrette into my hair to hold the waves off my face, 'why the police couldn't find the knife Arthur was stabbed with.'

'They certainly searched us all thoroughly,' Martin said, his voice dry. 'Perry Allison had a pocketknife, but it was perfectly clean. I don't think the wound could have been deep at all, if they suspected a pocketknife could've done it.'

'No blood on anyone . . .'

We shook our heads simultaneously at the opacity of the mystery surrounding the parking-lot stabbing of Arthur Smith, police detective.

Martin gave me a kiss and left to go to the hospital, and I finished preparing for church.

As I started a load of clothes in the washer on my way out the door, I reflected that this had been the best morning Martin and I had had in a while; longer than I liked to count up. For the past few months, Martin had been traveling more, had stayed in the office longer hours, had never let more than a day pass without going into the plant. Outside of work hours, the Athletic Club took up more time, and the meetings of all the boards and clubs he'd been asked to join – Community Charity Concern, Rotary, and so on and so on – ate into his lunchtimes and his evenings. I'd been increasingly on my own or thrown into the company of Angel and Shelby, with whom I had little in common, fond as I was of both of them.

As I retrieved my car keys from the hook by the south kitchen door, I realized Martin and I hadn't gone out together at night, except for four community functions, in maybe three months.

This was not the life the young wife of a handsome, older, wealthy man was supposed to lead, right? He should be hitting all the nightspots flaunting me, right?

I'd heard the stupid phrase 'trophy wife' behind my back on more than one occasion, and I thought it offensive and absurd. Of course I was quite a bit younger than Martin, and I was his second wife; but I was no voluptuous bimbo who'd married Martin for money and security. When Martin wanted to establish himself as the alpha male, he tended to challenge another man to racquetball rather than encourage me to wear low-cut dresses.

It might seem – to an outsider – that Martin, to some extent, had lost his taste for me. That our honeymoon was so far over that I was housekeeper and occasional companion to Martin, only. That I'd gone back to work because I was bored and unfulfilled as a full-time wife. Or that my married life was sterile because I'd found out I was.

Well, I'd certainly succeeded in ruining my morning, all by myself.

I yanked open the garage door and backed out my lowly car, blotting my tears and listening to country and western music all the way to St James's. I pulled into the parking lot at nine-thirty on the dot. Aubrey, our rector, to whom I'd once been nearly engaged, conducted another service in a nearby town at eleven, so we were his early Eucharist.

My eyes were still red, but I powdered over my makeup again to look passable. I could hear the organ playing, so I stuffed my handkerchief and compact back into my purse and slid out of my car. As I slammed the door behind me and began trotting to the church, I heard another car door slam and registered that someone else was even later than I.

Standing at the back of the church, I spotted a familiar head of carefully styled Clairol brown hair. My mother and John Queensland were ensconced in their usual pew in front of the pulpit (John had been having hearing difficulties the past two years). Aubrey, the lay reader, the chalice bearer, and two acolytes were already lined up behind the choir for the procession to the altar. Aubrey and I exchanged fleeting smiles as I scooted past to duck into the next-to-the-back pew, which happened to be empty.

I had no sooner pulled down the kneeler and slid to my sore knees, grimacing with the discomfort, than I became aware of a man falling to his knees beside me.

I finished my belated prayer, shot to my feet, grabbed the hymnbook, and began trying to find my place in the song all the rest of the congregation was singing as the procession went down the central aisle. Suddenly, a hymnbook was thrust in front of my face, open to the correct page. I took it automatically and glanced up.

Dryden was looking down at me, his face unreadable, his eyes expressionless behind his heavy glasses. We exchanged a long look, searching on his part, quite blank on mine, since I hadn't a thought in my head as to why Dryden would be here in my church juggling a prayer book with a hymnbook in the Episcopalian shuffle. He did not make the mistake of trying to establish a bogus rapport by sharing the hymnbook; but he pulled another one from the rack and joined in the singing with a great deal of enthusiasm.

Was this man *everywhere?* I couldn't throw a stick without hitting him.

As we were preparing to listen to the First Reading, he whispered, 'I put the Andersons on a plane this morning.'

I nodded curtly and kept my eyes straight forward. I couldn't think of any good reason why I should be the recipient of this information.

'She said to tell you good-bye, that she appreciated you listening.'

I gave him a quelling look, the look I saved for teenage boys cutting up in the library.

It seemed to work pretty well on Dryden, because he sat through the rest of the service in silence, affording me some much-needed peace. I wondered if he would follow me up the aisle to take communion, but he stayed in the pew.

As we pushed the kneeler up after the final 'Amen', Dryden said quietly, 'They're not coming back. After the incident last night, she's too afraid.'

I nodded acknowledgment. People were chatting all around us, and so far we weren't attracting too much attention. I tucked my purse under my arm and opened my mouth to say a firm good-bye.

'I kind of like you,' he said suddenly.

I wondered if the steam coming out of my ears was visible. I took a deep breath to suck my temper back in. 'I don't care,' I said in a low, deadly voice, goaded into absolutely sincere rudeness. I was furious, and I was also terrified that any moment a curious churchgoer would wander up to be introduced.

Luckily, the rest of the congregation was in line to shake hands with Aubrey, all anxious to get out into the beautiful weather and go home to prepare Sunday dinner. They were also providing a welcome cover of conversational buzz.

My mother was talking to Patty Cloud. The detestable Patty was looking absolutely appropriate, as always. By a *remarkable coincidence* Patty had begun attending St James's soon after Mother married John Queensland, who was a lifelong communicant. John was having a back-slapping conversation with one of his golfing cronies.

So I was safe for the moment; but any second now, Mother'd look around and then the questions would begin when she called me later, about why I was sharing a pew with one of the objectionable men she'd met at Bess Burns's house, and what he was saying to me.

'I got the punching bag out of the airplane for you,' was what he was saying.

I gaped at him.

I finally managed to say, 'How did you know?'

'I was watching. With binoculars. From the top of that ridge between the airport and the road. An experiment your reporter friend thought of, huh? Incidentally, we think she's right; that's probably how Jack Burns landed in your yard. In that little plane, all the pilot had to do was lean over, open the passenger's door, bank the plane, and out he went.'

'You were watching,' I said, unable to believe my ears. I recalled my long struggle with the bag going down the hill, the grueling process of getting it into the hangar and up into the plane, how I'd sworn and sweated.

'Yep. That was my job, till my bosses decided Jack's landing in your yard was incidental. After that they withdrew O'Riley and put me watching the Andersons. But I liked watching you better; I never know what you're going to do. Getting that bag down the hill was pretty hard.'

'Then why the *hell* didn't you come help me?'

It was the only thing I could think of to say, and I spun on my heel and stalked off down the aisle, the last to shake Aubrey's hand. He looked surprised at my expression, which must have been a picture. I said goodbye hastily and hurried out to my car, praying Mother wasn't waiting for me in the parking lot. I love my mother, but I just wasn't up to her today.

Somehow Dryden had gotten to his car quicker than I had, and he was pulling out of the parking lot as I unlocked the driver's door. The car felt oppressively warm and damp inside; I stood by the open door for a minute or two to let the atmosphere clear out.

I needed the time myself. I was stunned and shaken by Dryden's revelation. The thought of being watched when I thought myself unobserved gave me the cold creeps and a hot anger. Dryden must be good; I could believe I'd never spotted I was being followed, but I could scarcely believe Sally hadn't suspected.

But then, why on earth would she?

I quickly considered Dryden cast in the role of Angel's crazy admirer. I had to discard him, though only with great reluctance, after a little reasoning. But Dryden hadn't met Angel until he'd come out to the house to 'interview' me.

At least as far as I knew.

Angel's past was largely unknown territory to me. Angel was not a great one for talking about herself. I knew she'd grown up in Florida, that she'd met Shelby when he paid a condolence call to her folks. Shelby had been a Vietnam pal not only of Martin, but also of Angel's much older brother Jimmy Dell. Jimmy Dell had met his Maker after the war and far away from Vietnam, in the mountains of Central America.

Shelby had waited a few years for Angel to grow up, then he'd married her. They'd always been happy together, as far as I could see. Even the day or two Shelby had doubted Angel's pregnancy was his work had not, in the end, disrupted their relationship.

Maybe somewhere along the way she'd met Dryden. Maybe they'd both been acting cleverly the day I introduced them.

But what would have been the point in that?

Oh, this was all so confusing.

I looked at my watch. Martin had had plenty of time to pack up the invalid and take both Youngbloods home. The funeral wasn't until two. I turned the key in the ignition and put the car into drive.

Automatically, I turned toward home as I left the parking lot. But after a block, I realized I really didn't feel like seeing anyone right now. Perhaps I wanted to sulk awhile; maybe roll in a little self-pity. Sometimes I surfaced from my life to look at it in wonderment and irritation and also a certain amount of bafflement. I should have ended up in a house like my mother's, married to someone like Charlie Gorman, a perfectly nice boy I'd dated in high school. Charlie had always made class vice president; he was the salutatorian; he just missed being handsome. He would have been a good father for, say, two little girls; he'd done well in computers since he'd graduated from college. If I'd married Charlie, I would never have known anyone who died of murder; I would never have seen a dead person. We'd go to Walt Disney World, I dreamed, and we'd camp out . . .

Well, maybe that was going a little far.

But I still didn't feel like seeing anyone I knew, just at the moment.

I went where I often go when human companionship seems undesirable: to the Lawrenceton cemetery. I always park by my great-grandmother.

A narrow gravel driveway makes a figure eight inside the cemetery fence, to allow for parking at funerals and for easier access to the graves. My great-grandmother is one of the few people buried between the encircling driveway and the fence. She was from a farming family; maybe she wanted to be close to the surrounding fields.

Shady Rest is an old cemetery, maintained by a coalition of Lawrenceton's white churches. The segregation of death is much stricter than segregation is in life, now. The black cemetery, Mount Zion, is on the southern edge of town, while Shady Rest is a little out in the country on the west.

Shady Rest is a very ordinary cemetery, traditional, none of this flush-with-the-lawn marker stuff. The earliest tombstones date about twenty years before the Civil War, when Lawrenceton became more than a tiny settlement. There are live oaks and other hardwoods; there is close-clipped grass covering the gently rolling ground. Tiny iron fences interrupted by little gates surround some of the older family plots. There is a high, fancy, ironwork fence enclosing the whole cemetery; but there is no gate to close over the main entrance, though the two other back entrances are gated and usually locked, except during a funeral. There has never been vandalism at Shady Rest, though I'm sure some day there will be. Every now and then, someone donates a cement bench to sit beside one of the two narrow drives that cross through the graves, though I don't believe I've ever seen anyone sit on them but me.

After nodding to my great-grandmother, I go sit by Mr Early Lawrence, most times. Naturally, he was the man Lawrenceton was named after, and he earned it by hustle; an early entrepreneur, was Mr Early Lawrence. Though his descendants don't like to talk about it, somehow Early held on to his money and increased it after the War. Even today, none of the Lawrences are poor folks.

Early Lawrence had a magnificent tombstone, perhaps ten feet tall because it was topped with a stone angel whose hands were outstretched, palms up, pleading – perhaps urging passersby to feel sorry for Early? To remember to mow the grass? I had never quite understood that beseeching gesture, and I often pondered it when more immediate things gave me pain or anxiety.

After the heavy rain of the morning, the ground was soggy. I pulled out the old towel I kept in the trunk of my car, since the bench had a damp look. I picked my way to my chosen spot, spread my flowered towel, and sat down with a sigh.

Close to the center of the cemetery, the green tent was set up over the hole dug to receive Jack Burns, I noted approvingly; Jasper Funeral Home was on the ball. The chairs for the family were unfolded and ready with green covers slipped on. Artificial turf discreetly covered the mound of dirt at the back of the tent. The artificial green was gleaming with water droplets.

I wandered over to have a closer look, and found that the lowering device was in place over the grave, the green webbing stretched across to receive the casket. I wondered which of the levers on the side released the webbing to let the casket descend, but I was certainly not about to experiment. Sheer interest in the mechanism kept me there for a few moments, until I recollected that into this hole would descend the body of a man I knew, and I beat, a shamefaced retreat to Early Lawrence.

I looked up at the angel, again studying that calm face for some trace of a clue as to its intent. I wondered who had sculpted it; did he churn them out, or make each one as it was commissioned? He'd enjoyed doing the wings, I could tell . . . they were full and beautiful, as feathery as stone could look.

I thought the usual thoughts – what would they say, all these dead Lawrencetonians, if they could see the town now, look over the horizon and see Atlanta approaching, encroaching? What if my maternal grandmother, whom I could faintly remember (she was over there close to Great-grandmother, but within the driveway), could give judgment on her daughter's successes and her granddaughter's peculiar life?

We were not a fertile family; I was the only child of an only child, and according to the specialist, I could not even have that one my mother and grandmother had been granted. I'd known now for two months; but sometimes I still cried when I thought about it. I had to get over that. I began counting my breaths, slow and even; in, out, one, two, three, four . . . self-pity was a drug. I must not become addicted. Self-pity is like chocolate; as you get older, you can only afford a little bit.

I heard a robin, then a mockingbird. Bees did their thing among all the flowering bushes and a few premature Easter lilies, set by gravestones. Here and there was a red foil-covered pot filled with shriveled remains of poinsettias, but on the whole folks took better care of their dead than that.

So peaceful. I deliberately took off my watch and dropped it in my purse. After a while, my tears dried and I cut loose from my worries, letting my mind drift. It was as though the countless religious ceremonies held here had drenched the soil not with anguish, but with calm detachment, thoughts of eternity. Every now and then I'd see a car go by; Shady Rest was perilously close to one of the new housing developments.

When at last I rose I'd achieved peace, or at least calm.

I really wouldn't have had Charlie Gorman on a platter.

I was making my way back to my car, taking my time and reading headstones, when I actually began to think. It seemed to me I hadn't been asking the right questions. I'd been asking *why* these bizarre things were happening, *who* could be doing them, instead of *how*.

I was convinced that all the events of the past couple of weeks were related: the murders of Jack Burns and Beverly Rillington, the murderous attacks on Shelby and Arthur Smith.

Jack Burns had been dumped from an airplane, so the killer had to know how to fly. Jack had been killed by a blow to the head (last night's local paper had said), as had Beverly Rillington, so the killer was strong and not afraid of violence.

Since somehow the killer had approached Shelby, who still had no memory of the attack, either (for convenience's sake I'd term the killer male) he was someone known to Shelby, someone Shelby had no reason to fear; or he was used to stealth.

And if the stabbing of Arthur in the middle of a crowd was any indication, this person was getting increasingly reckless. The stabbing had to have been impulsive; the weapon was probably a lowly pocketknife, if the gossip I'd heard had been correct. So someone in the crowd around Arthur had been overwhelmed with fury so sudden and devastating that he'd risked all to injure Arthur.

And somehow, somewhere, he'd concealed the weapon so that

none of the police on the scene had been able to find a trace of it. Could a pocketknife be swallowed? I wondered wildly. We'd all been searched. Where the hell could it be? This was a crucial *how*. How had it been concealed?

It was the sort of puzzle that I eagerly moved on to find the answer to in every fictional mystery I read. I never tried to figure it out myself when I knew the writer would supply the solution in a page or two. But I couldn't flip to the end of the book now . . .

I rolled down the car window, letting the cool breeze toss my hair. I looked at the proper green tent-roof over Jack Burns's grave. On its surface I replayed the banquet's ending.

Martin and I walked out the door, and he took my hand. Arthur and his date were behind us. I remembered how irritated I'd been with Arthur; how he'd eyed me.

And when I remembered that, a little cold trickle started down my spine.

But I ignored it with a great effort of will. I was going to track this memory.

The cool, sweet evening. The parking lot. The little knot of people on the sidewalk. The quiet voices exchanging pleasantries. Jesse Prentiss introducing Verna, a stout sixty-year-old with a narrow mouth and a tight perm, to the anxious Andersons, who wanted only to be gone. Perry asking Jenny Tankersley if she wanted to go to his place for a drink . . . Paul with his hand in his pocket to retrieve his car keys, his date standing with her arms crossed on her chest; probably having circulation problems because her blue jeans were acting as tourniquets. Who else? Marnie Sands, groping in her purse, looking annoyed. I remembered thinking she couldn't find her keys.

We'd moved to the right, facing out into the parking lot, preparing to cross to Martin's Mercedes. The dog and the cat had provided the diversion necessary for the attacker to make up his mind; he'd try for Arthur . . . the idea of what extreme anger must be necessary to prompt such risk-taking made me shiver.

Then, of course, my fall to the pavement. I touched my bruised face; I had a blue bump on my right forehead, and a little scrape on my right cheek. I'd been lucky.

The confusion, the screaming, the moan and curse from Arthur. Martin helping me up, trying to find out where I'd been hurt. Jesse Prentiss, unexpectedly authoritative, telling Perry to run inside to call the ambulance . . . the sound of Perry taking off. There'd been running feet to and from the scene on the sidewalk: Dryden had run up to us, and Perry had run away.

Paul Allison had said, too late, that he'd called it in from his car already; Perry had been in the building by the time Paul had told us. Perry had had a perfect opportunity to get rid of the knife.

Okay, what about Dryden? His presence at the end of the parking lot was explainable; he was guarding the Andersons. But could he have thrown a knife, somehow? No, I decided reluctantly. Arthur had been facing Dryden's car, and the wound had been in the back of Arthur's shoulder.

Arthur's date, the little gal with the ponytail? Nope. Not only did it not ring true, but she'd been searched. So had Deena Cotton, who hadn't been carrying a purse; and if she'd had a gnat in the pocket of those jeans, I would've been able to count its legs. Jesse and Verna Prentiss had been standing too far away to reach Arthur, by any stretch of their arms or my imagination. Martin and I had been holding hands and had been in front of Arthur. Marnie Sands had been in the right position and had had her hand in her huge shoulder bag . . . but how could she have gotten through the search?

Paul had watched us every minute until his fellow officers had arrived, unless . . . yes, there'd been the seconds he'd knelt beside Arthur, his hand supporting Arthur's head; he'd been staring down at his wounded colleague. There'd been seconds, then.

But as I'd left the community center, I'd seen the police officers examining the area where Arthur had been stabbed. If the knife had been there – and it could only have been concealed hastily – they would've found it.

No. Somehow, some way, Perry had concealed the knife on his way into the community center. Had to be Perry.

I thought of my friend Sally, about how cheerful she'd been the day we took the punching bag to the airport. She'd already been through so much with Perry, his bouts with depression and his run-in with drugs; the prospect of Jenny Tankersley as a daughter-in-law had to look like Easy Street in comparison. It was inescapable, though, that Perry looked like the best bet for this series of horrible events. He'd looked at Angel with wanting eyes; he'd had a chance to hide the knife.

But that wasn't enough, even close to enough, evidence for an arrest.

I started the car and drove out of the cemetery slowly, not having the slightest idea of where I was going. It was noon, lunchtime. I bought a sandwich from our local barbecue place and ate it sitting in the car, a practice I normally detest. Maybe I should have called Martin. I thought of doing it, then I remembered the day before when I'd had to track him down, and I childishly thought it might do him good to wonder where *I* was for a while. But those were surface thoughts, ideas that just skated through the front of my brain.

I had the feeling you get when everyone begins roaring with laughter at a joke, and you sit anxiously waiting for the punch line to make sense. There was something big and obvious right in front of me, and I couldn't see it. It was like there was a hole in my glasses. In that spot, I was blind, though I could see clearly all around it.

Chapter Ten

I surprised myself by driving to the hospital and asking to see Arthur.

'He's got a police officer stationed outside his room, you'll have to ask her,' said the stout, elderly volunteer at the information desk. So I trudged through the uncomfortably familiar corridors, thinking that if this kept up, I might even learn the floor plan and figure out the reasoning behind it.

Arthur was in a room at the end of the hall so visitors could be seen coming for a long time. The officer in blue outside Arthur's room was indeed a woman, husky and tough in her uniform. 'C. Turlock' said her little name pin, and it seemed an unpromising sort of name.

Sure enough, Officer Turlock was determined to be the snarlingest watchdog a wounded fellow officer ever had, and she found me highly suspicious. Since my head was approximately as high as her elbow, and I offered to leave my purse out in the hall with her, I couldn't see the source of her suspicions – did she think my glasses concealed a hidden dagger?

If Arthur himself hadn't called out to C. Turlock to find out what she was in a lather about, I would have had to give up; but when he found out who was at the door, he ordered C. Turlock to let me in.

Arthur had one of those horrible gowns on. I could see the bandage at the back of his shoulder, where the material had pulled to one side. He looked as if he was in pain; and I was reminded that being stabbed, even with a pocketknife, is a very unpleasant experience.

I stood beside him, looking at him and wondering what to say. He looked right back.

'So, did Perry do it and drop the knife in a garbage can inside the building?' I asked finally.

Arthur's face went through the most amazing changes. First he looked stunned, then aghast, and at last he started laughing. It was a big laugh, from the belly, and C. Turlock stuck her head in to see what was so funny. Arthur made an imperious sweeping motion with his right hand, and she hastily shut the door.

That right hand kept on traveling and grasped mine, drawing me nearer to the bed. I looked steadily into the pale blue eyes that had once turned my legs to jelly.

'I should never have left you and married Lynn,' Arthur said.

'Yes, you should,' I said briskly. 'And you ought to go back to her now, if she'll have you.'

'Can't I detach you from that shady bastard you married?' Arthur's voice was light, but he was serious.

All the troubles Martin and I had flashed through my mind. I shrugged. 'Not with a crowbar,' I answered.

'I don't think Perry did it,' he said, after a moment, dropping my hand.

'Why?'

'Faron Henske hand-searched the garbage cans along the way to the office where Perry placed the call to 911,' Arthur said. 'He looked down drains. He took apart a sink. Faron isn't a ball of fire, but he's a very reliable searcher. And there were cleaning people still in the community center, plus a few guests who stayed to talk or take down some of the decorations, and they say Perry didn't stop on his way to the office.'

'And the office was taken apart.'

'Yes. Of course.' Arthur leaned back against his pillow; I'd only seen him look this bad once before, when I'd nursed him through a bout of flu.

'I'm real sorry you got hurt,' I said.

'I'm real sorry I fell on you,' he answered politely. 'Took you down to the ground, Paul says. Of course, it made the fall easier on *me*.' A shadow of his hard grin was on his face. 'Did you get hurt?'

He sounded rather as if he hoped I had.

'Just some bruises and scrapes.' I pulled back my hair to show him the bump on my forehead.

'Next time I'll try to fall on someone bigger, and land on her front and not her back,' he told me, trying for bawdy.

'Lynn's bigger than me.'

'Roe . . .'

'Okay, sorry. I don't know what went on with your marriage. But I'm not the escape hatch. I'll always have good memories of you, and I don't want them to get sour.'

'Straight from the hip, Roe.'

'Had to be,' I said.

'I love you.' Suddenly he looked twenty, vulnerable and yearning.

'You love what you remember. But you were screwing Lynn on the side for the last three or four months we were together. So I'd say your love wasn't ever an exclusive item.'

'Let me have it when I'm down.'

'Only time I can get you to listen.'

The corners of his mouth twitched in a smile. 'Okay, okay. You listen now,' and he reached for my hand again. 'You take care, Roe. I know you love Bartell, but since you told me what you think about my marriage, I'll tell you what I think about yours.'

Oh, boy, I didn't want to hear this.

'That guy is out of your league, Roe. He's tough and he's ruthless. He's a lot older. He'll never think you're his equal.'

That seemed a very strange charge to level at Martin, and I looked at Arthur in some surprise. I'd been scared, perhaps, that Arthur would tell me he'd kept Martin under surveillance and that Martin had a mistress. Or that Martin was engaged in some criminal activity. Arthur would just love to catch Martin in those situations, and he'd make sure I knew, because he'd warned me from the time I met Martin that I shouldn't marry him.

If Arthur hadn't caught him, Martin wasn't doing it, I suddenly realized. I hadn't known how worried I'd been until the relief spreading through my body made me giddy with cheer.

'I don't know if he thinks I'm his equal,' I said. 'We're so different I think "equal" would be hard to pin down. But he lets me be myself, and he's never tried to change me, and we enjoy each other very much.'

We looked at each other steadily. I thought of how wounded I'd felt at Arthur and Lynn's wedding, how betrayed. It seemed strange now, as though those emotions had been felt by some other person and only told to me.

'Good-bye, Arthur. I hope you get out of the hospital soon.'

'Bye, Roe. Thanks for visiting. I know you're curious about what happened. I'll get Paul to keep you filled in.'

I thought about being embarrassed, decided to skip it.

'Thanks. See you,' I said, and walked through the door.

'Officer Turlock,' I said, inclining my head. She nodded back grudgingly. I didn't feel I'd made a friend.

A glance at my watch told me it was almost time for the funeral. I brushed my hair and powdered my nose in one of the chemically scented hospital bathrooms, and drove to Western Hill Baptist Church.

Western Hill was easily the prettiest church in Lawrenceton, a town of many churches. It sat by itself on the top of a rolling hill in, obviously, the (north) western part of town, which consisted mostly of newer suburbs. The church overlooked Lawrenceton, a calm, white-spired presence that everyone enjoyed. Western Hill was landscaped to the nth degree, with flowers, shrubs, and grass that looked clipped with a level. In its rivalry with the larger Antioch Baptist, which actually possessed an indoor swimming pool, Western gained points with its parking lot, which surrounded the church on three sides; no long slog to the car at Western.

And Western was undoubtedly the best place to have a funeral, though I was sure that hadn't crossed Bess Burns's mind when she'd joined the church years before.

The long black hearse was parked at Western's massive front doors, on the semicircular drive that curved across the hill in a graceful arc. This was a driveway used only for ceremonies;

Western had provided back entrances and that wonderful parking lot for regular occasions. I used one of those smaller entrances, and wended my way through the day-care corridor to the sanctuary door. In the sanctuary, the ceiling was two stories high, and the walls and ceiling were dazzling white, giving the impression of light and sky. The sun streamed through the high arched windows and flung a bolt of dramatic light across Jack's dark gray coffin, topped with a large casket spray of white gladiolus, resting at the steps up to the altar.

Jack Burns was being buried on a beautiful day.

I had to walk to the back of the church, since I'd entered from the door to the west of the altar area; as I passed, I scanned the row of pallbearers on the left front pew. I knew all of them, from Jack's fellow officers – Paul Allison, Faron Henske, Chief of Police Tom Nash Vernon, Sheriff Padgett Lanier, and (amazingly) Lynn Liggett Smith – to his son, Jack Junior. I scurried by, not particularly wanting to meet the eyes of any of the people on that pew, especially Lynn.

The church was rapidly filling up, and I ducked into the first aisle space I saw, nodding to Sam and Marva Clerrick sitting in the pew behind me. I was closer to the front of the church than I liked to be, but I didn't want to sit on one of the folding chairs that had been lined up in the back. I got settled, tried to stick my purse under the pew, began to slide to my knees and just in time recalled I wasn't in a church with kneelers.

'Almost hit the ground again, didn't you?' murmured a voice in my ear.

I had a moment of sheer rage when I thought the speaker was Dryden. Was I going to be approached in every church I entered?

But Martin, perfectly appropriate in a quiet suit, sat down in the pew beside me. I took his hand and squeezed it, my heart thudding in a ridiculous way. I was so glad to see him I was in serious danger of crying, and that would have been noticed this early in the proceedings.

'You came anyway,' I whispered, knowing that was obvious but wanting to say it, nonetheless.

He looked at me sideways, and a little smile curved his lips. 'Missed you,' he said.

Then the organ music changed in tone, the funeral director from Jasper's appeared at the front of the church to signal the family had arrived, and Bess Burns and her daughter walked down the aisle as the congregation rose to its feet. In her black, Bess seemed to have lost ten pounds in a few days, and Romney's round face was bare of makeup and stained with tears. I knew Romney well from her teenage days, barely over, when she'd come into the library three or four times a week. It shocked me to see her look so adult.

I hastily revised my carnal thoughts for those more appropriate to the occasion; whatever Maker there was to meet, Jack Burns up yonder in the stainless-steel coffin had seen that Maker face-to-face. No more mysteries left to solve for that detective.

I wondered if the pall-bearing detectives on the front row had thought of that. I could see a slice of all their faces, as they looked to the right as the minister entered his pulpit. Paul was looking pale and resolute, Faron Henske solemn, and Lynn Liggett Smith was just blank. I'd never expected to see a female pallbearer, but I heard Marva hissing to Sam that Jack had specified Lynn in his will. Arthur was supposed to serve, too, but his wound had prevented it; Paul had replaced him.

The coffin remained closed after the minister's address. I could well believe that it had been impossible for the mortician to reconstruct Jack. So instead of viewing the deceased, a ritual I was glad to forgo, we all retreated to our cars and drove to Shady Rest. Though parking space at Shady Rest would be at a premium, I took my own car and Martin took his Mercedes; I didn't want to leave my Chevette at Western Hill, which was not exactly on the way home.

Martin and I stood in the sun, our heels sinking into the rain-softened ground, while the brief graveside service came to an end. The pallbearers laid their boutonnieres on the casket, and the minister, reminded by their action, did likewise.

The funeral director, a trim blond man I'd never met, bent

down to Bess and murmured something, and Bess, wakening from her thoughts, nodded and stood. The funeral was officially over.

Immediately, most of the attendees left to resume their regular Sunday afternoon pursuits.

Romney Burns went around saying hello to people she recognized while her mother had a quiet talk with the minister. I introduced Romney to Martin and we talked stiffly about the day and the service. Romney seemed remote, numb; I felt so sorry for her.

Jack Junior stood by himself, facing out over the adjacent field, smoking a cigarette, his expression savagely angry; I thought I would steer clear of Jack Junior, who was obviously in a very volatile state.

Not everyone had noticed this, however. Somehow uncued by Jack's stance, Faron Henske laid a big, brown would-be comforting hand on Jack's shoulder. Jack twitched away, threw down his cigarette, and abruptly lost control. Those of us looking in his direction could see him pop, and a collective wince ran through us.

The minister was pulling out of the main gate. He should have stayed a few minutes longer.

'One of you did it!' Jack shrieked. Those who'd not seen the windup froze in their tracks; and poor Faron looked devastated at having set off this firestorm.

'He wouldn't turn his back on someone he didn't know! One of you did it!'

Martin looked grim and hard. The blond funeral director, closest to the two, was considering whether to intervene; he thought the better of it, and I was sure he was right. The only person who could handle this came striding across the soft ground; Bess, in her black, wrapped her arms around her son and talked quietly in his ear, her eyes dry. Romney, round and sandy as her father had been, stood a few feet away, scared to join them.

'The tension seemed to seep out of Jack as we watched, and the few remaining people scattered to reach their cars, trying not to look as if they were hurrying. Jack was crying as Martin and I turned away. I glanced over my shoulder to see Bess, Romney, and her brother make their way to Jack's car, and leave.

I looked sideways at my husband. If there's anything Martin hates worse than watching strangers pour out strong emotion, I have yet to discover it; that's one reason I go to the movies with Sally or Angel. His lips were pressed together, his gaze straight ahead. Martin looked as if he were tempted to say, 'Thanks a lot, Roe,' but was trying to forbear.

'I'm sorry,' I said with a certain bite in my voice, 'for letting you know I wanted you to come.' I could hardly apologize for Jack's behavior. I eyed him cautiously, waiting to see what his mood was.

'How many years will Lawrenceton recall that little scene?' he asked. I relaxed.

'Forever and ever. Do you think Jack Junior was right?'

'Yes,' said Martin after a second. 'Yes, I think he was.'

I thought of the faces around the grave, all of them known, familiar. I shivered in the bright sun, and Martin put his arm around me.

'I have a feeling,' Martin said, looking straight ahead, 'that we haven't exactly been operating on the same wavelength lately.'

That seemed as good a way of putting it as any. I remembered Martin's first wife telling me that Martin was not a man to talk about problems, and I felt he was doing the best he could, considerably better than I had anticipated.

'I've been working a lot of hours, and when I thought about it on the way home from Chicago, I realized I hadn't been seeing you much, lately.'

This was going almost too well.

'I'll try to be at home more,' Martin said briefly, but not without effort. 'I guess I didn't like it when you went back to work without talking to me about it first.'

The shadow of an oak branch tossing in the wind played over Martin's face.

'Possibly,' I said very carefully, 'we should talk to each other a little more.' We looked at each other cautiously and stiffly, like creatures from different planets who basically bore each other good will, but who did not speak the same language to explain that.

After a long pause, Martin nodded in acknowledgment, and we resumed the walk to his car. As we reached the Mercedes, shining whitely against the green carpet of grass, Martin swung me around to face him, gripped both my arms, and to my astonishment leaned me against the car and kissed me thoroughly.

'Well,' I said when I came up for air, 'that was wonderful, but don't you think we really ought to postpone this until we get home?'

'Everyone has left,' Martin said breathlessly, and I saw that that was true, for the most part. On the other side of the cemetery, the group of pallbearers (minus Jack Junior) was deep in conversation by Paul's dark blue Chrysler, and I remembered all of them were police officers with murders to solve.

The funeral home staff had gone to work as soon as the widow had left. The casket was in the ground, the lowering device had been packed up, and the funeral director and another man were shoveling the dirt into place, while a third man loaded the folding chairs into the funeral home van. I knew from past experience that soon the dirt would be mounded, the flowers laid over it, the artificial turf removed. The tent would stay for a day or so. Then that would be gone; the cemetery would return to its slumber.

'I'll see you at the house,' I told Martin, and rested the palm of my hand against his cheek.

As I bumped the Chevette along the gravel road leading out of the main gates of the cemetery, I passed Paul's car. Paul and Lynn were the only ones left of the group that had been there a few moments ago; I raised my hand as I passed, and Lynn responded with a bob of her head, but she didn't stop talking to Paul. Paul's pallor and sharp features had never been more evident. I thought he was suffering from some distress. He had one hand extended, resting on the roof of his car, and that seemed to be the main thing holding him up. He didn't acknowledge me at all by wave or smile, but fixed me in a stare that seemed to pin me like a captured butterfly. I was glad when I was by him and on the road home; I couldn't imagine what he and Lynn could have been discussing that would make him look that distraught. I glanced once in my rearview mirror to see Lynn's car leaving the front gate of the cemetery, turning left instead of right as I had done.

Perhaps Lynn, too, had come to the conclusion that the person who'd attacked Arthur was Perry, Paul's former stepson and now his friend. That would account for the haggard expression on Paul's bony face.

I thought of how upset he'd been last night, when Arthur had been stabbed; I thought of his unexpected choice of female companion, a woman with poor taste and judgment, so different from Sally. And yet, this was the woman whose rump he'd groped in front of me. I felt again that flash of uneasiness. That hadn't really been Paul-like, had it? Paul had always been calm, controlled, and conservative.

He'd sure lost his calm the night before. His voice had certainly been ragged when he'd told Jesse he'd already radioed to the police station.

I braked and pulled over to the side of the road. Luckily, there was a shoulder; luckily, no one was behind me.

He'd called from his car.

There *was* someone else who'd had a chance to hide a knife. Paul. The detective who'd guarded us till the other officers could get there.

But why? I raised my hands in front of me to cover my face so I could concentrate.

Why would Paul stab Arthur? They'd never liked each other much, but they'd worked together for years without actually harming each other. What could have precipitated . . . ?

Arthur had separated from Lynn recently. So?

And Arthur had shown up at the Pan-Am Agra banquet with an obviously unsuitable date, as, indeed, had Paul. But Arthur had eyed me all during the banquet. My husband had certainly noticed, and if he had, others would have too . . . why would

Paul stab Arthur over Arthur's lust for me? It just didn't make sense.

Yes, it did. But it was hard to admit it to myself, because it seemed so bizarre, so ridiculous. It had been in front of me all the time, but I would not see it, I could not see myself as that kind of woman. Angel had suspected it all along: I remembered the look she'd given me the day Paul had deposited Beverly Rillington's purse on her car hood, mistaking it for mine.

Paul had stabbed Arthur because Arthur had 'dated' me for months, openly wanted me again.

Paul had attacked Beverly Rillington because Beverly threatened me in public, in front of Perry – who had relayed the scene to his former stepfather, uncle, and friend. Beverly's purse was the evidence of Paul's revenge for her slighting me.

Paul had hit Shelby over the head because Shelby was patrolling my yard when Paul wanted to – break in? Stare at my window? Serenade me in the rain with a mandolin?

I slapped myself in the cheek to keep concentrating, to keep from veering away from thoughts that made me sick. I laid my hands on the steering wheel. They were trembling violently. Think, Roe!

Jack Burns, my longtime enemy, a man known to publicly badmouth me, a man Paul had to see every day since he was Paul's boss. The first death.

I'd been so fixated on Angel's magnificence, I'd been unable to read the very clear message. Jack Burns, falling out of that airplane, head over heels, to land in my yard. Like the damn cat bringing me the mouse. A trophy.

See what I did for you?

Oh my God. And I'd left Martin at the cemetery with Paul. And in front of this obsessed man, Martin had just laid a kiss on me that had practically singed my hair.

Chapter Eleven

I did the most reckless U-turn ever performed on a country road in Spalding County. I went as fast as I could bring myself to drive, and prayed heartily that this day above all days a county patrolman had set up a speed trap on this remote little road.

Of course that didn't happen.

I had to think, I told myself frantically. I couldn't just drive in there and make everything all right.

I slowed the car as I reached the cemetery. I swerved the Chevette across the road and into the ditch and didn't care if it stayed there till it rotted. It was off the road.

As though my furious parking method hadn't made any noise, I got out quietly and shut the door with great care. My car had entered the ditch a little above the southeast corner of the rectangular cemetery tract. The main gate was in the middle of the long east side, the two auxiliary gates were on the west, opening out onto a rutted dirt track that ran along outside the length of the fence to tie back into the county road forming the eastern boundary of the property.

From this corner, the trees obscured my view, but I could catch a glimpse of gleaming white up close to the north part of the cemetery where Jack had been buried; Martin's Mercedes.

I shivered all over. I forced my brain to work, to plan.

The main gate on the east was too exposed, visible from most places in the cemetery. So I crept along the fence, through the high weeds, and tried not to let the thought of snakes cross my mind. Since church and funeral going had been the designated occasions when I'd dressed that morning, my clothes and shoes were hardly helpful in ditch-slogging or cemetery crawling. The rayon of the beige skirt caught on everything I passed, the low heels of the pumps sank into the wet earth, and my loose hair was collecting a fine assortment of seeds and burrs.

I reached the track at the southwest corner and followed it, ducking low while trying to run, one of the most difficult things I'd ever attempted.

Every three yards or so I'd stop to look and listen; I heard nothing, saw nothing, cursed the trees and bushes I'd thought so beautiful this morning.

I got to the first rear gate.

It was fairly exposed, though if Martin and Paul were still close to Jack's grave, there were several tall plantings and grave markers between them and me. But I dropped to my stomach and crawled. I reached a good vantage point behind one of the few raised vaults in Lawrenceton, and peered from behind it.

My heart sank. Paul's car was indeed still parked parallel to the west fence; I could see only the back of the tent left over Jack's grave, but I could tell the hearse and the funeral home employees were gone.

I sidled up closer, hugging the granite of the vault. I confirmed what I already suspected – there were no other cars. Paul and Martin, alone here.

And me.

Then I saw them. Martin's left side was toward me, his back against the thick trunk of a live oak, and he was looking several degrees whiter than he had when I'd left. His face was set in lines I'd seen only once before. This was how he must've looked in the war, I thought fleetingly.

Paul was standing with his right side to me, his back to his car, and he had a gun in his hand. He was talking to Martin; though I couldn't hear him, I could see his mouth moving, and I saw from the way Martin had his head cocked that he was listening.

No weapon. I had no weapon.

I couldn't run and tackle him; there wasn't enough cover between the vault and where he was standing.

Would he shoot me?

Maybe not; maybe. He was supposed to love me, after all. But what if he did shoot, and his shooting me didn't give Martin enough time to grab him? Neither of us would be saved.

I had to hurt Paul.

And by God, I wanted to.

But I hadn't anything except my hands, and I didn't think they'd do enough damage to stop him long enough.

What if the knife was still in his car? The thought burst on me like a beautiful firework.

After a moment I realized it was a stupid idea, but it was all I had. As I began my approach to his car, slightly to the rear of Paul's peripheral vision, I realized just how dumb it was. But I considered for a second: he'd had to leave it there during the investigation at the community center. He'd had to leave it in there this morning, when he'd been at the police station, presumably; and he'd had to leave it in there for the funeral, because he couldn't withdraw it during the service or later at the cemetery. So our whole salvation depended on whether or not Paul Allison had been too exhausted the night before to withdraw the knife and clean its hiding place.

He'd parked facing south on the little drive, so I had to creep up the passenger side, and pray the door was unlocked. I was afraid to look toward Paul and Martin, afraid that I would see Martin get shot, afraid that if my eyes met Martin's his face would change and Paul would turn to see me. I could hear Paul's voice ranting on and on and I made my way closer, but I shut out what he was saying.

Finally, I had used all the available cover, including Early Lawrence's angel. I had come to a point where I was blocked by graves or trees, and I had to cross the track that made a large figure eight within the cemetery, about at the cross-loop. I took off my shoes so they wouldn't crunch on the gravel, and tried to think light so my feet wouldn't make noise. I risked a glance; I had worked my way so close that I was nearly behind Paul now. Martin's eyes were focused on Paul. I didn't know if he'd seen me or not.

I had to chance it. I took a deep breath and stepped out into the open. I took one step across the gravel, then another, then I could regain the soft grass and walk quickly to the passenger side of the car.

I looked down at the door. I was so desperate that for a minute, my eyes refused to focus.

The door was unlocked.

Praise God, I thought; I gripped the handle. I had to look again now, and I fixed my gaze on Paul's back, trying not to see Martin over his shoulder. It helped that Paul was the taller of the two by a couple of inches. I did not want to see Martin's face, see the knowledge of my presence reflected in it. I willed Martin not to know I was here. And I pressed in the release button with my thumb.

It sounded like an explosion to me, but I knew the sound was small. I stopped breathing, the car door barely open, waiting to see if Paul would turn my way.

He didn't. He kept on talking. I inhaled deliberately. I was lightheaded with relief and oxygen deprivation.

Gently, gently, I pulled open the door. So slowly my thumb cramped, I eased it off the release knob. I unclenched my fingers from the handle. I wiggled them for a second or two, trying to restore circulation.

I crouched again, my sore knees protesting at a barely discernible level. The scabs had come off eons ago in the ditch; I could add blood to the list of items staining my skirt.

But I hadn't made that tiny stain on the blue cloth of the car seat. You'd only see it if you were thinking about blood.

Maybe he'd had it covered with the little notepad that was almost on top of it now; maybe he'd jostled the pad when he'd gotten out of the car.

I looked at the police radio longingly; but I had not the slightest idea how to operate it, and I was scared to death someone would radio Paul while I was crouched here beside the car. I looked over the front seat quickly. If the knife was here, it would have to be around this small area.

The quickest and easiest place to hide the knife would have been to slip it in the crack in the seat.

I slid my hand down into the crack, where I could see the tiny stain. I felt stickiness. I felt a hard shape.

The knife was still there.

My fingers examined it with caution; I didn't want to grab the blade. I gripped it and pulled it out. There was old, dark blood staining my fingers; the stickiness I'd felt. I stared at the knife, wishing I had time to be squeamish. There was dried blood on the little blade and on the hilt. Paul had driven it into Arthur as hard as he could.

It was just a little brown pocketknife, with handy attachments.

Unfortunately, the only one of use to me was the blade.

I stood. I had the knife gripped so the blade pointed upward; all the fictional crime I'd read told me that was the way to use it. I should try to come in under his ribs, I recalled.

I worked my way around the car and stood perhaps twelve feet behind Paul. I was curiously indecisive. Should I sneak up and stab him? Should I scream and run headlong over the grass? The nature of the ground, broken by headstones and footstones, pots of flowers, and a toddler's grave heartbreakingly decorated with a tiny baseball mitt, forbade the scream-and-run approach.

So I began to step quietly over the grass, not daring to look at Martin, focusing on the spot low in Paul's back where I would drive in the knife.

My bare feet made scarcely any sound, and Paul was still talking.

'You've never valued her enough, you can't give her the devotion she needs,' he was telling Martin. 'You go out of town all the time and leave her alone. A husband should stay with his wife. Leaving her with the hired help, you see now that couldn't work! And you let people hurt her. If you really loved Aurora, you wouldn't let these people hurt her!'

I was absolutely determined to kill this man and save Martin's life, but now that I was close to him, I realized I should have run full-tilt after all. This creeping, this planning, was making my soul sick. I could feel sweat pop out on my forehead. My hands were shaking.

I was a yard behind Paul now, and I registered the fact that he'd taken off his suit coat after the funeral – one less layer to penetrate. This was so much harder than I'd ever imagined.

I bit down on my lip, took the last step. My left hand went up to grip his shoulder as my right hand drew back, then plunged in the knife.

Paul made a horrible sound, and his shirt became reddened in a widening circle. I let go of the knife and jumped back to be out of his way when he fell, and he said, 'Walk around where I can see you or I'll shoot him this second.'

I wanted to throw up.

I'd done it. I'd stabbed a man I knew. And there he stood, not falling, not defeated. I did as he said, though my legs were trembling so much I didn't think I'd make it.

The knife, so much heavier at the handle than the blade, slid out of the wound and fell to the ground. I made a horrible noise, but not as horrible as the sound of that knife meeting the dirt.

For the first time I met Martin's eyes. His face was unreadable. He might have been made of stone.

Paul's face was more open. He'd been pouring himself out to Martin, and he hadn't closed the emotional doors yet. He was anguished when he saw his attacker was me.

'Oh, Aurora, how could you do this?' he said wonderingly.

I was so shaken, I found myself on the verge of apologizing.

'You have to spare Martin,' I said to him, willing him to be swallowed up in my intensity.

'Look over there, Aurora,' Paul said gently. 'See the bed of flowers I've got for you?'

The 'bed of flowers' was the funeral arrangements spread neatly on the freshly turned dirt.

'I'll kill him and we'll share the bed of flowers. You deserve something that beautiful, that fragile. You're so beautiful and fragile yourself.'

I shook my head hopelessly, not knowing what to say. Paul was crazy, but not so crazy he couldn't function in his job. I didn't think I could deceive him, since a large part of his work lay in detecting deception.

'Paul, I am willing to go with you if you'll let Martin go,' I said. The seepage of blood had slowed, but not stopped. I felt as if a dog had ripped me up and left pieces of me all over the clipped green grass. I felt the tears beginning to flow. I might not be able to save my husband or myself. I had one more chance.

I held out my arms to Paul Allison and I stepped a little closer. 'Paul, listen, you're – I'm so sorry,' and I began to cry in earnest, but I didn't cover my face, didn't let my arms drop.

'You have to stay where you are, honey,' said Paul. His voice was faltering. 'Please don't cry.'

'No,' I said, and kept on moving slowly, inch by inch, until I wrapped my arms around Paul, holding his to his sides. I laid my head against his chest; how strange it felt to be holding someone built differently from Martin; taller, thinner, less muscled. I could feel Paul's heart beating beneath my cheek. I had sunk a knife into this man's body. His blood was staining my left arm and hand.

And I felt his extended forearm fall to his side, the arm holding the gun. I heard the thud as the gun fell to the grass. I felt both his arms circling me, pulling me closer to him for the first and last time.

He buried his face in my hair.

'Sweet,' he said, and then Martin clipped him in the head with the gun butt.

We had a hard time getting ourselves believed, even after Lynn told the other cops that Paul, his heart overflowing under the emotional pressure of the funeral, had confided in her that day, following Jack's interment, that he was 'deeply involved' with me. He also told her some of the same points he'd raised against Martin: that Martin was an absentee husband, that Martin permitted slander against my name.

To say the least, Lynn was highly skeptical and dubious about all Paul's fantasies. And she knew me well enough to know that's just what they were.

But she wasn't happy to testify against a fellow officer. No one on the police force was delighted to be told that one of their number had murdered another officer, one female civilian, and attacked a male officer and a male civilian.

And Paul popped back into a more rational frame of mind to deny everything except that he had a real crush on me, not exactly an unknown situation. He said that Martin and I had attacked him unprovoked, that I'd misunderstood certain things he'd told me, and that Martin had then pulled Paul's gun from Paul's holster and hit him with it.

That was not exactly a sturdy defense, no matter how much the police wanted to believe one of their own. And there were stains matching Arthur's blood between the seat cushions of Paul's car. And there was a matching stain left on the handle, a stain not washed off by Paul's own blood. Then Jenny Tankersley, that tough flier, came forward to tell Lynn that she'd seen Paul practicing sharp banking moves in one of the small planes she rented, and that she'd noticed something odd: he was opening the passenger door of the little plane while he was flying, then banking to let the door slam shut.

'I knew it was someone after you,' Angel said one day, the day Paul finally confessed to Jack's murder.

'You did?' I said. 'Sure.'

'You thought it was me, but I knew it was you. You just weren't looking at it straight.'

'You seem much more a candidate for obsessive love than I,' I said stiffly.

'It's not your fault,' she said, shading her eyes against the sun. We were lying in our swimming suits on the sundeck, cold drinks at hand. I was trying desperately to feel as lighthearted as the day and the frivolous occupation should have made me. There was not a cloud in the sky. I glistened with oil as though I were going to be fried. I hadn't tried to get a tan in years, avoided the sun as I would the plague. And yet here I was, trying to lighten up my life.

Angel was lying on her back, and I stole a glimpse at her stomach. It was definitely convex.

'That's not *my* fault,' she said.

I closed my eyes and felt myself flushing.

'You gotta work that through, Roe. Or you'll go crazy. There are pregnant women everywhere.'

I nodded. I hoped she was watching.

'You know when the baby comes, Shelby and I gotta find somewhere else to live.'

'I figured,' I said quietly. I turned over on my stomach and buried my face in my arms.

'In fact, before. Because my mom told me after it comes, I'll be too busy to move.'

'So, have you looked at houses?'

'No. I want you to go with me.'

I pushed up on my elbows to look at her.

'Shelby found us this place. I want to find the next one,' she explained, as if every couple operated this way. 'But I've never bought a house, I don't know what to ask or look for, and you do. Will you come with me?'

'Sure.' I was glad I had on dark glasses.

Actually, I could call my mother and she could be on the lookout. They'd need at least three bedrooms; maybe they'd have another baby . . . or Angel's mom might come to help take care of this one . . . and they'd want a yard for the child to play in. I projected Shelby's income and I ran through the neighborhoods in Lawrenceton that would suit it.

'Would you want a pool?' I asked.

I saw Angel's mouth curve in her slow rare smile. 'Sure,' she said. 'Gotta get our exercise somehow.'

A shadow fell across Angel's legs.

'Martin!' I said in amazement. 'You're back early.'

'I told them they didn't really need me at that meeting. They could have asked me everything they needed to know on the phone,' he said, setting his leather briefcase down on the deck and loosening the knot of his tie, an act I never failed to find sexy.

Lately I'd been finding precious little sexy, and I hadn't been able to go back to the cemetery. I had a feeling I'd never sit there in peace again.

Angel said suddenly, 'I'm done to a crisp, and the doctor told me not to get too hot!' She gathered up her towel and lotion and strode off to her apartment without further ado. I heard her tromp up the stairs, and just a few seconds later, tromp down again. 'Gotta go to the store!' she yelled.

Surely that was a little peculiar?

I opened my eyes. Martin had taken off his starched white shirt, his shoes and socks, and was slipping down his pants.

'Good Lord!' I exclaimed.

'No, just me,' he said.

'Did you give Angel some signal?'

'Yes, this.' And Martin pointed at the chaise where Angel had been baking, pointed to the garage, and made a pantomime of hands on the steering wheel.

'What! Why?'

'Because I want to have sex with you on our sun-deck right here and now and I don't want Angel to watch,' Martin said.

'Oh.'

'Because you haven't seemed to want to do that lately, and I thought maybe an exotic locale would – stimulate your interest,' Martin continued, stimulating my interest right then and there, in front of God and the big blue sky.

'Martin! Don't do that!'

'Why not?'

'Well . . . I don't know . . .'

'Then why don't I do it a little longer?'

'Ahhh . . . okay.'

'Then maybe I could just move this chaise over by yours . . .'

'Oh. Urnhmm. And then?'

'I was thinking you could show me how you put that oil all over . . .'

'And then?'

'Roe, I may be too old for a "then"!'

'Oh, not you,' I said confidently.

And I was right.

A Fool and His Honey

For my family –
my mother, father, husband, and children –
who sustain me in all that I do.
Without you, it would hardly be worth doing.

Chapter One

The day everything went rotten was the day the woodman went crazy in my backyard.

My mother and her husband, John Queensland, were just leaving when Darius Quattermain rattled up my driveway, his battered blue pickup pulling a trailer full of split oak. Mother (Aida Brattle Teagarden Queensland) had taken a moment from her busy day to bring me a dress she'd bought for me in Florida, where she'd been attending a convention for real estate brokers who'd sold over a million dollars worth of property in a year. John, who's retired, had come out with Mother just because he likes being with her.

As Darius was getting out of his truck, Mother was hugging me and saying, 'John isn't feeling so well, Aurora, so we're going back to town.' She always made it sound as though Martin and I lived on the frontier, instead of just a mile out of Lawrenceton. In fact, since there are fields all around our property, on clear days I could see the roof of her house, sitting on the edge of Lawrenceton's nicest suburb.

I looked at John, concerned, and saw that he did indeed look puny. John golfs, and normally he looks like a hale and hearty sixty-four-year-old. Actually, John's a handsome man . . . and a good one. But at that moment he looked old and embarrassed, as men so often are by illness.

'You better go home and lie down,' I said, concerned. 'Call me if you need me, after Mother goes back to work?'

'Sure will, honey,' John said heavily, and eased into the front passenger seat of Mother's Lincoln.

Mother gave my cheek a little brush with her lips, I thanked her again for the dress, and then while they maneuvered through turning around to head down our long driveway, I strolled over to Darius, who was pulling on heavy gloves.

I didn't suspect it, but a perfectly ordinary day – getting Martin off to work, going to my own job at the library, coming home with nothing more than a little housework planned – was about to go spectacularly wrong.

It began slowly.

'Where you want me to unload this wood, Miz Bartell?' Darius Quattermain asked.

'This area under the stairs, I think,' I told him. We were standing by the garage, which is connected to the house by a covered walkway. On the side facing the house, there's a stairway going up to the little apartment over the garage.

'You not afraid of bugs getting into your siding there?' Darius asked dubiously.

I shrugged. 'Martin picked the spot, and if he doesn't like it, he can move it.'

Darius gave me a strange look, almost as if he'd never seen me before, which at the time I wrote off as conservative disapproval of my attitude toward my husband.

But he got down to work. After a brief conference, I'd given him the green light to pull the trailer as close as possible, and he began unloading rapidly in the chilly air. The sky was gray, and rain was supposed to start tonight. The wind began to pick up, blowing my long tangle of brown hair into my eyes. I shivered, and stuck my hands in the pockets of my heavy red sweater. As I turned to go inside, I looked over at the roses I'd planted at the corner of the concrete porch at the back of the house, outside my kitchen. They needed pruning, and I was trying to remember if I was supposed to do it now or wait until February, when a piece of wood flew by my head.

'Mr Quattermain?' I said, whirling around. 'You okay?'

Darius Quattermain, deacon of Antioch Holiness Church, began to sing 'She'll Be Comin' Round the Mountain' in a manic bellow. He also kept up with his task, with one big difference.

Instead of stacking the wood neatly under the stairs, Darius pitched split pieces of oak in all directions.

'Whoa!' I said loudly. Even to my own ears, I sounded panicky instead of authoritative. When the next piece of firewood missed my shoulder by only a foot or so, I retreated into the house, locking the door behind me. After a minute, I risked a peek out the window. Darius showed no signs of calming down, and there was still a lot of wood on the back of his pickup. I was thinking of it as ammunition now, instead of fuel.

I dialed the sheriff's department, since our house is outside the city limits.

'SPACOLEC,' said Doris Post. 'SPACOLEC' stands for Sparling County Law Enforcement Complex. It sounded like Doris was chewing a mouthful of gum. I figured she must be trying to quit smoking again.

'Doris, this is Aurora Teagarden.'

'Oh, hi, hon. How you doing?'

'Just fine, thank you, hope you're well. Ah – I have a situation here.'

'Is that right? What's happening?'

'You know Darius Quattermain?'

'The black man who delivers wood? Got six kids? Wife works at Food Fantastic?'

'Right.' I peered out the window, hoping that somehow the situation would have changed for the normal. Nope. 'He's gone crazy.'

'Whereabouts?'

'In my side yard. He seemed just fine when he got here, but all of a sudden he started singing and chunking wood.'

'He's still there?'

'Yes, he is. As a matter of fact . . .' I stared out the window in appalled fascination. 'Um, Doris, he's taking his clothes off now. And still singing. And chunking.'

'You locked in that house, Roe?'

'Yes, and I've set the security system.' Guiltily, I reached over and punched in the code. 'I don't think he means to hurt anyone,

Doris. He just can't help himself. It's like he took drugs, or had a seizure, or something. So whoever comes out here, if they could take it real easy?'

'I'll tell them what you said,' Doris told me. She didn't sound bored or lackadaisical anymore. 'You move away from the windows, Roe. A car's on the way.'

'Thanks, Doris.'

I hung up and hid behind a curtain, so I could check on Darius from time to time. I needn't have bothered to hide. I could have been on the surface of the moon for all Darius cared. He was one big brown goose pimple in the chilly breeze as he danced around buck naked, telling the sky that we would have the wedding supper when she came.

I wondered what Darius would do when he ran out of verses.

I didn't have to wait long. He switched to 'Turkey in the Straw'. Darius was having a flashback to elementary school music class, I decided.

He scampered around to his own music with an impressive light-footedness for a staid middle-aged man.

I decided to call my husband.

'There's a naked man in the backyard,' I said softly, because Darius had stopped singing and was hunting an imaginary deer.

'Anyone I know?' Martin's voice was cautious. He wasn't certain how seriously to take this.

'Darius Quattermain. The woodman.'

'I assume you've called the sheriff?'

'The car's here now.' The official car had just pulled up my driveway. I nodded approvingly. The siren wasn't on and the lights stopped flashing as I watched. 'Jimmy Henske and Levon Suit,' I told Martin.

'Jimmy Henske huh? Maybe I'd better come home.' And the phone was replaced firmly in its cradle. Martin has no high opinion of the sheriff's department in Sparling County, and Jimmy Henske, who is maybe twenty-five, gawky and diffident, has never inspired my husband with his competence.

But Jimmy's a nice guy, and Levon Suit (who went to high

school with me) is a very controlled deputy who is not only innately more intelligent than Jimmy but five years more experienced. I remembered that Levon had dated one of Darius's daughters when we were juniors.

I watched, fascinated, as Levon slowly approached Darius. I was a little surprised the deputy would brave walking right up to him – but then, it was completely obvious Darius wasn't carrying a weapon. It appeared that Darius had killed the deer and resumed singing and dancing in celebration. In fact, he was so glad to see Levon that he grabbed Levon's hands and capered off, and for a delirious minute or two Levon trotted right along with him.

With a patience that made me proud, the two deputies coaxed Darius into their car. Jimmy hurried back to pick up Darius's clothes, which he tossed in the front seat.

'Yes sir, we'll sing along with you all the way into town,' Jimmy was saying earnestly, as Martin parked beside the squad car. My husband emerged from the Mercedes looking, as he generally did, immaculate, prosperous, and handsome.

'Hey, Mr Bartell!' Darius called happily, as Jimmy was shutting the car door. 'I brought your wood!'

Martin stood on the covered sidewalk between our house and the garage and saw the pieces of oak scattered around the backyard, which we'd finally, expensively, had rolled and reseeded to make it smooth and grassy. Quite a few divots had been ripped out of the turf by Darius's impromptu log toss.

'Thanks a lot, Darius,' Martin said.

I came out after the squad car had departed, all three of the occupants singing away. I mentally filed away a decision to write a letter to Sheriff Padgett Lanier to commend Levon and Jimmy's restraint and good sense.

Martin was shedding his suit coat and pulling on his own heavy gloves from the toolshed built into the back of the garage. He got the wheelbarrow, too.

Besides my heavy red cardigan, I was still wearing my work clothes, a long sleeveless denim dress over a red T-shirt, but Martin was setting such a good example that my inappropriate clothes were no excuse to be idle. I found my own gloves and helped out. As we worked, we speculated on this bizarre event and whether Darius, though clearly not in his right mind, had actually broken a law by dancing naked in our yard.

'How was the library this morning?' Martin asked, after we'd stacked the last piece of wood. I stood back, feeling sweat bead on my forehead from the exertion though the air was bracingly chilly, and smiled at him. He knew I was happier now that I'd resumed part-time work at the Lawrenceton library.

'Sam decided patrons with overdue books would be more likely to return the books if they were called personally, rather than sent a postcard. This comes from him reading some study in a magazine, of course. So guess who got to make at least fifty phone calls this morning? Thank God for answering machines. I decided it wasn't cheating to leave a message on the machine.' I watched Martin pull off his heavy gloves. 'What about you?'

'I had my annual physical, followed by a morning-long meeting about implementing the new EPA regulations.' My husband Martin, who has a pirate gene stuck somewhere in his DNA, frequently gets frustrated with his job as vice president of manufacturing for Pan-Am Agra, an agricultural products company. He has not always done something so legitimate and safe.

'Sorry, honey.' I patted his shoulder sympathetically. We strolled back to return the things to our toolshed. Darius's pickup and small trailer were still parked blocking my car in, halfway on the gravel and halfway on the grass; when I'd okayed that, I'd only expected him to be there for a little while. The ground had been nice and dry, but as I turned to go back into the house, big drops of rain began to patter down. We simultaneously thought of the truck making troughs in the softened dirt, and hurried back to check the cab of the truck.

Martin said a heartfelt and obscene word. The ignition was empty.

I looked in the passenger side. Perhaps Darius had just withdrawn the keys and tossed them on the seat to silence the little beeper that reminds you your keys are in the ignition. I do that occasionally, if I have to run back into the house for a minute or two.

'Look, Martin.' I pointed. But not at a set of keys.

Martin stuck his head in the door.

There was an open bottle of generic pain reliever, acetaminophen, on the seat.

Martin raised one eyebrow at me. 'So?'

'He started acting so funny so fast, my first thought was that he'd taken a drug. And I don't think he's the kind of man who would ever think of doing something so dangerous.'

Martin said, 'We'd better call the sheriffs department again.'

So once again Jimmy and Levon drove the mile out of town that got them to our house, and Jimmy pulled on plastic gloves before he picked up the pill bottle. He poured its contents onto the gloved palm of his other hand. He didn't tell us to leave, so we watched.

Martin saw it first. He pointed.

Levon bent over Jimmy's palm.

'Damn,' he said in his deep voice.

One of the pills was a smidge smaller than the others, and not quite the same shade of white. It didn't have the manufacturer's initial on it as all the other pain relief tablets did. The difference was obvious when you were looking for it. But without some good reason to examine the medicine, who would think of doing so?

'We got another one,' Jimmy concluded, looking down at Levon.

'Someone else has been drugged?' I asked, trying to keep my voice casual and sort of insinuate the question.

'Yes'm,' Jimmy said, not catching the warning look Levon was trying to send him. 'Lady last week left her purse in the cart in the grocery while she walked over to the frozen section to get some Ore-Ida hash browns. When she was driving home, she took a pill from a fancy case in her purse, that she used to carry her – well, some prescription medicine – with her. Instead of getting tranquil, she went nuts.'

'What did she do?' I asked, fascinated.

'Well . . .' Jimmy began, treating me to a grin that told me the story was going to be a good one.

'We need to be getting this back to SPACOLEC,' Levon said pointedly.

'Huh? Oh, right.' Jimmy, aware he'd been on the verge of indiscretion, flushed to the roots of his reddish hair. 'When one of Darius's kids shows up, we'll tell them you'd appreciate them moving the truck. The keys were in Darius's pants. I coulda brought 'em out here if you'd mentioned them over the phone.'

I flushed guiltily. I'd been so excited over finding the pills, I had forgotten why we'd looked in Darius's truck in the first place.

I watched as their car turned out of our long driveway and began the short stretch into Lawrenceton, piqued that I hadn't gotten to hear the rest of Jimmy's story. I wondered if my friend Sally Allison, a reporter for our local paper, had heard anything.

'I have to go back to the plant for a little while,' Martin said unenthusiastically. 'I have a stack of letters to sign that need to go out.' He climbed back into his car, started it, and rolled down the window as I turned toward the kitchen door. 'Don't forget,' he called, 'we've got dinner at the Lowrys' house tonight.' The rain picked up a little momentum.

'I have it on the calendar,' I called back, trying not to sound dismal.

If there'd been a can in front of me, I'd have kicked it on my way into the house. It didn't seem like a good night to eat out with people I was (at best) on cordial terms with. Close friends and homemade chili sounded good; friendly acquaintances and dressing up didn't.

Catledge and Ellen Lowry were not soul mates of mine. But they were among the leading citizens of Lawrenceton. Catledge was the mayor for a second term and Ellen was on every board and a member of every club worth joining in our small town. Keeping the town government, ergo the Lowrys, pleased was important to Martin's business and therefore to a great many people in Lawrenceton who depended on Pan-Am Agra for a paycheck.

'They're not that bad,' I said out loud to my silent house. Even to me, I sounded sulky. I trudged upstairs to figure out what to wear, straightening one of the pictures hung by the staircase as I went up. Gradually the house warmed and cheered me, as it nearly always did. My house is at least sixty-five years old, and it has beautiful hardwood floors, tall windows that no standard curtains will fit correctly (so every single 'window treatment' has to be custom made), and a voracious appetite for electricity and gas. I love it dearly. We'd had it renovated when we married. Since we've been married less than three years and have no children and only one alleged pet, there's nothing to redo yet; at least not for a basically practical person like me. I still have space on the built-in bookshelves lining the hall, and now I can afford to buy hardbacks.

I showered and shampooed, once again going through the tedious process of combing and drying my mess of hair. At least curly, wavy hair was fashionable now. It was a pleasant change to have others actually envy me my abundance, rather than peer at it with pity in their eyes.

I flipped through the garments in my closet without much interest. The cerise wool dress my mother had brought me was too fancy for the occasion, so I finally decided I'd wear a long-sleeved garnet silk blouse, a black-and-garnet patterned skirt, and my black pumps. Looking at my collection of glasses – I'm very nearsighted – I had a wild impulse to select my purple-and-white-framed ones.

Oh, hell. The Lowrys would be offended if my glasses were frivolous. I got my new black-rimmed ones with the delicate gold wire-and-bead decoration and set them out on my vanity table. This morning I'd put on my favorite workday red specs, and I viewed them in the mirror with some satisfaction. They added a spark of liveliness to my unhappy face.

'So, why'm I sulking?' I asked the mirror.

That particular question never got answered because the front doorbell rang.

What a lot of visitors I was having today, if you counted the deputies coming twice.

Through the opaque oval glass pane in the front door, I saw the silhouette of a woman with a baby carrier in her arms. I assumed it was my friend Lizanne Buckley Sewell, who'd had her baby boy two months before. I disarmed the alarm and opened the door with a smile that collapsed in on itself. I stared blankly at the plump, dark, pretty young woman who stood on my front porch with a perfectly strange baby, who seemed smaller than Lizanne's infant.

'Aunt Roe!' said the dark young woman. She looked exhausted, and she also looked as if she expected a warm welcome.

I had not the slightest idea who she was.

The next instant everything clicked, and I would have thunked myself on the forehead with the heel of my hand if I'd been alone. I was aunt to only one young woman, and that was Martin's niece, the daughter of his sister Barby.

'Regina!' I said, hoping my recovery hadn't been too obvious.

'For a minute there, I didn't think you recognized me!' she said, laughing.

'Ha, ha. Come on in! And this is little . . .' Regina had had a baby? It was covered with a blue blanket and wore a red sleeper. Martin had a – great-nephew?

How could I have missed that? Granted, we don't often see Martin's sister and her daughter, but I would have expected a certain amount of phone calling to herald the new arrival.

'Oh, Aunt Roe! This is *Hayden*!'

'And you call him Hayden.' I nodded with a wise look. 'No nicknames.' I could hardly recall ever having been more at sea.

'No, me and Craig are set on him being called Hayden,' Regina said, trying to look firm and determined and failing completely.

Martin may not have gotten all the looks in the Bartell family – Barby and Regina are both pretty, in their way – but he'd surely gotten a disproportionate amount of the brains and resolution.

I craned out of the front door, trying to see if Craig Graham was maybe getting luggage out of the trunk. 'Where's your husband?' I asked, never imagining this would be a sensitive question.

'He didn't come,' Regina said. Her generous mouth clamped tight.

'Oh.' I hoped I didn't sound as blank as I felt. 'And how's your mother?' I was gesturing to Regina to come on in, still peering around in the hopes of spying a companion. She'd driven all the way from Corinth, Ohio, on her own?

'Mama's on a cruise,' Regina said, too gaily. This gal was having serious mood swings.

'Hmmm. Where to?' I repeated my 'come in' gesture, more emphatically.

'Oh, she's taking a long one,' Regina chattered, finally stepping over the threshold. 'The boat stops by some islands in the Caribbean, then over to two stops in Mexico of several days apiece, then back to Miami.'

'My goodness,' I said mildly. 'She's with a friend?'

'That guy,' Regina said, depositing the baby, still in his infant seat, on the coffee table in front of the couch and unslinging a huge diaper bag from her shoulder. There was still a fabric-care tag dangling from the shoulder strap of the diaper bag.

'That guy' was Barby's fiancé, investment banker Hubert Morris, whom the divorced Barby Lampton had met when she'd bought a condo in Pittsburgh, the closest major city and airport to Corinth, Ohio, Barby and Martin's childhood home. Though Barby hadn't lived in Corinth since her teenage years, Regina had met her husband-to-be while she and her mother were in Corinth visiting an old friend of Barby's. Regina had married the boy – I mean, young man – only two months later.

Martin and I had flown up to Pittsburgh for the wedding, maybe seven months ago. We'd gotten the impression that the young couple would be living in very straitened circumstances. Craig Graham had been a dark, lanky no-brainer, whose greatest apparent virtue had been that he cared for Regina. He was eighteen to Regina's twenty-one. The groom's share of the wedding duties and expenses had been borne by Barby, who had tried to be unobtrusive about it. Of course, Martin and I had noticed. But Barby had made it clear to us (to Martin, anyway, since she seldom talked to me directly) that after the wedding, the young couple was going to be financially independent, as far as she was concerned. She'd made some pointed remarks about who had made beds and who would be lying in them.

'Would you like a drink? Coffee or hot chocolate? Though maybe those things aren't good for the baby.' My friend Lizanne was breast-feeding and, though I hadn't asked, she'd generously given me a *very* thorough grounding on the subject. After being indoctrinated with Lizanne's opinions on the virtues of, and necessity for, mother's milk, I was taken aback when Regina gave me a blank look.

'Huh? No, I'm bottle-feeding,' she said, after a pause. 'Gosh, if I nursed him, it'd have to be me that fed him every time.'

I kept a smile planted on my face. 'So, some coffee?'

'Please.' She slumped back. 'I've been driving for hours.'

She *had* driven all the way from Ohio. This was very strange, and getting stranger.

I brewed some coffee, shuddering at Regina's protest that instant would have been fine. After I'd poured a cup for each of us, adding cream and sugar to Martin's niece's, I listened to Regina blather about the long drive, the baby, her mother's condo, her Aunt Cindy . . .

'Oh, I'm sorry!' she apologized. 'I shouldn't have said anything.'

'Aunt Cindy' was Martin's first wife, the mother of his only child, Regina's cousin Barrett. I sighed internally, *still* kept my smile pasted on, and assured Regina that she needn't apologize. A little corner of my brain repressed an urge to ask Regina why she wasn't at Aunt Cindy's instead of Uncle Martin's, if Aunt Cindy was so great.

'Did you see Barrett on TV the other night?' Regina said enthusiastically. 'Boy, didn't he look handsome? I always call all my friends when Barrett's going to be on television.'

Regina was digging at all my sore – or rather, sensitive – spots. Barrett had not come to our wedding. He'd been up for a big part, he'd told his dad, the implication clear that a new part for Barrett was more important than a new wife for his father.

And he hadn't visited Lawrenceton in the three-plus years Martin had lived here.

But he'd found the time to come to Regina's wedding, where he'd managed to dodge us with an almost unbelievable agility. Martin had told me he'd had a drink with Barrett in the hotel bar after I'd gone up to bed the night before the wedding, and that had been the contact he'd had with his son – whose career he'd been subsidizing.

I was beginning to wish Martin's only niece had stayed in Ohio. I was also beginning to puzzle at the reason behind her visit. She was being mighty evasive.

'Regina,' I said, when she'd finished blathering about Barrett's career, 'I'm delighted that you came to visit, but this evening, just for a couple of hours, may be a little awkward. Your uncle and I have a longstanding dinner engagement, and though we could call and tell the Lowrys we have to take a rain check, I'm afraid—'

Regina, who happened to be holding the baby (Hayden, I reminded myself), looked up with something approaching alarm. 'You two go on like you had planned. I'll be fine here. Just point me at the microwave and I'll be glad to fix my own supper. After all, I just appeared on your doorstep.'

It seemed to me – almost – that Regina was anxious to get us out of the house. I could feel my eyebrows draw together in a frown.

'Excuse me a minute,' I said. Regina, her attention focused on the baby, gave me an absent nod.

I went across the hall into the room we'd decorated as a study and a television room. Plucking the cordless phone from its stand, I plumped down on the red leather couch in front of the windows. Madeleine, the cat that lived with us, emerged from her favorite private place, the basket where we put newspapers after we'd read them. 'While I was punching in numbers with one hand, I was tickling Madeleine's head with the other. One part of my mind noted that I'd have to get Madeleine out of the study before Martin got home. He and the cat enjoyed a hate-hate relationship. It had started with Madeleine deciding Martin's Mercedes was her basking site of choice, especially when the ground was muddy and she could leave some nice footprints on the hood and windshield. Martin had retaliated by parking the Mercedes in the garage and closing the door every night. Since it was then her move in their little game, Madeleine (who ordinarily couldn't be bothered) caught a mouse, decapitated the rodent, and put the corpse in Martin's shoe. Then Martin . . . well, you get the idea.

'Martin Bartell's office,' Marnie Sands said. Her raspy voice was all business.

'Mrs Sands, this is Aurora. I need to speak to Martin.' It had taken me weeks to stop apologizing for disturbing him.

'I'm sorry,' Mrs Sands said, her voice several degrees warmer than it had been when I first married Martin, 'but Mr Bartell's out in the plant. Want me to page him?'

I thought of trying to tell Martin that his niece was here with an unexplained baby, over a telephone where he stood surrounded by employees. 'No, that's okay,' I told the secretary. 'Please ask him to call me before he starts for home.'

I hung up the phone. I made a face, the kind of face my mother always warned me would make my features stick in permanent disgust.

I strolled back across the hall to Regina. She was putting some bottles of formula in the refrigerator.

'I just made myself at home,' she said brightly. She'd gotten out a pan and boiled some water, and an empty can of formula powder was on the counter by the sink. 'It always helps to have plenty made up and ready to heat. Now, when I heat them up . . .' and she described the procedure at tedious length.

Hayden stared at me with the big round-eyed goggle some babies have. He was a cute little guy, with a pink mouth and rosy cheeks. In fact, he was strikingly fairer than Regina, who was pretty enough, but endowed with the dark complexion and wide hips her own mother'd bequeathed her. Hayden waved his arms and made a sudden gurgling sound, and Regina looked at him adoringly.

'Isn't he wonderful?' she asked.

'He's so cute,' I said, and tried not to sound yearning.

'Too bad Uncle Martin's too old to have another kid,' Regina said, actually giggling at the idea.

I could feel my back stiffen and I was sure my face had followed suit.

'We talked about it,' I said in a voice of pure ice. 'But unfortunately, I am not able.' Martin, who was staring fifty in the face, hadn't been able to work up any enthusiasm for starting another family, though at my just-turned birthday of thirty-six, I could still hear my biological clock ticking. Loudly.

However, it was ticking in a malformed womb, which let Martin off the hook as far as making a decision.

I began to empty the dishwasher, all the time telling myself I'd sounded hostile and I had to calm down. Regina, who really seemed to be remarkably tactless, had stuck a sharp stick into my tenderest grievance, my inability to conceive. She was staring at me now, trying to look properly cowed, but I detected a certain – what? Satisfaction? Her eyes had the same look I saw in Madeleine's when she'd left those footprints all over Martin's windshield. I had a sudden inspiration.

'Would it suit you if we put you and Hayden over in the garage apartment?' I asked, trying to make my voice light and friendly.

'That would be super. I wondered when I drove up if that was a separate apartment,' Regina said. Maybe she sounded a tad disappointed that I'd changed the subject. 'Hayden still gets up at night, and we'd be less likely to bother you.'

'Let's just take your things over there,' I suggested. Taking the keys from a hook by the back door, I grabbed the big diaper bag and Regina's purse and trotted across the covered walkway and up the stairs that ran up the side of the garage, the side toward our house. The heavy bag looped over my shoulder banged ponderously against my thigh. Though the air was colder and wetter, it wasn't actually raining at the moment.

The apartment smelled only slightly stale. Our friends Shelby and Angel had moved out about eight weeks ago. I had been keeping the heat on so nothing would freeze or mildew, and I turned it up and glanced around as I heard Regina open her car trunk below.

The garage apartment is one very big room, with a corner walled in for a bathroom and adjacent closet. There's a queen-sized bed, a chair and love seat and attendant tables, a television, and a small table for two in the kitchen area. It's as pleasant as basic apartment living gets.

Regina seemed pleased.

'Oh, Aunt Roe, this is so nice,' she said, throwing a suitcase on the bed. 'Before we got married, we lived in an apartment that was a lot smaller than this.'

I hated to think about that.

'Well, I hope you enjoy it,' I said at random. 'You and Hayden, that is. I'll leave you to unpack. Oh, do you have something for the baby to sleep in?' I had no idea what to do if she didn't. But Regina assured me she had a portable travel crib. That seemed a luxurious item for a poor mother to have, and I wondered a little.

I heard the crunch of gravel as I stood in the doorway. Martin emerged from his car and stood staring at Regina's car for a minute.

'Martin,' I called, 'come up here.' Evidently he hadn't returned to his office before he came home.

He passed under the walkway to stare up at me. 'What are you doing in the apartment?' he asked. No one had been in the apartment since Angel and Shelby had bought a house in town.

'Oh,' I said, feeling a pleasurable anticipation, perhaps tinged with a touch of malice, 'you won't *guess* who's come to visit, honey!'

Looking distinctly apprehensive, Martin came up the stairs. I stood aside so he could enter the apartment.

'Uncle Martin!' cried Regina. She faced the door with a big smile stretching her generous lips, the baby pressed to her chest like a bag of groceries.

Martin's face was priceless.

'Did we know she was coming?' he asked me in a low voice as we walked over to the house.

I shook my head.

'Did we know she'd had a baby?'

I shook my head again.

'Then Barby must not know it either,' he said. 'She wouldn't keep something like that to herself.'

I didn't think so either. I further thought that Barby would just hate the idea of being a grandmother. I was willing to bet Regina knew that, too.

'So, we don't know why she's here?' Martin, used to commanding information and having everything lined up and organized, was definitely on the frustrated side.

'It'd be easier to tell you what I don't know,' I said. 'I don't know why she came or how long she's staying. I don't know where Craig is. I have no idea what your sister knows.' And though I didn't say it out loud to spare Martin's feelings, I was far from certain of the provenance of the baby.

Martin stood in the kitchen drinking a glass of tea while he mulled this over. 'I've got to go back up there and speak to her again,' he said abruptly. 'Get some of this settled. We still going to the Lowrys'?'

'I don't think we can put it off. Regina seems all right about us going, and you know how touchy Catledge is.'

'Okay. I'll just be a minute or two with her, then I'll come in and shower.' Thunking his glass down on the counter, he marched out again into the gathering dark and dripping rain. His white hair gleamed through the darkness.

I went upstairs to finish getting ready. As I put on makeup and jewelry and pinned my hair out of my face with a pretty black-and-gold comb, I wondered if Martin would be able to winkle any more out of his niece than I had. Martin is far more likely to ask direct questions than I am.

But he didn't look satisfied when he trudged up the stairs twenty minutes later. He looked tired and worried.

After giving me a quick kiss on the neck, Martin unzipped his pants and sat on the bed to untie his shoes.

'Hey, sailor, how about it?' I asked, in my best Mae West voice.

Martin flashed me a smile. He glanced at the bedside clock.

'Afraid we don't have time,' he said regretfully. 'I have to shower. Two people in the meeting smoked.'

Martin hates the smell of smoke clinging to his hair and clothes.

'You could have asked them not to,' I said mildly. Martin's asking might as well be called telling: He was the boss.

'They're going to retire at the new year,' he said. 'If that weren't the case, I would have kicked their asses out into the hall. As of January one, I'm going to make the entire plant a smoke-free zone.'

We talked about how many smokers Pan-Am Agra employed, and mulled over other mundane topics as Martin stripped, showered, and re-dressed. Martin is almost thirteen years my senior, but he looks absolutely great without his clothes on, and he's just as attractive dressed. He has snowy white hair, but his eyebrows are still black, and his eyes are a light, light brown. He lifts weights and his racquetball games are endurance tests for the younger members of the management staff.

'Didn't you say you had your physical today?' Looking at Martin's physique had prompted another train of thought.

'Yes,' he said, rather shortly. My wifely antennae perked, tuned in to what he wasn't saying.

'Wasn't everything all right?' Martin had never had a bad physical. In fact, he was usually boastful after his annual checkup, required by the plant.

'Zelman wants me to have a full battery of tests. Just because I'm getting older,' Martin added hastily, before I could even fully develop my concerned expression.

'Did he find anything?' I asked, in the voice that said he better let me know everything.

'He said I was stressed. He just wants to run some more tests.' Martin was standing in front of his closet picking out his clothes for the evening. I understood from his tone that the subject was closed.

'We'll schedule those right away,' I suggested.

'Sure, I'll get Mrs Sands to do it tomorrow. Did I tell you she's going to be a grandmother?'

'Is she happy about it?'

'Oh, yes, she's already named the baby and picked out a preschool. Not that her daughter knows about that . . .'

All this chatter was a delaying tactic of Martin's, while he thought over whatever Regina had told him.

'What'd Regina say?' I asked, as he used his electric razor.

'Not much,' he admitted, sticking out his chin to shave under it. I was sitting on the toilet lid. Not for the first time, it occurred to me how much I enjoyed being married, just sitting in the bathroom with a man while he shaved, and all the little intimacies that entailed. 'I don't think she's going to tell us why she's here until she's ready.' He stretched his upper lip down over his front teeth. 'I hope nothing's happened to Craig.'

'If he'd been in a wreck or been ill, surely she'd let us know,' I said hesitantly, aware I wasn't on Martin's wavelength.

'I was thinking more of Craig being in trouble,' he said, pulling on a fresh shirt and tucking it in. 'Do you have your lipstick on yet?'

'No,' I said, surprised.

Martin pulled me to him and gave me one of those wonderful kisses that makes my pulse jump around like a drop of oil in a hot skillet. I responded enthusiastically, and let my fingers do the walking.

'Whoa! Whoa!' he said, gasping, holding me away. 'Oh, later! After we come home!'

'That better be a promise,' I said lightly, giving him a final pat and sitting at my vanity to twist the tube to apply Mad Rubies.

'Take it as sworn to,' he told me.

We should have taken twenty extra minutes and been late to the Lowrys'.

Chapter Two

Catledge Lowry met us at the door, his wide happy smile fixed in place.

Catledge was a politician through and through. He had a good-sounding set of goals, he had a good campaign manager, and he'd done some worthwhile things. I didn't trust him as far as I could throw him, and given Catledge's six-foot-four frame, that wasn't an inch. I just enjoyed Catledge for what he was.

'Hey, good lookin'!' he cried. 'If your husband would just turn his back a minute, I'd give you a kiss to curl your toes, you beautiful thing!'

'This beautiful thing would rather have a glass of wine, Catledge,' I said, smiling. 'Besides, I don't think you can bend down far enough.' I'm four-eleven.

'Honey, I'd amputate my legs for the chance,' Catledge said dramatically, and I laughed.

'Ellen might not care for that,' I said, handing him my coat. Martin reached past me to shake hands, and in a moment the men were deep in conversation about some yahoo's chance in the Georgia governor's race. I expected a flushed and harried Ellen to rush from the kitchen, but instead I saw her strolling through the garage door holding a brown paper bag containing, from its shape, a bottle of wine. She was groomed to a tee and in no great hurry, either. I had a moment of surprise and then Ellen was bending down to peck my cheek, and I was reconnecting with the bundle of nerves that was Ellen Dawson Lowry.

Ellen was maybe five-ten, as tall as Martin, and thin as a rail. She dressed beautifully, used minimal makeup, would be an unobtrusive blonde for the next twenty years with a little help, and had graduated with honors from Sophie Newcomb. She'd intended to be a CPA. Then she'd married Catledge, and all her mild ambition had been consumed in Catledge's flashy brilliance.

Ellen had told me she'd been happy when their sons had been young, and happy when she worked at the bank for a few years while the boys were in high school; but Catledge had wanted her to quit when he'd been elected mayor, and she had. At one time, when we'd had to work together on the board of a charity, we'd felt rather close. But after our year on the board was up, it had seemed harder and harder for us to meet, and our brief closeness faded.

'Roe, you just get prettier and prettier!' Ellen gushed.

'Oh, Ellen,' I mumbled, embarrassed at her strange manner.

Ellen's eyes had a glaze to them, and her hands moved nervously up and down the skirt of the dark blue-and-gold dress. The colors were becoming, but Ellen had lost even more weight and looked almost painfully thin.

'What do you hear from your boys?' I asked.

'Jefferson's tenth in the senior class at Georgia Tech, and Tally is . . . working on a special study in Tennessee.' Despite her hesitation over nineteen-year-old Tally's current occupation, Ellen was like most mothers in her pleasure in talking about her children, and my questions kept our conversation rolling along until Mrs Esther came in to announce dinner. Martin and I exchanged discreet glances.

Lucinda Esther is a notable personality in Lawrenceton, and the fact that the Lowrys had hired her to produce this meal surprised us. This was not a dinner on which some important deal depended; this was not a crucial social event. Hiring Mrs Esther always signaled that the meal was significant, perhaps when the parents of the bride entertained the parents of the groom for the first time, or when an important newcomer was welcomed into an affluent home.

Maybe, in this instance, it meant the hostess was not capable of producing a suitable meal.

Standing with massive dignity in a starched gray uniform with a white apron, Mrs Esther said, 'Dinner is served.' She did not meet our eyes or wait for a reaction, but strode back into the kitchen, her dark face still impassive, her chin proudly up. The heavy gold hoops in her pierced ears swayed as she walked.

Mrs Esther didn't serve. She placed the food ready on the table and remained in the kitchen until it was time to clean up. And she almost always prepared a menu she'd decided on herself. Tonight she'd picked chicken baked in a white sauce, green beans, home made rolls, sweet potato casserole, and a tossed salad. Calories and cholesterol were not considerations in Mrs Esther's catering business.

After we'd all passed the dishes around, which was a pretty effective icebreaker, Martin asked me to tell Catledge what had happened in our backyard that afternoon.

As I turned it into an amusing vignette, without the element of anxiety that had given the incident its edge, naturally I glanced from Catledge to Ellen and back. Catledge was at the end of the table to my left and Ellen was opposite me. Their reactions were more intriguing than the story. Catledge was shaken, visibly upset; Ellen thought the whole episode was vastly amusing. I'd have sworn Catledge would laugh and Ellen would worry. This reversal was very interesting.

To my further fascination, Catledge cut the ensuing discussion off at the knees. I was just sure as sure can be that ordinarily Catledge would spend a good fifteen minutes speculating about who'd 'spiked' Darius Quattermain's acetaminophen. Yet here he was, trying to shunt the conversation into the ongoing battle between two factions of the library board. I shot a significant look at Martin while Ellen was fetching more tea from the kitchen and Catledge had excused himself.

I can't let puzzling behavior go by without picking it apart to discover its cause. Suddenly I wondered if Ellen had been the unnamed woman who'd been sabotaged by the medicine switcher.

I was pleased with the idea, the more I hammered it out. Twitchy Ellen was very likely to have tranquilizers in her purse. She was certainly abnormally serene tonight. Perhaps Catledge feared staying on the subject of Darius Quattermain because he thought Ellen likely to reveal her own little episode of similarly bizarre behavior? He would hate it to be known Ellen took 'nerve pills'.

The silence that had fallen over the dinner table was so awkward that Martin felt compelled to break it.

'We had a surprise visitor today,' he said easily.

'Who was that?' Catledge asked, right on cue, relief easy to read in his voice.

'My niece came to visit, with her baby boy,' Martin said.

I cocked an eyebrow at him. We weren't going to mention Regina's visit, we'd decided.

'A boy,' Ellen said. 'I miss our boys. They were adorable babies. But all cute babies grow up and leave home, don't they?' That should have been said in a light tone, but it wasn't. Ellen's voice grew more and more edgy with every word. Once again, an uneasy silence fell over the table.

Ellen pushed her chair back and rose, maybe a little unsteadily. 'Excuse me, please,' she said, managing to sound almost normal. 'I'm being a bad hostess. I feel unwell.' And walking quickly, her backbone stiff, she was out of the room and going up the stairs, face carefully turned away.

'I'm so sorry Ellen is ill,' I said instantly. 'She should have canceled. We would have understood. Bless her heart, she worked so hard when she should have been in bed.' I hoped my chatter would fill the silence and smooth things over, and to some extent it did.

'Ellen never knows when to take things easy,' Catledge said gratefully. 'We'd love to have you back when she's well.'

'Oh, no, it's our turn,' Martin contributed. He was already up and retrieving my coat. 'We enjoyed the evening, I'm just sorry it ended this way.'

As Martin and Catledge kept up the social end of the evening, I stepped into the kitchen to tell Mrs Esther that I'd enjoyed the food and that she could clear the table. Mrs Esther was sitting at the small breakfast table in the bay window in the kitchen reading *How Stella Got Her Groove Back*. Just as I opened my mouth to speak, I saw that the kitchen door to the garage was being pulled shut, and I understood that Ellen had gone down the back stairs, stepped silently through the kitchen, and – this I definitely heard – was starting up the car in the garage.

When I looked from the garage door back to Mrs Esther, I saw that she was regarding me with an absolutely neutral expression. As clearly as if she'd spoken it, her face said, 'This is none of my business and I don't want to know.'

'Thanks for the delicious supper, Mrs Esther,' I said. I picked a dish at random. 'The chicken was especially good.'

'Thank you, Mrs Bartell.' Another one who didn't call me Ms. Teagarden. But it was not an issue I was going to fight over. It had never made any difference to me what people called me, as long as I knew who I was.

We exchanged good-byes, and I turned back to the dining room to find Martin and Catledge shaking hands. But then Catledge mentioned the Wednesday meeting of the zoning commission, and Martin remembered that Pan-Am Agra had bought some land adjacent to the plant that needed to be rezoned, and they started up all over again.

I couldn't fiddle with the table, not with Mrs Esther in the kitchen waiting to take care of it, and I couldn't wander around the house because that would be rude. So I fished around in my purse for a mint and surreptitiously popped it into my mouth, I got all my hair freed from the collar of my coat, and then I gently patted Martin's arm.

'You and Catledge will just have to call each other tomorrow, honey. We need to get home.'

Martin smiled down at me fondly. 'You're right, Roe. We need to check on Regina and the baby before we turn in.'

So, finally, finally, we were out the door and on our way. Even then, we had to stop to get gas, because Martin was low and didn't want to have to fill up on the way to work in the morning.

We'd had Ellen's wine with our meal, and a somewhat trying day, so we were quiet and (speaking for myself) sleepy on the drive home. Though I was still mildly concerned about Regina's visit and the unexplained baby, I was willing to put off worrying about it until the next morning. But I could tell from Martin's frown that he was brooding over it again.

As we turned up our long driveway, my pleasant drowsiness evaporated.

Though I couldn't tell much about it, there was a strange car parked in front of the garage. And Regina's car was gone.

The automatic security light at the back of the house showed, also, that someone had taken Darius's truck and trailer. I hoped it was one of his children.

We didn't have an automatic security light at the front of the house because it had shone in our bedroom window; we'd had it switched to manual, and we'd forgotten to leave it on when we'd left for the Lowrys' dinner. The brilliant light in the backyard gave the front some illumination, but it was faint and full of shadows.

So the front of the house and garage was relatively dark . . . but aside from the strange car and absence of Regina's, there was plenty visible to alarm us. I could see, and so could Martin by his grunt, that there was something lying on the stairs that mounted to the garage apartment.

Most worrying of all was the irregular fan of dark spots on the white siding of the garage.

'Martin,' I said sharply, as if he hadn't already noticed all these things for himself. We looked at each other as he switched off the Mercedes's engine.

'Stay here,' he said firmly, and opened his door.

'No,' I said, and opened mine. The cat was crouched in the azaleas, staring at the thing on the stairs. Madeleine didn't acknowledge our presence; she remained fixed and alert in her chosen spot. Somehow that made my skin crawl, and for the first time I was convinced this might be something bad, very bad.

It wasn't just very bad. It was absolutely horrible.

The dark stain on the white siding was a spray of blood. As I stared at it, one drop moved. Not completely dry.

The blood had shot from the long limp thing on the stairs, a man.

A hatchet had cleaved through his forehead. It was still embedded in his head. Blood had soaked into the dark hair. I thought about Regina and the baby, and if your heart could actually move within your body, mine would have fallen to the pit of my stomach. I suspected the dead man was Craig, Regina's husband.

Martin was looking up the stairs to the apartment door. There was a line of black where it should have met the frame. The door was ajar.

That realization was enough to propel me over to my husband. In the dim light, I could see that he looked old and ill, all the lines time had ironed into his face seeming deeper in the shadows. And since I knew him, I knew he was thinking he had to go up those stairs and find out what was in that apartment. But he was afraid of what he'd find. Regina and her baby were his family.

A light rain began to pelt down.

Wordlessly, I laid my hand on Martin's shoulder and squeezed it before edging by the dead thing sprawled on the stairs. I tried not to look down as I sidled up with my back to the railing. I didn't want to touch the blood on the wall, either. Once past the body, I went faster, but still my legs were heavy with reluctance and quivering with fear. It seemed an hour before I faced the door.

There was a little sound inside the apartment.

I bit down hard on my lip. I poked the door open with one fingertip. Reaching in, I flipped up the light switch by the door. A brilliant glare illuminated the apartment. I spent a long moment scanning for Regina's body, bloodstains, signs of a struggle.

Nothing.

The little sound went on and on. Finally I stepped in, looking repeatedly from side to side. Martin called from below, but I didn't answer. My breath was coming too unevenly. The rain began to fall more heavily and the drumming of the raindrops on the stairs made the little apartment feel more isolated.

The closet door was open. Clothes, I assumed Regina's, had been hung inside. Her suitcase was on the dining table, open. Clothes that appeared to have been tossed in rather than packed were flowing over the sides. The bathroom door was flung wide and I could see a jumble of makeup and toiletries on the counter by the sink.

The only area not visible from my position by the door was the floor on the far side of the bed. And that was where the sound was coming from.

I went around the bed, reasoning with one part of my mind that nothing could be worse than what I had already seen.

The floor was empty, but the folds of the quilted paisley bedspread were moving, down at carpet level. I dropped to my knees and bent over. Holding my breath, I lifted the skirt of the bedspread.

Under the bed, kicking his legs and waving his hands, was the baby. He was just beginning to get upset that his mother hadn't picked him up after his nap. He looked perfectly all right, and his red sleeper was pristine.

So Regina's car was missing, and Regina wasn't anywhere in the apartment.

I was certainly thinking without clarity. At first, I thought the baby's presence and wellness were good news. And they were good news, of course, but they were only part of Martin's concern. When I came to the top of the stairs and called down to him that the baby was fine but Regina was gone, the look on his face reminded me that someone had murdered the young man on the stairs, and the vanished Regina was by far the most likely person to have wielded the hatchet. Martin was standing passively, leaning against the garage, his arms crossed over his chest. His hair and his coat were dark with rain. His alien behavior struck me like a fist to the chest.

'You have to call the police,' I reminded him, and I saw the anger flare in my husband's face. He didn't like being told to do that. My presence obliged him to do the right thing. He'd been thinking of concealing this somehow, I could tell. It was the pirate side of him coming out.

There was something stuck under the windshield wiper blade

of the strange car, which I noticed had Ohio tags. I could hardly get much wetter, so I carefully eased down the stairs and over to the car. I touched the sodden mass with a finger. It was a folded piece of paper, a note. I could see the streaks that had been blue ink. A note: to whom, about what, I'd never know.

The baby began to scream. His cries carried on the chilly night air. I expected someone to pick him up and tend to his needs, and when that didn't happen, I had what Lizanne calls a Real Moment. Hayden's mother had vanished; Hayden's father, Craig (and I was pretty sure the corpse was Craig, though I'd only met him once at the wedding), was lying before me dead. The baby's grandmother, who ought to be willing to take charge, was on a cruise with her boyfriend. I, Aurora Teagarden, was (at least temporarily) responsible for this baby, unless Martin acted. Staring at my husband, I saw how unlikely that was. Instead of feeling elation – finally, a baby! – I felt an almost bottomless dismay.

The rain pattered to a halt.

I turned and once again mounted the stairs to the garage apartment. I squatted and eased Hayden out from under the bed. With effort, I rose from the floor holding him. It was shocking how much he could wiggle, how hard it was to hold on to him, especially when he arched his body with rage. I was trembling, and it wasn't for the dead man on the stairs. Somehow, I made it down the stairs and across the walkway, passing a still-silent Martin without saying anything.

After unlocking our house, I reached for the security pad, only to find that it had been turned off. Of course, we hadn't told Regina how to set it . . . at least, I hadn't. I called 911 from our kitchen telephone. I jiggled Hayden with one damp arm while I dialed with my free hand. I could barely hold him, but I couldn't put him on the kitchen floor. He was screaming so loudly by now that I had to repeat myself twice. At least Doris wasn't still on duty, and the dispatcher didn't seem to know that I'd already had county police at my house that day. After I hung up, I could put off tending to Hayden no longer.

I had no idea what to do.

As Hayden's need, whatever it was, wasn't met, he screamed more. Too frightened and uncertain to leave him by himself, I staggered back out into the night, toting the increasingly heavy baby, and edged once again past the awful thing on the stairs. Its horror was actually paling in comparison to my frenzied desire for Hayden to shut up.

I wished Martin would stir himself to help me, but he was standing with his hands on the Mercedes hood, looking out into the night, that odd introspective look still on his face.

The baby's diaper bag, feeling considerably lighter, was lying on its side in the middle of the floor. I was glad to see it. I looped the strap over my shoulder and carried the shrieking Hayden on yet another trek into our house. I was utterly unable to think of what to do next.

But Hayden wouldn't stop crying.

I tried to reason through all the noise. He must be wet or hungry, right? Or both. Wasn't that generally what was wrong with babies?

I opened his diaper bag and pulled out one of the disposable diapers Regina used. Then I had to figure it out, since I'd never even examined such an item, much less put one on a baby.

When I thought I understood the thing, I ripped a paper towel off the roll and spread it on the kitchen table, where we ate most of our meals. I plopped Hayden down on the middle of the towel and began to unsnap his sleeper, which seemed incredibly complicated. I extricated his kicking legs with great difficulty and peeled open the tabs holding the diaper shut.

Whew. He did need a fresh one.

I had to clean him off. What with? I couldn't take my hands off him. What if he rolled off the table? This problem absorbed me so thoroughly that the sirens of the arriving cars were only background noise. My free hand found a plastic box in the diaper bag. I flipped it open and found premoistened towelettes inside. Yahoo!

After a few more strenuous minutes, Hayden was clean and rediapered . . . more or less. He was whimpering now, and I knew he'd break out into screaming again if I didn't solve whatever other problems he had. Hunger seemed the most likely, and I remembered Regina preparing the bottles that afternoon. God bless her, I thought. If she left me bottles for this baby I'll forgive her, no matter what else she has done.

There were four bottles in the refrigerator. I heated one up in the microwave as Regina had shown me, and I wondered if she had foreseen her departure when she made such a point of telling me how to prepare the bottles, how to test them for temperature.

The idea that Regina might have known she'd be leaving was so unpleasant I was sorry I'd thought of it. I put Hayden in his infant seat, which I found in the living room and carried back into the kitchen, and held his bottle to his mouth. Hayden did the rest. I slumped in a chair, my forehead resting on my hand, my other hand holding the bottle in the right position (I hoped).

I heard feet tramping up the steps to the kitchen door, and I knew it was time to answer questions. I looked down at Hayden, who was pulling on the bottle as if it were the answer to all the troubles of the universe.

I wished I could have one.

Chapter Three

After an hour or two of the county cops coming in and out, I was so exhausted, angry, and horrified that I could hardly put two words together, much less come up with coherent answers. Martin was outside most of the time, but he came through the kitchen with Sheriff Padgett Lanier following close on his heels. They went into the study across the hall and didn't come out for ages.

I passed the dreary time trying to resnap Hayden's sleeper, holding him, and trying to burp him, something I recollected you were supposed to do to babies after you fed them.

'You need to hold him up a little,' said one husky young man in the khaki of the sheriffs department. 'I got a four-month-old,' he added, to establish his credentials. I shifted the warm bundle cautiously, offering it to him.

'And you need to have a diaper over your shoulder,' he continued helpfully. I passed him a cloth diaper from the bag just in time. Hayden smiled and burped formula all over the diaper. The young man smiled back at him and handed the child to me. I held out my arms reluctantly. I was unused to the baby's weight, and my shoulders were already aching.

Then I was horrified by how spoiled I must be, since I realized I was angry at Martin because he was not somehow making this baby go away, or at least commiserating with me, or at the *very* least giving me tips on what to do, because after all, he'd had one.

I resolutely made myself feel sympathy for Martin, who had found a horribly dead man on our property, who was missing a niece suspected of murder, who wasn't able to contact his sister and let her know about this situation; and on top of it all, he was still in wet clothes.

Once I rose out of my snit and channeled my thoughts in less emotional directions, I asked myself the obvious question: Was the dead man really Craig, Regina's husband? I hadn't seen Craig since the wedding. The dead man had been wearing jeans, a leather jacket . . . I couldn't remember any more than that, but I knew I'd see his face again in my dreams.

When I mentioned the soggy note under the windshield wiper to one of the officers who passed back and forth in a steady stream, he said it had disintegrated when they'd tried to extricate it.

Gradually all the men and women left, and all the cars reversed, and I understood that the body had been removed and the last question had been asked. At least for tonight. I looked up at the clock. It was midnight, only two and a half hours since we'd left the Lowrys' house. Hayden had at last gone to sleep, and I'd put him in the infant seat, grateful for the chance to rest my arms, which were definitely worn out from the unaccustomed burden.

I put my head down on the table. I must have dozed. When I looked at the clock again, it read twelve-thirty. Martin was standing by the table, looking at me.

'Let's go to bed,' he said, his voice empty.

'We have to get the portable crib for the baby,' I pointed out, trying to sound practical rather than aggrieved.

He stared at Hayden almost in astonishment, as if he'd assumed the police had taken the baby with them, too.

'Oh my God,' he said wearily.

I bit my tongue to keep from speaking.

After what I considered more than enough time for him to volunteer, I said in a tight voice, 'If you'll keep an eye on him, I'll go get it.'

'Okay,' said Martin, to my complete amazement. He sat in another chair and propped his chin on his hand, looking at the baby's face as if he'd never seen one.

Gritting my teeth and simply ducking under the crime scene tape, I went up those apartment stairs once more, maneuvering carefully around the bloodstains and wondering who the hell would clean them up. Probably me, I figured. I was building up a good head of grievance.

It was a shock to see how messy the apartment was. Of course, they'd searched for evidence about the crime and Regina's whereabouts. I don't know why I'd assumed they'd leave it neat. I shook my head in disgust with my own naiveté and snatched up a flattened contraption I assumed was the portable crib. There were assembly directions on a white rectangle attached to the pastel bumper sort of thing. I was pathetically grateful.

I was so scared I wouldn't hear the baby if he woke in the night that I laboriously assembled the crib right by our bed. Martin didn't comment. At least he carried the diaper bag up after me, and at least I managed to lay Hayden down without waking him. I perceived Hayden as a baby – instead of a massive problem – for one moment before exhaustion took over; for that moment, I saw the smooth pale skin, the tiny fingers, the sweet crease of the neck, and it took my breath away.

Then he was once more a terrifyingly fragile being, who was (it seemed) my sole responsibility, and I was totally ignorant of how to take care of him. I sighed, pulled off my clothes, and tossed them into the wicker basket in the bathroom. I pulled on my blue nightgown, brushed my teeth, and sank into bed. I registered that Martin was turning out the light before I retreated into sleep.

'Was it our hatchet?' Martin was asking me.

'Uhmm?'

'Roe, was that our hatchet?'

I considered, my head still pillowed on my arms. I felt warm and comfortable, but as soon as I really woke, misery was just waiting to pounce.

I rolled over, snuggled up to my husband.

'I don't know,' I said against his chest. Martin sleeps in pajama bottoms only.

He put his arm around me absently, his chin gently rubbing the top of my head. 'I hope it wasn't,' was all he said.

'She didn't do it.'

'Why do you think that?' He didn't sound upset, just curious.

'She wouldn't leave her baby, right? And she wouldn't leave all her stuff, either,' I said more firmly.

'But her car is gone, not the one Craig came in.'

'That was Craig's car?' Martin didn't bother answering. Of course, Craig had gotten here somehow; he hadn't dropped from the sky.

Not that the scenario was unknown to me; a body had dropped from the sky into my garden the year before. But it seemed unlikely it would happen twice, even to me.

So, I reasoned, Craig had come after Regina. He'd been in his own car. Maybe Regina had left him and Craig wanted her to come back. They quarreled and Regina took the hatchet that . . . How did the hatchet enter the picture? Where had it been before it landed in the middle of Craig's forehead?

Okay, ignore that mental image. Say Craig had been threatening Regina with a hatchet he'd gotten out of his own car – 'Come back to me or I'll kill you' – and she got it away from him and killed him with it.

While he stood passively below her on the stairs?

And then she wrote a note to her uncle and fled, leaving her baby to the care of whoever walked in the apartment door?

Okay.

Craig had brought a friend with him, who had taken a letch to Regina. This friend got a hatchet and killed Craig and abducted Regina, but didn't want to be burdened with Hayden. Or the friend didn't even know there was a baby, so to save the child, Regina had snatched a moment to stash Hayden under the bed.

I thought that scenario covered everything. I relayed my theory to Martin.

'That would exonerate Regina,' he said, sounding as if that were a very remote possibility. He seemed a smidge more hopeful, though. 'I'm sure she left because someone forced her to. I can't believe she'd leave the baby unless she was under duress.' Martin kissed my forehead to say thank you, but the arm beneath my neck felt like a log, it was so hard with tension.

I decided to relieve his stress in the happiest way. I nuzzled his nipple. He drew in his breath sharply and his unoccupied hand found something pleasant to do.

'Eh!' said a little voice behind me.

I shrieked.

'It's the baby,' Martin said, after a fraught moment. 'In the crib. By the bed.'

'Eh!' said Hayden. I rolled over to see two tiny hands waving in the air.

'Oh, no no no,' I moaned, all thoughts of sex flying out of my head like rats leaving a sinking ship. 'I don't know what to do. You had a baby, you have to help.'

'Cindy took care of Barrett when he was a baby.'

Why was I not surprised?

'I was always . . . too scared to do things for him. He was so little. He was three weeks premature. And by the time he was large enough, when I was sure I couldn't hurt him by accident, Cindy and I had gotten into the habit of her taking care of him, bathing and feeding and diapering.'

Absurdly, it was not Martin's ignorance of baby care that made tears spring to my eyes as I dragged myself from the bed. It was the thought of Martin and Cindy's shared experiences: the birth of Barrett, the concern about his health and fears for his survival after the premature birth, his slow growth and improvement with Martin and Cindy watching as parents. All this he'd had with her, and would never have with me.

I hadn't ever been jealous of Cindy before, and I'd certainly picked a bad time to start.

Already feeling tired, I hoisted Hayden from his portable crib – surely he'd gained weight during the night? – and laid him on the bed beside Martin while I found my bathrobe. When I turned back, Martin was propped up on one elbow, looking down at the baby, his finger extended for Hayden to grasp. The baby was regarding Martin solemnly. I stood for a long moment looking, feeling my heart break along several different fault lines.

I turned away to pull my mass of wavy hair back into a ponytail and secure it. Hayden had showed a tendency to grab and pull the night before, and I hadn't enjoyed the experience. I tied the sash of the black velour robe and cautiously bent down to lift the infant from the bed.

'How old do you reckon he is?' I asked, startled to think I didn't even know this child's age.

'I have no idea.' Martin stared at the baby, running some comparisons in his head. 'He seems a little smaller than Bubba and Lizanne's kid.'

He did to me, too. 'Maybe – a month?' I hazarded.

He shrugged his bare shoulders.

'People will ask,' I said, and to my own ears I already sounded tired. 'People always do.'

'Oh, God.' Martin rolled onto his back, pressing his hands against his face as if to guard it from the world.

'You'd better call Cindy,' I said, trying to sound matter-of-fact. 'Regina halfway implied they were close. Maybe she can tell us some more about this baby. Maybe she knows how to contact Barby.'

I went down the stairs carefully, holding up the nightgown and bathrobe with one hand while pressing Hayden to me with my free arm. I was relieved when I reached the bottom safely, and felt foolishly optimistic at this good omen.

There was a discreet tap at the kitchen door. Now, this knock was unmistakable. My mother.

I canceled the security and opened the door.

My mother, Aida Brattle Teagarden Queensland, is fifty-seven and stunning. She is Lauren Bacall on a good day. She is sharp, smart, and by her own efforts has amassed a small fortune. I love her. She loves me. We live on different planets.

'Have they found the girl?' Mother stepped inside.

'The girl' would be Regina. 'No. Not that we know of. I just got up,' I explained unnecessarily.

'Martin still in bed?' She glanced up at the clock. It was already nine-thirty.

'We had a late night,' I reminded her. I'd called Mother as soon as I could after the police arrived so she wouldn't hear our news from someone else.

Mother held out her arms and made a peremptory gesture. I gave her the baby. Mother had three step-grandchildren now, and to my amazement she was very fond of them.

Mother looked down at the boy, who looked back, for a wonder in silence.

'Maybe two, three weeks old,' she said briefly, and put him in his infant seat, still in the middle of the table. 'Got formula?'

'Regina mixed some up before she . . .' I trailed off into confusion. Before she murdered her husband and ran? Before she was abducted by aliens?

'You need a nurse for that baby,' my mother observed. Her voice was absolutely matter-of-fact; she judged me totally incompetent at child care, which wounded me somehow. But then, why should she have any faith in my ability to take care of a baby? I never had before.

It was funny what hurt and what bounced off. This really hurt.

'You'd better call your friends and see if you can find a temporary babysitter,' Mother suggested.

I stared at her. She wasn't offering to do it for me, or rather to have her office manager do it? It dawned on me that all was not well with Mother. I'd been so absorbed in my own problems that I hadn't even looked at her with much attention.

'What's wrong?' I asked. I hated the quaver in my voice.

'John had a mild . . . well, maybe a heart attack last night, about two hours after you called,' she said.

'Oh, no,' I said, my eyes filling with tears immediately. I was fond of John Queensland, having been his friend before he dated and married my mother. I took a deep breath. Mother wasn't crying, so I couldn't cry. 'How is he doing?'

'I've moved him to Atlanta. They're doing tests right now,' she said, and I could read the exhaustion in her face, and the fear.

'I'm so sorry,' I said quietly. 'What can I do to help you?'

'You have your hands full,' she said, looking out the kitchen window. It was another windy, overcast day; a leaf from the gum tree whirled past. 'It's just a lot of hospital sitting, and you can't help me sit.'

I thought of Martin, the baby, the missing woman, the dead man.

My mother finally needed me and I couldn't help.

'Are Avery and John David there?' I asked. These were John's two sons, both in their thirties and married.

'John David flies in this morning. Melinda's going to meet him at the airport and get him to the hospital. That's something she can do with the kids in the car,' she said. Mother smiled briefly, and I saw with a kind of unworthy pang that she had become very fond of Melinda, Avery's wife.

'What's the prognosis?' I asked, dreading the answer. Behind her back I noticed Martin standing in the doorway. I didn't know how long he'd been there.

'We don't know yet,' Mother said quietly. 'He's been conscious, off and on. He's in some pain.'

'Don't worry about us, Aida,' my husband said. He moved until he was by Mother's side, and he gripped her shoulder. Her hand came up briefly to cover his, and then they both retreated back into more comfortable personas. 'We'll be fine, we just have to get this straightened out.'

'Roe,' Mother said, as she picked up her purse and went to the door. 'This is just an *awful lot* of trouble at one time.'

I realized she was half apologizing for focusing on her husband, or at least extending her regrets that my trouble was not her only concern.

'We'll all get through it,' I said briskly, trying not to cry. 'I'll be checking with you later. Tell John I'm thinking of him.'

She nodded. She'd scrawled John's hospital room phone number on a sheet of paper, and she handed it to me.

After Mother left, I sank down into a chair and put my head in my hands. If the baby started crying, I just couldn't bear it.

The baby started crying.

I forced myself up and to the refrigerator, thinking (as I pulled a bottle from the shelf and popped it into the microwave) that I was almost willing to forgive Regina for everything if she would just return and leave again with the baby.

Martin had made coffee. I noticed he was dressed in khakis and a sweater, about as casual as Martin gets in day wear. He was staring out the window sipping from a mug, looking like a Lands' End ad. I was still in my velour robe, my hair was trailing down my back in a cascade of waves and tangles, and I was in a very tense mood. Hayden, still dressed in the same red sleeper and a diaper that was undoubtedly dirty, was yelling.

'Pick up the baby,' I said to Martin.

'What?' he said, turning to me with an automatic smile. 'I can't hear you, the baby's crying.'

I hadn't had a cup of coffee.

'Pick . . . up . . . the . . . baby,' I said.

Martin was so surprised he put down his mug and picked up the baby.

I took the bottle from the microwave and shook it. I tested some formula on my arm. It was the right temperature, as far as I could tell. I handed the bottle to Martin, who had to free his left hand to take it.

I left the room.

I stomped across the hall, or at least I tried to, but stomping is uphill work in fuzzy slippers. I stuck John's hospital phone number by the desk telephone. I flung myself down sideways on the red leather sofa, my back braced against one armrest, and stared out the window at the nasty gray cold windy day. That was exactly how I felt inside, I fumed, nasty and cold and gray. Maybe not *windy* . . . Then all my rage turned into something much more immediate as a head appeared between the back of the couch and the window. It was the head of a young man, a blond and handsome young man, and his expression was groggy.

'Hey,' he said. 'You're Aunty Roe? I thought you'd be old. Where's the kid?'

I shrieked and set a record for bounding off red leather couches.

Martin was hampered in his rescue attempt by the baby. He looked ready for action when he appeared in the doorway, but the effect was spoiled by the feeding Hayden. Martin shoved baby and bottle into my arms and stood waiting. He was spoiling for a fight, which the young man was just perceptive enough to see.

'Hey, man, it's okay, didn't Regina tell you I was here?'

We stared at him.

It gradually sank into his dim consciousness that something was drastically wrong.

'So, where's Craig?' he asked uncertainly, working his way out from behind the couch. He proved to be not much over five-eight, and he was wearing ancient blue jeans and a none-too-clean flannel shirt hanging open over a T-shirt. A golden stubble made his face look dirty. But he didn't look threatening. He had an aura of amiable stupidity that I came to learn was, to some extent, quite accurate.

Martin and I exchanged glances.

'Did you come here with Craig?' Martin asked, as if the answer were not important.

'Sure, didn't he tell you?'

'Was Regina expecting you?' I asked next.

'Well, no. She didn't expect Craig to get out early, but the jail got real crowded, and Craig really toes the line when he's in, so they released him early.'

There was so much in this sentence to absorb that we just stood and stared. Visibly unnerved, the stranger tried to fill the silence with chatter. 'See, after we stopped for some beer at that liquor store on the main drag, we had to help this lady who was having trouble with her car. And then we got here, but all of a sudden I was feeling really really tired. I never felt anything like that. So we came over here to this house, and Regina was in the kitchen with the baby, and she and Craig started fighting right away, you know, and I could see this couch across the hall while I was standing there listening to them, and I was so sleepy I just came in here and lay down. That's the last I remember, except I had a dream about hearing someone scream, and I musta hid.'

We exchanged glances again.

'Ain't you ever going to say nothing? You are Regina's aunt and uncle, right? Though I got to say, lady, you don't look old enough to be anyone's aunt.' He grinned at me, or tried to, but by now it was so obvious something was wrong that his grin was only a shadow of what it could be.

Martin scowled. I am less than thirteen years younger than he, but I look even younger than that. The same genes that are keeping my mother's skin smooth at fifty-seven are being equally kind to me, and I'll never be taller than my present inadequate height.

Hayden finished the bottle. I put him up to my shoulder to burp and began patting, trying to think of what to say next.

'Martin is Regina's uncle and I'm Martin's wife, Aurora,' I said cautiously. 'Last night some things happened here.'

'Don't tell me Craig hit Regina or nothing like that.'

'Could you tell us who you are?' Martin asked, trying to sound very calm.

'Sure, man. I'm Rory Brown, Craig's buddy. We've been best friends forever.'

'Then I have bad news for you . . . Rory.'

'Craig's back in jail?'

I had to sit down. This was going to be worse than I thought.

'No,' Martin said. 'He's dead.'

Chapter Four

I'm no psychic, but Rory Brown seemed genuinely stunned by this news. He sank back down to the couch, his face contorted with horror and disbelief. 'But he was alive just a few hours ago!' Rory protested, as if it took a long time to die.

'I'm sorry,' I said. 'He was killed last night. We found him lying on the steps to the apartment.'

'Where's Regina?' Rory's voice was hoarse with, I swear, unshed tears.

'She's nowhere to be found,' my husband told him. Martin was in his thinking posture, arms crossed over his chest, fingers tapping. As he reached a decision, Martin moved toward the telephone.

'You calling the police?' Rory slid onto his knees. 'Man, please don't! I'm violating my parole. They'll send me back to jail for sure. I'm not even supposed to see Craig, much less leave the state with him!'

'Parole.' Martin said it thoughtfully, as if parole were a common condition among his acquaintances. 'You were in jail with Craig?'

'Uh, well, yeah. You know. We, uh, we wrote a few bad cheques.'

So Rory wasn't any desperate felon. I hadn't known how tense I was until I relaxed.

'Whose name did you sign to the bad cheques?' Martin asked. I glanced at him admiringly, for making a point I'd never have considered.

'Well,' Rory said, trying on his charming grin, 'ours. Or it'd have been forgery. Much more serious.'

Rory seemed to know his way around the penal code.

'Craig's boss would have paid him that money at the end of the month; we just needed it a little earlier than that.'

Martin and I looked at each other with raised eyebrows. This sounded very weak to me. It was becoming all too clear that Regina had made a poor choice in the man she married. Of course, some people thought I had done the same when I married Martin. Ha! At least Martin had never been in jail! I *thought*. I opened my mouth to make what would have been a very ill-timed query, when we were interrupted.

The phone rang, startling all of us out of our skins. In Hayden's case, this naturally meant he started to cry. I began patting him more rapidly, saying 'Sshhhh, baby,' in an increasingly frantic whisper, as Martin grimaced at me while he tried to hear the caller.

'Give him his Binky,' suggested Rory.

'His what?' I patted faster.

'His pacifier.'

A lightbulb went on in my head as I remembered seeing Lizanne's baby sucking on a plastic thing.

'Where?' I asked eagerly. 'Where is one?'

'You didn't find one in the diaper bag?'

Martin's scowl increased in ferocity.

'No.' I scooted into the kitchen as fast as I could, burdened with Hayden, and returned with the diaper bag. I thrust it at Rory. 'Find one!' I told him.

The young man turned the bag around, opened a Velcroed flap, and reached in a pocket, one I hadn't even noticed. He pulled out a plastic and rubber object and offered it to me.

It looked like it had lint on it. I stuck it in Hayden's mouth anyway.

Blessed silence.

Rory beamed at me angelically. Hayden's face looked just as sweet, all of a sudden. Martin became my handsome husband instead of Ebenezer Scrooge. I felt as if the vise clamping my temples had been loosened a couple of turns. I sat down on the couch very carefully, easing Hayden onto his back. He looked up at me with hazy blue eyes, relaxed and content.

'Hello, sweetie,' I said softly, watching the baby's hands curl and straighten. His fingernails, his tiny fingernails, how would I ever cut them?

Martin said into the receiver, 'So you haven't found her or seen any sign of the car?'

I snapped back into our current situation with some reluctance.

'Umm-hmmm,' he said. 'I understand.'

Rory was looking down at the shabby boots on his feet, and I could practically feel the force of his hope that Martin would say nothing.

'She hasn't called here,' Martin said, as if he were confirming what the caller had already stated. 'No.' While he was talking, Martin was eyeing Rory with the same calculation he showed when he was hiring someone. Martin seemed to reach a conclusion. He turned his back on the boy. 'No, we don't know anything more than you do. Please keep us posted. Anything you find out, we want to know as soon as possible.' After another minute's worth of listening, Martin hung up.

'If you don't explain things to my satisfaction,' he told Rory grimly, 'I'll pick up the telephone in a minute. Now, when did Regina have this baby and why didn't anyone know about it?'

'Could I have something to eat and a little trip to your bathroom before I have to explain?' Rory asked.

'You're welcome to go to the bathroom,' Martin said, 'but before we feed you, we have to know more about you.'

The young man looked surprised at Martin's refusal. I was a little embarrassed at not offering hospitality right away, but I could see Martin's point. We'd probably already made a mistake in not calling the police the moment we'd seen him. We shouldn't compound that mistake by turning Rory into our welcome guest.

While Martin showed Rory the downstairs bathroom, I put Hayden upstairs in the portable crib and took a minute or two to get dressed. Jeans and a sweater, a vigorous tooth- and hair-brushing, and I felt like a better woman. I put on my red glasses to set off my navy sweater. After I ran a brush through my tight waves, my hair crackled with so much electricity that it flew around my head like an angry brown cloud.

This might be the only moment I had to myself today, I figured, so I called the hospital in Atlanta to ask about John.

Mother answered the phone in his room. She told me in that hushed voice people reserve for bedsides of the very ill that John was resting, that tests were ongoing, and that John had definitely had a cardiac incident, which I interpreted as 'heart attack'.

'What are his options?' I asked, and Mother said all those buzzwords like 'angioplasty' and 'stress tests'. I barely listened, because all I wanted was the bottom line: Was John likely to die soon or not? After I'd gathered that he was going to live, barring some sudden and drastic circumstance, I was content to save the details of his treatment until I could spare a portion of my brain to understand what was entailed.

Mother didn't say a word about the baby. She was preoccupied, too.

I tightened the laces on my high-tops and tried to tiptoe down the stairs. Martin and Rory were in the kitchen, and I saw that Martin had relented enough to pour the boy a cup of coffee and microwave a couple of cinnamon rolls for him. Rory looked up when I entered, and let a gleam of admiration show a little too obviously. So I didn't offer to fix him any bacon or eggs.

'Rory here was just telling me about Craig,' Martin said. He was sitting opposite our visitor, his arms crossed over his chest, his face relaxed and cool. Mr Skeptical.

'What was he saying?' I slipped into a chair at one end of the table. The back part of my brain was wondering if I could borrow a baby monitor from someone. Wasn't that what the surveillance thing was called?

'I was telling Mr Bartell, I've been Craig's friend since we were little. Our folks were friends, too. Then when Craig's mom and dad died, Craig moved in with his aunt and uncle, Mr and Mrs Harbor. His brother, Dylan, was old enough to be on his own but too young to keep an eye on Craig, and the Harbors were glad to have him.' Rory paused to take a bite of cinnamon roll, and I worked on keeping the relationships straight in my head.

'And that was the couple at Regina's wedding, the people who acted in the place of Craig's parents?'

'That was his aunt and uncle, Mr and Mrs Harbor,' Rory confirmed. 'They had raised four girls of their own. But now Mr Harbor, he's kind of sickly.'

Martin and I sat blinking at him like foolish owls.

'Would that be Hugh Harbor?' Martin asked, obviously dredging the name up from his distant memory.

'Yep,' Rory mumbled, caught with more sweet roll in his mouth. 'Mrs Harbor used to be a Thurlkill.'

'And your folks?'

'My mother, Cathy, used to be a Thurlkill, too,' Rory said, seeming rather proud of the fact. 'Me and Craig're kind of related. My dad is Chuck Brown, his dad was Ross Graham.'

Martin looked away from the table, letting his gaze light on the front of the refrigerator. I knew he was thinking deep thoughts because his fingers were twiddling, the way they do when he's having ideas he can't talk about.

'Craig's brother was at the wedding,' he said abruptly. 'He seemed like a nice enough guy.'

'Dylan's a great guy,' Rory agreed readily. 'And he and his wife, Shondra, they have the cutest little girl.'

Martin did a little more staring and twiddling.

I felt like I had to say something.

'Rory, when you feel like freshening up, there's a toothbrush in a plastic wrapper in the top drawer in the downstairs bathroom,' I told our surprise guest. 'There are extra towels in the closet by the sink, and I think I have shampoo and soap out and ready.'

Rory took the not-too-subtle hint in a jiffy. 'That was real good,' he told Martin sincerely, carrying his coffee cup and plate over to the sink.

I had another thought. 'If you'd like to set your clothes out the bathroom door, I'll throw 'em in the washer,' I offered. I rose to go upstairs to check on Hayden. 'I'll put a robe in the bathroom first.'

'Thank you, ma'am,' he said, smiling shyly.

Martin was staring at Rory as if he were an alien wearing an ill-fitting human suit. I padded out of the room and began taking the stairs at my usual pace, and then realized I'd have to go slower. The night before had taken its toll, and toting the baby around had already made my arms trembly. I was in no shape to be thrown into the role of mother.

It wasn't any trouble finding a robe for Rory to use, since when people can't think of anything to give Martin, they give him bathrobes. Some men get gloves, some men get ties; my husband gets bathrobes. Last year, my seldom-seen father had sent us matching green terry ones (which made us look like walking bundles of Astroturf). Martin's son, Barrett, had sent him a silk paisley, and my mother had given him a blue flannel. The year before that, Barby had presented him with the nicest one of all, gray polished cotton with his monogram in maroon.

I hung the green terry robe in the downstairs bathroom and Rory scooted in. A few minutes later, his clothes were deposited discreetly outside the bathroom door, and I went to the washer and dryer closet at the rear of the house in the kitchen to start a load. There was always something in the laundry basket I could throw in with a small bundle of clothes.

Martin had gotten the portable phone and was punching in a series of numbers, peering at a page in his personal address book. He looked up at the kitchen wall clock as he listened to the ringing at the other end.

'Hello,' he said. I thought he sounded uncertain, which was rare for Martin. 'Cindy Bartell, please.'

I began to load dishes into the dishwasher – anything to stay in the room and keep working without making it obvious I was determined to listen to this conversation.

'Cindy? This is Martin. Have you been doing well? Barrett told me you'd taken a partner on . . . yes, he called me at work last week.'

Barrett hated to call here because I might answer the phone.

'I'm glad you're finally getting some free time. Who'd you . . . ?'

Martin's face underwent the oddest change.

'Dennis Stinson,' he said. 'Hmmm.' He looked as if he were restraining all kinds of comments. I gathered Dennis Stinson was not unknown to Martin; but frankly, Cindy's business dealings were not my prime concern at this point in time.

I just barely heard Hayden whimper upstairs, and I cringed. I went up the stairs so fast I wished I'd had Martin clocking me. I stood by the portable crib and held my hands up in a soothing gesture, as if that would calm the baby back into sleep. I noticed that my hands were shaking, and I was saying, 'Sshhhh! Sshhhh!' in a kind of frantic way. Hayden's blue-veined eyelids fluttered once more before he settled back into sleep.

Feeling as though I'd just avoided a herd of stampeding buffalo, I shambled back down the stairs and collapsed into the chair across from Martin. I slumped over the table, burying my face in my folded arms. After a moment, I felt Martin's fingers in my hair. He stroked my head the way a man absently pats a dog, but I was so tired by my unusually prolonged turn at being the strong one that I found even an offhand caress comforting.

'So, have you seen Regina lately?' Martin said into the telephone.

I could hear a tinny buzz that was Cindy's answer.

'Not in five months? Did you notice, the last time you saw her, that she'd gained some weight?'

Buzz, buzz.

'She had a baby,' Martin said.

I heard a kind of shriek coming from the other end.

'Yes, really.'

I raised my head to look at Martin, but he was scowling at the stove while Cindy kept talking.

'I can imagine you'd want to talk to her, but the fact is . . . she's disappeared.'

Buzz.

'Well, no, I can't contact Craig to ask him where she is because

Craig is here. I guess the sheriff's department here will have arranged to tell his brother and the Harbors by now. This is bad news, Cindy. Craig is dead, murdered.'

Buzz, buzz.

'No, it wasn't over drugs.' Martin raised his eyebrows to me, indicating that we had learned another fact about the deceased Craig. 'We don't know what happened, exactly, but Regina is gone, Craig is dead, and we have the baby.'

Then Martin had to tell Cindy that Barby was out of touch on a cruise, and that we didn't know what to do with Hayden.

'Yes, I guess we could,' Martin said cautiously. Cindy was offering some advice, I gathered. 'Yes, I guess we could do that. Well, we'll talk about it, and if we decide to come, I'll give you a call when we get there.'

He hung up a moment later. 'Before Rory gets out of the shower,' he said, keeping his voice low, 'Cindy says she had no idea Regina was pregnant, and she bets no one in Corinth knew about it. Cindy said Craig had been in jail for one or two things: possession of marijuana, bad cheques, that kind of stuff. His friend Rory was almost always involved with Craig's law problems, too.'

'Are we going to call the sheriff about him?' I asked, tilting my head toward the bathroom door as if Martin had a choice of subjects. We could hear the pipes groan as hot water gushed out of the shower-head. The downstairs bathroom was the noisy one.

Martin stared across the hall to the door as if it could give him an answer.

'You're really thinking about not calling the sheriff,' I said, my voice full of incredulity.

'Cindy suggested we bring Hayden to Craig's aunt and uncle in Corinth, the ones who raised him,' Martin said. 'We might as well take Rory with us. Do you think he knows anything more than he told us?'

'I have no idea.' I drew myself upright in my chair, trying not to breathe fire at the stranger sitting across from me. 'But I don't think we're the best judges of that. I think we've been as kind as possible, feeding him and giving him a chance to clean up, but I think now he needs to go face the music.'

'You amaze me,' Martin said, with no evident amazement.

'You're giving me a surprise or two yourself,' I said, with equal grimness.

'Do you think that boy has brains enough to lie?'

'Just because he's stupid and sweet doesn't mean he's good,' I countered.

'But, Roe, if we turn him over, it'll make things that much worse for Regina.'

'How so?' If my eyebrows could've crawled up any higher, they would have been in Maine.

'Because he knows why Craig came to Lawrenceton,' Martin pointed out. 'And he's the only one.'

I gaped at him. I honestly tried to think that one through. Finally, I shook my head. 'I'm not following you at all,' I admitted.

The water had stopped in the bathroom.

'He's going to tell the police whatever puts him in the best light,' Martin said. He'd also noticed the water had quit pounding through the pipes. 'By his own admission, Rory's been in trouble with the law, in a minor way, for years. His dad and granddad before him have done jail time. I recognized his dad's name as soon as he told me. The Thurlkills, the mother's family, is just as bad if not worse. Rory isn't going to tell anyone anything he doesn't want to.'

'So what's the profit in taking him with us?'

'He may tell us. We may be able to tell, once we get on Craig and Regina's home ground, what they were doing. Find some way through this without Regina ending up in any more trouble than she's already . . .' His voice trailed off, as he realized it would be pretty hard to find more trouble for Regina.

'Why would he tell us?'

'I can only hope he will. Now that Craig's dead, why not? We can't revoke his parole or punish him for whatever he's done. Maybe if we leave him out of this as far as the law is concerned, he'll reciprocate with information.'

I could think of one word for this theory, and it wasn't a polite one.

What had happened to my incisive, figure-all-the-angles husband? He could only be this gullible because it concerned his family. Had Martin ever been foolish about me? I thought not. Did that mean he loved his sister and niece more? His son? What about his first wife? I had a moment of sheer irrational rage as I stared at Martin. Then, once again, I took a deep breath and made myself recall that he had had a terrible shock the night before, that he must in some sense feel responsible for Craig's death, that his niece was missing and might, for all we knew, be dead.

Be calm and patient, I advised myself. Calm and patient.

But I was pretty close to being clean out of calmness and patience.

I heard Hayden's little noises from upstairs, and once again I plodded up and back down, this time bringing him with me, wrapped in the only blanket Regina had brought. He was definitely awake. I sat at the table holding him, looking at the bundle in my arms.

The baby's hands fluttered, and his blue eyes were wide open. He began to make the little fussy sounds I was learning would develop into a full-blown wail. My nose told me he needed changing. And he'd want to eat after that; I was willing to put money on it. We had only one more prepared baby bottle. Where could you buy the formula? Anywhere?

'I wish we could go upstairs for a while,' Martin said wistfully. But he didn't look horny. He just looked like he wanted oblivion.

'Dream on,' I said, spitting out each word as though it were a hunk of poisoned apple. I tried to remember if the formula had been in powder form or concentrate. Had it been milk based? Soy? I'd have to dig the can out of the trash.

My husband was staring at me with bewilderment – if you can believe that – as I picked up Hayden and trudged into the living room to change him.

Rory was standing in the living room, the big diaper bag in his hands. I stopped short.

'Just seeing how many more diapers the little fella has,' he explained. He put the bag down on the low coffee table with some reluctance, and backed away.

'How many are there?'

'What?'

'How many diapers are left in the bag?' It sounded like one of those bizarre math problems you get in the lower school grades. *If it takes Suzy ten diapers a day to keep little Marge clean, and Suzy lends Tawan three diapers and uses two, how many more diapers will she need that day?*

'Six, at least, I think,' Rory said.

'Thanks.' When he didn't move, I said, 'Do you want to change Hayden?' I held out the baby to him.

'Oh, no!' he all but yelped, backing out of the room with great speed. 'No, that's okay.'

I now had all the products arranged in a line on the table, and a section of newspaper spread out to put the baby on. I managed this change with relative efficiency. All the while, watching Hayden wave around his arms and legs, hearing him fuss when his bottom was exposed to the cool air, clapping a paper towel over him quickly when he began an unexpected pee, I was wondering what Rory had been doing. When Hayden was reassembled, I looked to the left, to the wide opening to the entrance hall, and behind me to the open doors to the dining room. No one in sight.

While Hayden exercised, I undertook a real search of the diaper bag. It had, besides the big central cavity, lots and lots of pockets and pouches, zippered or Velcroed. I found two extra pacifiers; a big plastic fake key ring, which I handed to Hayden; four diapers; and a faded blue dish towel that I figured Regina had used to cover her shoulder when she burped him. I rummaged through all the little pouches until I found one I'd nearly missed, because it was on one end of the bag right under the shoulder strap clip.

I slid a finger in beside the little Velcro tab that held it shut, and broke the seal. Yep, there was something in this one. The pocket was so tight I could only insert two fingers, and I slid one behind and one in front of the object and pulled up.

'Oh no oh no oh no,' I breathed, and slid what I'd extracted into Hayden's receiving blanket, which I immediately wrapped around him. I lifted him and made a beeline for the kitchen, trying to act casual.

Martin and Rory were ensconced at the table with a map of the Southeast in front of them and more detailed maps of each state we'd pass through lying ready to hand.

Just as I was trying to think of a plausible reason to talk to Martin privately, the front doorbell rang. I started to hand the baby to my husband, realized that he would feel the bundle in the blanket, realized he might well haul it out in front of his companion. That wouldn't do at all. So I veered through the kitchen doorway to the hall, scooted back down the hall, and awkwardly opened the front door with one hand.

Ellen Lowry was waiting with a stack of blankets in her arms.

'Hey, Ellen,' I said, unable to keep the surprise out of my voice.

'I'm sorry to intrude, but I heard you had troubles, and I thought you could maybe use these,' she said, nodding at the stack. 'These are baby blankets I used when the boys were little, and I believe they're in perfect shape. I ran them through the washer and dryer this morning to freshen them up.'

'How kind of you! Please, come in,' I said, trying to summon some poise. I stood aside and ushered Ellen into the living room, where the square low table was covered with changing paraphernalia. Ellen smiled in a nostalgic sort of way.

'You'd think it had been so long I would've forgotten about changing the boys, but to me it seems like yesterday,' she said, shaking her head in disbelief.

I forced myself to respond. This was a very gracious gesture of Ellen's, and I needed to be gracious in return. I asked if she needed something to drink, or eat; she refused. I urged her strongly to sit down and stay a while; she said she only had a minute, and sat on the edge of a rather uncomfortable chair. She asked about John's heart and the health of the baby, and ran her fingertip over Hayden's soft cheek. I was afraid she'd offer to hold him. How could I explain a refusal? But the money in the blanket would be obvious to anyone who held the baby.

Luckily, Ellen stood after a brief conversation and began her good-byes. The weak winter sun streamed through the window to make her smooth blond hair glow like a halo as she bent over me and the baby to coo at him before she picked up her purse. Ellen looked like a model in a catalog for mature women.

She was elegant, thoughtful, intelligent, and kind: and I could hardly wait for her to be gone.

Finally I could watch her car go slowly down the driveway to the road. I whipped around and strode into the kitchen, as much as you can whip and stride with a baby in your arms. Martin and Rory were sitting at the table, having an earnest conversation. I abandoned any idea I'd had of concealing my discovery.

'Do you want to tell me about this?' I said, pulling the sheaf of bills from Hayden's blanket and tossing them on top of the map.

Rory looked as though I'd slapped him.

'I didn't have anything to do with that,' he said, as if he were sure I'd believe him, as if we were lifelong friends.

Martin's eyes closed, slowly. He opened them, sighed, picked up the sheaf of bills. He counted it silently. 'Five hundred,' he informed us.

Rory's eyes had never left the money. His face altered when Martin told us the total. I could swear I glimpsed naked rage on his face. But it softened immediately into a mask of puzzlement and anxiety.

'Would you like to tell me about this?' Martin asked him.

'That must be the money Craig stole,' his best friend said hesitantly. Then Rory fell silent, his eyes fixed on the money.

If there'd been a jug of water handy I'd have thrown it on him.

'Would you care to explain a little further?' Martin's voice was deceptively mild.

Rory looked pretty darn reluctant to start explaining, but we were both waiting and I think he knew we would not change the subject.

'When Regina was expecting,' Rory began, 'Craig began thinking of all the things the baby was gonna need, and I guess he just kinda went crazy, since he couldn't get them for her, so he robbed a convenience store.'

'In Corinth?' Martin asked.

I sat down with my burden to listen to this latest fairy tale. Hayden wasn't interested. He made little smacking noises. I looked down to discover he was asleep, with his tiny fist jammed into his mouth. I eased him into his infant seat to give my arms a rest.

'No, sir,' said Rory. 'He went across the state line into Pennsylvania somewhere. I don't know the exact town.'

For an appreciable length of time we just sat staring at Rory, who ducked his head and blushed at our critical scrutiny. I eyed the telephone, tempted once again to pick it up and call the sheriff to come get this fool.

But Martin shook his head, reading my thoughts.

'You were out of jail when Regina had the baby?' I asked.

Rory looked as though a lightbulb were appearing over his head.

'No, ma'am. I was in the jail.'

'Was Craig in jail when Regina had the baby?'

'No, ma'am. Craig got out a few days before I did.'

'But Craig was back in jail for the past . . . ?'

'Well, we got picked up again two weeks ago. About.'

I now understood why the police beat people who wouldn't confess. I knew somewhere in that cute, empty head lay the truth. And I wanted it badly enough to extract it with red-hot pincers, or at least so I told myself. I could tell by the way Martin was clenching his hands that he felt the same way, and I was willing to bet that under other circumstances Martin could make Rory talk.

'We'll have to talk about this more, later,' I told them both.

I've never been trained to be a detective of any kind, but I'm a reasonably observant person, and this money was not the jumble of rumpled bills of all denominations you'd get if you robbed a convenience store. This was the kind of money you'd get at a bank, two one-hundred-dollar bills, the rest in twenties: a compact little bundle, smooth and flat.

Chapter Five

Lunch that day was a real tense meal. I heated up soup and made grilled-cheese sandwiches, and we sat together at the kitchen table in uneasy silence. For once in my life, I wanted the phone to ring. Maybe the highway patrol would stop Regina's car. Martin had asked Cindy to try to discover the name of the cruise line with which Barby had sailed, and getting Barby here would be a great relief. Or my mother might tell me more about John's prognosis. I had so much to worry about, my thoughts were running around inside my head like hamsters.

Just as I began the dishes, I heard Hayden stirring, and this time he woke up ready to raise the roof.

I put a bottle in the microwave before I left the kitchen. I was getting numb from the unaccustomed responsibility for this baby. I had never been so tired in my life, and every time I heard him tune up to cry, I leaped into action to stave off any more wailing. My stomach clenched every time he made a noise.

An hour later, I had changed Hayden, fed Hayden, burped Hayden – in short, fulfilled my part of the bargain. But he wouldn't go back to sleep. In my opinion, he should be out of the picture until the next feeding-changing-burping cycle; but it was one he didn't seem to share. Not knowing what else to do, I was holding the baby, sitting on the couch in the library, staring down at the round face with more than a little frustration. Furthermore, I had an awful feeling that the half-done dishes were still sitting on the counter in the kitchen.

'Listen, you need to give me a break,' I said. 'Don't you know I only have so many interior resources?' I definitely felt the cupboard was pretty bare in my interior resources closet.

Hayden regarded me wonderingly. He didn't seem to be

concerned that he was at the mercy of a totally inadequate caregiver. His arms waved around. He made little noises, 'eh' and a kind of creaky grunt being the most popular. With my free finger I touched the round cheek. It was so soft. Through his thin down of fair hair, I could see the pulsing place on the top of his head where his skull had not yet joined, or so Lizanne had explained it to me. It made this small life seem incredibly vulnerable.

I had a sudden, strange impulse: I would call my friend and priest, Aubrey Scott, and have him baptize Hayden.

If my hands had been free, I'd have slapped myself after I ran that idea through my head a second time. Baptism wouldn't put a protective candy coating on Hayden. He wasn't an M&M. And to assume the responsibility of having this child baptized would indicate I had given up on Regina bobbing to the surface to reclaim him, a terrible admission.

But I knew I would've felt a lot better if I could have just eased into the church and sort of casually had Aubrey sprinkle some water over this kid. I figured that Hayden Graham, son of Craig and Regina – if that was indeed who this child was – needed all the help he could get.

Confident that no one could hear me, I whispered, 'You is booful baby.' Hayden's hazy blue eyes focused on me. He smiled. My heart pounded suddenly, as if I'd just fallen in love. I beamed back at him as exaggeratedly as a children's TV show host.

Sally Allison said, 'Your lips are gonna fall off if you keep that up.'

I jumped. 'Why'd you go and scare me like that, Sally? Good golly Miss Molly! You about made me jump out of my skin!'

'Sorry. You and Tiny Tim here just looked so cute.' Sally bent over to get a close look at my lapful.

'You heard about our predicament, I guess.'

'Mild-mannered reporter Sally Allison sees all, tells most.'

'Got any news?' Having had her look, Sally threw herself in Martin's luxurious chair while my blood pressure finally settled back down to normal.

'Hmmm. Well, police found Regina's car.'

'What?'

'You heard me.' Sally was carefully patting her right hand against her bronze curls, a gentle sort of pat that wouldn't disarrange the perfect arc they formed around her head. She was checking for holes. Next, she'd pull her compact out of her purse and powder her nose; then she'd rummage for a lipstick and redefine her mouth. This was Sally's personal checklist. As she opened her compact, she said, 'It was just across the state line in South Carolina.'

'Any sign of Regina?'

Sally shook her head. 'No, honey, I'm sorry. But on the big plus side, no bloodstains.' Sally carefully crossed her legs, smoothing the skirt of her expensive green suit.

Hayden smiled at me again, and it dawned on me that he didn't smell very good. In fact, that was putting it nicely.

'I can't imagine what happened,' I said absently, wriggling forward on the couch so I could stand with the baby. I managed this, and took him to the living room, which I'd definitely settled on as the best place to keep the diaper bag and the rubberized pad mat you put under Hayden before you took off his diaper. (Experience had taught me the use of the pad.) With scarcely a fumble and no missed snaps, I wiped Hayden's bottom and changed him. I dropped the soiled wipes in the dirty diaper before I rolled it up and retaped it shut, a refinement of which I was extremely proud.

'Good job,' Sally said approvingly, taking the used diaper from me and marching through the dining room to dispose of it in the kitchen. I heard the gush of running water as she washed her hands.

'I take it Martin knows about the car?' I called.

Sally gave me a funny look. I caught the tail end of it as she rejoined me in the living room. 'Yes, the sheriff came to tell him. They're out there talking in the yard.'

In the yard. Why would Martin talk to the sheriff outside? It was cold, and windy, and . . . oh shit. Where was our unwanted houseguest? That was why Martin was keeping the sheriff outside.

'What's wrong?' Sally was paying attention, as usual.

'Nothing!' I said brightly. I was darting little looks out to the hall, the dining room, the kitchen, to see if I could spy Rory. When I looked back at Sally, she was looking skeptical, to say the least.

'And you say,' she began, her voice an extension of that skeptical look, 'that you have no idea what happened out here? Excuse me, Roe, but that's hardly like you.'

'Listen here, Sally Allison, I have a lapful of trouble without you adding to it,' I said, to my own surprise. Then I burst into tears. If I'd been able to choose, I could hardly have picked a more effective diversion. While Hayden lay on his back on the coffee table, looking around him with increasingly heavy eyes, Sally patted my shoulder vigorously.

I found myself Telling Sally All About It, which means I was telling her my singular emotional reaction to the whole day yesterday, culminating with the appearance of my mother in the kitchen this morning with her own terrible news.

Sally's pats gradually grew less and less emphatic and more and more punitive.

'What?' I asked, when it dawned on me that she looked sour rather than sympathetic.

'Not about you, is it?' she asked brusquely.

'What?'

'All this. Your stepfather's sick, so your mother is preoccupied with him, as she should be. Your husband's niece is missing and her husband is dead, so Martin's thinking more about his family than he is about you, for once.'

I stared at Sally like a landed fish. Was I really that selfish? Or had Sally been so jealous of me all these years, and I hadn't noticed? I felt like I'd been negotiating a minefield and the soldier behind me had started chucking rocks over my shoulder.

'You know, Sally, this maybe isn't the best time to tell me about my character flaws,' I said in as even a voice as I could manage. 'I had in mind something like you telling me, "There, there, you poor thing," rather than implying I'm a selfish bitch who thinks I'm the center of the universe.'

Of course, no matter what I said, I was wondering how much of what Sally had said was true. Did everyone see me that way? Oh God, had all the friends I'd had all these years looked at me and thought, That Roe, she's okay, but talk about egocentric!

Sally looked stricken, thank God. But my relief faded when she said, 'Roe, my timing stinks, I apologize for that. But you've never known how lucky you've had it. Your mother does everything but wipe your rear for you, and your husband not only thinks he should protect and pamper you, but he has money!'

'And that's my fault?'

'No!' she said. 'No! But it's your – responsibility!' She looked at her watch and gasped. 'City council meeting! I have to go now, Roe, I'll see you soon.' And she grabbed her purse and flew out the door before I had a chance to respond.

I scooped up the sleeping Precious Burden and watched through the window as Sally crossed the yard, pausing to talk to Martin and the sheriff. I was glad to see Martin was wearing his waterproof jacket, since the day was overcast and every now and then the sky spit some rain. The sheriff strolled away from Martin and leaned on Sally's car, talking to her through the partly open window for a moment before Sally gave a quick wave and swung her car around.

I picked and puzzled at the scene with Sally, which had upset me deeply. I felt like I hadn't known the lion was within when I'd shut the village gates for the night. Gee whiz – Roe Teagarden, Monster of Selfishness?

I'd always thought of myself more as Roe Teagarden, the Incredibly Lucky. Well . . . sometimes. Maybe not a few years ago, when my steady boyfriend had suddenly married the woman he'd gotten pregnant while he was dating me . . . but then again, I'd been lucky I hadn't married him, right? And maybe I hadn't been so lucky when my father and stepmother had moved my half brother out of state, making it almost impossible for me to see him . . . but then again, I'd saved his life, and I'd gotten to fly out to California to visit Phillip twice since then.

This 'good luck' evaluation was just as helpful as opening the closet full of bridesmaids' dresses I'd kept in my storage closet before I'd met Martin. Time to shuffle off this coil of introspection and deal with a here-and-now situation.

Hayden was asleep. His eyelids were so pale the veins stood out clearly, making his skin look almost translucent. I lowered my head to inhale his scent.

'I cheated you,' Martin said. He was standing in the archway to the dining room. He hadn't shaved, and his hair was rumpled. The stubble on his cheeks was white, like his hair, not black, like his eyebrows.

I wasn't in the mood for any more deep emotional scenes.

'How do you figure that?' I asked, my voice hushed and level because of the baby.

'We could have explored other options,' he said, his voice equally subdued. 'Maybe your' – he nodded toward my mid-section to indicate my malformed womb – 'could have been corrected surgically or something. We could have adopted privately; we have enough money.'

I looked at my husband for a long, wake-up moment before I said, 'And these are new thoughts to you?'

I carried Hayden up the stairs and laid him in his crib.

Then I marched downstairs. Martin was standing right where I'd left him. I said, 'I shouldn't hop on you with both feet because something was more important to me than it was to you.'

It was like my words didn't register, as if Martin had become deaf to anything that didn't resonate with some mysterious pre-occupation. 'We should start out tomorrow morning,' he said. 'We'll have to drive. Given the circumstances. Maybe you should go to the store and get whatever the baby will need for the trip.'

Like I knew? I opened my mouth to protest, then shut it again. Sally's observation had stung me where it hurt, had made me doubt my every impulse. I went to the desk to make a list of things I might need, but instead I sat with my hand on the telephone.

Despite a nagging fear that somehow this conversation, too, would be dispiriting, I called the one person I could count on, my best friend, Amina.

Wife of a Houston lawyer, Amina was the mother (and I the godmother) of a lovely little girl, Megan. Amina, an only child, and her husband, oldest of two siblings, were happily indulging Megan (now a Terrible Two) and threatening her with a brother or sister.

'Amina,' I said, relief throbbing through my voice when my friend answered the phone.

'Roe,' she said, in a curiously hushed voice. 'I can't talk long, Megan's got the measles.'

Of course.

'Is she very sick?' I asked, trying to sound Deeply Concerned.

'Just the usual case, I guess.' Amina was trying to be brave, not doing a very good job of it. 'But she just needs me every minute, or at least she thinks she does. I've been taking her Popsicles and playing games with her all day. Do you think she's a little spoiled? That's what Hugh's mom says.'

'Only as much as any only child,' I told Amina, somewhat grimly. I had grown up as an only child.

'We'll take care of that soon,' Amina said, with the confidence that comes of getting pregnant on your honeymoon. 'Thank God I'm not pregnant now, since I have to take care of her and measles are so scary if you're expecting. Oh hell, I hear her calling. Again.'

I cocked an eyebrow. Amina was wearing a little thin in the nursing department. I wasn't surprised. Tall, energetic, and attractive, Amina had always been a person who had to keep moving, had always had a project in the wings and another to keep her currently occupied.

'I'll let you go in just a minute,' I promised, 'but I need some information first.'

'What can I help you with?' Amina's voice had fallen even lower.

'What supplies do you need to take care of an infant for maybe two or three days?'

After a moment's thoughtful silence, Amina began, 'Four sleepers, about twenty diapers . . .' I wrote furiously on the notepad I kept by the phone. Bless Amina, she didn't ask any questions. If I wasn't going to get to cry on her shoulder, I might as well not go through the whole explanation.

After I hung up and checked on Hayden, I found my coat slung over a chair in the dining room. I put it on and grabbed my purse. Martin and Rory had a football game on in the den. I didn't think either of them could have told me the score if I'd asked, but I wouldn't have put money on it. To make sure I had their attention, I stood in front of the screen.

'Martin,' I said, hoping I didn't sound like a total shrew, 'the dishes are still on the counter from lunch. Please do them by the time I come back. Rory, you listen for the baby. He's asleep upstairs.' They both stared at me groggily, so I didn't move until I had confirming nods from both of them.

It was a real pleasure to leave the house.

I turned a country music station up real loud as I drove to that new southern cultural center, Wal-Mart. Somehow, country music seemed to fit the low-down strangeness of the past two days. 'My Husband's Niece Done Hacked Her Man' – how would that play? Or 'Whose Baby Am I Feeding?' Nah, couldn't think of a chorus for that one. What about 'There's a Dead Man on My Stairs and a Baby 'Neath the Bed'?

That kept me smiling until I got past the greeter (who happened to be a cousin of my husband's secretary and always had to pass the time of day with me due to that connection), got my cart (known locally as a 'buggy'), and set off down the main aisle. I wheeled my buggy toward a corner I seldom visited, the corner full of baby paraphernalia. I had my little list with me, the list I'd scribbled while I was on the phone with Amina, and I studied it with care. I bought: a package of Pampers, a can of powdered formula, some baby bottles, three more sleepers in what I estimated was Hayden's weight range, one rubberized bib, another baby blanket, an extra set of fake keys, and four spare Binkys. I thought pacifiers were the most wonderful inventions on earth, and I planned to boil them and put them in little plastic bags and stow one in my purse, my coat, and Martin's coat, and keep the spare in the diaper bag.

I paused, my hand resting on a box of wet wipes. I looked down at the fuzzy sleepers in the buggy. Why did Hayden need clothes? I put the wet wipes in the buggy very slowly, wondering. I recalled the look of the apartment, the open suitcase, the spill of clothes.

Clothes for Regina. Not clothes for the baby.

Aimlessly, I began pushing the buggy around the store, trying to figure out what that meant. Regina had known she was going on a trip. But she hadn't planned on taking Hayden? Or – she hadn't had a baby when she started on the trip? That didn't make any sense.

Shaking my head, I realized I'd plowed into men's wear. I slipped a pair of jeans and a flannel shirt into the cart. They were smaller than Martin's usual, but I hoped no one would think of noticing. Probably Rory also needed underwear, but I'd be damned if I'd pick it out. I tucked the 'no clothes for Hayden' thought into a side pocket of my mind, to pull out and reexamine later.

While I was in the men's section, I was lucky enough to run into our closest neighbor, Clement Farmer. He was staring dubiously at a rack of silk boxer shorts. Clement was a small man, almost bald, with a few wisps of white hair over his ears. He had a red complexion and very white even teeth, which made him look overall like a Christmas elf.

'I told Padgett I saw a car pulling out of your drive the other night,' Clement said, without any preliminaries.

'Is that so?'

'Yes, it was a dark red car with Ohio plates.'

Regina's car.

'Who was in it?' I asked, dreading the answer.

'Two people. I couldn't see the driver very well, but the passenger was a dark-haired young woman.'

Sounded like Regina.

I was in more of a hurry than ever to get home and tell Martin.

I thanked Clement for telling me (though I wondered why he hadn't called us on the phone) and asked him to feed Madeleine for us while we were gone. She hated to be checked into the vet's almost as much as the vet's staff hated to see her coming.

'Sure!' Clement agreed, obviously pleased. He was the only person I'd ever met who seemed to genuinely like Madeleine. 'Think she'll need a brushing?'

'Oh, I'm sure it wouldn't hurt.' I'd made one person happy today, anyway.

I loaded my purchases into Martin's Mercedes and stopped by the filling station to top up the tank. Home again, this time to find the dishes done and in the drainer; Rory watching television in our den (still, or again); and Hayden continuing his nap. Martin was packing in his usual efficient pattern, and I noticed he'd gotten out his extreme-cold-weather gear, which he seldom needed in Lawrenceton.

It seemed grossly unfair that Hayden slept when he was alone with Martin.

I told Martin what Clement Farmer had seen the night before.

'So she's a hostage, if it was Regina Clement saw,' he said.

'Could be, Martin.' I wondered how he'd gotten that out of the story I'd told him, but shook my head and decided not to pursue it. I thought of sharing my wonderment about the lack of provision for Hayden with Martin, but he looked so distracted I decided I'd be wasting my breath. I turned and went downstairs.

I sat at the kitchen table studying the directions on the can of formula powder. I read them over and over, determined not to do Hayden harm with my ignorance. I assembled everything I'd need, down to the same pan I remembered Regina using. I had a hard time believing I'd talked to Regina while she prepared formula right here in this kitchen, less than twenty-four hours before.

While I waited for the water to boil, I called John's hospital again, talked to my mother once more, found out John was out of the room having a test.

Our telephone persisted in its curious silence. I did get a call or two from older friends of my mother's, asking about John; but other than our priest, Aubrey, no one seemed to want to know how Martin and I were handling our own little corner of Craig's tragedy. I wondered forlornly at that, but then I decided that no one knew quite what to say.

A brusque rap at the back door made me look up sharply while I was sealing bottles of formula to put in the refrigerator. I'd made enough to last us the trip to Ohio, I estimated, having no idea what I'd do if I'd figured wrong. Could you buy formula ready to serve? I hadn't remembered to check while I was at the store. I was so lost in worries about feeding Hayden that it took me a second to realize I was happy to see my friend and former employee Angel Youngblood and to translate that happiness into a smile.

Only the fact that Angel was preceded by a huge bulge kept me from hugging her, which would have surprised both of us. Angel is almost a foot taller than me, and golden and rangy as a leopard. Though now she looked like a really pregnant leopard, the effect was still striking. I couldn't remember exactly how old Angel was, but I was sure she was at least six years younger than I, and her husband, Shelby, was a few months older than Martin. Shelby and Martin had been buddies in Vietnam, and had met sporadically after the war and their covert activities in South America had concluded. Now Shelby worked for Martin as a crew leader at the Pan-Am Agra plant.

'Where's the baby?' Angel was always direct. I called up the stairs softly, to alert Martin, and led Angel up to have a look. Martin, who'd been reading a magazine (or at least staring at its open pages), rose when Angel came in, seemed to pull himself together a little. Angel just nodded at him. She was absorbed in the tiny face. She put her long fingers around the curve of Hayden's skull, and she laid her other hand on the mound of her pregnancy. The mound constricted – that's the best way I can describe it – and, after a long moment, relaxed.

Angel smiled at me. 'This one doesn't even have room to move around anymore,' she said, her voice quiet and smooth so as not to wake Hayden.

'Isn't it almost time for you?'

Angel nodded. 'Time, and a day over. But I'm feeling fine, so today's not the day, I guess. I'm sorry about your stepfather,' she added, jumping mentally from her own hospital stay to John's. 'How's he doing? How's your mother holding up?'

My mother and Angel had developed an arm's-length mutual respect.

'She's doing pretty well.' You know my mother, my voice said.

Angel nodded, her eyes back on the baby's face. 'There's something about them,' she said, the smooth low voice almost hypnotic. 'You'd kill for them.' Her hands caressed her own stomach again, and I saw it tighten again.

'If they're your own,' I said, a question in my tone.

'Maybe not just then. Look at him.' And Angel crouched over the pale-green-and-blue portable crib, her blond hair framing her narrow face.

'What are you gonna do with him, Roe? If I understand right, his dad is dead and his mother is missing,' Angel said, as we went back downstairs to the kitchen. She sat at the table while I poured her a glass of orange juice.

'We're planning on driving to Corinth, where Regina and her husband were living,' I explained. 'Then, I guess we'll see if Craig's family will keep him. Or maybe Regina will have turned up by then, and we'll know what happened. Or . . . we'll be able to get in touch with Barby, and when she flies back from her cruise, she'll be coming into Pittsburgh, which is the closest airport to Corinth.'

It sounded pretty thin and uncertain, even to me.

'Wouldn't it be better to stay put?' Angel drank her juice in one long gulp and set the glass down. She eased forward in her chair, and her hand rubbed her back absently. Her face tightened suddenly, then relaxed. 'After all,' Angel said slowly, with effort, 'if Regina does escape, or return . . .' Her face did that tightening and relaxing thing again. 'She'd come back here, for her baby . . .' This time Angel's face stayed tight for a while.

'Angel?'

'I think,' she said slowly and thoughtfully, 'that maybe it will be today, after all.'

I was on my feet in a flash. I'd seen one baby born, and I wasn't about to do that again. 'Let me drive you to the hospital,' I said. 'I'll get my jacket.'

'No, that would get the cars all confused,' Angel said, but as if she hardly knew what she was saying. All her attention seemed to be focused inward. 'My car would be out here, and who knows when I could come back to get it. I can drive home, and wait there for Shelby to get off work.'

'Call him from here.'

'Okay,' she said, to my surprise. My concern deepened. Easy capitulation was not one of Angel's characteristics. 'Let me use the bathroom first.'

I hovered outside the door.

When Angel emerged, she said, 'Today for sure.' Her voice was still calm and flat, but I sensed all kinds of suppressed excitement just trying to bubble to the surface. She went to the telephone on the kitchen wall, walking in a kind of tentative way, as if she expected something to grab her at every step. I bounced around her like a rubber ball, anxious to help, trying not to get in the way, scared to death she'd have the baby here.

Angel punched Shelby's work number, waited for an answer, all the while that inner-directed look on her face.

I heard a squawk from the other end of the line.

'Jason Arlington, that you? This is Angel. I need to talk to Shelby,' Angel said.

I could hear the tiny voice squawk some more.

'Yes, you can sound the siren,' Angel said, sounding as if she were holding on to her patience by a very taut leash. The siren's wail was audible from where I was standing.

'Shelby's crew think it's real funny that he's going to be a father for the first time,' Angel explained. 'They set up this siren to call him if he's far out in the plant when I phone to tell him the baby's on the way.' Her face tightened again, and her fingers clenched the receiver until they turned white. Then, gradually, she relaxed. She smiled into the telephone. Her husband was on the other end.

'Shelby,' Angel said. 'I'm going to leave right now to drive back into town. I'm at Martin and Roe's. Meet me at our house.'

This time I could hear Shelby's words. 'You stay right there,' he bellowed. 'I'll come get you. Don't you try to drive!'

To my amazement, Angel said, 'All right.'

I think Shelby was startled, too, because there was silence on the other end of the line. Then he said, 'I'll be right there,' and the line went dead.

I caught a glimpse of Rory Brown stepping quietly down the hall. Angel's back was turned, and frankly I don't think she'd have cared if a real leopard went through the house, at that point.

I went to the foot of the stairs and called Martin, who came down with a newly awake Hayden. Martin tried not to look dismayed when I explained the situation. He handed me the baby immediately.

Angel seemed to want to remain standing, so I tried not to fuss over her. I put a bottle in the microwave, and Angel said, 'That's not a safe way to heat bottles.'

'What?'

'Sometimes they have hot spots if you heat them that way. That's what the baby book said.'

Everyone's a critic. 'So far, we haven't had any problem,' I said. 'I'm testing it before I give it to him.'

Angel shrugged, as if she'd done her best and it wasn't her fault if I was misguided. I shook the bottle vigorously, tested the formula on my arm, and sat down to feed Hayden, who had just let out a few preliminary 'eh' noises.

Angel did the face-clenching routine again. This time she propped herself against the wall.

'Are they getting worse?' I asked, while Martin looked as if he wished he were on the moon.

'Maybe I should call the ambulance,' he suggested.

I noticed he didn't suggest taking Angel into town himself. I had a sneaking suspicion he was worried Angel's water would break in his Mercedes.

'No,' she said, shaking her head. Martin tried not to look relieved. 'I know this is going to take hours. I'm just trying to get used to the feeling. It's like a clamp. Then there's the release. Then, along after a while comes the next clamp.'

'Does it hurt?'

'Not yet, but it's on a roll downhill,' Angel said. 'I hope Shelby doesn't pass out in the labor room. He got sick when I broke my leg a few years ago.'

A battered car sped up our driveway, and Shelby, tall and pockmarked and burly with muscle, was out of the vehicle and in our kitchen door before you could say 'Having a baby'. His dark hair, liberally streaked with gray, was dented all around where his hard hat had rested, and his Fu Manchu mustache was going in all directions, as if he'd rubbed his hands over it.

Wordlessly, Shelby shook hands with Martin, kissed me on the forehead with nary a glance at the baby I was holding, and took his wife by the elbow to hustle her out the door. Angel gave us a nod and they were on their way, Shelby shepherding Angel as though she were the only woman who'd ever given birth. 'Jason said he'd get one of the guys to drive him out here to pick up Angel's car; I gave him a spare key,' Shelby called over his shoulder at the last minute. Then he buckled up and headed back into town to the Lawrenceton hospital.

Rory came out of the den when Shelby had turned out of the driveway. He was looking amused.

'So, she's gonna have a baby really soon,' he said agreeably. Listening at doors did not seem to present a moral dilemma for Rory Brown. 'Craig took Regina to a midwife.' Then the reminiscent smile faded from the boy's face as he remembered that his friend Craig was now dead. 'He told me it was a lot cheaper,' Rory added, with no smile at all.

'I have to pack,' I said, and both the men looked at me.

'Okay,' Rory said, after what I could only think of as a pregnant pause, 'I'll feed the little fella.'

I transferred baby and bottle to the young man, and spent a blessed hour alone upstairs, trying to assemble clothes suitable for an Ohio winter. A number of important questions bobbed to the surface of my mind as I folded and figured. Where would we stay in Corinth? The Holiday Inn I'd used before would certainly be cramped with a baby sharing the room. I wondered about the farmhouse Martin owned up there, the one in which he'd grown up. He'd had it restored from its near-derelict condition, he'd mentioned in passing.

'We could stay in the farmhouse,' Martin said from the doorway, and I jumped in my skin. 'I didn't mean to scare you,' he said.

'I was just thinking about the farmhouse,' I said, when my heart had stopped trying to make tracks out of my chest. 'You had it repaired?'

'Yes . . . and to confess something to you, Regina and Craig were living in it.'

'Why should you say "confess"?' I asked. I sat down on the end of the bed, two unopened packages of panty hose in my hands.

'I didn't tell you,' he said. He wandered across the room to stand looking out the window. His shoulders had an uncharacteristic slump. The bleak view of winter fields couldn't have helped his state of mind much. It was a gray day, and the clouds were full of rain . . . Pregnant with it, in fact, my brain told me chirpily. I dropped the hose on the floor and clutched my head with both hands.

'Why didn't you tell me, Martin? Why did that have to be such a big secret?'

He sat beside me on the foot of the bed. He put one arm around me, carefully, as though he realized there was a good chance I'd sock him in the nose.

'Cindy told me you would always keep secrets,' I said. 'She said you couldn't help it.' I'd never told Martin about the conversation I'd had with his first wife before Martin and I were married. I'd been convinced he'd learned his lesson during his first marriage, that with me he would not repeat the same mistake.

'I've never lied to you about anything,' Martin said now, and that was something else Cindy had told me.

I *hated* her being right.

'Martin, if there's something you know about this that you haven't told me, if there's anything about Craig and Regina and Rory and Cindy or your sister . . . *anything* you haven't told me, this is your last free pass.'

'After this I get penalized?' His face fell into more familiar lines, the uncertainty fading to be replaced with the intelligence and command he normally wore like his suit coat.

'After this, you get thrown out of the game.' I looked him straight in his pale brown eyes.

'But I'm still in?'

I nodded.

His mouth only had to move an inch to cover mine.

It was different, this time; we'd always been perfect together in bed, and this morning he still had the magic to make me lost in the act of love; but now he was rougher, more demanding. It was as if he were reasserting his exclusive right to me, daring some cosmic force to just try to separate us. You woman, me man, his body said, and mine gasped, Hoo boy.

Chapter Six

We started out in the dark early the next morning. We didn't want anyone to see Rory in the car with us. He was sitting in back with the baby for now, though I planned on switching seats with him later, at least for a little while. Martin would do the driving: He much preferred to be in the driver's seat. What a shock, right?

We didn't even go through a drive-through to get coffee until we'd been on the road an hour. Rory was asleep, and after a sip or two I woke up enough to want to talk to Martin.

'What did you do about Shelby and Angel?' he asked.

'I left a message on the answering machine at Buds 'N Blooms,' I said. I inhaled the coffee vapor. 'They'll take her a huge pink bouquet today.' Shelby had called at midnight to tell us that Angel had had a baby girl, a seven-pounder. He had been exhausted and elated; I could never have imagined hearing Shelby sound so *grateful.*

'Gift?' Martin asked tentatively, aware he was on shaky ground here.

'I gave her a baby shower,' I reminded him, noticing a warning edge in my voice. 'Mother and I gave her a playpen.'

'And how is John?'

'Mother called at ten last night to tell me John would be in the hospital for a day or two more. The doctors are sure he had a heart attack, and they're still talking about treatment options.'

'How's he feeling?'

'Scared.'

'And Aida?'

'She's scared, too, but you would find it hard to tell.'

Martin was closer to my mother's age than mine, but it still felt strange to hear him call her by her first name.

'I know how hard this is on you.' In the lightening gloom, I could tell Martin had turned briefly to look at me, before refocusing on the highway. 'I expected you to tell me any minute to take Hayden back up to Ohio myself, that you were staying with your mother.'

'Martin,' I said, 'it never occurred to me to do that.'

We rode in silence for at least half an hour after that.

A long car trip in the winter with a baby . . . when you've never had a baby . . . the formula for disaster, right?

The best I can say is, it could've been worse. For example, someone could have pulled out my eyelashes one by one.

We stopped to feed and change the baby . . . well, we stopped so I could feed and change the baby. Oddly enough, it wasn't the physical work of caring for Hayden that was so exhausting, though that was tough, too. What was most difficult was an unexpected aspect of traveling with a child: the observations of strangers. I hadn't realized every mother learns to discuss her child with every waitress; restroom customer; and Tom, Dick, and Harry who walks by. The restaurant where we stopped for lunch gave me my first sampling. I carried Hayden in his infant seat, found it was impossible to fit it anywhere on the table or on one chair, and finally discovered that if Martin and Rory sat on one side of a booth, I could put the infant seat and myself on the other side. This did not make Martin happy, but at that point, making Martin happy was low on my priority list.

The waitress, a plump black woman with gorgeous up-slanted eyes, gave me my first taste of what was to come. 'Oh, he's so cute!' she said, with apparent sincerity. 'How old is he?'

'A month,' I said, as Rory said, 'Two and a half weeks.'

She laughed as Rory and I glared at each other. 'He a big baby,' she said admiringly. 'How much was he?'

I stared at her blankly. Cost-wise?

'He weighed eight pounds, five ounces,' Rory said firmly.

So the correct answer was his birth weight. I'd try to remember that. I smiled at Rory.

'Oh, that's sweet,' the woman ('Candra' her name tag read) commented, handing us menus. 'The daddy knows the birth weight!'

'Oh, he's a great father,' I assured her, suddenly feeling quite giddy. 'He was there the whole time.'

As Candra absorbed the age difference between me and Rory, her eyes widened. 'Can I get you something to drink?' she asked in a subdued voice.

When we'd all ordered, I fished a bottle out of the cooler and asked Candra if she'd heat it up for us. That was another thing I learned on that trip: how to ask favors, some of them outrageous, of complete strangers. When you're functioning as a mom you have to. Would you heat this bottle? Bring extra napkins? Throw away this dirty diaper? Pretend not to hear my child screaming his head off?

My most humiliating moment came in Kentucky at a rest stop, when I carried Hayden into the ladies' room to change his diaper. I had the baby, the diaper bag, and my purse. I changed him somehow – at least that particular freezing rest room had a foldout tray to do the job on – but then I found I had to use the facilities myself quite urgently, and I had nowhere to put him and no time to carry him out to Martin. I don't think I've done anything as complicated in my life as try to pull down my slacks and underwear in a cubicle the size of a phone booth while holding a baby, a bulky diaper bag, and a purse, and wearing a coat.

It was humiliating. And though it probably would've made *America's Funniest Home Videos*, at the time it wasn't at all amusing to me. As a matter of fact, as I began wearily to reverse the process, I decided I'd *never* think it was funny.

And I knew for a fact that Martin would never get over being called 'Grandpa' by one well-meaning cashier. It was lucky for Rory that Martin hadn't noticed his suppressed smile, and lucky for me that my own face was too tired to form the grin I felt rising to my lips.

Most of our conversation on this trip consisted of Martin trying to get Rory to give us more specifics about Craig and the baby, Regina and the baby, the baby's birth, why Regina had driven down to Lawrenceton without Craig.

'Oh, well, she didn't expect us to get out of jail when we did,' Rory explained, when he saw he couldn't get away with waffling anymore. 'I expect she just wanted to show off the baby to you, since her mom is out of the country.'

'Does my sister know she's a grandmother?'

'Huh?'

'Does Regina's mother know Regina has had a baby?'

'Well, not to say so. Not really.'

Rory was sitting in front with Martin now, and I was buckled in the back with Hayden, whom I was amusing by dangling a toy for him to focus on. I considered flattening the receiving blanket that lay in my lap, twirling the ends until it formed a long rope, then looping it around Rory's narrow neck. He'd spit out the truth then! I told myself truculently, realizing I was somewhere beyond tired.

'Is this baby really Regina's?' I asked sharply. 'Or did she steal Hayden from someone?'

Martin closed his eyes briefly, then refocused on the road.

'Of course this baby is Regina's!' our companion said, as indignant as he could manage to be.

'How do you know?'

'Craig drove her to the midwife's!'

'And you watched the baby being born?'

'Hell, no!'

'But you were at the midwife's?'

'Well . . .' Rory seemed to be thinking deeply, and that seemed to be difficult for him. 'Not exactly, not me so much as Craig. I think I was in jail.'

I looped the ends of the receiving blanket around each hand so I'd have a good grip, just waiting for a nod from Martin to choke this goofball.

Martin glanced back to see what I was doing, then looked forward hastily, his face convulsing with suppressed laughter.

'Say the word,' I told him.

'Rory,' Martin tried again. 'Which one of you took Regina to the midwife's office?'

'Maybe I went part of the way,' Rory improvised. 'They dropped me off at the house on their way.'

'And this baby, Hayden, the one in the backseat, is the child of Regina and Craig?'

'Gosh, I don't know. They all look alike, don't they?'

Martin turned a little and directed his next words at me. 'You know, I'm actually tempted,' he said. 'Keep it handy.'

Like most horrible things – roller coaster rides, committee meetings, vaginal exams – the trip eventually came to an end. After thirteen hours on the road (during two and a half of which Hayden screamed), we got to Corinth. By that time I didn't like anyone in the Mercedes, myself included. Rory directed Martin to his family's home, in a section of Corinth as derelict as any I'd seen in Lawrenceton. When we pulled up in front of a tiny brick house set up on a hill, the steps up to it steep and crooked, Rory ejected himself from the car with unflattering speed. 'I'll give you a call,' he promised. 'Thanks for not turning me in. Take care of old Hayden, now.' He went up the steps two at a time, his extra clothes clutched to him in a paper bag, his hair sticking out all around from a knit watch cap he'd had stuck in his pocket. The streetlight gave the blond hair a tinge of green and his progress a definite touch of the surreptitious.

We watched him go with relief.

'If he had two thoughts at one time, they'd throw a surprise party,' Martin said mysteriously, and I nodded.

'The question is, is he bad or good underneath the stupidity?' I said.

'I don't think he's smart enough to be bad,' Martin said.

The same streetlight made my husband look hard and angry. Really, he was just tired and grumpy. Maybe.

'You don't have to be smart to be bad,' I reminded him.

It was too late, and we were too tired, to cope with any

surprises the farmhouse might have to offer. We checked into the Holiday Inn and staggered to our room with all the paraphernalia the baby required. Martin set up the portable crib while I changed Hayden, who rejected another bottle. There was a little refrigerator in the room, so I stuck the bottle in there, laid Hayden in the crib, and patted him on the back until he fell asleep. By that time, Martin was in bed. I felt like an elephant had rolled over on me and lain there for hours. I brushed my teeth, washed my face, and crawled in beside him.

Two hours later Hayden woke up.

I was standing beside the crib when I attained consciousness.

Hayden was hungry.

The formula was cold, and there was no way to heat it.

Finally, I tucked it in my nightgown next to my body – you can imagine how good that felt – and held Hayden and jiggled him in the room's straight chair, trying Binkys and bouncing and humming with no effect. When the formula was slightly less chilly, I stuck the nipple in Hayden's mouth, and after a brief protest, the baby began to suckle.

Martin slept all the way through this.

In the morning, when he shook me by the shoulder – very gently – I buried my face in the pillow.

'Roe,' he said, kissing me on the cheek, 'it's nine o'clock, and the baby's awake.'

'Take care of him.'

'I changed his diaper,' Martin observed, trying not to sound proud and failing. 'I think he's hungry, and there aren't any bottles.'

'Go to the store, and see if they sell formula already made up,' I advised. 'Or take him to Craig's aunt and uncle and let them worry about it.'

Martin heartlessly laid Hayden on the bed by me, and I raised my head enough to see his tiny finger waving. He made his little 'eh' sound. His cheek was close enough to kiss, so I did, inhaling the now-familiar baby smell. I could hear the diaper rustle, and knew Martin hadn't put it on snugly enough. Oh, hell.

I sat up, groggy as it is possible to be. 'I was up with him last night,' I said, fixing Martin with as baleful a stare as I could scrape together. 'While you slept,' I emphasized, in case he hadn't gotten the point. I could not find any trace of sympathy for Martin in my heart. It didn't make any difference that his niece was missing and her husband dead. He'd had what I hadn't – undisturbed sleep.

'I'll go look,' he said hastily. 'What kind should I get?'

I made him write it down. Hayden was beginning to escalate in his demands. 'And hurry,' I added, in case he hadn't gotten *that* point.

There was no going back to sleep. I found a Binky, stuck it in Hayden's mouth, rejoiced to find that pacified him at least for the moment. I dashed into the bathroom, took a hot and sketchy shower, scrubbed my teeth again, and was appalled at the amount of makeup I needed to make myself look healthy this morning. I pulled on tobacco-brown slacks and a sweater of a deep yellow that I believed was called goldenrod. I took a moment to sit down on the bed and do some research with the local phone book. Then I finished rigging myself out with my rings, a chain, some earrings, my gold-rimmed glasses, and socks and loafers . . . By the time I'd finally put myself together, Martin was coming back in the room with a bag. It contained clean bottles and a few cans of ready-made formula.

'You wouldn't believe what I had to pay for this,' he said with some indignation.

'I don't care. Did you get a can opener?' I asked tensely.

He produced one from the bag with an air of triumph, and I gave him a heartfelt kiss on the cheek. He was about to go for something more meaningful when I heard the warning tune-up behind me.

'He's getting serious,' I said, panicking. 'We've got to get the bottle ready now!'

Working together, we had a brand-new bottle full of brand-new formula ready in record time, and Hayden was gumming away on the nipple in blessed near-silence. While I aided and abetted, Martin checked the skinny Corinth telephone book for the address of Craig's family, the Harbors, who'd taken him in when his parents died.

'Maybe they're on their way to Lawrenceton,' I said, with a wave of horror. 'Maybe they're on their way there to collect Craig's body!'

'Nope,' Martin said, his eyes never leaving the columns of phone numbers. 'Padgett Lanier told me Craig's brother had asked him how to ship the body back to Corinth when the autopsy was over.'

I felt a tide of relief sweep over me. The people who had raised Craig for the past five years were here in Corinth. I was not thinking of the Harbors as bereaved; I was thinking of them as baby repositories. And I'd lost any shame I had about it, too.

'Here they are,' Martin said absently. 'Eighteen-fifty-six Gettysburg Street.' He closed the phone book and returned it to the drawer with a much more cheerful air.

'Who'd want to name a street after Gettysburg?' Obviously, I was talking right off the top of my head.

Martin looked up at me, his eyebrows raised and a patient look on his face.

'Oh,' I said, abashed. I'm not one of those unreconstructed southerners who refers to the War of Northern Aggression, but it seemed I'd been indoctrinated to some extent. I made a face at my Yankee husband. These people probably had an Appomattox Avenue, too.

We packed all the baby's things in his diaper bag, folded up the crib for the last time, and went carefully down the stairs to our car. We hadn't had coffee yet, or breakfast, and yet that seemed secondary to getting Hayden to qualified caregivers.

Since Corinth is only a little bigger than Lawrenceton, we found the Harbors' house quickly. To my silent dismay, it seemed like a darker shadow of the place where we'd dropped off Rory the night before. This house's once-white siding was peeling, and the front yard had not a blade of grass.

Martin and I avoided looking at each other. We slowly got out of the car, and I opened the back door to extract Hayden. He was sound asleep, and I pulled out Ellen Lowry's blue-and-white-striped blanket to drape over his head. A chill rain had begun to fall. Martin covered us with an umbrella. We picked our way across the yard to the door. My heart sank at the sight of the ripped shades at the two front windows. Who could have guessed, seeing the Harbors at the wedding, that this was how they lived?

Then I chided myself for my snobbery, reminded myself that children grew up healthy and cherished in the poorest of homes. But I knew it wasn't the poverty that bothered me. It was the air that the people who lived under this roof had given up. They no longer cared – about peeling paint, or the lack of bushes to soften the mean lines of the old house, or the absence of stepping stones to keep visitors' feet dry on messy days. There was not even a two-dollar doormat outside the front door to wipe my feet on.

But someone had put a big black bow on the door knocker, to show that this was a house of mourning.

Martin leaned forward to rap on the wood and slid his arm around me. I leaned into its warmth, my hand absently patting Hayden's round little bottom.

I hardly recognized the woman who answered the door as the same Lenore Harbor I'd met at the wedding. She'd put out a great effort then, I realized, seeing her now. Her hair had been done, her dress and shoes new. And she hadn't been smoking. A cigarette hung from the corner of her mouth now, jiggling when she spoke to us out of the other corner.

'I halfway expected you, Martin. Come on in, I guess. I haven't had a chance to clean up, I'm sure you know we've just been knocked on our butts by this news about Craig.'

Her voice was raspy, but she didn't sound exactly as I'd expected. Sad, yes . . . but not agonized. She wasn't Craig's blood mother, of course. My heart began to sink.

I tried my hardest not to look around the room, but it was impossible not to absorb the depression that hung over the ancient furniture and loose linoleum, the plethora of overflowing ashtrays and discarded magazines. The Harbors had received a couple of plants and some sympathy cards, and they were arranged on the shelf of a nasty maple hutch. The ribbons on the arrangements stood out in brilliant contrast to the rest of the material in the dingy living room. But it wasn't the age of the furnishings, or even the presence of the ashtrays; it was the lack of maintenance, or care, of these things that bothered me.

This wasn't what I had pictured as a temporary home for Hayden.

'And this is your wife?'

Lenore Harbor had met me at the wedding, but didn't seem to recall that. Martin reintroduced me, and Lenore waved her hand at the couch. We perched there uneasily after piling all Hayden's gear near the door.

Lenore turned her head toward the back of the house and called, 'Hugh! Martin and his little wife are here!'

There was a curious sound from the next room, a kind of long wheeze, and then Hugh Harbor made his way into the living room. He was preceded by the *thump! shuffle, thump! shuffle* of a person using a walker. Hugh was about Lenore's age, somewhere in his midfifties I estimated, and he was gaunt, with neutral coloring and light brown hair outlining a tonsure.

He greeted us in a wheezy voice. I noticed an oxygen tank sitting in the corner. Surely it was dangerous to smoke in a house with oxygen tanks? I remembered Rory saying that Hugh Harbor had been ill. I wished now I'd paid more attention, asked more questions. But in the rush to find someone to take Hayden off my hands, I hadn't thought enough . . . about anything.

'I'm so glad you made the drive to come back to Corinth,' Hugh Harbor said. I wondered how he knew we'd driven. He eased back into a green vinyl armchair with stuffing protruding from one arm. There was a towel spread over the seat. I suspected the towel covered worse depredations. 'We don't think that Gina could've hurt poor Craig.' Hugh wheezed. 'Musta been some thief, don't you think? Or some guy who just saw Gina, thought she looked good? Craig wouldn't a let anyone mess with Gina.'

'We're sure Regina didn't have anything to do with it,' Martin agreed firmly. I could tell he was mighty relieved. It would have been horrible if they'd believed Regina had killed Craig.

'I know Hayden will be a consolation to you,' I said, but I couldn't hear any excitement in my voice. I sort of extended the baby, who'd been lying in my arms.

They gave me a very peculiar look, and I could tell they'd been married many years. Their faces held almost identical degrees of puzzlement and surprise.

'Of course, babies are wonderful things to have,' Lenore said, with a distressing lack of enthusiasm. 'Hugh and I raised a houseful of them. We didn't know you and Martin was even expecting, young lady.'

Martin and I turned to look at each other. We probably had twin expressions too; and they were of sheer bafflement.

I didn't think I could talk, even if I could think of what to say. Martin looked down at Hayden, back at Lenore, who was taking advantage of the break in the conversation to light another cigarette.

'This isn't our baby,' Martin said, not sounding very sure about it. 'This is Craig and Regina's boy, Hayden.'

You would have thought we'd announced we were going to strip and have sex on the floor. The Harbors once again had twin expressions – this time, shock and fascination. After they'd absorbed what Martin had said, emotions scudded across their faces like clouds on a windy day.

'This is the first we've heard of it,' Lenore said finally. I could have sworn it wasn't the first thing she thought to say. Hugh nodded agreement, the top of his bald dome glinting in the overhead light as his head bobbed back and forth.

'You didn't know Craig and Regina were expecting a child?' Even knowing the answer, I had to ask. My heart couldn't have sunk further. It was at the level of my big toe.

'No,' Hugh said. 'They never said nothing about having a baby. Are you sure this boy is theirs?'

We did the Tweedledum and Tweedledee thing again, searching each other's faces. I gave a tiny shrug.

'That's what Regina told us,' Martin said carefully. I had expected Martin to be visibly upset again, but to my relief, he had returned to his more familiar persona of cagey businessman. His face was unreadable; his hands loosely clasped each other in a relaxed way.

I gathered Hayden closer to my chest. I understood that I would be taking him out of this house with me. I looked at his little pile of paraphernalia and gave a silent sigh. All to be hauled back up the motel stairs again.

'How much did you see of Regina and Craig?' I asked, my voice as soft and simple as I could make it. Didn't want to put them on the defensive.

'Well, I ain't been well,' Hugh said apologetically. 'I have good spells. I was having one about the time they got married. But I ain't been so good since about late July, and I'm afraid I take up most of Lenore's time.'

We had been fools to bring Hayden up here. I saw clearly that these people had not the resources, the legal obligation, or the slightest inclination to take care of Hayden even temporarily. How could we have been so blind? I had followed an anxious Martin's lead without a thought, consumed by my own conflicts. I should have listened to Angel; might have, if her baby hadn't decided that afternoon was the time to arrive. Angel had figured we should stay in Lawrenceton, and she'd been right.

I barely listened while the Harbors explained to Martin over and over again why they really hadn't had a chance to go visit the newlyweds since the wedding. The farm was far out in the country, they emphasized, and it was so hard for Hugh to get around. And, Lenore Harbor pointed out righteously, they hadn't been invited.

'Did Craig come to see you here?' Martin asked.

He'd dropped by once or twice, the Harbors admitted, usually with that friend of his, that Rory.

It took a few more questions from Martin to establish that the couple hadn't seen Regina – except across a store – since a week after the wedding. But they'd seen Craig quite often.

'You know,' Hugh said with an effort, his breathing increasingly difficult, 'we thought, when Craig got married – and we stood in as his folks at the wedding – we thought Craig's old ways were over. Gina being a little older than him, we thought she'd hold him down, make him toe the line. We were – well, I guess Lenore and I are maybe a little ashamed to say it – kind of relieved. Craig turned out to be a bigger responsibility than we ever dreamed, him getting into trouble so often. We was glad to take him in, Lenore being his aunt and so on, and we took care of him through high school, but I won't say it was all peaches and cream. We'd raised girls before, but that boy was a whole different kit and caboodle.' He shook his shiny head sadly. 'Nope, he and that Rory was always into trouble. We thought for a while that it was Rory who would marry Gina, when they began hanging around together.'

Martin began our closing remarks, so to speak, and after a little more strained conversation, we rose to leave. We began tucking Hayden's bits and pieces wherever we could, with Martin once again holding the umbrella.

I nuzzled Hayden's fuzzy head, and wondered what we should do next.

As we pulled away from the broken curb, the silence in the Mercedes might well be described as thick. And tense.

I looked out at the passing streets of this depressing little farming town. I had no idea what Martin was thinking, but I knew if he asked me if I liked having a baby now that I had one, I would pinch him where it hurt, because I was so bitterly amazed at myself. I'd wanted a baby. Now I had one. And I was trying with all my might to get rid of him.

Partly, I thought, this was because the care of him had been dumped on me. Partly, it was because I hadn't had the hormonal buildup that natural mothers get.

But mostly, it was because I knew – I just knew – that his mother would turn up sooner or later, and Hayden would be gone. If the claimant wasn't Regina, it would be someone else with a better title to this child than mine, which was almost nonexistent. What point was there in lining up more pain for myself?

I felt better once I'd admitted all this in my secret heart. While we waited on a red light, I looked over at Martin, who was staring out the window at the bare trees. The sky had that leaden gray look that often presages snow, at least in my very limited experience. 'I guess we should talk to Cindy, and then Craig's brother,' I said. I didn't sound excited about it.

'Yes, we need to,' my husband agreed, turning to look across the seat at me. 'And we need to track down Rory and see if we can get any more out of him. And we probably need to move our stuff out to the farmhouse. It'll be a lot easier with a stove and refrigerator. And more than one room.' 'It' being the care of Hayden, I gathered. I noticed we weren't saying one word about walking out of the Harbors' house with him, when we'd gone in with the resolve of leaving the baby with Craig's family.

'I wonder if the police have been out there, to the farm,' I said, the idea sort of slipping into my head sideways.

Martin looked surprised, then thoughtful. 'You'd think they'd want to see if anything Craig and Regina left out there could explain what happened,' he said. 'If the Lawrenceton sheriff's department called them. And I'm assuming they did.' Martin mulled it over a little. 'I know who to call. An old friend of mine named Karl Bagosian has a key to the house, and if anyone knows, he will.'

We parked in front of the florist's shop owned by Cindy Bartell. I'd been there once before. Then, there had been Easter decorations in the big window facing the sidewalk. Now it was filled with fall decorations. Through that window, over the top of a miniature corn sheaf, I could see Cindy's head of smooth black hair bent over a gift basket on the large worktable behind the counter.

Martin was opening my car door, which he'd somewhat fallen out of the habit of doing. I had never seen door opening as an issue, but I used his choice as a clue to his feelings. As Martin held out his hand to help me out of the Mercedes, he looked down as if he were trying to refresh his memory of my face. I was all too aware that my hair had been excited by the rain into separating into streamers, with waves and curls interrupting their wild flow. My London Fog was not exactly a sexy garment, and I was sure my nose was shiny. I couldn't remember what glasses I'd put on this morning, so I reached up to touch the frames. The gold-tone wire rims.

'I was right,' he said unexpectedly. Without further explanation, he unbuckled Hayden from the car seat in the back. He lifted the baby out, handed him to me, and in we went to interrupt his ex-wife's workday. The bell attached to the door ting-a-linged when we entered, and Cindy looked up.

'Martin, Aurora, how good to see you,' Cindy said with a minimum of enthusiasm. 'I see you survived the drive.' She laid down the dried flowers she'd been working with, dusted her hands on her apron, and came around the counter. She actually shook hands with us, which I thought was a bit much. After all, she'd been married to Martin. She could've given him a little hug or something.

Then I noticed the large man just rising from a desk behind the counter. He got up, and up, stopping finally at about six-foot-five. He had a full mustache and dark hair peppered with gray, clipped even shorter than Cindy's. He also possessed a notable set of shoulders, and hands as big as my face. I found myself hoping he'd turn around so I could have a peek at the rear view.

'This is Dennis Stinson, Aurora,' Cindy said, smiling. I'd never seen her smile. It made her look like a million dollars. I propped the baby over my shoulder so I could spare a hand for the hunk, and my fingers vanished in Dennis Stinson's. 'Martin, I know you remember Dennis from high school.'

'Of course. It's been a long time,' Martin said, and I had to fight not to grin at the coolness in his voice.

'I guess this is the baby you were telling me about?' Cindy held out her arms, and I gently eased Hayden into them. She looked down at his flushed face, her discreetly made-up eyes scanning him.

'Cute kid,' she said, and I exhaled silently. 'You sure he's Regina's? I'd have put money on her telling me if she was expecting, Martin. It just seems incredible that someone as – well – dependent as Regina would do something as monumental as having a baby without telling the people who care about her.'

I noticed Cindy didn't say it was unthinkable that Regina would stoop to such a deception.

'But we haven't seen her for the past few months, darling,' Dennis rumbled. He had a voice that matched his size. 'To tell you the truth, Martin, I didn't encourage Regina to come by here. She was always hitting Cindy up for money, or asking us to give Craig a job . . . you get the picture. And since Cindy wasn't exactly a family member any more . . .'

'Just the mother of Regina's cousin,' Martin interjected quietly.

'Well, that, but not really Regina's aunt . . .'

'How long had it been since you saw Craig or Regina?' I asked hastily, and Cindy looked a little surprised, as if she'd assumed I couldn't speak without permission.

'Oh . . . what? Three months or so?' Cindy looked up at Dennis. 'Regina came by the house,' she continued.

'That was about the Fourth of July, so it was at least four months ago,' Dennis said. 'We were getting ready for our pool party.'

'We were,' Cindy confirmed with a reminiscent grin, and I could feel my smile get broader. Cindy was apparently partnered with this hunk not only in a business sense, but also in a personal sense, and it certainly sounded like they were living together.

'She came by?' Martin prompted. 'To the house on Archibald Street?'

'No, I moved. We moved. Dennis and I live on Grant.'

I rolled my eyes. Gettysburg Street. Grant Street. 'You *people*,' I muttered into the fuzz on Hayden's head.

'Did you say something, Aurora?' Dennis asked, bending down to me.

'No,' I said, smiling with all the sugar in my system. 'We're just having us a time, taking care of this little baby.'

'Oh my gosh, Aurora, this must be awful for you!' I felt every muscle in my body tighten as her pitying tone alerted me to what she was about to say. 'Is it true that you can't have your own? Martin, I think Barby told me you'd said that?' Cindy asked, and right then and there I decided I would kill my husband slowly, painfully, maybe publicly.

'Of course, with us never seeing Barrett, Martin was thinking of having more children,' I said, as slowly and deliberately as I could manage. 'But I said, "No, Martin, that wouldn't hardly be fair to poor ol' Barrett. I know it doesn't look good, him never visiting you even though you've been sending him money for years, him never showing me the courtesy of shaking my hand – much less hugging my neck. But us having another child would just make Barrett feel so *bad*. So *displaced*".' I stopped then, afraid I was over the line into parody.

Cindy turned an uneven kind of red.

Martin was looking at me with a kind of horrified fascination. I hoped he had enough sense to keep his mouth shut.

'So, where are you staying while you're in Corinth?' Dennis asked hastily.

'Ah – out at the old farm,' Martin said, not taking his eyes off me. Evidently, he had enough sense. 'we've been at the Holiday Inn, but with the baby . . . I think we would be better off out at the farm.'

'It was nice of you to let Craig and Regina live there,' Dennis said, since I was elaborately fussing with the baby and I had the strong feeling that Cindy was still staring at me.

'Yes,' Martin said senselessly. 'Well, we better be on our way. You wouldn't happen to know where Craig's brother Dylan lives, would you?'

Dennis said, 'Let's step outside, Martin; I can give you better directions that way.' They were out the door with suspicious alacrity. As Dennis pointed down the street, apparently counting stoplights, Cindy and I gave each other quick glances.

'Barrett really hasn't come to see you at all?' she asked in a subdued way.

'No. He doesn't acknowledge that I'm alive.' To my pride, my voice was calm and dispassionate. 'Now, I can see that is loyalty to you, which of course you'd expect from a son. But it does make Martin feel bad that Barrett never visits him and seldom calls.'

His mother sighed heavily. 'Barrett has never been able to see the divorce as anything but Martin walking out on us, though Barrett was in high school when we separated. He never saw that if Martin needed to be away from me, I needed just as much to be away from him.'

I tried to look interested and understanding. I was, to some extent, but I was also thinking my arms would fall off at the shoulders from the burden of holding this baby. I sort of half laid Hayden on the glass-topped counter.

'Just before and after her marriage, Regina used to come talk to me,' Cindy went on in a low voice, while through the front window I observed Dennis and Martin continue their pantomime of checking the weather and kicking the tires, or whatever guys do when women have embarrassed them. 'Aurora, there's something wrong with that girl. She's got some moral blind spots. Craig's brushes with the law seemed to make no difference to her whatsoever, and the fact that Rory went everywhere with Craig – and I mean *everywhere* – didn't seem to give her any pause.'

Hayden's Binky rolled from his mouth. Even as he made some fussy protest, Cindy caught it in her hand before it hit the floor and popped it back into the little mouth. Hayden lapsed back into semiconsciousness.

'What do you mean?' I asked cautiously. 'Good catch, by the way.'

'Thanks. I guess I mean Regina never seemed to make a moral judgment about the trouble Craig got into, he and Rory. She never said, "Oh, no, my husband has done a bad thing, writing those worthless cheques." Or "My God, my husband uses illegal drugs!" And she never tried to defend him either . . . pretend he was set up, or he was simply innocent. It was like it was just a lark, you know? Just fun. And ah-oh, Craig got caught!'

I'd always just thought Regina was intellectually stupid. According to Cindy, she was morally stupid as well.

'Thanks for warning me, Cindy,' I said. I took a deep breath and tried a social smile. 'Dennis seems very nice.'

'Oh . . .' she paused, eyed me sideways in a significant way. 'He *is*.'

We both started laughing, and Cindy opened the door for me. At the sound of the bell, the men both turned with relief apparent on their faces. Martin unlocked the Mercedes.

'You might want to call Margaret and Luke Granberry when you get out to the farm,' Dennis suggested. 'They've owned the one next door for a few months. Luke pretends to farm, and Margaret pretends to farm right along with him. They're really living on income from a trust, but they're trying to put a back-to-nature spin on it.'

'They're very nice,' Cindy agreed. 'She's the kind of woman who loves to help out.'

Martin and I nodded our thanks for the information, went through the interminable process of buckling Hayden in his seat, and finally were back on the street.

I took a deep breath. 'Martin,' I began.

'Roe,' he forestalled me. 'Listen, I know, I'm sorry. I had no right to tell Barby your problems. I was just – unhappy that you were unhappy, and she asked me over the phone one night how you were. I just . . . overstepped my bounds.'

'Yes.'

'You and Cindy were having your difficulties, weren't you?'

'We're okay now, Martin. I don't want to go relate our whole conversation.'

'You and Cindy are at peace?'

'Yes.'

'What about you and me?'

'Unless you ask me first, never tell anyone about my female problems. Never.'

'I promise.'

'Okay. We're all right.'

'You don't sound altogether all right.'

'Don't push it.'

We stopped at Dylan Graham's house next. After the squalor of the Harbors' place, Craig's brother's home was almost painfully respectable. It was small, and on a street of small houses. But every yard was neat, and Dylan's house in particular was freshly painted and shiny. The only disorder, if you could call it that, was the scattering of toys visible in the little backyard. I remembered Rory telling us that Dylan and his wife had a little girl.

Rory, come to think of it, had been full of information, of the less-than-valuable-and-pertinent kind.

Martin went to the front door and knocked. After a long pause, the door opened, and a young woman began talking to Martin. At first her face looked suspicious and tight, but gradually she seemed to relax. She was plump and plain and friendly, with a small mouth, pale freckled skin, and crinkled light brown hair that was cut in bangs in the front and bushed out behind her shoulders.

Martin turned and gestured to me to come on, and I slipped out of the car and started to walk toward the little house.

And then I remembered the baby. I heaved a sigh, the theatrical kind, and turned around to go through the process of retrieving Hayden.

'Oh, isn't he beautiful!' the young woman said. 'Won't you come in?'

While we exchanged condolences on the death of her brother-in-law, she waved us into the tiny house, which reminded me of an apartment I'd had while I was in college. The complex had just been finished when I signed the lease, and everything in the small space had gleamed: kitchen cabinets, walls, countertops. Craig's older brother, Dylan, and his wife, Shondra, were obviously house-proud, and after a few days of taking care of an infant, I was impressed that Shondra, herself a new mother, was still keeping her standards high.

Shondra was just as spotless as her house; her face was

scrubbed, making me feel like a made-up tramp, her rose-tinted sweats were pristine, and even her sneakers were spanky white.

'Such a nice home,' I said quietly, after she'd talked about Craig a little, without much sorrow. Shondra beamed, her conventional expression of grief shucked in a second.

'Thank you,' she said, trying to sound offhand. 'Dylan did most of the work on it himself, in the evenings and on weekends.'

'That must have been hard,' Martin commented. He had taken off his coat and was holding the baby while I tugged mine at the sleeves.

'Well, I didn't get to see a lot of him. So I'd come over with his supper or a snack and just sit and watch, while I was expecting,' Shondra said, a little smile letting us know she'd enjoyed that.

'Where's your little girl?' I asked politely.

'Kelly. She's taking a nap,' Shondra said. 'Can I hold this little guy? My brother was just here, and I wanted to thank you for bringing him home.'

Martin and I glanced at each other. We were sure slow on the uptake.

Martin, who'd had more sleep, heard the shoe drop first. 'Rory? Rory Brown is your brother?'

Shondra looked down at the baby, rocking him gently in her round arms. 'Yes,' she admitted, less happily. 'Rory is my big brother. He's, ah, he's . . . a good-natured guy, and Dylan and I have been praying hard that he'll see the Lord's ways.'

I looked at the little table sitting in the exact middle of the kitchen. There were two mugs on it, one with a spoon beside it with a little circle of brown in the center. The coffee wasn't dry yet.

'We must have just missed him?' I held out my hands, offering to take Hayden back. Shondra noted my gesture but she stared down at his face for several more long seconds, as if she'd just noticed something that gave her pause.

'Oh, that's right. You just missed him,' she said absently. 'In fact, when we heard your car pull up, he went right out the back door.' Shondra glanced over at some pictures and a vase of dried flowers on top of the composite oak-colored TV cabinet, then back to the baby's face. She slowly returned Hayden to me. 'He's a beautiful baby,' she said soberly. Her small mouth pursed, as if she was thinking over a problem.

A little wail from the back of the house pulled at her attention like a tractor beam. 'My goodness, Kelly is up. Let me go see to her.'

While Shondra was out of the room, I strolled over to the TV cabinet as casually as I could manage. The framed baby pictures were old enough to be from Shondra's family album, or Dylan's, and in one grouping was a baby girl about a year old, a baby girl embedded in a ruffled dress with a little bow stuck in her wispy hair, and a baby boy in a tiny suit. 'Barf,' I muttered, and then the face of the baby caught my eye.

'Hmmm and double hmmm,' I muttered, turning away right before Shondra came back in carrying a much larger bundle than Hayden.

While we were doing the obligatory admiring of the child, I was nasty enough to be sorry this young couple already had a baby, so perfect would they be to leave Hayden with. And they were blood relations to the baby, one way or the other. Martin and I had not discussed the possibility of finding a temporary home for Hayden with Dylan and Shondra, and after the shock of the Harbors' house, I would've been scared to even mention it before I'd met them.

As it was, I hadn't met Dylan. After a few minutes' conversation with Shondra, I could see the steel beneath the sweetness and lack of worldliness that were undoubtedly genuine. So it was my impression that Shondra would not marry a charming ne'er-do-well like her brother, or a true rascal like her brother-in-law. But we'd have to check Dylan out, and we could hardly be sure that they'd agree to something as difficult as taking care of another baby.

Martin and I exchanged glances. He'd read my mind. He asked a few questions about Dylan's job at the John Deere dealership, which I knew would give him an idea about Dylan's income and hours, and he got more information out of Shondra about her brother than I would have thought possible.

'Shondra, excuse me, I was just wondering,' I interjected, when Martin showed signs of flagging and Shondra was asking us for the third time if she could get us a drink. 'Did you know your sister-in-law was pregnant?'

Shondra's face flooded with guilty color. 'Yes, ma'am,' she blurted, as though she'd been caught in a shameful position. 'She called me on the phone and told me, about a month before the baby was due.'

'Did you see her while she was pregnant?'

'No, ma'am.'

I felt as old as the hills because of that 'ma'am', and I had to nip at the inside of my mouth to keep from protesting.

'Did you know when she had the baby?'

'My brother said she had,' Shondra said, fussing unnecessarily with the baby's plastic keys. Her baby grabbed the ring and stuffed it into her mouth, gumming the toy enthusiastically. 'Oh, honey, that ain't real clean,' Shondra muttered to the baby, but let the child keep it.

I noted that Shondra had not said that she'd seen Regina when Regina was obviously pregnant. So far, no one reliable had admitted to that. 'Do you know where Regina had this baby?' I asked.

'You sure you couldn't drink some hot chocolate?'

'No, thank you,' Martin said, quite firmly. He was getting impatient, because he was accustomed to people telling him what he needed to know, telling him promptly and in detail. I sent him one of those looks that say *back off.*

'Did she have Hayden at the local hospital?' I asked, to get us back on the track.

'No, ma'am. Rory said she went to the midwife in Brook County.'

That was what he'd told us.

'And her name is?' I smiled at Shondra as coaxingly as I can smile.

'Her name is Bobbye Sunday,' Shondra said, looking down at the baby fixedly. She spoke so unwillingly that I knew she was telling us the truth.

'Thank you,' Martin said, letting out a pent-up breath and practically jumping up from his chair. He swept the diaper bag up with one hand and held out his other hand to me. I accepted a little yank, to get me up off the couch with Hayden. We said our good-byes and thanks in a flurry of goodwill and relief that this visit was over, and at Martin's request Shondra promised to send Dylan out to see us that afternoon when he got off work. Martin strongly suggested that Dylan bring Rory with him.

We returned to the Holiday Inn, gathered our belongings, and checked out, each separately reviewing our little visit mentally. Rory was avoiding us, which meant he had information he didn't want to give us. That wasn't exactly news, but it was interesting. Martin hadn't agreed to bring the young man back to Corinth, in direct violation of the law and common sense, just to have him skip out on us and avoid us at every turn, and I had to promise myself a new pair of glasses if I didn't let the phrase 'I told you so' cross my lips.

I ran into the grocery briefly, and while I shopped, Martin bravely took Hayden with him into K-Mart. Then we were on our way to the farm where Martin had grown up, where he'd lived until he'd gone to Vietnam. His father had died when Martin was a boy, and by the time Martin left Corinth, his mother had been married for years to another farmer, Joseph Flocken. It was the widowed Joseph I'd had to see in order to purchase the farm I'd given back to Martin as a wedding present.

The Bartell farm was south of town on Route 8, further out than I remembered. You could just see a bit of the roof from the road. 'Secluded' was the word for this property, if you were feeling charitable. Actually, the farm seemed forlorn and bleak, out here in the winter countryside. As we reached the end of the long gravel driveway, I saw that Martin had indeed had the house restored. It was trim and painted now, and the barn had been leveled, so there was no longer a blight on the landscape. The driveway had been regraveled, too, and we pulled up to the side of the house under a new carport. It was just a roof on four posts, but it would keep the worst of the snow and rain off the car.

As best I remembered, there were three ground-floor doors; the front door, covered by a tiny roof, the kitchen door to the side, and the back door, which led onto a small porch-cum-laundry room that was now glassed in. Martin had the door keys on his key ring – another surprise. I found it interesting and strange that the keys to the old farmhouse were always by his hand.

'Is there a phone?' I asked.

'I don't know. I should've called Karl before we left town. He'd know. I've always got the cell phone if we have to use it.'

I waited at the bottom of the kitchen steps, Hayden a bundle of blankets in my arms, while Martin fumbled with the key. Finally the door yielded, and we stepped into the house.

'How long has it been since you were here?' I asked cautiously, looking around at the room. The kitchen had been scrubbed and repainted, and the counters had new surfaces since I'd toured it so briefly years before. The overhead light was on, and there was a plate on the table. It still held food. It had been there for days. The glass beside it was half full of Coke, or one of the other dark cola drinks.

'Not since it was finished. I came to look at it once, when I had to be in Pittsburgh for business. And I got the cleaners and contractors out here to tell them what to do, though it was Karl who checked on their work for me. I haven't been in here since then, and I think that was at least a year and a half ago. I told Regina when she married Craig that the house was sitting empty and since they were going to be in Corinth for a while, they might as well use it. Barby had been hinting how hard up they were going to be.'

I wandered slowly through the downstairs, deciding the house was even older than ours in Georgia. The old window coverings – I remembered them as ragged blinds – had been thrown away, and Regina hadn't replaced them. The gray sky outside seemed to fill the rooms with gloom. While Martin brought in the rest of our things, I walked around with Hayden.

I had very little memory of the house, but today I discovered that in that memory I had minimized the size of the rooms and maximized the height of the ceiling. Martin's childhood home was an old two-storey farmhouse, with three large rooms downstairs and three up; a decent bathroom on each floor that had obviously been created from a small bedroom or large closet; a large original pantry off the kitchen; and a washer and dryer crammed on the added glassed-in back porch. I was betting that had first been called a mudroom.

If Joseph Flocken had left anything in the house, Martin had had it cleaned out.

The plaid couch and matching armchair in the family room were surely out of someone's attic, probably Barby's, and the lone bed upstairs with its matching night tables and chest of drawers had been Barby's wedding gift to the couple, I recalled. I opened the closet door. Clothes, not many. Mostly flannel shirts and blue jeans, for both Craig and Regina.

I wondered where Regina was now. It made me shiver, seeing those clothes hanging there.

But I shoved them over to one side of the closet, making room for our hanging bag. Awkwardly, one-handed due to Hayden, I stripped the sheets off the bed. I tossed them down the stairs so I could pick them up and wash them later.

I heard Martin rumbling around on the ground floor, doing God knows what. I thought of calling to him, but instead I wandered into the second bedroom upstairs, across the little landing.

There was a sleeping bag on the floor, with a pile of clothes beside it. More blue jeans and flannel shirts, and T-shirts, socks, underwear. A pair of heavy boots. There was a door between this bedroom and the next.

'Hmmm,' I said. 'Whose are those, Hayden?' Hayden made one of his favorite 'eh!' sounds in response, and waved his hands. Martin was standing beside me suddenly, but I was used to his quiet approaches and wasn't too startled. He had a box under his arm.

'Rory stayed here, I'll bet,' he said, and we exchanged looks. Hugh Harbor's remark about not knowing whether Regina would marry Craig or Rory had stuck with both of us. And while she and I were alone, Cindy had hinted pretty heavily that Craig and Rory did everything together. I saw no need to pass that little tidbit along to my husband.

'It probably wouldn't have done any good, but we should have asked him more questions when we had him,' I commented, and then bit my lip. I was getting mighty close to losing my new glasses.

'Yes,' said Martin heavily. 'We should. I'm going to try to track him down tomorrow, if Dylan doesn't bring him out this afternoon.'

When we moved on to the next room, which also opened onto the common landing as well as connecting with this bedroom, we found it contained a battered, aged crib (cadged from the Salvation Army or some garage sale, I was willing to bet) and an equally dilapidated rocking chair. There were none of the accouterments I'd seen in my friends' nurseries: no mobile, no changing table, no diaper pail. There was an old plastic garbage can, cracked and dirty, still with rolled-up dirty diapers inside. The sheet in the crib appeared to be a regular twin flat, sloppily folded and tucked to fit the small mattress.

'She didn't really plan on keeping a baby here.' I turned to face Martin. With reluctance, he met my eyes.

'There aren't any presents,' I said mercilessly. 'You always get presents when you have a baby. Even kids living on the poverty edge get presents when they have a baby – maybe just a crib sheet or a receiving blanket from the dollar store, but they get something pretty. This, this is *nothing*. There's no way on earth she planned on keeping this baby. I'll bet she wasn't ever really pregnant.'

'What about the things she brought to our house?'

'The diaper bag and the portable crib?' I took a deep breath.

'The tags were still on. I think on her way to our house, she stopped at the first discount store she came to and charged them or wrote a bad cheque for them,' I said. 'Or maybe she took those things from whoever she took this baby from.'

Martin flinched.

'We have to talk about it, Martin. No one knew she was pregnant. She didn't go the hospital. Rory just says Craig took her to a midwife. Did you notice how reluctant Shondra was to tell us what the midwife's name was? I'll bet if we ask this Bobbye Sunday, she'll tell us that Regina was never a patient. How do we know this baby is even Regina's? What if – well, what if the money in the diaper bag was ransom money?'

'Rory knew the birth weight,' Martin said. 'You remember, in the restaurant, when the waitress asked?'

I nodded. 'I also know Rory's a liar.' Hayden raised his head off my shoulder and goggled at the room. I turned my head slightly and kissed his cheek. His face wobbled around to mine. He banged his skull against my shoulder, and then came up again to look at me. We rubbed noses. His eyelids fluttered, and he laid his head down on my shoulder again.

'I don't know who bore this baby,' Martin said, his fingers brushing Hayden's wisp of hair. 'But I think Rory was around when it happened.'

'So, we need to talk to the midwife. And we need to find out if Craig's big brother knew more about it than his wife did.' I was swaying gently from side to side, assisting Hayden's slide into sleep. I eased over to the crib, glared down at the sheet, certain it was dirty. In a whisper, I asked Martin to lay one of our receiving blankets over it. When he'd done that, I eased the baby into the crib, propping him on his side with a small firm pillow at his back, and covering him with one of the blankets Ellen had given me.

I'd been aware Martin was still in the room, and I stepped quietly over to see what he was doing squatting on the floor.

Martin was plugging in a brand-new nursery monitor he'd extracted from the box he'd had under his arm. He untwisted the tie around the cord and moved the transmitter close to the crib.

Wordlessly, he handed me the receiver. He'd already put batteries inside. I looked up at him, and his face told me clearly I better not comment on his acquisition. He must have bought it on his trip to K-Mart this morning.

Martin and I left the room on tiptoe, and half closed the door behind us. The house had been cold when we entered. Since Craig and Regina had been paying their own gas bill, they'd kept the heat turned down, or maybe his friend Karl had lowered the thermostat, but Martin had gone straight to it and moved it up. He stood in the nearly bare living room, looking around him at the gleaming wood of the floors and the soft white of the walls. I knew the memories must be flooding in. As I watched him, I saw him change, the years erase. There were traces in his face of things I never saw on the man I'd married: uncertainty, unhappiness, doubt.

In three quick steps I'd reached him and put my arms around him. I wished I were taller so he could rest his head against my chest and feel protected, just for a moment. It was an awful thing, being a man, I thought; and I pitied Martin for the first time since I'd known him.

With Hayden asleep, we were able to explore the house a little more thoroughly. I opened cabinets and drawers, feeling like the worst kind of snoop, since Regina had arranged all these things in her own system. But I couldn't see a way around it. We'd be here for at least a few days, and we might as well use what was there; it was Martin's house, after all, and Regina's child was with us. Well, a child, maybe Regina's.

Craig and Regina's belongings fell into two categories, like most young married couples'. They had old things given them by relatives and friends who no longer wanted them, like the couch and chair in the living room and some rather battered pots and pans; and they had brand-spanking-new things they'd gotten for wedding presents. Regina's engraved thank-you notes were still sitting underneath an address book in the kitchen drawer that held the phone book and quick-phone list.

While Martin wandered around checking out the renovation job, and probably reminiscing, I located kitchen things I might need, figured out the stove, and started lunch. Corinth didn't have much in the way of restaurants, and I didn't feel like coping with Hayden in a public place again. Besides, I like to cook, especially when no one else is in the kitchen. I planned a large meal since we'd missed breakfast. When Martin saw me deboning chicken breasts, he pulled on his coat and scarf and went outside to take a walk. He returned with the welcome news that in case we needed it, there was a rack of firewood that looked dry.

I thought about Darius Quattermain when Martin mentioned the firewood. I wondered if he was all right, if he would ever feel like delivering wood to my house again. Maybe no one had told him he'd stripped in front of me, but he might remember all on his own. I didn't know what drug he'd taken, or what its after-effects would be. As I waited for the cooking oil to heat in the electric skillet, I wondered what kind of person would drug another; it was a kind of poisoning, wasn't it? Poisoners were supposed to be sly and patient, I recalled. Anyone could pick up a baseball bat and swing it out of frustration. Well, maybe not anyone, but many people. I was sure the number of potential poisoners in the population must be much lower.

'What are you thinking of?' Martin asked, and I jumped, dropping the chicken breast into the hot oil, which popped me. When he'd apologized and I'd taken my hand out from under the cold running water, I said, 'I was just thinking about Darius.'

'You were shaking your head, raising your eyebrows in this kind of amazed look, and got this *ew* expression on your face.'

I shook my head, feeling silly. I didn't want to explain my train of thought to Martin. A knock at the front door made me jump again. Martin went to answer it, and a second later a tall young man came with him into the kitchen. I had only to look at his face for a moment to know this was Craig's brother.

I wiped my hands on a dish towel and took Dylan's hand, telling him how sorry I was.

Dylan, who was wearing a John Deere green shirt and some

khakis, was dark like his brother, but his build wasn't reedy like Craig's had been. Dylan was more bull-like, solid and stolid, a man who saw his way from Point A to Point B and took the most direct route.

'I would sure like to see the baby,' he told me, and seemed surprised when Martin volunteered to take him upstairs to the makeshift nursery.

When they came back, Dylan looked like a man with a puzzle in front of him.

He accepted a seat at the old kitchen table, folded his hands on it, and began to say what he'd come to say.

'I couldn't set my hands on Rory to bring him with me. Shondra told me you wanted to talk to him.'

Since he said this primarily to Martin, Martin nodded. I kept on pottering around the kitchen, feeling this would make the younger man relax a little more. I opened a can of green beans, put them in a very nice saucepan, and began to cook the rice in the microwave (chipped Corningware casserole, aged small microwave).

'My brother, Craig,' Dylan began, and came to a difficult silence. We both kept our eyes down, waiting patiently. 'My brother, Craig, was not always a good man.'

Martin made a gesture that could be interpreted as 'Who is?' and I made a little noise that was meant to be commiserating. This seemed to encourage Dylan.

'Craig likes – liked – things to be easy. But being married and earning a living – being an adult – those aren't easy things.'

I nodded to myself. That was the absolute truth.

'I'm the last person Craig would have told, if he'd had plans to somehow make money off that poor little baby. But I can't help fearing somehow that was the case. Whatever Craig's plans were, Rory knows them. I hate to speak bad about my wife's brother, just like she didn't like to speak bad about Craig, but the fact is, Rory and Craig are two of a kind, and they deserved each other, just the way I hope Shondra and I deserve each other. If you had Rory in the car with you all the way here, I guess that was your best chance to find out what he knew. I don't pretend to understand why you let him go. Why didn't you turn him over to the police?'

Oooh, good question. I raised my eyebrows inquiringly and transferred my attention to Martin.

'At the time,' Martin answered, thinking as he spoke, 'I was sure that bringing him here would make things go easier on Regina if the police picked her up. I think – I know – I was sure Regina had killed Craig, and I didn't want to see her in jail, see her stand trial. Particularly since I couldn't understand why. Why she would do that, how she would do that. Regina is the most important thing in my sister's life, she's . . .' My husband seemed to run out of words.

'But letting her get away with murder ain't doing her a favor,' Dylan said.

Martin and I blinked and looked at him. There was not a thing to say.

He was absolutely right.

Chapter Seven

We had more company that evening. After a quiet afternoon, we'd had a light supper. I'd just washed the supper dishes. Martin, in between trying to get in touch with the midwife and with Rory Brown (we'd found a working phone), had boiled a used batch of bottles and nipples and set them out to drain on a clean towel. I'd put a load of linens and a few clothes through the washing-and-drying cycle. The isolated position of the farmhouse had begun to make me think of us as cut off from the world, a not-unpleasant idea; so the sound of the car and the knock at the front door came as something of a jolt.

Martin walked through the living room to the front door and switched on the outside light. There wasn't a peephole, and the door was solid wood with no glass window, so he just had to open the door on trust, a habit we'd discarded. Big-city crime was drifting from Atlanta through outlying suburbs like Lawrenceton at an alarming rate.

I don't think Martin could have looked very welcoming, but the couple on the steps didn't seem alarmed. They were smiling in a friendly way, and they maintained their smiles even when faced with Martin's stern expression.

I ventured out into the living room when I heard the man say, 'Hi! I'm Luke Granberry, and this is my wife, Margaret. We have the farm to the south of here.'

'Martin Bartell.' My husband held out his hand and Luke shook it exactly the right amount.

'We can just barely see the farm from our house, and we noticed more lights on tonight than there have been, so we felt we ought to check it out,' Margaret said. Luke Granberry seemed to be about thirty or so, and Margaret was within five years of that, more or less, I estimated. The closer I got to her, the stronger I was willing to bet on the 'more'.

Hers was the most beautiful skin I'd ever seen, pale and smooth as silk, with fine webbing at the corners of her eyes and mouth. Her hair was red, flaming red, bushy and full. She wore it pulled back from her forehead with a cheap barrette. As she bent to shake my hand, I noticed she wore no jewelry besides her plain wedding ring.

'Please come in,' I said. 'I'm Martin's wife, Aurora.'

Martin stood aside to let the neighbors in. As Luke Granberry edged past Martin, I could see that our visitor was the taller and broader. He had huge shoulders and a mildly handsome face, distinguished mostly by high cheekbones that made his small brown eyes seem perpetually scanning the distance for some adventure. His dark hair and brown eyes made his wife look even paler.

'Regina told us about you,' Margaret said. 'The aunt and uncle, right?'

'Yes, I'm Regina's mother's brother,' Martin said.

'Barby's brother,' Luke said. He looked at Martin as if trying to see a trace of Regina in his face. 'We heard a rumor that there was some problem . . . ?' Luke spread his big hands in a gesture that seemed to imply that the Granberrys wanted to help, if only they knew how.

'Regina is missing,' I said. Unfortunately, because I didn't know these people and so couldn't burden them with our emotions, I sounded like Regina's disappearance was just a little whim of hers. I was sorry the minute the words left my mouth.

'We're sure she'll turn up just any time,' Martin said, to give me some support. *We really do care, we just have a positive attitude*, his voice implied.

'Where are Craig and Rory?' Margaret asked, looking around the room as if she expected we'd stuck them in a corner.

'Please come in and have a seat,' I said, glancing anxiously at Martin. 'I'm afraid we have some bad news about Craig.' I had no idea if these neighbors had known Craig well, and could not gauge how much preparation they needed for the bad news.

Since there was only the couch and one chair in the living room, seating was a pretty cut-and-dried process. The Granberrys took the couch, which I indicated with a hostessy sweep of my hand, and I perched on the edge of the chair so my feet could touch the floor, Martin standing just behind me. I looked back at Martin, but his face gave away nothing.

'Ah . . . Craig is dead, I'm afraid.' I gave them my most serious expression, which Martin always said looked as though I suspected I was having a heart attack.

'Oh, it's true, he's dead!' Margaret said. She turned to her husband, the thick red hair sweeping across her shoulders. Her white hands clutched his. 'Luke!'

'I'm so sorry,' Luke Granberry said, in a slow and solemn voice that I thought would be perfect for reading Poe out loud. I hastily put a cap on that thought, since I'd actually opened my mouth to say it, and instead pursed my lips and shook my head, as if the tragedy were too horrible for words.

'So you'd already heard?' Martin asked.

'The counterman at the hardware store said he'd heard it from Hugh Harbor, yes. But we didn't think we knew the Harbors well enough to call and ask them what the facts were. We heard Hugh is really sick . . . – and we didn't see Craig's funeral announcement in the paper.'

'The body hasn't been released by the medical examiner yet,' I said, finally managing to strike the right tone. Sober concern, that was appropriate. For the first time, I realized I was sleep deprived in a serious way. As if hearing his psychic cue, Hayden began to make noises upstairs. It was amazing how clearly his little voice came over the receiver, which I was clutching in my left hand. I'd been afraid to put it down.

I half turned to Martin, said, 'I'll check, honey,' (as though Martin had moved). I plodded up the stairs, to see the little arms and legs flailing above the edge of the bumper pads.

He wasn't crying, so I figured he wasn't hungry. Maybe you

were supposed to hold off on the bottle until they asked for it? Since the only way for a baby to ask for a bottle was to cry, wasn't that kind of mean? On the other hand, sticking food in their mouth every time they were awake would create a bad pattern . . . Gosh, there was nothing easy about this. You might as well get your answers by interpreting the pattern of chicken bones tossed under the full moon. I propped Hayden back on his side and began to pat him. To my pleasure, he went back to sleep.

While I'd been tending to Hayden, the Granberrys had been establishing common ground with Martin. I'd hoped they'd be a source of information about Regina and Craig, but I knew we'd have to let a polite conversational time lapse before questioning them. They'd been talking about the possibility of snow during the night, and I came in on the tail end of the weather discussion.

Margaret liked babies. I could tell by the way her eyes latched onto the nursery monitor as I came into the room.

'I didn't realize you and Martin were parents,' she said slowly. 'How old is your baby?'

Martin, who'd gotten a straight chair from the kitchen, looked resigned.

I said, 'He isn't ours.' After they refused a drink, I eased back into the chair, tired as I'd ever been in my life.

'You're baby-sitting?'

'This is Regina's baby,' Martin said.

'*Regina's* baby?' If such a thing were possible, the pale Margaret, whom I was beginning to warm to, turned a shade whiter. She stared at us, stunned.

Even her next-door neighbors hadn't known Regina was going to have a baby? My doubt that Regina had ever given birth was beginning to consume me.

'Regina's baby?' Luke asked. He seemed just as startled as his wife. 'Where on earth has it been?'

'With Regina missing and Craig dead, we had to step in,' Martin said smoothly, as I opened my mouth to tell them the whole story.

'That was the best plan,' I said, just to justify my open mouth.

Obviously, the Granberrys were curious, but too polite to ask any more questions. After some idle talk about how long we might stay, and a polite offer on our visitors' part to help in any way they could, the Granberrys rose to leave. Margaret was holding Luke's hand, and I thought that was sweet. I love to see people who've been married a while still act like lovers.

Though, I considered, she might actually need the support. Margaret was looking a little shaky.

'We didn't know Regina was going to have a baby,' I said, kind of throwing out a line, as Luke and Martin were shaking hands.

Margaret nodded. 'She was very secretive about it, apparently. Listen, if you get lonely, give me a call? Our number's in the book. If Martin has catching up to do with friends here in town, you may be at loose ends. Or maybe you'll need me to baby-sit.'

'Thank you,' I said. 'I'll call you. And thanks for coming to check on the house. We appreciate your being concerned.'

'We've tried to keep an eye on the house since we heard about Craig,' Luke said. He looked from Martin to me, to make sure we both understood his sincerity. 'If you need anything, anything, while you're here, just let us know. We'll be glad to see you.'

As I gave Hayden his bottle later, I said, 'They seemed nice, Martin. I think we should try to get together with them again and see if they know any more about Craig and Regina than the little we know. It sounded to me like they saw them fairly often. What do you think?'

'They seem too damn trusting,' my husband said. 'Coming all the way over to what they think may be an empty house at night, to check on lights. What if we'd been burglars?'

'He had a rifle in the gun rack in the cab of his pickup,' I said, moving Hayden to my shoulder to burp him. 'I noticed, because it made me feel right at home.' In Lawrenceton, everyone seemed to own a gun, a rifle, or a shotgun, whether or not they hunted. Martin had a gun himself; Martin had not always been a business executive, as I would do well to remind myself.

This day had contained more than its fair share of hours. I was ready for it to be over. The ancient dryer was taking too long to dry the newly washed sheets. Martin occupied Hayden while I went in search of more. I was surprised and relieved to find another set in the upstairs bathroom closet, and it took me a minute or two to remake the bed. I had to put on the same blankets and bedspread, but I resolved to wash them in the morning.

I knew, as I scrubbed quickly in the ancient bathtub, that any mild obligatory affection I had had for Regina had ebbed away with this close examination of her marriage. I loathed her life. I loathed her little mysteries. But most of all, I loathed the nasty situation she'd dragged to our door, because I had a deep conviction that Regina had known exactly how imperiled she was when she'd driven from Corinth to Lawrenceton. If she'd been open with us, if she'd been frank, everything that had happened since then – and I visualized a long set of dominos, one toppling against the other – could have been prevented.

My distaste and disapproval for a member of Martin's family made me feel like a bad Christian and a bad wife. I'd often thought being a Christian meant by definition being a bad one, since nothing is more difficult than Christianity, so I was more or less used to that feeling. But I was not used to being a bad wife.

Maybe I could make it up to Martin, a little.

He was dozing when I crawled in bed next to him. I'd switched off the light in the bathroom off the landing, and making my way to the bed was something of an adventure. But once there, he wasn't hard to find. I slid down, down under the covers. Martin made a startled noise. But it was definitely on the happy-startled side.

Afterward, when he held me and kissed me, he murmured, 'Oh, honey, that was so good.'

'I hope I haven't made you crazy today,' I ventured.

'You've made me crazy from the moment I laid eyes on you,' he told me, his voice drowsy with sleep and satisfaction.

I snuggled into my pillow, praying for a Haydenless night.

'I love you,' Martin said suddenly. 'I have a feeling that's gotten shunted to a sidetrack the past few days.'

Past few months, more like.

'I know you love me,' I whispered.

'When we got married . . .'

I was so exhausted I had to force myself to listen. None of the Advice to the Lovelorn columns told you that some days you'd be too sleepy to listen to a declaration of love.

'. . . all I wanted was to protect you from any harm. To make you safe. Not to let anything worry you . . . frighten you . . . and make sure you never wanted for anything.'

Bless his heart, that was just not possible. But it was the most attractive illusion in the world, wasn't it? What had I wanted to give Martin in return? I remembered hazily that I'd resolved to help him in his career by being a good hostess and a good guest, attending every event promptly and in appropriate clothes, expressing appropriate sentiments. I'd wanted to provide him with a house that was a home: clean, comfortable, good cooking smells in the kitchen, laundered clothes.

But after a while I'd felt compelled to work at least part-time, to go back to the library, because I loved the job and the books and the people. And there were days I had indulged myself by reading rather than doing the laundry, talking to my mother and my friends rather than starting preparations for an elaborate meal. And since I had a big contrary streak running all the way through me, I had sometimes rebelled in my own tiny way by wearing bizarre glasses to a Pan-Am Agra wives dinner, or by saying what I actually thought rather than what people wanted to hear.

'So,' I said suddenly, 'have I been the wife you wanted?'

'I didn't want "a wife",' he muttered, clearly putting the phrase in quotation marks. 'When I saw you standing on the steps in front of that house with the wind blowing your hair, looking so anxious, in that suit . . . I remember the color . . .'

'You thought, Gosh, I want to marry her and keep her forever?'

'I thought, God, I want to get in her pants . . .'

I began to giggle, and Martin's hand came out of the darkness and stroked my cheek.

'Good night,' he said, on the edge of sleep. 'You have never disappointed me.'

'Good night,' I answered, and let go of the day.

My little traveling clock on the night table told me it was seven-thirty, and the wailing from next door told me Hayden had started his cycle.

I hopped out of bed before I was fully awake, and the cold of the floor gave me a nasty shock. Our house in Lawrenceton had hardwood floors too, but they never felt this cold. I slid my feet into slippers as I headed for the door, and I crossed over to the 'nursery' with the soles slapping the floor pleasantly. The house seemed very quiet except for Hayden, who was red faced and sobbing when I got to him.

He'd slept all night.

'Mama's here,' I said, my voice still thick with sleep. 'Don't cry, baby!' I scooped him up from the crib, after figuring out how to lower the side. I only knew cribs had sides that lowered because I'd watched my friend Lizanne do the honors on her baby's bed. For mothers less than five feet tall, the lowered side was an essential feature. Not that I was a mother! I warned myself, catching my error.

'Heat a bottle, please, Martin?' I called down the stairs as I changed Hayden on our bed. He definitely didn't like the cold air smacking his damp bottom, and I didn't blame him. He was overdue for a sponge bath, but I dreaded giving him one in this chilly house.

Down the stairs we went, Hayden still complaining but not as frantically.

The kitchen was empty. Far from coffee waiting for me and a bottle awaiting Hayden, everything looked boringly like it had the night before.

The door to the back porch opened. Martin stepped in, stamping his feet, and stood on a little rug by the back door to take off his boots. He stepped through to the kitchen in his stocking feet.

'Look outside, Roe!' he said, with the grin of a twelve-year-old.

For the first time I glanced out of the windows; and I realized why the house had seemed so silent. The fields and the driveway were covered with snow.

'Oh my God,' I said, stunned. I stared at the heavy white coating. 'Oh. Wow.' From one horizon to the next, it was the same. 'I've never seen that much snow in my life.'

'I almost wish we had a sled,' he said.

'I almost wish I had a cup of coffee.'

'Coming right up.' Martin was awful damn cheerful. Who could have guessed snow would have that effect? I sat there in a semiconscious lump while Martin heated the baby bottle, started the coffee, and made toast with a beautiful toaster that had to have been a wedding present for Regina and Craig.

Martin even hummed. He is not a hummer.

He took Hayden and gave him his bottle. 'Look out there, fella. Snow everywhere! When you get bigger you can bundle up and go out there and make snow angels and pee in the snow and make a snowman . . .'

I sensed a theme.

By the time Martin had wound down, I had had time to pour two cups of coffee down my throat and eat my toast, too.

'Can we get out of here?' I asked. I took my third cup with me to the window. 'I mean, can your car get out of the driveway?'

Martin looked serious, all of a sudden. He loves that Mercedes, for sure.

'I'll call Karl,' he said, and vanished.

I tried to remember Karl from our wedding, which Martin had assured me Karl attended. I was drawing a blank. Of course, I'd been so nervous I was surprised I'd gotten the responses right.

I occupied myself by spreading towels by the kitchen sink to give Hayden that quick sponge bath I felt obliged to give him. He hated it just as much as he had the last time I'd tried this process, maybe even objecting more loudly because it was so cold. I'd already had dark doubts about this little ritual, which Amina had assured me was obligatory. After all, how dirty could Hayden get? I cleaned his bottom every time I changed him.

But I dutifully soaped the hands that never grasped food and the feet that never took a step. At least, I told myself bracingly, all this complaining would surely wear out the baby, resulting in a good nap.

'Karl's coming out,' Martin told me.

'Great. Remind me about Karl?'

'Karl Bagosian, whose family was Armenian a couple of generations ago. He went to school with me, though he's a couple of years older.'

'So what does Karl do now?'

'He owns the Jeep place.'

I nodded wisely. It was all becoming clear.

'So you fellas were buddies through school?'

Martin shrugged. 'Yeah, we were. We were on the football team together. We went hunting together. He dated Barby for a while. We joined the army together.'

'Speaking of high school buddies, what's the story on Dennis Stinson?'

'I always hated that son of a bitch,' my husband said, with very little change in his voice.

'He seemed nice to me.' I tried to look innocent. 'Just because he's moved in on your ex-wife . . .'

'Cindy and I have been divorced for a long time,' Martin said. 'I don't think it's that . . . or maybe, not much. And he tried to copy off my paper in geometry.' I couldn't help it, I started laughing. Martin had the grace to look abashed. 'Dennis just . . . I wouldn't have minded Cindy living with someone, if it had been Karl. But Karl went and got himself married to a girl that just got out of college, right about the same time you and I got married. He's got kids older than her, I think.'

If the amazing Karl was going to bring us a Jeep, I needed to get dressed. Jeans, a sweater, and boots seemed to be the uniform of the day, judging by Martin, who seemed to be more relaxed than he'd been in days. He even laid Hayden in the middle of our bed and brushed my hair for me, a pleasant pastime we hadn't had a chance to indulge in lately.

Since Hayden remained content, I called my mother, but missed her both at her house and at the hospital. I left a message on her answering machine, and talked to John's oldest son at the hospital. He said his father was on the upswing, that they hoped to take him home the next day, and he knew my mother would want to tell me all the details. He further informed me that my mother was holding up just fine, which I hadn't doubted for a second.

Next I called Angel and Shelby to ask about the baby, found out little Joan was perfect in every respect, and Angel was recovering from the birth in record time.

I handed the phone to Martin so he could call the Pan-Am Agra plant, but he told me he'd already talked to his second-in-command that morning. I glanced at my watch and winced. If you wanted to work for Martin, you had to get up early and be bright the minute you slid from between your sheets.

'But I do need to talk to David in Receiving,' Martin decided. He punched in numbers wearing his business face, so I went downstairs and poured another cup of coffee.

Just then I heard a chugging noise, and looking out the window I saw a bright red Jeep coming through the snow. I could only assume it was on the driveway.

A man hopped out and began slogging his way to the front door.

Karl Bagosian was about Martin's height, maybe five-nine or five-ten. His head was bare, and I saw that his hair was very thick and coarse, and very dark, though graying, an attractive complement to his olive complexion. Martin was still on the phone, so I unlocked the door and threw it open.

'Hello,' Karl said, looking up at the sound. He gave me a comprehensive but brief scan, and lowered his eyes to make sure he'd stamped all the snow off his boots. Satisfied, he pulled off the boots and left them by the door, padding farther into the living room unselfconsciously, and I began to see this was the protocol in snow country.

'I'm Aurora. Thank you for bringing the Jeep. Martin says he's known you forever.'

'Just about.' Karl had finished divesting himself of several layers of outerwear and finally looked me in the eyes.

Karl Bagosian had the most beautiful eyes I'd ever seen on a man. On anyone. Large, oval, very dark, fringed by eyelashes most women could only dream of, those eyes could speak to you long enough to talk you right out of your clothes and into Karl's bed.

'Well, I feel like a female peacock,' I said, mildly disgruntled. 'Would you like some coffee?'

'Yes, please,' he said, after a surprised hesitation. Karl preceded me to the kitchen, and I had to remind myself he'd been here many times before . . . before I was born, no doubt. Karl had thickened a little with middle age, and he had white teeth that gleamed like an actor's. He sat at the kitchen table watching me, while I poured a mug of coffee and placed it before him, with milk and sugar handy.

'If you haven't had breakfast, I would be glad to make you some toast,' I offered. 'Martin's on the phone; he'll be down in just a minute.'

'This is southern hospitality, the kind I keep hearing about, I guess.'

'It's just hospitality. How else would I treat you?'

He had no answer for that. 'This is some mess about Regina, huh?' he asked, looking up at me with those gorgeous eyes. He poured sugar in his coffee with a liberal hand. I watched in amazement as he did the same with the milk. It hardly looked like coffee anymore.

I propped myself against the kitchen counter. 'Did you know Craig?'

'Yeah, he stole a car from my lot.'

'What did you do?'

'I went after him and got it back.' And the large dark eyes didn't look so gorgeous anymore. In fact, they looked downright scary. I realized I was very glad I hadn't been there when Karl had gotten his car back.

'Mr Vigilante,' Martin said from the doorway. He meant to be smiling when he said it, but the smile came off lame. He'd heard the whole conversation.

Karl got up and shook Martin's hand, and they did the shoulder-patting ritual. Deep affection.

'The little sumbitch—'scuse me, Aurora – is just lucky I didn't fix his wagon for good,' Karl said, white teeth gleaming. 'I only laid off because he was your niece's husband.'

'This was since they got married?'

'Yeah, in fact this was last week. Right before he showed up on your doorstep down in Georgia, dead. Maybe he wanted to drive down in a jeep.'

'The police know about this?'

'Yeah, I told 'em after I heard Craig got killed. Told 'em I had a key to the house here. They come out here to take a gander.'

Karl Bagosian looked so exotic I found I had expected him to have a foreign accent. It was a little shocking to hear a homely midwestern voice coming from his mouth. I thought of him in harem pants. I clamped my lips together.

'What are you smiling about?' Martin asked from my elbow. I jumped.

'Would you like some more coffee, honey?' I asked.

'Lord, she's no bigger than a flea, Martin.'

I particularly dislike to be talked about as if I weren't there. But this was Martin's friend.

'Small but mean,' Martin said. I looked up, startled, and he was smiling . . . Lucky for him.

'Was the house very different than it is now? When you brought the police out here?' I asked Karl.

He took a swallow of coffee, raised the cup to me in appreciation. Since Martin had made it, that compliment wasn't due me, but I nodded anyway.

'Yes, the house was a mess,' Karl said bluntly. 'All I did was hang up the clothes and vacuum, run the dishwasher. That made a big difference.'

'Thank you,' I said, impressed at his enterprise. 'Did the police seem to think anything had happened here in the house?'

'It was just like they'd gone shopping,' Karl said, shaking his head. 'Like they were both going to be back any moment. Oh, I forgot to empty the waste-baskets that day, I just recalled. Sorry. Darlene was with me, but that girl is bone lazy.'

'How old is Darlene now?' Martin pulled out a chair, settled in opposite his friend.

'She's twenty-six.'

Martin was seriously shocked. 'Not . . . your daughter Darlene? Is twenty-six?'

Karl nodded. 'And she's my youngest. Darlene is responsible for every one of these gray hairs.'

'How old are your others, now?' Martin sounded apprehensive.

Karl cast his eyes up, as if the answer would be written on the high ceiling. 'Lessee. Gil is thirty, 'bout to be thirty-one. Therese is twenty-nine.'

Martin looked at me, horrified. I shrugged, smiling. The difference in our ages had always bothered Martin more than me. Martin, who worked out and played killer racquetball, had always had the body of a younger man. Not that my experience was that broad . . . but he'd always pleased me, and he knew it. As far as mental attitudes went, Martin and I had our differences, but no more than any two people have.

'How old are you, Aurora? Martin's looking worried.' Karl was not a man who would miss much. 'My wife, Phoebe, is just a kid, too; she's twenty-five.'

'I'm older than your wife *and* your children.' I gestured toward his mug, asking if he wanted a refill.

'No, thanks,' Karl said. 'Martin, you ready to run me back into town?'

'Thanks for bringing the Jeep out, Karl,' I said. I perceived that it was *mano a mano* time, and I was being left behind.

'Do you need me to get anything while I'm in town, Roe?' Martin was already putting on his coat and sliding the cell phone into his pocket. I sighed, but tried to keep it silent. Tracking down a scrap of paper took a minute, but I quickly made a list of things we'd neglected to get the day before.

In the back of my mind was the fear the snow would get worse, and we'd be marooned out here. What if we lost our heat?

What if whoever had killed Craig came here looking for Regina?

This was a thought so sudden and shocking that I really regretted having it, especially since I was watching the bright red Jeep recede down the driveway with Martin and Karl inside when the idea came to full bloom in my mind.

I paced around the house distractedly, trying to rid myself of the fear. It hardly made sense that whoever killed Craig in Georgia would come looking here – and that was assuming the killer hadn't been Regina herself. I managed to talk myself out of the worst of my funk, but a quarter of an hour later I was still padding around the house in two pairs of socks; staring out the windows at the snow.

After checking on the now-napping Hayden, I pulled on my boots and stuffed the baby monitor in my coat pocket. Gloved and hatted, I stepped out the south-facing front door and watched my boots sink into the snow.

I'd seen ice, I'd seen sleet, and one memorable January we'd had three inches of snow and been out of school for two and a half days. But I'd never in my life seen white stuff this deep, probably six to eight inches. I knew from what Martin had said about his childhood that it was likely this snow wouldn't melt for weeks, but only be deepened by subsequent storms.

The sky was an oppressive leaden gray, just like yesterday. It seemed quite probable to me that – amazing though the thought was – it was going to snow again. If we'd been on a vacation in a ski lodge, with lots of fireplaces and smiling servers, that would've been one thing. But out here in Farm Country, with the fireplace in the living room that at least also served our bedroom upstairs, we'd have to do a lot of fetching and carrying if our electricity went out. The other rooms would be icy. I made a mental note to use the stove to prepare as many bottles of formula as I could while I had the wherewithal.

Since I wanted to stay close enough for the monitor to work, I'd been tramping around the house in a circle. I'd noted with relief that there was a woodpile in the western side yard, the one farthest from the road, and I'd even brushed some of the snow off the wood to check that the pile was as large as it seemed.

But as I prepared to slog off and finish my circuit, I spied something I hadn't noticed earlier. There were other footprints in the snow, prints that had been made some time in the night, since they were half filled in. Though it was a little hard to tell the heel end from the toe end, there was no mistaking these prints for deer tracks, or the trail of any other kind of wildlife.

Feeling like Hawkeye, I visually followed the marks. The prints approached the front-facing kitchen window from the south, across the fields, and then circled the house; just like my path, but closer to the windows, so the owner of the prints could look into the rooms.

Or maybe the steps left and returned? But that was crazy. Why would Martin climb out the window to leave the house? He'd entered at the back porch door this morning. I could see his tracks, still crisp and clear, and I recognized the tread of his boots. He'd come out that back door, tromped over to an oak tree, walked even farther west away from the road, rotated in a tight circle to take in the view, and made his way back to the same door.

I swallowed the lump of fear in my throat.

Someone else had been lurking around the farmhouse. I tried like hell to think of another reasonable – or even unreasonable – explanation, but I could think of none, not a single damn one.

The snow had done such a great job of cheering up Martin that I hated to deflate his balloon. But I decided I had to tell him about the tracks. I cut short my expedition and stomped my boots on the back steps as Martin had done, leaving mine on the little rug where his had rested earlier, right inside the door. On the kitchen counter close to the dining table, Martin had left the little Corinth phone book open to the yellow pages (Car Dealerships) and I spared a moment to be deeply thankful that Regina and Craig had had phone service.

The man who answered agreed to go see if Karl and Martin had made it into town yet.

'Yes?' Martin asked crisply, after a lengthy pause. He was using his business voice.

'Martin, someone was outside during the night,' I told him.

This was what I loved about Martin. He didn't say, 'Are you sure?' or 'That's ridiculous!' He asked, 'How did you find out?'

After I described the footprints and my line of reasoning, there was another appreciable pause.

'I guess the light wasn't good enough this morning for me to notice the tracks. You're locked up now?' he asked.

'Yes.'

'Baby asleep?'

'Yes.'

'Then go upstairs, look in my suitcase, and get out the gun.'

'Okay.' Jeez, I hated guns. But I was scared enough to listen.

'It's loaded. You remember how I showed you how to take off the safety, how to fire?'

'Yes.'

'If the footprints are blurry, there's nothing to worry about. Whoever made them is long gone. But just in case, it would be good if you had the gun handy. Wouldn't it make you feel better?'

'I guess so.'

'Okay, now. You call the woman who was over last night, Margaret what's-her-name, see if she can come stay with you. I'm going to do a couple things here in town and then I'll be right back out.'

'Okay.' What could he have to do in town? Maybe Martin had thought of something to improve the farm's security. What we needed out here was a large ferocious barking dog, I decided.

After a few more exchanges, we hung up. I hightailed it up the stairs and rummaged through Martin's suitcase for his automatic. I hated to even touch the thing, but stronger than that loathing was the desire to protect myself and the baby in this Ohio farmhouse.

Chapter Eight

Thirty minutes later, I was feeling much more secure. Martin's Ruger was near at hand but not obvious, stashed in an otherwise empty drawer in the kitchen, and Margaret Granberry, who'd been glad to come over, was having a cup of coffee at the kitchen table. She was also holding Hayden, who of course had woken up just as I was saying hello to Margaret.

I was ready to take him from her to give him his bottle.

'I'll do it,' she volunteered.

Oddly enough, I almost told her no. No, to the first offer of help I'd had with this baby. I had actually opened my mouth to demur, to say that I was used to it, to protest that this was my job.

I forced myself to smile and say, 'Here.'

Margaret pushed the coffee cup all the way across the table so she wouldn't spill hot liquid on the baby by some accident, and took Hayden gently in her arms. I'd shaken the bottle and tested the formula, so I handed it to her and she began to feed him.

'Have you had children yourself?' I asked, relaxing when it was evident the baby was fine.

She shook her head. 'Nope. I don't want to give you more of our history than you want, but Luke and I have been married for ten years. The first few years, we could afford hospitalization insurance, so getting fertility testing was just out of the question. About three years ago, Luke's mom passed away, and she left her money in a trust fund for us. But by that time . . . I'm quite a bit older than Luke, and though we went on with the fertility testing, we didn't have much hope. Rightly, as it turned out.'

Almost happy to have company in my predicament, since it made me feel not so inadequate, I told Margaret. 'I'm not fertile, either.' When she seemed interested, I told her about my unpleasant experiences with a top gynecologist in Atlanta, and Martin's indifference to our having our own baby. Suddenly I realized how much I was saying, and I apologized. 'I don't like to talk about my reproduction problems at home,' I said wryly. 'It's like people know I failed, and they look at you like you're lacking something. Getting pregnant is so easy for so many women.'

Margaret shifted Hayden slightly, held up the bottle to see how much was left. Hayden protested, and she smiled and slid the nipple back into his mouth. 'Luke can't understand how women can talk about something as personal as fertility problems,' Margaret said. The cold sun lit her red hair until it almost seemed to give off warmth. 'It does seem strange to think that in this day and age there are some medical problems beyond fixing.'

'I know,' I agreed fervently. 'You keep thinking that this can't be an end of it, there must be something else they can do. If they can accomplish so much in other fields, why can't they fix you so you can have a baby?'

'Martin was married before, right? To the Cindy who runs the flower shop?'

'Martin has a grown son. You might not know if you haven't been living in Corinth that long, but Barrett's an actor. He's got a recurring guest spot on one of those nighttime soap operas. That's why I think Martin had a kind of "been there, done that", attitude about having another baby.'

Margaret nodded. 'It's snowing again,' she observed, glancing out the curtainless window before turning her attention back to Hayden.

'I'm ready for Martin to get back. I live in the country at home, but somehow the snow makes this place feel even more isolated,' I confessed, thinking I sounded pretty whiney and should probably shut my mouth. Growing up in the same general area, maybe Margaret was accustomed to the deafening silence of the snowfall. Had it been very lonely for her out here? 'Did you see Craig and Regina much?' I asked.

'Not at first,' she answered, after a moment. 'We're so much older, and they were newlyweds. And Luke and I are both busy.

But they got bored playing house after a while, and then we saw them more and more.'

'What did you think of the marriage?'

'That's a big question.' Margaret Granberry hunched her head to her shoulder to push her flaming hair back behind her ear while she continued to feed the baby. 'Were – are – you and Regina close?'

'No. I hardly know her.'

'In that case . . . I'll tell you, I never could quite figure out why Regina and Craig got married. Their friend Rory was here all the time, and between you and me, I think there was something of a ménage à trois going on . . . strange though that is to think of in Ohio farming country!' She laughed, and I tried to politely join in.

Margaret noticed my lack of enthusiasm. 'I'm sorry,' she said, a smile belying her contrite words. 'We tried that Missionary Bible Church last weekend, and the people there were so fire-and-brimstone, the contrast with our lovebirds out here was really sharp.'

'Martin's parents went to that church,' I said. 'At least, his step-father made Martin and Barby go after he married their mother. They had a terrible experience there.'

'I heard about it from one of the women in my book readers' club,' Margaret said. 'His sister Barbara, Barby? She got pregnant, right? and they drove her out. I hope you don't mind me bringing it up. It's a famous piece of local history.'

'That was after Martin's mother died, and Barby was just sixteen or fifteen, very young. Isn't it just bitter, when you can't conceive, how easily, other women can?' I made myself drop that line of whine. 'Martin's stepdad got up in front of the church and denounced Barby and asked the congregation to pray for her.'

'What happened?' Margaret's light eyes were bright with interest.

'Martin punched out his stepfather,' I admitted. 'Then he joined the army.'

'What happened to his sister?'

'She was put in a home for unwed mothers, I believe.' When

Martin told me the story, and it was one he hated to remember, it was because he was explaining why his family farm was in the hands of a man who hated him.

'You don't know the rest of the story?'

'No. Martin was hazy on that part because he had left for boot camp. I never had the nerve to ask Barby. She and I aren't good friends. Besides which, I know that had to have been terribly painful.'

'Giving up your baby? I can't imagine that.'

'But then, what kind of childhood would that baby have had in a household run by Joseph Flocken? Mothered by a sixteen-year-old?'

'Good points. Ones I should've considered, since my own husband was an adopted child. His parents were just great.'

'I'm glad for him. It must be a consolation, to know you were wanted enough to be selected over others.'

Margaret shrugged.

'Where do you think the footprints lead?' I asked, standing up to look out the side window. I hadn't wanted to frighten Margaret, but it would have been wrong to ask her to come over because I was anxious without telling her why.

'Unless they go across the fields all the way to our farm, I think they'll end in that little grove of trees in that hollow,' she said. She'd gotten up with Hayden propped upright on her shoulder, and she was patting him so he'd burp.

'Why?'

'Because that's the only place big enough to hide a truck or car,' Margaret said practically.

I hadn't thought about it, but if a prowler didn't want to freeze his booty off, he'd have to have come in a vehicle, and that vehicle would have had to be parked somewhere unobtrusive. My neighbor was right.

'So how did the car, if there was one, get to the grove?'

'There's a little turnoff from the highway there, and a dirt lane runs between the fields.'

'Oh,' I said lamely. Margaret knew her local geography. 'Is that your land?'

'That's the boundary between the farms. Regina would walk from there and back to the house every day. I guess she was exercising because she was pregnant.'

'And you really didn't suspect?'

Margaret looked embarrassed. 'I never said I didn't know, exactly. I guess I did think she was expecting. But I had no idea she was as far along as she was.' Margaret wrinkled her classic nose. 'I guess now . . . I should have asked her about it. But I didn't think it was any of my business. The past three months, I didn't see her to talk to that often. Where shall I put the baby?' Hayden had fallen asleep.

'I'll carry him up.' Margaret eased the baby over to me, and I carefully navigated the stairs with his heavy little body clutched to my chest. My guest had helped herself to another cup of coffee by the time I came back down. She was looking out the window of the living room, and I joined her. The Granberrys' dark green Dodge pickup was parked to one side of the front door, and we stood side by side contemplating it. Margaret was about eight inches taller than I, and broad shouldered, but there was an air of feyness, of frailty, about her.

'I just can't understand why Regina wouldn't tell everyone she was pregnant,' Margaret said, her head moving gently from side to side in an amazed negative.

According to Margaret, Regina *had* been pregnant . . . so if the baby I was calling Hayden was indeed Regina's child, he hadn't been kidnapped, and at least that was a crime I could wipe off Regina's slate in my mind.

'Why indeed,' I murmured, mostly to myself. The only reason I could think of . . . Oh, ew, no. I winced.

'You had a thought?' Margaret asked. 'You look like you just ate a lemon.'

'What if she didn't plan to keep the baby?'

'You mean, give it up for adoption?'

'Maybe. But I was thinking . . .' I just hated to voice the

thought, and I couldn't even formulate why I found it so loathsome.

Margaret was looking down at me expectantly. 'What?'

'What if she was carrying the baby for someone else?'

'You mean, got pregnant on purpose? On commission, like?'

'Or got inseminated with someone else's sperm, so the baby would be the true child of half the couple.' At least Margaret seemed to be able to follow my sometimes fractured thinking process. She was nodding.

'You may have something there, Aurora,' she said. 'But I find it makes me think much less of Regina, that she would exploit someone's infertility for her own support.'

She began to clear the few dishes off the table, and I began running hot water to wash them. As we washed, rinsed, and dried, Margaret told me about an art exhibit she and Luke had driven into Pittsburgh to see the week before, but I was still thinking about Regina.

Chapter Nine

The surrogate-mother theory explained a great deal. Why Regina had stayed out of sight while she was pregnant. She wouldn't have wanted to answer a lot of questions.

Why she had money in the diaper bag. She would have been paid for her pregnancy, and presumably she would've received money for expenses during it. That would be why she and Craig had been able to afford to live without government aid, even though neither she nor Craig held a steady job.

'I'd been thinking,' I said slowly, 'that Craig had gotten involved with some drug deal or some scam of his that had gone wrong. But that didn't explain all the facts.'

Margaret shrugged. 'I've had a month or two to wonder about it. Regina's attitude seemed so strange.'

'But why would someone kill Craig? And take Regina?'

'Maybe nobody took Regina. Maybe she went.'

'Leaving her baby?'

'People leave babies all the time,' Margaret said, her face grim. 'Luke and I lived in Pittsburgh before we moved back here so Luke could help his mother out during her last illness. The first year we were married, before we were trying to have our own child, this woman in our apartment building left her baby right outside our door. She was thinking since we didn't have kids, we would be ecstatic, I guess.'

'Oh my gosh! What did you do?'

'Of course we called the police, and they called the child welfare people. They had to take the baby to a foster home.'

'That's so sad! What happened to the mother?'

Margaret shrugged. 'Jail time, I think.'

It had certainly become a morning of mysteries to ponder. Why a woman would have a baby she didn't want . . . why she'd leave that baby's life to chance . . . and where was the father of the baby, all this time, huh? Why did his responsibility get to be voluntary, while the mother's was mandatory? I thought of my father, who'd never sent child support; Regina's father, who had vanished the minute the divorce was final.

Boy, in a minute I was going to be spitting fire because I wasn't allowed in combat. I shook myself briskly and asked Margaret Granberry if she'd seen the latest Harrison Ford movie.

Our husbands lurched up the driveway in their separate vehicles. We had quite a convention in front of the house now, with Margaret's dark green pickup, Martin's (leased, rented, or borrowed) Jeep, and Luke's battered sort-of-white Bronco.

Luke hopped out of the Bronco and hurried to the front door, his face reddened by the cold. He was wearing a rugged coat that looked like sheepskin or some other animal hide, and he'd gone without a hat or gloves. Martin, who hated headgear – I suspected because it messed up his hair – was impressed enough by the cold to have put on a sort of Russian hat he'd had for years, and he'd worn the leather driving gloves I'd given him last Christmas. His arms were full of bags from the grocery.

'I got your message,' Luke told Margaret breathlessly. 'Is everything okay here?'

'Yes, honey,' she said. 'I didn't mean to scare you. I left Luke a note about why I'd come over here,' she explained to me in an aside. 'I didn't want Luke to think I'd just ducked out on the firewood we were supposed to split this morning!'

'Oh, I'm so sorry I interrupted your chores!' I had assumed that because it had snowed, everyone was on holiday, I realized. A legacy of my southern upbringing.

'No, no. We can just as well do it this afternoon. I've enjoyed the break in routine.'

Luke said to Martin, 'My wife tells me you've had a prowler.'

'You wouldn't think this was the weather for it, would you?'

'Mighty brave guy,' Luke commented, in agreement.

'Or desperate.'

Martin went to put the groceries in the kitchen, leaving this little chilling statement hanging in the air behind him like an icicle from the eaves.

I smiled at the Granberrys, but I felt it was an anxious sort of smile. 'I'll go see if we can find some hot chocolate,' I murmured, and scooted into the kitchen after Martin.

'What are you in such a snit about?' I breathed at him. He was standing in his 'I'm mad' pose, shoulders hunched up, hands in his pockets, staring out the window.

'I can't track down that slippery little bastard,' Martin growled back. I assumed he meant Rory Brown.

I started to point out that this was no big surprise, but my better sense came to my rescue. 'We'll talk about it later. Let's serve the Granberrys some hot chocolate. After all, they came to help when we needed it.'

Martin carried the tray with the four mugs out to the living room and set it on the battered table in front of the couch. The tray was clearly one of Regina and Craig's wedding presents, probably from Pier 1, a rattan and iron construction that would have looked charming in more congruent surroundings.

'Do you have any idea how long you'll stay?' Luke asked, taking a mug of chocolate and dropping some miniature marshmallows on top. He seemed like a different person now that he was sure his wife was safe – relaxed and secure, even physically larger somehow.

I let Martin field that one.

'We have no idea,' he confessed. 'If Regina is found, and under what circumstances . . . if we can track down my sister, Barby, and her fiancé . . . if we can find out if the baby is really Regina's . . . All that will have a bearing.'

'What a terrible set of circumstances,' Margaret said. She didn't seem inclined to repeat the ideas she'd voiced to me when we were alone, and I thought that was wise. I'd try to tell Martin when the Granberrys left.

Luke was the first to hear yet another vehicle coming up the driveway.

'Expecting anyone?' he asked Martin.

'No.' Martin went to the front window. 'Blue Dodge pickup.'

To my astonishment, our newest set of callers consisted of the hunky Dennis Stinson, Cindy Bartell, and our erstwhile trip companion, Rory.

This house *had* seemed isolated. Now it was beginning to feel like a social center. We should have charged for parking and hot beverages. I went to the kitchen to put some more water in the pot, found some cookies in the bags Martin had carried into the house, and put them on a plate.

'The shop's closed on Saturday afternoons, so we thought we'd come out to check on you,' Dennis said. He looked even larger in the layers of cold-weather wear. Cindy looked like one of Santa's elves next to him, with her pixie-cut hair and narrow face. She was in a red-and-green sweater, which heightened the impression. Rory wasn't smiling, or even wearing his usual look of amiable stupidity. On the contrary, he seemed sullen and stubborn. He didn't speak, but grabbed a cookie and ate it in one bite.

I sidled over next to him, since all the other people in the room were talking to each other and I had a little time on my own.

'How come you're here?'

'That Stinson guy grabbed me,' Rory said. He looked down at me, ran his tongue around his teeth to clean off the cookie remnants, and summoned back up his charm. 'I oughta call the police,' he said, all naughty. 'I was just walking around downtown, minding my own business. Then I cross in front of Cindy's Flowers and out comes this Stinson guy, and he grabs me and tells me your husband is looking for me and I gotta go with him. Then Mrs Bartell, she says I got to go, too. Since it was her, I came without giving them no trouble.'

'Thanks, Rory. We really do need to find out more about what happened to Craig and why.'

'I told you everything I know!'

'That's hard to believe,' I told him, surprised at my own

directness. 'You were living out here with Craig and Regina, weren't you? Isn't that your stuff up there, in one of the extra bedrooms?'

Rory gave me a fleeting look: bright eyed, hard. 'What we did here isn't any of your business,' he told me, with some justification.

'Don't speak to my wife like that,' Martin said coldly. He had appeared by my side with his usual silence. 'We don't care about your love life. We just want to find out where Regina is, and whose baby this is.'

'Whose?' Rory looked down at his feet. He didn't seem to understand what Martin meant, and I thought, That could mean two things. 'Well, as long as that baby is here, anyone could claim it, couldn't they? Anyone could say anything about that baby, who's gonna say no? Nobody knows nothing except me.'

That was a real conversation stopper, and it got the attention of almost everyone in the room.

The silence was broken by Karl Bagosian's entrance through the kitchen porch. I was so surprised to see him, I involuntarily said, 'Where'd you come from, Karl?' Then, shaking my head at my own rudeness, I said, 'Excuse me! It's good to see you again so soon! Would you like some coffee or hot chocolate?' I registered the fact that Karl wasn't wearing his prosperous midwestern car-salesman clothing anymore, but some very practical cold-weather wear.

Karl was looking at Rory Brown with the coldest, most assessing look I'd ever seen. If I'd been on the receiving end of it, I'd have been as silent as Rory, and just as scared.

'Hey, Mr Bagosian,' Rory said finally. 'How you doing? How's Therese?'

'Don't speak her name.' How theatrical the words sounded, and yet none of us even thought of laughing. Karl was deadly serious.

Therese? I searched around the corners of my brain, finally remembered Therese was Karl's middle child.

'I need to talk to you for a minute, Martin,' Karl said. 'In the kitchen.'

Talk about your social challenges.

'Rory,' I said brightly, 'wouldn't you like to go upstairs and gather your things together? Then you wouldn't have to make another trip out here!'

To my relief, he took the verbal shove and went up the steps. Somehow, Rory looked much more at home in the house than I did. I fetched a baggy old sweater with big pockets I'd draped over the back of one of the kitchen chairs. Karl and Martin were deep in conversation, so I didn't speak to them. I'd had the sweater on under my coat this morning when I'd gone out in the snow and seen the tracks, and the nursery monitor was still in the left-hand pocket.

I glanced back through the doorway at our uninvited guests, who took the hint and began making small talk. Hayden, who'd been up for a few minutes, had been deposited in his infant seat by Martin, and of course he came in for a share of the conversation. The nightfall of snow was another hot topic, and after that, odds and ends of town gossip that were as boring to me as Lawrenceton gossip would be to any of these people. I was able to gather from the snips I caught as I refreshed mugs and fetched napkins that Margaret had once been a schoolteacher, Dennis Stinson supported the Dallas Cowboys, and more snow was expected today.

The hoot of a horn attracted my attention, and I went to the front door to see an old black pickup with an attachable sign that said US MAIL sitting on the roof. The mail carrier was leaning out of the passenger window, a box and some envelopes in her hand.

'Hello,' I called, and stepped out with only my sweater for warmth. The receiver for the nursery monitor, stuffed down in one of the big pockets, banged as I walked. I was glad I had my boots on. I crossed my arms over my chest as the breathtaking cold dove into my lungs.

'You the new people?' the woman asked. She was round all over and had a very misguided haircut, kind of a poorly done old-fashioned shag. She reeked of cigarette smoke.

'We're staying here temporarily. We're the owners,' I said,

close enough to the windows to lower my voice. The chug of the engine was loud in the snow-induced hush.

'Just wanted to check. I have a package here for the renter. You want to accept it? You want me to hold it until she comes back?'

It was a box from Victoria's Secret. Good Lord.

'I'll keep it for her,' I said reluctantly, and tucked the box under my arm. The mail carrier had thoughtfully put a rubber band around the package to hold the envelopes to it.

'What's your name?' the carrier bellowed.

'Teagarden, and my husband's name is Bartell, but I don't think we'll be getting any mail here,' I explained. 'Do you just leave it in the mailbox out by the road?'

'Yes, normally, but this box wouldn't fit, and when I saw tracks going in, I thought I could be sure someone would be up here,' she said. 'Well, nice to meetcha.'

I thanked her, and clutching the package across my chest and shivering, the heavy pocket of my sweater banging against my stomach, I darted back into the house.

'That was Geraldine Clooney,' Margaret said with some amusement. 'What did you think?'

'She's one of a kind,' I said.

Cindy and Dennis laughed. Luke wasn't in the room. Karl was pouring himself another cup of coffee, and Martin was coming down the stairs. The baby wasn't in his infant seat. Martin must have put him in his crib.

I wondered why Rory hadn't come down with his things.

I wondered what Karl and Martin had been talking about in the kitchen.

I wondered at the officiousness of Dennis and Cindy. Telling Rory that we wanted to see him was one thing; bundling him up and practically kidnapping him was another. If Dylan or Karl had brought Rory out, I wouldn't have wondered, but Cindy and Dennis?

As often happens to me, my mind began drifting along its own path. There's nothing like being alone in a crowd to spark a really interesting little thought pattern. I wondered how the Corinthians dug graves in the snow. Did the ground actually freeze, like the tundra? Would I get to see a snowplow? Did snowplows clean driveways, too?

'Roe? Roe?'

'Yes?' I gasped.

'I'm sorry,' Margaret said, concern in her voice. 'But I was telling you that we were going to be going now. You seemed so out of it.'

'Just daydreaming, I'm afraid,' I said, trying to sound matter-of-fact. 'Thank you so much for coming to my rescue this morning.'

'I think I left my purse in the kitchen.'

'Of course, let me go get it.' I scooted into the kitchen. There was a rifle leaning against the wall by the back porch door. I absorbed all of this in one comprehensive glance, snatched up Margaret's purse from the counter, and handed it to her in the living room within seconds.

'I don't see Karl's transportation out there, Aurora,' Margaret said. I looked up at her and shrugged.

'You got me,' I said cheerfully. 'Men are strange.'

Amusement crossed the pale face. 'Come see me,' she said warmly, and waving good-bye to the others, she and her husband made their way through the rutted snow to their vehicles.

Well, that was two fewer things blocking the view down to the little copse. I was loading the tray with used cups when I heard a strange little rustling sound. The oddest thing about it was that the sound seemed to be issuing from my appendix.

I thought about it as I carried the tray to the kitchen, sliding it carefully onto the counter. I looked down anxiously, I admit, and felt like a total idiot when I realized the sound had been issuing from the nursery monitor. Hayden must be moving around in the crib, I figured.

But . . . rustling? Karl came in just then, politely bringing an empty Equal packet. He looked around, spied the trash can, and dropped in the bit of paper. Since he was a courteous and orderly person, he tried not to ask me what I was doing staring at a nursery monitor as if it were communicating with me, but since he was also the man who'd been outside toting a rifle, he had to ask. Picking up on my concentration, he simply pointed a finger and raised his eyebrows inquiringly.

'Listen,' I whispered, as if the receiver could also be broadcasting what I said. I held it up to his ear. Karl's dark face looked puzzled. The rustling had been succeeded by a series of baffling little noises, a little *whump*, a small rattling sound, the unmistakable tiny noises of a baby fussing in his sleep. Then footsteps, getting a little fainter.

'Eh!' said Hayden, so I knew he was all right. Following the sound of the footsteps, I looked out of the kitchen across the living room to the stairs, down which Rory Brown came, carrying his backpack and a paper bag full of clothes.

'He took something out of Hayden's room,' I said. I was across the rooms and up the stairs before I knew what I was doing, and passed Rory without so much as looking at him.

Hayden was still asleep, restlessly, and the sheet on his crib mattress had been taken off and then replaced. Since it had been a regular flat bedsheet, much folded to fit the crib mattress, I'd noticed how it'd been tucked before, and I knew that it had been removed and refolded. The receiving blanket I'd covered the sheet with had been placed back on top, but it was wrinkled and crooked. As long as Hayden was all right, I couldn't see that any harm had been done, but I was mighty puzzled.

When I came slowly down to the living room, I saw that Cindy and Dennis were about to go.

'Rory's going to stay here for a while,' Martin was saying, smilingly. 'I'll get him back into town.'

Cindy looked doubtful. 'Are you sure, Martin? It looks like it's going to let go any minute.' The sky looked heavy with snow, the fields and the sky blending into one big sheet of dirty white. Dennis, his hand holding Cindy's, was looking over his shoulder at the horizon, and he was clearly anxious to be gone.

'C'mon, Cindy, we'll see Martin later,' he said. 'And thank you, Aurora, for the coffee. You'll have to tell Cindy how you do it. Her coffee is not her strong point.'

I thought of barfing all over his boots, but decided that was a little extreme. Cindy was red. I met her eyes, and elaborately drew my finger across my throat and made a choking noise. She laughed, a little reluctantly, but laughed. This confused Dennis – of course, it would.

'See you!' Martin called from the kitchen, where he and Rory and Karl were standing in a somewhat strained grouping.

'Good-bye,' I said brightly, ready for them all to be gone. Something was fishy, and the sooner Dennis and Cindy pulled away, the sooner I'd find out what it was.

Chapter Ten

I went in the kitchen to face what looked like an interrogation. Martin and Karl had taken the paper bag from Rory, and as I entered they dumped it on the table.

I gasped. Besides the usual deodorant and razor, underpants and condoms, the bag contained packages of bills. Just like the one in the baby's diaper bag, the one I'd discovered in Lawrenceton.

'They were under the sheet on the crib,' I said, into the silence.

'It's mine,' Rory said sullenly. 'As long as you can't find Regina, it's mine. She shows up, I share it with her. But we owe some of it to the midwife.'

'Where'd it come from?' Martin asked. It was the opening salvo in a long bombardment.

An hour later, no one had gotten anywhere, except me. I'd looked up Bobbye Sunday's address in the telephone book, which covered several small towns in the area. The midwife lived in Bushmill, and she wasn't answering her phone. I'd tried her number several times while Martin and Karl questioned Rory. Rory, who was wily if not intelligent, had made up his mind he wasn't going to tell anyone anything. I felt like I was some kind of civil rights observer, there to make sure Rory wasn't thumped by an increasingly exasperated Martin. Karl seemed to consider this Martin's show, but he contributed to the atmosphere of menace by smoldering at Rory, with some effect.

'I never meant to hurt Therese,' the boy blurted out of the blue.

Karl slammed his palm against the kitchen table with explosive force. 'I told you never to say her name!' he said. Then he turned to me. 'Therese is simple,' he said bluntly. 'She can cope with life, but just barely. Then this guy shows up, tells her after one date he loves her, gets her knocked up. I have to take Therese for an abortion. Phoebe's young enough to have one of her own if she wants; we don't want to raise Therese's kid, and it's not our job. She can't raise a kid, he can't raise a kid, he doesn't even want to marry her. But he had a fit when she had the abortion, which left her crying for weeks. He had a use for the baby, but not for Therese, who hasn't seen or heard from him since.'

I looked at Rory in a new light. Rather than a passive accomplice to a plot not yet determined, he was an instigator of a subsidiary plot. Not a very efficient instigator, since Therese's father had taken care of the situation, and would have outfaced Rory under any circumstances . . .

I was sick of trying to figure out what had happened in this farmhouse in the past few months.

'I'm going to take a ride,' I said abruptly.

'You're going to drive in this snow?' My husband looked amazed, and that was all it took to make me grab my coat. I'd been dragged along on this, outvoted by my husband as to the wisdom of bringing Rory back to Corinth, stuck with the care of Hayden, forced to consort with Martin's ex-wife. I was in a royal snit compounded of grievance and self-pity.

'Yes, I am,' I replied briefly.

Even as my better sense – and I did have some – told me to stay at the farmhouse, I grabbed the keys from the counter and my purse from the table and rode the crest of my snit out to the Jeep. I climbed into it, and switched on the engine.

It would have served me right if the engine had refused to start or I had driven into the fields on my way to the county road, but to my surprise I got to Route 8 just fine. I paused at the end of the driveway for a minute or two, looking at the map I'd yanked out of the glove compartment.

It was the middle of the afternoon, and the sky outside was about to loose its load of snow. I wished I could close my eyes or wiggle my nose and make the kitchenful of men disappear. Then I could go back to the farmhouse without losing face.

But I turned right, on my way to the tiny town of Bushmill.

It was easy, after all, to find Bobbye Sunday's office. It was the little building with the snow all over the blackened and broken roof. The trailer parked behind it didn't look damaged, but the snow around it was unbroken.

I looked out of the foggy window of the Jeep, shivering despite its efficient heating.

The nearest convenience store was manned (and I'm using the word loosely) by an adolescent male with acne and chin-length hair parted down the middle. It was not a flattering style, but I told myself that was just because I was old, and feeling older by the minute.

I smiled as winningly as I could. 'Can you tell me what happened at the office down the street?' I asked.

'Which one?' he asked indifferently.

I will not snap, I told myself. I will not snap and snarl. 'The burned one,' I said gently.

'It burned,' he said, smirking at the points he was scoring off the old dame who was at least in her thirties. I wondered if he would think it was as funny if I kicked him in the groin. I took a deep breath. Over-reaction.

'When did it burn? Was anyone hurt?'

At least he didn't care why I wanted to know. 'I guess it was a couple nights ago,' he told me finally. 'Someone broke in after midnight, the police figure. Stole some computers and stuff, set a fire. I bet she had some painkillers and stuff in there, someone could sell around here.' He smirked again. I felt like giving him a little pain.

'But Miss Sunday is all right?'

'Yep. She was at home when the fire started. She went down there in her nightgown, I heard.' Another smirk.

I turned to leave the store, lost in thought.

'Don't you want to buy something?' the boy asked pointedly.

'I do want to find where Bobbye Sunday lives.'

'I already told you a lot of stuff,' he grumbled. 'You need some gas, some cigarettes?'

'No, thank you,' I told him, out of all the things I could have said.

It had just dawned on me that I probably knew where Bobbye Sunday lived; the small trailer behind the little office.

The woman that answered my knock was in her early thirties. She was plump and had hair the color of a rusty chrysanthemum. It was either a very inept or a very avant-garde dye job. Either way, it was notable. The cut itself was conventional, short and curly. But her ears were pierced at least four times apiece. Then again she was wearing nurse whites and orthopedic shoes.

Miss Mixed Signals.

'Bobbye Sunday?' I asked.

'Yes.' She didn't invite me in, but she didn't bar the door. 'Have you come about the fire, are you from the insurance office?'

'No, I'm afraid I'm not.' I tried smiling, but she didn't respond. 'Could you tell me what happened?'

'Why should I talk to you?' she asked. She slammed the trailer door in my face. Bushmill was chock-full of reticent people.

I trudged back to the Jeep through the snow, feeling my blue jeans brush against my boots with the heavy feel of wet material. My feet were warm and dry, at least, and I made myself stamp the snow out of the treads of my boots before I hoisted myself up into the Jeep.

'Wait!' Bobbye Sunday slogged through the snow, holding her hands out for balance.

'I'm sorry I was so short with you,' she said, when she'd reached the side of the Jeep. I'd shut myself in, but rolled down the window. 'I lost so much in that fire,' the midwife continued. 'My patient records, the computers and software I'd just gotten . . .'

'I'm sorry,' I said. 'I'm glad you weren't hurt.'

'I keep telling myself that.'

'Sometimes that's not much consolation, I guess.'

'If you aren't from the insurance company . . .'

'I just wanted to ask you about a patient you had, a baby you delivered, around three weeks ago? Here, at your office.'

'Oh, I can't tell you about that,' Bobbye Sunday said firmly. 'That's private.' She hesitated. 'I usually go to the mother's house for delivery, but every now and then I deliver a baby here. That's all I can say.'

I could tell she meant it, and I felt sorry for her.

'Good-bye,' I said, so she could get in out of the cold. 'I hope your insurance comes through for you, soon.'

She made a face at me, half doubting, half smiling. 'Thanks.' She turned and made her way through the yard, back to the trailer door.

So that was another door shut.

I found myself wondering about the so-timely fire, destroying the record of Regina's prenatal visits and delivery – if she had indeed delivered in Nurse Sunday's office – right after Rory came back to Corinth. When I thought of Rory's handsome young face, impossibly guileless, I heaved a long sigh. What would we do with Rory? Would he be safe, riding back into Corinth with Karl? Did I care? Would Martin be willing to keep the boy in the house overnight? I wasn't sure I would.

I was grateful to see the entrance to the farm, and even more grateful when I entered the kitchen to find Rory intact and Martin and Karl apparently holding on to their tempers. I tossed down the keys and my purse, realized I'd forgotten to take my boots off at the door, and knelt to dry them with a towel.

'So, what have you guys been talking about?' I asked. I looked up at Karl.

'This fool—' he began, and then the window exploded.

Since I'd been kneeling well away from it, I clearly saw the shards of glass flying into the kitchen, glinting in the fluorescent light. The glass sprayed Rory's left side as he sat slumped at the table, sprayed Martin's right side as he stood across from him, and grazed Karl, who was perched beyond Rory on one corner.

And the bullet that had broken the glass, that bullet hit Rory in the neck on the left side, punching a mortal hole and exiting on the right, causing a shower of blood and tissue that rained on Karl, as the same bullet struck Karl's thigh, hitched over the corner of the table.

At that moment, it seemed, Martin screamed, 'Down, down,

down!' and took a flying leap to land on top of me, flattening me to the floor. A heartbeat later – a heartbeat Rory didn't have – I was facedown on the floor amid the glass and blood, my heart racing at a terrifying pace. Karl was screaming, and Rory bonelessly slid out of his chair and landed two feet away from me, blood pouring out of the wounds in his neck to puddle under him. His eyes were open.

I shrieked without knowing I was going to do it. With Martin weighing me down, I lay shivering and shaking on the floor with Rory's blood spreading toward me.

And then the kitchen was silent.

After the longest minute I'd ever lived through, no more bullets punched through the window. Martin gradually eased off me. I made myself crawl over to Karl, who had begun to moan steadily. The floor was covered with glass, and I found myself thinking of brooms and dustpans – and mops – as the advancing pool of blood stopped inches from me.

'Martin?' I asked hoarsely.

'Yes,' he said, breathily.

'Honey, I think Karl has to have a tourniquet.'

'Rory?' he asked.

'Dead,' I said.

Trying not to sit up, I fumbled my belt out of its loops, and wound it around Karl's thigh. To my intense relief, Martin scooted on his elbows to the other side of the wounded man and drew the belt tight.

Karl became silent, and I risked looking at his face to see he was as pale as his complexion would permit him to get.

I glanced at Martin, wanting to see if Karl's poor condition had registered with him.

I made an incoherent sound, of horror. Martin was covered with blood.

My husband, the invincible and strong, the coper with crises.

'Oh, honey,' I said. 'Oh, honey, you're hurt.' Sometimes the obvious truth is the only one that fills your mind and you don't care if you sound smart or not.

'Cuts from the glass,' he said briefly. But he was breathing shallowly, and his color was as bad as Karl's.

Without wasting further breath, Martin reached up a cautious hand to get the telephone sitting on the counter.

From upstairs, Hayden began crying. It came over the monitor clearly. I made as if to rise, and Martin clamped a hand on my shoulder. His grip wasn't strong, but the force of his will was.

'Are you crazy?' he hissed. 'Stay down!' He dialed without holding the phone to his ear. I was closer to it, and I could see that the little light, the one that comes on to illuminate the numbers so you can dial in the dark, was off.

'Phone's dead,' I told him, unable to control the shaking of my voice. I followed the wire with my eyes, and when it came to the jack, I saw that the phone had not been cut off outside the house, but inside; the little plastic connector had been cut off. I pointed, and Martin followed the line of my finger. For the first time since I'd met him, I saw despair in his eyes.

Martin held it up to his ear to confirm what his eyes had already checked. One of the people who had been our visitors in the past two hours had done this. They'd all been in the kitchen. This was the only phone in the house.

'Where's the cell phone?' I asked.

'It's out in the Jeep.'

Of course. I'd seen it there minutes before.

'We'll have to get Karl into the Jeep. We'll call the hospital on our way into town.'

'You and the baby have to come.' Though he seemed barely conscious, Martin crawled over to the wall and got Karl's rifle.

I couldn't remember how close the Jeep was to the front door. 'Let me go check where I parked the Jeep,' I told Martin, and crept on my hands and knees to the front door. I stretched up a hand and opened the door, peering around the frame to keep as much of myself covered as possible.

The Jeep was wonderfully close. I felt a surge of hope. We'd get out of here, into town, to the little Corinth hospital.

Then I noticed that the Jeep was canted oddly to one side. My heart did something painful inside my chest when I realized that two of the tires were flat, the two on the side away from the door.

I shut the front door, ran in a crouch to the stairs. They weren't visible from any windows, or at least the angle would be quite acute. I sprinted up as fast as I could, reached the top safely. I stood and panted for a few seconds, trying to get my breathing rate down to something approximately normal, then scurried into Hayden's room, which was over the kitchen. It was safest for him right where he was, I made myself admit, though my every instinct was to pick him up and take him with me. But I couldn't stand the crying. I tried popping his pacifier into his mouth. That would hold him, I hoped.

I didn't want to tell Martin about the Jeep's being disabled, but I had to. He looked even worse than he had three minutes ago, and Karl, I thought, was unconscious.

Martin was still thinking clearly, though.

'Check to see if the phone's still in the Jeep,' he told me, though he clearly hadn't much hope. This silent admission that he was not capable of action was more terrifying than anything to me in that horrible kitchen. Martin, strong, dangerous, and brave, had been like a rock at my back for three years. I felt exposed and anguished. 'If the phone's not in the Jeep, Karl's pickup is parked behind that clump of trees down in the south field. He went out there to check to see what kind of vehicle whoever was looking in our windows had driven. Then he walked up to the house, following the tracks.'

'Okay,' I whispered, half distracted by the continuous sound of Hayden's renewed complaining. 'So?'

'You'll have to go get Karl's pickup.'

'How do we know someone's not out there?' I asked, thinking Martin was nuts. I wasn't about to leave him.

'No more shots,' Martin said succinctly.

'Unless they're waiting for us to stand up so they can shoot again,' I protested.

'He would've come closer by now and picked us off, if he was still out there. I'm assuming he just wanted Rory.'

I glanced over at Karl, whose face was a waxy color I associated with Madame Tussaud's. He was covered with sweat, and blood, and bits of stuff. He looked very bad. Martin had spots of blood on his shirt, mostly on the back where glass slivers had pierced the material as he lay covering me. There was one long cut over his right eye that looked particularly bad, but I reminded myself that head cuts bleed worse than anything. I couldn't give myself any comfort over his color, though, and I knew that something worse than a few cuts was wrong with Martin. I found myself too scared to ask him.

'Take the baby,' Martin said.

'What?' This was crazy. It had begun to snow again.

'Take the baby.'

'Are you serious?' I said savagely, because I was terrified. 'Out in the cold, and I don't know who's out there? I'll drive back here, we'll load Karl in the pickup bed so he can keep his leg stretched out. I'll get the baby then.'

'I'm thinking you should drive straight to town. Don't stop.'

'Martin, I can't leave you,' I began, unhappy all over again to hear how distraught I sounded.

'Go!' he said harshly. 'For once, don't think about it!'

He knew something I didn't.

'Okay,' I said, trying to sound less tearful than I felt. I accepted the keys he handed me, the ones he'd taken from Karl's pocket. I ran back up the stairs, bundled and wrapped up Hayden. Then I stood by the front door, terrified of stepping out. I looked into the kitchen at Martin sitting by his friend on the floor. From somewhere, Martin dredged up the strength to give me an encouraging nod.

In retrospect, my agreeing to leave him sounds crazy; but at the time I was so seriously upset that Martin's request made some kind of sense to me. Though I was absolutely terrified, I stepped out into the snow holding the baby.

The cold hit me in the face. But no bullet. I was at the Jeep in four steps, looking through the windows. No phone. It had been taken. There were footprints, sure, but in the gray dim light and falling snow they were surprisingly hard to follow, and there were many other footprints in the parking area now.

So I began my trek through the falling snow clasping Hayden, who at least at this moment was quiet. I scanned the whiteness, looking for some sign of life out here in the bleak fields, but I saw nothing. A bone-scraping wind sprang up and scoured my face, and flakes clung to the knit cap I'd pulled over my hair. Hayden snuffled against my chest. I clutched him closer.

It was no great distance to the copse, perhaps not even a half mile, but the ground was uneven and the contours concealed by the snow. Halfway there I became aware that I was crying, and I nuzzled the baby's cheek as if he could comfort me. I knew something was wrong with my husband, and yet he had told me to leave him. Did Martin think the shooter would come around the house to make sure of Rory, and therefore invent some reasoning to make sure I left?

And then I realized why Martin had told me to take Hayden.

Hayden was my insurance.

Martin knew the shooter wouldn't try for me if I was holding the baby. Hayden was the whole point of this. I wasn't even sure what 'this' was, but Hayden was the center. Now I had the protection of Hayden's presence: and Martin didn't.

I nearly decided to turn back twice, even stopped and physically began to reverse, but I couldn't seem to figure out anything. I was shocked and freezing and desperate, and the remembered urgency of Martin's tone kept me on my course.

The snow and the baby and the rough ground made the walk seem twice as long as it actually was, but finally I was among the trees. There was Karl's black pickup, carefully parked so it was unobtrusive. I got the keys from my pocket and climbed in awkwardly, the baby making an upset choky noise in protest at the continued cold.

I laid Hayden on the floor on the passenger side. That was the best I could do. Then I scooted the seat up so my feet could reach the pedals. The pickup started on the first turn of the key just like the Jeep had, which was a real blessing, and it had an automatic shift, which was another blessing. The heater roared into life, and after a few minutes I felt a sheer, pathetic gratitude for the onset of warmth. I began backing out of the trees. When I'd turned the truck to face the road, I saw a little track at least two vehicles had made. Under those tracks must be the dirt road Margaret had told me about.

I followed them up the gentle slope to the county road, figuring the smoothest ground would lie that way, and though the pickup lurched a couple of times, we reached the road in one piece.

I started to turn the wheel left, toward town. Then I thought longingly of the Granberrys to the right, so much closer.

But Martin had said to go to town, and Martin always had a reason for making a decision. So I prepared to turn left, and I peered both ways to see if anything was coming.

It surprised me that something was.

And to compound the surprise, the traveler was Margaret Granberry, in her Dodge pickup. She stopped when she saw me by the side of the road and lowered her window.

'What are you doing?' she called. 'Isn't that Karl's truck?'

'Margaret, you should get home and lock the doors!' I yelled. 'Someone came up to the house and shot him!'

'Shot *Karl*?' Margaret's pale face looked even whiter, and she jumped out of her truck, which she left running in the middle of the road, and made her way swiftly over the packed snow to my window, her hands shoved in her pockets.

'He's bad,' I told her. 'I have to get to town to get help.'

'What about Martin? And Rory?' Margaret asked.

'Rory's dead,' I said baldly.

'So you left the baby there?'

Just then Hayden began crying, and I looked down to the floorboard to make sure he was okay.

When I looked back to the window, Margaret had a gun in her hand.

'Oh shit,' I breathed. 'Don't shoot, Margaret.'

'I won't if you'll come without any trouble.'

'Sure,' I said instantly.

'Then you bend over and pick up my baby.'

I did, though it was difficult to maneuver both our bundled bodies in the cab of the pickup.

Margaret stepped back from the door. 'Now, get out holding the baby. And don't try anything like throwing him at me to get me to drop the gun.'

'I wouldn't dream of that,' I said indignantly, and then told myself it would be a good thing to keep my mouth shut.

Margaret's head was uncovered, and her red hair had caught a lot of snowflakes. She turned her head uneasily from side to side, like she was tracking movements invisible to me.

I slid down off the high seat, holding Hayden.

Margaret seemed to be thinking hard.

'Go get in my pickup,' she ordered. 'You're going to have to drive.'

So I struggled uphill to the road, praying for more traffic to come along. This wasn't the day for my prayers to be answered the way I wanted them to be. The road was empty as far as I could see, north to south.

Following Margaret's directions, I got in the driver's seat, having slid Hayden over to the passenger side. The truck, still running, was older than Karl's fancy pickup, and it had seen harder usage. Before I could do more than formulate the thought that I could throw the truck in drive and take off, Margaret had grabbed Hayden and was getting in herself, the gun pointed at me.

'Go up to your driveway,' she instructed.

I drove slowly, still hoping someone else would come along and read something strange into the situation, call the police. I turned in when she told me to, only to reverse and back out into the road again, this time pointed south.

'We've already turned into your driveway twice, so that ought to account for our tracks,' Margaret said. 'With more snow falling, it'll be hard to read the tracks anyway.'

I wondered what Martin had thought when he'd heard the

truck, near the house. He'd probably thought help had come quicker than he'd expected. He'd have felt proud of me . . .

Instead, I'd been tricked, and I hadn't gotten help.

Shame broke over me in a wave of blackness.

It was followed by a rage so overwhelming that I had trouble seeing the road ahead of me. I seldom lose my temper, and this was far beyond that, light years beyond. I knew I had blocked from my complete awareness, until this moment, just how bad Martin had looked, just how much he too needed a doctor.

Now this woman was keeping me from getting help for him, and Karl, too. I remembered Rory's empty eyes and the pool of blood around his head; but Rory was beyond human assistance, and I had no more grief for him. My sense of urgency vied with my terrible rage for supremacy in the limited emotional room I had to spare.

I tugged at my ear on my left side, away from Margaret. My earring slid out, the back rolling down my collar and into my shirt. The small earring, just a little gold knot design, went down in the deep crack of the seat. Some policeman would find it and nail Margaret Granberry, I hoped most devoutly.

Aurora Was Here.

I pressed my fingers to the wheel, the steering column, the seat adjuster, the window, as unobtrusively as possible, hoping she'd overlook a print when she wiped down the truck. Maybe I'd seen too many movies and too many episodes of *America's Most Wanted*, but I was doing the best I could for myself.

Margaret told me to turn into her driveway. It was the first time I'd seen the Granberrys' house. It was a farmhouse with extras added, in keeping with what Cindy had told me about their lifestyle. Gleaming white, with spanking green shutters and a hot tub in a sunroom to the south, it was farming deluxe.

Luke came running out the front door as we lurched to a stop, his face twisted with anxiety. There was a rifle in his hands.

'What happened?' he cried.

'Look, honey!' Margaret called, holding up the baby so he could see it.

Luke's face went slack with horror.

'What have you done, sweetheart?' he asked.

'Don't worry, she was heading to town in Karl's truck. He was parked down at the copse,' Margaret explained. 'But she was taking the baby with her, and I figured this might be our last chance.'

'But . . .'

'And sweetie, she says you hit Karl too,' Margaret interrupted.

'I only fired once,' he said, protesting.

'The bullet went through Rory,' I told them, hardly able to choke out the words through the rage.

'He's dead,' Margaret said, relief clear in her voice. 'So we don't have to worry about that anymore.'

Luke's shoulders slumped with the same relief. 'Let's get you all inside the house,' he said briskly.

'I can show Lucas his nursery,' Margaret said, delight coursing through her voice.

'Hayden,' I said.

'No, that's the nasty name *she* gave him,' Margaret told Hayden's scrunched little face. 'His real name is Lucas.'

While her attention was riveted on the baby, I risked a glance at Luke. He, too, was looking at Hayden. If he hadn't been armed, I would have had him, and at the moment I felt equal to a pro boxer. Nothing would have stopped me, if I hadn't known I had to ask him for something.

'You have to call an ambulance and send it to the farm,' I said, sounding as reasonable as I could, considering I was in a frenzy.

'Why? Rory's dead!'

'I realize he's beyond consideration,' I said, hardly knowing what words were issuing from my mouth, 'But Karl is very badly hurt and Martin is not well. I'm afraid he's . . . I'm afraid he's . . . really sick.' I was making a superhuman effort to sound calm and matter-of-fact.

The couple looked at each other, communing silently.

'Don't think we can risk it,' Luke said.

Margaret started into the house. 'No,' she threw over her shoulder, 'I don't see how we can.'

'You have to,' I said. I stood in the snow, looking up at Luke, whose brown eyes were clear and blank. 'You can't let my husband die. You can't.'

'Margaret? Maybe we could send an ambulance?' he called to her, though he kept his guard on me.

'I'll bet they can trace a nine-one-one call,' she said doubtfully. 'Let's get inside and think about it. I bet our baby is hungry.'

They weren't going to help.

That was the final straw.

I jumped him, rifle and all.

I woke up on a floor, a cold concrete floor. It was in a windowless room lit by a bulb hanging from a cord in the middle of the ceiling.

My mouth was dry as cotton and my head hurt like hell. I tried to lift it, and the effort left me shaken and nauseated. I satisfied myself with just shifting my eyes around. I thought of all the books I'd read, all the mysteries. Spenser wouldn't have ended up this way. Neither would Kinsey Milhone. Or Henry O. Or Stephanie Plum. Well, yeah, maybe Stephanie Plum.

'Hey.'

I found the source of the voice. A young woman, dark haired, was sitting on a straight-backed chair against the wall.

'Aunt Roe, are you all right?'

I hadn't realized I'd been sure Regina was dead until I saw her sitting there alive and well. But it wasn't possible for me to feel more shocked than I already did; I just accepted our niece's presence with no more than dull surprise. 'Regina,' I whispered.

'Yeah, it's me!' she said cheerfully. 'Hey, how are you feeling? And how's the baby? I've been going nuts down here.'

'Where is here?'

Regina thought that one over for a second. 'Oh, you mean, where are we right now?'

'Yes,' I said, without the energy to be exasperated.

'We're in the Granberrys' basement.'

I'd never had a full basement. Not that many houses in Georgia do. I'd only opened the door to the basement in Martin's old farmhouse, shuddered at the dark cold that rolled up the stairs, and shut the door with alacrity. Now here I was in a basement, a windowless, below-ground prison.

'How long have you been here?'

'Since that night at your place. Well, minus the trip back to Ohio, but I don't remember much of that. Margaret gave me a bunch of sleeping pills.'

I knew anguish was waiting just around the corner. When Luke Granberry had knocked me out, he'd done me a favor. I tried to stave off the misery for a few minutes. 'Tell me what happened,' I croaked.

'Oh, well, the Granberrys showed up,' Regina said, making a face as if Margaret and Luke were particularly undesirable party crashers.

'Why?'

'Well . . . you know . . . to get the baby. But Craig beat them there.'

'Why?'

'Well . . . to get the baby.'

I felt a tear roll down my cheek sideways on its way to the floor. Martin, alone with the dying Karl Bagosian, waiting for the ambulance I was supposed to send, the help I was supposed to bring . . . 'Tell me from the beginning,' I said, in a voice I didn't recognize as my own.

'When I got pregnant, it was like, a big disaster. You can imagine!'

No, I couldn't.

'I'd just married Craig. Well, it happened before we got married, if you can count you can figure that out, and you better believe the old ladies around here can count! Especially after my mother had that baby, you know, the big scandal.'

'Yes.'

'But we got married, so hey, everything was cool. But I still didn't tell anybody, because frankly, I was thinking about getting rid of it. I mean, I'm just too young to have a baby. Right?'

'Yes.'

'And the idea of Craig as a daddy, well, that just didn't feel right. But I wasn't throwing up or anything, felt great, so I just decided to wait a while and see how I felt. A baby might be kind of neat. They love you, right?'

A tear flowed down my other cheek.

'So, anyway, I began showing. Craig and Rory thought that was just amazing. Feeling the baby move. But I still thought about getting rid of it. Then the Granberrys showed up one night and told us they'd been thinking.'

'And?'

'Well, they said they really really wanted a baby and they couldn't have one, and they had noticed I was gonna have one, and they wondered since we were kind of strapped for money, if we would consider letting them adopt the kid? That seemed like a great idea the more we thought about it, Rory and Craig and me, so I told them, sure. They paid for me to go to the midwife, one in the next county so no one from Corinth would see me, and they asked me not to go to town, because they didn't want anyone telling the baby where he'd come from until they decided it was time. That seemed right to me, too, so I just hung out at the farm. It was boring, let me tell you!'

'I'm sure,' I murmured, feeling the hair on either side of my face grow damp as the tears flowed. The basement was lined with shelves and crowded with odds and ends. I saw that Regina had made a sort of nest for herself in one corner. There was an ancient easy chair, a lamp, and a board across two cement blocks that served as a table beside the chair. It was piled high with magazines. A mattress topped with a sleeping bag was pushed against the wall. There was a cubicle that I suspected hid a toilet and maybe a shower, close to the base of the stairs.

'Have you tried to escape yet?' I asked, interrupting Regina's account of the onset of her labor. She sounded exactly like she was the only woman in the world who'd ever had a baby.

Regina gaped at me. 'Are you kidding?' she asked incredulously. 'As soon as Craig and Rory show up with the baby, Margaret'll let me go. I'm just, like, a hostage! If I tried to escape, they might hurt me!'

Ah-oh. She didn't know. If I could have felt worse, I would have. 'What do you think happened in Lawrenceton?'

'See, I had the baby,' Regina said, and I sighed. She was not going to edit her adventures. 'And when I saw him, I just thought I couldn't give him up. And Craig got put in jail, so he couldn't make me. I told Margaret and Luke I had to breastfeed for the first few days, that the midwife had told me so, but really I'd had the shot to dry my boobs up. I just said that so I could take him home with me. But I knew the Granberrys were dying for me to give him up; they'd been pestering me from the hour I had him.'

'So you ran?'

'Yeah, man, I just took off. I didn't think that Craig and Rory would figure out where I'd gone. And I never thought they'd get out so quick. I mean, I missed them, Craig especially. But I couldn't make up my mind. And I had really thought the Granberrys would be great for the baby, but then I began thinking Margaret was a little weird, and she could make Luke do anything. So maybe she wouldn't be a good mother. And,' Regina's voice lost its bounce, 'I really loved the baby. I kind of wanted to keep him, even if we really needed the money. So one day when I knew the Granberrys had gone into the city for some art thing, I lit out.'

'The Granberrys had already paid you some?'

'Oh, yeah, they gave us half the cash when he was born. They were gonna give us the other half when we turned him over. I hid the money, except for some I took out for the trip.'

She'd hidden it in the crib mattress. Where Rory had found it.

'What about the legal part of it?'

'Margaret said she and Luke'd move as soon as the baby was old enough. She figured wherever she lived, no one would ask questions. She read a couple of books on how to get a birth certificate for him. You know you can get books that tell you how to do that? She was gonna change his name to Lucas. I just called him Hayden for my great-uncle on my father's side. He was my favorite when I was a little girl.'

I thought about all this. Finally, I told Regina I was thirsty, and she jumped up to bring me some water in a plastic cup. There was a sink on the wall, stained and ugly and old, but functional. Regina slid a hand under my head so I could raise it enough to sip from the cup.

'What's wrong with my head?' I asked, staving off the inevitable. Besides, I did want to know.

'I guess Luke hit you with the stock of his rifle. Margaret says you jumped him! That was kind of crazy, Aunt Roe.'

'Yes,' I agreed.

'Anyway, you have this big bruise and swollen place on your forehead, it goes up into your hair, and a little blood dried on your face. So, have you seen Craig? When's he coming to get me? Did Rory get sick in Lawrenceton? He sure was acting awful funny.'

'What do you remember about that night?' Hard to believe it had only been five days.

Regina looked down at me doubtfully. She was sitting on the floor beside me now, the cup still in her hand. I became aware I was lying on yet another sleeping bag, and she was crouched on the cold concrete. Her black hair was a mass of tangles and her eyes were puffy.

'After you guys left to go to that dinner, I was in your house fixing up some supper, one of those Healthy Choice microwave meals you had in the freezer.'

I would have nodded if my neck wouldnt've snapped.

'Then I heard a car pull up, and I knew it wasn't you because you guys were gonna be gone longer. So I look out, and it was a black kid. He was real polite, said a friend had brought him out to get his dad's truck. I thought I saw something fall out of the back of the trailer as he was turning it around, but I didn't tell him. I figured I'd go pick it up later. After he'd driven the truck out of your backyard, and the guy who'd given him a ride had followed him out of the driveway, Craig and Rory turned in. They came into the house with me, and we started fighting almost right away. I was mad. I'd left because I needed time to think, and here he was right on my tail.

'I began to get a little nervous, alone with the guys, them being so mad at me. Course Craig would never hurt me, but he was really furious, it was the worst fight we'd ever had.' Regina's face softened. 'He's usually so sweet,' she said almost tenderly. 'It was one reason I almost kept the baby.'

I had my serious doubts that Craig had been the baby's father. In my secret brain compartment where I keep a lot of thoughts I want to hide from myself, I'd stored the idea that the baby looked much more like Rory. Rory's baby picture, framed in his sister's house, had been the spitting image of Hayden. 'So Rory began feeling bad?' I asked weakly.

'Yeah, he was acting really strange. He said he was so sleepy he couldn't stand up, and I told him to go lie on the couch. He said some blond-haired woman, some older gal in a fancy car, had asked them to help her in the liquor store parking lot, and she gave them a couple of beers to say thank you, I think her car had gotten stuck in a dip or something, and they'd helped her rock it out. Rory thought there'd been something in the beer; he said when he got through there were some speckles in the bottom of the bottle.'

'So you went over to the garage apartment?'

'Yeah, actually, Craig and I . . .' And here Regina turned coy. In between quarrels, they'd wanted a passionate reunion, apparently.

'You took Hayden?'

'Yeah, sure, we couldn't leave him in the house over there, with Rory out of it! On the way over, Craig picked up something from the yard. It was a hatchet, from the back of the guy's pickup, and he put it on the steps so the guy would see it if he missed it and came back.'

That was where the hatchet had come from. One small question explained.

'So you took the baby over to the apartment.'

Regina turned a dull, unbecoming red. 'He was asleep,' she said defensively. 'We didn't have time to put up that crib thing, so I laid him in his infant seat in the recline position.'

'Then?'

'Well, before things got . . . serious, you know . . . we heard *another* car pull up, and Craig said, "Hey, what is this place, Grand Central Station?" and I looked out the front window and it was the Granberrys!' Regina shook her head. 'I said, "Craig, you're not gonna believe this!" and he says, "Hey, we're not letting them have our baby, cause here they are following us!" and I said, "You're right, let's keep Hayden".' Regina sighed, offered me some more water.

I started to shake my head no, then realized that was a very bad idea. 'No,' I said. 'Thanks.' I wondered if Regina had ever made a reasoned decision in her life.

'While Craig was zipping up, getting ready to go down the stairs, I took the baby and kind of slid him under the bed. He was so sound asleep, he didn't even peep. He's so good! I didn't want them to walk in and see him and get all grabby, like they did once before. I told Craig what to say.'

'Why didn't the Granberrys get there when Craig and Rory did?'

'Well, they'd stopped to eat. At the last gas station they'd stopped at, Craig and Rory had asked for directions to Lawrenceton, so Margaret and Luke knew where they were going. When they were talking later about following Craig, they said they'd been scared to follow too close. When they got to Lawrenceton, they just looked in the phone book for familiar names, came up with Bartell in five minutes.'

'So, what happened then?' I closed my eyes, listened to Regina's voice wash over me. She was glad to have someone to talk to, so glad she hadn't noticed I hadn't answered any of her questions.

'I heard Craig yelling at them, telling them he'd decided they couldn't have his boy after all. That he'd been willing because a deal was a deal, but now they'd tracked him down from Ohio and he didn't like that at all. So after a while, Margaret came in the room, she said Luke was down there talking to Craig, where was the baby?'

'And you told her—?'

'The same thing I'd told Craig to tell Luke. That you and Martin had the baby, that you'd taken him riding with you so he would go to sleep, that you wouldn't be coming back for a long time.'

'She want to know where Rory was?'

'I told her he was over in the house.'

'So?'

'So, she wrote him a long note and stuck it under the windshield wiper of their car. I don't know what it said, not everything, cause she had pulled a gun on me by that time. You could have knocked me over with a feather, Margaret Granberry pulling a gun on me! So I was sitting there, quiet, and I couldn't fight, because Hayden was there under the bed and who knew what would happen to him? And I was scared to death he'd wake up and make a noise.'

'But he didn't.'

'She looked around the room, but she never thought of looking under the bed,' Regina said. 'So she told me to get in my car, we were going to drive some.'

'And you went down the stairs?'

'Yes. It was hard to leave Hayden, but I knew once we left, Craig and Rory would search for him; Craig knew for sure he was in that room!' Regina beamed fondly.

'Where was Craig when you left?'

'Oh, he and Luke were still arguing. Craig didn't say anything when he saw me coming out without the baby, and I knew he'd take care of Hayden and come after me.'

I took a deep breath, and my head throbbed as though it were splitting.

'Aunt Roe,' she said suddenly, 'what are you and Uncle Martin doing in Corinth? Every now and then if Margaret and Luke are talking in this room right overhead I can hear them through the gap around the dryer vent, and I heard that you were at the farm.

Doesn't anyone know where I am? Aren't Craig and Rory looking for me? Why do you have Hayden?'

I had to tell her about us bringing the baby and Rory back to Corinth, about what had happened before we'd brought them here. It wasn't kind to let her ignorance go on any longer, though I still had lots of questions.

'So when you and Margaret drove off in your car,' I began, 'Luke was still arguing outside with Craig?'

'Yeah, they were standing on the steps.'

Where, Craig had left the hatchet. While the note to Rory began to disintegrate in the rain. What had Regina imagined the note said? Why hadn't Regina figured the Granberrys had no reason to leave Rory a note if they planned to leave Craig there alive?

'Regina,' I said, trying to sound gentle, succeeding only in sounding weary, 'after you left, Luke killed Craig.'

Regina stared down at me. 'Why would he do that?' she asked finally. Her voice had a tremor in it.

'I guess they fought,' I said. 'Craig didn't want Luke to have Hayden. You both had gone back on your agreement. Luke was mad.' Regina didn't seem to have much grasp of consequences.

'What about Rory? Did Luke go in the house and kill him too?'

'No. Luke needed him to stay, get the baby back, and return him to Corinth. I suppose in the note . . . Margaret promised him more money if he brought the baby to them. But we brought the baby, and we wouldn't have given him up to Rory. All Rory was, was a problem. So today, Luke shot Rory.'

I could see the whites all around Regina's irises.

'Both gone,' she whispered. 'Then why am I alive?'

That was a good question, and unexpectedly astute of Regina if she'd meant it literally. While she sat in disbelieving silence, I gave her the bare bones of our trip to Corinth, of what had happened at the farm this afternoon.

And I had to tell her that Margaret and Luke had the baby.

Regina began to cry, but I had no comfort to offer her. My own problems overwhelmed me. I couldn't move without waves of pain and nausea, and I could no longer put off my fear for Martin. I didn't have enough energy to worry about Karl Bagosian, too; I thought, obscurely, He's got plenty of family, and I did my best to dismiss him from my mind.

My thoughts wandered away from the chilly cellar and the stupid young woman beside me. I fantasized that maybe Martin had managed to make it to the road and was flagging down some passing car. That was the least taxing way to get help I could imagine. Even then, the struggle down the snowy driveway, the long cold wait . . . I remembered how sick Martin had looked, and I wondered what was wrong.

After a while, I admitted to myself that I figured it was his heart.

I recalled Martin's hesitance when I asked him about his physical, in what seemed the long-ago past. I suspected that Martin had learned then that something was going wrong inside him. But with the troubles of his family, and the troubles of my family, he'd thought it best to put off having that explored; that was what I would have done, and I was sure Martin would think that way.

'You think Uncle Martin will get us out?' Regina asked, in a voice worn limp with tears.

I lay there and hated her. 'He didn't look good when I last saw him,' I said. 'Over at the farmhouse.'

'We're on our own?' Regina sounded as if that were unbelievable. All her layers of backup, gone. I could sympathize. 'Have you heard from my mother?'

'Not a word.'

'So she's still on her cruise,' Regina said. She sat for a long time in silence, which I welcomed. When she finally spoke, it was hardly reassuring. 'So they'll kill us, now that they've got the baby,' she said, and I whispered, 'Yes.' She'd reasoned herself to the end of the line.

We fell silent. We waited.

Chapter Eleven

Later, I thought of asking Regina if the Granberrys kept any dogs.

'No,' she said, obviously thinking I was an utter loon.

'Good.' Any idea of escape would be complicated by dogs.

Once we heard Hayden crying upstairs, and both of us twitched as if we were going to rise and tend to him. (In my case, that meant my arm moved.) I knew that sooner or later I was going to have to get up and go to the bathroom, and I dreaded it . . . when I had any dread to spare.

Margaret and Luke didn't put in an appearance. Probably totally wrapped up with their new baby, I thought bitterly. Though I wanted them both to die in agony, if they were going to live I wanted them to bring me some Extra-Strength Tylenol.

I slept some, though it wasn't like normal sleep; it was suspiciously like falling unconscious. Regina moaned and wept. I couldn't blame her, but the noise grated at the terrible sore ache in my head. Finally my bladder couldn't hold out any longer, and I talked my niece into helping me up.

The trip to the little room at the foot of the stairs was about as much fun as I thought it'd be. At least I emptied myself completely in one trip, since I threw up. I knew I had a concussion, but people survived concussions – right? In mystery novels, the hero always checked out of the hospital when he had a concussion, and went on about solving the case. I knew what books I would throw across the room in the future, providing I had a future.

Also, detectives in books seemed to take as many aspirin as they wanted, without regard for the recommended adult dosage. Was I the only person in the world who watched the clock so I wouldn't take my pills too close together? Though at the moment, I would take anything anyone handed me. Please, knock me out.

You can see the quality of my thinking was not high. And those were only the good parts.

I tried to concern myself about escaping. I tried to pretend I was well, and resourceful, and determined. The truth was, I was sick in body and heart, and desperate.

There was an outside door to the basement, the kind I'd only seen in movies before now; almost flat to the ground, barred on the outside. No windows. Regina assured me she'd tried that door many times, and it was of course always barred. There was nothing like a saw in the basement; the Granberrys had removed the tools. What they'd left was extra stores of canned goods, luggage, and a pile of odds and ends of lumber.

One of them would have to bring us food eventually. And after some hours, Luke did. But Margaret stood above him on the stairs, her gun in her hand.

'How's Hayden?' Regina asked, beginning to sob yet again.

'Our baby's fine,' Luke said, briefly and pointedly.

I prayed Regina wouldn't ask them what they were going to do with us.

'What are you gonna do with me?' she asked. So I was only half disappointed.

Luke didn't answer, which was just as well. He set down a tray on Regina's makeshift table, and left. Margaret was vigilant the whole time. I looked as ill as possible, which was no stretch.

There was a bottle of Excedrin on the tray. Regina opened it for me, and though I was afraid it would make me sick again, I took four. What a rebel. I propped myself up on one elbow to try the soup, which was Campbell's chicken noodle, and I managed a couple of crackers and some water. I was exhausted when I lay back down.

But after about thirty minutes, I found I felt better.

'Help me up,' I told Regina.

'Need to go the girls' room?'

'No, I need to move a little.'

Regina had carried the tray up to the top step, which she said was normal routine. Margaret had opened the door, bent down, and removed it. It had looked to me like she was alone.

Now, after my cell mate had helped me stand, I managed to walk by myself, though 'walking' makes it sound more organized than it really was. I went over to the cellar storm doors. I had to push against them for myself. They gave only a fraction of an inch. There was a dead bolt inside the cellar, of course, but at some point Regina had unbolted it and left it that way.

'What's the bar outside made of?' I asked.

'Metal,' she answered gloomily. She had experimented more than she was letting on. 'I did think of breaking one of the jars, putting a straight piece of glass through the gap, and sawing at the bar, if it was wood. But it wasn't.'

'You were talking before like you were content just to wait down here.'

'I was trying to act like I thought everything would be okay.' Now that, I understood. 'And I guess I figured they were more likely to let me out if they saw me assuming they were going to let me out.' She shrugged. 'It couldn't hurt.' Her head tensed. 'Listen! There's someone here!'

After a second, I could hear it, too. The front door slammed, and there were more footsteps above us. Suddenly the basement door swung open a crack.

'If you say one word I'll kill this baby,' Margaret said. 'Don't scream, don't say anything.'

After she shut the door Regina and I stood looking at each other.

'She wouldn't hurt Hayden,' I said. 'Look at what she's done for him already!'

'I know . . . but . . .'

Suddenly deciding, I managed to get to the stairs, grabbed the wooden railing, began to haul myself up. Then I felt a hand gripping my pants leg.

'She might mean it,' Regina said.

'Martin may already be dead,' I told her. 'I have to get out of here and get help for him.' I was pleading.

'I'm sorry, Aunt Roe. Not if there's a chance she might hurt my baby.'

And Regina, bigger and stronger, clapped a hand over my mouth, held on to me, and would not let me go. I was hardly in any shape to offer much resistance.

We could hear voices right outside the door. Several male voices, one female. Margaret.

'Come over this way where we can hear,' Regina whispered, and dragged me off the stairs and over to a spot by the wall where the dryer vent fed into the basement.

I was adding my niece to the list of people I wanted to die. But for now that would have to wait, and I listened as she bid me.

'. . . his truck by the road,' a male voice was saying. 'His wife has been out looking for him.'

'Is he going to be all right?' Margaret asked, and I swear there was genuine concern in her voice.

'Well, he's lost a lot of blood,' the man said doubtfully. 'We'll just have to wait and see. One dead, two in bad shape. They can't tell us what happened. You didn't hear any shots?'

'. . . heard what might have been one, late this afternoon,' Luke said. His voice was much fainter.

'And you had already been down there? Everything was okay?'

'Oh, yes, fine!' Margaret. 'But – I hate to say this – Martin's first wife and her boyfriend were there, and there was some bad feeling in the air.'

'Dennis and Martin never did get along,' the male voice said thoughtfully.

'And I really don't like to say this,' Margaret said, 'but it seemed to me like Dennis was kind of making eyes at Martin's new wife.'

'. . . we don't know where she has . . .' the voice faded away.

If it wasn't for the baby, Regina would let me go.

If it wasn't for the baby, I would scream my head off.

If it wasn't for the baby, none of this would have happened.

No, no. If it wasn't for Regina . . .

No, even that was wrong. If it wasn't for the Granberrys and their desire to have what nature couldn't give them . . .

No, it was all of these things.

It was quiet upstairs. Our rescue had walked out the door.

Regina let me go.

I sank down on my sleeping bag, exhausted.

'I'm sorry,' Regina said, when she saw my face.

I started to tell her I would never forgive her, but I think she already knew that. At least I was certain that Martin had gotten help, though I had no idea what shape he was in. 'Tomorrow morning by surprise,' I said, 'we take them.' I outlined my plan, which was based on far too little data.

'I thought you were a nice lady,' Regina said, awed.

'Not anymore,' I told her.

In the morning, about eight o'clock, Luke brought our tray down, Margaret covering him as she had the night before. They looked glassy-eyed, and I hoped Hayden had kept them up all night. There were two cups of orange juice and two Toaster Strudels. No coffee. Well, good. That would make me meaner, having to go without my coffee.

We ate. I took more Excedrin. I felt about like you'd expect – hell warmed over – but at least I'd slept fitfully. After we'd used the bathroom and washed our faces in the sink, Regina carried the tray up the stairs and put it on the small landing right inside the door as she had the night before.

She came down and stood before me. 'You're sure you can do this?' she asked me. I could tell by the look on her face that I looked bad.

'I'm a lot more worried about you than me,' I said, with mis-timed bluntness. 'Do you want your baby back?'

'Yes,' she said fiercely. 'The people that killed his dad can't raise him.'

Discovering she was a widow had tempered Regina overnight. I looked in her eyes and saw only determination. It almost matched the desperation I felt, the absolute necessity of reaching my husband to find out what had happened to him. Only that desperation got me up off the sleeping bag, pushed me up the stairs.

I stood, one foot on the landing just inside the door and one foot on the next step down, with my back to the wall, looking over the wooden handrail at the open space of the basement, reviewing what I had to do. I glanced at my watch; it was nine o'clock.

Then there was only the waiting. If it were the much larger Luke instead of Margaret, if for once it were both of them retrieving the tray . . . then we were sunk. I was counting entirely on them being accustomed to Regina's passivity.

I had been hearing someone moving around in the room right outside the door, which Regina had told me was the kitchen. Now the footsteps became clearer.

The lock clicked, the door began to open, and I took a deep breath. A head appeared as the door swung open and touched the wall right by my hand.

Margaret had come alone for the tray.

She'd bent to pick it up before she noticed me flattened against the wall. And by then I'd reached up, grabbed that long red hair, and yanked with all my might.

Adrenaline had come to my aid, and since I pulled myself back sharply, Margaret shot past me at a good clip, unable even to get a sound out, which was great. She was hurt by the fall, but I don't know how badly, because when she reached the bottom of the steps, Regina lifted a board that had been part of the pile of lumber, and hit Margaret Granberry's head with all her might.

There was a slight crunching noise, and Margaret lay silent at the foot of the stairs.

'Ick,' said Regina, panting.

My thoughts exactly.

Regina came up the stairs behind me, having stepped over Margaret quite casually.

I picked up the tray to get it out of our way, and took a cautious step into the kitchen. Margaret had propped the rifle by the door, I noticed. Fat lot of good that had done her.

The kitchen was a beautiful sunny room floored with white linoleum. The sun was bouncing off the snow outside and into the room through gleaming windows. My eyes were dazzled by the brightness.

On my right there was an open door into a den or living room, to my left a closed door that I thought led to the outside. I'd have been in more of a mood to appreciate Margaret's decorating skills if Luke Granberry hadn't stomped in the back door just then with an armful of wood.

His face was almost funny when he saw me, and the fact that I had the tray in my hands, as he'd expected Margaret to have, seemed to compound his confusion. I threw the tray at him, and the kitchen was clean no longer.

He dropped his armful of logs and orange juice splattered his pants. He stared down at them in bewilderment.

And suddenly, as if I'd walked into a wall, I ran out of strength. I sank to my knees, and was hard put to it not to fall on my side. The pain in my head throbbed and pulsed, and my legs felt like Jell-O.

Luke looked up from his assessment of the stain to say, 'Regina, don't do that.' His eyes were fixed on a spot behind me and a little to his left.

'You killed my husband,' Regina said. 'You took my baby. Now you go get him and hand him to Aunt Roe.'

I managed to turn my head enough to see that Regina was holding the rifle. I wondered if she knew how to fire it.

Luke didn't move. 'You don't understand, Regina. Where's Margaret?' he asked, and I saw the beginning of panic on his face.

'I think I'll just go get Hayden myself,' Regina said, and shot Luke.

I sat on the floor, paralyzed and gaping. When Regina changed, she didn't mess around. She went full circle.

In the next second, I was aware that I was alone in the kitchen with the moaning Luke Granberry. He was curled in a ball just inside the still-open door. Cold air was pouring in and he was clutching his right shoulder. His coat was stained with blood.

I pulled myself up until I stood with my hands on the kitchen table. I wondered where the car keys were. Then I spied the telephone. I staggered over to it, took it off the wall. I was so sure it would be dead, it was an almost painful shock to find it worked perfectly.

Margaret had neatly posted emergency numbers on the wall beside the phone. I punched in the sheriff's number.

'Come get me,' I said to the man who answered. 'I've been hurt and I'm too weak to drive and I have to get to the hospital.'

'What's your location, ma'am?'

I hadn't the slightest idea.

'I'm at the Granberry farm,' I said.

'What's that route number?'

I remembered. 'Eight. It's right next to the old Bartell farm,' I said.

'Oh, all right, south of town, that would be.'

'Please hurry.'

'What's the nature of your emergency?'

'Oh, shit! Just come! There are dead people out here!' I said, and hung up. Stupid man. That would bring them, though the Granberrys might not be dead. Hurt bad, surely that would qualify.

'Here's Hayden,' Regina said, her voice almost a coo.

I scarcely looked at him. If I'd said, 'So?' Regina might've shot me. All my energy was bent on lasting, staying upright, until I could see Martin again. 'He looks fine,' I said. My voice came out more like a whisper. I was feeling more like my old self every minute, Aurora Teagarden the librarian, whereas Regina seemed permanently transformed into Iron Woman.

But maybe I would never be my old self, I reflected after a moment, since I seemed to be able to ignore Luke's moaning.

I thought of getting the keys and driving Margaret's pickup or Luke's Bronco into town, to save time, but then I had to admit to myself that I would probably pass out along the way. I sank into a chair and put my head on my arms. Regina sat next to me, holding her son, and together we waited for the sirens to get closer.

They even searched Hayden, to make sure he wasn't packing heat in his diaper, I guess.

'Take me to my husband,' I said, and I said it to every officer who came in the door.

It pleased me that they believed us pretty quickly, after they'd been down in the basement and seen the evidence of our imprisonment. But believing isn't the same as releasing, and it was all too long before the sheriff himself decided to drive me to the little hospital in Corinth.

'They're going to transfer Mr Bartell to Pittsburgh when he's stable enough,' the sheriff told me.

'He had a heart attack?' I asked.

'Yes,' the sheriff confirmed, his wide Slavic face looking so sorry for me that my heart sank.

I made myself ask about Karl.

'He's in critical condition, but he lasted this long,' Sheriff Brod told me. 'Karl Bagosian is a tough bird. He hasn't been able to tell us exactly what happened. Would you like to tell me?'

'My husband and Karl were standing in the kitchen with my niece's friend, Rory,' I said wearily, staring out the squad car window at the frozen fields. To me, it was an alien landscape. The cold sun made it gleam like the white linoleum in the Granberrys' kitchen. I saw the blood against it, heard Luke moaning again like an animal.

I got through the account of what had happened, yet again.

I could tell the sheriff had a hard time believing I'd started Margaret down the stairs. I was a librarian, for God's sake. I reached up and touched the dreadful bruise and swelling on my forehead. I'd gotten a good look in the Granberrys' bathroom mirror. Even touching as delicately as possible, my head rang with pain.

'You need to get checked out at the hospital,' the sheriff said. He was a big man, wide faced and heavy.

'After I see Martin,' I said, and didn't speak again until we were there.

'I just want you to know, ma'am, that the deputy that questioned the Granberrys last night . . . well, he won't go without an official reprimand.'

I shrugged. It didn't matter anymore.

Somehow I was in a wheelchair going down corridors freshly painted in a glossy beige. The rubberized flooring was a dark chocolate brown. The place smelled like a sure-enough hospital, the sharp odors of disinfectants and medicine and the bland smell of hospital food vying for supremacy.

Through the doors marked ICU we went, the nurse pushing me not offering any comment no matter how many questions I asked her. The tiny ICU unit had room for six patients, and Martin and Karl were the only two.

Cindy was in Martin's glass-sided room, and she stepped out when she saw me coming. She started to say something to me and then thought better of it. Her eyes were red.

The nurse wheeled me right up to Martin's bed. I looked at him in horror. His face had lost all its normal color, and everything that could be hooked up to a tube was. He looked twenty years older.

'He hasn't said much,' the young man in the shadows of the room told me, and I saw that it was Barrett.

I knew then that Martin was going to die.

'Sweetheart,' I said, trying to keep my voice from shaking. 'I'm here.' I stood and took his hand.

His eyes flickered open. He took in the bruise. 'You got hurt,' he said faintly. 'That's why you didn't come.'

'Yes.'

'I knew it.'

'Miss me?' I said, trying to smile, having no idea what to say.

'Oh, yes,' he breathed, almost smiling.

'I missed you, too,' I said, choking on the words. My eyes brimmed and welled over. I kissed him on his cheek, and wished with all my heart I was alone with him. But I couldn't tell his son to leave.

That meant Barrett was there when Martin gave a rattling breath five minutes later and alarms went off, and Barrett was there when the technicians hustled us out in the hall and worked over my husband, and Barrett was there when the old doctor came out minutes later to tell me that my husband had died.

I became a widow the same week as Regina, the same week Luke Granberry became a widower.

Regina had been deprived of both of the men she'd cared for; I'm not going to assume she loved them. Her mother had returned and promised to help her raise the baby, whom Barby claimed was the spitting image of a Bartell. I never held Hayden in my arms again. Somehow I never wanted to.

Regina faced only nominal charges in the death of Margaret Granberry, since Luke himself attested they had held Regina and me prisoner. Without Margaret, Luke seemed to lose all his resolve, to become indifferent to his own life. But he recovered from his bullet wound to face three charges of kidnapping (Regina, Hayden, and me), two counts of murder (Craig and Rory), one count of assault with a deadly weapon (Karl). Since Luke pled guilty, I didn't have to return to Corinth for the trial.

I would never go there again.

Two weeks after Craig's funeral, Craig's older brother, Dylan, charged Regina with being an unfit mother, citing her plan to sell her baby to the Granberrys. He and his wife, Shondra, wanted to raise Hayden along with their little girl.

But Regina and Barby together had too much Bartell determination for the judge. He ruled the baby should stay with his mother, but the judge did order Regina to take parenting classes.

She met an older man at the first session, a divorced thirty-year-old ordered to take the class after he'd slapped his child in a grocery store, and the next thing I knew, they were married. Regina seemed to slip into marriage easily, not seeing it as so different from any other state of being.

*

Of course that was months after I had brought Martin back to Lawrenceton for the funeral. Cindy had hinted that there was room in Martin's parents' plot, and Barby had done more than hint. But I can be mighty deaf when I feel like it. It was none of Cindy's business; ex was ex. And Barby had never been a favorite of mine.

Poor Mother. She had to try to tone down her joy at her husband John's complete recovery from his heart attack, and he was twenty years older than Martin. I saw her efforts and pitied her in a remote way.

Poor John stood by the graveside trying not to look guilty. John was a rock to me, and his children, too. I'd always resented them a little, maybe, having been the sole child of my mother until she remarried, but his two sons and their wives were so kind and tactful that my petty irritation seeped away.

I was still in the stunned shell of numbness when the letter came. I'd stopped at the mailbox on my way back from work, and I shuffled through its contents indifferently. Bills, catalogs, occupant mail. But there was one personal letter, hand-written, no return address.

I slit it open when I got into the house.

I glanced at the signature. It was from Luke Granberry.

I dropped it as if it were a loathsome spider. But seconds later, I picked it back up.

Dear Mrs Bartell,

I know you will never forgive me for what I have done but I wanted you to know why I even thought of it.

Margaret and I moved to Corinth because I had discovered my mother lived there. At least for a while.

I think Margaret told you I was adopted. I was lucky to be adopted by wonderful people. Not only loving, but rich. My dad had made a lot of money in the tire business.

Like most adopted children, I always wondered who my real mother and father were. I didn't want to ask my mom and dad. I knew it would upset them. But I always felt that they knew my mother's name, that they had met her at the unwed mothers' home, from something Dad let fall once. After I married Margaret, she became as determined as I was to find out, and she was a lot smarter than me at thinking of ways to do it. When my mother died, Margaret went through all her papers, thinking she might find some trace, and sure enough she found a private detective's report on a Barbara Bartell Lampton. My mom had kept track of my birth mother that way. 'Why, I don't know. I guess she wanted to know how Barbara turned out. When Margaret read the old story about Barby, the story about my mother getting thrown out of her stepfather's church because of an illegitimate pregnancy, Margaret knew she'd found my birth mother.

From the reports, we found out that Barbara didn't live in Corinth anymore, but my sister Regina did. So we bought the farm next to the one where Regina was living and set out to make friends with her. We'd always wanted a baby, and when we saw what a mess Regina was likely to make of her pregnancy, we felt like we had to take a hand. It seemed just exactly right since Margaret and I had tried so hard for so long. If we couldn't have one of our own, one that was partly ours by blood was next best. Margaret never got over that woman in our building thinking we would like to have her baby. She said she told you that story, about the woman leaving her baby at our door.

We did everything for Regina without telling her I was her brother. We made her go for her checkups. We paid for some of her groceries, so she'd eat the right food. We even went through Lamaze, hoping she'd let us be there at the birth, but she didn't want us there. She'd rather have those two thugs there. At least she was sure one of them was the father of the child.

We just wanted the baby. We couldn't kill Regina when it would have been so easy to. No one would have known. But she is my sister, and I just couldn't. We believed her that night when she told us you and your husband had the baby. Margaret never could have imagined that Regina would leave her baby, even for a moment, under a bed.

What I want to let you know is, we never planned for any of this to happen when we first found out who my mother is. I wanted to know that, and I wanted a child of my own and Margaret's. I had a right to those things. I still think so. If Craig and Rory had just stayed out of it, and I had been able to deal with Regina on my own, it would have worked out, since she's my sister.

I'm sorry.

Luke Granberry

I looked at this letter for a long time after I read it. I wondered if Regina and Barby needed to know about Luke. I decided that wasn't my responsibility.

I went outside into the cold dry air with a match from the box on the mantelpiece. I hadn't had the spirit to build a fire all winter, from the wood Darius Quattermain had strewn around the yard, the wood that Martin and I had gathered up and stacked . . . I headed my thoughts off before I could tear up. I struck the match against a brick, and it ignited beautifully. I set the letter on fire and, when I could no longer hold it, I dropped it into an empty flowerpot I'd never put away in the toolshed.

I thought about Darius again, though, about his singing and dancing in the chilly wind. I thought about the drug he'd been slipped, and about Rory's unexpected sleeping jag after the woman at the liquor store had bought them beers in exchange for their help in getting her car out of a trough.

I grabbed my keys and drove back into town. Mostly these days I just drove to work and back, and the spontaneous errand felt very odd.

I knocked on the Lowrys' door ten minutes later. As I'd hoped, Catledge hadn't gotten home yet. Ellen was by herself.

'Come in,' she said instantly, all graciousness. 'How've you been doing?' Everyone said that now. As if I'd tell them.

I stepped in, sure I was about to ruin my welcome for good, not caring. 'You were the one doing it,' I said without preamble. 'You put the pills in Mr Quattermain's bottle, and you drugged the beer you gave Rory Brown.'

'Rory Brown?' Ellen's smooth brow wrinkled in puzzlement. 'Oh, was he the scruffy blond boy at the liquor store?'

'Yes. He described you to me, and I remembered you coming in the garage door with that bottle of wine. You weren't acting like yourself.'

'That's funny,' Ellen said coolly. 'I thought I was acting very much like myself.'

'Are you that cruel?'

'For a time, I was.'

I stared at her with something like hatred. Who knew how things would have turned out if Rory hadn't been drugged?

'You're pathetic,' I said. It was the worst thing I could think of to say.

'Yes, I am. I found all those pills in my son's room this summer. I confiscated them. Of course, I should have flushed them down the toilet, but for some reason I didn't. Catledge and I checked Tally into a drug rehabilitation program. You are the only person in this town who knows where he really is.'

I took a deep breath, let it out. Some of the rage seeped out with it.

'I couldn't tell anyone. I couldn't talk to Catledge about it, he absolutely refused. The program Tally was in, the head therapist said it was important he not get any visitors for a while so he could concentrate on the agenda. Catledge didn't want me to work.' She threw her hands up in the air. See how the world had frustrated her?

'Don't give me that,' I said. My tone wasn't pleasant. 'You could have worked anyway, no matter what Catledge said. You could have flown to wherever your son is and told them you were paying for his stay and by God you wanted to see him. You could have taken space heaters to poor old people. Instead, you slipped drugs to the unwary.'

Ellen looked down at me coldly. 'I won't do it again,' she said. 'For one thing, I'm out of pills. But I've got to say, I kind of enjoyed it.' She gestured toward the door and I left.

Driving home tired me out. So many things seemed to tire me

these days. I spent a lot of time watching television in bed, which had involved buying another television, getting it installed in a special stand up in our bedroom, and paying a higher cable bill. Reading didn't seem as interesting to me . . . Nothing did.

Again, I pulled in the driveway and got out, looking around me at the familiar landscape.

The wind had picked up again and, as I watched, it snatched up the ashes of Luke Granberry's letter and began to scatter them from the flowerpot. I looked at the weather vane Martin had installed on the garage roof and saw that the wind was blowing the ashes west. Toward the cemetery.

Last Scene Alive

Chapter One

When I stopped at the end of the driveway to extract my letters and magazines from the mailbox, I never imagined that in five minutes I'd be sitting at my kitchen table reading an article about myself. But my entertainment magazine had had a fascinating teaser on the cover: 'Crusoe's Book Comes to the Screen (Finally) – WHIMSICAL MURDERS Goes On Location.' It had taken me only seconds to flip pages to the article, which was faced by a full-page picture of my former friend Robin Crusoe, his long frame folded into a chair behind a desk piled high with books. Then, with a much deeper sensation of shock, I realized that, in a green-shaded sidebar, the small woman walking to her car, head down, was me. Not surprisingly, I decided to read the sidebar first.

'It was a strangely jolting experience to see Aurora Teagarden in the flesh,' began the writer, one Marjory Bolton.

Strangely jolting, my tushy.

'The diminutive librarian, whose courage and perspicuity led to the discovery of the serial killers terrorizing Lawrenceton, Georgia, is no recluse.'

Why would I be?

'Though only in her thirties, she's experienced more excitement than most women have in their lifetimes,' I read, 'and though she became a widow last November, Aurora Teagarden could pass for someone ten years her junior.' Well, I kind of liked that. I could see the end of my thirties if I looked real hard. I wasn't looking.

'She comes to work at the Lawrenceton Library every day, driving her new Chevy.' Would I drive someone else's? 'Modest in dress and demeanor, Teagarden hardly appears to be the independently wealthy woman she is.' Why would I wear designer originals (an inexplicable waste of money anyway) to my job at the library? This was absurdity.

I skimmed the remaining paragraphs, hoping to see something that made sense. Actually, I wouldn't have minded another reference to my youthful appearance. But no. 'Though Teagarden refused to let the filmmakers use her name, the main female character in the script is widely held to be based on her persona. Teagarden's mother, Aida Queensland, a multimillion-dollar real estate salesperson, attributes her daughter's distancing herself from the project to Teagarden's aversion to the memories the incidents left and to Teagarden's deeply religious heritage.'

I brought the cordless phone into the kitchen and hit an auto-dial number. 'Mother, did you tell this Marjory Bolton that I came from a "deeply religious heritage"?' We hadn't even settled on the Episcopal Church until Mother had married John Queensland.

My mother had the grace to sound a little embarrassed as she said, 'Good evening, Aurora. She asked me if we went to church, and I said yes.'

I read through the paragraph again. 'And you told her you were a multimillion-dollar real estate broker?'

'Well, I am. And I thought I might as well get in a plug for the business.'

'Like you needed it!'

'Business could always be better. Besides, I'm trying to get into the best position for selling the firm. One of these days I'm going to retire.'

It wasn't the first time in the past couple of months Mother had said something about selling Select Realty. Since John had had a heart attack, my mother had cut back on her work hours. Apparently, she'd also begun to think about how much longer she wanted to work.

Two years ago, I'd have sworn she'd die while she was showing a house, but now I knew better. She'd gotten a wake-up call.

'Listen to this,' I said. '"Ms Teagarden, close friend of rising power-that-be Cartland Sewell, may have political plans. Some insiders regard her as a power behind the scenes in area politics." Who on earth could've told them that? What a bunch of . . .'

'Aurora!' Mother warned.

'Codswallop,' I finished. It was a word I'd never had occasion to say out loud before.

'I'm sure it was Bubba himself,' Mother said. She was more politically astute without trying than I would be if I had a fully briefed advisor.

'Really?' Even I could hear the wonderment in my voice.

She sighed. 'I hope you never remotely consider running for office or backing any candidate you really want to win,' she advised me. 'And I've got to try to remember to call him Cartland. After calling him Bubba for forty years, Cartland is a mouthful. He seems to think he has a better chance of getting elected if he goes by his christened name.'

Well, I might not be politically astute like Bubba Sewell – excuse me, *Cartland* Sewell – but I could see that even my own mother had had a self-serving reason for contributing a quote to a completely unwanted, unnecessary magazine article about me.

'Have you finished the whole article?' Mother asked, and her voice had taken on some anxiety.

'No.' That sounded ominous. I skipped over the last part of the sidebar, the part where my friend Angel Youngblood had shoved the photographer, and returned to the main body of the article, the reason for the revival of interest in yours truly.

'After a long and frustrating wait, the grisly tale of the murders upon which Robin Crusoe's book WHIMSICAL DEATH was based is coming to the small screen as a two-part miniseries. Filmmakers hope for a more successful pairing of true-crime book and movie than *Midnight in the Garden of Good and Evil.* Crusoe's sojourn in Hollywood has made him skeptical of the result. "I don't know how the natives of Lawrenceton will feel about the job we're doing," Crusoe admitted. "I plan to be there for the location shoot." Crusoe has another reason to be on the scene; he's the constant companion of actress Celia Shaw, who will play the Teagarden character.'

I flipped the page, just hoping. Yep, there it was – a small shot of Robin and Celia Shaw at some movie premiere party. Celia had done an Emmy-winning guest stint on *ER* as a sexually addicted med student, and in this picture she and Robin were whooping it up with three of the cast members. My mouth dropped open. It was one thing to have known for the past several years that Robin was in Hollywood, writing his mystery novels from there while he touted the screenplay of his book, but it was another thing entirely to see him being Hollywood.

I examined Celia Shaw's face, the size of a fingernail, with a fascination I found hard to explain to myself. Of course, she really didn't look much like me, even like the Aurora of a few years ago. She was short, and she had notable cleavage, and her eyes were brown; those were the only points of similarity. Her face was narrower, her lips were plumper, and she had more of a nose. (I could hardly be said to have a nose at all.) And, of course, she wasn't wearing glasses. She was wearing a dress I wouldn't even have given a second glance to as I flicked through a rack. It was deep emerald green, had a sequined top, and plunged low.

I glanced down at my own cleavage, modestly covered by the tobacco brown twin set I'd worn to work over khakis. I'd look good in that dress (I told myself loyally), but I'd be uncomfortable the entire time.

Not that I could imagine going to any occasion where that dress would be appropriate. A few Lawrencetonians mixed in Atlanta society, as our small town came closer and closer to being absorbed in the urban sprawl of the South's great city, but I was not one of them; nor had I ever wanted to be.

I'd never really enjoyed the social functions I had to attend or arrange as Martin's wife, and they'd been relatively modest. As the head of the large Pan-Am Agra plant, Martin had had many obligations, only some of them related to actually running the plant.

When I looked back on the two years we'd been married, the evenings seemed a blur of entertaining higher-ups from out of town, potential customers, and representatives from the bigger accounts. We'd been invited to every charity event in Lawrenceton, and not a few in Atlanta. I'd bought the appropriate clothes, worn them, and smiled through it all, but those social evenings hadn't been much fun. Coming home with Martin had been the good part.

Coming home with Martin had been worth every minute of that social tedium.

And with that memory, the heaviness I carried inside me every moment of every day came crashing back down. I actually felt the misery descend.

Until I'd thought about the article, been distracted for a few minutes, I hadn't realized how grievous a burden I was carrying: it was the weight of my widowhood.

As abruptly as it had engaged my interest, the magazine article repelled me. There would be strangers swarming around my hometown, strangers who were interested in me without caring about me. All the horror of those old deaths would be raked up. At least a few townspeople would be made miserable, as the deaths of their loved ones were reenacted for the titillation of whomever had a television set. There was no way to stop this from happening, apparently – no way to keep the curtain of privacy drawn around me. Already, in a national magazine, I was being depicted as mysterious, odd, and somewhat boring.

I didn't want this movie to be made, and I didn't want those people here.

As I'd thought, there were a few people in Lawrenceton who were as glum as I was over the prospect of entertaining a film company. One of them was the aforementioned Bubba – excuse me, Cartland – Sewell's wife, my friend Lizanne. Her parents were among the victims of the pair of serial killers who had caused us all tremendous grief. Lizanne, too, had read the magazine article, I discovered later that evening.

Lizanne said, 'Roe, I imagine Bubba's boosterism got in the way of his common sense.' Beautiful Lizanne has always been a tranquil woman, resolutely uninvolved in any town intrigues, and for the past two years her attention had been narrowly focused on her children, two boys she'd named Brandon and Davis. Brandon was eighteen months old, and Davis had just turned three months, so Lizanne had her hands full. In the course of our choppy telephone conversation, we were constantly interrupted. Bubba, Lizanne told me, was at a bar association meeting. I fumed at not being able to speak my mind to Bubba, but I would have settled for a nice chat with Lizanne. But in five minutes, Brandon's shrieking and the wails of the baby reached such a peak that Lizanne excused herself.

While I washed my few dishes that cool October evening, I found myself wondering which of the unfamiliar faces in the library in recent weeks had belonged to the magazine writer. You'd think a writer for an LA-based entertainment weekly would have stood out like a sore thumb in our library. But the dress of our culture has become so universal, it isn't as easy to spot outsiders as it used to be.

It struck me as particularly nasty that this woman had been able to come and stare at me and dissect me, while I'd been totally unaware. She'd said I'd turned down a request for an interview. That was so automatic that I actually might not have remembered it. But how could I have been oblivious to the fact that I was under observation? I must have been even more preoccupied than I'd thought.

Being a widow was a full-time occupation, at least emotionally.

Everyone (that is, my mother and her husband John, and most of my friends) had expected me to move back into town after my husband's death. Our house, a gift to me from Martin when we'd married, was a little isolated, and too large for one person. But from my point of view, I'd loved the man and I loved my home. I couldn't lose both at once.

So I stayed in the house that had been known for years as the Julius house. When Martin had given it to me, I'd renovated it from the bottom up, and I kept it up well, though now I had to have more help in that keeping. Shelby Youngblood, Angel's husband and a close friend of my husband's, had offered to come out and do the mowing, but I'd turned him down gently. I knew Shelby, with his own yard and house and baby, had plenty to do when he had a couple of days off work. I'd hired a yard service to do most of the heavier work, but every now and then I got out and put in bedding plants, or trimmed the roses.

With less justification than the yard service, I'd also hired a maid. Martin had always wanted me to have help in the house, but I'd felt perfectly capable of taking care of the house and cooking, though I was working at least part-time most of our marriage. Now, oddly, I was seized with the determination that the house should always look immaculate. It was as if I was going to show it to a prospective buyer any moment. I had even cleaned out all the closets. Where my new passion for absolute order and cleanliness had come from, why it possessed me, I could not tell you. The maid (whose identity kept changing – at the moment it was a heavy older woman named Catherine Quick) came in once a week and did all the heavy cleaning – the bathrooms, the kitchen, the dusting, and the vacuuming – while I did everything else. I didn't suffer a smudge on the kitchen floor or an unwashed sock. Even though only one upstairs bedroom, the downstairs study, one bathroom, and the kitchen were in any kind of regular use, I kept this regimen up month after month.

I guess I was a little crazy: or, since I could afford a slightly kinder word, eccentric.

As I trudged up the stairs to go to bed that night, I wondered, for the first time, if keeping the house hadn't been a mistake.

Opening the bedroom door still gave me a little shock. One thing I *had* changed, a couple of months after Martin died, was our bedroom. Once fairly masculine and centered around the king-sized bed, now the big room was peach and ivory and fawn, the bed was a queen, and the furniture was more ornate. Atop the chest of drawers, there was a picture of Martin and me at our wedding. That picture was all that was bearable.

I looked at it for a long moment as I pulled off my rings and put them in a pile in front of the frame. I added my watch to the little heap before I climbed into the high bed and switched on the lamp, stretching a little further to reach the switch to flick off the overhead light. I picked up the book I was reading (though for months I hadn't remembered a word of any book I read) and had completed just a page when the telephone rang. I glanced at the clock and frowned.

'Yes?' I said curtly into the receiver.

'Roe?' The voice was familiar, tentative and masculine.

'Who is this?' I asked,

'Ahhhh . . . it's Robin?'

'Oh, great. Just the guy I wanted to talk to,' I said, my voice saturated with sarcasm. But way down deep, I found I was really glad to hear his voice.

'You've seen the article. Listen, I didn't write that article, and I didn't know it was going to be in the magazine, and I had nothing to do with it.'

'Right.'

'I mean, it's good pre-publicity for the movie, but I didn't arrange it.'

'Right.'

'So, at least, you already know I'm coming back to Lawrenceton?'

'Yes.' If I could stick to one syllable at a time, I might be able to restrain myself. The anger had definitely dominated that little spurt of pleasure.

'The thing is; no matter what the article said about me and Celia, I want to see you again.'

To see how I'd aged, how I'd changed? Not for the better, I was sadly aware.

'I heard,' Robin said into my silence, 'you have a house out in the country now. I hope you'll let me visit you.'

'No,' I said, and hung up. It didn't really make a difference to which statement I was responding. 'No,' covered just about everything. Maybe, two years ago, I would have been appalled at my own rudeness. Somehow, marriage and widowhood had given me the indifference to be rude – at least from time to time.

I lay awake in the darkness for a while, thinking over the implications of Robin's call. Was he truly hoping to renew our friendship? I didn't know why; maybe he just wanted me to be fodder for the camera. Or maybe he was just calling because Celia Shaw had told him to call. I didn't like to think of the very young actress leading Robin around by his . . . nose.

Surely Robin was counting on finding the old Aurora: the one who, in her late twenties, had just discarded her high school wardrobe for something more adult; the one who was just learning to say what she thought; the one who was just on the verge of coming out of her shell. Robin had left town before that process had gotten up a head of steam.

Across the fields, my neighbor Clement Farmer's dog Robert began to bark – at the moon, at a coon, at a wandering cat or derelict dog . . . who knew? Robert (short for Robert E. Lee) had a barking episode just about every night. I didn't mind, this once; the noise was company for my thoughts.

I found myself wondering how Robin himself had changed. I remembered meeting Robin when he'd moved into the row of townhouses I managed for Mother. I figured that when I'd met Robin, I'd been twenty-nine. Now I'd turned thirty-six. Why, Robin must be forty!

When he first moved to the coast, he'd called me a lot, telling me this and that. His book had gone through three title changes, he'd had trouble getting some of the relatives of the victims and the murderers to talk to him, and one deal had been discarded in favor of another. He'd gone out to California with his agent, and I was pretty sure they'd been more to each other than agent and client but, somewhere along the way, that relationship had changed. His book, finally titled *Whimsical Murder*, had been finished while he was in California.

I'd been angry with him, even then. I'd always hated the idea of a book about the crimes in Lawrenceton. I'd tried to understand his need to write the book, the conviction he'd had that this was the book that would 'make' his career. Well, it had. Robin's fiction had all been reprinted in matching paperbacks, *Whimsical Murder* had been on the best-seller list for months, and the paperback was poised to be on the stands the week the movie opened.

My eyes fluttered shut, for just a second of sweet oblivion. My anger against Robin slid off my mind, replaced with a more familiar melancholy.

He'd been living in Hollywood, swimming with the sharks, off and on for the past few years. I would seem even more naïve and provincial to Robin now. I'd had a certain amount of awe for him when we met, because he'd been a fairly well-known mystery writer, teaching a writer-in-residence course at a college in Atlanta. I thought of the day I'd gone into the city to meet him for lunch . . . I'd worn that ivory blouse with the green ivy pattern . . .

I could sense sleep approaching now, could feel it stealing over me. I held onto the thought of Robin so I could slide under; if I looked directly at the sleep I needed, it would slip away. Tomorrow I'd check his picture in the magazine again, examine his hair for any signs of gray. I didn't have any yet, but when I spotted some, I'd have Bonita take care of it right away . . .

Perry and Lillian were in the library's employee lounge when I got to work, and their conversation ground to a guilty halt when I appeared. Lillian Schmidt beamed at me with her most insincere smile. Believe me, she's got quite a repertoire. Perry Allison just looked nervous, which was about par for the course for Perry. Perry is about half Lillian's age, bone thin and perpetually jumpy, while Lillian is as round and plain as a ball of coarse yarn. Perry, who's been in and out of mental facilities and drug treatment programs, is now on an even keel as long as he takes his medication. Lillian, with whom I have even less in common, is a self-centered member of a fundamentalist Christian church. These are my best work friends. Am I lucky? I stuffed my purse in one of the bright orange lockers while they covered the silence with a spate of chatter that wouldn't have deceived a reasonably intelligent child.

'Good weather for this time of year,' Lillian told Perry, who nodded his head in an alarming series of jerks.

'Uh, Roe. We just want you to know we didn't know anything about that writer, or the article, or anything.' Perry was trying an ingratiating smile, but it was sliding off the other side of his face. Perry had a difficult life, and he didn't want me mad at him.

'No, hon, we would've told you if we'd known a magazine writer was in the library.' Lillian's eyes were bright with excitement.

For all her gusto in the situation, which was the way she was born, I really believed Lillian. For that matter, I believed Perry, who could be quite devious. Other librarians came and went, but we three had been yoked, somewhat off and on for . . . oh, seven or eight years.

'Okay,' I said mildly, but in such a way as to close the subject. They were probably telling the truth, but *someone* had talked to the writer, Marjory Bolton. I thought I could pin the betrayal on the shoulders of the aide who'd been fired last week for stealing from other employees. I was willing to bet she was already out of town and beyond reach. I suggested this to Perry and Lillian, and they jumped on the idea with enthusiasm.

After a second or two of relaxing small talk, both put on their work faces and went through the door to the patron part of the library.

The employee lounge was a large open room with a couple of tables and matching chairs, a small kitchen, and a large worktable in one corner where we repaired books and prepared new ones to be placed on the shelves. Then there was a half-wall with glass in the top, through which you could see Sam Clerrick's secretary's office. Sam's was firmly walled. His secretary wasn't at her desk, but I could see the lights in Sam's office were on. If he wanted to ask me about the article, he'd call me in. Otherwise, I knew he'd appreciate not being disturbed. Sam was a whiz with the budget, could apply for grants with one hand tied behind his back, and he was an absolutely sound administrator.

But Sam was a dismal failure with people. Painfully aware of the fact, he tended to leave all the personnel interactions he possibly could to his secretary, a position he'd manufactured with some creative money managing. Though the job was only part-time, Patricia Bledsoe had made the most of it.

She was coming in the back door now, dressed, as always, in painstakingly matched and ironed clothes. They weren't expensive clothes, but she had good conservative taste and was an ardent shoe polisher. Patricia – not Pat, or Patsy, or Trish – was somewhere around fifty, with skin the color of a Brach's caramel. Her hair was tamed into a short pageboy – not for Patricia the weaves and beads of more trendy African-Americans. Patricia didn't like nail polish, or dark lipstick, or high heels. Her teenager, Jerome, was not allowed to wear clothing sporting a visible brand name: no Nike, no Fubu, and no Reebok. There was a reason behind everything Patricia Bledsoe did, and if she'd ever acted spontaneously, it had been a long time ago in a galaxy far, far, away.

Not too surprisingly, everyone depended on Patricia, but no one liked her very much. The great exception was Sam Clerrick, whom she guarded as though he was a wealthy industrial magnate.

Patricia said, 'Good morning, Ms Teagarden. How are you today?' Her voice was as crisp as if it'd been in the vegetable drawer overnight.

As always, I fought the terrible impulse to imitate her brisk enunciation. 'I'm fine, thank you, Patricia. Did you see the magazine with the article about the movie?'

Patricia knew what I was talking about since everyone in Lawrenceton had been buzzing about the movie company's arrival for weeks.

'No, is there something new?' She waited politely for my answer, her beige sweater half-off. Today she was wearing a solid yellow camp shirt with a khaki skirt and yellow espadrilles. It was that kind of weather, cool in the morning and evening but still awfully hot during the day; the kind of Southern weather that makes you think summer will never, ever, be over.

'People don't like to talk about it around me,' I said matter-of-factly. 'But as far as I could tell, the only thing that isn't common gossip around here is the name of the female lead, and the strange fact that there was someone in the library who was willing to talk to a reporter about me. I hate the idea that someone would do that without talking to me first,' I told her.

When her reaction came, it certainly wasn't one I'd been expecting.

Patricia's face tensed. She froze for a beat, and then she finished shrugging off the sweater and sat in her rolling chair in front of her computer.

'That does seem strange,' she said, but it seemed to me that she was picking words out of the air at random. The secretary was deeply upset. In fact, she seemed suddenly afraid.

I waited for a second more, but finally I knew that whatever comment Patricia had on news reporters, I wasn't going to hear it.

She did ask me for the name of the magazine. When I told her, she just nodded in thanks and switched on her computer. I'd been dismissed. Her composure was back in place.

Thinking of how perplexing Patricia was, I shrugged and left the staff area to start my working day in my favorite place in the whole world, the library. Any library would have done, but this one was dear to me because the shelves held some of my best friends. While I gathered the books that had come in through the afterhours book drop the night before, I puzzled over Patricia's odd reaction.

It was the first time I'd felt curiosity in months. When I realized how refreshing it felt, I knew that it was good.

Pushing a cart of books through the library, nodding to Mr Harmon (who came in every morning to read the papers), I had a flood of revelation. (What a time and place to review my life, past and future! But I suddenly realized that when I was alone, my life was the thing I worked hardest to avoid considering.)

As I dislodged one of the cart's rollers from a worn spot in the heavy-duty carpeting, I understood – abruptly and very clearly – that my life had not been bad before I married Martin Bartell. Maybe it hadn't been what I expected, or what anyone would have predicted for me, but it had been livable, with enough surprises and bits of happiness to make it worthwhile and, above all, interesting.

Grief was boring. This was a shallow thought about a deep subject, but it was a valid observation.

When my loss had been fresh, passing every hour had been like hiking through a rocky terrain with a monster hiding behind every other boulder. I'd get my bank statement and remember Martin wasn't there to balance our checkbook anymore. I'd cry. I'd go to the grocery store, and remember to get one chicken breast, not two. I'd suffer. There'd be no one in the house to share my day with, no one to take care of. That phase had been jagged, acute, draining, a shock wrapped around every daily occurrence. I missed Martin every day, every hour, sometimes every minute.

But that era had faded, worn thin, and dissipated. Without noting it, I'd entered another phase. The past few months – say, the past six – had been like slogging through a gray swamp. I'd been too exhausted to even open my eyes and look around me. I had routinely forgotten whole conversations, complete transactions, significant events. Nothing had seemed important but my loss.

Right now, just at this split second, I fully comprehended for a fact that my life would go on and there would be things in it I would enjoy.

For the first time, that didn't seem like a betrayal of Martin. Though he'd been the picture of health and his death had been the worst kind of shock, I'd always been aware of the fact that he was fifteen years older than me – that probably, in the natural course of things, I'd have some living to do without him. Events had taken an unnatural course, but the result was the same.

I was getting sniffly, so I concentrated really hard on checking in the books, getting them back to the shelves, returning the cart to its designated spot. Perry and Lillian were always very obviously tactful when my eyes looked red, God bless them, and they were again today.

Chapter Two

I looked up Celia Shaw on the Internet that night. My computer was less than two years old, bought by Martin so he could work at home from time to time. I'd learned to use it, at least enough to send and receive email and to search for information. The games bored me, I'd discovered, and my money was 'handled' by my accountant, so I only turned the machine on a couple of times a week.

Celia was supposed to be twenty-five, I learned, a figure I took with a grain of salt. She'd been born in Wilmington, North Carolina, where her mother had been working in a movie. I hadn't realized there were movie studios in Wilmington but, according to the article, it was quite a moviemaking center. Well, back to Celia. Her mother, Linda Shaw, a middle-aged minor actress, had been so long separated from her husband that the baby's parentage was in doubt. Linda Shaw had left the infant Celia with an aunt and uncle, and fled. Linda resurfaced in California a couple of years later, dead. She'd committed suicide in a motel – barbiturates and a razor combined.

What a tragic beginning.

Though my father had left when I was a teenager, my mother had been a rock. I'd never had aunts and uncles, since both my parents were only children (which may have contributed to their problems), but my mother had a whole network of friends, family connections, and co-workers on whom to call.

Having become more sympathetic to Celia Shaw, whom I'd been quite prepared to dislike, I continued scrolling along. I examined pictures of Celia in various movies I'd never seen. I paused to check out a dress Celia had worn to the Emmy Awards. Hmmm. I was more conservative sartorially than I'd realized.

I peered at the picture. Had she had to glue that bit into place? How had she planned to cope if she'd dropped her purse? Of course, someone would've picked it up for her gladly; Celia Shaw would never have to perform any little service for herself, at least not for the next ten years. Still, what if she'd forgotten her posture and slumped a little . . .

Well, she had nerve, anyway. I'd give her that.

According to her bio, Celia Shaw had won escalating parts in five minor films and two major television shows. However, *Whimsical Death*, a two-part made-for-TV movie, would constitute her first leading role. Chip Brodnax was taking the role of Robin. His face was familiar to me, but I couldn't remember where I'd seen him. I didn't watch a lot of television, but I was sure I'd noticed him in something before.

The same picture of Celia Shaw that had been in the magazine was on the website, the one of her with Robin at a party. There was another shot of Celia holding her Emmy. She was beautiful, no doubt about it. And even if her given age of twenty-five was literally less than the truth, there was no doubt in my mind that Celia Shaw was several years younger than me.

As I closed down the computer and went upstairs for my bath, I wondered why I'd bothered to search out this information. I told myself it was because she was going to play me – or someone at least as close to me as the movie could go, since I'd refused permission for a character to have my name. Surely it wasn't too surprising that I'd have an interest in the woman who was going to represent me?

I attended Evening Prayer that Wednesday night. This was by no means my normal schedule, I'm sorry to say. St Stephen's saw me on Sunday mornings, but that was the limit of my church attendance, and I'd dodged the altar guild, the vestry, and the annual Christmas bazaar committee with amazing agility. (I was beginning to have a slightly guilty feeling, as though I watched PBS every night yet didn't send in a dime at pledge time.) On this balmy evening, I scooted into an empty pew close to the back of the small church and let all my worries go while I moved through the ritual that meant so much to me.

As I was about to shake Father Aubrey Scott's hand while I was going out the door, he said, 'Could you stay for a minute? I'd like to have a few words.'

'Sure,' I said. I'd always been fond of Aubrey. In fact, I'd dated him for many months. Then I'd met Martin and he'd met Emily, and we'd parted amiably. The warmth of a pleasant companionship remained. I rummaged through my mind for any recent hot topics in the congregation that he'd need to discuss with me, but I couldn't come up with a one.

With a sense of mild expectation, I settled on a bench in the quiet churchyard while the other congregants got in their cars and switched on their headlights in the gathering dusk. Soon we'd have the time change. We'd be leaving in the full dark. Through the lighted windows I could see Aubrey's wife, Emily, blond and suburban, moving around the church. She was raising kneelers that had been left down, picking up programs discarded in the pews, and turning out lights. Elizabeth, Emily's daughter by her deceased first husband, hadn't been in church that night. She'd probably used homework to wriggle out of coming; Elizabeth, now ten, was quite a handful. But Aubrey never regretted adopting Elizabeth; he doted on her.

Having divested himself of his robe, Aubrey came to sit beside me in the half-darkness. Aubrey was a lot grayer than he'd been when he'd first come to Lawrenceton to take the helm of St Stephen's. Was Aubrey thirty-nine? Or closer to forty-two? I caught myself frowning: I was thinking about age far too often these days.

'I have something I need to ask you,' Aubrey said, sounding very grave.

'Ask ahead,' I told him. From the open church door came a *thwack!* as Emily raised the fourth kneeler from the back on the left, which was a little noisier than the others.

'Would it offend you if the movie company filmed some scenes here at the church?' he asked.

Whatever I'd expected, it wasn't this request. I was glad of the darkness, since I had no idea what my face looked like. I couldn't think of what to say.

'The vestry met with the film company representative last night. The thing is,' he continued, after a pause to offer me a chance to comment, 'they're offering enough in compensation to get a new roof put on St Stephen's – both the parish hall and the church. But if you have the slightest objection, we'll forego the money. It won't be worth it. You're one of ours. The vote on that was unanimous.'

So many comments came to my lips that I compressed them together to lock the words inside. There was only one answer I could possibly give. 'Of course,' I said. 'For a new roof, you have to say yes.' I knew my voice was much cooler than I wanted it to be, and I knew my words weren't exactly enthusiastic or even very civil, but that was the best I could do.

'You don't sound okay about it,' Aubrey said after a hesitation. 'You sound like you want me to go play in traffic.'

I smiled a little, a very little, but he couldn't see that.

'St Stephen's is beautiful. I'm not surprised they'd like to use it as a set. Nothing will be changed?'

'He promised not. He said everything would look just the same or better, since the film company will paint the sign on the corner for us.'

'Then you'd better do it.' It crossed my mind that I could pay for the new church roof, all by myself, and then the film company could go whistle. But that would draw even more attention to me, and that was the one thing I didn't want. I made sure to exchange another comment or two with Aubrey, so he wouldn't think I was leaving angry. He'd given me a choice and I'd picked, so I couldn't take the result of my decision out on him.

By the time Emily locked the door of the church, I was on my way to my car.

Madeleine was waiting at the kitchen door when I got home. Madeleine, golden and fat and increasingly slow, was the living part of the legacy an old friend had left me. Jane had left me the cat and a pot of money. Guess which I liked best? Madeleine was known and feared by every vet in the Lawrenceton area. Fortunately, except for the effects of old age, the cat had always been healthy. Her annual checkups were traumatic for everyone involved. Though I'd grown up without pets, thanks to a mother who thought having animal hair in your house was comparable to having lice, Madeleine and I had coexisted in reasonable harmony for several years now. I fed her, brushed her in the spring and summer, and scratched behind her ears. She ate the food, enjoyed the brushing, purred when I scratched her, and otherwise ignored me. It worked for us.

I watched the huge old cat launch into her kitty chow with gusto. When that palled, I wandered across the hall into the den, admiring the way the wooden floors gleamed and the books marched in even rows in the built-in bookcases in the hall. The answering machine light was blinking by my telephone and for a minute or two I thought about checking my messages.

Then I decided it didn't matter what other people wanted.

Smiling a little, I hiked up the stairs, spent some time in the bathroom on my minimal grooming ritual, and climbed into my high four-poster. I had lots of pillows, a comfortable bed, and a good book.

Martin hadn't really liked my reading in bed. To Martin, a bed was for sleeping in or making love on, not for reading or lolling of any kind. For the most part, I'd read downstairs in the den while we were married. Now, this was one of the moments of the day to which I actually looked forward; and if it was raining outside or cold, or both, and I could swathe myself in blankets, so much the better. The night was mild outside my windows this evening, but as I pulled up the clean sheet I came as close as I could, these days, to being happy. I was reading a new C. J. Songer, too, an added bonus.

Just when I was getting drowsy, the phone rang. I leaned forward to check my caller-ID device. I picked up the phone, already smiling.

Angel said, 'I got a question to ask you.'

Angel and Shelby Youngblood were both very direct, Angel more so than her husband. Shelby, a Vietnam vet and one of the toughest men I'd ever met, had learned to approach certain topics sideways rather than straight on, something I didn't think would ever occur to Angel. Their little girl Joan was going to have to be one sturdy kid. Already, at nearly a year old, Joan seemed more independent than most babies her age. At least Angel told me so.

'Shoot,' I told her.

'You mind if I work this movie? I got a call from a guy who asked if I wanted to do stunts.'

Everyone, *everyone*, wanted to work for the damn movie. I had a moment's flash of intense resentment, an irrational conviction that all the people of Lawrenceton should shun the movie and the moviemakers, not rent or sell to them, not be employed by them, and all for my sake, because I didn't want this film made.

'Of course you ought to,' I said calmly. 'I know it's been years since you got any stunt work, and you must miss it.'

'Thanks,' Angel said. She was so direct herself that it seldom occurred to her that people didn't exactly mean what they said. 'If you're sure. We're trying to save up for a swimming pool for Joan.'

'Above ground?'

'Nope, in-ground. So we got a ways to go.'

I silently exhaled. 'Well, you better get to it. Bye, Angel.'

'See you soon, Roe.'

I thought it was the perfect cap to a perfect day. *What could happen tomorrow*, I asked myself rhetorically, *that would make it any worse than today?*

I should have known better than to ask myself any such a thing.

Chapter Three

I didn't have to work that Thursday, so I didn't get up until about seven-thirty. Catherine Quick, the maid, was supposed to be coming in that afternoon, so I didn't have to make my bed; she'd be changing the sheets. I trotted down the stairs to put on the coffeepot, and I popped an English muffin in the toaster before I went to the living room at the front of the house to look out. Though the air was chilly that morning, making me glad I'd pulled on jeans and a sweater before I came downstairs, it was going to warm up and be a beautiful day. The air was crystal clear, the sky so blue it almost sparkled. I told myself I wouldn't worry that day, wouldn't think about the movie at all. Maybe I would call Sally Allison to see if she could have lunch with me. Since she was a reporter, Sally always knew what was going on in Lawrenceton.

The kitchen had two doors, the back one opening onto our patio, and the side one opening under the covered walkway leading to the garage. Madeleine's cat flap was in the patio door, and she made an entrance just about this time every morning, tired from her night's adventures and ready to eat her kibble. But this morning, though I filled her bowl and renewed her water, she didn't show. Maybe I'd see her when I went down the long driveway to fetch my newspaper.

I opened the side door and made a noise somewhere between a gasp and a shriek. The young man sitting on the steps jumped up, dumping Madeleine off his lap in the process.

'Hello, Aurora,' he said, and in that moment I recognized him.

'Hello, Barrett,' I said, trying hard not to sound as anxious and angry as I felt. It was all I could do not to blurt out, 'What do you want?' At six feet, Barrett was tall enough to cow me, and of course he was fit, since looking good was part of his stock in trade. His hair was a new color, a dark blond, and he was wearing glasses he didn't need.

It's an accurate measure of our relationship that I wondered, just in a flash, if Barrett had come disguised so no one would recognize him in the police lineup after my body was discovered.

'I didn't know you were in Lawrenceton,' I said, my voice much more shaky than I liked.

'Oh, yes. And I came to see you first thing, Step-mom.'

So it was going to be that way.

As if it had ever been any other way.

'Barrett, what are you doing here?' I was not stable enough emotionally to put up with all this parrying.

'Just wanted to come check in on you, see how you were enjoying my dad's money,' he said casually. The actor. I wondered how often he'd rehearsed tossing that line over to me.

I sighed. I considered several responses, most based on my new policy of rudeness, but a sudden deep exhaustion quenched anything I might have said.

'Frankly, Barrett, I don't enjoy much of anything.' My voice was as weary as I felt. It was time to speak plainly, and end this if it was possible. I stepped back and said, 'Come in, if you have to, and say whatever you have to say. I'm sorry we misunderstood each other so badly after your father died. I just wasn't at my most intelligent or sensitive.'

Barrett's face was already arranged to say something witty and cruel. But there was a subtle shift in his expression as he listened. He nearly relented, but at the last second his grievance settled back on his shoulders like a cape. 'Did your lawyer tell you to say that?' he sneered.

I could think of no response. 'Do you want some coffee? Have you had breakfast yet?' When in doubt, fall back on being a lady, as my mother had always advised me – though truly, it would feel better to kick Barrett in the butt.

Once again, Mother was proved right. Barrett had no idea how to pose himself. 'I'd like a cup of coffee,' he said after an appreciable pause. 'I take it black.' He looked around the kitchen with almost palpable surprise. What had he expected – marble countertops and a resident chef? It was just an ordinary kitchen. I got another cup from the cabinet and buttered my English muffin, which had popped up.

'So, what are you doing here in Lawrenceton?' I asked. 'I guess you came to visit your dad's grave? I got the headstone in about four months ago. It looks real nice.' I took a deep breath, trying unsuccessfully to repress the tears that welled up. I grabbed a tissue and blotted my eyes. I glanced over at my stepson as I put his coffee on the table, to surprise a look of shame on his face.

'You didn't even think of going out to the cemetery,' I said out loud. I was truly stunned.

'He's not really there,' Barrett said, scrambling for a defense. He sat down at the table and looked sullen.

'No, of course not,' I said numbly. I put half my muffin in front of Barrett. 'And I know I shouldn't have spent so much time out there at first, but somehow you just want to be close . . . I know that's stupid.' I shook my head. I could feel the trembles and weepies looming, like unpleasant relatives due for a visit.

Barrett was staring at me like he'd never seen me before. He took a sip of his coffee. 'You've lost weight,' he said at last.

I shrugged. 'Maybe a little.' It was my turn to drink some coffee. My eyes ached with tears. But this, too, would pass. 'I suppose your cheque got to you all right?' Martin's will had finally been probated; of course, money was at the root of Barrett's rancor.

'Yes,' he said.

The silence dragged uncomfortably. 'I'm sorry, again, about the – about the misunderstanding after Martin died.'

'No,' said Barrett sharply. 'Let's not talk about that.'

Which was fine with me. In the turmoil after Martin's death, I had simply forgotten that Martin's adult son had been in the habit of receiving handouts from Martin when acting jobs proved few and far between. For one thing, the largesse had been irregular; Martin had always thought it would be an insult to give Barrett a steady allowance, as though Barrett were still a child. So he waited until Barrett called and hinted that he needed a 'loan', and then Martin would mail a cheque. Once I'd become aware of this practice, I'd bitten my tongue to prevent myself commenting.

Most importantly, it was none of my business. I had my own money, and Martin's cheques to Barrett had not deprived me of anything at all. But in my opinion, if Martin thought it right to support an adult son, he should have made it a regular arrangement, so Barrett wouldn't have to ask.

My lips were sealed even more tightly because Barrett loathed me and always had. He'd dodged coming to our wedding, at family functions he never addressed me directly if he could avoid it, he'd only visited Lawrenceton when I was out of town, and he'd made it insultingly clear (out of his dad's hearing) that he thought I was marrying Martin for his money.

So in the months immediately after my husband's funeral, Barrett's financial state had been the last thing on my mind. But one night Barrett had called me, when he'd held out as long as he could for his legacy. Probate often takes much longer than it has any right to, and in the case of Martin's estate, which was a little complicated because of his diverse holdings – real estate, stock, insurance payments, and the retirement fund of Pan-Am Agra – well, settling Martin's affairs was a drawn-out process. That night, Barrett had stiffly demanded I mail him the money he was accustomed to getting.

I hadn't reacted well. I could tell how difficult it was for Barrett to call, but in my view, he should have been man enough to manage on his own rather than phone me. At the same time, I admit I was aware that Barrett must truly have his back to the wall financially to be driven to such a measure. But I was just too mired in my personal hell to care about Barrett's problems. He could have helped me in many ways when Martin had died – just being civil would have been a good way to start – and he had chosen not to do so. Now, I chose not to help him. I'd told him so, frankly and at length, being unable to think beyond the moment and see this from any other angle than the one in front of my face.

The next day I'd woken up sorry, but not because I hadn't

solved Barrett's financial problems. I'd been sorry because Martin had loved Barrett, and would have wanted me to send the money – no matter what it said about Barrett that he'd even asked me for it. So without calling or writing a note to enclose, I'd FedExed Barrett a cheque – my own money – for what he'd needed.

I'd never heard a word from him after that, until this moment. I'd sent him his share of Martin's estate when it had all been settled. I had not deducted what I'd already given him. That would have been businesslike, but he would have taken it as petty. I just didn't want to struggle with Barrett any more.

So here we were, not talking about the incident that lay between us, as big and smelly as a dead fish.

I cleared my throat and asked after his mother and aunt. Cindy's florist shop was doing well, Barrett said. In fact, Cindy and her partner were expanding the shop to include gifts and home-decorating items. 'They took out a loan,' Barrett made a point of telling me, I guess so I'd realize he couldn't have turned to his mother for money. 'She and Dennis plan to get married.'

'I'm glad for them,' I said, not caring one little bit.

'Aunt Barby has been keeping Regina's baby for a week or two, while Regina and her husband are on vacation in New York.'

While I was indifferent about Cindy, I actively disliked Martin's sister Barby and her daughter Regina, who was on her second marriage. I was confident that Regina would someday be on her fourth. Probably she would have had a few more babies along the way.

'Why didn't you and Dad have any children?' Barrett asked me. The question came from out of the blue and lodged in my heart.

'I can't have children,' I said. 'We talked about it a little, before we found out that I had some fertility problems. I sure wanted a baby, and sometimes he did too. But he was a little wary of starting a new family at his age.' I saw Martin, so clearly, leaning over Regina's baby when I'd placed him beside Martin on our bed. Tears trickled down my cheeks. I lowered my face and wiped it with a napkin. 'Can I get you some more coffee?' I asked politely.

'No, thank you. I need to be getting back.' Barrett and I both stood up. He scrabbled through his pockets for the car keys, and looked uncertain, not a normal Barrett state of mind.

He looked as though he were going to make some kind of pronouncement, but in the end, all he said was, 'Thanks for the coffee.' It wasn't until I watched his car turn onto the county road that I realized he'd never told me why he was in Lawrenceton.

It didn't take long for the other shoe to drop. While I was upstairs covering up the circles under my eyes and brushing my hair, it suddenly occurred to me that Barrett was in town because he had a part in the movie. I couldn't imagine why I hadn't made the connection earlier. He would be a natural choice for the cast, as the stepson of one of the real-life figures in our local drama. He'd even visited Lawrenceton before, when I'd been gone with my mother to a real estate convention in Orlando.

I collapsed ungracefully on the delicate peach-colored chair in the corner of the bedroom and further considered this likelihood. Barrett was an up-and-coming actor, whose longest running part had been on a popular soap. I think he played a seductive chauffeur. Since I never watch daytime television, I'd never seen him in it – which, now that I came to examine my conduct, was just as much stubbornness as his refusing to come to our wedding – but several women who knew of our connection had told me how good he was. They'd had their tongues hanging out as they said it, too.

I wondered what role Barrett would have. I wondered, for the first time, what the script was like; how close the movie would come to the reality.

I wished I hadn't hung up on Robin Crusoe.

Moved by an impulse I didn't even want to analyze, I decided to go shopping that morning. My friend Amina Day's mother owned a women's clothing store called Great Day. If I bought anything in Lawrenceton, rather than going to my favorite store in Atlanta, I bought it at Great Day. To my pleasure, Mrs Day had a younger partner now, and the selection had really improved as a result.

I had a closet full of good clothes already, but I needed something new, some voice deep within me advised. My coloring – brown hair, brown eyes, fair complexion – was pretty neutral, so my color field was wide open. As Barrett had noticed, I'd lost weight I'd never regained when Martin died, so my involuntarily smaller size was another excuse for shopping.

As I got out of my car at the strip mall that housed Great Day, a cluster of people emerged from the Crafts Consortium next door. Homemade quilts, candles, and all kinds of 'country' stuff formed the bulk of the store's goods, and crowds were not something I'd ever seen there. The center of the group seemed to be a short, thin, very young woman with artistically disheveled blond hair who was wearing the highest heels I'd ever seen on a woman who wasn't standing on a street corner. And these high heels were worn with jeans, the tightest jeans I'd ever seen. No, wait; Nadine Gortner had worn some just as tight to one of the Pan-Am Agra picnics, and her zipper had popped.

As if the heels and jeans weren't enough to mark her out, this woman had lips outlined in the darkest possible shade of red while the lipstick she'd filled in with was a creamy pink. She looked like a bee had been at her.

The people accompanying this creature were not as eye-popping, which was a relief. An older, grizzled man who might be from almost anywhere was carrying a bag (which I had to believe belonged to The Creature). A slightly less ornate woman in a modified version of The Creature's outfit was scrabbling in her outsize purse with fingernails like a Chinese emperor's. She pulled out some car keys, and immediately reached out to steady her flamboyant friend, who had stumbled on the irregular surface of the parking lot. No wonder, in those heels.

After absorbing this trio in a comprehensive glance, I passed them with my eyes straight forward. That was why I noticed Miss Joe Nell standing in the glass door of Great Day making an elaborate face at me, jabbing her finger vehemently in the direction of the little group. It was hard to keep a steady course forward, since Amina's mom was doing her best to get me to stop, turn, and stare.

'That was them!' she said excitedly, as soon as I came through the door. Miss Joe Nell and her partner, Mignon Derby, were flushed and practically panting.

'Them?' I said, trying not to sound as irritated as I felt.

'The movie people!' Without ever thinking that I might not be delighted to have come in close proximity with some 'movie people', the two women began speaking all at once. Miss Joe Nell and Mignon (who, at twenty-eight, had the kind of skin most women only dream of) were extremely revved up about the trio's just-concluded visit to Great Day, where the Starlet Lite (as opposed to the spike-heeled Full Starlet) had bought a white linen shell.

'I don't know what Celia Shaw bought at Crafts Consortium,' Mignon babbled. 'I'm gonna go call Teal and find out!'

So that had been Robin's girlfriend, at least according to the magazine article. I was almost proud for despising her before I had known. Then I was angry with myself for my lack of charity. This was not my day to be pleased with the way I conducted my life.

I am not exactly poker-faced, so Miss Joe Nell was picking up on my lack of enthusiasm.

'Well, that was fun, but we know who's going to be around when the movie people are gone,' she said, smiling. 'What can I show you today, Roe?'

Since I didn't know what I wanted, I felt even grumpier. I was rapidly getting to be the town killjoy. At that moment, I was sure I was the only person in Sparling County who wished everyone associated with the movie project would fall into a big hole.

I calmed down as I shopped, the familiar ritual and the renewed attentiveness of Mignon and Miss Joe Nell combining to make me feel once again that I had a legitimate place in the world.

Hmmm. Was I just full of sour grapes at not being Top Dog? Was I way too used to having people treat me with a little deference and a little extra attention because I was well-heeled and a widow?

Just could be.

A life unexamined is not a life lived, I reminded myself, and resolved to be a little less stuffy and a lot less grudging about the excitement the filmmaking was bringing to Lawrenceton. Maybe, despite my legitimate gripes about the movie's being made at all, what I was really doing was . . . pouting. Hmmm, indeed.

I left with a nice bulky bag and lots of news about Amina, since Miss Joe Nell and her husband were just back from a trip to Dallas to see Hugh, Amina, and their two-year-old, Megan, who was being taught to call me Aunt Roe.

Spending money always makes me feel better, so I drove to my lunch engagement with Sally Allison with a lighter heart. Sally was waiting in the foyer of the restaurant, wearing her usual solid colors – today she sported a bronze silk blouse under a tan pants suit – and groping in her huge shoulder bag. She pulled out a phone and dialed while I watched. Holding up a finger to let me know she'd just be a minute, Sally told her adult son Perry to be sure to take his clothes by the cleaners that day. I raised my eyebrows, and Sally had the self-awareness to look a little embarrassed.

'Once a mother, always a mother,' she said after she'd hung up.

'Let's get in line, unless you want to call someone else?'

'No, I'll turn it off during lunch,' she said bravely, and pressed a button. 'When are you going to join the twenty-first century?'

'I have a cell phone. I just don't turn it on unless I want to call someone.'

'But . . . but . . . it's to use!'

'Not if I don't want to,' I said.

Sally clearly loved her cell phone and, since she was a reporter, I could see that it would be a valuable tool for her. But to me, it was just a nuisance. I got too many phone calls as it was, without arranging for a way to get more.

Sally told me all about Perry's new girlfriend as we moved down the line. I got my tray from the stack, and my silverware, and ordered ice tea and beef tips over rice. I got my number and looked for a free table while Sally ordered. Beef 'N More seemed quite crowded, and I wondered a little at that – but it was a popular place, especially with the noon business crowd.

'See, these are movie people,' Sally hissed as she unloaded her tray and put her receipt faceup where the waitress could spot it when she brought our food. 'Isn't this something?'

Even Sally, the toughest woman I knew, was dizzy with excitement about the damn movie. I remembered my good resolutions, and I managed not to look sour.

'Where are they all staying?'

'The Ramada out by the interstate, most of them,' Sally said after she put down her little packet of sweetener and stirred the powder vigorously into her tea. 'That Celia Shaw has the Honeymoon Suite. But the director – Joel Park Brooks – is renting Pinky Zelman's house. I hope Pinky's asking a lot of money, because I bet it won't be in any great shape when he moves out.' Sally looked a little pleased, as if the prospect of writing a story about the director's damage to Dr Pincus Zelman's house was a treat Sally had in store.

Clearly, Sally was seeing stories, stories just lining up to be written. What a bonanza this was going to be for the *Sentinel*.

'Are you going to watch them filming?' I asked.

'Every chance I get. And they've hired me as a consultant.' Sally flushed with pride.

'That makes sense. You did the best series of stories on the murders, after all.' Those stories had nearly bumped Sally up to a bigger paper in a bigger city, but somehow it just hadn't happened. Now, Sally was in her late forties, and she no longer expected that someday she'd leave Lawrenceton, as far as I could tell.

'Thanks, Roe.' Sally looked pensive for a moment, her square, handsome face crumpling around the eyes and mouth. 'At least,' she said, less cheerfully, 'now I can finally finish paying all Perry's hospital bills.'

'That's great.' For the last few years, Perry had been doing very well, but I knew the bills for his treatment had been staggering.

Sally had been whittling away at this debt. 'Can we have a bill-burning, or some kind of celebration?'

'I'd love it, but it would make Perry feel bad,' she said regretfully. 'He hates to be reminded of the cost of all that help I gave him. As if I grudged it. It was worth every penny.'

'Did Perry pay for any of it?' I regretted the question as soon as it left my lips.

'No, it was my bill, and I paid it,' Sally said, after a moment's hesitation. 'And don't you say one word about it, Aurora. Perry's a young man; he doesn't need any burdens. He needed to put all his resources into the effort of getting well and staying well. And getting married!'

I clamped my mouth shut. After a moment, I asked Sally how her chef salad was.

And that was the way it went the rest of the meal. We stayed superficial.

In addition to Catherine's old car, there was a black Taurus parked in my driveway. The rental company must specialize in Tauruses. Tauri? Sitting on its gleaming hood was Robin Crusoe.

I got out of my car slowly, uncertain about how I felt about seeing Robin again after all these years. I'd forgotten how tall he was, at least six three. And he'd filled out quite a bit. I remembered Robin as being weedy thin when he'd lived in my mother's townhouse. His hair was as bright a red, and his mouth as quirky, and his nose was the same sharp beak. He was wearing dark glasses, which he whipped off and stuck in his pocket as I approached. He stood – and stood, and stood. I put the Great Day bag on the ground, and kept walking toward him, and he held out his arms. I walked right into them. I wrapped my own around him.

Robin said, 'I didn't know if you'd throw something at me or not.'

'It was a toss-up,' I admitted. I leaned back to look up at his face. 'I've been brooding and pouting.'

He smiled down at me, and I smiled back. It was hard to resist smiling at Robin.

'How was LA?' I asked.

Robin's mobile face darkened and all of a sudden he seemed ten years older. 'Unbelievable,' he said. 'I learned a lot. The thing is, I didn't want to know most of what I learned.'

'You'll have to tell me all about it.' I recalled his changed circumstances, his relationship with Celia Shaw. 'If you have any free time, that is.' I released him and stepped back.

'Will you show me your house?'

'Yes.' I unlocked the door and punched in the security code. I half-expected Robin to say something about the security system, but he must have gotten accustomed to them while he lived on the West Coast.

'Catherine!' I called. 'I'm here with a friend.'

'Hey, Roe,' she called from upstairs. 'I'm just about done.'

Robin looked at the bright kitchen, done in cream with orange touches, and went into the hall, admiring the built-in bookcases and the hardwood floors. The den, which was warm in dark blue and deep red, drew a compliment, and the dining room and living room got a nod. There was one smallish bedroom downstairs, and he glanced in its door.

'What's upstairs?' he asked.

'Two bedrooms and a small room Martin kept his workout stuff in,' I said.

'I'm sorry, Roe,' Robin said.

I kept my gaze averted. 'Thanks,' I said briefly. 'Would you like to see the patio? We added it on after we moved in, and I wonder sometimes if it wasn't a mistake.'

As I was about to open the kitchen door, the cat flap vibrated and Madeleine wriggled through. 'I've never seen that fat a cat,' Robin said, clearly impressed. 'Is this Madeleine?'

'The one and only.' I'd inherited Madeleine after Robin left Lawrenceton, but I remembered writing him about the big orange cat.

The patio forgotten, Robin bent to hold out his hand to

Madeline. She glared at him after she sniffed it. Pointedly, she turned her back to him and waddled off to her food bowl. It was empty, and she sat in front of it with the air of someone who could wait all day. She would, too. I got out her kibble and filled her bowl. When food was in front of her Madeleine ignored the rest of the world, and she dove in as eagerly as usual.

Catherine came downstairs, her feet heavy on the treads. Catherine was the most consistent 'help' I'd ever had. Mostly women came to work for me, showed up on time at first, and then drifted on to some other job. Sometimes they'd tell me; sometimes they just wouldn't show up. Cleaning houses is not for everyone. It's not high-paying, at least in Lawrenceton, and some people seem to feel it's degrading. So I was grateful for Catherine's consistency, and I tried hard to be a good employer.

'I'm fixing to leave,' she said, after I'd introduced her to Robin. 'You need to get some more Clorox and some more Bounce sheets. I put it on the list on the refrigerator.'

'Thanks, Catherine,' I said.

'See you next time.'

'Okay.'

We were never going to be best friends, but at least our exchanges were always civil. After she'd left, I poured some iced tea for Robin and we went into the study, den, downstairs room – I'd called it all three. There was a red leather couch with its back to the window. Robin settled on that, so he'd have plenty of room for his long legs. I had a low, comfortable armchair that allowed my feet to sit firmly on the floor. We looked at each other a little anxiously, not knowing what to say next.

'Are you very unhappy about the movie?' he asked abruptly.

'I was. I'm still not exactly thrilled.' I took a deep breath, exhaled. I was making an effort to be honest, with a little tact thrown in. 'But the town is very excited, and the money will be good for its economy.'

Robin nodded, and seemed to want to change the subject. He started playing 'How is?' and we went down a list of names rapidly. It was an unpleasant surprise to me to find how long it had been since I'd seen some of the people Robin asked about. There seemed no excuse for it in a town the size of Lawrenceton.

'Tell me about your husband,' Robin said out of the blue.

I sat and stared at my hands for a minute. 'Martin was . . . a senior executive at Pan-Am Agra,' I said carefully. 'He was older than me by almost fifteen years. He was a Vietnam vet. He was very . . . dynamic. He had done some shady things in his life. He was always looking for that to come back at him.' He loved me deeply. He was fantastic in bed. He was extremely competitive with other men. He was domineering even when he didn't think he was being so. He really listened to me. He broke my heart. I loved him very much, though our marriage had loose edges and rough patches. All this.

'I know you must have some hard times,' Robin said quietly. 'My mother lost my dad earlier this year, and she's been struggling.'

I nodded. Hard times, indeed. 'I'm sorry about your dad,' I told him, and for a minute we sat in silence.

'Are you going to marry the actress?' I asked brightly, trying to get us back on a less dangerous track. 'I saw you-all's picture in the magazine.'

'You can't believe the stories about me and Celia,' he said. 'At one time they had some truth to them, but not any more. We're just barely friends, now.'

I raised my eyebrows at him, making a skeptical face.

He grinned. 'No, really. She's full of ambition, she's really young, and she's got different priorities. Since she won the Emmy, in fact . . . well, the only reason she's doing this project is because she'd signed on for it prior to her win.' He looked like a different man when he said this, older and harder.

I gave his disenchantment a moment of respectful silence. Then I asked, 'So, what did you want from this visit to me?' He must want something, I was sure.

He paid me the compliment of not protesting he'd just wanted to see me again. 'I want you to come to the set, at least once. I want you to see this being filmed, read the script.'

'Why? Why on earth would you want that?'

'Because I want you . . . to approve. At least, not to hate it so much.'

'Does it really matter to you?'

'Yes.' Robin was dead serious.

For the life of me, I couldn't figure out why my approval made any difference at all. But what did I have to lose? I wasn't scheduled to work tomorrow until late afternoon.

'Okay, Robin. I'll come tomorrow to observe for a little while.'

'Great,' he said, brightening. 'I'll set it up.'

Chapter Four

You would've thought the circus had come to town. It was the biggest mess I'd ever seen, but I was pretty sure that was because I didn't understand what was happening. There were people everywhere, standing in clusters talking seriously or buzzing busily around the area that had been delineated with sawhorses. A sizeable number of the cast and crew found time to stop by a table laden with bagels and fruit and coffee, a table supervised by a stout, auburn-haired young woman in a white uniform with 'Molly's Moveable Feasts' embroidered on the chest.

It appeared that Robin himself was barely tolerated on the set, which surprised me. No one seemed pleased to see him or gave him more than a nod. Writing fame was no guarantee of special treatment here.

'How come they're not happy to have you on the spot?' I asked.

'Writers are just a pain on the set,' he explained. He didn't seem at all ruffled or surprised by the indifference shown him. I couldn't believe that Robin was being herded into a corner and practically treated as if he were invisible. To me, writers were the most important people around. I noticed that I was invisible by extension, and that was fine with me.

I only dared talk to Robin in whispers. I tried to figure out what I was seeing, and after a while I asked him to interpret the scene for me.

'That's the director,' he said in a low voice, nodding toward a tall, gawky man with five earrings on one ear, a shaved head, and an irritating black goatee. He was wearing an absolutely conventional oxford-cloth shirt and khakis, not only clean and pressed, but also starched. Somehow, with the shaved head and goatee, the shirt and khakis looked odder than a Limp Bizkit tee shirt and cutoffs would have. 'His name is Joel Park Brooks, and he's smart as hell. That's his assistant, Mark Chesney, to his right.' Mark Chesney was as sunny as Joel Park Brooks was grim, and he was wearing exactly the same kind of clothes. It just didn't look like a costume on Mark Chesney.

'Who's that?' I indicated the graying, rough-looking man I'd seen with Starlets One and Two yesterday.

'That's the head cameraman, Will Weir. He's worked everywhere,' Robin said admiringly. 'He's easy to work with, they say, and very good.'

'Is that Celia?' Starlet One had come out of a trailer and was striding toward the churchyard. She was recognizable only by her walk, as far as I was concerned. Her hair was tame, her makeup looked very moderate, her clothes were definitely more modest than yesterday's outfit. As I watched, she stumbled on something on the sidewalk, and righted herself with a little jerk. Joel Park Brooks didn't seem to notice, but the cameraman – Will Weir, I reminded myself – frowned as he observed the misstep.

'Yes,' Robin said, and he didn't sound glad, or unhappy – any reaction I would have expected from someone seeing the woman he'd dated until fairly recently. He sounded – worried, concerned. Odd. After all, anyone can stumble. I am no graceful swan myself.

Celia hadn't closed the door to her trailer, which was a sort of queenlike omission. I saw the wind blow in and ruffle the pile of papers on the floor, so I stepped closer to take care of the door; and, also, just to satisfy my curiosity. I saw a couch inside the tiny room, a little table sitting by that, and on top of a pile of what seemed to be a manuscript and some library books was an Emmy . . . the real, bonafide statue. I wondered if Celia would let me hold it, because surely I'd never in my life set eyes on one again. But Robin was looking at me strangely, so I swung the door closed.

Robin pointed out the producer, a wild-haired burly man dressed all in black. 'Jessie Bruckner. He's going to be catching an afternoon plane back to LA,' Robin told me. I had heard of Jessie Bruckner, so I was properly impressed. People seemed to be moving around more purposefully now, and Joel Park Brooks was shouting directions at top speed, so apparently something was about to happen. I was so engrossed in the scene around me that I didn't register my stepson's presence for a while, but then I noticed him waiting by the door of the church, dressed in a conservative suit and tie. He was wearing faux glasses and carrying a Bible. In character, I assumed.

'Who's Barrett playing?'

'Bankston.' Robin looked down at me to see if I thought that was funny, and I managed a smile. Of course, the real Bankston Waites had never worn glasses, or carried a Bible, as far as I could remember. He had gone to church, but not this one. Oh well, I guessed accuracy mattered only so much.

Fleetingly, I thought of how much Martin would have relished his son working in Lawrenceton. Then I thought of how happy it would make me if I never had to speak to Barrett again.

When I turned my attention back to what was happening around me, I could see that the actual area the cameras were trained on held no one but actors. Everyone seemed to be at his or her workstation. An amazing amount of food had vanished from the service table, and the stout young woman in white was cleaning away the remnants. She smiled and waved at Robin as he glanced her way.

Silence reigned. As two well-dressed extras took their places on the sidewalk facing away from the church door, I glanced up at Robin to see him absorbed in the scene before me. He draped a long arm around my shoulders as if that were automatic. I stood stiff and frozen, my own arms crossed across my ribs, trying not to be ridiculously self-conscious about a casual gesture.

At the director's signal, the scene began. It appeared this was supposed to be a Sunday morning, right after church was over. A silver-haired man in priest's robes was standing to the right of the open door, shaking hands as 'parishioners' came out. So warm and caring did he look, so saintly was his bearing, that he practically reeked of goodness. The couple already in the churchyard stepped briskly past the cameras. One or two other people came down the church steps. Then one of the 'churchgoers' swatted at a wasp, and Joel Park Brooks called the action to a halt.

'Again, without the swatting!' he called, and the actors obediently went back into the church. The couple resumed their place on the sidewalk. The priest's aura of Godliness wavered and then snapped back into place as the action began again.

This time, Celia Shaw (the 'me' composite) and Chip Brodnax (I gathered he was the Robin character) made it out of the church. They were positioned in the foreground, while the church emptied behind them.

'I hope you enjoy your stay in our little town,' Celia told Chip. Her accent was genetically southern. I rolled my eyes, all to myself. Why can't Hollywood comprehend that there are regional accents in the south, besides Cajun? 'Lawrenceton's always been so quiet, so safe,' she drawled.

'This is a fantastic town,' Chip said enthusiastically, staring down at Celia with transparent admiration. 'And I know I'm gonna love living here. What do you do for excitement?'

'Why don't you come to a meeting of our club tonight?' Celia said, smiling with delight at her own inspiration. Then she added naughtily, 'I'm the guest speaker tonight, and you'd better bone up on . . . murder!' Then she marched off, head triumphantly in the air, as Chip stared after her, cute bafflement written across his handsome features.

'Cut!' cried a hoarse male voice, and immediately Joel Park Brooks launched himself toward the waiting Chip and Celia.

'You wrote that?' I asked, trying not to sound too horrified.

'No. They hired a script doctor after I turned my version in.' Robin's cheeks were red with embarrassment. Or maybe it was just the heat.

The day was definitely getting warm. In October, our night temperatures drop down into the forties pretty often, but the day temperatures can march right back up into the eighties. People were discarding jackets all over the set. I was wearing a short-sleeved dark blue silk tee shirt and khakis, having decided to be cold for an hour rather than tote a sweater the rest of the day. I felt smug. Robin was equally practical in jeans and a green golfing shirt. The jeans made his butt look very nice.

'Interested?' Robin asked, and for an unnerving moment I misunderstood him. I looked up at him with wide eyes until I realized he was just asking if I was enjoying the controlled chaos around me. I nodded. Looking past Robin's shoulder, I saw someone waving in his direction. 'Hey, that gal wants to talk to you,' I said. It was the stout young woman who'd been overseeing the Molly's Moveable Feasts table.

Robin looked uncomfortable. 'What now?' he said, and strode off. I was left standing in the middle of a sea of busy people and mysterious cables. I was afraid to move for fear I'd go where I wasn't supposed to, or trip over something vital. It was hard to look nonchalant, under the circumstances, and I was relieved when the chief cameraman stopped to chat.

Though he might be on the unpolished side – his hair was rough and poorly cut, his face almost obscured by a huge graying mustache – he was really polite. 'Will Weir,' he said, extending a hand. I shook it and introduced myself.

'Oh, yeah, Robin said he was bringing you to the set,' Weir said. 'Celia's character is based on you, you know.'

'I'd heard,' I said dryly.

'Robin is a nice guy,' Weir said. 'I don't know how much of the script is autobiographical, but according to the book, you two dated for a while?'

It seemed a strange thing for this cameraman to ask. Why would he care? Our relationship was really none of his business. But there wasn't any reason for me to be touchy, either.

'We dated for a couple of months,' I said levelly. 'Then he went off to Los Angeles to seek his fame and fortune.'

Weir appeared to relax at that, and I wondered if he'd been worried that Robin would be distracted by me and thus upset the star of the movie.

Celia seemed upset by something, anyway. Weir heard her voice just as I did, raised in a sharp protest over something. The actress was just far enough away, in a little huddle with the director and Chip Brodnax, to be unintelligible from where we stood. But there was no mistaking the anger in her posture. Her right hand swung out almost as if she intended to slap the much taller director, but Joel Park Brooks proved quick on his feet. He dodged the swinging hand adroitly, and stared down at the actress with a stony face.

Celia herself seemed appalled at what she'd done. For a long moment she looked from Joel to Chip to her own hand, her mouth open in amazement. Then, her body language unmistakable, she apologized.

All three lowered their voices and bent their heads together, and then Joel was striding back to his chair, his shaved head shining in the sun. He'd have to put on a hat soon, or he'd be sorry tomorrow.

Chip and Celia moved back into their starting positions for the scene, as did the first couple, and then . . . everyone did the whole thing over again.

By the fifth time, Robin was back by my side, with a murmured apology that I didn't quite catch. I was bored, hot, and ready to leave, and I was none too happy with being dumped and reloaded by Robin so unceremoniously. As I whispered my own deliberately unintelligible farewell, my nose was probably as high in the air as Celia's when she did her 'pert' sentence.

'I'll call you,' he promised. He still seemed distracted. 'I think tomorrow we're doing street scenes.'

Well, the heck with him, I thought, making my path through the confusing tangle of cables and equipment. I was determined to reach my car and make my getaway. Just as I cleared the edges of the scene and stepped through the tape that held back onlookers, I heard a breathless voice call my name.

'Miss Teagarden!' The caller had a husky, sexy voice, and I turned to find Starlet Two hurrying after me.

'Yes?' I tried to sound more civil than I felt.

'Please, Miss Teagarden, I'm Meredith Askew.' She waited a moment, hoping I'd recognize the name. She gave a resigned little sigh when I didn't. 'Celia was hoping you could eat dinner with her tonight?' As though this were a great favor.

I bit back my first response, which was, 'For God's sake, why?' 'No, thanks,' I told the girl. It sounded lumpishly ungracious, even to me.

'Oh, but . . .' Meredith Askew looked disconcerted and unhappy. I looked up at her with more attention. I'd believe this one was twenty-six, or twenty-one, for that matter. 'Celia really wants to talk to you.'

'What about?'

'Well, about the script, I guess.'

'I don't know anything about the script,' I observed.

'She'd like to know what you felt when your mother opened the chocolate box and almost ate one. And it was poisoned.'

'What do you think I felt?' I asked incredulously.

'Oh, please come,' Meredith said pleadingly.

She was an actress herself, so I should've known better. This not-too-subtle show of terrified innocence, intended to convey that the seasoned and ruthless older actress would torture Meredith if she didn't produce me, couldn't be real. But, I admit, I was beginning to wonder what all this was really about. Besides, what else did I have on my schedule, besides another evening at home with Madeleine?

'All right,' I said, sounding as grumpy as I surely was. 'Where?'

'We made reservations in Atlanta at Heavenly Barbecue,' Meredith said, relaxing openly. 'We heard that was the best place to get a taste of the South.' I had to keep reminding myself that she was an actress, and that relaxing openly would be the reaction she selected, not necessarily her true feeling. 'You can drive over there with us in one of the Range Rovers. We'll leave at eight.'

That seemed mighty late to eat, but I nodded shortly and agreed to meet them at the Ramada right off the interstate, where most of the cast and crew were staying. 'Though Joel's renting his own house,' Meredith said, trying not to sound too envious.

I'd turned to leave when a sudden thought rambled through my head. 'Meredith,' I called. The young woman turned to look at me, forcing her features into Concerned. 'Will Barrett be coming?' I asked. She scanned my face to pick the answer I wanted.

'No,' Meredith said, finally. I was quite unsure if she were telling the truth or lying. Lying, I thought, and sighed as I thought of an evening of awkwardness. I'd accepted, though, and I would keep my word. Meredith turned away to go back to her business, whatever it was, and I plotted my route back to my car.

With some difficulty, I picked my way among the cables, trailers, and people. The fringe of the set was becoming heavily populated with Lawrencetonians who had nothing better to do, and I had to stop to meet and greet five or six people who had a thousand questions.

After staggering along the street for two blocks, I had to admit I'd lost my car. I pressed the Open button on my keypad, which would make the lights blink. I looked from side to side. Nothing.

Okay, time to drag out the big guns. I hit the red Panic button, and just like a charm, I heard *Honk! Honk! Honk!* just out of sight. A middle-aged couple turned to stare, and a dog began barking frantically. I just didn't care. I flew down the sidewalk to pass a clump of sesanquas, and there was my car, honking away faithfully. I pressed the Panic button again to silence the horn. Within seconds, I was buckled up and maneuvering the car out of the space I'd wedged it in, thinking all the while about the evening's excursion with the movie people. I was relieved they wouldn't be eating anywhere in town – but Heavenly Barbecue, a huge and popular place on the outskirts of the Lawrenceton side of Atlanta; was often aswarm with locals.

Through a haze of misgiving, I couldn't shake a certain sense of anticipation. I felt like I'd agreed to a date with a rough, sexy guy from the wrong side of the tracks.

It had been a long time since I'd had plans for the evening beyond a dinner with my mother and her new family, or renting a move to watch with Sally or the Youngbloods. As I worked at the library that afternoon, directing patrons to the right section of the stacks or dealing with the copier (which was at the stage of having to be nursed through every encounter with the public), I thought about my invitation from the movie people much too often. I just had time to shower and change when I left work.

I had to resist the temptation to buy more new clothes. I refused to spend more than five minutes deciding what to put on that evening, but I did check over my chosen shirt and slacks to decide if they needed ironing. As I was frowning at a little crease in my khakis, the telephone rang.

'Uh-huh?' I said into the receiver, my mind a thousand miles away.

'Ms Teagarden?' The crisp voice could only belong to Patricia Bledsoe, Sam Clerrick's secretary. Patricia the Paragon, as Perry Allison had taken to calling her after she'd found a mistake in his paycheck that cost him money.

'Yes, who's calling?' I didn't want to sound too sure. Why on earth would the woman phone me?

'This is Mrs Bledsoe,' she said, sounding as surprised to be calling as I was to be called.

'What can I do for you?' I asked, trying to modify my voice so my words wouldn't sound abrupt. I'd been at work for seven hours. Why hadn't she taken the opportunity to talk to me then?

'My son Jerome really wants to see the film crew on the job,' she said carefully. 'Mr Allison just now told me that you had visited the set this morning. So I was hoping that you could tell me where they are working now.'

Patricia Bledsoe also didn't like to use contractions.

I told her the crew had been working at the Episcopalian church that morning, and she checked the address to be sure she knew where that was (there are many, many churches in Lawrenceton, and I am sorry to say there is little racial mixing on Sundays). 'But I don't know about tomorrow,' I said firmly. 'I believe my friend said something about street scenes.'

'So they are not likely to be coming to the library?' she asked. I had the odd feeling that Patricia Bledsoe could see the surprised expression on my face, because she added hastily, 'That would be so convenient, you see, if he could just come here.'

'I have no idea what streets they're going to use,' I told her. 'I suppose if they wanted to film at the library they would've already asked Sam, either directly or through the City Council.'

'That's true,' she said. She sounded quite annoyed that she hadn't thought of that herself. 'Yes, thank you,' she said briskly, and I knew that Patricia was regretting she'd called me at all. 'I'm sorry I bothered you, just go back to whatever you were doing,' she continued, trying to sound chipper. 'Forget I even called.'

I thought, *She wishes*.

To my relief, I spotted a familiar tall form in the parking lot. Robin was included in the dinner invitation. I'd been a little anxious at the idea of being alone with a bunch of people I didn't know. Furthermore, they'd be people with whom I had nothing in common. It was pleasant to find out I was only four-sixths right.

Meredith Askew had indeed either lied or been mistaken, because Barrett was standing with the rest beside a rented van. That counterbalanced Robin's presence. Barrett smirked at me, and I felt weary already. The best I could do was to manage my entry into the van, so I climbed in the backseat with Meredith Askew and the assistant to the director, Mark Chesney. Celia was in the middle with Robin, who barely managed to fit his long legs in, and Barrett was in the front passenger seat. The head cameraman, Will Weir, drove. He seemed to be everywhere.

Despite what Meredith had said when she invited me, Celia didn't seem anxious to talk to me, at least not immediately. Mark asked her about her next project. 'I'm doing a movie about the sixties radicals,' she said. 'I play one of those bombers they had then.'

After some exclamations from Mark and Will, Celia twisted in her seat to face me directly. 'I was in your library the other day,' she said. 'I really wanted to meet you then, but I ended up checking out some books for research. Now I have my own Lawrenceton, Georgia, library card! Quite a souvenir of the role!'

I smiled faintly and agreed, glad I hadn't been in the library to witness the fuss when she had entered. Celia didn't address me directly after that. She and Meredith chattered back and forth about the industry, and Mark added a comment or two from time to time.

If I'd agreed to come because I wanted to observe *them*, I would have been in hog heaven. As it was, I couldn't escape the feeling that I was out of my element. I found myself thinking of a book I'd left half-read at home and wishing I'd stuck it in my purse so I could pull it out now. But I gave myself a little lecture to get 'up' for the occasion. After all, how many chances would I have again to ride in a van with a group of Hollywood insiders?

The answer, to my relief, appeared to be none.

The treatment we got at the restaurant was amazing. It was like – well, I don't know what it was like. Waiting to greet us at the door was the manager, whose embroidered pocket read 'Smoky'. Smoky was a short man with a thick thatch of curly, light hair. He was built like a tree trunk, and his heavy, hairy arms waved emphatically as he told us how pleased he was to have us in his establishment. Beaming with pride, he led us to a private room. We had to parade the length of the restaurant to get there. It may have been my imagination, but it seemed to me that Smoky walked quite slowly and mentioned Celia's name – and Barrett's – much more often than necessary.

Once we were seated at a large rectangular table, covered for the occasion with a red paper tablecloth, we were served instantly by a group of favored servers, all of whom yearned desperately to be noticed by someone, anyone, in the magic circle of Hollywood. I had never been waited on with such perkiness, such assiduity. I didn't know whether to jeer or weep.

'Is it always like this?' I whispered to Robin as we were studying our menus.

'Yes,' he said, quite matter-of-fact about the spectacle ordinarily normal people were making out of themselves.

There was already a lot to think about.

Robin was at my side because Celia had maneuvered so that that should happen. She sat directly across the table, flanked by Barrett and Will Weir. Meredith and Mark Chesney sat at the ends. The rest of the tables in the private room were empty. The voices of our group sounded unnaturally loud as the menu was discussed with exhaustive – and boring – thoroughness. Robin and I began to talk about our mothers. I'd never met his, but he'd talked about her often and with fondness, and of course he'd met my mother when he lived in Lawrenceton. We kept the conversation going while we placed our orders and received our drinks. That procedure took twice as long since the young people in the Heavenly Barbecue colors (sky blue and deep red) were determined to impress themselves on each and every member of the party; my choice of entrees had never received such attention.

I could see that this was all to impress Celia; somehow, though Celia was not remarkably famous, these young people could tell she was the alpha in our small group. After a few moments' observation, I decided the determining factor wasn't looks; it was attitude.

I acted like no one.

Celia and Meredith were playing the parts of dazzling celebrities who were being just folks, just like everyone else, no special treatment please! Will Weir, who, Robin had whispered, was actually one of the best known and most reliable cameramen in Hollywood, had a definite air of authority that put him firmly in the club, and Robin had a well-known face since he'd promoted his book on so many talk shows. Barrett was handsome, and he looked like an Actor. Mark Chesney and I were the nonentities.

I wish I could say that this was just fine with me, that I hardly noticed it. At least, after five minutes of being mildly chagrined, I worked around to laughing at myself. After that I felt much better. Mark Chesney and I exchanged a smile that let me know he was on my wavelength. Barrett was glowing. I'd never seen him look happier. This evening was apparently a significant one for him, and as I watched him speak to Celia, I wondered if Barrett was attempting a conquest. Robin's claim that he and Celia were no longer a couple seemed to be true; he didn't seem at all concerned that Barrett and Celia were flirting openly and outrageously.

Barrett mentioned his previous visit to Lawrenceton when he

was talking about the difficulty some of the cast was having in communicating with the locals. Our accent might be a little heavy to a Midwesterner's ear, I guess.

'You've been to Georgia before?' Meredith asked, as if our state was remote and inaccessible.

'I thought everyone knew,' Barrett said. He certainly looked genuinely surprised. 'My father lived here.'

'He doesn't any longer?' Celia sounded interested and quite innocent.

There was a moment's silence. Barrett and I looked at each other. 'No,' Barrett said. 'Unfortunately, we lost him last year.'

Though that made Martin sound like a misaddressed package, I appreciated Barrett's restraint, and I gave him a tiny nod. The subject was dropped, to my relief and, I'll bet, to Barrett's.

Robin and I were discussing the latest book by Robert Crais, whom Robin knew slightly – now, to me that was thrilling – when I became aware that I was being observed. It was like noticing that a mosquito is hovering around your face, a sensation you can't quite pin down and eliminate.

'But the Joe Pike character, how do you think he measures up compared to Hawk in the Parker books?' Robin asked. I was trying to formulate my reply when I glanced across the table and saw that Celia was silent and intent. She was observing me, and even as I looked at her I saw her hand move in a little hand twist that ended with the palm up. I hadn't realized it was a gesture I made often until I saw Celia imitate it.

In a flash, I understood the whole purpose of my being invited along this evening. I could only wonder, in that horrible moment, if Robin had known.

I wanted to get up and walk out of the room and never see any of these people again, because I felt that Celia Shaw had been stealing from me. But in a contrary way, I also wanted to minimize the situation, because I was raised to avoid direct confrontations. Besides, what could I say? 'You were copying me?' I hadn't accused anyone of that since the third grade. What could she reply? 'Was not!'

'Just trying to get your flavor,' Celia explained, looking Sheepish with a capital S. She was playing someone feeling sheepish, rather than actually feeling that way.

'I don't know how you've stood it,' I said to Robin, with more frankness than tact. Shoving back my chair and scooping up my purse, I excused myself to go to the Ladies'.

The ladies' room was supposed to look like a barn, God knows why. There were hay bales and corrals, and each 'stall' was only shoulder high. Talk about carrying a theme too far. There was no place to be private in there. I stood by the pay phone when I'd emerged, trying to decide who could come get me without asking too many questions. I'd just look like that dreaded thing, a Bad Sport, I finally decided, and stomped back to our private room.

Along the way, a starstruck girl asked me to get Celia Shaw's autograph for her and a man who was trying really hard to look like Johnny Depp told me he could give anyone in that room – male or female – an unforgettable sexual experience. I had no idea what to say to either of them, so I just shook my head.

The food had come while I was gone, and everyone was eating, but there was a testy silence in the room that tipped me off that something had gone wrong while I was out.

I slid into my place and spread my napkin, hoping this wouldn't be the time I'd spill barbecue sauce on my blouse. I don't think I've ever concentrated so hard on eating neatly. Every sixty seconds one of the servers would circulate around the table, asking each person individually if he or she had enough to drink, was satisfied in every way.

I was so self-conscious, thinking of the young woman across from me drinking in my every move and gesture, that I couldn't enjoy a thing. I wished I'd just said to hell with it, and walked right out of the restaurant. I could have called Shelby Youngblood or Sally Allison. Had I been under the spell of Hollywood glamour as much as everyone else? Was that why I'd agreed to come out with these people? I put down my fork with as little noise as I could manage, patted my lips with my napkin, and set it by my plate.

'Ready to leave?' Robin murmured.

'They're not through eating,' I whispered.

'We can go,' he said. 'I called a cab.'

'Thanks,' I said, realizing as he said it that I wanted to leave more than anything. In a regular speaking voice I thanked Celia for the meal, and though I sounded stiff and hostile I had fulfilled the letter of courtesy. Celia was sulky and on the verge of a tantrum. She muttered something at me. I didn't try to decipher it on the spot; nodding and getting the hell out seemed like the best thing to do.

Robin slid in the cab with me, told the driver where to go, and stared straight ahead.

'Thank you,' I said carefully.

'For being there while you were exposed to Celia at her worst?' His voice was dry and brittle. I realized there had been a serious quarrel when I'd left the room. I was petty enough to be glad.

'I guess she was just doing what an actress has to do,' I answered, hoping to make him feel less culpable. 'Anyway, that was certainly an experience.'

'They get so used to being the center of the universe,' Robin told me. 'I don't think I ever see it as clearly until I see them away from LA.'

I felt uncomfortable. There wasn't a response, so I didn't attempt one.

'She's gotten worse lately,' he continued. 'She's absentminded, and she forgets her lines. She's . . . it's like she's going off the tracks, somehow.'

I had to tread carefully. No matter if she and Robin had quarreled about how she'd treated me, this woman had been Robin's girlfriend. 'Does she use, ah, recreational stuff?' I asked, as delicately as possible.

'Drugs? No. Celia might take a hit off a joint if it's going around, but she doesn't buy it herself and she doesn't take pills.'

Somehow, discussing Celia's problems didn't interest me right now, but I felt obliged to listen if Robin wanted to discuss them. Up to a point. But Robin sat in brooding silence all the way to my house, where he told the cab to wait while he walked me to my door. I'd unlocked the door and punched in the security code, he took one step inside.

For a moment I felt awkward, in that lit-up kitchen with a man, alone. Then I thanked Robin for the ride home and for my interesting evening, and he gave a snort that suddenly made me feel at home with him. He seemed much more like my friend Robin than a stranger who'd been living in a strange land. Robin looped one long arm around my shoulders and stooped to give me a kiss on the cheek.

'I'll see you tomorrow,' he said.

'No, I have to work.'

'You don't want to come back to the set?' He sounded less surprised than he might have a couple of days ago. Robin was reorienting himself to my life.

'No.'

Robin looked down at me, his face inscrutable. 'Then I'll see you soon,' he said finally. I watched as he loped down the steps to cross the yard to the cab waiting on the driveway. There was a car passing by, out on the road, a little unusual for this time of night. Maybe my neighbor Clement had been out late.

What a strange evening it had been. I fed Madeleine and trudged up the stairs, yawning hard enough to make a cracking sound. As I got ready for bed, going through my usual skin and stretching routine, I wondered if I should have foregone my evening out with the movie people. Then I thought, *That's a once-in-a-lifetime experience. Even if I didn't enjoy it at all, it's a good thing to have done*. I was glad it was over, though, and as I composed myself to sleep I thought of Celia Shaw's clever, sulky, beautiful face. I wondered if she'd ever win an Oscar; I could say I'd known her when.

That would be more fun than knowing her now.

Chapter Five

Making a liar out of me, the next morning saw me on my way back to the movie set, which today, I'd discovered, was the Sparling County Courthouse. I was still blinking and trying to feel completely alert. Beside me in the front seat was my friend Angel Youngblood: mother, stunt-woman, and former bodyguard. Pregnancy and motherhood had not had any visible effect on Angel's long, sleek body.

When the phone had rung at the crack of dawn, Angel's was the last voice I'd expected to hear. 'Hey, Roe,' she'd said, her flat Florida drawl instantly recognizable. 'Listen, I need some help.'

'What?' I knew I sounded groggy, and I tried to focus on the clock. It was six, time for me to get up and get ready for work.

'Sorry I woke you up.'

'No, no, I have to get ready for work anyway. What can I do for you?' Angel never called without a reason; she wasn't a chatterer.

'Shelby's already at work with his car, mine won't start, and I need to leave the baby-sitter hers because Joan's got a doctor's appointment today. Can you give me a lift to the movie set?'

I ran a hand over my face, and recalled that Angel had told me she'd gotten work on the set. 'Sure,' I said. 'I'll be there in thirty minutes or less.'

'Thanks.' Angel hung up.

I washed my face and brushed my teeth, pulled on a long, pale orange tee-shirt style dress and a light sweater, slid into some clogs, powdered my face, and clattered down the stairs and out the front door before I had really attained consciousness. I was a little more alert by the time I beeped the horn outside Angel and Shelby's ranch-style home.

Angel slid out of the front door like a thief in the night, her

Capri-length black stretch pants and her white blouse emphasizing her golden colors and smooth body movements. Her thick blond hair was caught back in a ponytail, and she wore no makeup, which was Angel's norm.

'How's Joan?' I asked as Angel climbed into the car.

Angel grinned, and went from looking serious and possibly dangerous to looking like a mother who was proud as hell of the most wonderful baby in the world. 'She's into banging on pots and pans,' Angel told me, and we talked about Joan's progress for a minute or two. 'My neighbor is keeping her today. She has a little boy a couple of months older. Courthouse,' she reminded me, and as I pulled away from the curb to go to Lawrenceton's fake-antebellum edifice, she began to tell me about a civil confrontation Shelby had had with Martin's replacement at the Pan-Am Agra plant.

I was listening with great interest, when I stood back and gave myself a hard look. Was I that dreary cliché, the hometown honey? I found the Hollywood people boring, compared to Angel's fascinating account of little Joan's first crawling. Maybe I was pulling a double cross on myself, pretending enthrallment with family scenes of the Youngbloods to hide my secret lust for the Hollywood way of life?

It was both a relief and a slight disappointment to touch the bottom of my well of self-absorption and find I was absolutely sincere in my preference for the small details of home. And I was definitely getting a little too fond of my own navel, I concluded. So I concentrated on listening to every single thing Angel told me. I even volunteered to baby-sit Joan one evening so Angel and Shelby could go out together. Angel rolled her eyes at me doubtfully, but agreed to talk to Shelby about my offer.

Today the trailers and cables and cameras – all the paraphernalia I'd seen yesterday – had been set up in a new location, the front yard of the courthouse. Even the Molly's Moveable Feasts van was there, with its table set up and attended by the same auburn-headed young woman. (If she was actually Molly, who was doing the cooking?) Today the table was spread with pitchers of juice and doughnuts, and a plate of fruit. I wondered, for the first time, how long the movie people would actually have to stay in town.

Robin had told me that most of the shots filmed in Lawrenceton would be exteriors. Sets would be built back at the studio for interior scenes. So maybe scenes dealing with the trial were being shot today? I wondered why on earth they'd need a stuntwoman, and decided maybe it would be better not to ask.

For the first time, as Angel scanned the street for some safe parking spot, I thought of how difficult it would be to be an actor, to have to imagine how your character would've changed as a result of scenes you hadn't shot yet. You'd have to figure out how the character would react after some of the events in the film, before you'd ever emotionally experienced them. There was more to this acting than met the eye.

I had intended to drop Angel off and go on my way, but she knew one of the women working in the crew and wanted to introduce me. The friend, Carolina Venice, was one of the makeup artists working in a big trailer a little west of the courthouse. Angel's friend looked as exotic as her name. Easily five feet eleven, Carolina Venice had a smoking habit, cornrowed and beaded hair, and multiple piercings. The lip and tongue decorations made me a little queasy, I have to confess, though the woman was as warm and welcoming as she could be.

'Give me fifteen minutes,' she said. 'I have to finish this woman, and then I'll be with you. Here, settle into these chairs.' There were two cheap lawn chairs on the rolling platform (with steps built in) that had been pushed up to the makeup trailer.

I perched on one, looking around me to see if I could spy Robin. I felt a certain need to explain why I was where I'd said I would never go again. I was just yards away from Celia's trailer – at least I was pretty sure it was the same one Celia had used the day before. Will Weir, pulling on a lightweight jacket, was saying something over his shoulder to (I presumed) Celia, nodding, as he shut the door. Everyone I saw had the Styrofoam cups of coffee and juice that Molly's Moveable Feasts was handing out. Mark

Chesney went to the door of the trailer and knocked, but hurried away after a moment. I wasn't close enough to hear what response he'd gotten. A young woman I didn't know darted up to the door, cracked it slightly, and called something inside. Then she darted away as quickly as she'd come. I was interrupted in my study of movie location movement patterns by the emergence of Carolina, who'd had time to get pumped up about talking to her old friend.

She hugged Angel, shrieked at pictures of the baby, asked after Shelby, and behaved exactly like a happily reunited friend, gold hoops or no gold hoops. After a minute, it was easy to forget her bizarre appearance and respond to her warmth and cheer.

When the two were deep into reminiscence, I decided I could use some orange juice. I strolled over to the laden table.

'Can I pour you some coffee?' asked the young woman. She had discarded one white coat and was pulling on another. I was willing to bet that white coats had a high turnover. While I picked up a cup of juice, I noticed that she was prettier close-up. Her dark red hair was thick and smooth, her skin was clear, and her eyes were a nice blue. It was her heavy jaw that threw her face off balance and prevented her from being really attractive. The embroidered name on her white jacket read 'Tracy'.

'So you're not Molly,' I remarked.

She laughed. 'No, no. Molly's the genius. I'm just the server. When I clean this table up, it'll be time for Molly to come with the bag lunches for the crew. Then when I clear those away, it'll be afternoon snack time.'

'You must get to know everyone who works here.'

'By sight, anyway,' she agreed. 'They're all pretty cool. In this kind of weather, this is a great job.' Kind of a dead-end one, I would have thought, but on a beautiful clear day in October in a lovely town like Lawrenceton, with an interesting scene to watch, the idea didn't seem so terrible.

'Who do you like best?' I asked idly.

'Oh, the writer.' Tracy's face, already high-colored, flushed a deeper red. 'I've read everything Robin's ever written. I've got first editions of every book, all signed.'

She sounded like an ardent reader to me. 'He's good,' I agreed, trying not to smile.

'I saw you talking to him yesterday,' Tracy said. 'You known him long?'

'Yes, several years,' I said. 'Of course, Robin lived here at the time of the murders, and so did I.'

'You wouldn't be . . . you couldn't be . . . Aurora Teagarden?' She looked absolutely dazed.

'Yes, I am,' I said, trying not to flinch.

'OhmiGod, this is amazing,' she shrieked. 'To actually meet you!'

Oh, boy. High time to haul ass out of there, I figured. I finished my cup of juice, thanked Tracy, and tossed my cup into the large, lined garbage can, brimming over with identical cups and napkins and paper plates. Tracy immediately bundled up the contents, secured the bag with a twisty, and tossed it into the back of the catering van. By the time I went to say good-bye to Carolina and Angel, she had already relined the can and bundled her dirty coat and some dish towels into the van as well.

The two friends were still on the porch. They'd laid claim to the lawn chairs, and people who moved in and out of the makeup trailers had to work around them. Carolina was on her second or third cigarette, and she was telling Angel something between puffs. Angel was listening with some intensity. I was a little shy about interrupting, even though all I wanted to do was tell Angel I was leaving, so I looked around me, trying to look like I was content rather than impatient.

I was surprised to see Meredith Askew tripping along in my direction. She was smiling, a sort of conciliatory wincing lifting of the lips.

'Ms Teagarden,' she said while she was still a few feet away. 'Celia told me last night that if you showed up today, she hoped you would come talk to her a second.' She came to a halt below the porch.

'You're her messenger, now?' I asked, noting that my voice was appropriately cool.

Meredith's smile might have twitched a little, but she kept her composure up. 'Just doing a friend a favor,' she said, her voice level. 'Celia would like to apologize for her . . . for last night.'

Over Meredith's head I could see Barrett going into Celia's trailer. He'd knocked while he stood on the top step, and if he'd gotten an answer I hadn't been able to hear it from where I stood, maybe eighteen feet away. He looked puzzled, knocked again. He cracked the door, called 'Celia?' loudly enough for me to hear. He opened the door and stepped in, his face troubled.

I was just congratulating myself on Barrett's not noticing me when he stumbled right back out of Celia's trailer, his hand over his mouth. When I saw Barrett, I lost track of the conversations going on around me. I know trouble when I see it.

I glanced around the set, hoping someone else would come to Barrett's aid; he was so obviously sick, and something terrible had so obviously happened. I had a sinking feeling in the pit of my stomach that told me I wouldn't be getting to work on time today. As I watched, Barrett groped his way to the end of the trailer and bent over, one hand supporting himself against the side, retching.

For a second of blazing anger, I wondered if all these people weren't *acting* as though they hadn't seen Barrett. For all their attention to each other and their jobs, not one person appeared to have registered that there was a problem.

I went down the steps, bypassed Meredith, and approached my stepson warily. 'What's happened?' I asked him.

He didn't seem surprised to see me, or angry, so I knew with even more surety that something was very wrong.

'She's dead in there,' he gasped, and he began heaving again.

'Celia . . . is dead?' I could hear my own voice sharpen and rise with incredulity. I started to say, 'Are you sure?' but then I realized that was pretty damn insulting.

'Go get Joel,' he moaned.

I wondered if my stepson thought the director could actually bring his leading lady back to life.

'I'll get him,' Carolina said from behind me. 'I know where he is.'

'What did he say?' I heard Meredith ask her. 'What did Barrett say?'

I moved over to the open door of the trailer and peeked in. I didn't even put my foot on the concrete block that served as a step.

Celia was half-lying on the couch, up against one wall. The stack of books – including some library books – and the manuscript were tossed around her feet, which were flat on the floor. A dark red throw cushion, stained and nasty, lay on the couch beside her. Her tongue protruded a little from her mouth. It looked bruised, as well. There was a big dent in her forehead.

The Emmy was on the couch beside her. Its base was not clean.

Celia was definitely deceased. Feeling quite wobbly myself, I shut the door and leaned my back against it. I didn't want anyone else to see what I'd seen.

'What is it, Roe?' Angel had loped over and was looking at me quizzically. 'Don't tell me she's dead. That's what Barrett keeps saying.' Angel really, really didn't want anything to be wrong, but there was no help for it. I had to tell her.

Carolina returned. 'He's on the way,' she reported.

'You might want to call a doctor. Did the crew bring one?' I asked. She shook her head and her heavy earrings, too many to count, swayed as her head moved. Carolina's skull gleamed dully in the early-morning sun as she pulled a cell phone out of her pocket. It was the thinnest cell phone I'd ever seen. She dialed 911 as I watched. While she was speaking to the dispatcher who answered, Joel Park Brooks suddenly appeared in front of me as if he'd been expelled from another dimension. Mark Chesney was dogging his heels.

'What's this you say?' he asked, mad as hell at me.

In a cowardly way, I nodded my head toward Barrett.

'Oh my God, Joel,' Barrett said weakly. He'd dropped to his

knees and was pressing his face with both hands as if to force the grief out of it. 'Celia is dead. She died some awful way.'

As if I were a fly, Joel Park Brooks took me by the shoulder and shoved me aside. Before I could stop him, he flung open the trailer door. Leaping up the step into the trailer, he bent over Celia. Meredith and Mark were peering through the door, too. Both of them stood with one hand pressed against the door frame, on opposite sides. Altogether, the movie people were doing a great job of destroying evidence.

And I heard the voice I'd been dreading to hear, Robin's.

'What's wrong, Roe?' he asked.

'I'm so sorry,' I said, almost whispering. I wanted to be a hundred miles away.

'What's happened?' Robin's voice got louder as his fear mounted.

'She's dead,' Barrett said. 'I can't believe it, but she's dead. We spent last night together, and now she's dead.'

'What did you say?' Robin bellowed, and I crouched down.

'We . . .' All of a sudden, Barrett seemed to realize that this was neither the time nor the place nor the best choice of confidant. 'Forget it, man,' he muttered, but there were many ears clustering around by that point, including mine, and if Barrett had truly wanted to keep this intimate knowledge to himself, it was too late by thirty seconds.

That helped me pull myself together more than anything.

I moved over to my stepson, and laid my hand on his arm. He looked at me, too distraught to be hostile. 'Barrett,' I said, as quietly and earnestly as I could, 'don't say anything else. Everyone is listening. The police will be here soon.'

'An ambulance,' he began, and then closed his mouth with a snap.

'We called 911. But it's not gonna do her any good, and you know it. That woman was killed,' I told him, keeping my voice even and low.

'Murdered?' he said, way too loud. I could see cell phones spring up right, left, and sideways.

'Quiet, Barrett. Yes, she was murdered. I'd keep my mouth shut, if I were you.'

Anger flashed across his handsome face, followed by intense thought. Barrett was certainly good at projecting his changing emotions.

'What did you say?' Robin was standing to Barrett's side, his fists clenched.

'I was just talking. Ignore me.' Barrett turned to walk away.

As if I weren't there, Robin spun Barrett around and clamped both his hands on Barrett's shoulders. Barrett was younger than Robin by around fifteen years, but he was shorter, and Robin had a pretty good grip. I was going to have to believe Robin hadn't disengaged from his affair with Celia as much as he'd thought.

The movie people on the set were milling around, and I could hear sirens coming closer. But everyone there seemed to see his or her role as that of spectator, rather than participant. Robin opened his mouth to yell at Barrett, and Barrett's eyes ignited with anger, and I cast around for someone to help me.

Of course! Angel Youngblood met my eyes and moved behind Barrett, while I got behind Robin and circled him with my arms and pulled. Someone behind me actually laughed, and I resolved to track down who that was and kick him in the shins. I know I am small, and I know Robin is tall, but I was not in the mood for amusement.

Robin actually struggled for a minute, but I clung like a barnacle, and when he realized who it was had ahold of him, he relaxed. Blocked by his body from seeing what progress Angel had made with Barrett, I pulled gently on Robin's arms to get him to take a few steps away. He came willingly, and I could see that the anger had drained out of him. Robin wrapped his long arms around me and pulled me close, bowing his head over mine and crying.

For once I wished I were taller. I would put his face in the hollow of my neck and let him cry there, concealed, if only I could. I stood on tiptoes to let him lean on me more comfortably, and I patted his back. I wondered if I had any tissues in my purse, a soft mesh shoulder bag that was now banging uncomfortably on my bottom.

Will Weir was sitting on the curb of the sidewalk, his head buried in his hands. Meredith Askew was slumped by him, her makeup a mess, her hair all tangled. She was sitting as close to Will as she could get without climbing in his lap. Joel Park Brooks began shrieking at someone a few yards away. I recognized his voice, though I couldn't see him for the cloud of people, all chattering away on their phones.

'Hang up the damn cell phone,' he screamed, and a Motorola whizzed past me. Then a wafer-thin red phone. Everyone moved back in a hurry to protect their property from the director's hands, and there was a flurry of clicks as people hid their cells. I glimpsed Carolina sliding hers down the front of her tee shirt. Unless I missed my bet, Joel Park Brooks would be in no hurry to go after that one.

'Robin,' I said, hesitating to break into his grief.

He lifted his head and looked down at me. I reached up to rub a tear off his face. 'She was so fragile,' he said. 'She was such a mess.'

Not 'I loved her,' or 'What will I do without her?'

I pushed my glasses back on my nose and eyed him doubtfully.

'I'm really sorry, Robin, but the police are here. We need to find somewhere for you to wait, because they're going to want to talk to you.'

'Did you say,' he began slowly, disregarding what I'd told him, 'did you say Celia had been murdered?'

'I'm sorry, yes.'

He looked baffled. 'But that doesn't make any sense,' he said.

It seemed like a strange comment. But just as I opened my mouth to ask him what he'd meant, I heard a familiar voice.

And the day got even worse.

Chapter Six

His round blue eyes went from me, up to Robin, over to Barrett, and back again. 'Isn't this *fascinating*,' said Detective Arthur Smith. It was a moment pregnant with emotions, but those emotions were so snarled up it would have been hard to tease them apart.

If I just explain that my history with Arthur is long and complicated, it will spare us all a lot of tedium.

I hadn't seen Arthur (to speak to) in almost two years; of course, in a town the size of Lawrenceton, it would be hard to avoid glimpses of him, and I hadn't particularly been trying to do that.

Arthur was somewhat burlier than he had been in the days when we'd dated, and his hair was a little thinner, it seemed to me. He was still a solid block of a man, with hard blue eyes and curly pale hair. These past few months I'd been so far out of the loop that I realized I didn't even know if Lynn (Arthur's ex) and their little girl were still living in town.

'Who is this?' he asked me, as casually as if we'd had coffee together the hour before. He was pointing at my stepson.

'This is Barrett Bartell, Martin's son. He found her.'

Arthur squatted down in front of Barrett. Barrett met his eyes. I could tell Barrett was enough his father's son to dislike Arthur on sight – but Barrett was involved in a murder now, and couldn't afford such an emotion. I squeezed his arm to warn him. Barrett was definitely snapping back into his personality. He yanked away from me, and he didn't do it subtly.

I tried not to feel hurt, but it didn't work. I felt mostly . . . tired, I guess. I struggled to rise above it. Martin would want me to help Barrett, whether Barrett wanted to be helped or not.

'What brought you to Miss Shaw's trailer this morning?' Arthur said. His voice didn't sound particularly friendly.

'I needed to talk to her about . . .' And then Barrett stopped in mid-sentence.

'About what?'

He looked like he'd just seen the Ghost of You Better Shut Your Mouth over Arthur's shoulder, and it had shaken its finger at him.

'He was going to talk to Celia about the implications of their having spent the night together,' Robin said, his face absolutely expressionless. I had no idea what he was thinking or how he was feeling. Somehow he maintained his composure and straightened his slumped shoulders, his face now in profile to me and once more under guard. It was a 'man' thing to do, I thought wryly. But I admired him for holding on to his personality under the pressure of the shock and grief – and anger – he must be feeling. Even if he and Celia were no longer involved, it had to sting that she had so quickly found someone else to fill her bed.

Will Weir stepped over to Robin and put a hand on his shoulder. For a second the two men embraced, and if ever I had seen two miserable people, this was the occasion. Then they let each other go, and I was glad Robin had someone to comfort him, someone who'd known the dead girl well.

'Why are *you* here?' Arthur asked me. I had the feeling he'd said it more than once.

'Yeah, Mom,' Barrett said jeeringly. He'd recovered far more quickly than I'd hoped he would. His defenses were firmly back in place. 'You come to check up on me? I thought you'd had enough of us movie people last night.'

Martin had put up with a lot from Barrett, but if he'd heard Barrett speak to me this way, he would've knocked his son from here to kingdom come. I knew that as well as I knew my own name; and Barrett knew it, too. I met his eyes to see if there was any shame lurking there. There was, but it wasn't enough.

The guilt-engendered protective feeling I'd had for the young man – which I likened to temporary insanity – dropped right off my shoulders. Inside my head, I informed Martin that his son was just going to have to fend for himself. 'And it's about damn time,' I muttered, telling Martin a posthumous home truth.

'What?' Arthur looked startled, as well he might.

'I had hoped,' I said slowly, 'that you would make your father proud.' Barrett looked as if I'd kicked him in the jewels. 'Surely, Barrett, you're thinking more about this poor, dead young woman than you are about your little personal issues with me.' I turned my back on Martin's son. I felt thirty years older than Barrett, rather than ten.

I decided to pretend he wasn't there. 'Angel's car wouldn't start, so I brought her to work today,' I explained to Arthur, who'd been listening to my exchange with Barrett with great attention. 'She wanted me to meet her friend, the pretty woman with all the earrings, over there.' I inclined my head in Carolina's direction. 'Then, Celia's friend Meredith came to get me, to tell me Celia wanted to apologize for her behavior last night.'

'What behavior?' Arthur asked, which was a reasonable question. But I didn't want to talk about my vulnerability to Celia's particular sort of – well, maybe 'cruelty' was too severe a word – she'd *used* me . . . I got mad all over again, and lost my train of thought entirely.

'What did Celia Shaw do last night?' Arthur said gently. He had prompted me without being asked, an unpleasant reminder of how well he knew me. He reached out as if he were going to take my hand, and then changed the movement to a hair-smoothing gesture.

I cinched up my pride. 'She invited me to dinner so she could observe my mannerisms,' I said. I cut my eyes sideways to see if Barrett was going to comment, but he'd turned away.

'How did you find the deceased this morning?' Arthur asked. He'd gotten out his little notebook and the cheap Bic pen he preferred. He was still using the same model. Didn't make any difference if he lost it, he'd always told me.

'While I was talking to Meredith, I saw Barrett knock at the trailer door, open it, and go in. He came out looking sick.' I shrugged, letting him know that was that. 'Other people had come up to the trailer earlier and talked to her.'

'I'll talk to you later, Roe,' he said. 'You wait over there.' He pointed to one of the folding chairs on the porch of the makeup trailer. I didn't wait for a second offer. I sat in the chair and crossed my legs and took a few deep breaths. I was glad I'd worn a dress, a cool dress. The sun was coming up and the touch of it on my skin was beginning to show that little kiss of ferocity that said the temperature was going to reach the eighties. October is truly unpredictable in the South. I slid out of my sweater.

I got out my own cell phone and called the library to explain why I'd be late. Sam's assistant, Patricia Bledsoe, was at her desk, and as correct as ever. What a pain in the patootie that woman was, I thought absently, and then felt embarrassed at myself. Since when had dressing and speaking correctly, and acting professional, been a pain? 'I'll try to be in this afternoon,' I told Patricia and snapped my phone shut.

Well, it was a pain. She was a pain. And she was hiding something, my less correct self insisted on muttering to my nicer, more charitable persona. The last thing in the world Patricia Bledsoe would want was her Jerome hanging around on a movie set. That whole conversation had been fishy.

'I should have known not to bring you this morning,' a familiar voice said dryly, and Angel folded her long legs to sit beside my chair.

'It's not my fault stuff happens. Celia Shaw's dead,' I said.

'I heard tell.'

'I don't think it was a natural death. Unless she had fits or something. But then, someone whacked her with the Emmy.'

'Ummm.'

'Barrett found the body.'

'Time Barrett grew up.'

'I bet Barrett wouldn't be such a . . .' I groped for a nice way to say it.

'Asshole,' Angel supplied.

'Asshole, if Martin had stayed with Barrett's mother.' Sometimes the blunt term fits the bill best.

'I bet not.' Angel began braiding her hair, her slim muscular arms stretched back behind her head. 'I bet he would've been *worse*. Martin was miserable with his first wife. Named Cindy, right? Shelby met her – long, long time ago. I know you got to know her a little last winter, but I think she must have mellowed out by then.' Angel secured her braid with an elastic band.

'So it's not just me who thinks Barrett is hard to deal with?' I felt a little better.

'Oh, no.' Angel was matter-of-fact. 'Shelby, little as he knows him, can't stand to see that boy coming. And he *is* still a boy, when he should be a man.'

It was so refreshing to have a conversation with someone who agreed with me, and wouldn't think the less of me for detesting my stepson. I began to feel a few degrees less tense. Then I thought of the crumpled body just a few yards away, and realized that it was pretty darn likely someone had killed Celia Shaw while I was sitting in this very chair. I shuddered, despite the gathering heat.

'Wonder what this'll do to the movie schedule.' Angel took a sip from a bottle of water she'd snagged from the catering table.

'They won't cancel, surely?'

'No, they'll just hire someone else, I figure.'

'Meredith Askew?'

'That would be unusual,' Angel said. 'I think they'll hire someone just about Celia's level, and Celia was several steps higher on the food chain than Meredith.' I forgot, all too often, that Angel had an eclectic background that included considerable knowledge of the movie world. She was the most down-to-earth person I'd ever met, and I admired her many abilities immensely. And I would much rather think about that than the dent in Celia Shaw's forehead.

'Meredith's going to hope she'll be moved up,' Angel went on, spotting the young woman in the crowd, making the most of the 'friend of the deceased' role. 'But I doubt it.'

I thought about that a little. 'So, someone's going to be mighty happy about Celia dying.'

Angel nodded. 'But no telling who that is, though there may have been some other woman who's been on the back burner the whole time, some woman we don't know about. Carolina told me that Celia had been acting strange for the few days they'd been here.'

'Robin thought so, too,' I said after a moment. I had seen the perplexity on his face while he observed his former flame. I remembered the previous morning, when it had seemed for all the world as though Celia was going to slap the director.

'So that's Robin Crusoe, over there?' Angel had come to Lawrenceton after Robin left. She gestured with one bony finger, and I nodded, glad she'd spotted him for me.

Robin looked haggard, understandably enough, since he'd just discovered his former flame had been murdered, and that she'd spent the night before her death with another man. He'd put on dark glasses and was talking to a middle-aged woman with gray-streaked black hair. Robin pushed his fingers up under his glasses, and I knew he was brushing away tears. I pushed my own glasses up on my nose.

'You and him were tight?'

'Kind of,' I said, feeling unaccountably shy about it. 'But we're talking years ago. Right before I dated Arthur Smith.' I looked down at my hands, and began twisting my wedding band around on the finger it no longer fit.

Angel raised a blond eyebrow. 'So, what happened with Robin?'

'I was really fond of him. I think he was fond of me, too. But when he decided to write a book about the murders, and I realized there was no way he could leave me out of the book, I felt pretty unhappy about it. And when he went to Hollywood with his agent to push the book proposal, our connection just kind of tapered off.'

'He call you?'

'Oh . . . yeah. At first.'

'When did he quit?'

'When I told him I was marrying Martin.'

'And then he moved on to that Celia Shaw?'

'That's what the gossip magazines said. I think they had pretty much called it quits by the time they got here.'

'So he moved from the real you to the play you.' Angel looked amused at my wince. After a second of considering that unnerving idea, I shrugged.

We fell silent and watched the unfolding panorama together. Joel Park Brooks, shaved head flashing in the sun, was being attended by paramedics, by Mark, and by several other people whose names and functions I had not yet learned. He seemed to feel that the FBI should be brought in to investigate the death of an important actress like Celia Shaw. The Hollywood dispensation, I guess.

Robin had found a chair and sunk down onto it, his hands on his knees, lost in thought. I wondered if I should go to him.

Meredith Askew, still looking properly distraught, was resting her face on the shoulder of Chip Brodnax, the tall young man who was portraying Robin. His back was to me, so I had a good view of Meredith's face. As I watched, I saw her expression change to one of intense speculation. She was staring into the distance, unaware that anyone was observing her. As if she'd turned to me and spoken her thoughts out loud, I could tell that she was wondering if she had a chance of replacing Celia in the main role.

This was depressing. If anyone in this crowd (besides possibly Robin) was simply grieving for Celia Shaw, I could see no sign of it.

'Let's us go,' I suggested to Angel.

'Won't the police get us?'

'I have a feeling I can get around that.'

I made my way through the crowd to Arthur, who was issuing instructions to three other cops. I waited until he'd finished speaking, and as soon as they scattered to do his bidding, I knew he would turn to me.

'What can I do for you?' he asked.

'Can Angel and I go home?'

'Will you stay at your house until I come later? Will you not talk to anyone else?'

'I promise.'

'Okay, then. You and Angel can go.'

'Thanks.' I tried to dredge up a smile for him, but I couldn't.

I trudged back to Angel and gave her the thumbs-up. We made our way to my car and climbed back in. Though it was only nine o'clock, it seemed like a lifetime since we'd gotten to the set. The day was getting hotter by the minute. The car was stuffy. The streets around the movie site were almost chaotic; I had never in my life seen traffic this disordered in Lawrenceton. I figured all the police had been grabbed off traffic control and shifted to the murder scene. It wouldn't take the news crews long to get there, especially with all the busy cell phones on the set. I was willing to bet CNN already knew about it, had maybe aired a bulletin, if Celia rated that high.

I decided not to turn on the radio. I didn't want to hear anything about the murder, I didn't want to listen to any music, I didn't want to know the weather report. I just wanted to get out of here. With Angel helping me avoid cars and people, all going places they shouldn't go, I finally drove out of the area. I made a huge effort to obey every traffic rule. I was so grateful to Arthur for letting us leave, I was determined to be no trouble at all.

Once I got away from the town center, traffic thinned out dramatically. I took the county highway that led northeast out of town, past the very nice suburb where my mother and her husband live. My house is about a mile out of town, on a road that turns into farms pretty much right after it leaves the city limits.

The house waited for me, silent and dim, perfectly clean.

Angel hadn't been out to the house in a while. She looked around, a curious expression on her narrow face. She moved down the hall with her quiet grace, looking from side to side like a cat exploring unfamiliar territory.

'Geez,' she said finally, 'I want to kick the walls just to make a scuff mark. How can you live like this?'

'I don't know how to live any other way,' I said. And it was the first time that way struck me as odd. I stood in the middle of the long hall that runs from the front door and past the stairs down to a closet door, looked to the left into the formal living room, and I felt weirdly isolated. I stood, in my orange knit dress, feeling the coolness of the house, the shadows cast by the bright morning sun streaming in the windows, the sudden lack of contrast when clouds floated across the sun. I felt time passing.

'Do you ever have company?' she asked.

'No. At least, very seldom. But you know,' I said, pondering this idea through, 'that's not actually my fault. People don't come to see me. Even when I say, "Come by and see me", they don't.'

'You need to move back into town,' Angel said, her voice flat and definite.

I gaped at her. 'Like that would be easy! Like moving isn't incredibly stressful!'

She cocked her head, her blond braid trailing to one side.

'Is living like this *relaxing*? This place is a tomb.'

I stared at her, shocked.

She was absolutely right.

It was the second revelatory moment I'd had in two days.

'I would help,' she offered. 'I could bring Joan's playpen and set it up, and she'd be good for a while.'

'But this house,' I said, feeling my tears spring up. 'I was so happy here. Martin bought it for me.'

'You think Martin would like you being here by yourself? You think Martin would ever live in a place this . . . dead?'

That cut me to the quick. Martin had surrounded himself with energy, with projects, with life. I felt instantly that I had failed him, yet again.

'You didn't die with Martin,' Angel said brutally.

I gasped in surprise at the way her thought chimed in on what I was thinking. 'This house has so many memories,' I said feebly.

'You have the memories inside you. This house is stifling you. It's too big, it's out of the way, and it's . . . unwelcoming.'

'Enough,' I said.

Wisely, Angel did keep silent. We went to the kitchen, and I got out two glasses and filled them with ice while Angel got the pitcher of tea out of the refrigerator. Angel poured, and I put a package of Sweet 'N Low in mine.

In a desperate way, it hurt to even consider leaving this house. I had sure had enough hurting. But, with very little inner debate, I found I was thinking that Angel was right.

To effect such a change seemed incredibly daunting. I began to break it down into steps.

I would have to find a house in town. That would be easy, with a mother in real estate.

I'd have to have everything in this house packed and ready to move. I could afford to have that done for me.

I would have to sell this house. Well, part of keeping the house perfect was having its contents pared down to the minimum. This house was ready to show, as it was. With all the improvements I'd made, I had no doubt it would find a buyer sooner or later.

I'd have to pay someone to move all the furniture and boxes to the new house. So, the biggest exertion would be unpacking in the new house.

When I'd first met Angel and Shelby, they'd been hired by Martin to help bring this house to renovated life. They'd helped make the move into the house as smooth and painless as such a major upheaval could be. Now, Angel was offering to help me move out of the house. Somehow, tying the two events together made me cry. In the past year, I'd become used to sudden outbreaks of tears, but it startled Angel. I had to wave a reassuring hand at her, to let her know I was going to be all right. She eyed me doubtfully, but she relaxed when she realized she didn't have to figure out how to comfort me.

She indicated the phone and raised her eyebrows, and I nodded. Shelby now had his own office at Pan-Am Agra, and she was busy relating the events of the morning to him as I strolled out of the room and across the hall into the den to get a Kleenex. I kicked off my sandals, put my ice-tinkling glass on the small table by my current book. I folded my legs under me as I settled in the large leather armchair that had been Martin's favorite. I hadn't slept well the night before, and the day so far had been exhausting. When the air-conditioning came on again, with its relaxing drone, it seemed only natural to lay my head against the wing of the chair and close my eyes.

Chapter Seven

There was a hand holding mine. It felt comfortable; long, thin, fingers twined through my short ones. I opened my eyes to see Robin in front of me, sitting on the ottoman that matched the chair.

'Was I snoring?' I asked.

'No, actually. Just sitting there like you were resting your eyes for a minute.'

I pushed my glasses up with one finger. 'Where's Angel?'

'She's out spraying a wasp nest. What an energetic woman. If I were left alone in this house, I'd head for the bookshelves.' The shelves I'd had put in all up and down the hall were my favorite feature, too.

'Angel's not much one for reading,' I said. 'You're welcome to go to the shelves if you want. How come you're here? I'm glad you are,' I added hastily, not wanting to be rude, 'but I'm kind of surprised Arthur let you come.'

'Luckily for me, I had an alibi for this morning.'

'Oh?'

'First, I ate breakfast in the hotel restaurant at the same time as at least ten other people. It's quite the local watering hole, huh? Then, I was on the phone with my agent for thirty minutes. We were talking about this film, and the contract for my next two books. Then, after I got to the set, Joel grabbed me to discuss some dialogue changes. So I think I'm pretty well covered.'

'That's lucky for you. So Arthur said you could come out here?'

'No, I just came out here on my own.' There was a pause, not an uncomfortable one.

'Angel was telling me I should move,' I said.

'How do you feel about that?'

'I was thinking I was staying here because I had been happy here.' I was still a little simple from my nap.

'And now you think?'

'I think Angel is maybe right.' I wiggled straight in the chair, untwisted my legs. I was too old to fall asleep in such a position without paying a penalty. 'I loved this house the moment I saw it, and I've loved living in it. And I've spent a mint on it. But now it just feels . . . empty.' I made a face. 'Like I'm not even here any more.'

'Would you live somewhere else?'

'You mean, leave Lawrenceton?' I'd wondered what would happen if Martin got transferred, so this wasn't a new idea. 'Not likely. Not if I don't have to.'

'So you'd look for another house in town?'

'Yes.' Come to think of it, it was true that I could live anywhere in the world I wanted. I could live in England. I could travel to Italy. But that idea of moving out of my normal orbit scared the heck out of me. I was okay, right here in Lawrenceton. I knew who I was, here. And the time might be coming when my mother would need me; she never had, but it was always possible.

I'd always had the feeling I was a frill, rather than a necessity, for my mother.

Robin was looking thoughtful, but not as traumatized as I'd expected.

'Do you feel very bad?' I asked, trying to keep my voice small and level. After all, his former companion had just been murdered, and she'd spent the night with someone else before that, to boot. A punch in the stomach and a kick in the privates, all at the same time.

'I don't feel like you'd think,' Robin said ambiguously. He took his hand back and raked it through his hair, which was long enough to get seriously rumpled.

'Oh? And how would I think you'd feel?'

'You'd think I'd feel like you did when you lost Martin.'

'No, I wouldn't.'

'Why not?'

'Because I really loved Martin, and you didn't love Celia.' And then I closed my eyes and put my hand over my mouth, because I never should have said that.

Robin didn't speak, and I opened my eyes just a sliver to take a peek at his face. He looked sad. He didn't look heartbroken.

'I guess not,' he said, looking down at his hands, dangling between his knees. 'It was great for a while, but the last few months, I've been feeling like she was keeping secrets from me.'

'Secrets? What kind?'

Robin raised his eyebrows at me so I'd elaborate.

'Like . . . an "I'm pregnant" kind of secret, or an "I know who stole the nuclear warhead", or "I was witness to a mob rubout"?'

Robin almost smiled. 'I think it was more in the personal category.'

'Did you notice anything different about her?'

'Yes,' he said, as though he'd just realized that. 'Yes, there was a lot different about her. Sometimes she seemed like she was staring into space, not even in the same dimension. Sometimes she'd fall.'

I remembered seeing Celia stumble in the parking lot of Great Day.

'It was like she wasn't always in control of her own body. I suspected she was using drugs, for a while, but I'd never seen a recreational drug affect anyone quite like that. And I never saw her using, never.'

Her hand flying out to graze Joel's cheek, her horrified face . . .

'So maybe she was ill. Maybe she did die of some natural cause?' That would be great for those of us among the living. Though it sure hadn't looked natural to me. Could she have had some kind of fit?

'The police don't think so. But maybe they just have to act like it's a homicide, until they know different.'

'Did you tell Arthur all this that we've talked about?'

'No, he was more interested in establishing where I'd been all morning. He did tell me he wanted to talk to me again later, not to leave town. As if I would.'

I sat forward in my chair, preparatory to getting up to head to the bathroom. Not only did I need the facilities, I needed to rinse out my mouth and brush my hair. I had that sticky feeling I always get when I fall asleep in the daytime.

'Go pour yourself some tea,' I said. 'I have to excuse myself for a minute.' The downstairs bathroom didn't have a window, so I had to switch on the light to examine myself. I looked exactly like I'd just woken from a nap: rumpled hair, smudged makeup, sticky mouth. Yuck. I cleaned up, polished my glasses, and felt much more alert when I joined Robin in the kitchen. Angel had come in, and the two were in conversation about Angel's previous movie experiences and Robin's loathing of Hollywood.

'I thought you loved it out there,' I said, surprised.

'I did at first,' he admitted. 'I liked being somebody to people I thought were important. I liked being a noteworthy person. Writers don't get that too much, even in Hollywood, where you'd think they'd be revered. Those beautiful faces have to have words to say, after all. When I first arrived out there, I had a desirable property – my unfinished book – that several studios wanted. At first a really famous actress had an option on it. She wanted to play you.' He grimaced, an expression I really couldn't interpret. 'But then she went into rehab, and the option lapsed, and enthusiasm was cooling. The book actually came out, hit the best-seller list for a month, and interest built back up. A studio optioned it for one of its up-and-coming boy actors. They were going to beef up the role of Phillip.'

Phillip, my half-brother, had been staying with me when the murderer was arrested.

'Go on,' I said.

Robin looked weary, but he did offer me a little smile. 'Then the boy wonder backed out because he got a chance to do the new musical version of *Treasure Island*, and he wanted some stage credentials. In the meantime, the book went off the best-seller list, naturally. So, after all the hills and valleys, this production company optioned it for a made-for-cable miniseries, and hired Celia for it a few months before she won the Emmy.'

'Was that when you met her?'

'Yes,' he said, and wiped a big hand across his eyes. 'That was when I met her.'

'I'm sorry,' Angel said. I nodded.

'Like I said,' Robin told us, visibly pulling himself together, 'it was really over. There was a lot to admire in Celia, a lot of talent, but she also had a full measure of the selfishness actresses sometimes have. And there was definitely something going on with her these past few weeks.'

'Someone coming,' Angel said.

Then I heard the crunch of the gravel as a car made its way up the driveway.

Arthur was here, as he'd said earlier. I sighed. I just couldn't help it. I wondered how Lynn, his ex, was doing, raising their little girl. I'd heard Arthur took the child every chance he got, but still . . .

By the time Arthur knocked on the front door, Angel was making some coffee and I'd put some cookies on a plate. It was my attempt to soften the edges of an official visit. It didn't work, of course. Arthur was glad of the coffee, turned down a cookie with a pat of his waistline to explain the refusal, and got immediately down to business.

Angel and I went over our morning in detail, including approximate times and whom we'd seen and when we'd seen them. Arthur was particularly interested in my account of who I'd noticed at Celia's trailer door, but I pointed out that I hadn't been watching every second, and I'd only observed the door for maybe ten minutes. You had to figure that the murder had happened after Will, Mark, and the unknown woman (Arthur thought she must be a sort of sub-assistant director named Sarah Feathers) had spoken to Celia. That would have been while Angel and I were talking to Carolina.

'That Tracy girl who works for Molly's Moveable Feasts had as good a view of the door as I did, and for far longer,' I said.

'Yeah, but her attention was constantly distracted by people coming up and wanting juice, coffee, a pastry, to pass the time of day . . .'

I nodded. I could believe that.

Arthur wrote everything down and asked me and Angel a million questions. Robin sat silently and listened. Just when I thought we must be through, he said, 'Do you live out here alone, Roe?'

'Yes.'

'Do you think that's a good idea?'

I could feel my eyebrows draw together in a frown. 'If I weren't comfortable with it, I wouldn't do it, Arthur,' I said, in a final tone.

Because I'm short, some people think I'm helpless, or feeble, or silly. Arthur had known me for years; Arthur had even told me he loved me on more than one occasion. Why he would love a woman who would live in a place that terrified her when she had adequate means to move, I don't know, but he had that little smile that made me nuts. Patronizing.

'Do you really think you're safe out here?' he asked, trying ever so hard to sound gentle.

'Hell, Arthur, I've got a security system that's hooked up to the police department switchboard!' I could feel my face getting hot. Arthur had an amazing ability to make me angry. I was not about to tell him that this very day I had made up my mind to move.

'Okay, okay!' He held up a hand, palm outward, placatingly. 'But for a woman alone, living in town is safer.'

Much more of this, and I'd feel the steam coming out of my ears. 'If you've gotten all you need from Angel and me . . .' I said, making sure there was a nudge in my voice.

'I ought to be going, too,' Robin said. 'They may need me back at the motel. I'm sure Joel is having a meeting this afternoon to decide what to do.'

'I have to pick up Joan at the sitter's,' Angel said apologetically. 'Roe, would you like to come back to town with me? Spend the evening?'

There was no way in hell I was going to admit I wanted to be with someone, not while Arthur was standing there looking sorry for me. 'I have a lot to catch up on here,' I said, keeping my face calm as a pond. 'Thanks for visiting, Robin. I'll talk to you later, Angel. Tell me when you need me to take you to pick up your car.' Angel patted me on the shoulder. She'd asked Robin for a ride back into town, and he'd seemed glad to oblige. If I'd been him, I wouldn't have been too enthusiastic about getting back to the motel to face Joel Park Brooks, either.

To my dismay, somehow Arthur managed to linger while Angel and Robin left.

'How is Lorna?' I asked brightly, fishing the little girl's name out of my memory with a desperate yank.

'She's great,' Arthur said, his eyes focused on my face. Not too many people look at you so directly, but Arthur had always been a forceful and direct man. Except when he'd been dating me, and sleeping with Lynn Liggett. And asking her to marry him, when she was pregnant. Except for that. 'She's in the first grade.'

'Oh gosh,' I said, the impact of the years that had gone by hitting me between the eyes. I remembered how jealous Martin had been of Arthur, when he found Arthur pursuing me after Arthur divorced Lynn. All that emotional energy, wasted.

'Yes, I know.' Arthur laughed a little. 'They've moved into Atlanta. Lynn wanted to put Lorna into a private school, so she took a job with a big company that installs security systems for businesses. She's pulling in the big bucks.'

'How often do you manage to see Lorna?' I was struggling to keep the conversation going.

'I have her two weekends a month,' Arthur said. 'And some holidays.'

'Did you remarry?' I asked, all too aware that my voice was too bright and social.

'You know damn good and well I didn't,' he said. He didn't sound angry – just as if he were dusting off my pretense of ignorance. 'You would have known. I've dated a lot, come close to being that serious once.'

I automatically wanted to know who the close call had been, but that wasn't something I could ask.

'How are you recovering?' he asked.

I bit my lower lip and looked down at the hardwood floor. 'I'm probably doing better than I thought I would,' I said.

'That sounds pretty uncertain.'

I considered that. 'I thought I'd really collapse,' I said. 'Then I thought I was just being brave for a while and I'd collapse after that. But I guess I won't ever.'

'You seem surprised.'

I nodded.

'He never was . . .' Arthur began, and I held up a warning hand. There was a long silence.

'I'm leaving,' Arthur said. He rose wearily from the couch, ran a hand over his pale hair. 'Do you – would you like someone to stay out here at night with you?'

'You offering?' I was trying to get a little lightness into the conversation.

'I'd do it in a minute,' he said flatly, and I was sorry I'd spoken.

'Thanks, but I'm used to being by myself at night.' I did appreciate his thinking of my feelings. But the habit of turning Arthur away had gotten so strong I couldn't break it, and it would really be bad for me to begin asking someone to spend the night at the house to keep me company – not to mention what it'd do to my reputation, though I was pleased to find that consideration was strictly secondary.

'If you need me, you call,' Arthur said. 'But I know I make you rattled.' He looked resigned to that. 'There's someone who'd love to stay out here with you, and she needs money, if a paying situation would be more comfortable for you. The new young patrol-woman is just panting to meet you. She'd be glad to keep you company, especially if there was money involved.'

'Oh, she's on the poor side?' Why on earth would anyone want to meet me? Oh . . . the movie. Someday, I'd quit being completely naïve.

'Her husband ran up all their credit cards as high as he could before he left,' Arthur said, carefully showing no expression.

'He ran off with someone?'

'Her stepbrother.'

I let that soak in for a minute, until I was sure I had understood Arthur correctly. 'I guess my own problems aren't too bad,' I muttered, and Arthur nodded.

'That does put your life in perspective,' he agreed. 'Plus, the SOB took their car.'

'That's one of the worst stories I've ever heard,' I said after I'd thought it over.

'Tell me about it. So, if you want Susan to stay with you, give me a call.' Arthur patted me on the shoulder walked across the front porch, and opened the screen door. 'And call me if you think of anything about this morning, or about last night. Anything that might have happened while you were having dinner with the movie people.'

'I will,' I said, feeling sure I'd already told Arthur everything that could have a bearing on the murder of Celia Shaw.

I stood in the living room, all alone, and looked at the clock on the table. Amazingly, it was only noon. Equally amazingly, I was due at work.

Breakfast (two pieces of toast) had been an eon ago. I got some chicken salad out of the refrigerator and ate it out of the bowl, with crackers to scoop it up. I was glad I had a job where I was due, glad something had broken into the dreary pattern of my life . . .

Where had *that* come from?

I wasn't glad Celia was dead, was I?

No, not really. I was just glad something had happened to change things, jolt me out of my misery, cause people to treat me as something other than pitiful.

Because I wasn't, I told myself crisply. I was not pitiful, and I was not just a forlorn rich widow. I was no tragic figure to be wrapped in cotton batting, either. I was a *kick-butt* rich widow. I began to feel better and better as I cleared away the cracker crumbs and the glass, and by the time I got in my car to go back to town, I was in a mood to take on a grizzly.

No one looking at my four-eleven exterior could tell I was loaded for bear, and it was a considerable surprise to Lillian and

Perry when I told Janie Finstermeyer that her son had way too many overdue books, that it was getting to be a real habit of his, and that she'd better energize him into getting to the library with those books before the day was over or we'd yank his card.

I turned away from the telephone to find them staring at me as if I'd dyed my hair green.

'Can we even do that?' Lillian asked.

'You just watch me.' But it wasn't necessary to put the threat to the test, because Josh Finstermeyer flew into the library as if propelled within an hour, money in hand and an apology on his lips. He even took his baseball cap off in the library.

I tried to be equally gracious.

Chapter Eight

Of course, I heard from my mother that night. My mother, tall and elegant and reminiscent of Lauren Bacall at her coolest, might as well have been born on a different planet from me; I cannot imagine her carrying me in her womb, no matter what evidence there is to the contrary. I am an only child, and I've seen pictures of her pregnant, so I guess I'm really hers.

I was never much a child of my father, except biologically. He left when I was in my teens, my early teens. My mother, in her excellent vengeance, became a real estate tycoon in a modest way – if a tycoon can be modest – and we lived in more affluence than I ever would have if I'd stayed with my newspaperman father. He'd remarried, and had a son named Phillip, my half-brother. I hadn't seen Phillip in years. My father had decided I reminded the boy of a traumatic incident, and that seeing me was bad for Phillip.

When he got his own computer, Phillip began emailing me. I could tell, in his first messages, Phillip considered himself daring, contacting his dangerous older sister. I replied so calmly and matter-of-factly that it made my teeth ache, but at the same time I tried to make it clear that I was very happy to hear from him. Now we exchanged news once or twice a week. I hadn't had much to tell him since Martin died (Phillip had sent me the biggest, most sentimental card he could find, covered with a glittery substance). That wasn't the case tonight.

When the phone rang I was busy trying to tell Phillip about the excitement of the movie shoot, without dwelling on the death of Celia Shaw. Seeing the movie set and the movie people through different eyes made me feel better about the whole thing, myself.

I picked up the phone absently, my mind still on my composition.

'I hear you met up with Arthur Smith today,' my mother said.

'It's the first time I'd seen him in years,' I said. 'He looked pretty much the same.'

'Not dating anyone now,' my mother informed me, and I didn't ask her why she'd bothered to find that out. She wasn't giving me information about an opportunity, she was warning me. She'd never forgiven Arthur for dating Lynn while he was dating me, and especially for getting Lynn pregnant while I should have been. Mother's slacked off on the grandkid issue since she has some step-grandchildren through her husband, John Queensland. Especially once I told her that I had a malformation of the womb, and it was very unlikely that I would ever be able to have a baby: I'd tried to keep that to myself as long as I could.

But even if I told her I was dying to present her with a grandchild, she wouldn't want Arthur to be the father – not any more. In her opinion, he'd publicly humiliated me. (Actually, that was true. But I had given up minding.)

'So, that poor girl who died was the one who was going to play you in the movie?'

'Yeah, the composite me. Weird feeling.'

'Do you know Robin Crusoe is here?'

'Yes, I've seen him.'

'How does he look?'

'Much the same. He dresses better. His hair's still red.'

'Are you coming to dinner tomorrow night?'

'Oh . . . oh, sure.' I rolled my eyes at the computer screen. The last thing I wanted was to go to a family dinner with all John's kids, their spouses, and the children. But I'd agreed a few days ago, guilted out because I'd skipped the last two such gatherings.

'I'll see you tomorrow night, then, at six. Please don't be late. You can bring someone if you want.'

She always said that.

'I won't be late,' I said firmly. I never was: Roe Teagarden, punctual librarian. Didn't I sound exciting? I sighed after we'd said good-bye, pretty much standard ritual after a phone conversation with Aida Teagarden Queensland.

But my mother had always done her best by me, and she loved me. I loved her too. It would have been nice if I hadn't had to constantly remind myself of that. Abruptly, I was fed up with my own whininess, and decided it was high time I went to bed.

This had certainly been a highly eventful Saturday, compared with my normal weekend routine. I suppressed the memory of Celia's appearance when she was dead, and instead spun myself a fantasy in which Joel Park Brooks came to my door and begged me to take her place in the movie, and I did so with completely unexpected talent and grace, and some incredibly attractive actor – not anybody obvious like George Clooney or Mel Gibson, but someone more cerebral, like John Cusack – came to my door and begged me to return to Hollywood with him and tan by his pool and be his love goddess, since I was far more genuine and original than the shallow movie beauties surrounding him . . .

There's no age limit or personality conflict in fantasies, and this one merged pleasantly into sleep.

Next morning was a good Sunday for church. I attend on most Sundays, but sometimes I'm more enthusiastic than others. I wasn't sure what was happening to me, what process had been set in motion this past week, but I was relieved to feel better. I didn't realize how long a dark cloud had hung around me until it began to lift. I slicked my hair back and put it up as smoothly as I manage, and I wore a fall suit of a russet color. I put on my gold-rimmed glasses, and I had suede pumps and a purse to match. Amber earrings, I decided, and a dab of perfume.

'You look good,' I told my mirror earnestly. 'Pretty *darn* good.'

I got to St Stephen's about nine-fifteen. We had an early service, since Aubrey also preached at another church about thirty miles away at eleven o'clock. I slipped into the pew I usually used, noticed my mother and John hadn't gotten there yet, and slid to my knees to pray. Our church is small and beautiful, and just breathing the air of it makes me feel better. The organist began her playing before I'd finished, and I eased back into the pew and listened with my eyes closed. I don't have much of an ear for music, but I thought I was listening to Handel. The pew creaked as someone sat by me, and I opened my eyes after listening a little longer. Robin was on his knees next to me, wearing a perfectly proper suit and tie. He sat back by me, and began the business of book-marking his hymnal and turning to the proper place in the Book of Common Prayer. When he was arranged to his satisfaction, one of his long, slender hands reached over and patted mine. I turned my hand palm up so he could clasp it, and he gave my fingers a squeeze. His untidy hair was freshly washed and floating around his head in a coppery nimbus, and I averted my face so he couldn't see me smile.

Robin released my hand with another pat, and the processional began. We stood to observe it, and bowed at the passage of the cross. I was reminded all over again of how much taller he was than I. As Aubrey, the lector, and the two acolytes disposed themselves at the front of the church, I saw Will Weir, the cameraman, scuttle into the back pew on the other side. He was wearing a sports jacket, a white shirt, and jeans; not standard churchgoing garb in Lawrenceton, but he was a visitor, after all. My mother and her husband had slipped in late, as well.

The sun poured in the windows of the church and I watched dust motes dance in the beams. The ritual unfolded exactly as it ought, and as the congregation knelt and stood in unison, I felt a deep calm wash over me.

Will scuttled out of the church as fast as he'd scuttled in, so he apparently didn't want to meet and greet. Astonishingly, Robin went through the whole ritual. I gave him every opportunity to detach himself from me, because I was naturally aware that there was going to be speculation. But with the greatest tenacity, Robin stuck to my side and walked me to my car.

'My mother wonders if you'd like to come to dinner tonight,' I heard myself saying. Actually, that was true. She'd yanked me aside and ordered me to extend the invitation.

'How would you feel about that?'

I looked up at his small hazel eyes, fringed with rusty lashes. I looked down at my feet. 'If you'd like to come, that would be fine, of course.'

'Come by and pick me up at the hotel?'

'All right. Five-thirty okay?'

'Sure. Casual dress?'

'Oh, yes. I'll go home and change to pants and a shirt.'

'Will you let your hair down?'

'I don't know. I hadn't thought about it,' I said, more than a little surprised. I started to ask him why he wanted to know, but reined myself in. I also felt an impulse to ask him if he wanted to come home with me for lunch, and zapped that idea, too. Instead, I gave Robin a small smile and wave, and got in my car to go back to the house.

What an interesting morning it had turned out to be.

Arthur was parked in my driveway when I got back.

'I like the hair,' he called.

I sorted through my keys and nodded in reply as I went to the side door. 'Come on in,' I called, unlocking the door and deactivating the alarm.

Arthur was wearing a suit, and he was clean-shaven, but I was fairly sure he hadn't been at church.

'You're dressed up,' I said tentatively.

'I was on the news.' He looked embarrassed. 'You wouldn't believe how many news people are down at the station.'

'I haven't been watching the television. I guess it was everywhere on the news.' Arthur nodded. I was standing in the middle of my kitchen, tucking my keys back into my purse, and thinking as hard as I could. 'Oh, this is bad. They'll be coming around again.'

'Soon as they get directions to your house.'

I said a very unladylike word.

Arthur laughed. 'You can say that again. You know if it gets bad you can come stay with me.'

'I think not,' I said, smiling. 'Notorious Widow in Cop's Love Shack?'

Arthur took a deep breath. 'Listen, Roe, who in that movie crew was especially close to Celia Shaw?'

'Almost anyone would know more about that than I know.' I slung the purse onto the counter, slid out of my pumps, and made some fresh coffee. I got a mug out of the cabinet and put it by the coffeepot, and I got out some sugar and milk for Arthur's coffee. Funny, if you'd asked me how he took it, I wouldn't have thought I remembered – but here I was, setting out the things he took.

'I have reasons for asking you.'

'I'm sure you do. Well, of course, Robin dated her . . . though there were signs that the relationship was over.'

'Like her going to bed with your stepson?'

'Yeah, like that. No, really, there were indications before that.'

'Who else?'

'She seemed to be big buddies with Meredith Askew. I'm not sure how two-way that was, but Celia used Meredith to deliver her messages.'

'What about other crew members?'

'Will Weir was with her when I ran into them while they were shopping.'

Arthur consulted his notes. 'He would be the head cameraman. I understand he's more famous in his field than Celia Shaw had gotten to be in hers.'

'Well, he has a few years on her.'

'Anyone else?'

'When we went out to dinner at Heavenly Barbecue, Mark Chesney went.'

'He the assistant director? The gay one?'

'Right. Well, that is, he's the assistant director. I don't know about the gay part.' Actually, that was a conclusion I'd reached myself. I found that I was unwillingly impressed. There was no telling how many people Arthur had interviewed yesterday. He was definitely on top of this investigation.

'Did you notice anything peculiar about this actress?'

'Peculiar? How so? Mentally?' I'd seldom seen anyone more focused than Celia Shaw.

'Physically.'

'Yes, I had noticed some things. She stumbled a lot,' I said.

'Stumbled.' Arthur looked . . . not exactly excited, but intent.

'Yes, she was a little clumsy on her feet. And once she slapped at the director and looked surprised, like she didn't know she was going to do it.'

Arthur looked down at his feet. He didn't want me to see his face.

'So, are you going to explain?' I am as curious as the next person, and this was truly aggravating of Arthur.

'It'll be in the papers,' he said, more to himself than to me. He looked up. 'No, I just can't. We're trying to keep it quiet as long as we can.'

He had done this on purpose, I figured, to punish me for my lack of interest in him.

'Of course,' said Arthur, his hard blue eyes fixed on my face, 'if you were to butter up the lead detective sufficiently . . .'

'Define "butter up",' I said, my voice tart. I hoped he didn't mean what I thought he meant.

'A cup of that coffee would be nice.'

I flushed, and poured him the coffee. It smelled so good, I decided I'd have more, too.

'You didn't open your paper this morning.'

'No, I save the big Sunday paper for the afternoons.'

Arthur slipped off the rubber band and unrolled the paper. Celia's murder was the below-the-fold story on the front page. I blinked at the amount of coverage. The picture of Celia was one taken at the Emmys, when she'd been hanging on Robin's arm. She looked fabulous, and very young. Robin looked awfully mature, compared to Celia.

I motioned at a chair at the table, and Arthur sat. I slid into the chair across from him and began reading. The more I read the hotter my cheeks got. There were several references to the age difference between Robin and Celia. There were several references to Barrett. You didn't have to be Miss Marple to read between the lines.

When I'd finished, I couldn't look up at Arthur. This time it was I who didn't want him to read my face. I was wondering who was responsible for the slant of the story. Was it this individual reporter? Was this the way Arthur had read the situation, and had the facts he'd released to the papers been selected because they followed Arthur's reading? Or had this reporter been talking to Barrett?

I was willing to bet on some combination of all these elements. There were details about the evening at Heavenly Barbecue that had 'Barrett' stamped all over them, especially the inclusion of my name. It could easily have been left out of the story, and my presence at that awful meal clearly had no bearing on Celia's death – or at least, none that I could fathom. Barrett wanted to cause me discomfort and inconvenience, and he had.

The phone rang while I was thinking, and before I could answer it, Arthur picked it up. I felt rage prickle at the backs of my eyes while I waited for him to hand over my own telephone to me.

'Sure, she's right here,' Arthur was saying, and as he gave me the receiver he got a good look at my face. I don't think he'd quite realized that he was upsetting me, but he sure knew now.

'Roe?' It was Robin.

'Yes.'

'Have you . . . are you too busy to talk?'

'No, not at all.'

'You sound kind of funny.'

'I'm in a mood,' I said, with self-control.

'Yes, I can tell. With me?'

'Oh, no.'

'Have you read the paper?'

'Yes. It was just brought to my attention.'

'Do you . . . are we still on for tonight?'

'Definitely.'

'Good.' He sounded flatteringly relieved. 'This may be hard to arrange, because I'm besieged here at the motel.'

'Let me think. I'll call you back.'

He gave me his room number which he'd forgotten to do at the church, and I said good-bye. I hung up and swung around to face Arthur.

'Don't answer the telephone in my home.'

'I apologize. I was out of line. It was a reflex. I should have thought.'

'Now, I need you to go. I have things I have to do this afternoon.' I wondered what I would do if Arthur wouldn't leave, but I pushed that thought down into a corner as hard as I could. It wouldn't do to sound the least uncertain.

'All right,' he said. 'I'm sorry to have bothered you.' Now he was getting all stiff and huffy. Screw it. No more Ms Nice Widow.

I stared at him, unrelenting, until he stuffed his pad back into his pocket and stomped out. I set the alarm behind him. I watched from the window as he drove away. Again, I felt the isolation of this house. It was definitely time to move.

I wondered, as I turned away from the window, what big secret he had been going to tell me. I was proud of myself for not softening, but at the same time it was irritating to be left hanging that way.

As Robin and I had eventually arranged, I picked up a key at the desk and then pulled around to the back of the motel about two hours before my mother's dinner. We'd allowed plenty of time in case something went wrong.

Though they weren't in the front, where the office was, there were lots of reporters camped out in the side parking lot of the motel, and some television news vans. It had been easy for them to find out where the movie crew was staying. The men and women of the media were milling around on the pavement. Some of them had brought deck chairs, and some of them were playing cards.

I shook my head. I would not make a living as a reporter for any amount of money. No one could pay me enough to sit in a motel parking lot just in case someone should stick his head out of a door long enough to be photographed or interviewed.

I still had my hair up and I was wearing dark glasses, a

rudimentary camouflage move. I scooted up the stairs to a room on the second floor, not even glancing out over the railing to see if I was being observed. I had noticed Shelby's car parked two slots down, and that was one big relief. Shelby had rented the room I'd just entered under his own name, and left the key at the desk for me.

I called up to Robin's room. Shelby answered.

'He's ready,' Shelby said when he recognized my voice. He sounded amused.

'Okay. The door's unlocked.'

Shelby hung up; he was a man of few words.

In less than two minutes, the door swung open, and Robin walked in dressed in Shelby's blue padded Pan-Am Agra winter jumpsuit. It was what the men out in the plant wore when the temperatures dropped. Shelby was not as tall as Robin, but he was wider, and the poor fit was not so noticeable. The day was just barely cool enough to make the heavy garment reasonable.

'Can I take it off, now?' Robin asked. 'It's cutting me in a, uh, tender area.'

'Sure, take it off till it's time for us to leave,' I said, trying not to smile too broadly. I hadn't figured that Shelby's suit would be too short in the crotch for a long man like Robin. I perched on the end of the bed to watch.

'I see that smile,' Robin said, his voice muffled by his attempts to take off the jumpsuit while he faced away from me.

His nice clothes were somewhat rumpled by the experience, and his hair was disheveled, but he emerged from the heavy jumpsuit looking relieved. 'I'll put it back on before we go. You're sure your friend doesn't mind doing this?'

'Not as long as he gets his jumpsuit back. I owe them two hours babysitting now.'

'That doesn't seem too bad. I'll help.'

'You won't be around,' I said. 'You'll be back in Hollywood.'

'No. I don't think so.'

He sat beside me on the end of the bed, and what you might

call a significant silence fell. I was scared to look up at him, but eventually I just had to.

But I couldn't ask him what he meant.

He kissed me.

I can't say it was totally unexpected, but it was still a sort of shock. I hadn't kissed anyone since Martin died. And I hadn't kissed Robin, of course, in many years. But there was a familiarity to it, a kind of renewal, instead of the shock of something new.

Maybe because we were in a motel room, and I didn't have anything of my former life around me, maybe because I had that pleasant zingy feeling that I'd put one over on a lot of people with my plan to sneak Robin out for an innocent dinner at my mother's, maybe just because I hadn't had sex in a hell of a long time, but I went up in flames. It was all I could do to keep from grabbing him and throwing him to the bed. This was not my usual style. I was trembling with the effort of suppressing my reaction to his mouth.

'Roe?' he said, almost whispering.

He had put his hands on either side of my face.

'A little more,' I said.

'Aren't we a little mature to be making out?'

'You want to go sit on that chair over there?'

'Oh, hell, no.'

'Then mind.'

'Let's lie down as our next step,' he suggested.

'Okay.' I scooted up on the bed after kicking off my shoes, and Robin did the same.

'It's a lot easier to kiss you when we're lying down,' he observed, after a minute or two.

'I had noticed that.'

'Let's do that some more.'

So we did. It was like being teenagers again. We were thoroughly frustrated when I called a halt to the proceedings. But I just couldn't take that step. I just wasn't quite ready. Though God knows, my body was.

Robin vanished into the bathroom, and reappeared a few

minutes later, looking more relaxed. He wedged back into the jumpsuit. My blouse was buttoned and tucked, and I'd put on my shoes.

'Is your mother just as formidable as she was a few years ago?' he asked, watching me brush my hair, which I'd taken down. With a little help. I carefully pinned it in a knot.

'She's softer around the edges. Marriage and having grandchildren by way of John's kids has really fulfilled her.' I was still enjoying the pleasant sense of having been naughty.

'Remind me to take you to a motel room more often,' Robin said as we trotted down the stairs and scrambled into my car. No one called out to us. The jumpsuit and the hairstyle evidently were enough camouflage. 'If we'd stayed a little longer, maybe I could have had my wicked way with you.' He had jammed a baseball cap over his telltale red hair, and I turned my face away to hide my smile. Every man I knew wore a cap at some time or another and looked quite natural, but not Robin. He looked like an ostrich dressed up for Halloween. I was relieved when he pulled it off when we got into downtown Lawrenceton.

The scene at my mother's house was chaotic. John's two sons and their wives and their children made the two-storey four-bedroom seem positively tight. I had always liked John: warming up to his sons Avery and John David had taken a little longer. They'd been a little wary of my mother and me, too. The fact that John and my mother had signed a prenuptial agreement that was very clear on who got what when they passed away had been a great help, and my mother's cordiality and courtesy had won over her new stepdaughters-in-laws.

Melinda, Avery's wife, was braiding her toddler's hair in the foyer when I stepped in. Her infant, Charles, was in one of those portable carriers, which was on the floor where she could keep an eye on him. Charles was awake and watching his mother and sister with wide eyes.

'Hold still, Marcy!' Melinda was saying, her temper obviously at the breaking point. Marcy, of course, picked the entrance of a stranger (Robin) to spring into her worst behavior. 'No!' she shrieked. 'It hurts! Daddy do it! Daddy do it!'

'No, your daddy's busy. I'm going to braid your hair,' Melinda said firmly. My respect for her mounted. I would have gone searching for Daddy instantly.

'Melinda, this is my friend Robin,' I said, when Melinda's hands had begun dividing Marcy's fine brown hair into three parts.

'Hi, Robin! I'd shake your hand, but I'm busy right now. I think your mom is in the den, Roe.' Melinda's fingers flew, braiding like hell while Marcy was standing still.

'Hey, Aunt Roe,' Marcy said, looking up at us. She eyed Robin. He must have seemed huge to her.

We located my mother in the den, as Melinda had said. She was serving glasses of wine, but she put the tray down so Robin could give her a small hug (nicely calibrated on Robin's part). Then there was a round of handshaking among the men. John had recovered from his heart attack, but he was thinner and didn't move as quickly as before. He was still a handsome man, and he'd passed his looks to Avery and John David, tall brown-haired men with blue eyes. They were golfers like John, and they were both confident men who did well at their chosen careers. Other than those similarities, they were quite different, and their wives weren't anything like each other.

Avery, Melinda's husband, was an accountant. Avery was very traditional, and people who weren't also completely buttoned down were somewhat suspect in his book. He'd never been really sure about me. Melinda herself, though pleasant, was none too bright. But she seemed to have this raising kids thing down pat, and she was active in community work.

John David, the younger brother, had been a wild child. There was still a gleam in his eyes that said he was anticipating the unexpected. His wife, Poppy, had also made a name for herself as a teenager, but now she seemed quite settled into her role as a suburban wife and mother. She still enjoyed an evening out every now and then, and I would not have put money on either of them maintaining fidelity during their marriage, but I liked both of them quite a bit. Their new son, Brandon Chase Queensland, was the most placid baby I had ever encountered.

As I might have predicted, Avery questioned Robin cautiously about his means of making a living, his future plans, and his upbringing. John David wanted to hear stories of the famous people Robin knew, and instantly treated Robin as if he was my acknowledged companion.

'Not too surprising, since you have a hickey on your neck,' my mother murmured into my ear, and I jumped a mile.

'Oh, hell,' I said, clapping a hand over the spot she touched with one cool finger.

'Everyone's already seen it,' she said with a shrug. 'You and Robin seem to have picked up where you left off.' My mother's graying brown hair was beautifully styled, as always, and her tailored blouse and gray slacks were as informal as she got.

I took her arm and we stepped into the dining room, which so far was empty of Queenslands.

'The only thing is,' I said, with the frankness you can only show your family, 'I think about Martin and I just feel so guilty.'

My mother took a deep breath. Her eyes looked old, suddenly. 'You listen to me right now, Roe. Your husband is *beyond* all that.'

I sucked in my breath.

'Martin – yes, while he was here he truly loved you – but Martin has *passed beyond* those emotions that plague living people – jealousy, possessiveness, selfishness. He's not here, he doesn't worry about worldly things any more, and he should not affect your decisions.'

I was silent – mostly from the shock of her frankness – as I pondered my mother's pronouncements. 'You're sure you believe this,' I said, half-asking a question. 'Because you know . . . Martin, as he was, would rather have killed Robin, and maybe me, too . . .'

'And that wasn't Martin's best side,' my mother said calmly. 'But these things are no longer his concern.'

That idea caused a painful ache. It detached my life even further from Martin's. And yet, I could not deny that I felt a lightening of my heart, as if the fact that it was still emotionally tied to Martin's had been dragging it down.

'You are the best mother I've ever had,' I said, and my voice came out shaky. She laughed, and I laughed, and I gave her a hug, and then she went back to her company. 'Melinda, have you got that girl's hair braided?' I heard her asking as she went into the living room.

A mumble from Melinda, then Marcy's voice, shrill and piercing, 'Is that big man with Aunt Roe a giant?'

The whole house seemed to hold its breath for a second before laughter came from at least three different rooms.

Chapter Nine

'She had Huntington's chorea,' Sally Allison said. This was big news, and Sally relished big news.

It was eight in the morning, and I'd just finished getting dressed for work when the phone rang. Sally had called to ask me the same questions Arthur had asked me the day before: had I noticed Celia Shaw exhibit any of a list of symptoms?

'Yes, yes, yes,' I had answered. I detailed once again what I had observed. 'Now, what does that mean?'

When Sally told me, I was just as ignorant. 'What is that?'

'It's a disease, a horrible hereditary disease of the central nervous system,' Sally said. She sounded almost awed by the horror of it.

I would have expected a certain amount of zest to Sally's words; after all, reporting on the horrible was her bread and butter. But whatever Huntington's chorea was, Sally truly thought it was awful.

'So, what's the bottom line?'

'The bottom line is inevitable death with your mind reduced to vegetable status. You have no control over your body at all.'

'Oh. Oh, gosh.' That hardly seemed adequate, but then I didn't know what would.

'There can be lots of symptoms, and it can progress at different speeds in different individuals. Mostly, you begin showing signs in your thirties, and though it may lie almost still for a few years, it begins sinking its teeth into you.'

'Oh, that poor girl.' I wouldn't wish such an end on my worst enemy, and Celia had hardly been that.

'Well, actually, she was somewhat older than her official bio says,' Sally told me.

'I kind of guessed that.'

'Yeah, she was at least thirty. That's still young for Huntington's to have manifested itself, I gather, but it happens.'

'Do you think she knew?'

There was a long silence.

'Maybe,' Sally said. 'Maybe she . . . I don't know. If she began wondering why she was getting so clumsy – I think she must have known something was wrong, if not exactly what.'

'What about her mother?'

'That's it. I called the town where her mother died, as listed in her bio, and though Linda Shaw committed suicide, fairly advanced Huntington's was found at the autopsy.'

'Oh, my Lord. That's awful.'

'But, we have to ask ourselves,' Sally said wisely, 'is her mother's death related to Celia's murder at all?'

'How could it not be?'

'It doesn't have to be.'

I held the phone away from my face and stared at it. 'Sally, are you serious? The mother has Huntington's and dies young, a suicide. The daughter has Huntington's, and dies young, an apparent murder victim. No connection?'

'You didn't realize she was ill. I don't know who did. Maybe the people around her all the time were well aware something was wrong with her – our old friend Robin Crusoe, for example. Wouldn't someone as smart as Robin Crusoe realize his girlfriend had some severe problems? Wouldn't her self-proclaimed best friend Meredith know? Wouldn't you at least suspect something was wrong if you saw me begin to make involuntary movements, begin to show unusual clumsiness? Maybe say something completely off the wall?'

'Yes,' I said reluctantly. And you're not even my best friend, I added silently.

I just didn't want to believe that Robin had to have realized that something was up with the woman he'd been sleeping with. But I had to face the facts.

'I just don't see why anyone would kill her. So, she's sick. It's not her fault, and it's not catching, am I right?' I began doodling with a pencil on the pad I kept by the phone in the kitchen. Robin had said he didn't think he was going back to Hollywood. So where would he go?

'No, it's not contagious,' Sally said, as if the very idea was stupid. 'It's hereditary.'

'And it came through her mom. So, who's her dad?'

'No one knows. Linda Shaw didn't list anyone on the birth certificate, but her sister, the one who raised Celia, said Linda was not promiscuous, so she would have known, presumably. And furthermore, the sister says the guy was out in California with Linda when she died, from what Linda would say when she called.'

'So finding him would provide a lot of information.'

'At least. Maybe he and Celia had been in touch, who knows? She didn't talk about her family life to anyone.'

I could see why. A tough way to start your life, with no dad and a doomed and distant mother: I couldn't even imagine it.

'But what was the actual cause of Celia's death?' I asked. 'Surely someone killed her?'

'Oh, she was smothered with a pillow,' Sally said, almost as an afterthought. 'After being drugged with some tranquilizers, probably ground up in her coffee. Maybe she was already unconscious when she was smothered. Maybe she didn't even know. And then, a little later, someone brained her with the Emmy. There again, she didn't know.'

But maybe she had, my morbid imagination insisted. To be too drowsy to defend yourself, to feel the pillow against your face, to want air so desperately . . . I shuddered, and tried to think of something else. A lot had been happening to Celia's body. 'So she was dead when she was hit with the Emmy?' I asked, just to hear it again.

'Yes. She was killed three different ways. The pills, the smothering, the statue.'

'That was sure a quick autopsy.'

'Since there's so much media interest, she got moved to the head of the class,' Sally said cheerfully.

I found this all too depressing. I was just beginning to take a lighter look at my life, and I could not bear to be pulled down. I'd woken up looking forward to the day ahead – a mindset I'd once taken for granted – and I was selfish enough to want to hold on to the feeling. I had brushed my hair back in a ponytail, then rolled it up into a ball and pinned it, topping the whole with a bow low on my neck. I was wearing rust-colored pants and a light sweater, tan with rust-and-green patterns on it. My tortoiseshell glasses coordinated. Before Sally had called, I had been feeling a distinct glow.

It was difficult to believe that my whole balloon of happiness had been inflated by the simple fact that I'd given a man an erection. But when I tracked my new attitude down to its source, this was what I found. Well, what the hey. I'd settle. It wasn't the erection per se. It was the fact that I still *had it*. Okay, granted, to excite the human male was fairly easy (sometimes just the state of breathing was enough). But Robin had standards above that, I told myself stoutly. He'd had a high-powered agent, he'd had women in Hollywood (where beautiful women were a dime a dozen), and still, yours truly had excited him. I had a suspicion that if I examined my line of reasoning I would find many flaws, but that wasn't the kind of mood I was in.

I was determined not to brood on Celia Shaw's terrible end. I told myself briskly that Arthur was on the case and he was a good detective, and I should leave it at that. I took another rotation in front of the mirror, deciding that my bottom looked real good in these pants. I dabbed on some perfume. I'd managed to cheer myself up to my former level by the time I breezed through the employees' entrance into the library, slung my purse into my little locker and pocketed the key, and collected my usual pile of memos and mailings from my pigeonhole in Patricia Bledsoe's office.

She looked up from her computer, gave me a brisk nod, and returned to her work. I nodded right back, and began flipping through the medley of garbage that was my daily tree consumption. Lying between memos from the regional director about how many hours of course work were required to keep one's library degree current, and the seasonal reminder detailing the symptoms of head lice, was a plain dime-store envelope (in these days, you should call it a plain Wal-Mart envelope, I guess) with a folded sheet inside. I never got personal mail at the library. Only my name was written on the outside, in neat block capitals.

'Patricia, who brought this in?' I asked, holding it up so she could get a look at it.

'I don't know. It was on the floor by the checkout desk this morning, Perry said. He brought it back here,' Patricia said. She didn't seem too interested. As usual, she was ironed, starched, aligned, and every other straight-and-narrow adjective I could recall.

'Well, hmph,' I said. I put everything else down and borrowed Patricia's letter opener, which seemed to irritate the woman. Tough. I tapped the letter out of the envelope; a plain sheet of five-by-eight white lined paper, torn from a tablet.

It said, 'You Whore she's not even buried and your after her boyfriend.'

I stared at it as if it were a poisonous snake. I wanted it to go away, or to say anything other than what it actually said. I took a deep breath and tried to think what to do next. An almost irresistible impulse seized me, told me to rip the paper to shreds and burn those shreds. I didn't want to admit to myself that someone had directed words so venomous to me, much less admit to anyone else that I had received such a message. But Duty is practically my middle name – well, maybe Conventional, or Law-abiding – anyway, I had to call the police.

Of course, the cop who answered the call was Arthur Smith.

He held the paper with a pair of tweezers as he read it. His face remained blank. 'This is very interesting,' Arthur said, in a voice that would've sounded genuinely detached if I hadn't known him so well. He asked Patricia the same questions I had about the letter's provenance, plus about twenty more, all designed to elicit any detail she might have omitted.

It was interesting to watch Arthur with Patricia. She answered his questions clearly and in detail, but she never looked directly at him, and she didn't elaborate. It was like she was counting out the words she had to use to get her message delivered, and that was the number she would utter – that many, and no more. To my alert eyes, Patricia looked absolutely relieved when Arthur drew me from her little office into the employee lounge, which was deserted.

'You've been with the writer with the stupid name?' he asked.

He knew quite well who Robin was.

'Depends on what you mean by "been with",' I replied. 'If you're talking biblical, that's none of your business. But my mother asked him over to dinner last night, and we had to sneak him out of the motel so the reporters wouldn't follow. So, yes, I've spent time with him. I've known him for years.' It was remarkable how defensive I sounded for someone without a guilty conscience.

'Who knew this?' Arthur was nothing if not tenacious.

'Any of the movie people at the hotel, I guess,' I said slowly, thinking as I spoke. 'My family – my mother and John's family, that is. And Shelby helped me get Robin out of the motel, so Shelby and Angel knew.' I detailed the little plot to Arthur. It all sounded silly today, though yesterday it had seemed to make perfect sense.

'A lot of people,' Arthur said. He looked at the letter again, frowning. 'I don't want to alarm you, Roe, but you should do some thinking. The last woman who dated Robin Crusoe got smothered. Now you've gotten a nasty letter.'

I was flabbergasted. 'There's a great distinction between being killed and getting an anonymous letter,' I said, trying to sound tart and undaunted. But I was turning over what he'd told me, and I was dismayed; and that was what Arthur had wanted, for whatever reason.

'What was the name of the secretary?' he asked me, out of the blue.

'The lady you just met? Patricia Bledsoe,' I said.

'Is she new to Lawrenceton?'

'Comparatively. She's lived here maybe a year.'

'She have family?' he asked idly.

'She's got a son, Jerome. He's in the fifth or sixth grade, I think.'

Arthur stared at the wall of her office as if it would open to reveal Patricia Bledsoe. He shook his head as though whatever he was trying to recall just wouldn't pop into his head, a feeling with which I was all too familiar.

'Where's she from?' he asked, as if he were losing interest.

'She never talks about herself.' That was a remarkable thing all by itself. 'I only know from seeing her application that she moved here from Savannah.'

'Savannah. Okay, let me get this back to the station, send it off to the crime lab. You get any other mail like this, you call me right away. You did the right thing.' He sounded a little surprised.

'Yes, I know,' I said, taken aback by all this unnecessary chatter. This wasn't like Arthur.

'I'd stay away from Robin Crusoe,' he threw over his shoulder, which was far more Arthur-esque. Suddenly, he turned around, marched over to me with purpose in every step, and kissed me. I could not have been more surprised if he'd unzipped his pants. Stunned and unhappy, but anxious not to hurt Arthur's feelings – we'd hurt each other enough over the years – I endured the pressure of his lips, my hands hanging limp at my sides.

Then it was over, and he stepped back, giving me a baffled, angry look that I didn't know how to interpret. He walked out without looking back.

Arthur was like a dog with a favorite old bone, I decided as I wiped my mouth and set my mind in the right mode for work. He couldn't quite forget about it, and he couldn't quite abandon it. He kept digging it up and chewing on it, then putting it back in the ground.

That was where our long-ago affair should stay; dead and buried.

Mondays are always iffy at the library. Some Mondays are just dead; people are running errands and shopping and picking their work week back up after the weekend. But then, we have regulars who finish their library books on the weekend and come in Monday for a new supply. Teachers are fond of assigning term papers on Monday, and there are kids who come in to check out all the available books on a certain subject so they'll be sure of a resource.

This Monday was one of the quiet ones. Of course. I really wanted to be busy, to take my mind off the confusing events of the past week, but the most exciting thing that happened was catching a twelve-year-old girl trying to sneak out a copy of a new magazine that featured a cover article about her favorite boy band. I caught her on the way out the door, explained her options to her, and gave her a Kleenex when she started crying. Josh Finstermeyer of the overdue books saw me standing with the weeping girl, and hid behind the stacks to see if I'd stick bamboo under her fingernails. He clearly regarded me as the devil incarnate. I had to confess, it sort of gave me a thrill to be considered so formidable.

Tracy, the young woman from Molly's Moveable Feasts, came in. She waved to me while giving me a brilliant smile, and settled in a chair to read some newspapers. I guessed nothing was happening at the movie set yet.

About ten minutes before five o'clock, Robin loped through the glass doors. His long legs ate up yards of carpet like nobody's business. His hair was more of a mess than usual, and he was wearing khakis, a sharply pressed shirt obviously fresh from the laundry, and an old corduroy jacket. All he needed was a pipe clenched between his teeth, or maybe a golden retriever on a leash.

I was shelving books and, after he located me, he followed me as I trundled the little cart.

'When do you get off today?' he asked in a low, library voice. He pressed his hand against my back at my waist and left it there, while I put a Lauren Henderson book back on the shelf. His hand felt very warm. After a second or two, *I* began to feel a little warm.

'At five,' I said, glad to hear my voice come out cool and controlled.

The next book on the cart was Linda Howard's, and she was on the top shelf. I stretched up as far as I could and still could not quite slide Ms Howard into the right slot. Robin stepped closer to help, and after the book was in place, he stayed right behind me . . . in fact, so right behind me that he was sort of nudging me.

'Robin,' I said, a little question in my voice. Spooned, that was what we were. My curves . . . his – oh.

'Mmmm?'

'The book is where it's supposed to be.'

'And?'

'You should move.'

He sighed. 'If I must,' he said, and stepped back a little.

I smiled at the books in front of me. 'I assume you had a purpose in coming to the library?' I resumed rolling the cart. I may have headed down a deserted row. In fact, there was nothing to shelve at all in this area.

'I heard there was a *very* strict librarian here,' he said innocently.

I half-turned to give him a look, my eyes wide. This was a whole new ball game, one I'd never played. Hmmm.

'Oh, yes, very strict,' I said, trying to sound calm and assured. I wasn't sure where this was going, but I found myself quite interested in finding out.

'One who might punish me severely for having an overdue book,' Robin said.

'Have you been talking to Josh Finstermeyer?' I blurted.

Robin looked disconcerted. 'Who's he?' he asked.

'That boy in the corner who's trying to hide behind the shelves.'

Robin looked as if he was having trouble suppressing a laugh. 'Robbing the cradle, are we?'

I sighed. 'Can we get back on track here?'

'I don't know; if Josh Finstermeyer is your beverage of choice . . .'

'Robin!' I growled. I felt that everyone in the library was watching us, and I was right. Perry was taking a gander, as was young Josh, to say nothing of Tracy, who'd lowered her newspaper to stare. I felt my face turning red.

'I have two overdue books,' Robin said, his face suddenly serious. His voice was soft and significant. I looked up at him. 'Two,' he emphasized. He waggled his eyebrows.

'That's . . . *very* bad.' I narrowed my eyes. For the first time in my life, I wished I had a riding crop. I would flick it against my boot.

He bent down to my ear. 'I turned down the corners of some of the pages,' he whispered.

'You do need to be punished. At length,' I said. I raised my eyebrows to make sure he'd get it, 'At *length*,' I repeated.

He was a little pink himself.

'Maybe you should come to my room tonight,' he said, very low. 'To collect my fine.'

I decided to escalate.

'Why not now?' I said coolly. I glanced at the clock. 'I'm off work.' I gave him a challenging look.

His eyes widened behind his glasses. He ran a hand through his hair, which looked as if he'd been doing that all day.

'Can you hold this mood on the drive out to the motel?' he whispered in my ear. Very close.

'It's entirely possible.' My house was a lot closer, but I knew without considering the idea closely that my house was out. I cast a blessing at him for not suggesting it.

'Then let's go.'

'I'll go clock out.'

'You remember my room number?'

'Yes.'

'I'll be waiting for you.'

'You'd better be,' I said, in my stern librarian persona.

'Ooooh,' he breathed, giving me a look that let me know for sure he was into this.

I clocked out and retrieved my purse in record time, and was getting into my car in the employee parking lot behind the library when I saw Tracy approaching. Oh, heck, no! I was in a mood, and I didn't want to get out.

I decided if I were behaving uncharacteristically, I'd just go all the way. I pretended I didn't see her and pulled out of the parking lot when she was just a few feet away.

I had other fish to fry.

Robin, probably as uncertain as I was, was still fully dressed when I knocked on his door. But he had lit some candles and drawn the curtains tight.

'On your back, miscreant,' I said sternly. I had always wanted to say 'miscreant'.

There was delight in the crooked smile, quickly smothered by a very well assumed expression of fear. 'It was just two books,' he pled, stepping out of his shoes and socks and lying on his back on the bed. Yep, he was excited, all right.

'That's two books too many,' I told him. 'You have to learn your lesson.' With an expression of severity, I began unbuttoning my blouse. 'What's the worst punishment you can think of, you . . . scofflaw?'

Robin winced, and I could tell I would pay for that one, later. 'The worst punishment,' he said thoughtfully. 'The worst punishment would be to have to perform sexually, again and again – with only the briefest breaks for naps and food – for a small naked woman with . . .' His eyes widened. I'd taken off my bra. 'Oh, boy,' he breathed.

I climbed on the bed and straddled him. As I looked down at him, his eyes darkened. I took his glasses off and put them by mine on the bedside table. 'Can you think of anything that would make that punishment worse?' I murmured, bending down to him. My lips were an inch from his. My hair fell around his face.

'I would be forced to make you come twice for every one time I do,' he said, his voice rough and deep.

'Then I guess you better get started.'

Chapter Ten

I was changing my clothes when the phone rang. Almost without looking at my caller ID, I was sure my mother was on the other end of the line.

'Where were you last night?' she said, considerably agitated.

'I spent the night with a friend,' I said with commendable restraint. 'Now I have about fifteen minutes to get to work.'

'A friend? Who?'

I let the silence hang.

'Oh,' she said slowly. 'That kind of friend.'

More silence.

'Oh, sorry. Well, that's just . . . I didn't mean to intrude. I just wanted to make sure you're okay.' I could practically hear the questions seething over the line. I was proud of Mother's self-control.

'I'm fine, thank you.' In fact, more than fine. I was relaxed and mellow to an extent I could hardly believe. Except for the discomfort when I walked. Or sat. Or crouched.

I picked through my sweaters, looking for a turtleneck. Surely it was cool enough to make a turtleneck not unreasonable? I glanced into the full-length mirror on the closet door. Definitely needed the turtleneck. 'Oh, Mom, I need to look for a house in town and put this one on the market.'

Quite a silence on the other end. 'Aren't you rushing into this?'

'I'm not rushing. I had already decided to move back into town.' The last thing in the world I needed today was to have to defend myself to my mother.

There may have been a little edge in my tone, because she immediately said she'd list the house that very day. 'Who would you like to be your realtor?' she asked, keeping her voice scrupulously neutral. I'd had Eileen Norris the last time I'd been house hunting, but I had a better idea this morning.

'Why, the head honcho, of course.'

'Really? You think we can gee and haw together?'

'Sure. After all, this is your area of expertise.'

'Well, tell me what you want, and I'll line some things up.'

'I have no idea.' I tried not to wonder if Robin really meant to stick around in Lawrenceton, if he planned to buy a house or rent, should I be thinking of getting a house that would hold another person – and his books. No, no point in thinking of that. Jumping the gun, for sure. 'I guess I want a three-bedroom, but I need a room for a library, and a dining room, and a living room. And you know how I feel about plenty of kitchen counter space. On the other hand, I don't want much yard to take care of.'

'Your house is ready to show, I'll bet,' Mother said.

'Yes. Isn't that scary? All I'd have to do is pick up the floor of my closet.'

'I'll list it today,' she promised. 'I hope this is the start of a new era for you, honey.'

'I guess it is,' I said, after turning that over in my mind. 'I think it is.' We discussed the price I should set on my house and what I was willing to spend on my next one. I was once again grateful for my financial health. The independence it afforded me was absolutely blissful.

'What's your work schedule like the rest of the week?' my mother asked.

'I work this morning, but I'm free this afternoon.'

'Let me see what I can line up by then.'

'Wow. So quickly?'

'I didn't get where I am by letting my feet drag,' she said.

'Okay. I'll come by Select when I get off work.'

'Good, I'll see you then.'

The movie crew had resumed its activity at the courthouse this morning. I could tell from the traffic snarls in the area. Robin had said they would be shooting the scenes that didn't include Celia's character, until the recasting of the role was accomplished. He didn't expect that to take long.

I glimpsed the Molly's Moveable Feasts van parked a block away from the courthouse, and saw the familiar table set up further down the street. A man was in charge of it today. I wondered where Tracy had gone, and what she had wanted with me the day before. I could feel my cheeks burn as I thought of what had followed the little scene in the library. Just when you think you know yourself . . . well, it had been the most fun I'd had in a long, long year.

'Patricia,' I said, trying not to sound disgustingly cheerful. 'How are you today?' She was taking the cover off her computer and making little preliminary movements of things on her desk. Her pencil had to be just so, her little magnetic bowl of paper clips in a specific location, her chair exactly the right height.

'Just fine, thank you, Ms Teagarden,' Patricia said in a clipped voice. 'What do you think the police are up to, with Celia Shaw's death?'

'I have no idea. I haven't talked to anyone in the police department since the day it happened.'

She looked disappointed. 'Oh,' she said. 'I understood you were a particular friend of Detective Smith's.'

'No, that's not correct.' I could do clipped, too. 'As far as I know, they could be coming to arrest you any minute.'

My mildly belligerent comment had an amazing result. Patricia Bledsoe stared at me as though I'd grown a second head. She turned absolutely green.

'What do you mean?' she said, her voice faltering.

'I was just, ah, emphasizing how little I know about the investigation,' I said, convinced I'd gone over a line somehow. I felt knee-high to a grasshopper. 'Patricia! You, of all people . . . I mean, I bet you iron your *underwear*.'

Patricia looked at me with loathing. 'Go work,' she said.

She'd crossed the boundary into open rudeness in a great rush. What on earth had I done? I felt pretty truculent myself, by now. I couldn't think of anything to say that wouldn't escalate the hostility in the room, so I spun on my heel and left, my excellent mood stuffed in a sack for at least a little while.

My boss, Sam Clerrick, came in the employee door as I was stuffing my purse into my little locker.

'Good morning, Roe,' he said. His heavy glasses reflected the overhead light. He was carrying his briefcase, which was as much a part of Sam as his white shirt and tie. You'd think he carried nuclear warhead firing codes in it instead of library paperwork.

'Watch out for Patricia today,' I said.

'Something's wrong with Patricia?' Sam was as protective of his prize secretary as if she'd been a pedigreed bitch.

'She's a mite testy,' I said, trying not to sound spiteful.

'Have you gone and upset her?' Sam sounded calm, but I knew better. A good secretary, one who meshes perfectly with her boss's moods and personality, is worth rubies. Sam would much rather see me quit than lose Patricia.

'She went and upset herself,' I said in my own defense.

'You obviously didn't know that the day Celia Shaw came in here and checked out some books, I gave Ms Shaw a brief tour of the library,' Sam said.

Oh, I bet that had just made Celia's day. 'I'm sure she enjoyed it,' I muttered.

'And she met Patricia then, shook hands with her,' Sam went on. 'So naturally Patricia is upset by the news of Ms Shaw's murder.'

'I see that I shouldn't have brought it up,' I said, and that was the truth.

Casting me a hostile look, Sam stomped into Patricia's cubicle. I could see him saying soothing things through the clear upper panels.

So much for senior employee loyalty, I told myself, now just as frazzled as Patricia. I'd been working for the library for ten years or more, and Patricia had been here less than a year.

I stomped out to the main desk, emotionally loaded for bear. Luckily for my coworkers, about ten minutes after the library opened, the heavier of the two ladies who worked at Flower

Fantasies brought in a beautiful flower arrangement and carefully set it on the desk in front of me, as I was beginning to telephone the people who had overdue books. Chrysanthemums, daisies, and other flowers I couldn't identify mixed in a medley of warm colors against their dark green background.

'It's for me?' How long had it been since anyone had sent me flowers?

'Yes, ma'am,' the woman said, beaming at my pleasure. 'First order of the day.'

I took the card out of the little plastic prongs and opened the envelope.

'You are beyond beautiful,' the card said. It was signed 'Robin.'

I didn't melt on the spot, but it was a near thing. Tears welled in my eyes, which I kept very wide open.

'It's lovely,' I said. 'Thank you.'

'Enjoy,' she said, waving a casual hand, and returned to her van, parked illegally outside the main library doors.

I held the card to my chest like a schoolgirl, while I beamed at the arrangement. If Robin had planned a blitz attack on my body and heart, he was going about it exactly right. I could only be glad he'd decided to proceed with his campaign.

After the freezing-cold misery of the last year, I had the feeling I was sitting by a warm fire. That glow lasted all morning, with the exception of the few minutes it took to roust a reporter who came into the library to ask me how it felt to have been murdered by proxy, so to speak. Sam took care of him pretty quickly, and I was grateful.

The incident did set me to thinking back to that morning at the courthouse. I recalled sitting in the sun, waiting for Angel. I watched Will speak to Celia, shove the door shut with one hand while he carried a cup of coffee in the other. I watched Mark knock at the door in vain. Had Celia been angry with him? Had she already had the drugged coffee, begun feeling drowsy? Had she just been in the bathroom and unable to come to the door? Then the woman – Sarah Feathers, Arthur had told me – just barely opening the trailer door and speaking a few words, shutting it again. Then I'd lost a few minutes of surveillance while I talked to Carolina. Then I'd gone to Tracy's table in front of the Molly's van, watched her change jackets, had the orange juice. All trivial stuff.

I opened my eyes and focused on my flowers again. I'd been standing there with my eyes shut while I thought, probably a bad habit to get into. For the first time, I wondered if Sarah Feathers had heard a reply from Celia to whatever she had said. I didn't know Sarah Feathers, and I couldn't ask her, but I knew who could.

Sure enough, Angel had gotten Carolina's cell phone number.

'Hello!' Carolina said, after two rings. I asked my question, and she said, 'I don't know why you want to know, but it's easy enough to find out. I see Sarah all the time.'

Carolina agreed to call me back that evening. I went back to calling patrons about overdue books.

At noon, I trotted out of the employee door with my flowers held carefully in front of me. I was so busy planning how to place them in my car so they didn't fall over that I never saw the shadow behind me until it was too late.

'Roe! Roe! Are you all right?' A silhouette was between me and the bright fall sun, right overhead.

'What happened?' I asked, my voice weak and shaky.

'Someone ran up behind you and hit you,' Perry Allison said. 'Someone in a coat with the hood pulled over his head, so I couldn't see who it was. I called the police on my cell phone. They're coming.'

'My flowers,' I said, and I began to cry. That was why I felt wet. My flowers were all around me on the pavement of the parking lot, and the water in the vase had soaked my pants.

'I'm sorry,' Perry said. 'Are you hurt?'

'I'm okay,' I said, trying to convince myself. A patrol car was turning into the library parking lot already, and a patrol officer I didn't know leaped out of it as though the car had an ejector seat.

She was a small woman with short, dark hair, and she was already talking over her shoulder-rig thing.

'Which way did the assailant go?' she asked Perry.

Perry, trying not to gawk (he is a big fan of authoritative women) pointed in the direction of the heavily planted slope that divided the parking lot from the lower street. 'He went in the bushes after he pushed Roe down,' Perry called to the officer's back.

'Wow,' Perry said, deeply impressed.

I sighed, glad I wasn't one of those self-centered people who think getting attacked is all about them. This was my day for people ruining 'Aurora' moments.

Perry looked back down at me, maybe hearing something exasperated in my exhalation. 'Can you sit up, Roe?' he asked. He slid an arm underneath me and I was upright. I'd never been this close to Perry before, and it felt funny. I would just as soon he let me handle this on my own, but there was no way I could say 'back off' without sounding incredibly rude.

'This is good,' I said, more or less to myself. My head felt fine. After a second or two of thinking about it and getting my breath back, I decided I wasn't really hurt, just astonished.

The patrol officer came back through the bushes. 'I'm afraid the assailant has escaped,' she said seriously. 'There are other officers patrolling the area right now.' I wondered if she always talked like that, or if she'd acquired the habit since she joined the force.

'I'd like to stand up if you would give me a hand,' I said, giving Perry my right hand and extending my left to her.

'You sure you're okay for that?' she asked. 'Did you hit your head?'

'No, I took a spill when she shoved me,' I said.

'She? This man,' she inclined her head toward Perry, 'said your attacker was a "he".'

'Why did I say that?' I asked myself, while they pulled me to my feet. I thought it over. 'Perfume,' I said.

'The person who pushed you had a on a woman's fragrance?'

'Yes, officer,' I said. 'But I didn't see her coming at all. She just ran up behind and pushed me down and I dropped my flowers.' Embarrassingly, I began crying again.

'Who were they from, Roe?' Perry asked, probably hoping I'd stop with the waterworks.

'Robin,' I sobbed.

'Way to go,' he said. 'I'm Perry Allison,' he added to the patrolwoman.

'Uh-huh. Susan Crawford.'

'Pleasure to meet you.'

'How you doing, Miss?'

'Thank you, I'm okay.' I was still drizzling tears, but physically I felt all right. 'I'm Aurora Teagarden.'

'You *are*?' Now she was fully engaged. I looked up into her face, and realized that Patrol Officer Susan Crawford must be the young woman Arthur had told me about, the new officer whose husband had left her. 'I've wanted to meet you for ages,' she said. 'I'm sorry it's under these circumstances.'

She pulled off her dark glasses, and I saw her eyes were clear and gray. She wasn't wearing a speck of makeup, and she looked just fine. 'Thanks for coming so quickly,' I said, not really sure how to proceed. 'What do we do now?'

'I'll write up a report,' she said. 'Mr Allison, how was the assailant clothed?'

'What?' he asked, as if he'd been jogged out of a daydream. 'Well, this man – or woman – was wearing a hunter green coat with a zipper in the front and one of those hoods you can drawstring shut right around your face. He had on gloves and gray sweat pants, I think.'

'Thank you. Is this your place of employment?'

'Yes, ma'am,' Perry said. 'Any time you need me, I'm right here.'

'I'll bear that in mind.' She wrote a few lines in a notebook, talked into her radio, and then began to look around the parking lot, which was not very large to start with. Perry and I began picking up the scattered remnants of my arrangement, and I began inwardly gathering myself back together. After all, the flowers could be rearranged. My clothes needed changing, that was all. I wasn't even hurt to any appreciable extent; bruises and scrapes only.

The attack had been malicious rather than harmful.

I half-expected Arthur to show up. Any time anything had happened to me in the past few years, he'd been there immediately. A police detective has no great problem keeping tabs on someone. But Arthur was a no-show, and I was really relieved. Sally walked down from the newspaper office (she had a scanner on, full-time) and took the incident as casually as I could have hoped.

I left in my car after I'd talked to the humorless Officer Crawford again. I stopped by the florist, where I explained I'd dropped the arrangement, and could she be an angel and reconstruct it? At my cost, of course.

She would be an angel, she agreed. And within the hour.

I ran out to my house and changed, searching out my only other turtleneck. Luckily, it was cream colored and I could wear it with anything. Anything, today, turned out to be forest green pants. I pitched the soiled clothes into the washer. This was no time to abandon my ultraclean habits, considering my mother had left a message on my answering machine to tell me she'd be showing my house at three in the afternoon.

Quick work, even for Mother.

My face was bruised, as I discovered when I went to the mirror to brush my hair. Apparently I hadn't quite been able to stop myself from banging the pavement. Well, my hands had been full, and I hadn't thrown them up in time. It could have been much worse. What if my attacker had had a knife?

A thought skittered across my mind, and returned to take a deeper look out of my eyes.

Robin's last girlfriend was lying on a slab in Atlanta.

Robin's current girlfriend – and I guess that would be me – had just been shoved down in a public parking lot in broad daylight.

The two incidents weren't exactly comparable, were they? Still . . . food for thought.

Robin called the library before I got off work to ask if he could come out to the house. I appreciated him not assuming he could show up, and I said I'd be glad to see him. Which was true. But I would've been more glad if I could've seen him somewhere else.

I was still uneasy at having another man out to the house I'd shared with Martin. Surely that was natural? And I could tell my mother was debating whether I was moving because of Robin's reappearance in Lawrenceton. That would be nuts, I knew. Robin said he wasn't leaving town when the movie shoot was finished, but men said a lot of things under the sway of lust. My experience with Arthur had taught me nothing, if not that.

I wasn't moving because of Robin, I assured myself. I was moving because I was ready to rejoin life. And if that life included Robin right now, so much the better.

I was carrying the arrangement when I got out of my car, and he came over to me to help.

'They're beautiful,' I said. 'Thank you so much.'

A little awkward, he bent to kiss me, his hands full with the bowl of flowers. The minute his lips met mine, I felt a sort of solar flare. It was unexpected and violent, and I thought the damn flowers would end up on the ground again.

When we broke for air, I took a deep breath.

'This seems, I don't know, a little precipitous,' I said.

Robin's eyes were shut behind his glasses. He was breathing raggedly.

'Feels good, though,' he said.

'You're coming off a relationship and a loss, I'm coming off a relationship and a loss,' I pointed out. My relationship, and my loss, had been far greater, but he knew that already. We walked over to the house.

'What happened to your face?' Robin said. It was dark already, and I'd just disarmed the security and flicked on the kitchen lights.

'Does it look very bad? I've been dodging mirrors since noon,' I said. My fingers anxiously patted the darkened area. I trotted to the downstairs bathroom, Robin at my heels. I leaned across the sink, my glasses folded on the counter, and peered at my right cheek. Not too bad – a dark center and a lighter ring of bruising. It would be gone in a week.

'You want to tell me what happened?' Robin asked.

It crossed my mind that Robin had not expected me to call him about this. He was waiting for me to tell him – not angry at not knowing already. This was a different reaction from the one to which I'd grown accustomed. Robin definitely approached life differently from Martin, and his expectations were different, too. I shook my head at myself. I should not compare.

'You don't want to tell me?' His voice sounded mildly teasing, nothing more. But I could tell from the way he stood that he was more serious, now.

'Someone ran up behind me in the library parking lot and pushed me down. The flowers were in my hands, and I couldn't drop them fast enough – I didn't *want* to drop them – so I kind of hit the pavement hard.'

'Someone attacked you?' Robin was quite rightly astonished. 'In the library parking lot?'

'Yeah. Strange, huh? Right out in daylight.'

'The police didn't catch him?'

'Or her. No, the police didn't.'

'Why "her"?' Robin's face was involved in thought, suddenly. I could practically see the lightbulb over his head.

'I thought I smelled perfume.' I eyed him. 'Does this ring some kind of bell with you?'

Robin looked profoundly embarrassed. 'Ah, maybe.' He did everything but look up at the ceiling and whistle. 'But I . . . maybe if I went and talked to her . . . I hate to say anything unless I'm sure.'

'That's what people in mysteries say right before they get killed. "Yes, I think I know the killer, but I have to check a few things before I talk to the police". Next scene, they're toast.'

Robin was struck by this observation, which as a mystery writer should have occurred to him first. 'That's true,' he murmured. We'd drifted from the bathroom into the kitchen, and I'd gotten out a pitcher of tea. He nodded when I lifted it, a question on my face.

'Okay, well. This is really . . . there's this girl. She . . .' Robin turned a dark red. He took a big swallow of tea. 'She has this big thing about me. Like a superfan. She took this job to be . . .' Robin was overwhelmed with chagrin, shook his head speechlessly. Hollywood had not made him completely egocentric, I thought, smiling at him.

'She's nuts about you?' I suggested.

He nodded morosely. 'You know how I found out about Celia and Barrett spending the night together? I knew already when I came to the trailer. I got an anonymous note. I'm about ninety percent sure it was from her.'

I began to put two and two together, myself. 'Tracy,' I said. 'Tracy, from the Molly's Moveable Feasts catering company.'

'Yep.' Robin finished his tea in one long gulp.

I thought this over. 'Did you tell the police about Tracy?' I asked.

'No,' he said, horror written all over his face. 'This isn't exactly something I want to talk about, Roe.'

'Robin, didn't you consider the fact that the woman murdered was your girlfriend?'

'Former,' he corrected. He looked at me almost angrily. 'Of course, Roe. What are you . . . ?' His face cleared. 'Oh.'

I saw the tide of realization pour over him. 'Oh, no,' he said. 'Oh, no.'

'I hope not,' I told him. 'But you have to say something.'

He fumed and fussed, but he was just postponing the inevitable. 'You think she may have attacked you today, too?' he asked, as he pulled his coat back on to drive to the police station.

I shrugged. I remembered Tracy's face, after (I now realized) she had seen Robin and me together in the library, obviously close, obviously in lust. I wondered what would have happened if I hadn't pulled out of the parking lot, if I'd waited to talk to her as she'd wanted.

I was really glad I hadn't stopped to find out.

Chapter Eleven

I met my mother in front of a house on Oak Street. How perfect could that be? Every town has an Oak Street. Hearts of oak, the Old Oaken Bucket, Tie a Yellow Ribbon Round the Old Oak Tree.

The street name would have been perfect. The house wasn't. The living room was an awkward rectangle, the bathrooms tiny and inconvenient.

As I might have anticipated, my mother was less than patient with my quibbles. If she'd been more of a stranger, she'd have had to listen quietly. As it was, she argued – until I commented that I could easily switch realtors. 'In fact,' I said, 'I could go to Russell & Dietrich. They'd laugh all the way to the closing.' After that, Mother seemed to understand that if I said I just didn't like the house, it wouldn't do to quarrel with that feeling.

So our first evening out, we came up with zip. Mother had lined up four houses to see; and I had objections to all of them.

'The couple I showed your house to this afternoon seemed to like it,' she said, before climbing into her new Cadillac. But by that time all I could think of was getting back to that house.

As I let myself in, I was shivering. The evening had cooled down very quickly, and I knew our warm weather was about to end for the season. As I tickled Madeleine behind the ears, I admitted to myself that our failure was actually a relief to me. If the house-hunting process had been too easy, I would have mistrusted it. It would take forever to sell this place, anyway.

I was sure of that until about eight o'clock the next morning, when Mother phoned to tell me that the people who'd seen my house the afternoon before had called her with an offer.

'What?' I gaped at the telephone.

'What can I say? They saw it, they liked it, they made an offer.

It isn't even an insulting offer.' It wasn't. It was actually a little more than I had been willing to settle for.

Suddenly, I felt as if the ground were falling out beneath my feet. I was terrified. I was losing my life.

'Roe?'

'Sorry. Just . . . having misgivings.'

'You don't want to withdraw the house?' Mother was trying not to sound outraged.

'No. No,' I said, trying to stiffen my spine. 'No, I need to move. I just . . . when do we let them know?'

'You mean, you accept the offer?'

'I guess I do,' I said, surprised to hear my voice saying the words. 'I can't think of how not to. I just thought it would take months to sell this house. Months.'

'Me, too,' my mother said. 'But this couple wants to live in the country. The house looks beautiful now. They have a son who loves to hunt. The man's father is coming to live with them, and he needs the apartment above the garage.'

'Well. Counteroffer for two thousand more dollars,' I said, hearing my voice as if it were coming out of someone else's mouth. 'If they'll come up with that, I guess we've got a deal.'

'There is one snag.'

My heart gave a lurch of hope. 'Oh?'

'They need it now.'

'What?'

'They need the house as soon as you can get out of it. If that's before we can arrange a closing, they'll pay rent. It's a domino situation. They've sold their house, the grandfather has just retired and is driving down in a van full of his stuff, and they have nowhere to put him when he gets here.'

'He can't just drive up and settle here in the yard.'

'No, Roe, what I meant was that he can sleep on their couch, but that's going to be pretty unsatisfactory for more than a week or two.'

'So, I need to find an empty house. And buy it.'

'Or we need to work something else out. Of course, you can

stay with me and John for as long as you need to, but I know you don't want to put your things into storage if you can help it.'

We discussed the situation for a few more minutes, and Mother agreed to get together another lineup of houses to see that afternoon. I thought I'd calmed down, but I was still shaky when I hung up.

I thought of calling Robin.

No, I would not lean.

To my disgust, I began crying. I'd done fine on my own, just fine, until I'd met Martin and decided to marry him. Now, here I was, aching to have a man to talk to, used to having someone around to consult with, used to having a companion to share every little thing. I had missed that acutely over the past year.

The phone rang again. I was almost scared to answer it. But I did, since I am an optimist.

'Hey, this is Carolina,' said her accentless California voice.

'How are you?'

'Busy as hell. I just wanted to let you know I did talk to Sarah, and she says she just opened the door, said, "Thirty minutes till you're due on the set, Miss Shaw", and shut the door again.'

'No reply?'

'No, she didn't hear Celia say anything, and the light wasn't on in the trailer.'

No, it wasn't until Barrett had opened the door wide enough to let in sunlight that he'd seen the body. I thanked Carolina and hung up.

The clock was telling me I'd be late for work. I finished yanking my clothes on, determined to go in to work as usual. I brushed my hair carefully, hoping its length and volume would obscure my bruised face and my hickeyed neck. As I hurried out to my car, unlocking it with a click of my keypad, it did cross my mind to wonder if I *had* managed so splendidly before I got married. Hadn't I always been looking? Hadn't I always longed to have someone to share my life with? Hadn't I always assumed I would find that person, sooner or later?

I had. And he'd violated the dream by dying on me.

*

I was back on a more or less even keel after I'd been at work for an hour.

Probably it was inevitable that I'd have emotional spasms of grief for some time to come, right? For the first time, I wondered if it would ever be over. Surely I'd grieved and raged enough. I'd waited almost a year to even look at another man. Granted, when I'd looked it had been more like an immersion, but I had not even thought about men until Robin reentered my life.

I was broody and worried about the house situation, but not tearful, when Robin called.

I seldom get calls at work, of course, and I was a little surprised to hear Robin's voice on the other end of the phone.

'Roe, hey, I'm back at the motel. Listen, are you free for lunch? I need to talk to you.'

'Um, I guess so. Beef 'N More?'

'No.' I could practically hear him shudder. 'There's a pizza place on Kenneth Road. It used to be okay.'

'Yeah, Trixie's. That would be all right. I get off work at twelve-thirty. Is that convenient?' It wasn't Robin's fault I'd spent the morning castigating myself for my longing to throw myself into his life.

'Sure. Is something wrong?' He didn't sound as though he really wanted to ask. I guess I hadn't been as successful as I'd hoped in keeping my voice neutral.

'I'm just fine,' I said independently. 'I'll see you then.'

He might have sounded a little puzzled as he said goodbye, but that was okay.

As I was working the return desk, Mark Chesney came in. He was looking good today, wearing what seemed to be his work uniform of pressed blue jeans and an oxford-cloth shirt. He was carrying a small box.

'Aurora!' he said, looking as astonished to see me as I was to see him. 'What are you doing here?'

'I work here,' I said, trying not to sound too 'duh'. 'You knew that, Mark. It's in the script.'

'Sure,' he said. 'So, in real life, you really do . . .'

'Work in the library,' I finished, trying to sound as matter-of-fact as possible.

'Okay,' he said, still faintly stunned. 'Here, ah, these are books that Celia had in her trailer. I guess she checked these out before we started shooting. And I brought some paperbacks that were lying around, in case the library can use them.'

I glanced at the hardbacks, and then looked again. *The Seventies Bombers. Political Violence in the US. The Black Panthers.* And, sadly, *Diagnosing Your Own Illness.*

'She was doing research,' I said, carefully balancing my voice between question and statement.

'Oh, yeah, remember? She talked about it while we were out at supper that night, I think. Her next project was a movie set in the late sixties, early seventies, about violence in the hippy era. She was playing a middle-class girl turned radical who builds a bomb in her basement with the help of an African-American friend. Based on a true story.'

I nodded, as if I'd remembered all that. The truth was, I'd barely listened. I rummaged through the books. The paperbacks were an undistinguished batch of popular fiction, but we can always use books in good condition. 'Thanks for bringing these in,' I said. Mark turned his attention back to me. He'd been giving Perry the once-over. Perry hadn't noticed, for which I was grateful. Perry was not exactly Mr Stable, and I couldn't ever gauge his reactions, even to more ordinary occurrences.

'Hope you get to come back to the set,' Mark said politely. 'We've got our new leading lady. She's flying in tonight, and we should resume shooting scenes with her tomorrow.'

That must be why they'd gotten the trailer cleaned out so quickly. The new lead would need it. 'Jumping into a part must be incredibly hard for an actor,' I said, focusing on what he was telling me, rather than on my random thoughts. 'How can anyone learn lines that fast?'

'That's the business,' Mark said briskly. 'She'll be studying on the plane.'

'Not Meredith,' I observed. He looked blank. 'Meredith Askew didn't get the job.'

'Oh, gosh, no. Meredith doesn't have the star quality Celia did. And that's what we need.'

'Kind of hard on Meredith.'

'That's the business, too,' he said, shrugging. He smiled at Perry, who happened to be looking in his direction, and gave me a little wave before he left.

I picked up the medical book. A strip of paper had been inserted between the pages in the H's. Huntington's Chorea had been underlined. So the police knew, as I did now, that Celia had been aware of her problem. I wondered if she'd gone to a doctor when her symptoms had become obvious, or if she'd had some other kind of warning.

Poor thing. She'd known, and she had to have dreaded the disease's progress. But she should have been given the choice of how to deal with her death sentence. She should not have had that snatched away from her. Someone had drugged Celia, someone had strangled her, and someone had hit her in the head. She'd been killed so many ways. Had three different people wanted her to die? Or had one person caused so much damage? If so, why?

The plastic cover on *The Black Panthers* was torn, so I carried the whole box back to the repair area. That was a corner of the employees' lounge, the corner right by Patricia's cubicle. Nothing closed to view, here. We like to check up on each other, here at the Lawrenceton Library. The donated books would have to be processed back here, too.

After I'd placed the box on the table, I noticed that a thin manuscript was at the bottom. I fished it out. Mark had packed the script of the movie Celia had been signed up to shoot after *Whimsical Death*. I'd have to call him to ask if he would like to come by and retrieve it. I stuck it back in the box.

I examined our torn cover more closely. If Celia hadn't been dead, I would've had a sharp conversation with her about this book. She'd been underlining, though I admitted to myself I couldn't be sure that had been Celia. There were slips of paper stuck here and there through the pages. I flipped through, removing the slips. One had been inserted in the center of the volume, where there were pages of pictures. I glanced down at the Afros with that kind of superior amusement we give to past fads. I thought of showing some of the more outrageous ones to Patricia, as a kind of peace offering, and I looked over to her cubicle to see if she was overwhelmingly busy.

She was staring at me with the blankest face I'd ever seen. I couldn't tell if she was broadcasting fear, or anger, or just a feeling of stunned inevitability, but the emotion was strong and directed at me. Puzzled, I gave her a little wave like the one Mark Chesney had given me, and went back to weeding out the makeshift bookmarks. I risked a glance in Patricia's direction after a minute or two, and she was still sitting at her desk, but her head was bowed. I had never imagined Patricia looking defeated, or even cowed, but that was in her posture. I thought about going to speak to her. But since she was Patricia, and she didn't like me, and frankly I'd never particularly liked her, I just didn't.

The book looked like new, I thought proudly, after I'd finished replacing the cover. As I taped the last flap of plastic in place, Patricia walked by me, heels tapping on the linoleum, her trench coat belted around her tightly. She never looked in my direction. Her purse was hanging from her shoulder. She was talking rapidly into her cell phone.

'Please have him in the office by the time I get there. He's late for his orthodontist appointment,' Patricia said precisely. Her eyes met mine as she pulled open the employee door and she registered nothing. I might as well have been invisible.

This was weird.

A second later Sam came out of his office, which opened into Patricia's. He looked at her desk and then he looked through the glass at me. He pointed at his secretary's empty chair and raised his hands, palms up, to ask a question.

I shrugged. I pointed to the back door and made walking motions with my fingers.

Looking unhappy and disturbed, Sam wandered back into his

office. He left the door open, so he could see his paragon returning. Pale, fair, and losing hair at an alarming rate, Sam seemed an unlikely poster boy, but there was no doubt that he and Patricia had formed a mutual admiration society.

I was back at the return desk when I remembered an odd fact.

Patricia's son didn't have braces. In fact, Jerome was blessed with teeth so even and white I had remarked them. So how come she was taking him to the orthodontist?

Robin was waiting for me at Trixie's. We ordered, and while we waited for our food I told him about my house situation. Somehow it didn't seem so dire after I'd told him, and I could feel myself begin to relax. When our pizza was in front of us, he carefully wriggled a piece onto his plate and said, 'We need to talk about what the police told me this morning.'

This wasn't a happy opening. 'Okay,' I said. 'Shoot.'

Tracy, it turned out, was on probation . . . in California. She'd just gotten out of jail for another stalking incident with another mystery writer, Carl Sonnheim. Her pursuit of him and her jealousy of his girlfriend had ended up with Carl in the hospital, his girlfriend on a plane to Canada to put some distance between her and Tracy, and Tracy in jail. While she'd been in jail, Tracy had trolled through the prison library and ended up with all of Robin's books. She'd transferred her attentions to Robin.

'Lucky you,' I said.

'Right.' He looked grim.

'So she came to Georgia, and got a job with Molly's? How'd she find out Molly was going to be the caterer?'

'She'd done catering work in the past and still had some professional connections. They didn't know about her troubles.'

'Sheesh.'

'Molly couldn't believe it, Arthur Smith kept telling me. Said Tracy was one of the best employees she'd ever had.'

'Do they think Tracy killed Celia?' I had to ask.

'The drugs, the pillow . . . they say that doesn't sound like Tracy.'

'The Emmy does?'

'Well, it's more in line with what she did to Carl. She's been spotted around town. They don't think she'll leave.'

Now I felt cold all over. 'Then why don't they grab her?'

'Various people have seen her, but none of those various people happen to have been cops.'

'Oh.'

'So . . . you're going to be careful, right?' He put his hand over mine.

'I'm thinking it's you who should be scared,' I said.

'I'm thinking it's both of us.'

On my way to rendezvous with my mother, I remembered that when I'd walked up to the catering table the morning of Celia's murder, Tracy had been changing into a fresh jacket.

What if the soiled jacket had had Celia's blood on it? I shuddered again, and found myself looking at everyone I passed, on foot or in vehicles, trying to spot a head of auburn hair.

But it's not my way to keep scaring myself. I didn't see Tracy, and I told myself that the odds were good I never would again.

I met my mother in front of a house on Andrews Street. This was a fancier house than the others I'd looked at, and the price reflected that. But it looked good from the curb, and I was feeling optimistic.

Thirty minutes later, I was disillusioned. How could people put so much emphasis on floor space in a bathroom, and so little on kitchen room? The master bath would have held a Third World family, while the kitchen existed to rotate around the microwave. However, it was a pretty house in other respects, and I needed a house in the worst way. I mentally short-listed this one.

The ranch on Swanson Street was beautifully decorated, but too small. Poky.

McBride Street was full of trees. Even in the October night, I could tell that both sides were lined with oaks. I'd known someone who lived here – who was it? One of my girlhood friends, I thought. When I got out on the sidewalk in front of the house, the memories poured over me. This had been her house! I couldn't quite recall her name, but it would pop into my head soon. I had always loved spending the night with her.

'Who owns this now?' I asked my mother.

'David and Laurie Martinez,' she said, peering at the fact sheet in the light from the streetlight. 'They got transferred to Colorado. So the house is empty.'

'How much?'

Mother told me.

'Okay,' I said, 'that's not too scary.'

Mother had unlocked the door while I hung back, trying to recall what had made the house so special.

We stepped into the entrance. It was floored with red tiles. The carpeted area to the left was the formal living room. The red tiles ran down the hall to culminate in the kitchen, a large room with an eat-in area. Along the hall were doors to a formal dining room, a bathroom, and two large closets.

The kitchen had just been updated with new cabinets and a new dishwasher. There was a large walk-in pantry. It lay open to a sizable family room with a fireplace. There were sliding glass doors to a patio. I was remembering as I looked. Debbie, the girl who'd lived here, had had an older brother who made my heart throb with adolescent passion. I smiled as I thought of his utter obliviousness to my adoration.

'Okay,' I said again, sounding, to my own ears, cautiously positive. I didn't like the carpet in the family area, but that was easy to change. Not cheap, but easy. I pointed out its poor condition, and Mother nodded.

To the right, off the kitchen and family room, were three bedrooms. One was a huge master bedroom with its own bath, and the other two, somewhat smaller, bedrooms shared a bath.

Then – and this was the neat part – a hall ran from the kitchen further back into the property. There were cabinets on both sides of the hall, making it into an elongated storage area. At the end of the hall, with its own door, was an office lined with built-in bookcases. Debbie's dad had been an architect, and he'd done a lot of work at home. I didn't need a home office myself, but . . . I stood in the office door, suppressing every thought that popped into my head.

I looked at everything again. I looked at the huge windows in the master bedroom, wishing the house weren't in town. It would be necessary to keep the curtains drawn most of the time. Though I thought I remembered extensive planting outside the window – that would certainly help.

'Is there a fence?' I asked. Mother stepped to the light switch panel by the door of the bedroom, and began flicking. The outside lights came on. Yes, the backyard was fenced and the enclosed area included that outside the side master-bedroom windows. Yay!

'There's another couple who say they're going to make an offer on this house after they sleep on it tonight,' Mother warned. She sat on the window seat and reached up to smooth her hair. It must have been a full working day for her, but she looked, as always, smooth and composed.

'No, I think I'll take it now.'

Mother's head snapped up as though I'd popped her with a rubber band.

'Let me see the utilities,' I said, holding out my hand. She put the fact sheet into it somewhat dazedly.

The electric bills were a little high. I wondered how long it had been since someone had blown insulation into the attic. 'Where's the attic access?' I asked, and Mother told me it was out in the garage. We trailed out to the garage, to the west side of the house, which more or less faced south. The room was just a big old bare garage with the usual oil stains and battered cabinets, but it did have a door that raised and lowered. 'Is the attic floored?' I asked, and Mother had to confess she didn't know. I let down the attic access steps and mounted. There were planks over about a third of the available area.

'Who are the next-door neighbors?' Back on the ground, I dusted off my hands on my pants.

'Ah, the Cohens on one side; they're retired, they have grandchildren. On the other side the Herman sisters. They're in their forties. Both widows. I forget their married names.'

Sounded quiet.

I really liked the house and its layout. The square footage was comparable to the house I had now; a little less, but I didn't need any more. This house was in a good part of town, and I would have no trouble selling it if it didn't suit. I loved the red tile floors, and the redecorating would be minimal. The paint in almost every room looked as though it had just been redone.

'I'll take it.'

Mother said, 'It's not a coat, Roe.'

'I believe I understand that.'

She sighed. 'You're right. You're a smart girl, and you know what you want. You always have.'

Haven't always been able to *get* it, I told myself.

Mother pulled out her cell phone, consulted a list from her purse, and punched in some number. 'David? Hi, good evening. This is Aida Queensland.'

Mother listened. 'Yes, I do have some good news. I have a client who's made an offer.' She looked at me with one eyebrow raised. I tapped the selling price with my finger, then held up three fingers. I pointed down with my thumb.

'Three thousand less than the asking price,' Mother said into the phone. 'She said she'd need to replace the carpet in the family room.' Pause.

'I can always counteroffer,' Mother said next.

I wondered how many people had owned the house between Debbie's family and the Martinezes. I wondered where Debbie was now. Mother was doing some more listening.

'She doesn't have to wait for a loan,' Mother said. 'In case you think later that I was being devious, I have to tell you that the buyer is my daughter, Aurora Teagarden. She plans to pay for the house directly.

'Yes, I know, she's lucky to have that much available cash.

'Yes, it'll take a few days to get the paperwork done. But with no loan to apply for . . . I'll FedEx the agreement to you.

'Okay, we have a deal.'

Those were my favorite words.

She hung up and nodded.

I took a deep breath.

Well, there was nothing like jumping off a cliff. In fact, I'd gotten a running start.

Chapter Twelve

Robin called Thursday morning, while I was lying in bed trying not to be terrified at the magnitude of what I'd just done.

'What are you doing this morning?' he asked. 'I called the library and they said you weren't scheduled to work this morning.'

'No, I go in this afternoon and work this evening. I'm just lying here trying to make a list of what I need to do. I bought a house last night.'

'You what?' He sounded as though he thought he'd misheard me.

I explained.

'Wow. I just called to see how you were feeling after being knocked down in the parking lot. I didn't expect to find out you were changing your life.'

'Yet again. Oh, I have a bruise on my face, and my knees are a little sore, but I think I'm going to live,' I said, scaling my news to a more expectable level. 'Have you heard from the police again?'

'No more sightings,' he said. 'That's good. That Detective Smith, he can hardly stop asking me questions. Um, I'm not trying to imply anything, but was he formerly some significant male to you?'

'That's a nice way to put it. Yes, he was, briefly. Until he got another detective pregnant and invited me to the wedding.'

'Ouch. Painful.'

'It was, at the time. I'm over it.' Though I was beginning to wonder if Arthur Smith ever would be; his continued emotional absorption with me seemed strange, since I'd been the injured party in our little triangle. Of course, I hadn't known I'd been in a triangle. Oblivious me.

'When do I get to see the new house?'

'Right now, if you want. I need to go make a list, have a look in the daylight.'

'Give me the address.'

Forty-five minutes later, I was walking up my new sidewalk, carrying two cups of coffee I'd picked up at the drive-through of one of Lawrenceton's fast-food places. I had some cholesterol-packed sausage biscuits in a bag. Luckily, Robin pulled up right behind me, and was able to take the bags while I unlocked the front door. My mother had given me the key, not without a sharp look or two, since she really wasn't supposed to be doing this. The privileges of being a realtor's daughter are few and far between.

Robin looked around curiously while I put our breakfast on the counter.

'How come you're not at the set?' I asked.

'They don't want me,' he said casually. 'The new actress is having her first morning of shooting, and she's pretty nervous. Actually, they never want me to be there, but they have to put up with me, from time to time.'

'Then why did you come to Lawrenceton at all?'

He swung around to face me. His hair was as much of a mess as usual, and his glasses sat on his face crookedly. His cheeks were as smooth as a baby's bottom, and he smelled good.

His silence made me move restlessly. 'What?'

'I came because of you.'

I didn't know what to say. I didn't know how I felt.

'I wanted to see you again. I wanted to see if I really felt so comfortable with you, or if I was remembering it as better than it was. I had never slept with you; I hadn't seen you in years. You'd been married. What if it had all been something I made up when I couldn't find anything better?'

This was almost too much honesty.

'What do you want?' I asked hesitantly. 'From me?'

'I want us to date,' he said simply. 'I want to go to bed with you sometimes. I want us to have a chance. If it doesn't work out, so be it. I can move back to California, I can get another teaching job, anything. I'm self-supporting, and I can work anywhere. So right now, I want to work here in Lawrenceton.'

I couldn't seem to move. After a year of feeling empty, suddenly I felt full. After a year of grief, suddenly I felt a secret sort of joy. And I was terrified. I never could seem to do relationships like anyone else.

'Go look down the hall,' I said. I pointed to the cabinet-lined hall leading out of the family room. He obediently strolled in that direction. I followed him. He looked at the cabinets approvingly, and then he opened the door at the end of the hall. The room had windows on three sides, and the morning light dazzled the eyes. The built-in book-cases that took up the remaining wall space were blindingly white with new paint. There were electric plugs in the floor where a desk would logically be placed, for a convenient computer plug-in.

A huge smile lit up Robin's face, and he spun to face me. 'Come here,' he said, falling to his knees and opening his arms. I crept over to him. He wrapped his arms around my waist, hugging me so tightly it almost hurt. I laughed and laughed. Then he kissed me, and I stopped laughing.

The phone rang about thirty minutes later. I had forgotten my cell phone was in my purse, and the little tune it played jogged me out of a lovely fog. Robin reached one long arm over to hook the shoulder strap of the purse. He dragged it over. I rummaged in it and fished out the phone.

'Yes?' I said.

'Roe, this is Sam,' my boss said.

I tried to focus. I put my glasses on; everyone knows you can hear better over the phone if you're wearing your specs. 'What can I do for you, Sam?' I asked.

'You sound funny,' he said. 'Were you asleep?'

'Oh, no,' I said, my voice relaxed and slow. 'No. Not asleep.'

'I need you to do me a favor,' Sam said.

'What's the matter?' I asked, finally picking up on the worry in his voice.

'It's Patricia. She didn't come in to work this morning, and she doesn't answer my calls.'

'Gosh, that's not like her.'

'No, it's not. She hasn't missed a day of work since I hired her. Her son's not in school, either. The school called here, looking for her.'

'So what do you want me to do?'

'I want you to go over to her house and make sure everything's all right there.'

'So, if there's a dead body, you don't care if I find it!'

'Roe,' he protested, obviously offended. 'I can't leave. It's work hours.'

I sighed, not making any attempt to cover up my exasperation. Robin bent over me, doing something that made me bite my lip to keep in a gasp. 'In a few minutes,' I said, to get Sam off the phone. 'I'll go, Sam, in a few minutes.'

'Good,' he said, obviously surprised I'd caved so quickly. He gave me the address. 'Then let me know.'

I hung up without saying good-bye. Sam wouldn't even notice.

Robin went with me, once I'd explained the circumstances to him.

I'd never known where Patricia lived before today. Of course I'd known where the street was. It was on the upper end of the scale for the largely black area of Lawrenceton that ran on the northwest side of town, literally following the old railroad tracks. Patricia's rental was a small, square house with minimal yard and no carport. Patricia's little car was nowhere in sight. There were two newspapers lying by the front steps.

I knocked, of course, but I didn't expect an answer, and I got none. I tried to peer in the windows but, literally, I wasn't up to that. Robin obligingly undertook the task, and he reported that the house looked very clean, but a little disordered – as though the Bledsoes had packed very quickly. The kitchen counter held none of the usual small appliances. A set of keys lay on the counter along with a sheaf of money.

'Like she left the keys and the next month's rent so the landlord wouldn't feel any need to track her down,' Robin said.

'Oh, *man*,' I muttered, trying not to moan. 'This isn't going to be pretty,' I told Robin as I punched in the library number.

Of course, Sam was distraught when I told him Patricia was gone. He could not believe she would just cut and run with no warning.

'Did you do something to her?' he said accusingly.

I'd had enough. 'Sam,' I said sharply into the phone, 'Patricia may have been the perfect secretary, but I am the one who's worked for you for ten years. I think you should have a little faith in me.' We hung up on each other, equally unhappy. I was cudgeling my brain to think of what could have happened to Patricia and Jerome. It was eerie and frightening to admit that she had evidently packed up her clothes and some small goods, and vanished.

'Come to think of it,' I said to Robin, 'she's been acting funny for days. Ever since she found out that the movie people attracted the media, and Celia came into the library and actually checked out books, Patricia's been asking questions like crazy about where the filming was going to be every day, whether the movie people would be coming to the library, like that.'

'Do you think she's running from something? Maybe she knows someone on the crew,' Robin said. 'Someone she didn't want to recognize her?'

I considered. 'Maybe,' I said. 'Or maybe she was scared she'd be noticed by one of the media people here to watch the filming and do interviews.'

'Did you say anything about the film yesterday?'

'Nope,' I said. 'But she practically fainted when she saw me repairing a book. As a matter of fact, it was right after that that she left the library in a mighty big hurry.'

'What was the book?'

'It was one Celia had checked out. You know, when she came to the library after she first got to Lawrenceton. I think she was looking for me, to have a peek at me. But she thrilled Sam by taking out a library card and checking out some books to do research for her next movie.'

'The sixties-radical movie,' Robin said.

'Right. *Bell-bottoms and Bombs*, or something like that.'

'Can you find the book again?'

'Sure. Let's go to the library.'

I tracked down the book in record time. It had been reshelved. I flipped it open, Robin looking over my shoulder. I turned to the picture section and began to really examine the old pictures. Lots of Afros and jeans, dashikis and beads. Peace signs. And photographs of wires and bits of hardware that were used in the making of bombs. What an incongruous blend, the philosophy of world peace, disarmament, and the construction of bombs to blow a hole in the consciousness of middle America.

The next picture was of a group of radicals at some rally. *Right to left*, read the caption, *suspected bomb makers Joanne Cheney, Ralph 'Coco' Defarge, his teenage sister Anita, Maxwell Brand, and Barbara 'Africa' Palley.*

'Anything ring a bell?' Robin asked in my ear, making me twitch.

'No. Yes,' I said suddenly. I put my index finger on the picture of the radicals. 'Look at the little sister.'

'I never met Patricia Bledsoe,' Robin reminded me.

'This is her,' I said breathlessly. 'Oh my God. Patricia the perfect helped her big brother make bombs in the sixties.' I had to put my hands over my mouth to stifle a totally inappropriate laugh. Patricia, the rigorously traditional woman whose middle name was conservative! Patricia, who wouldn't even let her son wear Nike! 'This is just going to kill Sam Clerrick,' I said, suppressing a snort with great difficulty.

'This is funny, how?' Robin asked.

I tried to explain.

'Are you going to tell someone?' he asked.

'I have to, don't I?' I asked. 'Don't I have to tell someone? She obviously picked up and ran because she thought I'd smoked her out. It couldn't have been further from the truth. If she'd just stayed put, I'd never have known.'

'All the way back in the sixties,' Robin said gently.

'Yeah, I know,' I said, reluctant to debate my duty. 'I have a lot of sympathy for her, even if she was the biggest pain in the patootie I've ever encountered. Except maybe Sam himself. But you know – if she did help build that bomb – I'm not trying to be Rhonda Righteous, but a security guard got killed, Robin. Besides, obviously Patricia was panicked by the idea of Celia seeing this picture and noticing the likeness, just like we did. What if Patricia somehow made her way onto the set and killed Celia, thinking Celia had spotted her and was going to tell?'

'Can't take that lightly,' he agreed. 'Will you tell Sam?'

'Oh, you bet,' I said instantly. Then I reconsidered. 'At least about our suspecting she's Anita Defarge.'

'Not about her connection with Celia?'

'I know the papers this morning said it would have been easy for someone to have sneaked up to her trailer and killed her because there were a lot of people around. I just don't see it happening,' I said. 'Do you agree? There were a lot of people, but none of them looked or dressed like Patricia. And Celia had never talked to her, that I know of. They'd just glimpsed each other when Sam gave Celia a tour of the library. Wouldn't Celia have raised a fuss if someone she didn't know entered her trailer? She wouldn't have just sat there and waited for something bad to happen.'

'I agree, for the most part,' Robin said. 'Just mention the fact you're most sure of; that the picture looks like his secretary.'

'That's what I'll do,' I said resolutely. I folded immediately. 'In fact, maybe I'll leave calling the police up to him.'

Robin waited out in the employee break room while I went in to Sam's office and broke the news. The fluorescent lights glinted off Sam's thick glasses as he looked hopelessly down at the black-and-white picture. 'She was so great,' he all but whimpered. 'She took all my calls. I never had to talk to anybody. She understood the paperwork. She was never late. She was never sick. Her son was respectful and quiet.'

'I'm sorry, Sam,' I said as gently as I could. 'I'll just leave it up to you what to do.'

'Oh, there's no doubt about what to do,' he said gloomily. 'She may have been on the run all these years, always looking over her shoulder. And with the boy, too – I wonder what she told him. But I have to call the FBI. That's the law, and I have to uphold the law.'

I felt like a second-class moral citizen compared to Sam's straightforward conviction. It must be wonderful to always know what was right to do.

At the back of my mind, I kept hoping that Patricia would walk in with some explanation of where she'd been and what she'd been doing. It wouldn't take much to satisfy Sam. If she just said, 'What a coincidence, that girl looks like a young me,' that would probably do it. But the combined evidence of the flight and the picture – well, at least that should be investigated.

With a grim face, Sam picked up his phone to call the local police. He said, 'I guess they can give me the right number to call.' Then he put the phone back on its cradle. 'But you know . . . maybe I don't have to call right now. After all, she still might show up. Maybe there's a sick relative she had to visit.'

Maybe there was an elephant in my locker. I didn't know whether to laugh or cry. 'Excuse me, Sam,' I said. 'I'll leave. You do what you think is right.'

'Aren't you supposed to come in for the afternoon?'

'Yes.'

'Then I'll see you later.'

No 'thank you', no 'I appreciate it'. Well, that was Sam. No people skills.

Robin was still waiting for me. He opened his mouth to ask a question, but I lifted a finger to my lips. When we were safely out in the parking lot, I told him what had transpired. He shook his head doubtfully, but agreed that Sam should be the one to make the phone call that would set law enforcement on Patricia's – Anita's – trail.

I had two hours before I was due back at the library, and we trailed over to Mother's office to sign some paperwork.

Mother greeted Robin quite matter-of-factly, but she was not overwhelmingly friendly, even when he asked her to find him a modest rental. She looked relieved, but not enthralled. She'd have to have warm-up time, I guessed. I wasn't going to push it.

My mother saw Robin as a potential threat to my peace of mind, a possible dumper of her vulnerable daughter, the potential dumpee. His fame and fortune made no difference at all to her. But a couple of the other realtors were more impressed. I thought Patty Cloud, now a partner and divorced twice, was going to come clean across her desk and tackle Robin, she was so enraptured with having a real celebrity in the office. She made a determined attempt to impress him with her attractiveness and her business acumen, and I was pleased to see that she didn't make a dent. Patty had always played one-up with me – a one-sided game, since I had never had a competitive bone in my body. I hoped Patty had gotten something out of it, because it had never made a bit of difference to me.

'I'll be glad to take you around town, get you set up with the bank and a dry cleaner and so forth,' she offered, her eyes gleaming. Robin reached over to take my hand, very casually. 'Roe is taking care of me,' he said. Patty's face was just wonderful. She could think of about twelve bitchy things to say, but she couldn't, because, after all, I was the boss's daughter.

'Thanks,' I said, when we were returning to my car.

He knew full well what I meant, but he just smiled his crooked smile. 'It was my pleasure,' he said, wiggling his eyebrows, and I laughed out loud.

He went back to his motel room to work, and I went home to make phone calls. Mother had worked it so I could move out of this house and into the house on McBride in a week. I called a company on the outskirts of Atlanta, made a definite date for them to come pack up this house on one day, and move the contents to the new place the next. It only cost me an arm and a leg and one kidney. I tried to ignore the stab of pain I felt as I thought of leaving this house empty. I tried instead to focus on the incoming family, with their son who would love living out in the country. He might make friends with my neighbor's dog Robert. Maybe Robert would stop his nighttime howling when the new family moved in. Speaking of Robert, he was doing some daytime howling now.

As I was pulling on some nicer pants to wear to work, I thought I heard a noise downstairs. I stopped breathing to listen better, while my fingers automatically pushed the button through the hole. I took some silent steps to the top of the stairs and listened. There it was again, a step in the hall.

I knew it was not Robin or my mother or anyone who had a reason to be there. I thought of Tracy, her angry face, and I stepped back into the bedroom and lifted the phone. I heard a familiar *beep beep beep* – somewhere downstairs, a receiver was off the hook. I needed my cell phone.

It was in my purse, which was on the counter in the kitchen downstairs.

'Aurora!' called a familiar voice from downstairs.

My breath gushed out in a sigh of sheer relief. Catherine Quick. It was her afternoon. Oh, thank God.

'Catherine,' I called, trotting down the stairs, half-angry and half-delighted, 'why did you come in so quiet? You could tell I was home.'

I came into the kitchen to get yet another shock. Tracy, Robin's biggest fan, was holding a knife to Catherine's neck.

'Oh,' I said quietly. 'Oh.'

Catherine's face was contorted with fear, and tears were running down her cheeks. I didn't blame her. The knife Tracy was gripping was a Swiss Army type thing, as far as I could tell – not a butcher knife, or a Bowie knife. But the blade looked plenty long enough to penetrate a vital area. It would never make it through airport security, for example, I told myself crazily. My thoughts were trying to escape from the here and now.

'You ruined it,' Tracy said. 'He was just on the verge, I could tell! He was just on the verge of asking me out.'

'You're right,' I said instantly. She had to be made to let go of Catherine. That Catherine should be involved in this at all was simply atrocious. Catherine was in her sixties, had high blood pressure, and should not be subjected to this deranged woman.

Of course, I shouldn't be, either.

My purse was on the counter, right by the side door, where I had a habit of dropping it. Tracy, her auburn hair falling in snakes around her head, was between my purse and me.

'Did you kill Celia?' I asked, before I thought. Obviously.

She laughed. 'I hit her with the statue. She earned her own death.'

'But she was already dead,' I said, compounding my error.

'She was asleep,' said Tracy, frowning. Her face was dirty. She was a far cry from the spic-and-span food provider in her spotless white, the woman I'd met such a few days ago. Could people really crumble that quickly?

'Right,' I said hastily. Tracy wanted to take credit for Celia. And if I lived, I'd be glad to tell the police she'd done her best to kill Celia. It was just that someone had beaten her to it.

'For months, I've been planning this,' Tracy said.

'Planning . . . ?'

'Meeting Robin Crusoe. Getting him to love me. Ever since I saw the picture on his Web site.'

It was news to me that Robin had a Web site. 'Which picture? The picture of Robin and Celia at the Emmys?'

'Yes, right when it first came out. Did you notice the way she was ignoring him? She didn't even care that she was out with a brilliant writer. She's a slut; there's a million actresses in the world who can do what she does. But Robin's a writer in a million. I've read every single book he's ever written. Ten times apiece, I bet!' Her face was soft and dreamy, but the knife looked just as sharp. 'I've got every short story, in every language. I've got every interview, on-line and in print.'

'You probably know more about Robin than I'll ever know.' I

was quite willing to concede that. I edged a little forward and to one side. The kitchen table was no longer between us, which I regretted, but I was a little closer to the cell phone.

'You're damn straight I do. So what are you doing going to bed with him?'

It was dumb to be embarrassed in front of Catherine, but I was. As if she cared, at this point. 'How do you know what I'm doing?' I asked instead.

'I was in the backyard of your new house this morning,' she said, so choked with fury I was terrified all over again.

It made me sick to think of her watching Robin and me. I also felt a little surprised she hadn't broken in on us then.

'He wouldn't like me if he saw me kill you,' she said, as if she'd heard my thoughts.

'No, he wouldn't.' Let's make that perfectly clear.

'But then, if no one finds out, I would get to comfort him when you die.'

Okay, so this wasn't getting any better. 'Don't you think Robin would know?' I asked.

'He doesn't know about Celia.' She looked smug.

'He went to the police, to tell them he suspected you.'

I didn't know if saying that was smart or not, but to tell the truth, I needed to find something that worked, and in a hurry.

'Did he really? But I did it for him.' She looked more than a little confused. 'I'm glad I didn't go back home last night. I got a room in the motel where he's staying. I couldn't get a room on the same floor, because all the movie people are taking up that floor, but I got a room right below him.' She sighed. 'I lay awake all night, thinking about him.'

Hoo, boy. This gal would be spending some time in the loony bin, for sure. I had eased more than a foot closer during her meanderings.

'He's very attractive,' I said sincerely, 'but I'll bet you need some sleep.'

'I can't sleep,' she told me, sounding peeved about it. 'I just keep waking up. And I know he's there, just out of reach. I need him. I deserve him.' She gestured with the knife, and Catherine made a strangled sound.

'And I'm gonna have him,' Tracy said quietly.

Quick as a wink, she shoved Catherine to one side and lunged for me with the knife.

Even in those few short minutes, I'd accepted a status quo, and the sudden change in threat caught me off guard. Catherine went reeling across the kitchen, and I yelled, 'The phone! It's in my purse!' before Tracy grabbed me by the hair and began trying to stab me. I screamed and ducked, and she missed me with her first attempt. My scalp stung with the pull on my hair. She swung again, and this time she cut me below my shoulder. My knees folded from the shock of it.

The blood was immediate and it distracted her long enough for me to yank away from her – leaving her in possession of a handful of my hair – and drop to the floor. I rolled under the kitchen table, knocking the chairs out of the way. She staggered a little as a chair rocked against her and then fell to the floor with a huge clatter. She was still trying to get her balance. Without any planning on my part, my hands shot out from under the table to grab Tracy's ankles, and I yanked with all my strength. Down she crashed, with a shriek of her own, and then she gave a low moan and lay still.

After a long, shocked second of watching Tracy's blood flow onto my kitchen floor, I realized she'd fallen on her knife. I backed out from under the table so I'd be on the other side. I pelted out of that kitchen so fast I don't think my feet hit the steps down to the walkway. Catherine was outside, already talking to the dispatcher, though she was almost incoherent with shock.

'Where is she?' Catherine screamed.

'She's hurt, she's on the floor!'

'Oh my Lord! Did you hear that?' she demanded, and I heard the raised voice on the other end of the line.

'I have to go now, she might get up,' Catherine said. She turned off the phone. But she managed to tell me the cops were on the way, and she helped me scramble into her car. We locked the doors while we waited.

We had about three minutes before the police could get there, and at first we didn't say a word to each other, being occupied with important things like breathing and praying. Oh, and I was bleeding. Catherine grabbed a kitchen towel from a basket of wash in the backseat and folded it into a pad, and I pressed it to my wound. Finally, when our gasps were down to pants, Catherine said, 'I didn't have any choice but to bring her in, Aurora. She held that knife on me, and I just thought about my kids and grandkids, and I let her in with my key.'

'I don't blame you one bit,' I said sincerely. 'I would have done the same thing.'

'I tried to make a little noise,' Catherine said. 'To warn you. As much as I could.'

'Thank you. At least I suspected something was wrong when I came down the stairs.'

'Praise God we lived through that,' Catherine said, sounding surprised by the fact.

'I don't know if she did,' I said in a small voice. 'I think she hurt herself pretty bad, falling on that knife.'

'I know I will have to pray God for forgiveness, but right now, I just don't give a damn.'

'Actually, I vote along with you,' I said.

'Can't you stay out of trouble?' bellowed the new sheriff as he drew his gun and eased up to the side of the house. I rolled down the window to point at the open kitchen door, as if Sheriff Coffey couldn't see it himself.

Padgett Lanier had had a massive heart attack in his office (some said while he was receiving the personal attentions of an attractive prisoner) the previous spring, and his newly elected successor was a politically savvy African-American named Davis Coffey. Coffey, who was six feet tall and massive, had been out here a couple of times before during his years as deputy.

Jimmy Henske and Levon Suit, who had also paid visits to my house before, gave me disapproving headshakes as they followed their leader. Levon winked at me, though.

After calling into the house and getting no response, Davis Coffey hurled his large body into the doorway we'd left open, gun at the ready. After a few minutes, I could see through the kitchen window that he'd lowered his gun and was looking down at the floor.

The ambulance came up the drive just as Catherine and I scrambled out of her car, an aged Buick. It was for Tracy, Davis not having noticed I was wounded. Levon and Jimmy had stepped out of the house to wait in the yard, and Levon winced when he saw the blood dripping down my left arm. Jimmy raised his radio to his mouth and, in only a few minutes, another ambulance arrived for me. I knew my wound wasn't anywhere near life-threatening – it was probably pretty minor – but it hurt like hell, and I couldn't seem to stop the bleeding.

Tracy was alive, I could tell. Her mouth was moving when they were loading her into the ambulance, and though I couldn't hear what she was saying, I was sure it was about Robin.

Who, by the way, I should call. He picked up the phone at the motel and said, 'Yes?' abstractedly. It was his working voice. Well, he'd just have to put it aside for now.

I explained the situation to him briefly. There was a moment of silence, a silence I couldn't characterize. Then he said, 'I'll meet you at the hospital,' and the phone went dead.

By the time we got there, I was feeling a little spacey. Loss of blood and shock, I guess. Plus, the EMT who rode in back with me took my glasses off, for some reason, and I am never at my most alert when the whole world is a blur. He was a handsome young man, whose family had emigrated from El Salvador, he told me. He had a crewcut and a large tattoo, but I was willing to love him nonetheless. I had to admit our romance was doomed when he passed the time on our ride to the hospital by telling me about his motorcycle.

I would have been glad to ride into town in Catherine's car instead of the ambulance, but (a) I didn't want to get blood all over it, and (b) she didn't offer. It was possible Catherine had had enough of me for one day and, frankly, I couldn't blame her.

Robin was already at the emergency room entrance, and he behaved in a gratifyingly loverlike way. Not a disappointment, like my EMT. Robin was even a practical help, which I hadn't expected. He fished my insurance cards out of my purse and showed them to the admitting clerk.

'Thank you,' I said, wondering if my voice was as fuzzy as my vision. 'This is above and beyond the . . .' And then I didn't know how to finish the sentence.

'Obligation of a new boyfriend?' Robin suggested.

'Something like that,' I agreed, trying to smile. 'I started to throw you over for the cute Hispanic guy who rode with me in the ambulance, but I think you'll do.'

'Glad to hear it.'

The emergency room doctor was a gruff young woman employed by one of the big health-care systems. She had one of the worst haircuts I'd ever seen, but she had a massive assurance that I really liked. She let you know that she was not about to make a mistake, and you would get worse at your peril.

'Don't see too many knife wounds in Lawrenceton,' she commented. I had my head turned away, since I just didn't want to look.

'Mmmm,' she said after a painful few moments. 'Well, I'm gonna numb you up; you need some stitches.'

Robin winced. 'You can leave,' I told him, wishing I could, too. 'There's no need for you to watch this.'

'Are you the husband?' the doctor asked.

I opened my mouth to say my husband was dead, and then I shut it.

'I'm the boyfriend,' Robin said. His charm was such that she grinned at him before she strode out of the room.

'That what you are?' I asked weakly.

'I don't know what to call what I am, so that'll do.'

A nurse came in and gave me a shot, with the customary warning about me feeling a little pinch. I rolled my eyes at Robin. Whatever getting a shot felt like, a little pinch was not it.

'This really hurts,' I told Robin, 'and I'm really ready for the shot to work.'

'Do you need to think about something else?' he asked.

'That would help. I wonder how Tracy is. She tried to kill me!' I said, amazed all over again. 'Did I tell you she was watching this morning?'

Robin turned red. 'While we . . . ?'

'Yes, while we.'

'Oh, God.' His face scrunched with revulsion.

'Yeah, me too.'

'But it was great, wasn't it?' he said, bending closer. 'You want to think about that while the doctor takes these stitches?'

'It would be better than thinking about someone actually sewing on me.'

'Do you remember how you . . .' he whispered in my ear, and then the doctor came in. She began her work, chatting all the time to Robin, but I kept my eyes fixed on his face, and I knew he was thinking about that morning, too.

When she was through she gave me a list of instructions and told me I could go. Robin rescued my glasses and we left the hospital. I glanced at Robin doubtfully from time to time. This was surely a lot of trouble for a fragile new relationship.

Robin opened his car door for me, and went around to the driver's side. After he got in, he put the key in the ignition, but then he paused. 'I know you're tired right now, but I need to talk to you.'

Oh, no. Here it came. 'Sure,' I said, my voice empty of emotion.

'I feel guilty as hell. Tracy said she hit Celia with the Emmy?'

'Yeah.'

'And she attacked you. It seems like I bring nothing but trouble to a relationship.'

'I was just thinking the same thing about myself.'

His eyebrows raised in a question.

'My first long-term boyfriend marries someone else and then

divorces, my first husband dies, my short-term boyfriend shows back up and there's a killer stalking him.'

He laughed. When Robin laughed, his whole thin face was involved. 'I left my short-term girlfriend behind, hooked up with my agent, had a disastrous relationship with her, dated an actress who was strictly out for herself, then went back to my short-term girlfriend to get her stabbed, apparently.'

'Can we actually date without killing each other?'

'I think we have to try,' he said.

'I think I need to go to sleep,' I said.

Robin took me back home, and helped me undress and get into bed. Okay, maybe that was overdoing it a little, but I think a woman deserves some bed rest after she's been stabbed. I called the library to tell Sam I wouldn't be coming in on time. I explained why in as few words as I could manage. He was so miserable he hardly seemed to care.

Robin said he'd be downstairs with his laptop, and I snuggled down in the bed. I could hardly believe it was only early afternoon. The morning had been packed with more incidents than I usually encountered in a week. Maybe two weeks. I'd had great sex, found out a co-worker was a terrorist, started buying a house, and been stabbed in my kitchen. Busy day.

And it wasn't over yet.

I woke up about four. My arm was very sore, but it was bearable as long as I didn't move it too vigorously. I got some pants on by myself, and actually zipped and buttoned them. Getting the nightgown off over my head was much worse, and pulling on a knit shirt was just as bad. But finally I managed, and crept downstairs very slowly.

Robin was asleep on my couch, his laptop plugged in on my desk. He'd carried my phone to the couch with him, and it was moving up and down with the gentle rise and fall of his chest. He snored, like a big cat. It was a large noise, but oddly delicate.

I padded into the kitchen barefoot, and made some coffee. I looked outside to see a day that had gone gray and windy. Rain was coming up. I watched a swirl of gum leaves sweep past the window, yellow and red and brown. Indian summer was definitely over. I looked at the thermometer mounted outside the window. It had dropped twenty degrees since this morning.

While the coffee perked, I found a notepad with messages in Robin's slanted, narrow handwriting. My mother had called, which was no surprise. I should have called her. My sister-in-law – well, my stepsister-in-law – had called, too. So had Sally. And Arthur.

The last name Robin had written was 'Will Weir'. I wondered what the cameraman could have to say to me. Though everyone else deserved to be called back before Will, his was the number I dialed first, out of sheer curiosity.

'Weir,' he answered. I knew he must be on a cell phone, but it was the best connection I'd ever had. No crackling, no distant buzz.

'You called me?' I asked, after I identified myself.

'Right. The newspaper reporter who was here today, doing a story for your local paper . . . she said that a woman who claims to have killed Celia had attacked you. Is that true?'

'Yes,' I said, promising myself I'd grab Sally Allison and stuff her head in a food processor. Violent images were coming easily to me today. 'It was Tracy, the young woman who served the food at the caterer's truck?'

'The reddish-haired girl,' he said, after waiting a second for his memory to kick in, I assumed.

'That's her.'

'Why did she say that?'

I looked at the phone. I was glad Will couldn't see that look. 'Well, because she had a bee in her bonnet about Robin Crusoe, and she was resentful of Celia's former relationship with him.'

'But why would she attack you?'

This had me stumped. 'She thinks that Robin and I have a relationship now,' I said, feeling very awkward.

'That is a little quick,' he said, his voice as dry as toast.

'Robin and I are old friends,' I said, as neutrally as possible.

'I remember, from the book. Well, Mark and Joel wanted to know if it was because of something that happened on the set . . .'

'No,' I said, not following his line of reasoning, but willing to dismiss it as my own woolly-headedness.

'Mark brought some books by the library yesterday,' Will was saying.

'Yes.'

'Some books Celia had borrowed?'

'Yes.'

'They were in her trailer when she was killed?'

Were we playing twenty questions here? Robin slouched into the kitchen, his hair rumpled and his face creased from the throw pillow on the couch. He came up behind me and wrapped his long arms around me. I snuggled back against him.

'Yes,' I said again, hoping he'd get to the point soon. I tapped his name on the list with my finger, so Robin would know to whom I was speaking. I could feel him nod.

'The thing is, she'd borrowed some books from me,' Will was saying.

'Oh, gosh. No wonder you want to know about the books.' I never loaned books, myself. You never got them back, or if you did they had peanut-butter fingerprints on them, or smelled of other people's cigarettes or pets. 'Aside from a batch of paperbacks, there were two hardbacks about the sixties, and one home health book. Those were Lawrenceton library books, though. I'm really sure.'

'A home health book?' His voice sounded weaker.

'Yeah, the kind that you use when you want to diagnose your own illness. Poor thing.'

'You think she figured out what she had?' Weir sounded horrified.

'I know she had. There was a bookmark on the page for Huntington's chorea.'

A long silence fell. Robin poured himself a mug of coffee, asked me in mime if I wanted one, too. I nodded emphatically.

'She knew,' Will repeated, his voice just as shocked as it had been the first time. 'Oh, my God.'

'I'm sorry if I've upset you,' I said, actually feeling a little on the impatient side. 'What books were you trying to find?' I took a sip of coffee. The groggy nap hangover began to fade. My eyes strayed to my other phone messages. I had a lot of things to do, and my arm was burning.

'Books,' he said blankly. 'Oh, right, I'd loaned her some paperbacks. You said Mark also brought a few paperbacks to the library.'

'Yes, that's what I said.' He could have asked Mark before he called me.

'I'll drop by the library and have a look through those books,' he said. 'They're not important, but I stuck a letter in one of them, and I need it. When will you be working?'

'Tonight, six to nine,' I said. I'd told Sam I'd try to at least make the evening part of my shift, if I could. I didn't feel too bad.

'If we finish filming, I'll drop by,' he said.

'Okay,' I said doubtfully. 'They're in a box in the back. By the employee entrance, but it'll be locked, so come to the main doors. I can show you.' I was sure no one had had a chance to get to them in the past twenty-four hours.

'Good, maybe I'll get there tonight.' He sounded much more relaxed than he had at the beginning of the conversation.

'You're going in to work tonight?' Robin asked after I'd hung up.

'I ought to,' I said. 'I really don't hurt too bad, and with Patricia missing, I feel like I should keep things as even as possible. I'll call Sam to tell him as soon as I finish my coffee.'

'I was hoping you'd stay with me,' Robin said, doing his best to look pitiful.

'We've had our time today,' I reminded him. 'I think after work I'll need to come home and sleep some more. My arm is sore.' Plus other things.

He kissed my shoulder. 'Did that make it feel better?'

I tried not to smile, failed. 'A little.'

'Can we plan on tomorrow night?'

'Oh, yes. And I don't have to work the next day.'

He smiled at me. Robin had a radiant smile.

We talked about the move for a while, and the book Robin was working on, while I returned the rest of my phone calls.

Sam was glad to hear I was coming in, since he hadn't found anyone to replace me yet. After an incident a few years ago, librarians weren't allowed to work by themselves, no matter how few patrons showed up in the evening. My mother was glad to hear I was all right, and she had some rental units to show Robin. My stepsister-in-law Poppy was glad, too, and she wanted me to know that Brandon had his very first tooth. Arthur wanted me to know that law-enforcement gossip had it that Tracy was talking at great length about everything: her long-standing obsession with Robin, beginning with reading his books and escalating to focus on his personal life, her careful maneuvering to get the job with Molly's Moveable Feasts, her visit to Celia's trailer with a tray of croissants as camouflage, her subsequent movements . . .

'That's good,' I said, puzzled.

'She's telling us everything,' he repeated, significantly. 'In detail.'

I could feel my face turn red as I realized Arthur was telling me that everyone in the SPACOLEC (Spalding County Law Enforcement Complex) was aware that Robin and I had had sex on the carpet in the office of the house I was buying.

'Oh,' I said. My voice sounded small and embarrassed to my own ears.

'Oh,' he said. Angry.

'Um, Well, I'll talk to you later, thanks for letting me know – I think.'

'Roe, you realize this woman did not really kill Celia Shaw?'

'Yes, I know that.' Point?

'You want to know what I think.'

'No.'

'I think your new boyfriend did it. I think he knew what disease she had and killed her out of mercy.'

'I think you're *nuts*,' I said furiously, and slammed the phone down.

But when Robin asked me what I'd gotten upset about, I didn't look him in the face. And I didn't explain. No one could have persuaded me to believe Robin murdered someone – anyone – out of malice. But out of pity . . . it was almost conceivable. A lovely young woman, once beloved, facing a horrible fate – it was just barely possible. Didn't the fact that she'd been drugged argue that whoever had killed her didn't want her to feel the pain? Didn't the pillow pressed over her face give her a comparatively gentle end? Celia Shaw had had a merciful murder, if you believed such a thing was possible.

I didn't know Robin well enough, really, to completely rule out such a possibility. I needed to be by myself: to think, to recover my equilibrium. I reminded myself vigorously that Robin had a practically ironclad alibi.

He left a few minutes later, and we planned on seeing each other the next day, and I smiled at him, but when I locked the door behind him, I have to confess I felt some relief. When I thought of him not only coming to the hospital, but taking such good care of me afterward, I knew I was being one horrible woman to even doubt him for a second. But the tiny thread of doubt made me miserable, and I didn't need to be around him for a while.

I could not have a relationship with someone who could do such a thing. On the other hand, when I thought of the dreadful disease that would have killed Celia slowly, maybe her death had been a favor to her. That didn't mean I could cohabit with the one who'd granted it.

I pottered around, cleaning our mugs and the coffeepot, taking some extra-strength pain reliever the hospital had sent home with me, cleaning myself up a little for work. By five-thirty, I was at least presentable and functioning, though at a low level. Jeans and a long-sleeved tee were not my usual working gear, but I was not about to try to change again. I put on my red-framed glasses, to give me pep, and brushed my hair awkwardly. With the damp and cold in the air, my hair was on its worst behavior. It made a cloud around me, crackling with electricity.

It was already dark when I used my key to enter the employee door of the library, always kept locked after dark. The lights were on in the employee lounge, and I glanced over to see the books Mark Chesney had brought in, still in their box on the repair table. Patricia's office was still dark. I wondered how far away she'd gotten by now, and I felt sorry for Jerome. As I slung my purse into my locker, I thought of how long Patricia had kept such a big secret, and how careful she must have had to be for many years. A slip of the tongue, and her new life and her son would be gone.

Celia had had a massive secret, too. I wondered if she had known that her mother had died of the same disease she was developing. I wondered how she'd gone to work the first few days of filming, knowing what she was facing and how terrible her end would be: that surely her disease would become apparent to everyone in the course of time. I found myself thinking that Celia had surely had a theatrical flair, and she would have appreciated being a colorful True Crime episode rather than a disease of the week.

Lindsey Russell, a very young woman who'd just recently begun working as the children's librarian, passed through on her way out the back door. She gave me a cheerful wave, and told me the library had been really quiet all afternoon. Lindsey wasn't in the gossip loop yet, I gathered. I smiled back at her, and told her to have a good evening.

I strolled into the main part of the library, and discovered I was working with Perry. A few years before, it would have made me quite nervous to be alone with him. The money Sally had spent on him, or Perry's own determination to get well, or time itself, had gone far toward curing Perry of his many problems.

Perry was thin and nervous, but he was also a lot more sociable than he'd been, and he'd licked his drug problems. His relationships with women didn't seem to last too long, but wasn't that always the case until you found the One? I didn't always believe that there's a mate for every individual, but some days it was a real convenient and comforting concept.

'Hey, girl,' Perry said. 'I heard about your unexpected visitor. Was that the red-headed woman who was in here the other day, reading the magazines?'

'That was Tracy, all right. And she was the one who knocked me down in the parking lot, I'm sure.'

'It was a woman, after all. You were right. How's the arm?'

'It's sore, but I'm going to be fine. No muscle damage to speak of.'

'That's good. I can't believe you came in to work.'

'I hated to stress Sam out any more than he's already stressed.'

'So, you know Patricia left?'

I nodded cautiously. I didn't know what story Sam had told to give her a head start.

'Sam thinks she'll come back. If he wasn't already married, and if doing a mixed-race relationship wouldn't be so out of Sam's league, I'd say he was in love with that woman.'

Immediately, I felt something click, and I knew Perry was right.

Ultraconventional, ultraconservative lily white Sam Clerrick, married and the father of two, was in love with African-American left-wing former-bombmaker Anita Defarge. If she was his soul-mate, God truly had a sense of humor.

I shook my head to clear it. 'Perry,' I said, 'do we actually have any work to do?'

'I guess you could be entering the patron requests,' he said, with a sigh. That was a nothing job, recording the patron requests for specific books so we could fit them into our budget. 'There's only one patron in the building, Josh Finstermeyer. He's over in periodicals.'

I grinned at Josh's name, and Perry looked at me oddly. 'Oh, by the way, Roe,' he said, and he sounded so elaborately casual that I went on the alert immediately. 'You know the man who brought those books in yesterday?'

'Mark Chesney?'

'One of the movie people.'

'Yes, the assistant director.'

'Do you know him very well?'

'Hardly at all. He seems nice enough. I don't think working for Joel Park Brooks would be a job for the fainthearted.'

Perry was fiddling with some reserved books. I waited to see what he'd say, with some curiosity.

'He came back in this morning,' Perry said.

I tried to think of a neutral response. 'Oh?' was all I could come up with. I had a feeling I was about to be confided in. Perry fiddled with the books some more. 'Had he found some books he'd overlooked?' I prompted him.

'More things she'd checked out? No,' Perry said. 'He, ah, wanted to know if I'd go have a drink with him after work tonight.'

'Okay.' I shrugged. 'Are you going?'

'I'd love to talk to him,' Perry confessed. 'Someone who lives and works in Hollywood. God, that would be so interesting. You know, I've always loved to be in the community theater plays, and I've done a couple of things in Atlanta.'

Actually, I had forgotten all about Perry's obsession with the theater.

'I'd always hoped I'd get a chance to talk to your stepson,' Perry went on, 'but he was only in town so briefly when he came, and I could tell you two didn't have a good relationship.'

'That's putting it mildly.'

'So now this Mark, wanting to talk to me, it just seems so . . . exciting.'

'So go.'

'But at the same time, it seems like a . . . date.' Perry flushed dark red. 'I mean, why me? Would a regular guy just make a point of coming in and inviting another guy out for a drink?'

In my opinion, no. But I felt totally unqualified to give Perry advice on this issue. I had long suspected Perry had so much trouble maintaining relationships with women because he was backing the wrong horse, orientation-wise – but I sure wasn't going to suggest that to him.

'If you want to go, go. It doesn't commit you to anything,' I said at last. 'If you don't have a good time, if something happens that – doesn't interest you, that you don't feel comfortable with, get up and leave.' I shrugged again.

He brightened as if I'd given the date my blessing. 'That's the right way to look at it,' he said. 'You're so wise, Roe.'

That was me – the wise librarian of Lawrenceton, Georgia.

Our evening dragged. We were supposed to get off at nine, and at eight-thirty Perry excused himself to go through his getting-ready ritual, whatever that consisted of. I heard the drone of an electric razor from the men's restroom.

No one had shown a face in the library for the past hour, when Josh had left. I'd heard some books thud down into the book drop, but that was the most action we'd had. I began straightening the desk for the morning people. My arm was hurting, and I was looking forward to another pain pill and my own bed. The energy I'd recouped from the nap had long been used up, and I was very tired. I wondered where Robin was, what he was doing, whether he knew suspicion had crossed my mind. I wondered how Barrett was feeling, if he'd gotten over the shock of finding Celia dead. I wondered if he was a serious suspect in Celia's death.

While I was pondering all these things, I found a book with a number of loose pages. One of the day workers had put it on the cart to return to the stacks. I snorted with indignation. That book had to go back to the repair area.

'Mark's here!' Perry called. I turned to look at the front doors. Perry was wearing a black leather jacket and he looked really good. Mark was wearing a fresh shirt and creased khakis. 'I'm going to go on and leave if that's okay with you, Roe.'

It lacked only ten minutes till closing time. 'Sure. All I have to do is lock the back door on my way out.' I'd closed the library many times.

Perry and Mark waved as I locked the double glass doors behind them, and they strode off into the night. I began turning out lights in the main room. Of course, we kept some on all night, but that still left plenty to do. I looked around the big room, took one big inhalation of eau de book, and opened the heavy door that led to the new wing of the library. The employee lounge still smelled of Perry's cologne, and I decided that if Perry was putting on cologne and shaving for a drink with a guy, he wasn't as totally clueless of his own nature as he'd tried to appear. I got my purse out of my locker, extracted my keys, and spotted a light still burning in Sam's office. I went to switch it off. Now the employee lounge was the only lit room.

The building suddenly felt very empty, uncomfortably empty.

I heard someone fumbling at the lock outside and I stood in the middle of the floor, paralyzed with sudden fear. The door flew open, picked up by the wind outside. I realized as a leaf gusted in that it was beginning to rain again outside.

Patricia Bledsoe – I could not think of her by her real name – stepped in from the dark. She was as astonished to see me as I was to see her.

'He hasn't called the police,' I said instantly.

She gave a sigh. I thought it was of relief. 'I saw your car in the parking lot, but I noticed two people came out the front. I thought you'd gone somewhere with Perry,' she said. 'Jerome's out in the car. We had to turn back halfway to . . . well, halfway, and come back. I forgot something important.'

'Get whatever it is, don't mind me,' I said. 'I'm not even here.' I'd dropped my purse on a table, and now I picked it up again. Patricia sped into her office, pulling a drawer out all the way and fumbling under it. Her hand came up clutching an envelope, and I realized she'd had it taped to the bottom of her drawer. How the paranoid live. Though, in Patricia's case, the paranoia was justified.

'Where will you go?' I asked. 'Wait a minute, forget I asked that.'

And we both heard the back door begin to open. Patricia hadn't locked it behind her.

With a desperate expression on her face, Patricia ducked down below her desk. I stepped out of her office, hoping the light in there didn't show anything suspicious over the half-wall.

To my surprise, Will Weir stepped in. I'd half-forgotten our conversation. His timing was awful.

'What are you doing here?' I asked, not caring if I sounded rude or not.

'I'm glad I caught you,' he said, smiling. 'I'm sorry if I scared you. Is it illegal, coming in the back way? The front was locked, and it's not nine yet.'

No, it was all of 8:58. I felt abruptly uneasy. 'You're not supposed to come in this door,' I said. I didn't smile back. 'You're going to have to wait to come to the library tomorrow. I've shut everything down.'

'I just needed to see the books Mark brought in,' he said, still smiling. 'I see they're over here in the box.'

'It's too late. You have to come back tomorrow.'

'I have to work tomorrow. Let me just take a minute, and I'll be all through.' He'd made his voice soothing, as though I was being childish.

I know when someone's trying to get away with something. I've sure been a librarian long enough for that.

'Will, what's in those books that's so important? That can't wait?'

He smiled again, made a 'wait' gesture with his hand, and began riffling through the pile of books. The wind was whooshing through the cracked door, and it fluttered the pages of the book he held, the book about diagnosing your own illness. Will shook it. Nothing happened. He followed that procedure with every book in the box. As book after book proved a disappointment, he tossed them to one side. I almost protested, and then caught myself.

He kept talking the whole time, meaningless phrases like, 'I'll be out of your hair in just a second,' and 'I just need to check these books.' He was just trying to keep me sedated, I realized, and then he lifted the bound movie script that Mark had brought by accident. I'd completely forgotten it. Will turned it upside down, and shook it, and from its pages flew a folded piece of paper. The wind picked up the paper and blew it in my direction, and it landed on the table to my right.

Without a single thought in my head I picked it up and unfolded it. It was a yellowed letter, and it began, 'Dearest Celia, the lawyer should give you this when you turn twenty-nine. I think you should know who your father is . . .' and then the paper was snatched out of my hand.

'You don't need that. It's mine.' Will was smiling again, that warm and homey smile that had made me feel relaxed and comfortable in his company.

'Were you Celia's dad?' I asked, incredulous. 'Did she know?'

'She did after the lawyer delivered that letter,' Will said. 'She turned twenty-nine last week, and the package came Federal Express from the lawyer in Wilmington.'

'Why did Celia's mom leave her a letter?'

'She knew she wasn't going to be around to talk to Celia in person.'

'She knew she had Huntington's.'

'Yeah, she knew. 'Course, I didn't, until it was too late. I would never have risked a relationship with a woman who had a disease like that. I would have known my heart would get broken.'

'So you knew Linda Shaw after her divorce?'

'Yeah, she came out to California to find me. She'd felt the first symptoms, and the Huntington's had been diagnosed in North Carolina. She wanted to see Celia placed before she got any worse, and she wanted to do a little living before she got too sick. So she left Celia with her sister, and she followed me out to California. She wanted to do that living with me. The only thing is, she didn't tell me. She didn't tell me she'd had my child, and she didn't tell me she was going to die.' He was bitter all over: voice, stance, words.

'That was really wrong of her,' I said softly. I began to edge a little closer to the door. He was still to my left, by the book-mending area, but with one leap he could be between me and freedom.

'Damn right.' He looked as though he was going to cry. 'Then, when she got really sick, she begged me to help her. She begged me to kill her. Finally, I helped her out.'

'She wasn't a suicide.'

'Not strictly speaking.'

'It was you.'

'Yes, it was me. She asked me. I couldn't stand to see her suffer any longer, lose her personality, her muscle control, everything that made Linda a person.'

'What about Celia?'

He was scanning the letter. 'I met up with her when she came out to California after she got a bit part in a TV series I was filming. She looked so much like her mother that I followed her the first time I saw her. Then I arranged to meet her. She was Linda's daughter, all right, and she was my daughter, too. At first she tried to make friends with me – she didn't know, of course. She just knew I was an important guy.'

Oh. *That* was the kind of 'friends' she'd tried to make.

'Luckily, I'd told her I was her dad before the letter came.'

'You know, I really don't need to know any more,' I said cheerfully. 'You can take your letter and go now.'

'I think you know a little more than you need to,' he said. 'I've taken care of the women I loved. I've done the right thing by them. I don't love you, and I don't care any more if I do the right thing or not. I like my job, and I like to work, and I don't want you to stop me doing that. Celia never told anyone we were kin.'

'Who your family is, is your business.'

'I don't think for one second that you're that naïve, Aurora. I think you know I killed Celia.'

'Why?' I asked desperately. 'Why would you do that?'

'You could tell she was getting it,' he said. 'You could tell. It was just like Linda. She was beginning to stumble around. She was beginning to make these sudden movements without knowing she was doing it. She was having trouble remembering her lines. In a year, she'd be just another starlet who'd caught a bad disease, and she'd be forgotten in two years. This way, she'll always be remembered. She'll always be brought up in the magazines. Like Brandon Lee. Freak accident; they still print his name, his picture, what might have been. Celia, they'll do the same.'

The thing I hated most – media attention – he'd sought out as being preeminently desirable. More valuable than life. And yet, hadn't I had the same thought hours before? Better a provocative whodunit than a disease of the week?

'What would Celia have thought about that?'

'You can't tell me she didn't know,' he said defensively. 'I brought her the coffee with the Valium in it, a whopping dose; she must have tasted something funny about it. She just looked at me while she was drinking it. Then she closed her eyes and waited.'

Then she fell unconscious.

'She'd had a good night before with that stepson of yours,' Will Weir said. 'He was good-looking enough, and self-serving enough, to show her a good time.'

I wanted to throw up. The Celia Shaw pre-death lay.

'And she was on the set of her very own movie, her very first starring role. Her Emmy was beside her. She had her own trailer.'

'So you put a pillow over her face.'

'She didn't struggle. She was at peace. No disease, at the top of her form. And then I carried off the coffee cup.'

I put a hand over my mouth. He explained what he'd done so plausibly, but it was wrong, wrong, wrong.

'Did you ask Celia what she wanted? Did you tell her about her mom's Huntington's?'

'Not before she read it in the letter.' He shrugged. 'I didn't know about the letter.'

'Would you have told her?'

'No.' He looked surprised. 'No, I would never have told her. We'd have had to go through the whole emotional scene, then, the crying and shit.'

The crying and shit. What an inconvenience.

'Did you get this job with the idea of watching over her?'

He said, 'More or less.'

Meaning, no. He'd been hired by chance, observed the beginnings of Celia's disease by chance, revealed his identity to her only when she'd made a play for him. And then, he thought he'd kill her. After all, he was her dad. He had the right to choose for her.

I don't think I've ever loathed anyone so much in my life.

'What are you going to do now?' I asked, cutting to the chase. I might as well know.

'I guess I'm going to take this letter with me. I guess, if you say anything about it, I'll just say you lied.'

Hope flickered in me for a minute, to be extinguished when I considered the overwhelming selfishness of this man's life. He had no intention of leaving me alive with his secret. After all, there were blood tests that could prove whether or not he'd been Celia's father. And there was the lawyer who could testify he'd had a letter sent to Celia on her birthday, even if he couldn't say what the contents of that letter had been.

I had no idea what I could do to stop him. I don't go around armed. You'd be surprised how many Southern belles have a gun in their purse, but I wasn't one of them. I didn't have a stun gun, or a blackjack . . . hey. I had a panic button! It was on the keyless entry pad for my car. I'd gotten my keys out and now they were clutched in my hand. Was my car close enough to the back door to pick up the signal? I hadn't the slightest idea how the damn thing worked. I probably had to be closer. So, before I could have second thoughts, I made a dash for the back door, managed to get my hand out of it, and pressed the panic button.

Beep! Beep! Beep! My car responded in a wonderful way, lights flashing and horn blaring. But I feared it was too little, too late, because now Will had hold of me around the waist and was pulling me back into the library. I held on to the doorknob of the open door as long as I could, but he was a strong man and my grip was weak.

Who would be driving past the library anyway, at nine o'clock on a weeknight? Downtown Lawrenceton was pretty much deserted even on the weekends, much less on a Thursday night.

My heart sank, even as I kicked backwards at him, hoping to land a blow south of the waist.

I got him in the shin instead, not nearly as effective, but enough to raise a 'Huh!' of surprise. I shrieked, hoping to add to the din of the horn and addle his brain, but all that did was make him mad. He whopped me upside the head with an open hand. If he'd fisted it, it would have knocked me out or broken my neck, but I guess he wasn't used to victims who actually fought back. He couldn't control both my hands, so I went for his face, hoping to scratch him conspicuously, and I dug in. My nails are always short, so I didn't make as much of a gouge as I'd hoped for, but he was bleeding and cursing up a storm. He hit me again, and this time he did a better job of it.

'Help!' I screamed, and someone actually did.

I had completely forgotten Patricia Bledsoe.

Patricia was dancing behind him with a gun in her hand.

If she shot him, she'd get me.

Before I could give my opinion, she seemed to realize that, too, and turned the gun around in her hand. Holding it by the barrel, she poised herself, and swung the butt with all her might. She connected solidly with his head, right above his right ear. There was an awful little noise, like stepping on wet peanut shells, and then he collapsed in a heap.

We stood there and breathed heavily for a minute, Patricia's chest heaving just as hard as mine.

'Oh, thank you,' I babbled. 'Oh, Patricia, thank you thank you.'

'I've got to get out of here,' she said precisely, clipping off her words like they were the end of a cigar.

'Yes, sure.'

'What are you going to tell them?'

'I'll make up something, you get gone. I won't tell anyone.'

'I believe you,' she said, sounding a little surprised.

'He could've hit the corner of that table,' I said. 'It's wood.' I wasn't sure if that would make a difference or not, but it sounded good.

'Better put some blood on the corner, then,' Patricia advised.

She had her envelope still clutched in her hand, and now she tucked it into her skirt pocket.

'Good luck to you and Jerome,' I said, and then Patricia Bledsoe – Anita Defarge – was out of the Lawrenceton Library for the very last time, and over the sound of my car honking, I never heard her pull away.

I had a couple of things to do before I called 911. Feeling my whole face pucker with distaste, I touched my fingers to Will Weir's depressed wound, and I rubbed the blood and hair on the corner of the table nearest him. I thought briefly of trying to move him closer to the table, but I was afraid of screwing up things even more. Better leave it simple.

I didn't think I'd ever concealed a crime before in my life. It was kind of exhilarating. I rinsed my hands off in the employee sink, and then poured some cold coffee that had been sitting in the pot down the drain after the tinged water. I left the pot in the sink.

I dialed 911 on the phone in Patricia's office. While I was there, I checked to make sure everything had been left in order. I wondered what had been in the envelope she'd needed so badly – money? Documents? Whatever it was, she had saved my life by coming back to get it.

As I waited for the police to come, I wondered what would have happened if Patricia hadn't believed I would keep silent. After all, she'd had a gun in her purse, and she'd showed she wasn't afraid to use it. Then I decided there were paths I didn't need to walk, and that was one of them.

It was actually lucky for me that Will had hit me. By the time the room was swarming with police and emergency and library people, the whole left side of my face was swollen and blackening. The bruising had hardly healed from my mishap in the parking lot. I was going to forget what I really looked like. Blood and saliva had made a track down my chin where a tooth had cut the inside of my cheek. In the face of such graphic evidence, and the letter (which I never got to read all the way through) and Mark Chesney's testimony that Will had tried more than once to get Mark to give him the books to bring to the library, I was home free.

Airlifted to an Atlanta hospital, Will Weir lingered in a coma for four days. Then he died.

I had to endure a lot of silent sympathy from people who were sure a gentle woman like me would be harboring lots of guilt at having indirectly caused a death, even the death of someone who was trying to kill me.

I guess they just didn't know me very well.

If it ever crossed my mind to tell anyone about Patricia/Anita, I sat on the thought as heavily as I could. I imagined her building a new life somewhere else, but I hoped in this new life she would cut Jerome some slack and let him wear Nikes.

Sam waited three more days, griping loudly about Patricia's inexplicable absence, before he called the police, who weren't too swift about telling the FBI. The FBI hopped right on it, fingerprinted the rental house (which had been cleaned, in the interim, by professional cleaners who'd been hired and paid in cash through the mail), fingerprinted the whole office (though by then the library janitor had done a jim-dandy job of cleaning the desk, under Sam's direction) and questioned the whole staff. In the end, they still weren't a hundred percent sure we'd encountered Anita Defarge.

How did Robin handle all this? After all, he'd been with me when I saw the picture. Somehow Robin realized that identifying Patricia Bledsoe was no high priority of mine. I may have whispered something to him to that effect in the dark of the night, the night I moved into my new house. And since he had his plate full testifying against Tracy, moving his stuff from California to the small house on Oak my mother found for him, and doing some rewrites on the script of *Whimsical Death*, Robin didn't ask any questions.

I like that in a man.

Poppy Done to Death

Prologue

I paid almost no attention at all to the last conversation I had with my stepsister-in-law, Poppy Queensland. Though I liked Poppy – more or less – my main feeling when she called was one of irritation. I was only five years older than Poppy, but she made me feel like a Victorian grandmother, and when she told me she was going to foul up our plans, I felt very . . . miffed. Doesn't that sound grumpy?

'Listen,' said Poppy. As always, she sounded imperative and excited. Poppy always made her own life sound more important and exciting than anyone else's (mine, for example). 'I'm going to be late this morning, so you two just go on. I'll meet you there. Save me a place.'

Later, I figured that Poppy called me about 10:30, because I was almost ready to leave my house to get her, and then Melinda. Poppy and Melinda were the wives of my stepbrothers. Since I'd acquired my new family well into my adulthood, we didn't have any shared history, and it was taking us a long time to get comfortable. I generally just introduced Poppy and Melinda as my sisters-in-law, to avoid this complicated explanation. In our small Georgia town, Lawrenceton, most often no explanation was required. Lawrenceton is gradually being swallowed by the Atlanta metroplex, but here we still generally know all our family histories.

With the portable phone clasped to my ear, I peered into my bathroom mirror to see if I'd gotten my cheeks evenly pink. But I was too busy thinking that this change of plans was inexplicable and exasperating. 'Everything okay?' I asked, wondering if maybe little Chase was sick, or Poppy's hot-water heater had exploded. Surely only something pretty serious would keep Poppy from this meeting of the Uppity Women, because Poppy was supposed to be inducted into the club this morning. That was a big event in the life of a Lawrenceton woman. Poppy, though not a native, had lived in Lawrenceton since she was a teen, and she surely understood the honor being done her.

Even my mother had never been asked to be an Uppity Woman, though my grandmother had been a member. My mother had always been deemed too focused on her business. (At least that was how my mother explained it.) I was trying awful hard not to be even a little bit smug. It wasn't often I did anything that made my successful and authoritative mother look at me admiringly.

I think my mother had worked so hard to establish herself – in a business dominated by men – that she didn't really see the use in lobbying to join an organization made up mostly of homemaking women. Those were the conditions that had existed when she plunged into the workforce to make a living for her tiny family – me. Things had changed now. But you were tapped to join Uppity Women before you were forty-five, or you didn't join.

What did it take to be an Uppity Woman? The qualifications weren't exactly spelled out. It was more like they were generally understood. You had to have demonstrated strong-mindedness, and a high degree of resilience. You had to be intelligent, or at least shrewd. You had to be willing to speak out, though that was not an absolute requirement. You couldn't have any big attitude about what you were: Jewish, or black, or Presbyterian. You didn't have to have money, but you had to be willing to make an effort to dress appropriately for the meetings. (You would think an organization that encouraged independent women would be really flexible about clothing, but such was not the case.)

You didn't have to be absolutely Nice. The southern standard of niceness was this: You'd never been convicted of anything, you didn't look at other's women's husbands too openly. You wrote your thank-you notes and were polite to your elders. You had to take a keen interest in your children's upbringing. And you made sure your family was fed adequately. There were sideways and byways in this 'nice' thing, but those were the general have-tos. Poppy was teetering on the edge of not being 'nice' enough for the club, and since there had been an Uppity Woman in the forties who'd been just barely acquitted of murdering her husband, that was really saying something.

I shuddered. It was time to think of the positive.

At least we didn't have to wear hats, as Uppity Women had in the fifties. I would have drawn the line at wearing a hat. Nothing makes me look sillier, whether I wear my hair down (because it's long and really curly and wavy) or whether I wear it up (which makes my head look huge). I was glad that the Episcopal church no longer required women to wear hats or veils to Sunday service. I would have had to look like an idiot every week.

I'd been mentally digressing, and I'd missed what Poppy said. 'What? What was that?' I asked.

But Poppy said, 'It's not important. We're all fine; I just have to take care of something before I get there. See you later.'

'See you,' I said cheerfully. 'What are you wearing to the meeting?' Melinda had asked me to check, because Poppy had a proclivity toward flamboyance in her clothing taste. But I could hardly make Poppy change outfits, as I'd pointed out to Melinda. So I'm not sure why I stretched the conversation out a little more. Maybe I felt guilty for having tuned her out, however briefly; maybe it would have made a difference if I'd listened carefully.

Maybe not.

'Oh, I guess I'll wear that olive green dress with the matching sweater? And my brown heels. I swear, I think whoever invented panty hose was in league with the devil. I won't let John David in the room when I'm putting them on. You look like an idiot when you're wiggling around, trying to get them to stretch enough.'

'I agree. Well, we'll see you at the meeting.' She wasn't even dressed yet, I noted.

'Okay, you and Melinda hold up the family banner till I get there.'

That felt strange, but almost good, having a family banner to hold up, even though my inclusion was artificial. My long-divorced mother, Aida Brattle Teagarden, had married widower

John Queensland four years ago. Now Melinda and Poppy were her daughters-in-law, married to John's two sons, Avery and John David. I liked all of the Queenslands, though they certainly were a diverse group.

Probably John's oldest son, Avery, was my least favorite. But Melinda, Avery's wife and mother of their two little Queenslands, was becoming a true friend. At first, I had tended to prefer Poppy, of my two new step in-laws. She was entertaining, bright, and had an original and lively mind. But Melinda, much more prosaic and occasionally given to dim moments, had improved on acquaintance, while Poppy and the way she lived her life had begun to give me pause. Melinda had matured and focused, and she'd broken through her shyness to express her opinions. She was no longer so intimidated by my mother, either. Poppy, who didn't seem to be scared of anything, took chances, big chances. Unpleasant chances.

So, while I enjoyed Poppy's company – she could have made the Devil laugh – I held part of myself away from her, afraid of the intimacy that would make her loss even more painful. Frankly, I figured she and John David would divorce within the next year or so.

What actually happened was much worse.

Chapter One

Melinda sat next to me at the table nearest the door. We'd kept a chair open for Poppy the whole meeting, but she'd never shown up. The room was full of Uppity Women, and they'd all turned to look at us when Poppy's name had been called and we'd had to say she wasn't there. The other Uppities saw a very short woman in her mid-thirties with a ridiculous amount of brown hair and a wonderful pair of green-rimmed glasses, and a taller, very slim, black-haired woman of the same age, who had a narrow and agreeable face. (I was the shorter of the two.) I am sure all the Uppities who could see that far noticed that we had matching expressions, compounded of social smiles and grim eyes. I, personally, planned to rake Poppy over the hottest coals I could find. The president of Uppity Women, Teresa Stanton, was giving us a basilisk glare.

'Then we'll continue the meeting with our book discussion,' Teresa said, her voice clipped and businesslike. Teresa, aggressively well groomed, had that chin-length haircut that swings forward when you bend your head, as she did now to check the agenda. Her hair always did what it was told, in sharp contrast to mine. I was sure Teresa's hair was scared not to mind.

Melinda and I sat through the book discussion in mortified silence, but we tried to look interested and as though we were thinking deep thoughts. I don't know what Melinda's policy was, but mine was to keep silent so I wouldn't draw any more attention. I looked around the room, at the circular tables filled with well-dressed, intelligent women, and I decided that if none of them had ever been disappointed by a relative, they were a lucky bunch. After all, a woman hadn't shown up for a big-deal, high-pressure social engagement. Surely that was not such a rarity.

I muttered as much to Melinda, between the book discussion and lunch, and she widened her dark eyes at me. 'You're right,' she said instantly, sounding relieved. 'We'll go by and see her after this is over, though. She can't do this to us again.'

See? Even Melinda was taking it personally, and she's much more well balanced than I.

We scooted out of the dining room as quickly as we politely could after Teresa had dismissed the meeting. But we were waylaid by Mrs Cole Stewart, who inquired in her deep southern voice where Poppy was. We could only shake our heads in ignorance and mutter a lame excuse. Mrs Cole Stewart was seventy-five, white-haired, and all of a hundred pounds, and she was absolutely terrifying. From her affronted stare, we clearly received the message that we were being charged with guilt by association.

When we got to my Volvo, Melinda said, 'We're going over there and have a few words with her.'

I didn't say no. In fact, I'd never considered any other course of action. 'Oh, yeah,' I said grimly. I was so focused on having a few choice words with Poppy that I couldn't enjoy the clear, chilly November day, and November is one of my favorites. If we passed anyone we should have waved at, we never noticed it.

'It isn't as if she does a lot of work around the house,' Melinda said suddenly, apropos of nothing. But I nodded, understanding the extended thought. Poppy didn't work outside the home anymore, she had one baby, and she didn't even take very good care of the house, though she did take good care of the baby. She should have been able to manage what was on her plate, as my mother would have put it.

As I'd half-expected, when we got to Poppy's and saw that her car was still parked in the carport, Melinda quailed. 'You go in there, Roe,' she said. 'I'm liable to get so mad, I might mention a whole lot of other things besides the topic at hand.'

We exchanged a meaningful glance, the kind that encompassed a whole conversation.

I swung my legs out of the car. I noticed something on the ground by my feet, two long straps of embroidered cloth.

'Oh crap,' I said, glad only Melinda was there to hear me. I tossed them into the car for Melinda to look at, and I marched to the front door. I was mentally loaded for bear. 'Poppy!' I called as I turned the doorknob of the front door of the house. The door opened. Unlocked. Since by now I knew Poppy had already had company that morning, I was not so startled by this.

I stepped into the foyer and called again. But the house was quiet. Moosie, Poppy's cat, came to see what was happening. Moosie was a pale sylph compared to my huge feline basketball, Madeleine. The cat meowed in an agitated way and ran from hall to kitchen and back again. I'd never seen Moosie act so jittery. He was Poppy's pampered pet, a declawed half Siamese she'd adopted from the animal shelter. Moosie was not allowed out the front door, only out the sliding glass back door, which led into a backyard enclosed all the way around with a six-foot-high privacy fence. After Moosie stropped my ankles a couple of times, I registered the fact that the sensation was sticky. I looked down and saw that my hose were stained.

'Moosie, what have you been into?' I asked. Several unpleasant possibilities crossed my mind. The cat began cleaning himself vigorously, licking at the dark patch on his side. He didn't seem hurt or anything, just, well, catty. 'Where's Poppy?' I asked. 'Where's your momma?' I know that's disgusting, but when you're alone with animals, you get that way.

Poppy and John David actually had a human child, Chase, as well as the cat, but they'd had the cat longer.

'Hey, Poppy!' I yelled up the stairs. Maybe she'd gotten in the shower after her visitor left. But why would she? Even for Poppy, missing such an important engagement was very unusual. And if she'd been up to her usual shenanigans . . . I had to press my lips together to hold in my anger.

I stomped up the stairs, yelling Poppy's name the whole time. She'd missed Uppity Women, and she'd missed lunch, and, by golly, I wanted to know why.

The master bedroom looked as though she'd just stepped out. The bed was made and her bathrobe was tossed across the foot of the bed. Poppy's bedroom slippers, the slide-in kind, were in a little heap on the floor. Her brush was tossed down on her dressing table, clogged with red-gold hair.

'Poppy?' I said, less certainly this time. The bathroom door was wide open, and I could see the shower enclosure. The wall was dry. It had been quite awhile since Poppy had showered. I could see my reflection in the huge mirror that topped the two sinks, and I looked scared. My glasses were sliding down my nose, which is a very insignificant feature of my face. I'd worn the green-rimmed ones today to offset my bronze-colored jacket and tobacco brown sheath, and I took a little moment to reflect that autumn colors were really my best.

Well, I could think about myself any old time, but right now I needed to be searching. I went back down the stairs faster than I'd gone up. Melinda, waiting out in my Volvo, would be wondering what had happened to me. I, however, was wondering why the central heating was roaring away on this cool but moderate day, and why I was feeling a draft of chilly air despite the heating system's best attempts.

I muttered a less ladylike word under my breath as I strode farther down the entrance hall to the kitchen, though *striding* is a moot word to use when you're four eleven. Moosie wove in and out between my ankles and darted ahead when it suited him. The kitchen was a mess; although big and bright, it was scattered with dishes and crumbs and pieces of mail and baby bottles and car keys and the St James Altar Guild schedule – a normal kitchen, in other words. To my left, dividing the room in half, was a breakfast bar. On the other side of it was a family dining table, positioned by the sliding glass doors so Poppy and John David could look outside while they ate. A mug of coffee was on the breakfast bar. It was full. I laid my finger against the side of it. Cold.

Over the top of the breakfast bar, I could see that the sliding glass door was open. This was the source of the intruding cool air. A sharp-edged wind from the east was gusting into the kitchen.

My scalp began to prickle.

I stepped through the narrow passage between the end of the breakfast bar and the refrigerator and looked to my right. Poppy was lying on the floor just inside the open sliding glass door. One of her brown pumps had fallen off her narrow foot. Her sweater and skirt were covered in blotches.

A spray of blood had dried on the glass of the doors.

I could hear a radio playing from the house behind Poppy's. The tune wafted over the high privacy fence. I could hear someone splashing through the water of a pool: Cara Embler, doing her laps, as she did every day, unless her pool was actually frozen. Poppy, who had laughed about Cara's adherence to such an uncomfortable regimen, would never laugh again. The processes of life and living, continuing in the houses all around us, had come to a dead stop here in this house on Swanson Lane.

Moosie sat by Poppy's pathetic, horrible body. He said, 'Reow.' He pressed against her side. His food bowl, on a mat by the breakfast bar, was empty.

Now I knew how Moosie's fur had gotten stained. He'd been trying to rouse Poppy, maybe so she would feed him.

Suddenly, I had to escape from that suburban kitchen with its horrible secret. I flew out of the house, slamming the front door behind me. I had a fleeting impulse to scoop up Moosie, but taking charge of him was too much for me at that second. I dashed down the sidewalk to the curb, where Melinda was waiting. I was making the 'phone' signal as I hurried, little finger and thumb pointing to mouth and ear, respectively. Melinda had turned on the cell phone by the time I got to her car.

'Nine one one,' I said, gasping for breath. Melinda gave me a sharp look, but she punched in the number as I'd asked and then passed the phone to me. Did I mention that Melinda has a ton of good sense?

'The nature of your emergency?' said a distant voice.

'I'm at Eight-oh-eight Swanson Lane,' I said. 'This is Aurora Teagarden. My sister-in-law has been killed.'

I never did remember the rest of that conversation. When I was sure they were coming, I pressed the button that ended the conversation, and I began to try to explain to Melinda.

But instead, I flashed on the deep wounds on Poppy's hands, wounds incurred when she was defending her life, and I leaned over to avoid the car, my dress, and the phone while I threw up.

For the sixth or seventh time, I explained very carefully why Melinda and I had gone to Poppy's house. Because the city police made the house off-limits instantly, Melinda and I drove right down to the police station, and from there I called my mother at Select Realty, her agency. It was a difficult conversation, over my cell phone in a public place, but one that had to be completed. Her husband, John, had had one heart attack already. Mother was terrified of another, and the news about his favorite daughter-in-law might trigger one. Mother was right to worry about that, and she thought of a few more things to worry her before we'd finished our conversation.

'Who'll tell John David?' Mother asked. 'Tell me it doesn't have to be John.' John David was John's second son, and the husband of the late Poppy.

'Where is he, Mother? Do you know?' The police had been asking me that quite persistently. If John David wasn't at his company headquarters in Atlanta, I didn't know where he'd be. He'd been a pharmaceuticals salesman for the first few years of his marriage, but recently he'd gotten a job at company headquarters in the Public Relations division. John David had always been good at turning an attractive face to the world.

'John David? He's at work, I guess. Two o'clock on a Monday afternoon, where else would he be?'

'Do you have that phone number and address handy?'

I could hear little efficient sounds as Mother wheeled through her Rolodex. She rattled off a number, and I wrote it on a scrap of paper and handed it to the policewoman sitting across the desk. 'That's the same number,' the detective said, and I nodded.

'Will they let you go tell him?' Mother asked.

'I think the police will tell John David,' I said. 'If they can find him.'

'What do you mean?'

'I already gave them that number. The police called, and the people there told the police that John David left work early today. Before noon.'

'Then where could he be?'

'I guess they'd like to know that, too,' I said, figuring a number of other shoes were about to drop.

After an appreciable pause, my mother said, 'That would kill John.' Another pause: I could practically hear her thinking. 'Aurora, I've got to go, before he hears about this some other way. You know someone's bound to call the house and tell him there are a lot of police cars around John David's house. Wait! Roe, where's the baby?'

My face must have changed dramatically, because the detective stood up abruptly, sending her chair skidding a couple of feet. 'I don't know where the baby is,' I said numbly. I couldn't believe I'd forgotten about Chase, who was only eleven months old. 'I don't know. Maybe Melinda . . .' I swiveled on the hard chair, looking for my remaining sister-in-law. The next instant, I was on my feet. The detective said something, but I didn't listen as I searched for Melinda, my heels click-clacking on the linoleum floor.

She was in a cubicle with Detective Arthur Smith, whom I knew all too well. I stuck my head in. 'Roe?' she said, already apprehensive.

'Where's the baby? Where's Chase?'

She looked at me blankly. 'Why, John David dropped him off at my house this morning. My sitter is keeping my two and Chase, so Poppy and I . . .' And then her face crumpled all over again.

I hotfooted it back to the telephone, which I'd stupidly left on the desk. 'Chase is at Melinda's,' I told my mother. I was limp with relief. 'Evidently, John David took him over there this morning.'

'So John David was in town this morning. At least we know

that.' My mother had already absorbed Chase's safety and was moving on to other ramifications. 'Listen, Roe, you've got my cell-phone number.' I had it all right, tattooed on my brain. 'Call me the *minute* you know where John David is. I've got to get to your stepfather.'

I thought my mother was a wee bit affected in calling John my stepfather, and she did on every possible occasion. After all, I'd been in my early thirties when John, a widower, had married Mother. He'd been a friend of mine before he'd dated my mother, and I felt a mixture of different obligations and attitudes toward John. I certainly never addressed him as 'Stepdad'.

I hung up and faced the woman who'd been taking my statement. Her name was Cathy Trumble, and I'd never met her before. Detective Trumble was stocky and graying, with an easy-care curly hairdo and sharp, pale eyes behind rimless glasses. She was a real professional, I guess; I had no clue as to how she felt about the information I was giving her – the death of Poppy Queensland, my brother-in-law's absence – or anything at all. It was like talking to a piece of stainless steel.

'How come you don't have a cubicle?' I asked. I had been wandering off in my own mental world while Detective Trumble was typing into a computer, and she was a little nonplussed by my question. The Sparling County Law Enforcement Center housed the sheriff's office, the town police, and the jail. In the world of SPACOLEC, detectives got their own little space with head-high carpeted dividers.

'I just got hired,' she explained. She seemed startled into answering the question.

I recalled Sally Allison's story in the paper about the county having to increase its law-enforcement budget because of increased population, which had led directly to increased crime. Okay, Detective Cathy Trumble was the result. 'Where do you live?' I asked, trying to be sociable. With a mother who made a living in real estate, it was a question that was second nature.

'And you had planned this lunch date with your sisters for how long?' she asked pointedly.

Okay, we weren't going to be best friends.

'They're my sisters-in-law, sort of once removed,' I said for what felt like the millionth time. 'We've been planning to go to the Uppity Women together for a month. Melinda just joined three months ago, and I've been a member for about half a year.'

'And Poppy?'

'Oh, she'd gone as our guest twice. But today she was going to be inducted. Somebody had died to let her in,' I explained.

The clear eyes fixed me in their stare. I felt like I'd been caught in the headlights. 'Somebody had died?' she said.

For the first time, I regretted not being questioned by Arthur. 'Well, to get in Uppity Women – it's really the Uppity Women's Reading and Lunch Club, but everyone calls it Uppity Women – you have to fill a vacancy, because the bylaws limit membership to thirty,' I told Cathy Trumble. 'You have to be nominated, and if they vote yes, you get on the list. The list is limited to five. Then when a member dies, the top person on the list replaces that member. Etheline Plummer died for me.'

'I understand,' Detective Trumble said unwillingly. She looked a little dazed.

'So when Linda Burdine Buckle died two weeks ago,' I said, 'it was Poppy's turn.' I patted at my cheeks with a soggy Kleenex.

'What do Uppity Women do?' Detective Trumble asked, though she sounded as though she didn't want to hear the answer.

'Well, we talk about local politics and then we decide how we're going to handle local issues. We have representatives at every city council meeting and school board meeting, and they give reports to the club. We decide whom we're going to back in the primaries, and how we're going to do it. And then we have a book we've all read that we discuss, and then we eat lunch.'

This didn't seem extraordinary to me, but Trumble gave a kind of sigh and looked down at her desk. 'So, you have a political agenda, and a literary agenda, and a social . . .'

I nodded.

'You all read, what? Like from the Oprah Book Club? Like *The Lovely Bones*?'

'Um, no.'

'Well, what was this month's book?'

'*The Sublime and the Ridiculous: Economic Currents in the South-east*. By a professor at the University of Georgia? She was supposed to come down to speak to us about it, but she got the flu.' I had read every word, but it hadn't been easy.

The look Trumble gave me would have frozen a pond. 'Could you just tell me what you've been doing, say last evening and this morning?' Detective Trumble asked, her voice hard despite the thinnest overlay of courtesy.

'Last night won't do you any good,' I said, surprised she'd even tack that on. 'She wasn't killed till this morning.'

'How do you know that?' Trumble leaned forward, her eyes sharp and intent.

'About twenty different ways. First off, I talked to her this morning. Then, her clothes. She was wearing the right clothes.'

' "The right clothes"?'

'For the meeting. Poppy usually dressed a little extreme for Lawrenceton, and Melinda and I warned her that she had to look like Missy Matron for this crowd, at least till they got to know her. So I wanted to check on what she was planning on wearing. And she told me. And it was the outfit I found her in.'

Trumble nodded. Good. This was the kind of fact she liked.

'So, this *morning*, I got up at six-thirty, showered, had coffee, read the paper, got a phone call from Melinda.' I inclined my head toward the cubicle where Arthur was 'interviewing' Melinda. 'We talked for maybe five minutes. I got dressed. Then I called the vet to make an appointment for my cat, and I called Sears because the ice maker on my refrigerator is acting up, and I called work to find out when I could pick up my schedule for this month, and I called my friend Sally to ask her out for her birthday.'

Detective Trumble was gaping at me. 'You made all those calls this morning?'

'Well, yes. It's my phone-call morning.'

'Your "phone-call morning".'

Gosh, she seemed big on repetition. 'Yes, my phone-call

morning. I don't go to work till the afternoon on most Mondays, so I make all my phone calls early. I have a list.'

She shook her head slightly, as if she were shaking off raindrops. 'Okay,' she said. 'So, when would you estimate these phone calls were finished?'

'Let's see. The vet opens at eight-thirty, so I probably began around then.' Though I found it hard to believe, I again wished I were being questioned by Arthur. He knew Lawrenceton, and he knew me, and he would not make such heavy weather out of this. 'You know, they don't want to see Madeleine, so making the appointment takes awhile. The new receptionist is better about it than the old one, though.'

'Madeleine.'

I am not a ditz – at least I don't think I am; I just daydream a lot – so I was getting a wee bit tired of feeling like an airhead. 'My cat. Madeleine. Had to go to the vet.'

'Your cat's a real handful?' Comprehension was dawning. Perhaps she was a cat owner. I thought of Moosie, and wondered who was watching him. He wasn't supposed to go out of the house. I was willing to bet the police had let him out. I was mad at myself for not telling them Moosie had been declawed before Poppy adopted her, so she wasn't an outdoors kind of cat. I explained to the detective. To my surprise, she called the house right away.

When she hung up, she looked concerned. 'Our team searching the house says none of them has seen a cat.'

'Oh no. That's awful. That cat is declawed; he can't make it outside that fence.'

'I'll have the patrol cars look out for him, and I'll alert the pound in case anyone brings him in. Give me a description before you leave. Now, let's get back to this morning. You said your sister-in-law called you later, after you'd finished making all your phone calls?'

'Yes. The phone rang while I was getting ready to go. Poppy said Melinda and I should go on ahead, that she'd meet us there.'

'And she gave no reason for this?'

'No.' I hesitated. 'She said there was something she had to take care of, and she sounded as though it was something unexpected, but other than that, no.' There'd been the moments of my inattention, but that was for my conscience alone, not for Detective Trumble's consumption. Nothing could be done about it now. 'She just said there was something she had to take care of,' I repeated.

Arthur came out of his cubicle and beckoned to Detective Trumble, who pushed up from her desk and met him on middle ground. Possibly she thought I couldn't hear her because I was rooting around in my purse.

'Is this a fair example of a southern belle?' she murmured to my former boyfriend. I glanced up, to see her tilting her head toward me.

'Aurora?' Surprise made him a little louder than he'd intended.

'She's a moron. Her brains are scattered over several miles of bad road.'

'Then she's hiding something,' he said flatly.

Darn that Arthur.

I saw Melinda leaning out of Arthur's cubicle, making little gestures at me behind his back. So far, the new detective hadn't caught sight of Melinda, but she would soon. I shook my head violently then pasted a sweet smile on my face as Arthur leaned to one side to fix me with a glare. The minute my lips moved, I realized a sweet smile was wildly inappropriate, and I wiped my face clean, trying to come up with an expression that wouldn't be worse.

Arthur made his way through desks and chairs on the way to Trumble's area, and even I could read the reluctance in his gait. His whole demeanor was that of a man who'd just quit smoking but was obliged to tour the Marlboro factory.

The Marlboro factory would be me.

I should have been pleased, because God knows I'd hoped for years Arthur would get over his confused feelings about me, and he definitely had. I just didn't know why I had to be categorized as 'bad' in the process. Possibly this was a childish thought and I would be ashamed of it later. I hoped so.

'What are you up to?' he asked without preamble.

'My sister-in-law got killed, Arthur. I'm not "up to" anything.'

'Uh-huh. Anytime you pull that fluff-headed southern eccentric routine, you're putting out a smoke screen. I take this real serious, Roe. There's no give in this.'

I considered my options. I looked over at Melinda again. I shrugged. She looked relieved. I was taking the burden of concealment away from her.

'We found something in the driveway when we were sitting and waiting,' I said. I looked up. Why on earth couldn't Arthur sit down in Detective Trumble's seat, so I wouldn't have to strain like this? I looked down at my hands clasped on my purse, rotated my head to ease my neck.

'What did you find?'

'Ah, a baby pacifier.'

'Whose was it?' Arthur asked, his voice quite gentle. I could believe he wasn't mad until I looked back up at him.

'I'm not sure,' I said.

'You're sure.'

'No, I'm not.'

'Your sister-in-law Melinda saw it, too.'

'Yes.'

'And you agreed not to tell us?'

'No,' I protested. 'We just don't know for sure whose it was.'

'I think you have a real good idea.'

This was the part that was impossible to explain. I tried to think of how to get around it. I had a stroke of genius – at least it seemed to be at that moment. 'It's just a Binky,' I said. I pulled it out of my purse and handed it to Arthur.

He turned it over and over in his fingers. It was a blue Binky, and there were millions just like it.

'It could even be her baby's,' he said. 'Maybe it fell out of one of the family cars.'

Melinda had left the cubicle and inched closer to hear all this, and she looked profoundly relieved. Arthur was fairly irritated to see her when he turned around. He sighed. 'Do you confirm this, Mrs Queensland?' he asked. Melinda nodded.

'That's where we found it. It could have come from anywhere. Roe just picked it up on her way into the house because she assumed it was Chase's.'

Bless Melinda's heart. I couldn't have done better myself.

Then Melinda almost ruined it by shooting me a triumphant glance that practically screamed, But there's more that we've concealed! I felt as if my purse were smoking, the contents were so hot.

'If that's all, Detectives, we need to go to our family,' I said quickly. 'Melinda's got the baby at her house with her kids, and we have to see to John, and Avery will want to know all about it.'

'Where will you be going? In case we need to talk to you again?' Arthur was nothing if not tenacious.

'We'll be going to my house first, to check in on the kids and the babysitter,' Melinda said briskly. She was glad to be back on familiar ground, where she knew what was what and she could be her normal efficient self. 'Then we'll go over to John and Aida's house, I'm sure. You have Roe's cell number and mine, and the house numbers, so we'd like to hear as soon as possible if you find out anything.'

The next thing I knew, we were in the parking lot of the SPACOLEC complex, and Melinda and I were hugging each other and crying. This was unprecedented, and maybe we were both a little relieved when we separated to dig in our purses for tissues.

'They'll find out,' Melinda said.

'Yes, they will. But at least it won't have been us who told them.'

'I don't know why that makes me feel better,' Melinda said, giving a few hiccupping sobs, 'but it does. You know if that Arthur Smith finds out we're lying, he'll make it hard on us, and Avery will never forgive me.'

I nodded grimly. If Melinda thought Avery was the most frightening thing facing her, she'd never seen my mother angry.

'What should we do with them?'

I pulled the cloth straps out of my purse and glared at them. They were cute as the dickens. They'd been embroidered by Poppy, who was fond of needlework, for the sons of Cartland ('Bubba') Sewell and my friend Lizanne. The boys, Brandon and Davis, were now – well, Brandon was a toddler, and Davis was sitting up. The straps, which snapped into a circle, were designed to run through the plastic loop on a pacifier, so when the baby dropped the pacifier, it wouldn't fall to the floor. You could run the strap around the baby's neck, or around the brace of a car seat, or whatever. Brandon's had his name and little bunnies embroidered on it, while Davis's had footballs and his initials. Lizanne had loved them when Poppy had given them to her; I remembered the day she'd opened the little package. And I'd found them on the ground in Poppy's driveway. Melinda and I exchanged a long glance, and I stuffed them back into my purse.

I drove to Melinda and Avery's house, trying to be extra careful, because I was all too aware of how dazed I was. I waited out in the driveway while Melinda ran in to check on the kids, tell the babysitter what had happened, and change shoes. Highly polished flats replaced the pumps she'd been wearing. I liked Melinda more and more as I spent time with her, and not the smallest reason was her practical nature.

'Where's Robin?' she asked as we parked in front of my mother's house.

'He's in Austin,' I explained. 'He got nominated for some award, so he's going to the mystery writers' convention where they give it out. He asked me if I wanted to go, but . . .' I shrugged. 'The convention's over, but he's doing some signings on the way back. He should be home on Wednesday, in time to pick up his mother at the airport.'

'You didn't want to go with him?' she asked shyly. My relationship with Robin Crusoe, fiction and true crime writer, was new enough that the family was delicate about making any assumptions.

'I kind of did,' I said. 'But he was going to be with a lot of people he knows really well, and I haven't been with him very long.'

She nodded. You had to have a pretty firm footing in a relationship to be dragged into a massive 'meet the friends' situation. 'Still, he asked,' she said.

It was my turn to nod. We both knew what that meant too.

That was our last pleasant moment for the rest of the day. Our sister-in-law had died a terrible death, a violent death, and John David still hadn't been located. Poppy's parents had to be called, which awful job Avery agreed to undertake. All the Queensland men were tall and attractive. Avery was certainly the most handsome CPA in Lawrenceton, but his personality did not live up to his face, which could have been devilish if there'd been any spark in it. Avery was one of those men always described as 'steady', which is what you want in an accountant, of course. He was the older brother, and had been a year ahead of me in high school. Instead of playing football like John David, Avery had played tennis; instead of being elected class president, Avery had been editor of the school paper. He'd added to the local gene pool by marrying Melinda, who'd grown up in Groton, a few miles away.

Poppy had gone to high school in Lawrenceton. She and John David had been five years behind me at the local school, which in those days had meant I was hardly aware of their existence. Her parents, who'd had her late in life, had moved to a retirement community a couple of hours' drive away after she'd graduated. Poppy's father, Marvin Wynn, had been the local Lutheran minister, and his wife, Sandy, had worked in the registrar's office at the local junior college. The whole community had pitied these righteous people when Poppy, their only child, reached her teen years.

But she'd never been arrested or gotten pregnant, those two grim incidents typical of wild teen years. And by the time she'd gone to college, she'd more or less settled into a relationship with John David Queensland. It had been a tumultuous one, and they'd broken up and reconciled more times than any onlooker could count. Neither Poppy nor John David had been faithful during the off-seasons, and maybe not even when they were supposed to be going steady. This pattern seemed to have continued even after they'd eventually married, five years after they'd graduated from college and begun pursuing their careers. Amazingly, Poppy had been a great elementary school teacher. I'd heard how good she was from more than one set of parents. And John David seemed to be able to talk almost any doctor into buying his company's pharmaceuticals.

After Poppy had had Chase, almost any onlooker would have been excused for assuming that life had settled down for these two former wild kids.

Not so.

Though I'd always liked Poppy, and had often admired her terrifying habit of saying exactly what she thought, I didn't approve of some aspects of her marriage. To me, marriage is the chance to put away the trappings of a single life and concentrate on making one good thing work really well. The cornerstone of this would have to be – in my view – faithfulness. There have to be some assumptions you make when you agree to bind your life to another person's, and the basic assumption and maybe the most important of all is that this person will get your exclusive attention.

Poppy had had at least two flings that I knew about, and I would not have been surprised to hear there had been more. I had tried – real hard – not to judge Poppy, to enjoy the part of her I liked and ignore the part that made me queasy. I behaved this way for several reasons. The most important reason was that I was also bound to her by marriage, my mother's marriage, and to make a family work, you have to be willing to keep your mouth shut and park your judgments by the door. The last thing in the world I wanted to do was complicate my mother's life by causing trouble in our new family.

Another reason was my attempt to live my religion. When I'd

dated our priest, Aubrey, he'd commented once or twice on my ardent wish not to cause trouble by speaking up about other people's behavior. 'You have to take a stand for what you believe,' he'd said. Well, that was true. What was the point of having beliefs if you didn't express them and live them?

'I don't have to take a stand by telling other people they're wrong,' I'd protested. 'What business is it of mine?'

'If you love them, it's your business,' he'd said firmly. 'If their misbehavior is intruding on the happiness and well-being of others, it's your business.'

I don't know what Aubrey would have said about Poppy and John David, because I never asked him. I always felt I had so many weaknesses myself that the last thing I should do was point out other people's flaws to them. So I never mentioned their infidelities to John David or Poppy, and I didn't want them to discuss those affairs with me.

For sure, I didn't want that.

When other people would try to tell me what my in-laws were doing, I'd just hurry the subject right past my nose.

Avery interrupted these unwelcome memories to tell us that Poppy's parents were on their way to Lawrenceton. John, my mother, Melinda, and I were sitting around the table in the kitchen, coffee mugs in front of us . . . trying. Trying to think what to do next. Trying not to talk about where John David might be. Trying not to think about what to do with Chase, a baby with a dead mother and a missing father.

'At least he's weaned,' Melinda muttered to herself.

I raised an eyebrow at her,

'I bet Avery and I end up with him,' she said, then tried to sound happier about it. 'He's a sweet baby, but . . .' She struggled to keep the words 'I already have my hands full' locked down in her throat. 'Poppy's parents are too old, Avery's dad and your mom are too old, and I can't picture John David raising a kid by himself, can you?'

No, I couldn't.

'Poppy was a good mother,' Melinda said quietly. 'You wouldn't think so, but she was.'

I nodded. 'Poppy had a lot of good qualities.'

'What – excuse me, Roe, but I need to know – what actually happened to her?' Melinda asked, keeping her voice hushed.

'I think someone stabbed her,' I said, not meeting Melinda's dark eyes. I was actually quite sure about that, but I'm no coroner, and I wasn't going to give any final judgment on Poppy's death.

Melinda made a little sound of horror, and I winced in sympathy. How scared Poppy must have been . . . how much it must have hurt. Had she hoped Melinda and I would come to save her, arrive in the nick of time?

I snatched my mind away from this fruitless conjecture and gave myself a good scolding. Poppy must have died very quickly, perhaps within a scant few seconds. Melinda pushed back from the table and left the room. Avery followed her. After a moment, I could hear the murmur of their voices coming from the living room.

My mother was watching John like a hawk, on the alert for signs of heart trouble. John was staring down at the table, studying a tablet open to a blank page. He'd stated his intention of starting a list of people he needed to contact, like the funeral home and the church, but he'd stalled. I knew that couldn't wait any longer. I went upstairs, carrying the cordless phone into my old bedroom. I called Aubrey's house.

'Hello.' It was the cool, composed voice of Emily, Aubrey's wife.

'Emily, this is Aurora.' I sounded just as calm and sweet. We couldn't stand each other.

'Hey, how are you?'

'Well, I'm fine, thanks, but we have a family trouble, and if Aubrey is handy . . .'

'Roe, he's over at the country club, playing golf. Jeff Mayo asked him to make up a foursome. You know, Monday's supposed to be his day off . . .' Her voice trailed away delicately.

Bitch.

'Yes, and if my sister-in-law hadn't been murdered, I wouldn't dream of disturbing him,' I said somewhat less sweetly.

A long silence.

'He has his cell phone,' Emily admitted. 'Let me give you that number.'

'Thank you so much,' I said with no expression at all. Why couldn't I have dated a vet, or a bartender, or a farmer? Why had I dated a cop and a minister before I met my first and now deceased husband, Martin Bartell?

Who shows up in emergencies? Policemen and preachers!

I repeated the number to make sure I'd gotten it right, then bid Emily good-bye. I knew she would set the drums beating to alert the Women of the Church to the imminence of a funeral meal. Emily always did her duty.

I took a deep breath and called Aubrey before I could change my mind.

I don't like cell phones, and I almost never turn mine on; to me, it's an emergency tool, like a car jack or a rifle. But today I was really glad our priest had one.

He said he'd be at the house in thirty minutes.

Chapter Two

Aubrey made it in forty minutes, and he was wearing his black shirt and dog collar when he rang the doorbell. Aubrey had had very dark hair when I met him, and he was graying heavily now. He'd shaved his mustache the year before, which had changed his appearance drastically. And he'd gained a few pounds, even though he played golf, tennis, and ran three times a week. Still, Aubrey was an attractive man, and Emily was very watchful around the single female members of the congregation – and some of the married ones, for that matter.

Take Poppy, for example. Emily had always been markedly cold toward Poppy, who had laughed it off.

I took a ragged breath and hugged Aubrey out of sheer thankfulness for his presence. Then I took him into the kitchen.

Somehow, the appearance of the priest gave weight and substance to the fact of Poppy's death. If the priest showed up, it had to be true. Aubrey's arrival was both a shock and a relief.

I wandered in and out of the kitchen, keeping a sharp eye on John. He looked good, considering the horror of the day. He was practically vibrating with worry over John David's absence. I thought he would not feel the impact of Poppy's death until he could be sure of his son's whereabouts and safety.

John had to be aware that we were all thinking that until John David showed up to establish his innocence, he was the chief suspect in his wife's murder.

Even John had to be thinking that.

Where the hell could John David be? I walked through the kitchen, the dining room, the formal living room, back through the family room. Then I made the circuit again. I noticed my pattern was irritating the hell out of Avery, but that was just his bad luck. It helped me think.

If I were John David, and I'd left work early, and my wife was busy, and my son was safely at his aunt's house . . . I'd go visit my mistress. The answer popped into my mind with the air of finality your subconscious reserves for sure things. Whom had John David been seeing lately? I could feel my upper lip wrinkle with faint disgust at even considering such a question. I made myself comb through the half-heard rumors.

There was Patty Cloud, who'd worked for my mother for several years before becoming Mother's second in command. I'd never cared for Patty, who was a cold and manipulative woman. There was Romney Burns, the daughter of a murdered detective in the Lawrenceton Police Department. There was Linda Pocock Erhardt, whose bridesmaid I'd been; Linda, divorced for many years, had two daughters in high school, and I knew she should be at work today. She was a nurse for my doctor, Pincus Zelman.

I felt much better now that I had a mission. I slipped out of my mother's house and into my car and began touring the town. I'd never driven through Lawrenceton hunting down love nests before, and I felt queasy about doing it now. I know I'm not such a wonderful moral person. But somehow, the slipping and creeping, the surreptitiousness of it, the deceiving . . . well, I had to shrug and sigh all over again at my own censoriousness.

Linda's car, as I'd expected, was parked behind the doctor's office. And there was a phalanx of vehicles in the parking lot. I was 98 percent sure that Linda was inside taking temperatures and blood pressures, just as she ought to be. I called my mother's office and asked for Patty, and when she came to the phone, I told her my mother wouldn't be in for the rest of the day. Patty replied in a puzzled sort of way, saying that my mother had already called her to let her know that very thing, and I laughed weakly. 'Guess we got our signals crossed in all the confusion,' I said, and Patty said, 'Um-hum' in a loathsomely skeptical way.

That left the least palatable alternative.

Linda and Patty were both strong women, veterans of the

divorce wars, and both quite capable of making their own decisions. Romney Burns was neither of those things. Romney's apartment was a duplex, and I spotted John David's car immediately, parked in the neighbor's driveway. I assumed the neighbors were at work and that this was John David's way of casting up a smoke screen. How subtle.

Romney was a lot younger than John David. Romney was – well, she had to be less than twenty-six, I rapidly figured. And she'd lost her father less than two years before. Sandy-haired and fair, Romney had shed the weight she'd carried in high school by the time she graduated from college and returned to Lawrenceton, where she'd gotten a poor-paying white-collar job in the financial aid office of the junior college. Mother had told me Romney was the financial aid officer's assistant.

I hoped they didn't have any loan emergencies at Sparling Junior College today, because it looked like Romney was home.

I took a deep and unwilling breath before knocking on the shabby door. I would rather have been pulling my eyebrow hairs out one by one than doing this.

Naturally, Romney answered. Her light hair was a real mess, and she was clothed only in a bathrobe. It took her a second to recognize me, and when she did, she looked disgruntled. I hadn't been her father's favorite person, either.

'What are you doing here?' she snapped. She had to realize that seeing John David's sister-in-law at her door meant bad things.

'John David needs to get his clothes on and get out here right now,' I said, abandoning any attempt to put a polite gloss on the situation.

'Who?' she blustered, but she discarded that quickly. Then she straightened. 'Well, maybe I better come, too, since I might be a member of the family before too long,' she said, both defensive and proud.

'Oh bull,' I said. 'This is the third place I tried to find John David, honey. Not the first.'

I saw comprehension leak into her eyes as she struggled to maintain her position. 'He loves me,' she said.

'Right, that's why you two are walking down Main Street arm in arm,' I said, and turned my back on her. The door slammed behind me. Big surprise.

'What the hell is this about?' John David said when he joined me. He was put back together pretty well, as far as clothing goes, but his composure had big holes in it. John David had a more florid coloring than his father and brother, and fairer hair. He was a powerfully built man, and a handsome one. But I didn't like him anymore, and in my eyes, he would always be ugly.

'John David,' I said slowly, suddenly realizing I'd condemned myself to breaking the news. 'How long have you been here?'

'What business is it of yours?'

We faced each other, standing by my car.

'Believe me, it's my business. Tell me.'

John David was no fool, and he'd picked up on the undertone.

'I've been here since I drove back from the office at eleven,' he said. His voice was even. 'Now, you tell me what's happened.'

'It's Poppy.' I met his eyes squarely.

His face began to crumple. I swear that he looked as though this were news to him.

'Poppy was attacked in your house after you left this morning.'

'So she's in the hospital?' There was a desperate hopefulness on his face.

'No,' I said. No point stringing this out. I took a deep breath. 'She didn't survive.'

He scanned my face for any sign that what I was saying wasn't true, that my words might have some other meaning.

He knew before he asked, but I guess he had to. 'You mean she's dead,' he said.

'Yes,' I said. 'When Melinda and I went to check on her, she was gone. I called the police. I'm very sorry.'

Then I had to hold this man I didn't even like anymore. I had to put my arms around him and keep him from sinking to the ground while he wept. I could smell the scents of his deodorant and his aftershave, the laundry detergent that Poppy had used on his clothes – and the smell of Romney. It was intimate and disgusting.

There really was nothing more to say.

When he calmed a little bit, I told him he had to go to the police.

'Why?' he said blankly.

'They're looking for you.'

'Well, now you've found me.'

'They're looking for you.'

That got his attention.

'You mean that they think I might have killed her?'

'They need to rule it out,' I said, which was as diplomatically as I could phrase it.

'I'll have to tell them where I was.'

'Yes, absolutely.'

'You think I need a lawyer before I go in?' he asked, which was the most sensible thought he'd voiced.

'I think it wouldn't hurt,' I said slowly.

'I'll call Bubba,' he said, and whipped his cell phone out of his pocket.

'Oh no,' I said without thinking.

He stared at me.

I shook my head vehemently.

'You just call someone else, not Cartland Sewell,' I said. I was hoping the earth would open up and swallow not me but John David.

If he could look any worse, he did. 'All right,' he said after a deadly silence. 'I'll call Bryan Pascoe.'

Bryan Pascoe was the toughest, meanest criminal lawyer in the county. I don't know how much that was saying, but Bryan was local, and he was tough, and he knew his law. He was around Avery's age, I thought, which meant he was a year or so older than I. I knew him only by sight. Many of the Uppity Women hoped that Bryan would become a judge in the next couple of years.

Luckily, Pascoe was not in court, and his secretary put John

David through. John David tried to explain the situation, but he broke down in tears. To my acute discomfort, he pressed the telephone into my hands.

'Mr Pascoe,' I said, because I had no choice. 'This is John David's sister-in-law, Aurora Teagarden.'

'Of course, I remember you. I hope your mother is well?' The lawyer had one of those wonderful voices – deep, smooth, authoritative.

'She's fine,' I assured him. 'But we have trouble.'

'People who call me always do. What can I do for you on this beautiful fall day?'

'Um. Well, this is the situation.' I explained it to him as rapidly and concisely as I could while John David lay over the hood of my car, weeping. I was so glad Romney didn't come out of her duplex that I could hardly contain myself. Staying inside was incredibly smart of the girl, because I would have pounded her into a pulp. I didn't have any sympathy or tact to spare.

'Good summary,' Bryan said, and I felt like he'd poured syrup on my pancakes and cut them up for me. 'Lucky for both of us, I just had a client cancellation. I can meet John David at SPACOLEC in forty-five minutes.'

I started to ask Bryan Pascoe what the hell I was supposed to do with my brother-in-law in the meantime, but that was hardly the lawyer's problem. 'See you there in forty-five minutes, right outside the front doors,' I said, and hung up.

'Okay, John David.' I tried to sound bracing and authoritative. I turned off his phone and stuck it into his pocket. 'We need to get into my car, now.' I worried about leaving John David's car where it was, but I figured I couldn't take care of every little thing. I'd have to get Melinda or Avery to come pick it up pretty quick, because as soon as the news of Poppy's death was widely known, that car in that location might as well have a big scarlet A printed on the trunk. I fished John David's keys out of his pants, got his car key off his key ring, and slipped it under the floor mat on the driver's side. Then I called Avery and gave him the heads-up on the car. At least Avery understood completely without me having to explain every little detail.

I wrangled John David into the front seat of my car, fastened his seat belt, and ran around to get in the driver's seat. It would take me all of fifteen minutes, if I drove slowly, to get to the SPACOLEC complex. What could I do for thirty minutes?

'I need to go by the house,' John David said. 'I need to see where it happened.'

'No,' I said. 'You don't need to go there right now. For one thing, the police are sure to still be there. For another thing, the site needs to be cleaned up before you get in. I can tell you about it. It happened in your patio doorway. Someone came to your back door. He probably got into your backyard through one of the gates.' Or maybe Poppy was trying to flee into the backyard when her attacker caught up with her, having entered from the front door? But wouldn't she have pitched forward in that case? She'd been lying on her back with her legs outside the door. No, the attack had come from in front of her when she was facing out the glass door. 'She died real quick. She was stabbed.'

John David insisted again that he wanted to go home, and I told him flatly that I wouldn't take him, that the first place he was going was to SPACOLEC, and that he better tell them all the truth. I listened to the words coming out of my mouth, and to my terrified delight, I sounded exactly like my mother.

'This will ruin Romney,' he said, speaking so quietly, it was almost to himself.

'Poppy is more important right now than Romney Burns's reputation.'

'I'm just saying,' he said, placating me with a gesture of his hand that meant, Level out.

I had taken so many deep breaths, I thought I might hyperventilate. I drove very slowly and took the longest route I could imagine, but still we arrived at SPACOLEC before thirty minutes had elapsed.

Scared a policeman would spot John David in my car before the lawyer arrived, I drove out to Fuller Gospel Church and parked for a moment under the huge live oak in the old church's parking lot. The sun danced through the changing leaves as they flickered in a chilly wind. It was an oddly beautiful moment, and one I knew I would never forget – the grieving and faithless man beside me, the country church, the light among the dancing leaves.

Bryan Pascoe wasn't at all what I'd expected. Since everyone seems tall to me, I was surprised to notice that next to John David, he was actually a small man, perhaps five seven. He shook hands with me gravely and then turned all his attention to my brother-in-law.

While the lawyer listened to John David, I was able to examine him more closely. Bryan Pascoe had ash-blond hair and light blue eyes. He had the narrowest, straightest nose I'd ever seen in my life; it made him look sharp and arrogant. I didn't know him well enough to know if that was true. Right away, he told us to call him Bryan, and then he asked John David to tell him exactly what he'd done today.

'Got up at six-forty-five, usual time,' John David began. His voice was dull. 'Poppy stayed in bed until Chase started crying about seven. She fed him and changed him and packed his diaper bag for the day. We didn't talk much. She wasn't much of a morning person. I knew I was supposed to take Chase over to Melinda and Avery's, because it was Poppy's club day. Poppy asked me if I was going to be home on time today, because she was thinking of fixing pork chops for supper. She didn't often feel like that.' For a minute, John David's mouth twisted. 'She took Chase in to brush his teeth; he doesn't have many, so it just takes a second.' He clamped his lips shut, and his eyes, too, holding the memory in or blocking it out – I wasn't sure which. 'Poppy said since she didn't have to get ready until nine, she might get back in bed and snooze awhile longer. Since I was taking care of Chase this morning, I had to leave at seven-forty-five to get to work before nine, so I had to go then. I put Chase in my car – we've got a car seat in both cars – and I dropped him off at my brother's house. You know Avery and Melinda?'

Bryan Pascoe nodded. 'I've met Avery,' he said. 'Go on.'

'I talked to Melinda for a minute. Avery had already left for work. Melinda was worried because the sitter was late, and she couldn't leave the kids alone long enough to shower. I drove into Atlanta to work, usual terrible traffic. I got to work right at nine. I worked until about eleven.' His faced reddened. 'Then I told them I was feeling sick and needed to go home, so I drove back to Lawrenceton. I didn't go home. I went over to Romney Burns's house. She'd taken the afternoon off, too. I've been there ever since I got back to town, which would have been about eleven-forty-five, give or take a little. Traffic was a lot lighter coming back.'

This was certainly a simple-enough account.

Bryan took John David through the morning's activities and their timetable once more, quickly. Maybe the contrast was clearer because John David and I were so stunned, but I had to admire the lawyer's clarity and focus.

Then Bryan, took my hand, much to my surprise. 'And you, young lady,' he said gravely, though I was sure he was only a year or two older than I, 'tell me what your part in all this was.'

Once again, I told him a compressed version.

'The Uppity Women,' he said with a smile. 'My ex-wife is an Uppity Woman.'

By that time, he was shepherding us into the building, and I took a step back. 'I'm not going in,' I said.

'Of course, you need to get back to the family,' Bryan Pascoe said, his voice warm and understanding, but his thick blond eyebrows flew up.

'I need *not* to go in here with him,' I said emphatically, though unclearly. 'I'm a widow,' I pointed out, and though John David still looked dazed and uncomprehending, Bryan Pascoe immediately grasped my point. Any unmarried woman would be doubly suspect if she accompanied John David on this day, of all days. 'Good thinking. I'll talk to you later,' he said, and he and John David marched into the complex, ready to plunge into the business of justice.

Since I had to go back to the house and explain all this to John Queensland, I wondered who would have the easier time of it.

On my way back to Mother's, I stopped by the library to explain the situation and beg for some time off. Still in my nice dress, with my good pumps on, I was much admired before the condolences started rolling in. Perry Allison and Lillian Schmidt both gave me hugs, which I appreciated. After I'd accepted the first wave of sympathy, Perry said, 'Oh, by the way, there's a young man here waiting for you.'

Those words were not exactly the thrill they might have been. 'Not my stepson?' I asked, peering in all directions so I could hide if I saw Barrett coming.

'No, no, this one's younger.' Perry, who was resplendent today in deep green cargo pants and a chocolate brown shirt, pointed at the magazine area, and I looked at the young man sitting at the round table with a *Gaming* magazine in front of him. He was easily five nine, and he was broad-shouldered. His teenage-chic clothes had started out expensive, but now they were definitely on the grimy side. His skin was not perfect – teenage spottiness had hit him pretty hard – but it was deeply tan, and his hair had been dyed a bright metallic gold. His face looked familiar; there was something about the nose and mouth that made alarm bells sound in my head.

'I know him,' I muttered. 'Who is he?'

He glanced up, and his gaze returned to me after passing me over once. He got up slowly, closing the magazine and tossing it back on the rack.

'Want me to stay?' Perry asked as the teenager came over. I didn't answer him, because a hope had begun to grow in me, one I could scarcely bring myself to admit.

'Sis?' the boy said.

Oh my God – his voice had changed.

Peering up at him, I said, 'Phillip?'

The next instant, muscular arms lifted me into the air and the oddly familiar face was grinning up at me.

'My brother,' I said proudly to the gaping Perry. 'This is my brother.'

Once Phillip had replaced me on the floor, I pushed my glasses up on the bridge of my nose and grinned back at him.

'Are my dad and Betty Jo here in Lawrenceton?' I asked, amazed that I hadn't known of such a trip.

'Ah, no.' He might as well have had the word *apprehensive* tattooed on his forehead. Hmmm.

My coworker reminded me he was present by making a little noise in his throat. 'Phillip, this is Perry,' I said, sure I was making Perry's day. The arrival of a long-unseen brother was great news for Lawrenceton's gossip mill.

Perry shook Phillip's hand solemnly, said he was glad to meet any brother of mine, and then found something to do on the other side of the library. Perry was not insensitive to atmosphere. After an awkward moment, I suggested to my brother that we go outside to the employees' parking lot to have a little talk. It was cooler, and gusty; I was sure it was going to rain. Phillip was wearing a tank top under an unbuttoned flannel shirt, and the breeze was way too brisk for his ensemble. His flesh looked goosey.

'I'm truly happy to see you, but you better explain why you're here,' I said, trying not to sound too stern.

'Things haven't been going too good at home,' he admitted, shoving his hands down in his pockets. He'd hinted as much in his e-mails, so I shouldn't have been surprised.

'Dad couldn't keep his—' I stopped abruptly and substituted a milder phrase. 'Dad was not faithful to Betty Jo?'

'Right,' my half brother mumbled.

'I guess some things don't change.' I tried not to sound bitter. 'Listen, Phillip, please tell me they know where you are.'

'Ah, not exactly.' He tried to smile at me, but it didn't work.

'How'd you get here?'

'Well, a friend of mine's big brother was driving to Dallas, so I told him if he'd take me along, I'd split the gas.'

'This brother didn't know how old you are?'

'Uh, no.'

Sure he had. He had helped a fourteen-year-old runaway. Or was Phillip fifteen now? Yes, just barely.

'And after you got to Dallas?'

'I, uh, hitched a ride with a truck driver to Texarkana.'

'He was okay?' Phillip wasn't meeting my eyes.

'He was okay. The next guy wasn't.' Phillip was just shivering from cold, I hoped. After giving him a good look, I was sure.

I took a deep, deep breath, trying to keep it silent. 'Do I need to take you to the doctor?' I asked very gently. 'There're lots of specialists in Atlanta; they don't know you or me, and they'd never see us again.'

'No,' Phillip said, his face brick red. 'I get what you're saying, but it didn't come to that. It was pretty intense, though.' He may have thought he was smiling, but it was a grimace, compounded of fear, embarrassment, and humiliation.

'Where'd you end up?'

'I just made it partway to Memphis with the bad guy. I got another ride into the city.'

'Okay.' I was biting the inside of my mouth to keep my face calm. 'What then?'

'Uh, I went to the college campus – you know, the University of Memphis? And I found the Student Center, and I read the notices on the bulletin board.'

I wondered how he had learned to do that.

'And in those notices, there was one from two girls who needed a guy to ride with them to Birmingham. They were scared they'd have a flat tire or something, and I can at least change a flat tire. I think. Anyway, Britta never had one.'

Britta. Hmm. 'So they took you as far as Birmingham.'

'Yeah.' If possible, Phillip's face was an even deeper red. I was willing to bet those girls hadn't known his true age, either, and I was thinking even more grimly that Phillip might need a blood test. 'So from Birmingham, I just rode the bus.'

'I'm glad you had the money left for that.'

'Uh, Britta and Margery chipped in on it.'

'You had a lot of adventures,' I said, smiling so I wouldn't scream. He was lucky to be alive.

'Yeah. I think, you know, I did okay.' He seemed to know that sounding any more boastful than that would get him a good slap on the wrist.

'And all this time your parents haven't known where you were?'

He nodded.

I could not even imagine how they were feeling.

'How long has that been?' I asked in a voice I just barely managed to keep even.

'Uh, let's see. Two and a half days to Dallas, a half day to get the ride with Mr Hammond, then the ride to Texarkana, where I helped him unload the truck, and then the other guy, the one in the pickup, that lasted about two hours, and I hid in the woods . . .'

I could feel all the blood draining from my face, and I sat down on the hood of Perry's car, which was the closest.

'Hey, Roe, don't look so . . . It wasn't as bad as you're probably thinking. I'd just . . . I'd never imagined . . . He probably wouldn't have actually, uh, forced me . . . I just freaked.'

'That's okay. That's what people do when they're faced with a scary situation. Hiding was the best way to make sure you were safe,' I said reasonably, thinking I would even try calling the Psychic Friends hotline to find out who this individual was who had ripped a hole out of my brother's life. And then I'd rip a hole out of his.

'Now,' I said briskly, 'I think you've gotten up to four days?'

'I think so. Anyway, I did get a ride with a chartered busload of people who were going to the gambling boats at Tunica – you know, right below Memphis? But I got them to drop me off in Memphis, because I thought I probably had a better chance at getting a ride in a city. And then I met Britta and Margery.'

'So, your mom and dad haven't known where you were for six days, give or take a day?'

'Uh, well, I called them, you know.'

I closed my eyes. Thank God.

'I called them with my phone card, from pay phones. I'm almost out of minutes on it now. I just told them I was okay. I didn't tell them I was coming to you.'

And it had never occurred to them, because they hadn't called me to ask me to be on the lookout. For some reason, that made me angry. My half brother is missing, and my own father can't call me and let me know?

I realized, looking up at his young face, that Phillip was exhausted. Though I hadn't been around for much of Phillip's youth, due to my father's taking him far away from me – on purpose – when Phillip was in elementary school, I was sure that Phillip had had as sheltered and middle-class an upbringing as his parents could provide in Southern California.

'Maybe they'll let you stay for a while,' I said. 'I sure would like that.'

'I'm sorry they wouldn't come to your wedding, or your husband's funeral,' Phillip said miserably. 'I really liked Mr Bartell, when I met him. I tried to make them let me come by myself, but they wouldn't listen.'

'Hey, bud, that's okay,' I said. Of course it hadn't been, but his parents' bad behavior wasn't Phillip's fault. Martin had uncomfortably excused his son, Barrett, who had done pretty much the same thing, but Martin had been quick to become angry with my father and Betty Jo: Of course, he could see that my father had hurt me. Martin and I had stopped in to see them when we'd taken a trip to California. The visit had been very uncomfortable; the only highlight had been seeing Phillip.

That had been what – a year and a half ago? I figured Phillip had grown five inches in that time.

'We need to talk a little more about your trip later, and we need to call your folks, and we need to put your clothes in the wash, and you, too. You don't have any other clothes?' I was trying to sound mature and in charge, but I'd used up a lot of whatever authority I possessed when I was dealing with my errant brother-in-law.

'Uh, I left my backpack when I got out of the truck so fast,' he confessed, his eyes sliding away.

'Then we'll take care of the clothes situation.'

'Uh, Roe, you dating now? Mom said there was something in a gossip column in one of the movie magazines.'

'Ugh. I didn't know that. I'm sure not important enough to rate that, so it must be because of Robin Crusoe, the man I'm dating. He's a writer. I knew him a long time ago, and he came back to Lawrenceton a couple of months back and we started going out.'

'I read *Whimsical Death*.' That was Robin's non-fiction book, which had made a lot of money and spread his name everywhere. 'So I can just hang somewhere else when he's staying over,' Phillip told me with a man-of-the-world air.

'We'll talk about that later. It's not going to be a problem. And Robin's out of town right now anyway.' But I had to call him, and right away. Robin would be hurt if I didn't tell him about Poppy as soon as possible. 'Now, let me go inside and let them know I have to take the rest of the afternoon off, and we'll go over to my new house. I told you I moved, right?'

'Sure.'

'Okay, then.' I still had my purse clutched in my left hand. I dug out my car keys and pointed out the Volvo to my brother. 'You go wait in there while I run in for just a second.'

'Okay,' he said.

I started in the back door of the library, wondering what kind of fool I was to give my car keys to a wandering teenager, and I prayed with all my heart that he would be there when I came back.

Explaining to Sam wasn't easy, but then talking to Sam was becoming increasingly difficult. Sam was getting crankier as he got older, and since he was only in his early fifties, he had a lot of room to spare. He'd lost his perfect secretary a few months before, and he hadn't replaced her. He couldn't find anyone who even gave a hint that someday she might be almost as good as the lamented Patricia. I wondered how Sam's wife was taking his prolonged grief. I didn't know her very well, but Marva had been a junior high algebra teacher a long time, and I didn't think she'd put up with much foolishness.

To my overwhelming relief, Phillip was in the car when I opened the door. Not only was he in the car but he was sound asleep. His head was tilted back on the cushion, and when I slid into the driver's seat, I noticed that Phillip had a few long hairs on his chin. I almost burst into tears, and that would have been terrible. I drove to my house as gently as anyone can drive, and when we got there, I maneuvered my little brother (now only chronologically smaller) into the kitchen from the garage, and then into the guest bedroom. He was just barely awake.

'You get into the shower, and then you climb in the bed. I'll wash your clothes while you're asleep,' I said. 'I'll even call your mother for you, if that's okay.'

'Would you?' Phillip was transparently grateful for that. I probably should not have offered, but I couldn't let them worry a minute longer than necessary about their son, and he was clearly in no shape for an emotional confrontation.

I kept a robe hanging in the closet in the guest room. I pointed it out to Phillip, who looked at it as if he'd never seen such a garment before. I left to give him a little privacy, and in a short time I heard the shower running – and running, and running, and running. Just when I was about to go into the bathroom to see if he'd drowned, the water cut off. I caught a glimpse of Phillip shuffling from the bathroom back into the bedroom, the robe swathed around him. His clothes – and two towels – were in a heap on the floor of the steamy bathroom, and I automatically went through the pockets of his grimy blue jeans so I wouldn't wash anything I wasn't supposed to.

I fished out his wallet, a couple of wadded tissues, a pocketknife, some loose change, and two sealed condoms.

Okay, I was horrified. Legally, my brother couldn't even drive by himself!

I had to sit down and collect myself for a minute. I was reacting as if I were Phillip's mother – and I was old enough to be Phillip's mother – but I *wasn't*. I was his big sister. Phillip had a perfectly functional mother, who admittedly thought I was the devil incarnate, but other than that, she seemed to be a reasonable woman.

I realized that in all the fluster of his arrival I hadn't asked Phillip exactly why he'd turned up on my doorstep. He'd said that my dad had cheated on his mother, which was all too easy to imagine, but that just didn't seem like a motivation for hitchhiking across the country. I thought something more must have happened for Phillip to have taken such drastic action . . . though it probably hadn't seemed as scary to Phillip as it would to me, I suddenly realized. At his age, maybe Phillip didn't appreciate the evils of the world.

On the other hand, he had discovered at the age of six that bad things could and did happen to him, and I didn't know if that was a lesson that could be forgotten, no matter how young the learner. When he'd lived in Atlanta, I'd kept him for the weekend fairly often, so my dad and Betty Jo could have some couple time. And I'd enjoyed that a lot. But one weekend, Phillip had been abducted while he'd been staying with me, and he would have been killed in a horrible way if I hadn't shown up when I did; actually, if it hadn't been for Robin, Phillip and I both would have been killed. I'd bought us a little time, and the crisis had passed, but since then, my dad and Betty Jo had acted as though I'd caused the incident. They'd maintained that seeing me would further traumatize Phillip, and by moving to California and finding jobs there, they'd made sure I'd have to keep my distance. I'd only renewed unmonitored contact with my brother when he'd gotten his own computer. The first person he'd sent an e-mail to – after about twenty of his best friends – had been me. I'd been so proud.

It was time to face the music, whatever tune might be playing today. I looked up my dad's home number and punched it in.

'Hello?' The voice was Betty Jo's, and she was strung tightly.

'It's Aurora,' I said. 'I have Phillip.'

'Oh thank God!' Betty Jo burst into tears. 'Phil, pick up the other phone. Phillip's at your daughter's!'

'Is he okay?' my father asked.

'He seems to be fine. He's asleep right now.' I hesitated, then decided Phillip's adventures were his to relate. 'I told him I was calling you.'

'How did he get there? What – did you ask him to come see you? We checked his computer, and we found out he'd been sending you e-mails.'

Strike. I rolled my eyes, though no one was there to get the effect. 'Then you know that I didn't invite him here. I would never do that without talking to you first. As far as I can tell, this was completely his idea. He said there was trouble at home.' Counterstrike.

There was a long period of silence, way over there in California.

'Well, not to get into it now,' my dad began, and Betty Jo said sharply, 'He walked in on Phil while Phil was sticking it to another woman. Well, not even a woman. A *girl.*'

This was more than I wanted to know, but it did explain Phillip's extreme reaction. I was willing to bet Phillip knew the girl.

'You two have to work out your own problems. I don't want to hear the graphic details,' I said flatly. 'Let Phillip stay here for a while, okay? I'd love to have him, and this house is big.'

'But you have a boyfriend now,' Betty Jo protested.

'If you're accusing me of setting a bad example by perhaps, sleeping with my steady friend from time to time, well, I think Phillip already knows about the birds and the bees. Especially in view of what you just told me.' Hell, he already *engages* in sex, I thought.

'He would have this week off for Thanksgiving anyway,' Betty Jo said. For once, she sounded subdued. 'So, maybe if he could stay for a week . . . we may work things out, at least decide what we're going to do.'

'That might be a good thing,' my father said cautiously. 'Thanks, Doll.'

I hated being called 'Doll'. But he'd always called me that, and he wasn't going to change now.

'If you need longer, he can go to school here,' I said, as if accomplishing that would be a snap of the fingers. Of course, I hadn't the faintest clue how to enroll a teenager for school, but how hard could it be?

'Okay,' said Betty Jo. 'Okay.' She sounded as though she were trying to persuade herself that this was a good idea. 'I can't believe he went all the way across the country on his own. When I think of what could have happened to him . . .'

'Roe, thanks,' my father said. For the first time, he talked to me like I was an adult. 'I know you'll take care of him. I bet he just needs someone to talk to.'

'I'll bet that's it,' I said, trying to sound reassuring. 'He'll be fine. I'll watch out for him.'

'No new murders, right?' my father asked nervously. Not since this morning.

'No, Dad,' I said, as if that was the silliest idea I'd ever heard. 'Ha ha ha.'

'Say hello to your mother for us,' Betty Jo said, a sop toward courtesy. 'And have Phillip call us himself the minute he gets up.'

'He has a lot to answer for,' my father said grimly.

'So do you!' Betty Jo told him. 'Good-bye, Roe.'

I was so glad to end the conversation, I almost danced.

Chapter Three

The rest of my family was probably wondering where I was. I made a face in my bedroom mirror. When I'd gotten up that morning, my most pressing problem had been whether or not my only pair of intact panty hose was clean.

While Phillip slept, I'd checked Robin's itinerary and then called him at a store called Murder by the Book, in Houston. The young man who'd answered the phone had been very civil about getting Robin to the phone as soon as he'd been convinced I actually knew Robin and was not a crazed fan who'd dreamed up a clever way to talk to him.

'Did you win?' I asked him.

'No,' Robin said, though he sounded cheerful. 'But the panel was standing room only, and my signing line went out of the room. Awards are nice, but sales are better.'

'How's your signing at the bookstore going?'

'Just about to get under way. I'm signing with Margaret Maron, and the store is jam-packed.'

So he had a group of people waiting for him.

'I just have some things I had to tell you,' I said anxiously.

'You're all right?' His voice was suddenly sharp. 'Your step-father okay?'

'I'm fine, Robin,' I said, my voice soft. 'And John is healthy. But John David's wife, Poppy? She got killed this morning.'

'In a car?' he said cautiously.

'No, she was murdered.'

'Oh, I'm so sorry. From your voice, I'm betting you found her.'

'I'm afraid so.'

'Shall I come home right now?'

'Bless you for offering. But there's more.'

A long pause. 'I'm listening,' he said, just when I was about to ask if he'd hung up. 'Did you get arrested?' He wasn't entirely joking.

'My brother Phillip is here.'

'Your brother? Oh, sure! The little guy who was staying with you all those years ago! Hasn't he been living in Pomona? What's he doing in Lawrenceton?'

'He's at least five eight or nine now,' I said. 'And he got here by running away from home.'

'Uh-oh. You talked to your dad and the new wife?'

'She's not so new now, and my dad cheated on her. Phillip walked in on this little episode,' I said. 'That's supposed to be the reason he ran away, but I'm finding that a little, I don't know, extreme.'

'So, what do you think the real reason is?'

'Maybe time will tell. He's going to stay here for at least a week.'

'Hmm. Okay.'

'Yeah, I know,' I said. 'He needs this right now.'

'No problem. If you don't need me instantly, I'll just do two more signings tomorrow, one in Austin and one in Dallas, and then I'll fly home from there.'

'I sure will be glad to see you,' I said. 'But you keep up with your signing schedule.' I was flattered and delighted that Robin would offer to do that, but at the same time, it scared me. Had we rushed into this comfortable intimacy? I had just adjusted to being alone in my widowhood when Robin had unexpectedly returned to Lawrenceton. It hadn't taken long to resume our relationship of a few years ago. Though I hadn't yet brought myself to discuss my doubts with Robin, I had been thinking the past couple of weeks that we might have hurried things too much. But the minute Robin had left for his convention, I'd missed him. Now I found myself looking forward to his return, not only for the pleasure of his physical presence but because I'd be glad to have his support and his insight – especially in matters regarding Phillip. After all, Robin had been a teenage boy once upon a time.

'I have to go sign some books,' Robin said gently.

The doorbell chimed. 'And I have to go answer the door,' I told him. 'Just let me know when you're coming in, and I'll pick you up at the airport.'

'I left my car there so I could bring my mother back with me,' he reminded me. 'Her plane gets in right after mine. I'll call you when I'm back.'

When I remembered that Robin would not exactly be at my disposal when he returned, I was so distracted by my disappointment that I answered the door without looking through the peephole. That was a bad habit, and one I'd have to break. When I'd lived out in the country, I'd heard every visitor before they'd gotten to the door, and I'd had time to look out the window to find out who it was. Town living was different.

Bubba Sewell, my lawyer (and possibly my next state representative), was looming in my doorway. Cartland Sewell was a big man anyway, and he'd put on the pounds since he'd married my beautiful friend Lizanne.

'Is it true?' he asked.

'Hello. Glad to see you. Why don't you come in,' I said, waving my hand down the hall. I knew I sounded pissed off, and I was.

'I'm a little too upset for the amenities, Aurora,' he said. When he was in the house, I got a better look at him. Bubba had been crying. I reminded myself to call him Cartland; since he'd gotten into politics, Cartland had been the name of choice.

'What's put a bee in your bonnet?'

'Poppy,' he said. He seemed to have trouble getting the name out.

I looked at him for a long moment. 'So the rumor is true.'

'Yeah, it's true. I was actually thinking of . . .'

'You weren't going to leave Lizanne?' I sounded every bit as horrified as I felt. 'You idiot!'

Cartland looked as though he was thinking of slapping me. And I would almost have deserved it if he had; not that I think hitting is ever excusable, but I'd been unbearably tactless.

'Poppy was so wonderful,' he said. 'She was so beautiful, and she was . . . in intimate moments . . . she, ah . . .'

'Don't want to know,' I said. 'Too much information!'

He looked a little embarrassed. 'Sorry. But you just don't know,' he said. 'She was everything to me. I wanted her to run off with me.'

'Meaning an end to your political ambitions, your marriage, and your relationship with your children?'

'I could have patched things up politically, eventually,' he said, sounding as if he really believed it. 'Lizanne and I don't get along anyway. And how could she stop me from having a relationship with my own sons?'

'There's still a lot you don't know about Lizanne, if you believe that.'

'Roe, Lizanne is a great woman, and she's beautiful and peaceful and she's a good mother to the boys, but . . .' He waved his hands in frustration.

'But what?' I snapped.

'But Lizanne's so *dumb!*' he said. It was as if the words had been ripped out of him.

I opened my mouth to rebut his blunt assessment, but I made myself think over what he'd said. Poppy hadn't exactly been a rocket scientist, but she was shrewd, and practical, and a follower of world and local events. And she was articulate in voicing her ideas and opinions. That's why she'd been tapped to be an Uppity Woman. Poppy was – had been – a very different animal than Lizanne, who admittedly had very limited interests. Lizanne's intellectual boundaries had never seemed to bother any man before, as I reminded Cartland now.

'You know as well as I know, Roe, that being attracted to someone physically is not the same as being her constant companion.'

'But you're not Lizanne's constant companion. You go out almost every night to this or that meeting, and everyone knows you're counting on a political future.'

'And the reason I did all that was at least partly to get away from Lizanne.'

'I've never heard of anyone running for office to avoid a spouse.' Cartland wanted to be our next state representative.

'I've done a lot of things lately I never thought I'd do.'

I didn't like the sound of that. I took a step away from him. 'When did you last see Poppy?'

'I saw her last night. John David was going to be at some meeting, so I stopped by.'

'How'd you get in?'

'Went to the front door. I figured it might as well be an open visit, since it wasn't going to last that long, not with John David due back within the hour. I helped her bathe Chase,' he said tenderly.

I could have beaten him on the head with a baseball bat. I was willing to bet Lizanne could have used some help bathing Brandon and Davis. Why did this man think he was any smarter than his wife? And I'd been considering voting for this jerk!

'When did you leave?' I asked after an appreciable pause to regain control.

'I guess about . . . eight-thirty. She was wearing a bathrobe, since she'd gotten wet bathing Chase,' he said dreamily. 'Her hair was all curly from the humidity in the bathroom. She told me she'd think about divorcing John David. I think she would have done it.'

'And who do you think killed her?' I asked, conversationally throwing cold water on his fantasies.

'Her husband,' Cartland said, and he didn't look like an overweight lawyer anymore. He looked dangerous. 'I know it was John David.'

'And how do you know that?'

'She must have told him,' Cartland said reasonably. 'She must have told him she was going to leave him for me, and he killed her for it.'

'Where were you all morning?'

'Oh for God's sake, Roe! I went to my office and worked until about eleven, when I left to speak at the Rotary Club in

Mecklinburg.' Mecklinburg was about fifteen miles away. 'I was there, in front of about forty people, for the next hour and a half.'

I was going to have to talk to Lizanne soon, and I dreaded it. Those embroidered straps were still stuffed into my purse, and if Lizanne hadn't gone to Poppy's house and thrown them down in the driveway to let Poppy know she knew the situation, I was a Jersey girl.

'Okay, get out.'

'What?'

'Get out. I've listened to as much as I'm going to.'

Cartland looked stunned. 'But Roe, I was trying to explain—'

'Go to hell. You've just told me you've been cheating on your wife, who is a good friend of mine, with the wife of my brother-in-law; and you are evidently assuming that your wife would be happy to raise two sons of yours on her own, while you raise John David's boy! You actually think Poppy would have left John David? You're a moron! Get out! And keep your grief to yourself!'

I had herded Cartland to the front door, snapping at his heels like a sheepdog, and now he left in something of a hurry. I slammed the door shut and glowered at it.

For a few minutes, I hovered outside Phillip's door, afraid we might have wakened him. But there was no movement from the room, no rustle of sheets. Struck with the sudden fear that he'd crawled out of the window, I opened the door a crack, and was reassured by the sight of a big bare foot hanging off the end of the bed.

I eased the door shut as silently as I could, then I hovered in the hall, trying to think of what I should do next.

Amazingly, it was only 5:00 p.m. Since it was November, the daylight was almost gone, but I thought of some errands I needed to run. I hastily wrote a note and stuck it to Phillip's doorknob. After checking his clean clothes for sizes, I pitched them back in the dryer and set off for the small branch of Davidson's that Lawrenceton was proud to have. I got my brother a package of underwear, a bundle of socks, a pair of jeans and a pair of khakis, and two shirts, a T-shirt and a nice sports shirt, and a jacket.

Crossing over to Wal-Mart, I quickly purchased a comb and brush, a toothbrush, and a razor and some shaving cream. I grabbed some gloves, too; his hands had been bare.

Satisfied that I could clothe and clean him, I made one more stop, at the grocery store. I had a dim awareness that teenage boys ate a lot, but I wasn't really sure what they ate a lot of. I got some frozen pizzas, some Bagel Bites, and some egg rolls. I got some milk, too, and a bottle of soda.

By the time I'd unloaded all this booty and folded Phillip's dry clothes, it was seven o'clock. I called Mother to find out what was happening. She sounded exhausted and tearful, and she said John wasn't feeling very well. After a long, long 'interview' with Arthur Smith, John David had arrived at the house to assume his role as chief mourner. Mother thanked me from the heart for running him to ground and getting him to go into SPACOLEC with Bryan Pascoe. 'Avery was really angry for a while, but I think he sees now that you were right,' Mother said.

'I'm sorry if you've had to take the fallout from people who were really mad at me,' I said. The thought did cross my mind that it seemed to take very little to make Avery angry with me. 'I had to stay with Phillip, to get him straightened out.'

'I do wish all this hadn't happened at the same time.' I knew Mother had to have been really distressed even, to voice that much complaint about something that simply couldn't be helped. 'John told Avery that you'd done more practical things to help our family than had even occurred to him. John, that is.'

'That was sweet of John,' I said, abruptly aware of how fond I was of my stepfather. He was a better man than my real father. I felt cold and disloyal for that thought instantly, but I made myself face it and admit it was true. God wasn't going to strike me dead for admitting my own father wasn't a perfect man.

'How long is the boy staying?' my mother asked. Her voice was a little stiff. She had always had a hard time with the existence of another child of my father's, but I hoped she would get over it right now.

'I think at least for this week. He's out for Thanksgiving break now. I got the impression that things are going pretty badly between Dad and Betty Jo.' No point in spelling out my father's peccadilloes. As far as my mother was concerned, it was an old story. 'Phillip got caught up in the middle of that. He made his way over here, and I hope he can stay for a while. He's so big now, Mother, you wouldn't recognize him.'

'Just like Phil, messing up a second chance to get it right,' my mother said.

This was such a vulnerable way to put it, and her voice was so unhappy, it was hard for me to believe I was listening to the same stiff-backed woman who had created her own fortune after my dad had left her. The shock of Poppy's death had cracked Mother wide open.

'Have Poppy's parents come in yet?'

'No, they'll be here in about an hour, I think. Then poor John will have to go through another emotional scene.'

'Why?'

'Well, he feels obligated.'

'No, Mother. John David is obligated, not his dad. You make John go to bed, tell him John David and Avery can handle the Wynns. In fact, they can all go to Avery and Melinda's. For that matter, I can put the Wynns up. I have another bedroom, and all I have to do is go make the bed.'

That would make my life even more confusing, but I wanted to help my mother any way I could.

'I'll give you a call back on that. But you're right,' she said resolutely. 'John needs to rest more than he needs to worry. Avery and Melinda are perfectly capable of handling whatever comes up. And poor John, he keeps thinking that he and John David are so alike because John lost his first wife and now John David's lost his . . . but the situation is totally different. Tell me, where was John David when you tracked him down?'

'Ah, he was visiting a friend.' I closed my eyes at my own stupidity. That had sounded pretty lame.

'Visiting a friend, in the afternoon of a workday.' My mother's eyebrows were probably arched clear up to her hairline. 'I'll be willing to bet the friend is pretty and female and wasn't wearing work clothes when she opened the door.'

I winced. 'Well . . .'

'You don't need to say anything else,' Mother said. 'And Poppy, bless her heart, was just as bad. People these days are just like rabbits. Everything's sex. No duty, no loyalty. By the way, where's Robin?'

I didn't like her thought association there, and she was not the first person who'd asked me today where Robin was. We weren't engaged and we weren't talking about marriage. We weren't a locked-in official couple.

'He's in Houston. He'll be back day after tomorrow,' I said, sounding just as stiff as my mother.

'Do you think he and Phillip will get along?'

'Mother, you have enough to worry about right now. I believe I can handle Phillip and Robin.'

'You're right. Well, let me go. I have to convince John he's not responsible for the whole social process surrounding Poppy's death, and I have to remind John David that he is.'

'Good luck, Mother. I'll be there when I can. Remember, if the Wynns need a place to stay, the door is open. Just let me know thirty minutes ahead of time.'

'Thanks, baby. I'll talk to you soon.'

Because I couldn't seem to sit still, I went to the third bedroom and made the bed, just in case. If the Wynns drove in from their retirement community in the next hour, it would be at least another hour after that before they'd be ready to retire, and they might well want to go see Poppy's body. Could they? Or would her body have already been sent to Atlanta for autopsy?

I just didn't know.

I yawned, a big jaw-cracking yawn. I'd run out of steam.

Phillip shambled into the living room and plopped down on the couch opposite my chair. He was looking much better, and he was smiling.

'Thanks for the clothes and stuff,' he said. 'It was neat to find the bags in the room when I woke up.'

I was glad I'd passed a rack of those drawstring flannel pants at Wal-Mart, because that was what Phillip was wearing, the pants and the sleeveless T-shirt he'd had on under his flannel shirt.

'I was glad to do it.'

'Listen, what's happening about your sister-in-law?' he asked.

I told him what the situation was, and he was open-mouthed at the awfulness of the adult world. Moments like this reminded me how young my brother really was.

'I'll bet you're hungry,' I said.

'Oh,' he said. 'Oh, yes. Just point me at the kitchen. I can fix stuff myself.'

'Has your mom been working these past few years?' I felt guilty for not knowing this basic fact about Phillip's life.

'Yeah, ever since we moved to Pomona, she's worked at an insurance company as a clerk.'

'I talked to her.'

He froze in the act of turning on the oven. He'd already found the box of Bagel Bites in the freezer compartment. 'Um, how is she?' There were so many layers to his voice – guilt, anger, grief – it was hard to pick the dominant emotion.

'Glad you're okay. Relieved she knows where you are. Not too happy that you're with me.'

'I'm sorry,' he mumbled.

'You don't have to apologize. She wants you to be safe and happy more than anything.'

'Then why can't they act like it?' he said furiously. 'Why can't they act like parents, instead of switching partners-like they were kids?'

This was a complex bunch of ideas. I was beginning to get the feeling that there was no simple way to raise a teenager, or even to answer the questions one might ask you. Was every conversation with my brother going to be as loaded as this one? The prospect was exhausting.

'People don't always do what I wish they would, either,' I said. In fact, people stubbornly lived their lives as they wanted, without regard to me, to an amazing degree. I suppressed this observation, as I expected it wouldn't find favor with Phillip.

We talked for over an hour while Phillip ate (and ate, and ate). I told him about the possible arrival of Poppy's parents and introduced him to Madeleine, who came in while he was wiping his mouth with a napkin.

'Is that a cat?' he asked, regarding Madeleine with startled eyes.

'Sure,' I said, trying not to sound offended. 'She's really old, I know . . .'

'She's really *fat*.'

'Well, that, too. She doesn't get as much exercise as she used to, now that we live in town.'

'She probably can't walk more than five feet,' Phillip said scornfully.

'I guess she is a little dumpy,' I said, wondering how long it had been since I'd actually looked at Madeleine and really evaluated her. 'You know, she must be – let's see, when my friend Jane died and left me Madeleine, she was at least six years old. That was at least seven years ago. Wow, Madeleine, you *are* really old.' I tended to forget between vet appointments.

'Almost as old as I am,' my brother said.

That was a startling thought. I wondered if any of Madeleine's kittens were still alive. I scrabbled around in my memory for the names of the kind people who'd adopted them. That led to another thought, one I should have mentioned earlier.

'Oh, your mom said it was okay for you to stay this week,' I told him.

Phillip hadn't asked, but he'd been anxious; I could see his shoulders relax. I scolded myself for not having told him sooner. A deep sigh left him, as if the weight of the world had squeezed the air out of his lungs.

'I'll clean up the kitchen this time,' I told my brother, 'but from now on, when you use it, you wash it. That's the rule.'

'Thanks,' he said. 'I clean up at home, honest. Sometimes I vacuum and stuff, when it's on my list.'

I'd done the few dishes, wiped down the kitchen surfaces, and straightened up the living room a little, when Phillip, who'd been wandering around, said, 'He doesn't really look that different.' He was looking at a newspaper article about Robin's latest book. I'd clipped it to give Robin when he returned.

'I don't think so, either,' I said, trying to sound casual.

'And you guys are dating.'

'Yes.'

'Are you . . . um . . . really tight?'

'We're not dating each other exclusively,' I said, though I hadn't dated anyone else since Robin had returned to town. On the other hand, I hadn't dated anyone before then, either. But we hadn't talked about exclusivity.

'If he asked you to marry him, what would you say?'

'I would say it's none of your business,' I said, stating it more harshly than I'd intended. 'No, I'm sorry I said that.' Phillip's face had flushed. 'Truly, Phillip, I married Martin really quickly, and though I'm not sorry and never have been, I guess now I feel a little . . . cautious about doing the same thing again.' Then I felt like a hypocrite. I was as quick in making up my mind as I ever had been. I was just trying to put a mature face on for Phillip's benefit. But I knew I would never stop making up my mind quickly. That was my nature.

The Wynns pulled to the curb twenty minutes later. Avery, who'd called me to announce their arrival, had led them over in his car. He came inside for just a minute to reintroduce us. Avery looked awful, but then, I was sure I looked no better.

'The police are really asking questions,' he whispered as he gave me a hug.

'Well, sure,' I said, surprised. 'That would be the way to find out who did such an awful thing to Poppy.' Avery was speaking as though asking questions would lead to unpleasant revelations, when what we wanted, as a family, was the truth. But I was grateful to him for escorting the Wynns in and easing the way, so I tried to be friendly.

I had known the Wynns only slightly, and that when I was

more or less a child, so it was almost like meeting them for the first time. Sandy and Marvin Wynn were into their seventies, but they were both healthy and lean as whips. They'd always eaten correctly, walked four miles a day, and done things like taking square-dancing classes, or tai chi for beginners. Poppy, their late-in-life and unexpected child, had not had a chance of being included in this harmonious twosome. As much as they seemed to care for their daughter when she'd begun to act out in high school, the Wynns hadn't had a clue how to handle the problem. They'd clung to their sanity and hoped that Hurricane Poppy would lose its impetus in time.

Tonight, they were exhausted and grief-stricken and stunned. Somehow or other, they'd seen Poppy steered safely into the harbor of marriage and motherhood in suburbia, and now she had been killed in a horrible way, despite her achievement of a smooth life.

I had no idea what the Wynns needed. I didn't know whether to try to get them to talk, to hustle them into their bedroom, or to feed them . . . I'd had enough experience with grief to know that its effects can be unpredictable.

Phillip shook their hands, though I don't think he registered with them. Sandy hugged me as though we were very close, which we had never been, and Marvin hugged me, too, murmuring into my ear that he was so grateful to me for putting them up; the drive had been so long and confusing . . .

'Have you eaten?' I asked.

'Yes, I think we stopped a couple of hours ago,' Sandy said. 'I think we ate. I'm not hungry. Are you, Marvin?'

I remembered Marvin Wynn's hair as being red. Now it was snowy white. His face was lean and lined, and he had broad shoulders. He looked as though normally he could climb a mountain without breathing hard, and Sandy could probably drag a sled through the snow for a few miles. But right now, their faces were gray and sagging. Marvin shook his head. 'No, not hungry.'

I showed them the bathroom they would share with Phillip

(which I had restored to its orderly state) and then their bedroom. I'd opened boxes of tissues and left them on the bedside tables. There was free closet space and a couple of free drawers, extra blankets at the foot of the bed.

'If you need anything during the night, just come get me,' I said, showing them where my bedroom was. 'Otherwise, there are cold drinks in the refrigerator, muffins in the bread box, and the coffeepot is right here.'

'We don't drink coffee,' Sandy said earnestly. 'But thank you. We'll just wash up and go to bed, if that's okay.'

'Anything you want is fine with me,' I said. 'Here's a key to the house. You may need it tomorrow.' I put it out on the counter, making sure they couldn't miss it in the morning.

'You're being so kind,' Sandy said, and her eyes overflowed. 'Everyone is being so kind.' Marvin had put their suitcases in the bedroom, and now he put his arm around his wife. They went into the small room I'd prepared for them. I heard the door close.

I stared after them, the memory of the misery I'd plumbed after my husband died yawning wide at my feet. I would be useless the next day if I let myself step over the brink back into that awful time. With all the will I had, I wrenched myself back into the here and now. My brother's alarmed face was staring at me. He really did look only fifteen at that second.

'Phillip, everything I told them – coffeepot, muffins, if you need me – I would have told you before we went to bed. Anything you want to ask?'

'Is there anything in the refrigerator you don't want me to eat? Anything you're saving for supper tomorrow night or something?'

'No, feel free. Eat me out of hearth and home.' I could tell he was trying to be a great houseguest, and that touched me.

'What do we do tomorrow?' he asked.

'Tomorrow, I'm going to have to do stuff connected with poor Poppy dying,' I said. 'And I have to work, too. In fact, I have to get up early in the morning and go to work. I'll leave a note here with my phone number on it. Why don't you use the computer in the study to send your folks an e-mail? The password is on a slip of pink paper in the drawer.'

'The study? The room with all the windows and books?'

'Right. Sometimes Robin works in there, if his apartment gets to feeling too small. So don't rearrange the piles of books.'

He snorted, as if that was ludicrous. 'I'm not that much of a reader,' he explained. 'That book of Robin's was the first one I'd read in months. I'm not much on school, either.'

Meaning, I gathered, that the day he touched books voluntarily was a day that should be marked on the calendar. I suppressed a sigh. It was hard to believe a brother of mine wasn't a reader. I had never been able to figure out what nonreaders *did*. Maybe, during Phillip's stay, I'd find out.

I knew he had other pastimes. I was thinking, of course, of the condoms, and I thought about health issues. I tried to smile at him. 'Tomorrow, you and I are going to talk about some stuff.'

His smile faded. 'Uh-oh.'

'It won't be as bad as all that,' I said. I hugged him, and just when I was about to let him go, I pulled him tighter instead. 'Phillip, I'm so glad to see you. I was wondering if I'd ever get to see you again. I'm sorry you've been having a tough time. I'm happy you're here.'

He patted my back awkwardly and made some indeterminate noises. I'd embarrassed the hell out of him, and he was fifteen and didn't know what to do about it. After a second or two, I realized he was crying. I could only guess at the correct response. I remained still, my arms around him, rubbing his back gently. He wiped his eyes on the shoulder of my sweater, a childish gesture that somehow won me over completely.

'Good night,' he said in a clogged voice, then retreated to his room so quickly, I only glimpsed a reddened face.

'Good night!' I called after him, keeping my voice low so I wouldn't disturb Marvin and Sandy Wynn.

The silence sank into my bones. With a deep sense of relief, I went into my own bedroom. It had been a very long day, maybe twice as long as my days usually were, at least in terms of emotional content. Either Poppy's death or Phillip's arrival would have given me a full slate of thoughts and feelings, and to have both at one time had sent me into overload. I needed to sleep more than I needed anything, and the only thing that would have made my bed look more welcoming would have been a shock of red hair on the other pillow.

I sat on the side of the bed and realized that what I missed was not Robin exactly, and not sex exactly. And it wasn't missing Martin, either, though still at rare moments I felt I was being stabbed, the flash of grief was so intense. What I was missing at this moment was the state of being married. I missed having someone there to share the little moments of my day. I missed having someone to whom I was the most important person on earth. I missed being part of a team, whose job was always to back each other up.

Even the least perfect marriage has moments that are wonderful, and mine had been far from the least perfect.

I made myself go into my bathroom and begin my nightly routine. I was being ridiculous. My sister-in-law had died an awful death this morning, and here I was, blubbering about not having anyone to sleep with tonight. I was a ridiculous human being. I should know better, I told myself. There were far more terrifying things in the world, and one of those things was very close.

Somewhere in our town, tonight, a person was talking, or brushing his teeth, or making love to a spouse. Yet that person knew he – or she – had committed murder. That person had knocked Poppy down with vicious blows. That person had watched the life drain out of one of the most vital women I'd ever known . . . and done nothing to help her.

Now that was something to brood about.

Chapter Four

I woke up when my alarm went off the next morning. It was 6:30, and the glass doors onto the patio showed me it was a beautiful day. I felt wonderful for about thirty seconds, until I remembered the events of the previous day, which had been a Monday.

The rest of the week wasn't going to be good.

Look on it as a challenge, I told myself briskly. Something rebellious within me muttered back that it was sick of challenges.

But I was now an official Uppity Woman, and I would not let a bad Monday ruin the rest of my week.

This new point of view got me through my morning shower and my simple hair/makeup/clothes routine. After I'd made my bed, I went out to see what I could do for my company before I left for work. I was only a part-time employee, but today I had to work six hours, and tomorrow, too.

A glance into Phillip's room told me he was still asleep. The Wynns were already up and gone, their bedroom door left half-open. They'd positioned a note where I'd left the key, telling me that they were going out for breakfast, then over to my mother's, and probably from there to the police department.

John David should be with them, and I hoped he had realized that, too. I wondered if the police were going to let them into the house anytime soon. I also wondered if they had arranged for anyone to clean up the mess in Poppy's kitchen. I knew there were professional crime-scene cleanup teams in Los Angeles and other big cities, but there sure wasn't one in Lawrenceton, and I didn't think there was such a company in Atlanta. But if there was, would they come out to Lawrenceton? Wouldn't such a service cost a great deal?

I poured myself a cup of just-perked coffee and buttered my

slice of toast, so deep in my thoughts that I hardly noticed what I was doing. I was really hooked on the idea of getting that house cleaned.

I decided I would be willing to pay the fee as my way of easing the burden on my mother's family. How could I find out? My Atlanta telephone book was an old one, scrounged from a friend in the city who'd been about to toss it. I wasn't sure what the Yellow Pages listing would be under. I would call SPACOLEC and ask Arthur if he'd heard about any such service. I wasn't real excited about initiating any contact with Arthur, in case he had a relapse into thinking he was in love with me, but it was probably the quickest way to get that information. I looked up the general number and punched it in. It was very early, but with a murder case going, Arthur would be at his desk, I was fairly sure.

While I was talking to the dispatcher, I spotted a small crumpled wad of paper on my polished wooden floor, under one of the barstools at the breakfast bar. I stooped to pick it up, frowning. I don't like littering, either inside or outside. In fact, I've become kind of a crank about neatness, which my mother thinks is hilarious. While Arthur's extension rang, I flattened the little ball out.

The small piece of paper was a receipt from a gas station, the Grabbit Kwik, which was on the highway between Lawrenceton and the interstate. I shrugged, then walked around the counter so I could toss the slip into the garbage. I was mostly thinking about the phone call.

Then the time printed on the slip registered. Whoever had dropped it had gotten gas the morning before at 10:22, right about when I'd been talking to Poppy on the phone.

My fingers closed around the slip of paper. It had a slick feel, and the wrinkles in it looked gray.

'Hello?' Arthur's voice.

'Arthur, this is Roe.'

After a moment's silence, Arthur said, 'You call to confess?'

I laughed. I hoped that was the correct response. On the other hand, laughing about my sister-in-law's death was really outrageous. 'No, it's not that easy,' I said, trying to sound very sober. 'I wanted to ask you if you knew of a crime-scene cleanup business in Atlanta? And if I could find someone willing to do that, when could they get into the house?'

'Yes, there's a crime cleanup business there,' Arthur said. 'The guy who started it up came by the office last week and left some cards. It's called Scene Clean, and this guy named Zachary Lee is the one who owns it. For all I know, he's the sole employee, too. He used to be a lab tech for the Atlanta Police Department.'

'Thanks. Can you give me his number?'

Arthur dug up the card and read the information to me.

'Probably later this afternoon will be okay, as far as him getting in,' Arthur said. 'I think your hiring him is a good idea, if what I've read about crime-scene cleanup teams applies to Zach Lee. It could very well be that John David's insurance will pay for the bill, or maybe crime victims' compensation.'

'I never thought of that.' I'd made up my mind to shoulder the cost, but if insurance would cover it, all to the good.

'I hope they can get the . . . well, the stains . . . out of that rug by the back door,' Arthur said.

I found that comment somewhat odd. It was a second before I responded, 'The one Poppy liked so much, the one she found at some flea market? Ah . . . I guess that would be a good thing. But all I care about is getting John David and Chase back into the house so they can get clothes and things they need.'

'Sure.' Arthur seemed to be coming out of his little fugue. 'Well, let me know how it goes with Zachary Lee.'

'Thanks,' I said again. 'I'll give this man a call after I check with John David.' I started to say something about the Grabbit Kwik charge slip, and then I realized that by itself, it was meaningless. So, someone had stopped for gas between Atlanta and Lawrenceton? Lots of people did that every day. I needed to sit down and think of exactly who had been in my house, before this piece of paper acquired any significance.

'Roe, you're not close to John David, are you?'

I thought about it for a few seconds. 'Nope, I guess not.'

'If you knew something about him, in relation to Poppy's death, you'd tell me, wouldn't you?'

'Sure,' I said promptly, before I could think twice. If I held back, it wouldn't be for the sake of John David, but for his father – as it happened, though, my conscience was clear. That's what I told Arthur.

He made a sort of noise in his throat, an unconvinced sound. 'I'll let John David know about getting back in the house,' he said. I thanked him again for the Scene Clean information, and my mind had already moved on to the slip on the counter in front of me before I hung up the phone, though I reminded myself to go back over that conversation when I didn't have anything else to worry about.

Who'd been in my house yesterday?

Marvin and Sandy Wynn, my brother, Phillip, and Cartland Sewell – the lawyer formerly known as Bubba. Oh, and Avery; he'd come in briefly, too. Could I have acquired the slip somehow? I pick up things all the time, because I hate litter. My purse is always full of other people's grocery store receipts, rubber bands, paper clips – all sorts of detritus that people leave lying around. It was faintly possible that I'd picked up the receipt myself, stuck it in my pocket or purse for later disposal.

But I tended to discount that theory. For one thing, I would not have rolled it into a ball. I would have folded it. That's just what I do. For another thing, yesterday had been kind of a tense day, what with the newness of being an Uppity Woman, Poppy's tardiness, and then the awful shock of finding her body, and I didn't think my mind had even registered litter all day long.

So, most likely, one of the people who'd come into my house had dropped the receipt. And none of them was supposed to have been anywhere around Grabbit Kwik at that hour of the morning. Marvin and Sandy Wynn were supposedly in their retirement condominium, almost three hours away. Melinda was with me. Cartland was in Mecklinburg, making a speech. Avery was – where had Avery been? At work, exactly where he was supposed to be, most likely. At least Melinda hadn't mentioned Avery being scheduled to do anything out of the ordinary.

But without saying anything to anyone else, I needed to check on all these people, just for my own peace of mind. I could think of no reason why anyone would have wanted Poppy dead, not any reason that made sense to me. I didn't really think John David would marry Romney Burns, now that he was a widower, no matter what Romney might imagine. It was somewhat easier to believe Cartland would have divorced Liz to marry Poppy (which reminded me that I was going to have to have another unpleasant conversation today). But I found myself reluctant to believe that such activity would have been reciprocated: Would Poppy have left John David, cleaved to Cartland? That was hard to imagine.

And Poppy's parents – having gone through so much hell to bring her up, it was highly unlikely they'd have snuffed her out.

My brother Phillip had been on a bus. Or so he said. No witnesses, at least none that he could produce quickly, I was sure. But why on earth would he have been interested in killing Poppy, a woman he didn't even know? Besides, he wouldn't have needed a receipt for gas. He had no vehicle.

Avery seemed happy enough with Melinda. Why would he have laid a hand on his sister-in-law?

But just at a surface level, Avery had had a better chance than anyone to be on that road at that time. He had a secretary, but she only came in in the afternoon. Avery shared a suite of offices, and the secretary, with another CPA, but essentially he worked by himself.

Someone had dropped that receipt on my floor, and none of the people who could have done it should have done it. I just didn't want to imagine that one of them was capable of driving a knife into Poppy.

As I dialed the Atlanta number, I realized something else was bothering me, but for the life of me, I couldn't put my finger on it.

'Scene Clean,' said a happy male voice.

I introduced myself and explained the situation.

'Of course, I'd be glad to help you out,' Zachary Lee said

enthusiastically. I wondered if I were his first customer. 'But I have to have the home owner's written permission, you understand. And the responsibility for the bill?'

'I'll be responsible,' I said firmly. I could ask John David about the insurance coverage some other time. 'Mr Queensland can give you written permission, and I'll meet you there this afternoon at four, unless I call you and tell you otherwise.' I gave the cheerful Mr Lee my phone numbers, house and cell, John David's number, and the address on Swanson Lane.

Phillip staggered into the bathroom as I hung up. I was relieved to see him, because I had to go to work and we had to discuss what he would do while I was gone. I began to make a list while I waited for him to emerge; he seemed to be taking yet another marathon shower.

I scrawled a number of items on an old envelope. I'd number them later. 'When Memorial Service or Funeral?' I wrote, and then, 'T'giving'. Entries under that included, 'turkey', 'celery', 'sweet pot.', 'cran sauce'. Mother had invited me over to have Thanksgiving dinner with her and John, Melinda and Avery had been scheduled to go to Melinda's parents' home in Groton, and Poppy and John David had been wavering between accepting an invitation from some college friends or throwing in with my mother's plans. Now, of course, all these arrangements would be in disarray. Poppy's murder – and, to a much lesser extent, the unexpected presence of Phillip – naturally would alter the next few days beyond all recognition. No one in the family would want to think about the holiday, but we would all have to.

I was supposed to work today and tomorrow, though the library would be closed Thursday and Friday. Lawrenceton more or less shuts down on Thanksgiving, though not as much as it used to when I was a kid.

Phillip emerged from the steamy bathroom, wearing the bathrobe again. I was glad to see he looked pretty alert. When I offered toast or cereal, he said he didn't normally eat breakfast right after he rose. I bit my tongue to keep from pointing out he'd been up for a good thirty minutes in the shower, and he poured a glass of orange juice and sat by me on one of the high stools at the counter.

'You look ready for work,' he observed. 'So, what's my agenda for today?'

'If you left the bathroom in a mess, you need to go in and clean it. Remember, the Wynns are staying here,' I said. Phillip looked distinctly alarmed and unhappy at continuing to live in such close proximity to unknown old people who were in the middle of such a crisis. Tough.

'Also,' I said, 'here is a pad and a pen. There are going to be lots of phone calls today. Please write down each one: the time, the caller, and the message. Here's my phone number at work. Every two hours, call me and let me hear the list. Some of these I'll have to act on pretty quickly. Now, there's a remote possibility people will bring food by here if they hear the Wynns are staying with me. You accept the dish, write down any instructions about heating or refrigerating it, and who brought it.'

Phillip nodded. He seemed a little dazed.

'Here's the remote control for the TV. Here's the remote for the DVD player.' I went over to the television cabinet and opened a door. 'Here are my DVDs.' I went into the kitchen, opened a drawer, extracted a key from a plastic tray. 'Here's another key to the house. If you leave, please write a note saying where you've gone and when you'll be back. Do you have a watch?'

Phillip shook his head.

'Okay.' I handed him a watch that had been Martin's. I'd come across it that morning when I was putting on my makeup. It wasn't an expensive watch; it was the one he'd been wearing when we got married, and I'd given him a fancier one our first Christmas together. Martin had chucked this watch in a drawer and I'd automatically packed it when I moved. It was just a mass-produced watch; there were probably millions identical to it. It was absurd to feel a pang over a bit of assembly-line metal that ran on a battery.

Phillip gave me a sharp look as he slid the watch on his arm. 'I won't break it,' he said defensively. My face must have been showing more than I'd thought.

'I don't think you will,' I said, and hugged him, much to his surprise. 'And the world won't end if you do.' I hoped I wasn't being too demanding. Not only would someone performing all those little tasks be genuinely helpful; I would know where Phillip was. I'd given him a key because I wanted to show I trusted him. I wasn't sure I really did. I could not stop Phillip if he decided to leave while I was at work, and it would be ludicrous to try to find a babysitter for him. No, this was sink-or-swim time for my brother and me.

I just hoped we'd both survive.

Janie Spellman was working the check-in desk when I came out of the employees' lounge, my lipstick fresh and my mind pre-occupied. Janie gave me a brilliant smile as she loaded books on the cart. I regarded our newest staff member with both grudging admiration and envy. When Janie had gone to school, she'd learned computer systems as a matter of course, and she could help younger patrons far more knowledgeably than I. But Janie should have gotten a job somewhere else for a couple of years before she came back to Lawrenceton. She was always getting shocked. People who had been her revered elders when she'd been in high school and college were always startling her by checking out reading material that didn't jibe with her idea of what they should be reading. People she'd gone to high school with were not always particularly happy to see her. And children said and did things that could horrify the most jaded librarian, much less a young woman who'd so recently been a child herself.

Janie was also quite anxious about her single status. Though there was no discernible reason for her to be desperate, she was, and spread her nets unwisely. For one thing, Janie had cast her eyes at Perry Allison. Perry was at least fifteen years older, and I knew he was gay, but this was something Janie had not yet figured out – to be honest, it was fairly recent news to Perry himself.

Perry wasn't the only male Janie had set her sights on. Robin Crusoe was another. I was getting a little miffed about that. In fact, I was miffed at this very moment. Robin, who was supposed to be completing his postconvention book tour, was standing with his elbows on the desk behind which Janie stood, and he was smiling at her entirely too broadly. And she was simpering back at him.

I felt a rush of irritation, chased by a big dash of insecurity. I turned on my heel and went back into the employees' lounge. My hands were balled into fists and I was breathing deeply. I was being childish and unreasonable. Jealousy was beneath my dignity, and it was unattractive, too. What was wrong with me? I was one big emotional storm. This truly didn't seem like me, yet I was undeniably enraged. Janie's and Robin's shared smile had given me an utterly baseless sense of betrayal. I was so angry that I wished, not for the first time, that I were a lesbian. But a female couple probably had their share of lovers' spats, too. After all, it wasn't *men* I was unhappy with; it was vulnerability. I'd just had enough pain for a while.

I knew that I had a better life than maybe 90 percent of the women in the world, and I wasn't trying to be Pitiful Pearl. But after the little hurts of life that almost everyone sustains, I'd more or less just gotten through the staggering shock of losing my husband. More pain was something I hadn't signed up for when I'd succumbed to – okay, welcomed – the revival of my relationship with Robin.

'Eff him,' I said. My spine straightened. That felt good. I swung a fist up and shook it. '*Eff* him.' That felt better. I was pleasurably shocked at myself.

'Eff who?' asked my boss.

'Robin,' I said after I'd jumped maybe a mile. 'He's out there flirting with Janie. I just don't need that today. Actually, I don't need that any day. I need *security*. I need *devotion*.' I couldn't believe I was saying this to my boss. I had known Sam forever, and I won't say we hadn't experienced some mind-to-mind talks, because we had. But he had never been anywhere close to the top of my list of confidants.

Sam patted me awkwardly on the shoulder. 'Sorry about your

sister-in-law,' he said. I came out of my selfish absorption to register Sam's appearance. He looked awful. He was drawn and pale, and he'd visibly lost weight.

'What's up with you, Sam?' I asked with well-merited concern. I realized for the first time that Sam's problems amounted to more than missing his secretary. Sam looked really sick. In a way, I wasn't surprised.

Sam, who was in the neighborhood of fifty, had to juggle more balls than I could ever keep in the air. The city, the county, the state, the employees, the patrons – all of them had a stake in the library, and all wanted to have their say. The building maintenance, the book budget, hiring and firing . . . and on the home front, two girls who must be in their early twenties by now, and a wife named Marva, who could do simply anything, which I found almost unforgivable.

'I didn't sleep well,' Sam said. Maybe if he hadn't slept well for a month, I might have accepted his appearance, but not after one night. 'Marva is stenciling a design around the top of our bedroom walls, which she just finished painting.'

See what I mean?

'So I had to sleep in the guest bedroom, and the bed there leaves a lot to be desired. Plus, even with the bedroom door closed, I could still smell the paint, and it just makes me sick.'

Marva had been married to Sam for thirty years, so I was willing to bet she knew that. And yet she'd painted the bedroom in November, when the windows couldn't be opened. Big message there.

'I don't expect we can give each other any advice,' I said, for lack of anything else to say.

'I guess not,' he said. 'Good luck to you, and again, I'm sorry about Poppy. She taught with Marva for a while and came over to the house from time to time. I liked her, no matter what anyone said.'

That was typical Sam. Mr Tactful.

I trailed back out into the library, determined to earn my money. I was supposed to be checking people in and out as they used our computers, and giving them extra direction if this was needed. I'd also be filling out the paperwork for our next book order while I sat at the desk. That part was fun, the little gush of excitement at all those wonderful books coming into our library, just waiting to be picked up and read. (See, I really am a librarian at heart.) But someone had to deal with questions like how much would be charged for printing out information our patrons had found on the Internet, or how to find out the greatest ocean depth recorded, or the best way to look up whether dromedaries have two humps and camels one (or vice versa).

Robin was still there, still leaning on the desk. See, this is why I believe in gun control; because if I'd had a gun, I wouldn't have had much control over my actions.

'Roe,' he said, aiming his beautiful crinkly smile at me. It would have meant more – in fact, it would have melted my heart – if I hadn't seen him grinning at Janie just moments before. 'I canceled the rest of my signings and came home last night.'

'Robin,' I said coolly. True librarians stay calm in the face of adversity.

He looked considerably taken aback.

'I thought you'd be happier to see me,' he said uncertainly. 'I thought I'd surprise you.'

Janie was checking out books a little farther down the big desk.

'You seem to have found a way to keep busy while you waited,' I remarked, and picked up the ringing phone. Porter Ziegler wanted to know how to get scum off the surface of his pond. I told him I'd find out, but I was registering Robin's reaction.

Robin looked a little guilty instantly. Not my imagination, then.

'Just passing the time till you came in,' he said. 'I know I shouldn't just come in and chatter to the librarians when they're at work. I guess I don't know that many people here in Lawrenceton yet.'

And he was in Lawrenceton because of me was the subtext to that subtle plea for sympathy.

'Here I am,' I said after considering several possible responses.

'Are you okay?'

He was sounding so sympathetic and caring, I felt like I was being a big idiot. Then Janie, having finished with the patron, sidled over and reached across the desk to finger Robin's coat, which was a very nice suede. In what I could only characterize as a coo, Janie said, 'You're so snuggly in that coat!'

Gun control, I thought. Gun control.

'Let me leave you two to your discussion,' I said lightly. I smiled at both of them with all the warmth of an alligator, then went to ask the reference librarian if she could find out about pond-scum removal. She thought for a minute and then gave me the phone number of the county agent. Porter Ziegler would surely find the answer from that individual, a man who seemed to know everything about the out-of-doors.

When I went back to the main desk, Robin was gone. Janie, looking a little sullen, was checking out some books for a bearded man who had made the library his second home. We had often speculated about Horton Aldrich. He was clean, and he never smelled, but he was noticeably shabby, and gaunt. The address he'd listed when he'd gotten his library card had turned out to be the address of the local Salvation Army store. Mr Aldrich was prone to laugh to himself while he read the paper, which was maybe not so odd, considering the state of the world. He seldom talked directly to anyone, staff or patron, but he was nearly always through the doors right after they were unlocked, and he trotted out of them when the closing employee walked toward them with the key.

Today, Mr Aldrich seemed to be in a jittery mood. I wondered what had happened to upset him. But he was so peculiar, I would have asked about his well-being only if he'd been bleeding or sobbing. My policy – my chickenhearted policy – about Mr Aldrich was, Let him be. I always tried to smile at him, I tried not to look nervous when he decided to have a conversation with me, and I made sure no other patron hogged the Atlanta paper, thus preventing Mr Horton from reading it right away, because I'd noticed that really made his day bad.

Everyone in the world wanted to use our computers today, and the phone rang every time I put it down. I got about halfway through filling out the book order, when it should have taken me thirty minutes to do the whole thing. Phillip called at eleven o'clock, right on time, to tell me who'd phoned the house. He'd met Sandy and Marvin Wynn, who had come in briefly to retrieve an address book. Kind people had dropped off a cold-cut platter so the Wynns could have sandwiches whenever they were hungry, and a pie, though Phillip anxiously told me he didn't know what kind it was. But he swore he had the name and a description of the dish written down.

'You better have a sandwich and a piece of pie. Then you'll know what kind it is,' I said.

'Shouldn't I save all this for Mr and Mrs Wynn?'

'Honey, I would say "sure" if I had any idea they were going to be eating, or caring what they ate,' I said. 'And you know there's no way two skinny older people like the Wynns are going to eat a whole platter of cold cuts, or a whole pie.'

'Okay, that'll be lunch for me.'

'Good. Who's called?'

There was a long list, including my mother (naturally), Melinda (no surprise), and Sally Allison, my friend, who was also a newspaper reporter. (Maybe I should say Sally Allison, the newspaper reporter, who was sometimes also my friend. That was definitely more accurate.) I remembered that I'd called Sally to ask her out to lunch, and I'd left a message for her to call me back. Cara Embler, Poppy's back-fence neighbor, and Teresa Stanton, president of the Uppity Women, had also tried to reach me. And, to my surprise, so had Bryan Pascoe.

Phillip seemed to be pleased that he'd been useful, and he was also happy to have HBO and MTV and lots of food. When I asked him about the state of the bathroom, there was a long moment of silence.

'Um, it'll be picked up within about ten minutes,' he said defensively.

'Okay,' I said, reminding myself again that I was not his mom.

However, I was his older sister, and he needed to do what I asked of him. But for now, I backed off.

'I hope it's okay that I made a long-distance call on your phone?' he asked.

'Did you call your mother?'

'Okay, make that two long-distance calls.'

'You called your mother and who else?'

'Um, Britta – you know, the girl who gave me a ride?'

I tried to give a mature, balanced answer. 'Hell no' would not do. 'Phillip, unless you're calling your parents, I don't think you should run up my phone bill,' I said, keeping my voice calm and even.

'Hey, if I had any money, I'd pay you back!'

Okay, hostility alert.

'I know you would.' Keep the voice calm and even, Roe. 'But since you don't, you'd better hold off on the phone calls. Does Britta have an e-mail address?'

'Yeah.'

'Okay, fine. E-mail her to your heart's content, but don't visit any Web sites you have to pay for.'

After a silence, Phillip said, 'Okay, I'll do that from now on.'

I smiled at the patron standing at the counter, who beamed back. So that was a double-purpose smile. I was really pleased at ending the conversation with Phillip on a good note.

I noticed that Janie was staying away from me, which made me happy. I figured she wasn't as oblivious as she seemed. Perry came in to begin his work hours, and he gave me a pat on the shoulder.

'Sorry about Poppy,' he said. Perry had had a troubled life, but he seemed to have found his foothold now. To my surprise, I'd become his buddy, especially since his recent acknowledgment of his sexual orientation. I felt a little uncomfortable in the role, but I was so happy for Perry – and for his mother, Sally – when I watched his attitude grow more positive and cheerful, his demeanor more confident, I became resigned to assuming it.

'Had a great date last night,' he said casually but very quietly.

'Local?'

'Yes,' he said. 'We went to the movies.'

We talked about the film they'd seen, without Perry telling me his date's name. That was the norm in our conversations.

About fifteen minutes later, Perry's mom showed up. My friend Sally, who had always been incredibly put together, was beginning to look older. Although her hair color had once been easy to accept as natural, now that seemed increasingly unlikely. I didn't think she'd gained weight, but what she had was redistributing. She'd saved up for a face-lift, much to my surprise, but I had to wonder if she'd been to the right doctor. Her face looked smooth all right. But somehow, her skin didn't look like real skin.

Well, bless her heart. Sally had had a hard life, and she was doing her best.

'Son,' she said coldly, looking at Perry.

'Hey, Mom,' he said.

Uh-oh, trouble in paradise.

Sally asked me if I was ready to go to lunch. It was about 11:15, early for lunch.

'I didn't know we had a date,' I said. 'I called you to ask you out for your birthday, but we didn't ever get to set a date and time.' Sally stared at me blankly. I became flustered. 'Did I just forget? I can't believe it! I don't think I've ever just out-and-out forgotten a lunch date before.' I rummaged around in my memory, trying to dredge up any conversation I'd had recently with Sally.

'Didn't we set up lunch for today when we talked yesterday?' Sally looked as surprised as I was.

'Sally, we didn't talk yesterday.' I was sure of that. 'I called you at work. You weren't at your desk. I left a voice-mail message.'

'Of course we talked,' Sally said. She looked more upset than the situation warranted. 'I called you here, and you told me we would go to lunch on Tuesday, that you had something you wanted to tell me.'

'Sally, that was weeks ago,' I said, finally recalling the conversation. 'That was right after I'd bought the new house, and I wanted to tell you I was moving.'

Sally looked angry and frightened.

I turned to look at Perry, just because I had to put my eyes somewhere, and I couldn't bear to look at Sally. What on earth was happening?

Perry's face gave me a big hint.

'But today would be great,' I said brightly. 'Just let me go get my purse. I'll bet you did call, and I just got so upset with everything that's been happening to my family that I got all mixed up. You know me,' I babbled on, walking rapidly back to the employee lounge. 'I can't keep anything straight to save my soul.'

I had planned on going home to lay eyes on my brother. I didn't think it was such a great idea, leaving him by himself all day. I wondered if I could combine two events in one.

I got my purse from my locker and went back out to the check-out desk, to find Sally glaring at Perry, who was looking miserable and defiant.

'I guess you know my son thinks he's gay,' Sally said to me after we got in my car.

'Yes,' I said cautiously.

'I must have been a terrible mother. I guess I shouldn't have divorced Steve. Or maybe Paul.' Sally had been married to both Allison brothers. I'd hardly known Steve, but Paul had been a mine of emotional problems.

'No, I think you did the right thing there,' I said, trying to sound calming and positive. This wasn't easy. 'And I think you tried as hard as you could to be a good mother. Perry being gay doesn't mean you were a bad mother.'

'I got him through the emotional problems and the drug abuse,' she said plaintively. 'It seems to me it ought to be time for him to settle down like everyone else.'

I was speechless. Since Perry and I had discussed the orientation he'd finally revealed to himself, I had been wondering if maybe his emotional upheavals and substance abuse had been attempts to obscure it from himself. I had no idea what to say to Sally.

'Perry's a good guy,' I told her. 'He's well into adulthood, and he has to make his own life. You know he loves you.'

Those were true things. I wasn't sure that they all tied together, but Sally seemed to gain some comfort.

She began to talk about other topics, and everything Sally said was absolutely lucid and intelligent. I began to wonder if that episode in the library had really happened.

I invited Sally in to meet my brother, and she looked over the house with interest while I talked to Phillip.

'That Pascoe guy called again,' Phillip said. My brother seemed to be getting a little restless, which was what I had feared. He'd caught up on his sleeping and eating, he'd watched television and answered the phone, and now boredom was setting in.

I thought hard while I sat there, supposedly studying the list of callers. Phillip had spiky, tight handwriting, but it was legible after you'd looked at it for a minute.

I got out the Lawrenceton phone book and looked up a number I'd called several times before, but always in an official capacity. Josh Finstermeyer answered the phone, which was lucky for me.

'Josh, this is Ms Teagarden,' I began.

'I don't have a single overdue book!' Josh said anxiously. 'I swear!'

'I know that,' I said, trying not to sound irritable. 'I have a favor to ask. If your mother doesn't have anything for you to do today, that is.' Parental tasks took precedence over anything else.

'No, ma'am, my mom's at work anyway,' Josh said. He sounded curious.

'You have a car, right?' He'd just earned the right to drive by himself.

'Yes, ma'am.' Now he was even more curious. The good thing about Josh, whom I'd known from birth, was that he was a voracious reader. The bad thing was that he forgot to return books. We'd had our ups and downs

'My brother is here with me, and I need to send him shopping,' I told Josh. 'I have to go back to work, so I was hoping you could take Phillip to the grocery store and to Wal-Mart. And if there's anything on at the Global you haven't seen already, that would be okay, too.'

'So who's paying?' Josh was nothing if not businesslike.

'Gas money and movie money.'

'Done. How old is this dude?'

'He's fifteen,' I said.

'He's not weird looking, right?' Obviously, Josh wanted to know if Phillip was going to be an embarrassment.

'Not at all,' I said gravely. 'In fact, you might want to bring your sister.' Josh had a twin sister, Jocelyn, called Joss. She wasn't much of a reader; unlike her brother, but she had seemed okay when she was in the library doing research for school.

'Okay. When?'

'Anytime. You know where I live? On McBride?'

'Yes, ma'am. Where's your brother from?'

'The Los Angeles area,' I said grandly.

'Oh. Cool.'

'So I'll leave him the money.'

'Gotcha.'

Of course Phillip had been listening to my conversation, and he seemed half-excited and half-scared at the idea of spending the rest of the afternoon with kids his own age who didn't know him. I could understand that. But I knew what Phillip was capable of – taking off cross-country alone – and I wanted him busy. I peeled some money out of my purse, and while Sally and Phillip talked about southern accents, I worked on a grocery list.

After Phillip vanished into the bathroom to spruce himself up, Sally and I made sandwiches from the cold-cut tray, which had enough processed meat and cheese for maybe ten people. I rummaged in the refrigerator for mayonnaise, mustard, and pickles; meanwhile, Sally was being complimentary about Phillip's manners and looks. We had a pleasant conversation while we ate, though it was strangely nonspecific. I noticed that Sally said things like 'my boss' for Macon Turner, whom I knew well, and 'last week' instead of Wednesday or Thursday. But this was hardly conclusive. I was just thinking maybe I had imagined Sally's earlier reality blip, when she said, 'I really ought to be getting back to work.' We had put all the food away, and I fished my keys out of my purse.

'Okay,' I said. I needed to be getting back to work, too. 'Where's your car?'

Sally's face went blank.

For a moment, I thought she just didn't understand me. 'I mean, is it at the newspaper, or did you drive down to the library?' I asked.

For one horrible moment, Sally looked frightened.

'Oh, just take me back to the library,' she said with a nonchalance assumed so swiftly and smoothly that I almost didn't catch that moment. If my back had been turned, I would have swallowed her act.

Sally really didn't know where her car was.

Chapter Five

I had taken a circuitous route to make sure Sally's car was indeed at the library. It was, and I dropped her off right by it with some relief. I watched her unlock it and climb in the driver's seat. I wondered what to do, and then I realized that it wasn't up to me to do anything. This situation was Perry's responsibility, and all I could do was be a friend to him so he could talk if he needed to.

I patted him on the shoulder when I passed him in the employees' lounge, and he looked up at me and nodded, a short, jerky nod of acknowledgment.

'I made an appointment with Dr Zelman for her next week,' he said. 'She tries to cover it up, and she's pretty good at it, but it's getting worse and worse.'

There really wasn't anything else to say.

The two remaining hours of work flew by. There were lots of people coming in and out, lots of computer use, and the book order to complete. When it was time for me to clock out, I was actually glad. There were so many ways for me to go, I couldn't pick one.

My plans for the rest of the afternoon took an unexpected turn when I went to the employee parking lot and found Bryan Pascoe leaning on my car. His office was within easy walking distance of the library; it was in the old, ambience-laden, inconvenient Jasper Building, which also held Cartland Sewell's office. So it had been easy for Bryan Pascoe to get where he was. The question was why he was there.

'Ms Teagarden,' he said.

'Hello, Mr Pascoe,' I said, and even I could hear the question clearly in my voice. It was a relief not to have to tilt my head back to look Bryan Pascoe in the eyes.

He held out his hand, and I shook it. He had fine bones. 'Please call me Bryan,' he said politely.

'Bryan,' I murmured, and retrieved my hand. 'Aurora,' I said after a moment.

He nodded.

'My brother, Phillip, said you tried to call me? I would have returned your calls.' I wanted to be sure Bryan Pascoe marked the fact that he was pushing.

'Yes, but I wanted to talk to you face-to-face.'

'All right,' I said hesitantly when he'd been at a full stop for a long moment. 'Did you want to go to your office?'

'Can we walk around the block? I've been shut in my office all day.'

It was brisk, but not truly cold. 'Certainly,' I said after an uncertain pause. What the heck was going on here? 'My legs are short, I don't go at a very quick pace.' Robin always seemed to be two paces ahead of me. Thinking about Robin instantly made me feel bad.

'Your legs are fine,' he said, again catching me off balance, and off we went.

'Has something come up about John David?'

'Of course I've talked to Miss Burns. For the moment, she backs up John David a hundred percent. She says he was doing legal work for her.'

I glanced sideways at Bryan, and he smiled at me. He had gleaming white teeth. 'She's been drawing up her will, she says,' Bryan added in an absolutely neutral way.

'If Poppy were alive, Romney Burns'd need it.' I found myself smiling back.

'That's interesting. Did you see your sister-in-law as a jealous woman?'

I mulled that over. 'I don't think she would have wanted to be humiliated, if John David decided to divorce her, or something about his little relationships became flagrant. Like him taking Romney to the company Christmas party, or something like that,' I said finally. 'I guess that's different from being gut-jealous.'

'How do you feel about that?' the lawyer asked.

I felt like that was a strange question.

I stopped and faced him. Luckily, we were on the sidewalk by the side of the little downtown movie theater, and no one was going in or out at the moment.

'What difference does that make?' I could feel my eyebrows drawing together in a frown.

'Personal curiosity,' he said.

'I don't know why you want to know.' But I could see no reason to refuse to tell him, either. 'I thought it was really . . . distasteful,' I said, selecting the mildest word that would fit. 'Though I'm not an angel myself, for sure.'

'Why are you giving me your opinion in such a tentative way? You don't have to attach disclaimers.'

'I don't know you. For all I know, you cheat on your wife every day,' I said bluntly. 'I hate to sound holier-than-thou.'

'Why did you call me yesterday?'

'John David thought of you. You're the best, I hear.'

'I am, Aurora.'

I felt like I was missing something here. 'I'm glad to know you're so confident,' I said a little dubiously.

'I was glad to hear your voice on the phone yesterday. I've had my eye on you for quite some time.'

'You think I've done something illegal?'

'No, I want to date you.'

'I thought you were married, Bryan,' I said, genuinely astonished. Come to think of it, he had mentioned 'ex-wife' yesterday.

'I was, for five years. We got divorced over a year ago.'

'Uh-huh,' I said, feeling like he'd just smacked me in the head with a dead fish, or something equally startling. 'Well, Bryan, I'm real flattered, but I've been dating Robin Crusoe.'

'I know.' He smiled again. His smile managed to be confident, predatory, and hopeful, all at the same time. 'But my sources tell me he's been flirting with Janie Spellman.'

'Ouch,' I said sharply. 'That was below the belt. Who's your source?'

'I'm not bound by law to cover for her. My source is Janie Spellman herself, who is my cousin once removed.'

'Janie is not too particular about whom she flirts with.'

'I'm sorry you're angry, but you can't deny it,' Bryan said unequivocally.

'I don't have to reply any way at all, deny or admit or any which thing.' I glared up at him. 'In fact, this part of our conversation is over.' Suddenly, I thought of the gas station receipt in my purse. I couldn't let anything slip by just because I was irritated with Bryan. 'Now, I need to talk business.'

'Talk away.' If I'd in any way ruffled Bryan, he wasn't letting it show.

I explained about finding the receipt that morning, about its significance, and told him the names of the people who'd been in my house. Then I looked at my watch and exclaimed, 'Oh no! I have to be at Poppy's right now!'

'What for?' Bryan had listened to my account very carefully, which had made me feel better about him.

'The Scene Clean guy is supposed to be at John David and Poppy's house,' I explained. 'Someone called from SPACOLEC to say the house had been . . . well, released. So I called Zachary Lee and confirmed.'

'I need to see the crime scene anyway. Can I come with you?'

'I guess so,' I said ungraciously. We walked back to the library parking lot and I unlocked my Volvo. Bryan talked about local politics all the way over to Swanson Lane. I felt the touch of his attention every time he looked at me, and he looked at me a lot. My cheeks were hot by the time we parked behind a bright yellow van with SCENE CLEAN and a logo on the side. At least there were no macabre graphics. I fussed with my keys, yanked at my purse, anything to avoid looking into the eyes of the man beside me. We got out of the car and stood at the end of the walkway leading up to the front door. A young man with Asian features was waiting for us. He was absorbed in a book.

I was nervous about going into the house again. 'I'm glad Arthur released the house,' I said, just to say something.

'I'll bet Arthur has had a rough couple of days,' Bryan said, clearly inviting me to ask why.

'Any murder investigation . . .' I said slowly. 'But that's not what you're implying, is it?'

'I'm sure you have heard that Poppy used to see him. A couple of years ago?'

I thought I was going to pass right out. I could actually feel the blood rush from my head. Bryan put his left arm around me and held on to my right hand with his.

'Good God,' I said, trying to gain some time. 'But then he should be the last man on earth to be involved in investigating her death!'

Bryan said, 'Do you feel all right? Wasn't he your fiancé at one time?'

'No,' I said, shaking my head to clear it out. 'No, we never . . . Did you do that on purpose? Spring that on me? Why?'

'You did date him.'

'About a million years ago. Way before I married Martin.' I gave him an incredulous look.

'I wondered if Arthur had a thing for the women in your family.'

'You're confusing me.' I stepped away from his arm and walked up the sidewalk to the door, just as I'd done yesterday. I faltered for a moment as that comparison hit me, then picked up my stride.

Bryan was beside me by then. 'Hello,' he said to the young man waiting on the ornamental bench outside Poppy's front door.

'Zachary Lee?' I asked as he rose. Zachary Lee was much taller than I'd expected, maybe six feet, and looked, like a very happy mix of Caucasian and Asian.

'That's me,' he said happily. 'Zachary Lee, Scene Clean, at your service. I'm a certified crime-scene cleaner, and I've had extensive experience with the Atlanta Police Department. I took a course to learn how to do this properly, and I follow all safety and health regulations.'

He beamed at us. Apparently, Zachary Lee enjoyed his work.

'Did the police give you the okay?' I asked.

'Yes, ma'am, and Mr Queensland, the husband of the deceased, gave me his permission to do the job. By the way, he said to tell you thanks.' Zachary's teeth were perfectly straight and white, and his eyes tilted pleasantly when he smiled, which seemed to be most of the time.

'I'm Aurora Teagarden,' I said, 'and this is Bryan Pascoe, Mr Queensland's lawyer.'

'Pleased to meet you' was said all around.

'Let me just show you the, um, site,' I said, fumbling with the words. 'Mr Pascoe wants to have a look before you clean it. I'll wait here until you're through, then lock up after you.'

For the first time, Zachary Lee looked less than happy, probably at the idea of us sitting around the crime scene while he worked. But I wanted to see him off the premises, and just generally keep an eye on him. The young man was probably perfectly all right, but we knew very little about him.

The house had been closed, and it smelled less than wonderful. Poppy would have been embarrassed. There was the awful smell of blood, and the more mundane odor of a much-used litter box. Once again, I was distressed that Moosie hadn't been found. Somehow, the cat's disappearance was an insult to Poppy.

'Tell me what you did yesterday when you came in,' Bryan said, and I thought maybe he was distracting me, I was grateful.

'I went upstairs,' I said. 'No one was there. I came back down and went toward the kitchen.' I guided him down the short hall into the kitchen, where everything was the same as it had been, except for fingerprint powder. We stepped around the counter, and I waved a hand weakly toward the spot where Poppy had lain. The gesture was hardly necessary. The blood was a powerful testimony. In fact, seeing it like this – dried and dark – made its impact somehow more violent.

While Zachary Lee went over to the sliding glass door to have a look outside, I felt that my head was buzzing just a bit. I put a hand out to Poppy's breakfast bar, which was laden with bright cookbooks and dried flowers, to steady myself.

Instantly, Bryan steered me out of the kitchen/dining room and into the living room. Instead of depositing me on the couch, he put his arms around me. And he didn't say a word. His left hand stroked my hair.

I really liked that silence. Robin, since words were his livelihood, never quite seemed to know when they weren't necessary.

'So, there's nothing upstairs?' Zachary Lee asked from the doorway.

I began to pull away, but Bryan Pascoe's arms tightened. 'The fingerprint dust,' he said. 'No blood.'

'Okay,' the cleanup guy said, happy once again. 'Why don't you two sit out by the pool? It's a beautiful day. I've got to go suit up and bring in my gear.'

Bizarre as it seemed at first, that turned out to be excellent advice. As we walked out the front door and around to the gate at the side of the house (rather than crossing the bloody threshold of the sliding glass door), Bryan gave me rather unnecessary help. I have to confess I enjoyed it, after coping with Phillip and the assorted shocks of the past twenty-four hours. Sometimes I just didn't understand myself. Half of me wanted to stand upright and independent, and half of me wanted to lean against someone stronger. Possibly the answer could be found in a good partnership, in which one could take turns leaning.

In one of those unexpected little moments of clarity that make life so frightening, I realized (as I sat by the pool of a murdered woman, being comforted by an attentive lawyer) that my first marriage had not been such a partnership.

'All right?' Bryan was saying anxiously.

'Yes, I'm fine.' I sounded like a polite robot. I shook myself a little. 'Thank you for asking.'

At that awkward juncture, another presence made itself known. Teresa Stanton, Uppity Woman par excellence, swept through the patio gate.

'Poor Aurora!' Teresa called. Teresa was a terrifying woman. I hadn't known that a pantsuit with matching jacket was the appropriate outfit to wear to the house of a murdered woman;

until I saw Teresa, that is. She wore one, dark burgundy with golden brown touches, and so that was exactly the right thing. Teresa's dark hair was beautifully cut and blow-dried, so the short sides fanned back from her face, her makeup was discreet, and her teeth were perfectly white. Intelligence gleamed through her contact lenses.

'Teresa,' I muttered. Bryan, of course, stood. I suddenly remembered that the woman to whom Bryan had been married was the newly rewed Teresa Stanton. Teresa Pascoe Stanton.

'I've had the devil's own time catching up to you,' Teresa said.

I hardly felt I needed to apologize. 'This has been a very busy day,' I said noncommittally.

'Oh, of course! No doubt! Hello, Bryan.' Teresa made sure we knew she was adding the greeting as an elaborate afterthought.

'Teresa, good to see you,' he said, his voice cool and uninflected.

I tried real hard to think of a good excuse to get up and run away, but none popped to mind.

'What's that man doing there?' Teresa asked, distracted by Zachary Lee, who appeared to be wearing a space suit. He was working right inside the sliding glass door.

'He's cleaning up the blood,' I said. Of course, that didn't faze Teresa.

'I'm so glad you were able to find someone who does that sort of thing,' she said conversationally. 'Where's your Mr Crusoe?'

'I don't know.' I refused to explain or elaborate. I wondered what she would do if I asked her where Shorty Stanton was. I was so powerfully tempted that I actually opened my mouth, but then common sense prevailed.

'Of course, all the women in the club want to know what we can do to help,' Teresa said.

'Maybe Melinda needs some babysitting,' I suggested. 'Since she's got her own two kids and Poppy's boy, too.'

Teresa wrote this down on her little pocket notebook. 'What else?' she asked. 'We've already taken food to your mother's house.'

'I'd rethink backing Bubba Sewell for representative.'

'Do you think he is involved with Poppy's death?' Teresa was nothing if not direct, if she thought directness would serve her purposes best.

'No, actually, I don't, but I think his reputation may take a beating if the investigation ends in a trial.'

'So it's true: He was messing around with Poppy.' Teresa looked very cross.

I didn't meet her eyes.

'Someone who can't keep his pants zipped,' Teresa said flatly. 'We don't want that in a public servant. I think we've all seen enough of that.'

'True,' I said.

We all fell silent, and in that sudden hush I could hear the splash of the pool across the privacy fence. Some music was playing, too; it sounded like Handel.

'Cara!' Teresa called. 'Are you doing your laps? Can you take a break?'

'Is that Teresa?' a high voice hooted back.

'Yes, girl. Come over here!'

There was a little-used gate in the high privacy fence between the two properties. It made a high-pitched squeak as Cara Embler pushed it open. Cara was pulling off a swim cap as she walked toward us, and she'd wrapped a big towel around her because it was a brisk, cool day. Her hairstyle had been chosen to complement her athleticism; she wore her blond hair (now mixed with gray) short and straight. Cara had been a champion swimmer in high school and college, and someone had told me that she was training for a seniors competition. Lawrenceton people were bemused by Cara – swimming in all temperatures, goal-oriented – but they respected her dedication and her excellent physical condition. Married to a cardiologist who seemed always to be on call, Cara had a lot of time to shape as she pleased.

Though the Emblers had a son, who was studying to be an environmental engineer or something equally laudable, he was in college in northern California and seldom came home. So Cara swam, ran, dabbled in political causes, tutored kids at the junior high, and organized the annual fund-raising drive for the United Way. She had a couple of dogs, schnauzers; she was famous locally for going to any lengths to help the pound raise money, and she was ferocious about turning in animal abusers.

I couldn't understand why she hadn't been on the list for Uppity Women years ago, but I figured that by now she should be fairly close to the top of the list.

'How's John David?' Cara asked me. She plopped down into one of the lawn chairs, draping her head and neck with yet another towel. The day was cool enough that I would have been shivering had I been wet, but Cara seemed impervious to the temperature.

'About like you'd expect.' Actually, I hadn't seen John David since yesterday, and I had no idea how he was holding up. But somehow, that didn't seem the right thing to confess. I was a little surprised that Cara asked. I hadn't been aware she'd ever had a conversation with John David.

'This is just awful, and in the house right behind me,' Cara went on.

I hadn't thought of that. I would sure be scared, too. In fact, I'd be shaking in my shoes. But Cara seemed concerned, not frightened.

'Did you hear anything peculiar?' Teresa asked.

Cara, who was somewhere between forty and fifty, shrugged her muscular shoulders. 'No, the day was just as usual. Swam in the morning, decorated the house for Thanksgiving, went to lunch with a friend, came back, did my second set of laps – that's when I heard a lot of coming and going over here – and then in the late afternoon, I made plans for a Christmas party my husband and I are giving.'

I was sure that Cara Embler's plans for a party would be somewhat more sophisticated and complex than mine would be. Probably the guests would be more sophisticated, too, if they were from her husband's workplace. Did you entertain cardiologists and hospital administrators the same way you did, oh, say realtors and librarians? The wine would have to be better for the hospital people . . .

'Aurora,' Teresa was saying none too gently. 'Are you listening to me?'

'No,' I said. I saw Bryan turn hastily to one side to conceal a smile. Maybe I had been a tad blunt. 'Sorry, I was drifting,' I murmured. 'What were you saying?'

'I was reminding Cara that she was next on the list.'

The day after Poppy had died.

Teresa was not Ms Sensitive, but this was callous, even for her. We all regarded her in a long moment of silence.

'What?' she said.

'The circumstances take most of the zest out of becoming an Uppity Woman,' Cara said finally, looking past Teresa's shoulder as she spoke. 'Give me a call to let me know the time and place. If you leave it on my machine, I'll write it down. I can't remember anything if you tell me away from a pad and pencil.'

'I know how that is,' Teresa agreed. 'I live by my Day Planner.' She was quite oblivious to her offense.

'Who on earth is that?' Cara asked. She, too, had caught a glimpse of Zachary Lee in his space suit.

Bryan took on the duty of explaining.

What a long day it had been. And there was more to come. But I roused myself to ask Cara if she'd seen Moosie.

'I'll keep an eye out for him,' she promised. 'He's a cute cat. I personally don't believe in declawing, but I know the rationale was that declawing would keep him from climbing the fence and wandering the neighborhood. I guess Poppy's heart was in the right place.'

'She didn't have Moosie declawed,' I told her. 'She adopted him like that. He was in the animal shelter. Just give me a call if you catch sight of him. I know John David would like to know Moosie is safe.' If John David had had a chance to think about the cat at all: In his place, I wasn't sure I would.

Cara excused herself and went back to her side of the fence.

Before she left, she glanced once more at Zachary Lee, who'd opened the sliding door to clean its runners.

'You know,' Teresa said in the hushed voice you reserve for passing along scandal, 'Stuart Embler used to drop by to see Poppy before he headed home, at least before Poppy had the baby.'

I hadn't heard Cara splashing in the water, and I hoped she was not standing right on the other side of the fence, listening. To my relief, I heard her dogs barking as she slid open her own glass patio door. They were welcoming her back into the house with rapture, it sounded like. Maybe I should get a dog, I thought. Then I thought about what Madeleine would do to a dog, and I canceled the idea.

Bryan had a certain amount of distaste in his face as he looked at his former wife, but he also looked interested. 'I wonder where Stuart was yesterday around eleven,' he said.

'That should be easy enough to find out. But I'd be extremely surprised if Stuart had anything to do with this. His affair with Poppy was stale, and he wouldn't care if there was a little scandal anyway. Cardiologists can call the shots. I mean, if you had a sick heart, and this guy was the best chance of your surviving, would you care if you heard he'd had an extramarital roll in the hay?'

I could see Teresa's point.

'By the way, Aurora, speaking of extramarital affairs,' Teresa began, and my eyes fixed on her. 'Rumor has it that you saw someone leaving this house yesterday as you pulled up.'

How the hell had such a story started making the rounds?

'I'll bet it was a man. Or the wife of some man she'd been carrying on with.' Teresa's face was avid.

'No,' I said, my voice as cold as a Tastee-Freez Coke slush. 'That is not true.'

'Well, my goodness, I'm sorry, I didn't realize I was hitting a nerve. We all figured you'd about got this solved.'

I don't think I blinked at all as I glared at her.

Bryan said, 'Isn't there somewhere you need to be, Teresa?'

She stopped dead, her mouth open.

'You've come by, you've given your condolences, and you've gotten some suggestions of ways the Uppities can help. I'm sure you have another errand or appointment?'

'I do need to stop by the store, and phone the committee members,' she said slowly. Her face was red. 'Good-bye, Aurora.'

Gosh, I just *loved* seeing Teresa upbraided. Not the most pleasant side of my character, I'm afraid. 'Good-bye,' I said politely and distantly, and Bryan stood as Teresa did, then opened the gate to the front yard for her.

'She can't help it, you know,' he said when he sat in the chair beside mine.

'I realize that she has many fine qualities.'

He raised one eyebrow.

'She runs the Uppity Women smooth as a whistle,' I told him. 'She's organized and focused, and we do a lot of good under her leadership.'

'I was married to her. I know just how organized and focused she can be.'

'You said you've been divorced for a year?' Was it tacky to mention that?

'She married Shorty Stanton about seven months ago.'

'He works at one of the banks, right?'

'He's the president of Southern Security,' Bryan said a little dryly.

'Oh.'

'Yes, big money.'

I forbore remarking that Bryan himself couldn't be hurting for a healthy cash flow, unless he had a secret vice like gambling or drugs.

'Tell me about the car.' His voice was quiet.

I stared at the crouching, dim figure of the crime-scene cleaner. He was working on the glass again now. I considered and discarded several responses.

'I didn't see any car,' I said very carefully. 'But I did find evidence that someone had been here before we got here.'

'You know who it was,' Bryan said.

I looked at him sideways. 'No wonder you have such a good reputation as a lawyer.'

'It's deserved, I promise you. Who was it?'

'I can't tell you that right now.'

'Do you care more about this person than about your sister-in-law?'

'Yes.'

That took him aback, but the lawyer rallied.

'You don't trust me?'

'I told you about the receipt,' I remarked mildly. 'And I'll tell you something else.'

He turned his hand palm up, meaning, Give.

'Someone's been in the house since yesterday.'

'This house?' He pointed at it, startled.

'Yes.'

'How do you know?'

'The upstairs curtains are closed. They were open yesterday when I was up there.'

Bryan stared at the curtains in the master bedroom as if they could tell him why they were pulled together. 'Maybe the police closed them last night, so no one could see what they were doing,' he suggested.

I shrugged. 'Maybe.'

Bryan seemed to give up. 'Let's go check it out. I believe the man is telling you he's finished.'

In fact, Zachary Lee had emerged from the house, unsuited, looking cheerful as ever. 'I've got the rug rolled up and in my van; here's a receipt,' he said. 'I'm going to take it back to the shop and work on it. Everything else is done. You'll need to call a regular housecleaning service to get everything else back to normal.'

I could feel that little frown of confusion contracting my brows. 'Excuse me?'

'The upstairs. I went up to clean up the fingerprint powder.'

'What about the upstairs?' I cast a sideways glance at Bryan.

'This wasn't a homicide during a burglary?'

'You had better show us what you mean,' Bryan said.

This time, I walked through every room of the ground floor, and it all looked normal. Upstairs, though, was a different story. The room that had received the most attention was the master bedroom. Everything was tossed around, as if a demented child had had a field day.

'It didn't look like this when you found the body?' Bryan asked, his eyes missing nothing.

'No, it looked like a home.' I couldn't think of anything else to say. 'Surely the police wouldn't do this?'

'They would take the bedding to check for evidence,' Bryan said. And they had. 'But they wouldn't do this.' Drawers were pulled out of the chest of drawers, the dressing table, the lingerie chest, the jewelry chest. Poppy's side of the small walk-in closet was demolished. Out-of-season shoes had been dumped from their neat stack of boxes, and a set of stacked cubes that had held sweaters had been disassembled and lay strewn on the floor.

This was horrible. I felt like Poppy had been violated all over again.

I told myself instantly that this was a dumb reaction. What I was seeing was just a rummage through her things, not nearly as bad as sinking a knife into her, for goodness sake! But the invasiveness of it . . . I thought of how much I would hate someone going through my personal stuff, and I had to sit down abruptly on the needlepoint-covered stool that was intended to occupy the kneehole of the dressing table.

Bryan did a big production number about how I was feeling – asking if he should call the paramedics (which horrified me considerably) and muttering various things about how terrible a shock I had sustained. He had called the police already, so I let him run on for a bit. Was he trying to impress me with his empathy, with his regard for me as a delicate southern flower? I was a pretty wilted blossom, if so.

I wished Robin were there. Then I slapped myself mentally. No point wishing for that. He was flirting with Janie.

Anger stiffened my spine once more.

Chapter Six

I was fit company for neither man nor beast.

It was already late afternoon, and I suggested to Bryan that we wait until the next morning to find the gas station that had issued the receipt. That way, I pointed out, probably the same attendant would be on duty – if you could talk about attendants being on duty at gas stations anymore, which was doubtful. I could tell that for about a half cent, Bryan would take the receipt and ask the questions all by himself. I tried to impress on him how dimly I would view such behavior.

I drove Bryan back to his office, then stopped by my mother's to check on the well-being of my extended family. Melinda and Avery were at their house, and Poppy's baby was with them, just as Melinda had predicted. John David was sitting in a morose heap in Mother's den. Across from him was Arthur Smith.

What was he doing? Obviously, he was still on the case, which I found incomprehensible. Granted, Lawrenceton is a smallish town, and the police force is probably pretty stretched, especially considering murders are not the norm in our town. But you would think, even in Lawrenceton, the chief of police would remove the deceased's former lover from the list of investigating officers in a homicide case. No one had whispered in his ear yet, I presumed.

'Can you think of any reason someone might have broken into your home?' Arthur was asking. 'Do you know of any particular hiding place your wife used, for important papers or—?' This was certainly a quick response to Bryan's phone call.

'No,' John David interrupted. 'No, Poppy had nothing to hide.'

My mother was standing at the kitchen counter, reading the heating instructions on the casserole Teresa had brought by that afternoon. I knew the writing at a glance. When John David made his amazing statement, my mother's eyebrows flew up, expressing exactly the same incredulity as mine did. If John David believed what he was saying, he was a fool. If he believed he was fooling anyone else about Poppy's true character, he was also a fool.

I drifted around the counter so I could stand across from my mother. She was, as always, perfectly groomed, but she looked weary and worried.

'The bad thing is,' she said in a low conversational tone, 'that Poppy was a lot of good things, too, but no one's thinking about that.'

'It does seem as though the, ah, negative side of her character is probably what got her killed,' I said. 'But I agree, Poppy had a lot that was good in her. She was intelligent, she was entertaining, she loved Chase – oh, did she love that baby – and she was willing to work hard on projects she believed in.' There were a lot of people with better reputations than Poppy's, but it would be hard to think of so much good to say about them, I realized.

'Have you had a falling-out with Robin?' Mother asked. The question was so abrupt and so out of character for her that I hesitated before answering.

'Yes,' I said. 'He didn't call me to tell me he'd gotten back early from his book tour, and he was flirting with Janie Spellman.'

'Flirting,' my mother said, her voice blank.

'Yes,' I replied, feeling my cheeks redden. 'Practically holding hands.'

'In the library?'

'Yes, in the library!'

'Where nothing could possibly happen, under the eyes of a dozen people.'

'But why would he do that?'

'Maybe Janie wanted to flirt a little. You're not the only woman in the world who finds Robin attractive, Roe. Maybe Robin felt like flirting back, just a little. Did he ask her out? Did he kiss her? Did he tell you he didn't want to see you any more?'

'No.'

'Did you give him a chance to talk to you about it?'

'No.'

'Have I miscounted the days, or did he not cut short his tour to get back to you early?'

'Yes.' I felt embarrassment creep up my cheeks in a red tide.

'Um, um, um.' My mother shook her head. 'That evil, evil man. He's been mistreating you so badly, I may have to slap him.'

'Okay, you made your point.'

'I'd have thought you would know the difference, after that one.' Mother nodded toward the den. She meant Arthur, not John David. Mother would never forgive Arthur for humiliating me so publicly. He could save ten kids from drowning and foil a dozen bank robberies, and she'd still loathe him. It was kind of nice, having someone that firmly on your side, no matter how mistaken she might be.

After I'd spoken to John and patted his hand and seen for myself that he was better today than yesterday, I left without speaking to John David or Arthur, who were still deep in conversation.

On the short drive home, I thought about what Poppy might have hidden. If it could have been in a shoe box, obviously it was something small. Would Poppy have blackmailed anyone? I thought not, even as disillusioned as I was about her proclivities. But something she had had in her keeping had scared the hell out of someone. Perhaps the searcher had found the item in the upstairs bedroom, perhaps not.

So, we had a mysterious gas station receipt, a murdered woman, a philandering lawyer, a philandering husband, a past lover or three, a searcher, and a detective who shouldn't be on the case at all.

I wasn't surprised at all to walk into my house and find my brother and Robin waiting for me. They turned almost-accusing eyes to watch me come into the room. They'd been watching football. What a surprise.

'Hello,' I said, keeping my voice cool. 'How long have you been back, Phillip?'

'About thirty minutes. Robin was waiting for you.'

'Out in the driveway?'

'Yes.' Phillip had clearly switched his allegiance, based on his thirty minutes of renewed acquaintance with Robin. 'In the cold.'

'Was I expecting you, Robin?' I sure didn't remember inviting him over. I made an effort to draw my righteous indignation back around me. Robin had a key, but I suppose he hadn't felt welcome to use it.

'Um, no. I was just hoping I could talk to you. I missed you.'

'Let's go in the office. Phillip, did you eat? Do you need anything?'

'Josh and his sister took me to a Pizza Hut,' he said. 'I'm stuffed. Robin, the Broncos are ahead by seven!'

'I'll be back,' Robin assured him. He glanced sideways at me and added, 'I think.'

We trailed down the little hall to the office, a wonderful room lined with bookshelves. Robin had been working over here quite a bit, since he had a neighbor working the four-to-midnight shift at Pan-Am Agra, and this neighbor got up at nine o'clock expressly to tune his truck.

And before I'd even moved into the house, right here on the rug, Robin and I had . . . I blocked the thought.

We sat in the two wing-backed chairs after Robin had pulled his around to face mine.

'Tell me what all this is about,' he said. He didn't look angry, or guilty. He looked determined.

I was too grown-up to keep hugging my grievance.

'Robin, I've been up to here—' I made a gesture across my throat '—with the infidelity of Poppy and John David. I hate cheating anyway, and the last two days have just been full of it. So when I saw Janie flirting with you, and you flirting back, I just got . . . very angry.' It still troubled me to think of the wave of unreasoning anger that had swamped me. When I stood back and looked at it from a distance, that huge rage just seemed . . . odd.

'Janie is a cute girl. But she's a girl, and she's ready to flirt with anyone. Being rude to Janie would be like being mean to a fuzzy puppy.'

I raised an eyebrow.

'All right, I flirted back.'

I raised the other eyebrow.

'You're a *woman*,' Robin said firmly. 'Janie's a girl. I'm way too old for Janie. I wouldn't know what to do with her even if I was interested.'

I had nothing left to raise, so I tried a skeptical sneer.

'Okay, I flirted back a lot.' Robin looked down at his big hands. 'When I go on tour, my ego inflates, and I was nominated for the Anthony, and I was thinking big thoughts about myself.'

I waited.

'But now I'm regrounded.' He looked up at me directly.

'You sure?'

'Yeah.'

'So what you're saying is . . .'

'I'm supposed to make a mission statement?'

'It would help.'

'I'm not planning on seeing anyone else.'

'Bryan Pascoe asked me out,' I said, though Bryan had actually just indicated that sometime in the future he wanted to ask me out. However, I couldn't think of a way to turn that into a concrete statement.

'Are you going to go?' Robin's face was all shut down. 'I don't know Bryan Pascoe. He might be the guy for you.'

I thought about that. 'He'd be more in the category of a fixer-upper,' I said. 'I think it might be safer to say that I only want to date you right now.'

Robin seemed bigger suddenly, as if he'd been holding himself in a smaller space than he normally occupied.

'I like your brother,' he said. 'He seems like a pretty independent young man.'

'He's definitely feeling his new manliness,' I said. I lowered my voice and told Robin about the two girls Phillip had hitched a ride with on the last leg of his journey, and the condoms I'd found in his wallet.

'Better he have them and use them than not have them and

need them,' Robin said wisely. 'Maybe he was just carrying them because he wanted to need them.'

I worked that through. It was an interesting idea. 'What I'm hoping is that he didn't buy them after the fact,' I admitted. 'I mean, maybe he had sex and enjoyed it and then thought, Gee, if I'm going to have some more, I better be prepared.'

'I'll try to find out, in a very manly way,' Robin said. 'If you have to work tomorrow, I'll take Phillip out to eat or over to my apartment or something.'

'Sounds good. I don't have to work, but I'm supposed to go to a gas station tomorrow with Bryan Pascoe.'

'An original first date,' Robin said.

'Not a date. A clue.' I told Robin about the receipt I'd found on the floor, and then I told him about what had happened to the upstairs of John David and Poppy's house.

'That's mysterious,' Robin said. 'The house wasn't broken into?'

'No, and that makes it even stranger. I unlocked the front door for the Scene Clean guy myself. The sliding glass door uses the same key. It was locked, too, or at least I guess it was. Zachary Lee just had to turn the latch inside and open it while he was cleaning. I never thought to check to see if it was locked to begin with. I never asked him, after he showed us the state of the upstairs.'

'So the patio door may have been unlocked all along.'

'Well, it might have been left unlocked by whoever rifled through the upstairs. I'm sure the police wouldn't have left the back door unlocked. If I were breaking in, I'd pick the back door. You wouldn't even have to show your face on Swanson Lane. You could creep through the Emblers' backyard, and Cara is on the phone in her home office half the time. You'd have to check to make sure she wasn't using the pool. Her husband's hardly ever home. You'd just have to make sure the dogs were shut up in the house.

'Or, if you didn't mind a higher risk of being seen, you could cross Poppy's front yard and enter the back by the patio gate to the side of the house. The point is, once you're in the backyard, the privacy fence is so high, you're practically invisible.'

'Didn't you say Dr Embler had spent time with Poppy?'

'That's what I heard.'

'But not recently.'

'You're saying that passions would have had time to cool?'

'I would think so. I mean, even if Cara had discovered her husband's little fling with Poppy, she had to know by now that it meant nothing, in terms of consequences in her own life.'

I felt that we'd left my brother by himself long enough, so we moved back to the family room, to find him asleep on the couch, with the game still blaring.

I managed to wake Phillip up enough to send him to his own room. He stumbled off, mumbling that he'd see me in the morning. Robin and I were left looking at each other.

'Would you like to stay the night?' I asked, just as Robin said, 'So, can I stay awhile?'

We laughed a little, but then he put his arms around me, and it wasn't time for laughing anymore.

Chapter Seven

Robin was sitting on the side of the bed, pulling the sleeves of his shirt back through the right way when I opened my eyes. I reached over and trailed my fingers down his long, bare back, making him shiver.

'Morning,' I said, my voice still hazy with sleep.

He turned and bent to kiss me.

'Morning, Roe.'

His hair looked like a haystack. He hadn't put on his glasses yet, and his eyes were blue and soft. He looked good enough to eat.

'Are you in a particular hurry?' I asked.

'Just wanted to get out of the way before your company wakes up,' he said.

Oh hell. I'd forgotten all about Phillip's presence in my house, to say nothing of the Wynns. I gave a big, windy sigh.

'I'll come get him about eleven-thirty, after I've worked a few hours, and take Phillip to lunch.' Robin stroked my hair back from my face. 'You know, tomorrow's Thanksgiving.'

'You're going to eat here, right?'

'We planned that, didn't we? Remember, my mother's flying in this afternoon?'

I pulled a pillow over my head. I didn't want to think about meeting Robin's mother for the first time on a national holiday, when food was the main focus of the day. I wasn't that confident in my cooking.

I'd just have to suck it up and act like a woman.

'She wasn't planning on flying in and cooking, I hope?' I asked, just to make sure, not wanting to start out beholden to the woman.

'No, I told her I had made plans for us.' Robin looked hopeful. 'What can I bring?'

I laughed and pulled the pillow away. 'Oh, okay, I guess I'm up to it. Let me think. I picked up a turkey breast at the store the other day, thank God. I thought a whole turkey would be too much for just us. So that leaves sweet potatoes, peas, rolls, and cranberry sauce. And dessert.'

'I can get rolls and the peas,' Robin offered helpfully. 'And I can bring some wine.'

'That's good. Okay, I'll get the sweet potatoes and fix them, and the cranberries, and I'll make a pie or two. That'll work out.'

'What about your mother and her family?'

'I don't know what on earth they're going to do. I think Melissa and Avery are going to Melissa's parents, and I guess they'll take their kids and the baby with them. John David will probably go to my mother's, whatever she's up to doing. They have enough food there to last them through the winter, I think.' When I'd been at the house this afternoon, the refrigerator had been full to overflowing.

'You'd better check. Maybe your folks could come over here for a glass of wine after dinner?'

'You want my mother to meet your mother,' I said, suddenly getting his drift.

'Yes.'

I couldn't think of a thing to say. 'Oh. Okay.' I looked anywhere but at Robin. 'Um, how long is your mom staying?'

'Until Monday,' he said. 'I'll bet by then she'll be ready to leave. In fact, she'll be anxious.'

'I'm glad she's got other children besides you,' I said, laughing.

'She loves all of us, but she's most comfortable in her own home with her dogs, and her buddies,' he said.

A plaintive meow outside the door told me that Madeleine was waiting for her breakfast. She wasn't used to the bedroom door being closed.

'I have to go feed the Mongol horde,' I said, making myself get up from the warm bed and pull on a bathrobe. It was an effort, because I wasn't feeling so great. An overload of emotion? I was a little achy, a little tired.

'I'll call you later today,' he said. 'After I feed Phillip and plumb his darkest depths, I'll go get my mother at the airport. Then we'll talk about tomorrow.'

'Sounds good,' I said, thinking of all the things I had to do today. I had to run the strange errand with Bryan Pascoe. I was supposed to work for a few hours. I had to go to the grocery store again. I wanted to spend some brain time thinking of what could have been hidden in Poppy's closet, something so valuable that it was worth breaking into the murdered woman's house before it had even been cleaned of her blood.

And, most of all, I needed to talk to Lizanne, who had been outside Poppy's house the day she was killed.

Melinda and I had kept silent about Lizanne's presence at Poppy's that day, and we'd struggled with our decision for all of thirty seconds. Both of us believed that there was simply no chance at all that Lizanne had stabbed Poppy. But we did need to talk to her about why she'd been there. I guess I had a tiny, tiny sliver of doubt that needed to be erased by hearing Lizanne tell me, in person, what had happened that day.

I called Melinda to ask her to go with me. She was very busy, as you can imagine, but she agreed to go. She wanted to hear what Lizanne had to say as much as I did.

The yard had not been put to bed for winter at the sprawling ranch Cartland had bought when his practice had begun flourishing. The flower beds needed weeding and more mulch, and the grass hadn't gotten its final mowing. Someone had given up just a little too soon. A fenced-in area was strewn with little kids' toys, bright plastics that would crack in the coming cold. But the smell of corn bread rolled out of the back door when Lizanne answered our knock.

'Come in,' Lizanne said placidly, her arms full of baby. 'Let me just pop Brandon in his playpen, and Davis is already taking a nap. Then I can get the corn bread out of the oven, and we can talk.'

Melinda and I came in cautiously; I thought we were both

taken aback by Lizanne's casual air. She had to know why we were there.

Brandon was deposited in his playpen with absolutely no fuss, and he sat up and watched with interest as his mother, still one of the most beautiful women I'd ever known, despite having popped out two babies in almost instant succession, slid a pan of corn bread out of the oven and set it on top to cool.

'For the dressing,' Lizanne explained, poking it with a finger to test its doneness. I figured that might be a sign of nerves; she certainly didn't need to tell us that. In a bassinet against the wall, Davis gave a little sound and went back to sleep.

'Do you fix yours in a separate pan or in the bird?' Melinda was serious when she asked this burning question. Melinda had been on the quest for the perfect dressing for the past two years.

'Both. There isn't enough, if you just stuff the turkey. And I put some sausage in.'

Melinda's eyes lighted up with interest, and she began to talk apples, oysters, and chestnuts. They might have been sitting there for an hour, talking food, if I hadn't interrupted.

'Listen, Lizanne, we found the straps.'

'Oh.' She looked quite unsurprised. 'Why didn't you give them to the police? You should have.'

'What were you doing there?'

'Well, I was getting tired of Bubba going out at night and making these silly excuses,' Lizanne said. She would never call her husband Cartland, not in a million years.

'So, you confronted Poppy?'

'I was ready to.' I watched Lizanne's hands, long and thin, clench into fists. 'I didn't get the chance. She never came to the door. And the kids got hungry, and they started crying. I couldn't stand to have anything of hers, so I took the pacifier straps and threw them down in the driveway so she'd know what I thought of her. And I came on home.'

'What were you going to say to her if she'd come to the door?' I asked out of sheer curiosity.

'I was going to remind her that since, at Bubba's request, I quit my job after we got married, he is the boys' and my sole support. I was going to point out to her that there are better fish in the sea than Bubba.'

Melinda and I exchanged glances. 'What do you mean?' Melinda asked. Lizanne was measuring sugar into water to make cranberry sauce.

'Poppy was more serious about Bubba than she was about the other men,' Lizanne said after a long pause. 'I don't think she wanted to divorce John David and marry Bubba, but I don't think she'd completely dismissed the idea, either. But she might have just been stringing him along. I don't understand people like that.' Lizanne turned to us, a half-cup measure in her hand. Her face was white and disturbed.

'She just didn't seem to care whom she hurt. She would have what she wanted, and everyone else could just go to hell.'

Had Poppy really been that careless, that conscienceless? I had never crossed Poppy. I had never had anything she wanted. Melinda, I noticed, did not look shocked at all.

I was dismayed and a little mortified by my lack of acuity.

'So you just pulled up to the house . . .' I said, hoping to prod her into a more complete account of her actions.

Lizanne poured a whole bag of cranberries into the pot. She was going to have a lot of sauce, and a lot of dressing, too. I wondered how much company she was having. It reminded me that I needed to get home and start working in my own kitchen.

Lizanne, having given the berries a stir, turned back to face us. 'You all want a drink of something?' she asked politely.

'No thanks,' we said in chorus. She laughed, and we all relaxed a little.

'I pulled up to the house, and the boys were in their car seats in the back of the minivan,' she said. 'I knew Bubba was going to be giving a speech that day, out of town, so there wouldn't be any danger of him driving by and seeing me. John David would be at work. I figured it would be a good time to talk to Poppy. I just wanted to let her know that I knew all about . . . them, and that I wasn't going to divorce Bubba without as much stink as I could raise.' Lizanne said this with absolute sincerity. 'I know Bubba thinks I'm dumb, and I am about some things.' And you could tell she didn't care. 'But I know how it'd look in the papers. Mother of twins, orphan of murdered parents, abandoned by her lawyer husband for another woman. And you know what else?'

A little stunned, Melinda and I shook our heads.

'The second I learned about this affair, I started taking the kids to church every single Sunday. I wasn't so consistent before, but I haven't missed a sermon in five months. Wednesday nights, too. And Bubba hasn't gone with me twice, I bet.'

Lizanne was going to use God as a character witness.

'*And* I go to the same Sunday school class as Terry McCloud.' Terry was another attorney in Lawrenceton. He was my mother's lawyer, so he would be conservatively excellent. 'I speak to Terry every Sunday. I make a point of it.'

By this time, I was gaping at the woman I'd thought I'd known. I didn't know if I admired her or if I was horrified. I didn't dare look over at Melinda.

'But I don't really want to get a divorce,' Lizanne explained, never stopping her little tasks around the stove and sink. 'I get along okay with Bubba, and we have everything we need. I'd have to go back to work if we got divorced, and I like being home with the boys.' She beamed over at Brandon, who smiled back. He seemed to have inherited his mother's placid nature. 'So I went to see Poppy, to try to talk some sense into her. I knew Poppy was at home because her car was in the garage. But she never came to the door.' Lizanne blew on a spoonful of cranberry sauce, then held it away to examine the color and consistency. 'After a minute, I went over to the fence, thinking I'd go through the gate and knock on the sliding glass door on the patio.'

'And did you go into the backyard?' I asked, sitting on the edge of the kitchen chair.

'Oh, no,' Lizanne said, her voice once more serene. 'There was already someone there, so I went back to the car.'

'There was someone there,' I repeated.

'Yes, I could hear them talking.'

'Them?' Melinda said in a croak.

'Yes, them. Poppy and someone else.'

'Who was it?' I felt as if the air in the kitchen were vibrating.

'Oh. I don't know. The radio was on, so I couldn't hear very well, but I could hear two voices, and the louder one was Poppy's.'

'What did you do?'

'I went back and sat in the car. After about ten minutes, I went and knocked on the door again. But she still didn't come. So after a little bit longer, I threw the straps out of the van and drove away.' Lizanne turned back to the stove and stirred.

'You heard her killer,' Melinda said.

'What?'

'You heard the voice of the person who killed Poppy,' I said.

'Oh, that's . . .' On the verge of saying 'ridiculous', Lizanne stopped speaking, stopped moving. Her lips lost their color.

'I could have saved her,' Lizanne said finally. 'I could have saved her life, and instead I went back to the van and sat.'

'Or,' I said, not liking the way her color had changed, 'you could have gotten killed right along with her, and your children would have been left out in the van all by their lonesome selves.'

Lizanne sat down across the table from us. She looked positively punchy with shock.

'Oh,' she said, and that was all, but it spoke volumes.

I'd been sure that Lizanne wasn't as hard-hearted as she'd been letting on, and I was right. But she'd felt better when she'd acted tough.

'Could you make out who it was?' I asked after a pause to let Lizanne gather herself.

'No, I was so wrought up, and the radio was playing, and I was so angry . . .'

'Could you tell if the voice was a man's or a woman's?'

Lizanne's large dark eyes focused on me. 'Surely it must have been a man's?'

'Look at how angry you were,' I said. 'Do you think you were the only angry woman?'

'No, I reckon not,' she said. 'I assumed at the time it was a man's voice. Poppy's radio was on so loud – she was listening to NPR, like my daddy used to. Remember, Roe?'

Truthfully, I didn't remember what radio station Lizanne's dad had listened to, though I remembered Arnie with great fondness. But I nodded anyway.

'So, I guess I'll have to go to the police,' she said after a moment. 'I mean, if I really did hear . . .'

'You ought to,' Melinda said, trying to make her voice gentle. Davis squawked, and Lizanne got up and handed him the pacifier that had fallen from his mouth. He resumed sucking and fell back to sleep. Brandon watched us as if we were performing in a soap opera. To my eyes, both children looked like little Bubbas. If Lizanne did divorce Cartland Sewell, his face was still going to be right in front of her for the next sixteen-plus years.

'I guess I wouldn't be telling anyone anything they didn't already know,' Lizanne said. I thought she was backing out of going to the police, but finally I decided she was thinking of having to tell the police that her husband was cheating on her. 'The way things spread in a small town. Why did Bubba think he was fooling anyone?'

There were probably people in Lawrenceton who hadn't known that Cartland Sewell and Poppy Queensland had been having an affair (me, for example). But while I told myself that I enjoyed juicy gossip as much as the next person, this wasn't entirely true. Illnesses, inheritances, land transactions, job promotions – I was interested in all these bits of information. But sexual misdeeds, no, I didn't want to hear about them. I only knew the cast of John David's couch because Melinda had told me one afternoon when we were driving to Atlanta to shop, and I couldn't get away.

'Do you want Arthur to come here?' I asked, trying to sound offhand.

'That would be good. I have a lot of cooking to do; plus, I don't want to take the boys down to the police station,' Lizanne said. She brightened considerably. 'Oh, do you think he would?'

'Yes, I bet so,' I said. Melinda handed me the phone, and I placed the call. Arthur didn't sound very glad to hear from me, which I could understand. I explained as neutrally as I could.

As I expected, he was angry with me. 'You knew all along that Lizanne had been there that day,' he said unequivocally. After all, that was the absolute truth.

'Well, we suspected.' I was trying to sound mild and intractable, but that's hard to pull off. I just sounded stubborn.

'You're lucky I don't put you both in jail for obstructing an investigation.'

Melinda was leaning close enough to hear that, and she looked at me with alarm written large in her brown eyes. I shook my head. No way was Arthur going to do anything like that. 'On the other hand,' I said, still trying for mild, 'we happen to be over at Lizanne's right now, and we happen to know she has some information for you.'

'Maybe I'll just arrest her,' Arthur said. 'She had plenty of reason to kill Poppy.'

'Well, if she loved her husband, that would be so. But that's not the case,' I snapped. I had run out of mild. 'Arthur Smith, you know a woman with two babies in her van is not going to go in and stab someone to death!'

'Still waters run deep,' Arthur said portentously.

'Still waters, my round rear end.' Now I was sounding like a real Uppity Woman. But as I thought twice, I looked at Lizanne's placid and beautiful face, and read nothing there but polite interest in the outcome of my conference with the detective. Maybe Lizanne was deep water, and maybe she was only a shallow, still, pond. Either way, she was my friend.

'Are you coming?' I tried to sound more moderate.

He sighed, a deep and unhappy exhalation. 'Yes, I am. But I'm going to pretend she called me herself, instead of you, and I want you and Melinda gone by the time I get there.'

'Okay,' I said unhappily. 'Let's try to make it a trade-off.' I didn't want Lizanne to be alone for very long at all. She was having a tough time, and being alone might sap her good resolution to come clean.

'I'm bringing Trumble with me,' he said, and for a second I drew a blank. Then I remembered that was the name of the detective who'd interviewed me. 'I'm leaving here in five minutes.'

So Melinda and I talked babies with Lizanne for the next ten minutes. That was easy for Melinda, but not for me. I've never had a baby, and I never will. The elderly OB-GYN I'd consulted in Atlanta had been pretty clear that the chances of me conceiving were infinitesimal. I have a tilted womb (charming, huh?) and I don't always produce eggs, which makes me feel like an inferior chicken.

I suppressed a familiar ache and listened with a smile to their swapped stories about teething, walking, crawling, and sleeping patterns. This is the small talk of women of a certain age, and not only was I getting past that age; I'd never learned the language.

I quit feeling sorry for myself when I passed Arthur and Cathy Trumble on the sidewalk to Lizanne's front door, and reflected on how much I had to do between now and tomorrow. It was incredibly fortunate that I had to work only three hours today, and the library would be closed tomorrow and through the weekend for the Thanksgiving holiday.

When I pulled up to Melinda's house, she persuaded me to come in for a minute and talk to John David. He didn't want to go back to the house he'd shared with Poppy, cleaned or not, and he was taking very little care of his son. Melinda hadn't spoken to him about it yet, but she was going to, she told me. 'It's not that I don't care for the little guy; he's cute as he can be,' she said, guilt written large on her face. 'I just feel like I have enough to do.'

'Of course,' I agreed promptly, because to do less would have been insulting. I realized that no one had suggested that I should take Chase. And I realized that I was relieved. A couple of years before, I'd had the care of a baby, with absolutely no preparation or warning. Going into it cold was simply terrifying. 'John David should be able to take care of his own son, especially if he hires a nanny,' I said cautiously.

'Avery could cope with the situation,' Melinda said. 'He took as much care of Marcy as I did, when he was home . . . which wasn't as much as I was, of course. And he was so excited when Charles was born!' Melinda's face was transformed by a huge smile. 'Avery's a good dad,' she said, wrapping up a whole bundle of memories.

'I guess John David got a big bundle of charm but none of the moral fiber,' I said.

She considered. 'I think he likes to do the right thing, as long as it's not too much trouble.'

That summed up John David pretty accurately. But maybe we both would be proved wrong.

Melinda seemed relieved to get out at her own home, where she could follow her own normal round of activities. She'd deposited the children at Mother's Day Out at the Methodist church so she could finalize the preparations for driving to her parents' home for Thanksgiving, and she told me she was determined to go no matter what happened. 'It's been awful and tense the past few days,' she said. I couldn't argue with that. 'We don't know when the funeral will be, because Poppy's body hasn't been released yet, and this is a good time to get away, at least for a day. The kids need some downtime.' I wasn't sure who needed it more, but obviously Melinda was looking forward to seeing her family, and I wished her a happy day before leaving to put in my hours at the library.

It was absolutely dead at work. A few patrons dashed in to return books, and one or two checked out audio-books for the long drives to holiday destinations. But no one was browsing, and precious few were even using the computers. I had no compunction at all about leaving a little early for my appointment with Bryan Pascoe.

Bryan drove a Cadillac, which surprised me. He was wearing a very nice suit, and he looked as though he'd gotten a haircut. When he held the car door open for me, I smelled his cologne. It was something classic and masculine, like Old Spice – another surprise. I would have predicted a Mustang convertible, a Calvin

Klein cologne, and bikini underwear. I couldn't ask him about that, but I amused myself on our ride to the service station named on the receipt by trying to imagine a conversation in which that question would occur naturally.

'I understand that Cartland Sewell has a cast-iron alibi,' he said out of the blue. Bryan sounded as if that were a bad thing, and since he was representing John David, I guess it was. The more viable suspects, the better, particularly for my brother-in-law.

'I'm glad for Lizanne's sake,' I said. I know this was dumb of me, but I hadn't realized I ought to tell Bryan what had happened with Lizanne the day of Poppy's murder. Now I told him in as few words as possible. After questioning me closely about the probable time of all the events Lizanne had described, the lawyer lapsed back into a silence that I chose to characterize as thoughtful.

The Cadillac was so comfortable and the heat so effective, I was nearly drowsy by the time we reached the Grabbit Kwik. Bryan came around the car to open my door just as I was about to open it myself, so I held still and let him. This world is so devoid of courtesy, I never mind receiving a little, even if it's misplaced.

He offered me his hand, and I took that, too. I was wearing off-white pants, a fuzzy blue sweater, and blue suede moccasins, so I didn't have to worry about getting out of the car modestly. He gave a little pull, and up I popped, just like a cork.

The outside of the Grabbit Kwik was like any other convenience store/gas station along any highway. Grabbits are all painted a bright green, and this one had all its tawdry Christmas regalia in place. It had probably been up since the Halloween ghosts and pumpkins had come down. The concrete outside the door was dirty, but the glass doors were gleaming. We were the only customers at the moment, which I chose to regard as a good sign.

Inside, everything was as you'd expect, too – the racks of junk food and the refrigerated cases of drinks, the raised counter, the woman in the red smock behind the cash register. Her hair was a construction of elaborate and rigid ringlets, and she was generously round. Her heavily lined eyes looked like raisins sunk in gingerbread dough.

'Can I help you folks?' she asked cheerfully. On a tiny television behind her, a talk show was in progress.

Bryan produced a card immediately and introduced himself. She told him her name was Emma McKibbon and that she'd worked there two years. Her eyes flicked over to me curiously, but Bryan didn't include me in this dialogue. He'd been so absolutely correct and polite up to now; it made me as curious as Emma apparently was. But there must be a reason, so I kept quiet.

The woman's face looked really familiar, though, and I kept examining her, hoping I'd make the connection.

Bryan was asking her if there was any way she could remember a particular customer who'd come by two days before, and Emma confirmed that she'd been right there behind the counter on Monday. But Emma was wary of Bryan, for whatever reason – maybe just because he was an affluent white male. Watching her face seal itself off, I had a sinking feeling that any information we could have gathered was being chucked down a well inside the clerk.

'We were pretty busy that morning, same as always on Monday,' she said grudgingly. 'Let me see the receipt, but I ain't holding out much hope.'

I pulled the receipt out of my pocket and handed it to her. As our eyes met, a little *click* sounded in my ears. 'Emma!' I said. 'You were three years behind me in high school, right?'

'I sure was,' she said, relieved to track down her own elusive memory. 'I'm Jane's sister – Jane Pocket she was then.'

'Oh, sure. How is Jane?'

'Well, she's gotten married twice now, and she has four kids in school and another one on the way. I have two myself. I married Dante McKibbon right after we graduated. My girls – one's in high school, and the other's in junior high.'

'Oh, how nice,' I said, smiling as brightly as I could.

'Now, you still live in town, don't you? I'm sure I saw you at the store last month.'

'I do. I have a house over on McBride.'

'You married?'

A black pit opened abruptly, right in front of me, and I took a deep breath, gathered my composure, and stepped right over it. 'I'm a widow,' I said, maintaining my smile.

'Oh, too bad! You got any babies?'

'No, I'm all on my lonesome,' I said.

Emma obviously regarded this as the worst of all possible situations and cast around in her brain desperately for something upbeat to say to me. 'Well, you look great,' she told me. 'You don't look a day older than you did when you graduated. Those kids'll put the years on you, for sure.'

Bryan opened his mouth, but I got in there first. I knew what I was doing now. 'You remember my mom?' I asked. Emma nodded. No one forgot my mother. 'She married John Queensland, John David's dad? I know you remember John David.' He would be a little younger than Emma, but he'd had a lot of success on the football field, and that would have made his name more familiar.

'Oh, sure,' Emma said, relieved to be on a different topic. 'That John David, he speaks every time he comes in here.'

'Oh, he gets his gas here?' I leaned on the counter, as if I had all the time in the world.

'Sometimes,' she said. 'He was in here the other morning, the morning you were asking about, unless I'm real confused. But I think it was early, not at the time on this receipt. This says ten-twenty-two, and he always comes in before eight, on his way to Atlanta.'

'You remember Bubba?'

'Which one?' she said with a big laugh, and I had to laugh right along with her. 'You mean the big black Bubba who played center on the football team, or the Chinese Bubba who was so smart, or that Bubba who's a lawyer in town?'

'Lawyer Bubba.'

'He comes in here, too, but not so often,' she said, thinking back. 'He's always in a hurry, don't talk to me.'

'You remember Poppy?'

'Yeah, I hear she's dead.'

'Yeah. She married John David.'

'Yeah, after they fought all through high school. Were you in the cafeteria that day she slapped him upside the head?'

'I had already graduated, but I heard about it.'

'She didn't hold back none, either. She let him have it. Maybe that's why somebody killed her, she mighta whomped on them like that.'

'Her mom and dad are here,' I said.

'Yeah, her dad is that preacher,' Emma said. 'My mama used to clean house for them. I was over to see Mama the other day when the radio said that about Poppy. My mama said, "Like father, like daughter, I guess".'

'Oh my gosh,' I said, 'did he make a pass at your mother?' I am sure I looked as disgusted as I felt. Somehow, you're always a child when you hear about the peccadilloes of those who represented authority to you when you were young.

Emma looked sardonic. 'He don't like my skin tone,' she said, as if adding another mark against Marvin Wynn's tally of bad taste. 'But all those women who came to him for counseling, you can bet a bunch of them got more than prayers. Especially the really young ones.'

'Ew,' I said, and Emma laughed.

'I like a man with more meat to him than that,' she said. 'His wife is like that, too, all thin and bony. Now *she* was in here Monday around the right time, and I was surprised, because I hadn't seen that woman in a coon's age. Did they move back into town?'

I leaned more heavily against the counter, suddenly weak. Bingo. What the hell had Sandy Wynn been doing anywhere in the vicinity? I stuffed that thought away for later examination. I hoped that no one else would come in, since we were on such a roll. 'Well, I won't take up too much more of your time. I know you're at work. I don't know if you remember this, but I have a brother.'

She looked puzzled.

'He's a half brother. You may not recall that my mom was divorced when I was pretty young?'

'I knew something happened, since he wasn't around anymore.'

'Yeah, well, my dad remarried, so I have this brother, Phillip, who lives in California. He just hitchhiked over here to see me, and he met these girls along the way.'

'I can't believe he got here alive,' Emma said frankly.

'Me either. It was dumb, but he's a kid.' I shrugged. 'Anyway, he may have been here that morning, Monday morning. The car he was in stopped here for gas. It would have been my brother – he's about as tall as this lawyer here – and two girls, both older than he is.' I dredged my memory. 'He says they were in a green Impala.' Though Phillip had told me he'd caught a bus into Lawrenceton, I thought it would be unfair of me not to check on him, too.

'Can't remember,' Emma said after she'd turned it over in her head. 'So many kids, and if they're that young and white, I don't know 'em, so I just don't recall.'

'Thanks for taking the time to help,' I said. 'I enjoyed talking to you. You tell Jane I said hello, okay? And Dante.'

'Sure will,' Emma said. She smiled, but she also looked at me as though she was sorry for me.

Well, I just had to swallow that. I kept my smile steady, and Bryan and I left the store after he'd asked me if I wanted a cup of coffee, then bought me one and paid for it.

He handed me into the car as ceremoniously as he'd gotten me out of it, and I found that was a tiny bit tiresome. But I was glad to sink back into the leather seat and feel the heat blowing around me as we started back to town.

'That was a stroke of luck.' I was thinking of Emma's face as it was now, trying to picture the way it had been in our high school days. I was thanking my lucky stars I'd remembered the woman, since she was a few years younger. In high school, that makes a big difference.

'That was very smooth,' Bryan said, interrupting what I suddenly realized had been a long silence.

'Smooth? What?'

'Your questioning. Are you sure you don't want to be a lawyer? Or maybe join the police force?'

'I'm sure,' I said, smiling. He'd sounded almost miffed, but I was going to ignore that. I had a feeling Bryan was unhappy because his own questioning had proved unproductive. 'If you know someone, it's just easier to ask the right questions.'

'So. Mrs Wynn was there, Bubba may have been, although probably not, John David was there earlier, and she couldn't remember your brother,' Bryan summarized.

'That's about it.'

'Sandy Wynn.' He shook his head, looking as stunned as I felt.

'Yes. She's so – well, she seemed so devastated when they came to my house Monday night. I could have sworn all that grief was genuine.'

'But it's hard to understand how she could have just skipped telling the police she'd been in the area that morning.'

'Yes, of course. Well, maybe Emma made a mistake.' I'd heard older women complain before that young people seemed to regard them as interchangeable. Maybe Emma had seen another thin, fit older woman and identified her mentally as Poppy's mom, after she'd heard Poppy had been killed. That would be natural. But Emma had sounded so certain, and she had struck me as a good observer. And after all, *someone* had dropped that receipt on my floor.

'What are you going to do about Mrs Wynn?' I asked. 'Will you talk to her yourself, or will you sic Arthur on her?'

Bryan looked gloomy. 'I should tell the police,' he said after a thoughtful pause. 'I wonder if she was the visitor Poppy was expecting, the reason she didn't ride to Uppity Women with you.'

'Mrs Wynn's phone records would show if she'd phoned Poppy,' I said hesitantly. 'Would Poppy's phone record show incoming calls as well as outgoing? Can you look at those?'

'After the police have . . . if they arrest John David, I can. Other than that, I haven't any legal right to see them. They're John David's records, too. He could request them, give me permission . . . I'll think about it.'

We were silent during the rest of the drive. I guess both of us had plenty to think about. But I don't think we were pondering the same things.

Chapter Eight

By the time I got back to my house, Phillip was home and more than willing to help me unload the groceries – so he could find out what I'd gotten that he wanted to eat. I'd seen about half the people I knew dashing frantically through the grocery store, and all of them looked as scatterbrained as I felt, but I hadn't been so frantic that I'd forgotten to buy some snack stuff.

I told Phillip he was going to help me cook, and he stared longingly at the television before he agreed.

'How was your lunch with Robin?' I asked.

'We had ham sandwiches,' Phillip said, which was not exactly the information I was after. 'He's pretty cool,' Phillip added almost grudgingly after I'd put away the contents of one bag. 'We had a long talk about stuff. The only dumb thing about him is his name.'

'I'm glad you two are getting along,' I said. I was very curious to hear Robin's account of their conversation.

'You gonna marry him?'

It would be beyond coy to pretend I'd never thought of it. 'If he asks me, I'll think about it,' I said.

'You could ask him.'

Hmmm. 'No,' I said. 'I just don't think I could do that.' Though I was a raving liberal compared to 50 percent of the people I knew in Lawrenceton, I knew asking Robin to marry me was way beyond my possibility level, even though I was now an Uppity Woman.

'Chicken,' Phillip said fondly.

'Yep,' I said. 'That's me. Oh, by the way, I found a gas receipt on the floor Monday night. Did your friend stop for gas on her way into Lawrenceton?'

His face turned red just at the mention. 'No,' he said. 'We stopped for gas in Rome. Remember, I took a bus into Lawrenceton.'

Phillip had no reason to lie, and he'd never known Poppy. I had enough confirmation to drop him from my list. Though Emma had narrowed the list down, I needed to talk to the other people who might have dropped the receipt. I wanted to hear their stories with my own ears.

Opening the refrigerator, I poked the turkey breast with an anxious finger. It was close to being thawed. I got the package of ready-made piecrust out so it could be reaching room temperature, then took the pecans out of the freezer for the pecan pie. I handed my little brother a recipe for pumpkin pie and a can of pumpkin. 'Put all of this stuff in there,' I said. I got everything required out of the cabinet and put it in a clump on the counter. I pulled out my little electric mixer and a mixing bowl and set them on the counter by his stuff. 'There you go,' I said briskly. I turned on both of my ovens, yanked two pie plates out of the cabinet, and patted the piecrusts into place. Then I threw together the pecan pie.

Phillip worked quite a bit slower, but once he found out where the measuring spoons were and so on, he did a creditable job of preparing the pumpkin filling.

Since Robin's mom was coming, I felt obliged to follow Lizanne's example in making my own cranberry sauce, but that's the easiest thing in the world, and I got that ready while the pies were baking. Phillip ran the vacuum for me while I cooked the sweet potatoes and put them through the food processor for the sweet potato casserole, and I decided after that was done, we could rest. Every dish went into the dishwasher, I started it running, and then Phillip and I watched a stupid game show on television. We competed with each other to see who could shout out the answer the fastest, and in general we had a silly good time.

I called out for Chinese – we considered ourselves on the cutting edge, in Lawrenceton, having a Chinese restaurant that delivered – and though it was late in the evening to be eating, I was feeling relaxed, since the house looked good, I'd gotten a head start on the cooking, and, most of all, my brother just couldn't be involved in any way in Poppy's death.

Tomorrow, I would meet Robin's mother, and while I was a bit anxious about that, I figured since Robin spoke so lovingly of her, she couldn't be too formidable . . . And after all, I'd been a grown woman, married and widowed, for many years now.

Just when I was feeling fairly saturated with satisfaction, the phone rang. I reached over to the table by my chair, gestured to Phillip to turn down the volume on the television, and answered it.

'Aurora,' Mother said.

'Hi, Mother. How are things at your house?'

'John is doing fairly well,' she said, giving me the most important news first. 'John David hasn't been arrested, thank God. Melinda called. He was over at her house, and he announced he was taking the baby and they were spending the night in a motel. He said he felt like he'd been enough trouble to people and that he should spend some time with his son.'

I held the phone away and gaped at it. Would wonders never cease? 'That's amazing,' I said, finally realizing I had to say something.

'Yes,' she said a little dryly. 'I thought so, too.'

'Can you and John come over tomorrow to have a glass of wine with Phillip and Robin and Robin's mother?'

'His mother? His mother's in town?' Mother was shocked out of her weariness. 'Oh my Lord, you should have told me!'

'Yes, she's over at his apartment now. She's coming to Thanksgiving here tomorrow.' I knew Mother had too much on her shoulders right now, but it was good to hear her sounding more like her normal self. 'What about you and John? If you want to come here to eat, I'll have plenty. Did John David tell you any plans he might have? Should I invite him?' Three extra adults would be stretching it, but I could manage. I had assumed that John David would be staying with John and my mother and that they'd be eating together, though celebrating would be impossible.

'Of course John and I will come over for a glass of wine, and to meet Robin's mother. But I don't think we'd be exactly up to a festive meal. I'm feeding us out of the refrigerator tomorrow, since I just couldn't work up the energy for anything else. I think we have enough food here to last us for two weeks, and we actually have a smoked turkey breast and a ham. John David is coming over here. What time would you like us to drop by?'

I had planned to serve the holiday meal at one, so we settled on three o'clock. I told mother I'd call John David at his motel and at least invite him to come eat (no matter how much I secretly hoped he would decline). I remembered one more question for my mother before I hung up.

'Has John David heard from the police about when he's going to get Poppy's body back to bury?'

'It seems as though there's a backlog in Atlanta, so it won't be until Monday at the earliest.'

'Oh no.' Though in a way it was a relief that Poppy's funeral wouldn't be within the next couple of days, I didn't want to think about that backlog.

'I'm so glad the Wynns decided to go back home,' Mother continued. 'I know they had things to take care of, because they left to come over here in such a hurry. It'll be much better if they just come back when the funeral's settled. I think they assumed they'd be making the arrangements, and it took them aback when John David told them what he was going to do.'

'The Wynns are leaving? Where are they now?' I had actually forgotten about the Wynns, and to my shame, my Thanksgiving plans had never included them. I carried the cordless phone over to the door of the room the Wynns had been using and glanced inside. Their things were still there. Hmm.

'Why, I don't know.' Mother sounded surprised. 'Aren't they – they haven't come to your house and gotten their bags?'

'No,' I said, anxiety making my voice sharp. 'I haven't seen them since last night.'

'I talked to them about four today,' Mother said, 'and they told me they were leaving. Where do you suppose they could be?'

'I don't know.' I had a shameful, petulant moment of wishing someone would just do the predictable thing. I don't deal well with prolonged upheaval. 'Do they have any good friends left in town?'

'You know, they didn't have a lot even when they lived here.'

That was true, though I'd never posed it to myself that way. The Wynns, tall and thin and aggressively healthy, bright and articulate, had never been the most popular ministerial couple in town. The church youth group had been popular, though, because Marvin Wynn, awkward with his own belated child, was a whiz with other people's children.

I sighed, trying to aim it away from the phone. All I wanted to do was go to bed. But I had to track down my guests, and I had to relieve my mother of this anxiety.

'I'll call around a little,' I said. 'I'll get back to you. Maybe they're with John David, playing with the baby. Which motel?'

I called the Lawrenceton Best Western, and John David was in.

'Poppy's folks didn't leave our key with you?' John David sounded tired, and numb. I could hear the baby crying in the background. 'They wanted to get some family heirloom to take back to their house with them – something of Sandy's mother's. I told them I had no idea where it was but said they were welcome to go over there and look. They were supposed to leave my house key with you.'

'How long ago was that?'

'Hours. I thought they were long gone back home.'

'I guess I'll go over there and check,' I said. It was the last thing in the world I wanted to do, but it was what I should do.

'Please do.' There was a long pause. John David said, 'I don't know what they could be doing in our house for so long. Poppy always had a very tense relationship with her parents. If you'd do this, I'd really appreciate it. I'm just not up to dealing with them tonight. This little guy is missing Poppy.' I knew my stepbrother was referring to Chase, but I think he was also talking about himself.

It was pitch-black, and I didn't know what I would find over at the house on Swanson. I wanted someone to go with me, preferably someone bigger than I, or at least well armed. My dad and his wife would kill me if I took Phillip to a place where he might have *any* sort of bad experience. Robin's mother was at his place, and I hated to butt in on their time together; plus, it wouldn't make a good impression, would it – calling Robin to come help me, when his mom was in residence? Calling the police seemed a little over the top. I thought of Angel or Shelby Youngblood, who used to work for Martin and me – and then I remembered they'd gone to Florida. That left only one possibility on my list. Reluctantly, I called Bryan Pascoe. That was better than calling Arthur anyway. Why'd I call a guy? Politically incorrect, huh? Because I was scared, that's why. And I figured Melinda was busy with her kids. And I didn't like Avery.

Bryan, to my near dismay, was delighted to hear from me, and willing to go to Poppy's and meet me there.

Phillip, engrossed in his TV show, gave me an off-hand wave as I left. It took only five minutes to get to Poppy and John David's place, but the lawyer was already there. Bryan was wearing jeans and a sweater, which for him was really letting his hair down.

I apologized again for getting him out of his house so late in the evening.

'No problem,' he said. 'I'm a full-service lawyer. Besides, all I had to do was sit around and watch a tape of *Buffy the Vampire Slayer!*'

I laughed, much to my own surprise.

'What are you doing for the holiday?' I asked, just to stave off going up that sidewalk and into the house. Sure enough, the house wasn't dark; even though it ought to have been. Sandy and Marvin Wynn were apparently still there. What on earth were they doing?

'I'm going to have dinner with my mother at the Assisted Living Center,' Bryan said.

Again I was surprised. Somehow, I couldn't picture Bryan with his mother. 'Your dad's gone?' I asked.

'Nope, he's living in Atlanta with his second wife, a very nice woman he met in his nursing home. He and my mother have been divorced for the past twenty years or so.'

'And he remarried. I guess you're never too old for romance.'

'Definitely not,' Bryan said. 'Now, what are we doing here?'

'The Wynns are in the house. They borrowed John David's key. They were supposed to come by and get their bags and leave for their home. They told my mother they'd return when the funeral was definitely scheduled. They told John David they wanted to retrieve something of Sandy's mother's, some family heirloom Poppy had. I don't believe he asked or cared what it was. They've been here much longer than that should take. And we're almost certain that Sandy was in the area the morning Poppy was killed.'

Bryan considered for a minute. 'So, am I here as John David's lawyer or as your bodyguard?'

I smiled again, though I don't know if he could make it out in the gloom. Poppy and John David lived in the middle of the block, and the streetlights on the corners didn't really illuminate their yard. 'A bit of both,' I said. 'I'm worried about them. But if they're okay, I plan on being mad at them. They've been here way too long.' I took a deep breath. 'Mostly, this is just weird and needs to be looked into. John David asked me to do that for him.'

'Clear as a bell,' Bryan said.

We went up the flagstones to the front door, and after a moment's hesitation, I opened it without knocking. This wasn't the Wynns' house, after all.

Bryan shut the door behind us, and we stood in the hallway at the foot of the stairs leading up to the bedrooms, trying to make sense, of what we saw. Marvin Wynn was crouched by Poppy's rolltop desk, in the small room to the right of the stairs, the room originally intended for a dining room. Both Poppy and John David used it as an office, and they each had a computer there. A large bookshelf covered one wall, and it was crammed with all kinds of books and knickknacks. Now the room was in an utter jumble. Half the books were on the floor. Marvin, crouched on the floor, was pulling the drawers out of the roll-top desk and turning them over to examine the bottoms.

He was so startled when he looked up and discovered two people observing him that he jumped, visibly. He gasped and dropped the drawer, which landed painfully on his thighs. He made another noise, this one surprising from a minister.

Poppy would not have taped a family heirloom to the bottom of the drawer.

'What are you doing?' I asked, and I didn't sound polite.

'What is it, Marv?' Sandy called from the top of the stairs. She froze when she saw us. Her large brown eyes, magnified many times by her outsize brown-framed glasses, were wide and shocked.

'What are you two doing?' I said again, with even more of an edge to my voice now. Someone had already helped himself to searching the contents of Poppy's closet and her bedroom. Now Poppy's mom and dad were ransacking the house under the guise of parental love. I was very unhappy with them. I was also angry that people I'd always respected were making a mockery of that respect by their behavior.

The Wynns appeared to be groping for an answer to my abrupt question.

'We, ah, we were looking for something. We asked John David if he'd mind.'

'You told John David you were looking for an heirloom Mrs Wynn's mom had left her,' I said bluntly. 'You've been here for hours, searching this house, as far as I can see. And I'm sure whatever precious heirloom it was, Poppy wouldn't have taped it to the bottom of a drawer, or stuffed it into a book!'

The Wynns didn't seem to be able to come up with a response. Finally, Marvin said, 'Who is this man with you?'

'I'm Bryan Pascoe, John David's attorney.'

Sandy Wynn came farther down the stairs, the first time she'd moved since she'd called to her husband. She exchanged glances with Marvin.

'Surely you didn't need to bring a *lawyer*,' Marvin said in his best ministerial voice. 'After all, we're family here.'

He could not have said anything more calculated to make my neck crawl.

'We are *not* family,' I said clearly. 'Please explain yourselves.'

'Listen, missy,' Sandy said. 'We are thirty years older than you are, and you will treat us with some respect.'

'When you deserve it.'

Sandy's face sagged on its bones, making her look much older in an instant. 'We were just looking for some old family things,' she insisted. 'We haven't found them. Since you're in such a snit, missy, we'll just leave.' She said this as if it was a big threat. 'We'll stop by your house and get our bags and go home. You'll excuse me, under the circumstances, if I don't write a thank-you note.'

'It's very late for you to start home,' Bryan said, sounding irritatingly reasonable. 'Why don't you check into the motel here in town, instead, and start back in the morning?'

'No, young man,' Marvin Wynn said. 'I'm not too old to drive at night, and we want to get out of this town. The day I retired from my job here was one of the best days of my life.'

I'd learned, years ago, that being a pastor is a *job* – a difficult and stressful one at that – but nonetheless, I found it shocking to hear the former Reverend Wynn speak in such a vicious way.

Bryan didn't respond, which was a relief. I didn't want to hear any more discussion. I just wanted the absence of the Wynns. I nudged an open book with my foot. The house was in a terrible state now. I sighed, already guessing whose task it would be to set it to rights.

Sandy and Marvin took some time getting their coats; with Bryan and me standing there, there was little opportunity for them to take anything. I hated being so suspicious, but I knew I had to be alert. This situation was completely fishy. Sandy had seemed so broken up on Monday night, but now I knew she'd already been in Lawrenceton that morning. Marvin, too, had appeared grief-stricken and miserable, at least to my eyes. And yet here they were, trashing their daughter's home.

Finally, they were at the door. Swaddled in all their winter gear (pretty much not necessary, for the night was in the fifties), the older couple looked harmless and beneficent with their silver hair and glasses.

Sandy opened her mouth to say something else insulting, but I preempted her. 'What were you doing out at the Grabbit Kwik getting gas Monday morning? Have you told the police about your little trip to Lawrenceton before Poppy's body was found?'

'We never came here Monday morning,' Marvin said with dignity. 'I went to get my annual physical, and Sandy went to do some comparison shopping for a new stove.'

'Good cover story,' I said to Sandy. 'Something you could spend a long time doing, with no tangible results.'

If Sandy had looked tense before, she looked beleaguered now. But her lips stayed pressed together. I couldn't have wiggled one bit of truth between them.

'Key,' I said tersely, holding out my hand. Sandy fished in her pocket and dropped the key on my palm, which closed around it instantly. But then I had a thought, and I opened my palm to compare this key to the one John David had loaned me. They matched.

The Wynns gave us twin glares as they left.

I sat down on the stairs when the door shut behind them. This had shaken me more than I'd realized. I was actually surprised at how much the week's events were depleting my normal energy. I'd had several of these shaky spells. Bryan sat by me. He put his arm around me, which I could have done without, but it was okay. It didn't feel sexual, not until his fingers started playing with my hair, that is.

'Do you want to call John David from here?'

'Would you?' I was just plain being weak.

'Sure,' he said, but he didn't move. 'What do you think they were looking for?' he asked after a moment or two.

'I don't know. Something small. And the person who was searching Poppy's closet was looking for something small, too. Something that could be hidden in a book, or a shoe box.'

'Jewelry?'

'That would fit. Or documents.'

'What kind of documents? She left a will. Poppy and John David both made wills when Poppy found out she was pregnant.'

'John David tell you that?'

'Yes. But it wasn't the first thing he said. He didn't come out with it until I asked him that specifically.'

I thought Bryan was telling me that in his opinion, John David hadn't been thinking of his possible financial gain from Poppy's death. I had never considered the fact that Poppy might have some money stashed away, and I couldn't imagine where such a stash could have come from. Her dad was a minister, so his pay had been low, and he and his wife were still very much alive. If Poppy had ever gotten any substantial inheritance from another relative, I'd never heard of it. And Poppy had worked for a few years, but working for a few years as a teacher and living off the proceeds were almost a guarantee you didn't have a lot left over. 'What lawyer drew up the wills?' I asked.

'Bubba Sewell.'

'Hmm. You know what I wonder? I wonder if Poppy gave Bubba a key during the course of their affair.'

'I hope I don't have to ask him that in court.' Bryan's hand kept combing through my hair. I moved a little farther from him, and his hand dropped into his lap.

'I can ask him.' Especially after our confrontation the day before (or had it been Monday?), Bubba and I were quite ready to be rude to each other. My mind moved on ahead. 'Do you think . . . do you suppose . . . that Poppy gave a key to each of her, um, men friends?'

'There'd be quite a few around, if that's the case.' Bryan looked thoughtful.

'Yes.' I had a lot of unpleasant thoughts circling in my tired brain. 'But Bubba . . .'

'Yes?'

Suddenly, I didn't want to continue. 'Nothing,' I said. 'While I check out the house, why don't you call John David and let him know what happened? Then we can go. I really appreciate your doing this.'

'This is just the kind of thing a good lawyer does for his clients,' Bryan said with a wide, sharklike smile.

'There must be a lot I don't know about good lawyers.' I smiled back. I went up the stairs. The closet, of course, was still in disarray. This time, even John David's clothes and ties and coats and sweaters had been gone through. What the hell were people looking for? I was assuming that two different people (or groups of people) had gone through the house. The first intruder, the one who'd confined the search to Poppy's half of the closet, had had a specific idea of where the object – whatever it was – had been stashed. In contrast, the Wynns had used a shotgun approach.

'You could find out,' Bryan said, and I looked at him blankly. I'd been lost in my thoughts. I didn't even realize for a few seconds that he had followed me and was continuing the conversation. I was too slow responding. Bryan's face wasn't too happy. 'Excuse me,' I said. 'I was wondering what they could be looking for.'

'Okay. Anything else you want to do here tonight?'

'No. I'll clean it up Friday. I'll see if my sister-in-law will help.'

'Then I'll call John David.' Bryan went off to use the telephone.

I sat where I was and eyed the devastation around me. I didn't see how the Wynns could have hoped to conceal their depredations. They'd have had to work all night to put things back. I wondered how they'd hoped to explain it. This looked like a go-for-broke situation. If they'd found what they needed, they wouldn't *care* if they couldn't explain it. For a couple who placed tremendous importance on community opinion, they were acting recklessly. That meant they were desperate.

So, they were searching for something of vital importance, something so significant to their future that their need for it eclipsed their daughter's death.

I could not understand parents like that, though I reminded myself of the notorious struggles between the Wynns and Poppy when she was in her teens. And I recalled what Emma McKibbon had told me about the Reverend Wynn's predilection for young women. Was there proof of the retired minister's dalliance with female members of his congregation? Maybe such proof was what Poppy had concealed in her home.

I shook my head, all to myself. Why would she do that? What leverage would it give her with her parents? I couldn't imagine what she would want from them; want it so badly that she'd keep such unpleasant things. And what could those things be? Pictures? I swallowed hard, disgusted at downing such an indigestible idea.

'Are you going to be sick?' Bryan, having returned from calling John David, sounded terrified at the prospect.

'No, just thinking bad thoughts.'

'I talked to John David. He's baffled. I told him they said they were going home until they heard from him about the funeral – they're reverting to the original plan – and he seemed relieved. I also called Arthur Smith again and left yet another message on his voice mail at work. So far, he hasn't responded to any of my calls. I want to tell him what we found out about Sandy Wynn, and I want to tell him that the Wynns were here tonight.'

'I hope he calls back soon,' I said dutifully, though in truth I found it hard to care. I felt very tired, which seemed about par lately. I dragged myself to my feet. I didn't want to ask Bryan for help. My stomach curdled with anxiety. Oh boy. Maybe I *was* going to be sick.

I managed to get to my car without disgracing myself, and after thanking Bryan for coming out and providing moral and tactical assistance, I drove home.

Phillip was on the phone when I walked in, and he was smiling broadly, so I figured the person on the other end was a female. After a minute, I deduced it was Josh Finstermeyer's sister, Joss. After ten more minutes, I grew a wee bit exasperated and gestured to Phillip to wind up the conversation. He did so willingly enough, then told me all about what the Finstermeyers were doing for their Thanksgiving celebration – remarkably, almost exactly what we would be doing. He asked if he could go over to their house tomorrow afternoon, after we'd eaten, and I told him that would probably be okay. He beamed at me.

It was the first time I'd seen Phillip look carefree, and it made him very attractive. I felt sorry for Joss. I hoped she was a self-sufficient young woman.

'What happened with the Wynns?' Phillip asked. 'I was sitting here watching TV when they came stomping in like someone had stuck a cattle prod up their – like they were really fired up. They didn't even speak.'

'They were mad at me,' I said, realizing I should have called ahead and warned Phillip what to expect. He didn't seem unduly shaken by the incident, and I reminded myself all over again that Phillip had been raised in a different world from the one I'd been reared in. (That made me feel old, by the way.)

Robin had learned something about Phillip over lunch, I hoped, something worth telling me. I couldn't picture my dad telling Phillip about the facts of life – well, Phillip knew the facts. What I meant, I decided, was the responsibilities.

I was aware that I was absolutely exhausted. 'Phillip, I have to go to bed,' I said.

'Sure, Roe. Anything you need me to do?'

'No. I just hope I'm not catching anything.'

'You look kind of, ah, tired.'

Nice way of saying I looked like warm Jell-O. 'Yeah, I am. I'm going to call it a day. Come get me if you need me.' I went into my bedroom, and after a trip to my bathroom, I pulled on my nightgown and crawled into bed. No Robin to join me tonight, I reflected as I began to get drowsy (which was almost immediately). Maybe that was good. I didn't feel up to making whoopee. I felt achy all over, my skin extra sensitive. As I drifted into sleep, I prayed that I wasn't getting the flu.

Chapter Nine

I wasn't running a fever in the morning when I woke up, and I felt a lot better. Of course, I'd slept an hour and a half later than I'd planned, but somehow it was impossible to get out of bed in any hurry. I was sure Phillip wouldn't be up yet. Sure enough, when I went into the kitchen in my fuzzy slippers and bathrobe, he was nowhere in sight. I made some coffee and put out some coffee cake I'd gotten the day before. It was pretty close to time to put in the turkey, so I preheated the oven before I sat down with my breakfast. It was a beautiful day, sunny, and the temperature was expected to reach the sixties, though it was about forty outside at the moment.

I sat gazing dreamily out the window into my backyard, ignoring a magazine lying by my mug on the table. A list of things I had to do was there, too, and not one item crossed off. I found it hard to care. I finished the coffee and a piece of the coffee cake. As a matter of habit, I went to pour my second cup. But I just didn't want it today. Maybe this was the way my body was trying to get my mind to agree to get up and work. Actually, I needed to go to the bathroom anyway, so I figured I might as well get dressed.

In a matter of minutes, I was in my nice suede pants and orange sweater, my tortoise-rimmed glasses on to coordinate, all made up and ready – and with lots of messy kitchen work to do. I was just going to have a backward day. Normally, I wouldn't have put on my good clothes until the kitchen had been cleaned right before my guests' arrival. But I couldn't bring myself to care about my impracticality.

I scooted up my sleeves, found the apron that provided the most coverage, and turned on the Macy's parade to watch while I worked. I like that about my kitchen and den area; and that was another change from my former life, when I'd had no desire whatsoever for anyone to watch me while I was cooking, and I'd been glad my kitchen was just a kitchen. Now, I just didn't care. My kitchen/den/informal dining area seemed just great. I enjoyed glancing at the parade while I worked, and I enjoyed the sun coming in through the big windows on either side of the fireplace. Cooking took me away from Poppy's death and the mess and chaos surrounding it. Two hours flew by before I knew it. I glanced at the clock with some surprise.

Time to take stock.

Pies ready. Cranberry sauce ready. Dressing ready, prepared with canned chicken stock just so I'd save myself last-minute rushing. I'd gotten the turkey greased and into the baking bag, and now I slid the big pan into the warm oven. Robin would bring the English peas, which just required heating with some butter, and the rolls, which only had to brown – so nothing to do on that front. He'd have the wine, and he would open that. I got out the corkscrew and the wineglasses. Only the sweet potato casserole needed some more fixing.

The sugar was already mixed in, and I tasted to make sure I'd added enough. I'd finished adding the spices and eggs when Phillip at last emerged from the guest bathroom, shiny and dressed. He poured himself a huge glass of juice and cut a piece of coffee cake. He gave me a sleepy smile and settled on a stool at the breakfast bar to watch the parade. After a minute, he flipped open the *TV Guide* and started looking at the football listings.

Once Phillip had finished breakfast, I asked him to help me with the big tablecloth for the nicer table in the dining room. I set the table slowly, trying to make it look correct . . . but not ridiculously so. This was not an imposing formal occasion. If I turned it into that, I'd have to go put on panty hose and a dress. Yuck.

Good silver, good china. (I'd be doing dishes all day.) I kept checking the table. Salt, pepper. I got out the gravy boat. Glasses for iced tea. Sugar. Dish for lemon wedges. Serving spoons. The smaller turkey platter.

I'd be cleaning up at *midnight*.

Suddenly, my energy seemed to leak out through my fingertips, as though my night's sleep had simply evaporated. I pulled out a chair and sat down with an ungraceful thud.

Could the prospect of meeting Robin's mother really be that frightening? Martin's mother and father had been long dead when we'd become engaged, and I'd already known his sister Barby. Arthur had been my only other halfway-serious suitor. I'd known Mindy and Coll Smith, Arthur's folks, since I was little, at least by sight. So, though I was thirty-six, this was my first 'meet the parent' situation.

I rose and pushed the chair back into place, though I hardly felt better. I went back into the den and unwisely sat in my favorite old chair, close to Phillip, who was watching some sports show. In about thirty seconds, I actually dozed off. Phillip woke me up at quarter to one.

'You want to go put some lipstick on or something?' he asked a little anxiously. 'It's almost time for them to be here. The timer for the turkey breast went off thirty minutes ago, and the little red thing was sticking up out of the turkey, so I got it out of the oven. I put the sweet potatoes in. Was that okay?'

'More than okay,' I assured him. 'You saved my life, brother.'

He looked justifiably pleased with himself. Groggy with sleep, I had to absolutely push myself into the kitchen. I put ice in the glasses, a stick of margarine on a butter dish to pass around with the rolls – oh my God, the rolls! I told myself sternly to calm down. Robin was bringing them; they'd only take a few minutes. The rolls could go in after I'd gotten the sweet potatoes out. The dressing was baking in the other oven. (Following my mother's tradition, I always baked it separately.) All I had to do was make the gravy. But first, a look in my bedroom mirror was in order.

Phillip had been optimistic when he suggested I needed only lipstick. But I looked all right after brushing my hair, cleaning my glasses, and slapping on a little fresh makeup. Back in the kitchen, I buzzed around doing tiny things. I asked Phillip if he'd give some attention to his own hair, and with a dark glance, he retired to the bathroom to look in the mirror.

'And it better be perfectly picked up in there!' I called through the door.

'Yes, Mom!' he yelled back.

I stuck my tongue out, since he couldn't see me. Mom indeed.

And then the doorbell rang.

As I went to the front door, I said a little prayer, which basically went: 'Don't let me do anything really stupid.'

Robin's mother was really tall. That was my first impression. And she was smiling. That was my second.

Corinne Crusoe was as elegant as . . . well, as *my* mother. All I could think was, Damn. Her thick, perfectly white hair was pulled back into an elegant roll. Mrs Crusoe wore subtle makeup, discreet gold jewelry, and a gorgeous pantsuit of some heavy, smooth blue knit that hung like a designer dress. It matched her eyes to a tee.

'Roe, this is my mother,' Robin said, since you have to state the obvious some times. 'Mother, this is my . . .' Robin and I stared at each other, stymied, for a long second. 'This is Aurora.'

'Please come in,' I said, floundering for my composure in the face of such elegance. You'd think I'd be used to it, but no.

Mrs Crusoe was careful not to stare around too obviously, but I knew she hadn't missed a detail of me, or the house. Phillip, thank God, had come out of the bathroom and was looking very creditable.

'My brother, Phillip,' I said proudly, and he beamed at me. 'Phillip, this is Robin's mother, Mrs Crusoe.'

'Please call me Corinne,' she said smoothly, nodding at both of us.

Phillip stood a little straighter. I wasn't about to tell him he was too young to call an older lady by her first name, not in front of the older lady.

'Corinne, can I pour you a glass of wine?' Phillip said with perfect composure, and I glowed.

'That would be lovely.'

'We have . . .' and Phillip faltered.

I inspected the bottles Robin was carrying. 'Robin's brought a zinfandel and a shiraz,' I said. 'Or, if you prefer, we have some vodka and orange juice.'

'No, the zinfandel, thanks.'

We got that all settled, then sat in the small formal living room after I'd put the peas on. Corinne was a past mistress of small talk, and we set about getting to know one another through the accumulation of little facts – or, more accurately, tiny indicators of those facts. Corinne, I learned, was well-off, a widow who had no intention of remarrying. She was very involved with her grandchildren by her two daughters, and she was active in her church (Episcopal).

Corinne learned I was also a widow, also financially secure, still working, had two live parents, and was a steady church attendant.

Corinne learned that Phillip normally lived in California. He was here on a visit, I told her, not mentioning his method of arrival. And I hoped Phillip wouldn't, either, but if he did, so be it.

I excused myself to make the gravy and heat the rolls, and Corinne promptly asked if she could help in any way.

'If you don't mind, I'll borrow Robin, to help me with the turkey,' I said. 'We'll be in the kitchen. Would you like to come offer advice?'

'I'll be glad to come,' Corinne said, standing gracefully with her barely touched glass of zinfandel. 'But I'll just observe silently.'

I laughed and led the way. We've been formal long enough, I thought. True to her word, Corinne offered almost no observations on how she prepared Thanksgiving herself, which I thought was just wonderful and amazing.

After the usual flurry of getting everything on the table, and getting everyone to sit and relax, the meal went very well. Robin carved the turkey with enthusiasm and a total lack of expertise, Corinne seemed to enjoy her food, and Phillip had seconds of everything. Robin kept casting little glances at me that I couldn't interpret.

'What are you doing tomorrow?' he asked later, when we were all sitting, replete and sleepy, our forks laid down for good.

'Oh.' My contented feeling almost vanished. 'I have to

straighten up Poppy's house tomorrow.' Robin looked surprised. I hated to explain about the Wynns in front of Corinne.

'Who's going to help you?'

'I don't know. If Melinda can get a babysitter, I'm sure she will.' Even more than I, Melinda would not want the whole town to know what had happened, though I was sure that sooner or later the news would travel.

'I could help you,' he offered.

'That's so nice of you.' I was genuinely touched. Robin was no slob, but picking up and cleaning were hardly his favorite activities, and he had a houseguest. 'But I expect we can handle it. If we need anything too strenuous done, I'll give you a call.'

'Is there anything I can do?' Corinne asked, out of courtesy.

'Oh, no, thank you,' I said quickly. 'I'm sure Robin told you that my sister-in-law was killed a few days ago. As if that wasn't awful enough, someone came into her house and ransacked it. My brother-in-law just shouldn't be faced with dealing with a mess, in addition to everything else.'

We all laid out some platitudes about how dreadful the world was nowadays, and no one was safe, even in a small town like Lawrenceton, where people used to leave their doors unlocked year-round. I certainly didn't remember such a time myself, but my mother had assured me that was so.

My company all helped carry the food and dirty dishes into the kitchen, and to my embarrassment and gratitude, Corinne and Robin insisted on doing the dishes. My good china couldn't go in the dishwasher, so this was a bigger task than usual. Phillip and Corinne dried while Robin washed, and I put away all the leftovers. My pants felt a little tight around the waist, and though that wasn't unusual after a large meal, I realized that they'd felt a little snug when I'd put them on that morning. Even my bra felt tight. I decided tomorrow would certainly be early enough to worry about weight gain, but tomorrow I'd definitely need to cut back.

We decided to stay in the less formal den, cozier and more comfortable and right by the kitchen. Of course, a football game was on, and Phillip and Robin talked sports while Corinne and I discussed Thanksgiving customs, Christmas shopping, how long I'd lived in my present house, Corinne's grandchildren. Maybe she wouldn't mind so much, me not being able to have any, since she already had some. The minute the thought crossed my mind, I was sorry.

I was about to ruin my own day, and I slammed a mental door on that subject and turned to more pleasant ones.

'My mother and her husband are coming to share a glass of wine in a short while,' I said. 'I hope that you'll stay and meet them.'

'Oh, that would be wonderful,' Corinne said instantly. She seemed positively delighted at the prospect.

With Corinne, Phillip, and Robin settled down in front of the television, I excused myself. When I emerged from the bathroom off my bedroom, Robin was standing there waiting. Without saying a word, he kissed me. At first, it was a sweet sort of kiss, a 'You just met my mom and she likes you' kind of kiss, but abruptly it turned into a hormonal lip lock, that had more to do with ripping off underwear than Mom. In about one minute flat, we were ready to land on the bed.

'Whoa,' I gasped, pulling my lips away from his.

His mouth followed mine, and for a second we dallied with resuming the pleasurable activity, but sanity prevailed. My brother and Robin's mom were in the next room, and the television volume wasn't *that* loud.

'Can I come over tonight?' he whispered.

'Your mom!'

'She won't miss me for a couple of hours.'

'But she'll know, and that makes me feel creepy. I know she knows anyway, but still . . .'

'I'll think of a very good excuse. Remember, I'm a professional writer.'

'Okay,' I said, giving in without a further thought.

'By the way,' the professional writer said, 'your brother is a normal teenager who's just gotten lucky very recently and was safe about it.'

'That's all I want to know,' I said, making a stop sign by holding my hand up, palm facing him. 'No gory details. Brothers and sisters don't need to know too much.'

Robin decided we should kiss again. It was even harder to pull apart this time, and I was still feeling a little dazed by lust as we went back into the den, where Corinne was catnapping in an ever-so-ladylike way, and Phillip was talking on the phone again.

'Can I go?' he whispered. 'Josh and Joss have finished eating, and his mom says it's okay. They live about two blocks over, so I can walk. He's got a PlayStation 2 and some games I haven't tried yet.'

I glanced at my watch. I wondered whether my mother would be relieved or disappointed to miss seeing him, then decided that relieved would more fit the bill today, and gave Phillip my blessing, along with an injunction to be home in two hours, or I'd be calling the Finstermeyers.

Phillip waved good-bye to Robin, grabbed his jacket, and was gone before I could count to fifteen. Robin and I settled on the love seat and I leaned my head against his shoulder. Our hands were twined together. It was nice and warm, and I was full. I joined Corinne in dreamland for a few minutes, and then I heard my mother's distinctive knock on the door. I couldn't believe I'd missed all the worrying about the 'Aida meets Corinne' scenario, and I couldn't believe I'd fallen asleep twice in one day.

Corinne was sitting up straight, her eyes fixed on the television, so she was already alert. Good. She'd need it.

My mother was dressed in a discreet plaid skirt and a red blouse, with some gorgeous red pumps on. John was wearing a dress shirt and a tweed jacket but no tie. He looked very bluff and hearty, which was not John at all, but it made a good first impression.

The introductions went well, though Mother raised her eyebrows at me for having my company in the den instead of in the formal living room. Tough, Mom. We'd migrated naturally.

'Bryan called you at our house today,' Mother said to me directly during a lull in the chitchat. 'He seemed to assume you'd be at our house. I told him you'd been cooking your own Thanksgiving dinners for a while now.'

Okay. Mother wanted Robin to know other men found me attractive, she wanted me to know she didn't mind me not having Thanksgiving with them, and she wanted Corinne to know that she respected my independence.

Mission accomplished, Mom.

'I'll call him back tomorrow. Today's a holiday,' I said instantly, stating that my relationship with Bryan Pascoe was Business with a capital *B*. But in the next instant, I found myself wondering if he'd discovered something about the Wynns.

The visit went well, on the whole. John was not too talkative, seeming abstracted most of the time, but I was sure Corinne would understand. John had wonderful manners and was always able to think of something pleasant to say, so I knew he would improve on Corinne's acquaintance. Robin had an excellent rapport with my mother; the thought crossed my mind that he was better with her than my late husband, Martin, had ever been. Martin and Mother had always been so conscious they were close to the same age – in fact, if Martin had married Mother instead of me, it wouldn't have raised many eyebrows at all.

I tried not to compare other men to Martin, but sometimes ideas popped into my head whether I wanted them to or not.

I opened my mouth to interrogate my mother about Poppy's parents – if she remembered any specific scandal about Marvin Wynn – but I realized just in time that there was no way she'd discuss that in front of Corinne Crusoe.

'Where's the boy?' Mother asked as Corinne and Robin were telling John a long golfing story about Robin's late father.

'He's gone over to Josh's house,' I explained. 'You know, the Finstermeyers. Josh and his twin sister, Joss, took Phillip around the other day, to the movies and so on.'

'Well, that's nice,' Mother said unconvincingly. 'What do you think of the boy? How long is he going to stay?'

'Dad and Betty Jo want him to come back after Thanksgiving,' I said, suddenly aware that I hadn't talked to them in two days – or had it been longer? Surely they ought to have made some travel plans for Phillip by now. But how on earth would they get airline reservations this late? Weren't the airports full on the weekend after Thanksgiving? 'Maybe he can stay longer,' I added hastily so Mother would never think I was tired of Phillip. I didn't exactly want to get rid of him. I loved my brother, though I realized I didn't know him that well. My problem was the extent of my responsibility. If Phillip were to stay for a while, I would have to be a little stricter; I couldn't be an indulgent big sister if he was going to be with me for weeks.

Right after my mother and John gathered their coats and left (after drinking two cups of coffee apiece, instead of wine, and each having a piece of pumpkin pie), Phillip called and asked if he could spend the night at Josh's.

What I wanted to say was, Yes, if you can keep your hands off Joss! Don't even *think* about laying a finger on her in her own house! What I actually said was, 'Why don't you let me talk to Josh's mom, Phillip? Staying would probably be okay.'

Beth Finstermeyer put my mind at ease by letting me know casually that her daughter was off spending the night with her best friend, so the boys could have the run of the house. And she laughed after she said that, so I knew the boys would no more 'have the run of the house' than I would swallow a goldfish.

After I hung up, I could tell that Corinne was ready to go back to Robin's apartment and put her feet up. I urged them to take some pie with them, told them my brother was going to be away for the night but that he had surely enjoyed meeting Corinne, and fetched their jackets from the guest bedroom.

Robin's eyes had lighted up when he'd heard Phillip was going to be gone, and he dropped a chaste kiss on my cheek when he was saying good-bye, even as he was whispering, 'See you later.'

When the door closed behind them and I was finally alone, the relief was enormous. It was five o'clock, and no one wanted anything of me. The dusk was closing in outside, and I wandered around my house, pulling curtains to and picking up the odd crumpled napkin or used glass. I got out the carpet sweeper and ran it over the area rug, then swept the tiled floor that ran down the hall and into the kitchen and den.

There, that was it. All I was going to do today.

Thanksgiving was over.

I had a turkey sandwich while I watched reruns from a million years ago of a show I'd been too young to catch the first time around. I read a little, having a hard time truly engaging my mind in the convolutions of the book, a complicated psychological mystery. In another hour, I was yawning.

A discreet knock at the front door came just in time. It was followed by the sound of a key turning. I'd originally given Robin a key in case he wanted to work in my office while I was gone. A lot of his reference books were on the shelves that lined the office walls, because his apartment just didn't have room for all his books.

'Are you sleepy?' Robin asked, kneeling by my chair.

'I could probably be roused.'

'Your brother really at the Fin-whatevers for the night?'

'Uh-huh.'

'Oh . . . goody.'

It was one of those encounters where each person seemed to want something different. I was looking for a slow, sweet session, undemanding but satisfying. Robin was feeling more fiery and acrobatic. It took a while to get in sync, but when we did, the climax was the most intense I'd ever experienced. I lay in the dark of my bedroom with Robin's long arms wrapped around me, and I felt content and safe and loved. Though I'd been drowsy before, when I felt Robin relax into sleep, my eyes were open to the darkness.

I thought about Robin and how I felt about him. I thought about how Bryan Pascoe's interest in me didn't spark any feeling in me at all, except mild discomfort. I thought of how amazing it was that I was alive and well, able to experience lying here in the arms of a tall, thin man named Robin Crusoe, whose wild red hair was even now tangling with mine on the pillow. I had this, this wonderful moment, while Poppy, a woman vibrating with life, had had it all taken away.

What had happened to Poppy along her way? What had made her so two-faced? The loving, besotted mother, the well-dressed matron and dutiful wife had also been a promiscuous and sly female. The intelligent college graduate had deliberately wed a man she knew would not be faithful to her – probably in the sure expectation that she would not be faithful to him, either. Or had John David and Poppy married in the belief they'd cleave only to each other? They must have known, even then, that faithfulness was an ideal rather than a reality, given their natures.

Maybe blind optimism could carry you further than you ever meant to go.

I turned to look at Robin's sleeping face. I lay on my side, propped up on one elbow. The night-light in the bathroom provided a faint glow, just enough to see the disheveled head and beaky nose. When I tried to imagine his head lying on someone else's pillow, it hurt deep inside me. And then I felt the surge of anger, the backlash of that pain, just at his *imagined* infidelity.

Had it been that kind of anger that had motivated the hand that had stabbed Poppy over and over? But the evidence of the search through Poppy's closet and the odd activities of her parents added another layer of complexity to the question of Poppy's death.

'Robin, wake up,' I said. I folded his hand in mine.

'What? You okay?'

'Promise me something.'

'What?'

'Promise me you'll never cheat on me while we're together. If we break up, okay, anything then. But while we're . . . a couple . . . no one else.'

I sounded more like seventeen than thirty-six, but I was dead serious.

'Had you thought I might?' he asked with some difficulty. 'I mean, have you seen me looking at anyone? You know Janie isn't anyone I'd ever really date. She's just a goofy girl.' He clearly didn't want to have to go over the Janie Spellman ground again.

'I know,' I said hastily. 'That was just a . . . momentary craziness. I'm not saying I've seen you look at anyone specific. No. But I just want to hear you say it.'

'I have no intention of going to bed with anyone but you,' Robin said clearly. 'I think it's completely obvious that I love you.'

Well. I should wake Robin up more often.

I bent and nuzzled his neck. 'I love you, too,' I said, the words coming more easily than I had thought they would.

'I was hoping,' he mumbled. 'Now, can I go back to sleep? Talk tomorrow?'

'Sure,' I said, reversing again so my back was snuggled up to his front. 'Sure.'

Chapter Ten

I called Melinda after I got up the next morning. It was late. Robin had gotten dressed and left about 1:00 a.m., giving me a kiss and a pat. He'd left a note on my coffeepot to tell me that he'd talk to me later. He'd signed it, 'Love, your Robin.'

I had to wait awhile before I had my coffee that morning. Something I'd eaten the day before, or maybe just the volume of the food, had made me a little queasy. When I had a piece of toast, I felt much better, and by the time nine o'clock rolled around, I figured Melinda would be up and dressed and safely into her morning. I poured some kibble into Madeleine's bowl while I waited for Melinda to pick up the phone. I wondered why Madeleine didn't come in, and realized I hadn't seen her the evening before, either. But that wasn't especially significant. I often missed her little visits to her food bowl.

Melinda had had a good time at her parents' home, she reported. She'd seen her brother and her sister, and their children had played with her children. She sounded as though she hadn't been ready for that little reunion to end.

'We'd been thinking of staying until Sunday, but with everything happening, Avery thought we'd better come back last night,' she said drearily. 'So, here we are. At least the kids slept most of the way back, and they went right to bed when we got home. But this morning, I think Marcy is coming down with a cold, damn it. Did anything happen while we were gone? Have you heard anything else about the funeral?'

'Not a word. So it looks like Poppy's body isn't going to be released until Monday, if then,' I said. 'In the meantime, in addition to someone searching Poppy's closet and making a big mess in there and in her bedroom, the Wynns were looking for something all over the house and tossed it around worse than the first burglar.'

Melinda was stunned. I could hear her choking on whatever she was drinking. 'Poppy's dad, the minister?' she asked incredulously. 'Poppy's *mom*? Trashed her place? I can't believe it!' She went on like that for a few more minutes, though I knew she did believe me. It was a way to handle the unpleasant shock.

Melinda got to the bottom line quickly, as I knew she would. 'So, we need to clean it up,' she said. She sounded gloomy at the prospect. 'Well, let me call around and see if I can get a teenager to babysit. They're all out of school, and maybe one of them wants to do something as boring as watching kids. Speaking of babies, where has John David stashed Chase?'

'I hope you're sitting down. John David's still in the motel with Chase, and there he stays, taking care of the little fellow.'

That was just as shocking to Melinda as the vandalism of Poppy's house.

'I'll call him,' she said when she had recovered. 'I'll just check on them. This is a good thing, but I'm just not confident of his ability to take care of that child.'

'Wasn't he a help before?'

'Not as much as *I* would've liked, though I can't say Poppy complained. As I told you, Avery has been great with both of ours. Of course, everyone takes it for granted that the mom will do everything for the kids, but if a dad does a lot for them, it's a big deal.' I could picture Melinda's shrug.

'I'm proud of John David,' I said. 'I thought he'd fold.'

'Me, too. Goes to show.'

I wasn't sure what it went to show, but I grunted agreeably and we fixed a time to meet at the house on Swanson, if Melinda was lucky enough to get a sitter.

As I brushed my teeth, I found myself thinking of Sally. I felt a strong impulse to call her, just to check up on her. But what would I say? 'Forgotten anything important lately, Sally?' 'Do you remember who I am, Sally?' I wondered if perhaps a complete physical could turn up some problem that was solvable, and not just expose the explanation Perry dreaded – that Sally was in the early stages of Alzheimer's. I made a note to myself to call Perry or take him out to lunch so we could talk about it without being interrupted, which we would be at the library.

Melinda called back to tell me she'd gotten a sitter, and she sounded much more cheerful. I got the impression Marcy's cold was making her daughter a little difficult and that Melinda definitely wouldn't mind a break. We agreed to meet at the house on Swanson at 10:00 a.m.

I wrote Phillip a note about my plans, including the number for my cell phone and the number at John David's. After I got dressed in grubby old jeans and a faded Christmas sweatshirt, both a little loose to allow me some comfort, I started out on my morning errands.

Somewhere along the way, I yielded to an irresistible impulse and drove over to the Best Western. John David was on the first floor, and I could hear Chase shrieking from outside the door.

John David looked bleary-eyed when he opened it, but he was dressed, and not surprised to have company. 'Melinda already called this morning,' he said, moving aside to let me in. 'Listen, help me think of something to get him calmed down.'

'I have almost no experience,' I warned him.

'I've tried feeding him, burping him, changing him, and singing to him.'

The idea of John David singing to that baby just did something to me. I'm a sucker for a man who can take care of a baby, or a man who's at least trying to take care of a baby. To cover up the fact that my eyes were full of tears, I held out my arms and he put Chase in them. Chase was a wriggling bundle of misery, and he was making such a whirlwind of his little arms and legs that I was scared I wouldn't be able to hold him. I sat down in the room's one comfortable chair and held Chase so his chest was against mine, his head resting against my shoulder. The chair wouldn't rock, so I rocked for it, back and forth, back and forth, murmuring to the baby.

Chase began to relax some, and the shrieks died down to

whimpers. Suddenly, there was silence. He was sound asleep, but I kept up with my movement.

'He's all I've got left to love,' John David said in a near whisper. He looked thinner after only a few days of being a widower. He had shaved, and he had tucked in his shirt and combed his hair, but the spark was not in his eyes anymore.

'How can you say you loved her?' I asked. My voice was strained with the effort of containing my anger and speaking in a low, calm voice. 'I found you at Romney's, and it wasn't the first place I looked.'

'I always loved Poppy. I got mad at her a lot. She was a woman with a lot of secrets,' he said, his voice just as low and controlled. 'But I loved her. Just not the way *you* think people ought to love. You're such a straight arrow. Life has no spice unless you have adventures.' He even smiled, just a faint one, but a smile nonetheless.

If my hands had been free at that moment, I might have tried to throttle him. 'You're right,' I said, so furiously that Chase whimpered. 'I don't understand. I'll never understand.' I fought to keep my voice under control. 'I am really glad you're taking care of Chase. But it is beyond my comprehension, how you and Poppy could live like you did.'

'She was a complicated woman. She had some bad breaks when she was in her early teens,' John David said. 'I would have liked it if we'd been different, I swear I would. I didn't set out to be . . . like I am. But we made a pattern, and it was one that let us live together, and I thought it would be okay.'

It was like we had both taken a little truth serum. I had never imagined having such a conversation. But it was actually kind of refreshing to openly acknowledge their fractured marriage.

'So,' I began, then paused. 'You both always knew? When the other was seeing someone else?'

He nodded, and I felt my mouth twist with distaste. Abruptly, I was nauseated by the idea of such a union, and baffled by the point of it.

The baby was getting heavier and heavier. I got up very slowly and carefully and placed him in the bassinet that had been set up by the bed. Whether John David had brought it from the house or the motel had rolled it in, I didn't know, but I was glad it was there so I could put Chase down without my back positively breaking.

'John David,' I said very softly, looking down at the sleeping child, 'who do you think killed her?'

'I think maybe it was her mother,' he said, his voice a hoarse whisper. 'I'd hate to think Sandy would do something like that, but you don't know that family. Let me tell you, any sick pattern you think Poppy and I had, she learned it from her own mom and dad. She'd never get into details, but she never wanted them here. She'd be pretty open about everything else.'

'She talked about the other men?'

'Arthur most of all. He was always obsessive about her. I think it's pretty damn peculiar that the police chief has Arthur on the case, unless Arthur's persuaded him he's found a possible suspect. Arthur kind of transferred all those feelings he had about you to Poppy. He even talked to Poppy about you, all the time at first.'

This was more than I wanted to know.

'And then there were others.'

I shook my head. 'I can't understand.'

'She used them, you know,' he said. He leaned forward, his hands between his knees. I wondered if he'd be able to build a healthy relationship with anyone after this. 'They were always some use to her. Or after it was over, she made them useful in some way.'

'What about you?' I asked, not able to think about Poppy anymore. 'Is that the way you picked your . . . friends?'

'No.' He shrugged. 'I just wanted something *simple*.' After a minute, I realized that he was crying, and I patted him on the shoulder, gave him a little peck on the forehead, and left to search his house.

'We could have hired someone to do this,' Melinda said. We were standing in the middle of the chaos in what had once been a perfectly ordinary suburban home.

'Yes,' I agreed. 'We could have. But whatever's hidden here, it's us that needs to find it.' Ungrammatically and inelegantly as I'd put it, Melinda's dark eyes widened as she considered what I'd said.

She nodded. 'Whatever it is.'

'It's not going to be easy. The Wynns would have found it, if it were easy. And when we do find it, no one needs to see it but us.'

'The police?'

'We'll see.'

'So we're like detectives?' Melinda smiled weakly. 'Well, that's a new role for me. I already have so many hats, I can't wear them all at one time.'

'Hey, we're more than detectives,' I said, trying to make my voice bracing and hearty. 'We're Uppity Women.'

'So we are.'

By 10:30, we were putting books back on the shelves in the study. We dusted the books first, since neither of us was capable of reshelving anything that needed a runover with a rag. And we checked each book for enclosures, too.

Nothing fell from the pages, no matter how hard we shook. The desks were absolutely normal, too. Melinda and I were neat and methodical in our search. We didn't talk much at first, because we were intent on what we were doing, and because we were trying to move quickly.

Melinda balked after forty minutes. 'It's not the work I mind,' she said abruptly; 'it's the fact that you think we ought to judge whether or not the police get whatever we find.'

'You know that Arthur Smith was Poppy's lover?'

She nodded.

'You want him to decide whether or not something's relevant?'

'I've been wondering . . .' she said after a moment. 'I've been wondering if Arthur didn't actually . . . If he might . . .'

'You think Arthur might have killed Poppy?' I was shocked, but not as shocked as I might have been. 'He's got an obsessive personality,' I admitted. 'He's got lots of know-how.' Who was better qualified to be a murderer than a policeman?

I dusted the same book (a pharmaceutical dictionary of John David's) over and over as I thought about Arthur. 'But you know, Melinda . . . their affair was long over. If he'd still been involved with her, I would say it might even be likely.' I thought some more, trying to picture Arthur knocking on Poppy's glass door.

'I don't know,' I said, not wanting to picture that any longer. 'But that's why I think we need to talk about just burning whatever we find. However, first, we've got to find something.'

After an hour and a half, we had the office picked up, dusted, vacuumed, and searched. We had found absolutely nothing besides the usual detritus of any home filled with busy people. Poppy had an overdue bill from Davidson's that I knew I should bring to John David's attention (it had gotten stuck to another paper with some jelly), and she hadn't sent in her latest book club notice, so I put that on top of the little pile of due bills so John David would see it first.

The most exciting thing Melinda had found was one of a pair of earrings that Poppy had been trying to find for a month or more. I remembered her telling us, in her dramatic way, how she would just cry if she didn't find the missing earring. We cried a little ourselves when Melinda held it up.

Figuring John David wouldn't mind, we got some sliced ham out of the refrigerator and made sandwiches, in the process throwing out some leftovers that were obviously way past their prime. Cleaning out the refrigerator hadn't been high on Poppy's priority list. I took the first full garbage bag out the sliding glass door to the large garbage can Poppy kept there. After I tossed it in, I breathed in the clear, chilly air for a minute. My lungs felt dusty from all the books. Standing there looking at the back fence jogged a memory. I turned back into the kitchen and looked around. Yes, there on the counter was a radio. I examined it to locate the on button, then punched it. The music that came into the room, admittedly on the loud side, was not the classical or jazz music I usually heard on NPR, but a classic rock station based in Lawrenceton.

Well, there was another puzzle. Lizanne had said that when

she'd approached the gate to the backyard, she'd heard the radio playing loudly, loudly enough to obscure the voices at Poppy's back door. And that was when Poppy must have been murdered. But Poppy's radio wasn't on NPR.

Perhaps the crime-scene cleaner – nope, that was ridiculous. Sealed in his hazmat suit, he couldn't have heard music clearly at all; no reason for him to turn on the radio. That was as ludicrous as the idea of Marvin Wynn, right-wing preacher, turning on a classic rock station while he conducted an illegal search of his dead daughter's house.

Of course, Lizanne might have been lying. But her account had been so believable, so detailed. Why would she have lied about the radio station? It was something so easy to check.

And yet, no one had checked it until now.

Probably that was next on Arthur's list of things to do. Right?

Selfishly, I shared my worries with Melinda. She shrugged, not too interested in solving a puzzle with so many missing pieces. We'd been eating at the dining table by the sliding glass door, and I'd pulled the curtain back as far as it could go so the sun could brighten the room. Suddenly, it seemed confining, sitting in the chair. I pushed back from the table and went to stand by the glass door. I half-turned, easing a finger around the waistband of my slacks. I realized I must have horribly overeaten the day before. I felt swollen.

Should we have reported the Wynns' activities to Arthur?

I turned my head to say something to Melinda, only to catch her staring at me in a strange way.

'What?' I asked defensively.

'Aurora . . . don't get me wrong, here . . .We're friends, right?'

'Sure.' Confused and bewildered, that's how I sounded.

'You and Robin are really close, right? Really, really close?'

I understood what Melinda was trying to ask.

'Yes. Really, really close.'

'How long has it been since you had your period?' she said bluntly.

'Oh . . . I'd have to look at my calendar.' I tried to remember.

'Let's see, I was cutting out ghost silhouettes to put up for Halloween, and we decorate the library the second week in October, but I did those early . . .' I shrugged. 'I'm not always real regular.'

'So you're not on the pill.'

'No.' Boy, when Melinda decided to get personal, she didn't mess around.

'But you are using birth control?'

'Melinda! Well . . . mostly.' I felt my face redden as I thought of one evening a few weeks ago when we hadn't had time. In fact, we'd been in the bathroom upstairs at my mother's. It made me feel hot all over when I thought about it. 'You know I can't have kids, Melinda.' Robin had used condoms all the same, except for that once. Well, maybe one or two others. But it hadn't seemed like such a big deal; since I'd dated at least one man who didn't want me if I couldn't have children, I'd been very up-front with Robin about my infertility. This was a very sore subject with me, and I'd thought Melinda would respect that.

'I know Dr Mendelssohn, whom I think is an overpriced jerk, said so. Are your boobs sore?'

I was startled all over again. 'Well, sensitive,' I said, thinking of how I'd had to caution Robin to be gentler the night before.

'Have you looked at yourself in the mirror?'

'What are you driving at, Melinda?'

'I'll bet your bosom is really tender, not just a little sensitive.'

I nodded reluctantly.

'You've skipped using birth control at least one time, and I'd bet more often than that, and you're having sex. Your last period was six weeks ago.'

Well, that had been a long time, come to think of it.

'I'll bet you've been exhausted the past few days, been dropping off to sleep whenever you sat down. You have big rings under your eyes. Did you know that? Have you been queasy in the morning?'

I covered my mouth with both hands, feeling a wave of absolute terror and delight sweep over me.

Melinda waited for me to answer, then went on when I didn't. 'I've been pregnant twice, and I'd swear you should have a pregnancy test.'

'Don't even say it,' I told her. 'Don't even *think* it.' I waved my hands to erase her words from the air. I cursed the hope that sprang up in my heart. This was false and cruel.

'I'm sorry,' Melinda said, looking as though she was going to cry. And she damn well ought to, I thought. 'I just think . . .' Then she looked at me and canned whatever she'd been going to say. 'Okay, Roe. Subject closed.'

'Let's work on the bedroom,' I said, holding my eyes wide so the tears wouldn't spill out of them.

'Sure.' She grabbed a fresh dust cloth, a garbage bag, and the handle of the Dirt Devil. 'Let's go.'

It seems to be a universally held truth that people conceal their secrets in their bedrooms. If I had to hide something, I had to admit that I, too, would probably start looking for a good place in the room that was most mine, the room where I slept. Maybe Poppy, who had single-handedly organized the Christmas food drive at St James's, had had a smarter idea, but I planned to be even more meticulous in my search of this room than I had been in our reconstruction of the study. I had observed that Sandy Wynn had picked Poppy's bedroom to begin her own search, while relegating Marvin to the downstairs room.

Unfortunately, it was a large bedroom and the closet hadn't been cleaned in a long time. Poppy'd had a lot of clothes, and so did John David, since he had the kind of job that required suits. Melinda had a problem with small spaces, and though it was a big closet, it was still a closet. So I volunteered, then went back down the stairs to fetch a step stool. I was all in favor of a job that would keep me out of Melinda's sight for a while. I needed to work around what had happened downstairs. I was so conflicted that I pretty much felt numb. Doing something physical was exactly what I needed.

In no time, I was coughing at the dust I raised. The original searcher, the one who'd been in soon after Poppy died, had left a big jumble, and Sandy Wynn had added to the mess. But I could discern Poppy's storage method easily enough. She'd kept all her dress shoes in their original shoe boxes. Those had been stacked on the shelf above her hanging clothes, with the outer end of the box labeled – 'navy pumps,' for example, or 'black patent 2-in.' I dusted the shelf, and then I began examining the boxes and shoes as I dusted and replaced them. It was time-consuming and tedious. Poppy's everyday shoes had been on a rack on the floor of the closet, and there was a section of cube-shaped storage units toward the back that held Poppy's sweaters and purses. I restacked them, examining each one. I'd do her stuff first, then try to restore order to John David's side.

I could hear Melinda sliding out drawers to look at the bottoms and backs, checking to see if something had been taped in a hard-to-find place. She was also replacing the strewn contents of the drawers as she went, throwing away things like ancient prescriptions, odd socks, hose with runs. We had to walk a fine line here: returning things to order and neatness without interfering too much. We'd agreed to return Poppy's things to their hangers and boxes; her clothing and paraphernalia would have to be given away someday, but that wasn't up to us.

The top part of the closet was finally done, and I was hanging slacks when Melinda gave a sort of odd choking noise.

With some relief, I stepped out of the closet to check on her progress. My sister-in-law was standing by the bed, her eyes fixed on something she held in her hand. Her cheeks were flaming red.

'Melinda?'

She opened her mouth to speak, then shut it again. She shook her head violently.

'Melinda?' I reached around her to take the object from her hand.

It was a photograph. It actually took me a few seconds to comprehend what I was seeing. In this photograph, Poppy was giving someone a blow job. The picture had been taken from so close that you couldn't tell who the male was.

I can't describe what a shock it was to see a picture of someone

I knew performing a sex act. In this floral suburban bedroom, the picture was even more obscene than it would have been if I'd chanced upon it in a magazine.

'I wonder who it is,' I said once I could speak. 'I mean, possibly this is some loving record of her and John David?'

'Oh, it *never* is!' Melinda said. She was absolutely outraged. 'The Queensland brothers, I know from Avery, are both uncircumcised. This . . . individual, as you can see, is *not*.'

'At least she didn't keep it as blackmail.' I was looking for reassurance; 'I mean, you can't tell who it is, and the thing itself looks pretty anonymous, doesn't it? No big freckles, or, ah, anything unusual.'

Melinda looked at the picture again, her lips pursed with distaste. 'No, just a regular old wienie,' she said.

We looked at each other and burst into laughter. 'Look at it this way. You know it's not Avery,' I said.

'And look at the hair. Couldn't be Robin,' she pointed out.

True. Robin was redheaded all over, so to speak.

'I refuse to guess,' I said after one final inspection. 'But whoever it is, we agree that John David should not see this.'

'Absolutely.'

'Where was it?'

'It was taped to the bottom of this little drawer.' Melinda pointed to Poppy's jewelry box, which was filled to overflowing with inexpensive necklaces and earrings. There was a pullout drawer at the bottom, so you could lay your chains inside and they wouldn't tangle. Melinda had pulled it all the way out and flipped it.

'Aren't you smart to think of that!' I said admiringly.

Melinda looked modest.

'Well, no telling how much else we'll find,' I said, unable to suppress a sigh. 'I guess we'd better get back to work.'

The next find was mine. Taped into the lining of a spring coat Poppy had worn maybe twice a year was a letter. The letter was from the Reverend Wynn to Poppy. It was signed and dated. In the letter, he admitted he had had 'relations' with Poppy when she was thirteen.

For a few minutes, Melinda and I could not even look at each other.

'Relations with a relation,' Melinda said in an effort to pull us out of our nauseated reaction. She dropped that effort when it rang false. 'Poor Poppy,' she said sadly.

'No wonder she was so wild,' I said. 'No wonder she was so . . .'

'Promiscuous,' Melinda supplied.

'Yeah.'

'This is the nastiest thing I have ever read. I wonder why he wrote it?'

'I guess this was insurance,' I said, having thought it over for a minute or two. 'Maybe this was her way of keeping him away from her kids. Keeping him out of her life. She must have told him she'd tell his bishop, or whoever stands in place of a bishop in the Lutheran church.' I made a mental note to check on that later.

'Do you think his wife knows about this?'

I started to deny that instantly. Then I reconsidered.

'She was searching,' I admitted. I told Melinda about the gas station receipt. 'She could have come here that morning and questioned Poppy about it.'

'Then you'd have to assume she knows her husband did this to her daughter.' Melinda brandished the letter. 'If she does, how can she live with him?'

'This is a question I can't answer. Another one is, Would she have killed Poppy to conceal this? Bryan left a message for Arthur to call him back, so he could tell Arthur about the receipt. Maybe Arthur already knows.'

We began a little pile.

I had to rethink Poppy's character as I worked and searched. My sister-in-law had shown me only the tip of the iceberg, as far as letting me know her true self. I had to realize that I had seen the better, but less complex, portion of Poppy's personality. Beneath had lain monsters.

We were determined to find everything. It was not conceivable that we would let anything slip by us, to fall into the hands of a stranger, or, worse yet, someone who knew Poppy. Sooner or later, John David would give away Poppy's things to some local charity or to a friend. Or he'd search himself. He mustn't see these – what? Souvenirs? Insurance policies? Totems?

Bubba Sewell would definitely never make representative, I decided when I found the picture of him buck naked on Poppy's – and John David's – bed. He was real excited, and hardly looked like a lawmaker. In a beige photo album, that picture was slid in behind a snap of Poppy and John David on vacation in Florida. Definitely done in an 'Up yours, John David' moment.

'Idiot,' I muttered, and tossed it on the pile.

'Who's that?' Melinda looked up from her examination of Poppy's lingerie drawer.

'Cartland Sewell.'

Melinda shook her head in disgust, not even bothering to look at the picture. She continued with her search, and made the next discovery. She found an ID tag stuck in a rectangular Playtex box with a new bra – the kind of tag you clip to your lapel. The picture on it was of a bearded, thin man, who just happened to be Cara Embler's heart surgeon husband. It was his hospital identification.

'I guess Stuart got it replaced,' Melinda said. 'Her back-door neighbor! Poppy had never heard about not fouling your own nest, I guess.'

'He's one of John's doctors,' I said.

'Daddy John?' This was Melinda's pet name for John Queensland.

I nodded.

She sighed, a huge exhalation of exasperation. 'I'm sorry, heart surgeons don't get sex lives,' she said. 'Not with the daughters-in-law of their patients.'

'Who knows which came first, though, the heart attack or the affair? If you can term it an affair, that is. Maybe it was just a – you know.'

'Just a fling,' Melinda said.

That hadn't been the word I was thinking of, but . . . Oh well.

'That's right, we can't know.' This actually made her feel better.

'What I'm wondering is, What're we missing. If we're finding this much, what did the other searchers find? Can there be stuff that's worse?' We stared at each other, sunk in gloom.

And we heard a door open downstairs.

I don't know how I looked, but Melinda's dark eyes grew as wide and dark as tablespoons full of molasses.

'Who's there?' called a deep male voice, and we could hear heavy footsteps as someone began ascending the stairs. 'Aurora, are you all right? I saw your car.'

Melinda and I stared at the little pile, and, obeying an irresistible impulse, I sat on it.

We were perched side by side on the bed, looking guilty as hell, when Detective Arthur Smith came into the bedroom.

'What are you two doing?' he asked gently. He could tell he'd given us a scare.

'It's okay for us to be here, right?' Melinda's voice was high and squeaky.

'Yes, we told John David he could come back to the house anytime he wanted. But what are you doing?'

'We're cleaning up,' I said, all too aware that I sounded just as nervous as my partner in crime. 'Have you talked to Bryan Pascoe?' I wanted to change the subject.

'And you started with the study downstairs?' Arthur asked, ignoring my question. 'Surely it didn't look like that the other day?'

Arthur was far too observant. 'No, no, it didn't,' I gabbled. 'The fact is . . .' I looked at Melinda, desperately needing some help.

'The fact is,' Melinda said, glaring at me, 'that Roe caught Poppy's mom and dad going through everything Wednesday night, and she threw them out. So we had to clean up the study first.'

I hadn't expected Melinda to tell the truth, and I'm sure my startled face told Arthur more than I wanted him to know.

He pulled over a chair that Poppy had placed in the corner of the room, a pretty little wooden chair with a bright needlepoint cushion, more of Poppy's work. I hadn't noticed it before, at least in the sense of imagining its possibilities, and I found myself planning to check out the cushion later.

Arthur plunked himself down in front of us, looking up at us as we perched awkwardly on the high antique bed. My legs were sticking out at an odd angle, and Melinda's feet were just barely touching the floor.

'What explanation did they give?' he asked. His voice was reasonable, but his expression wasn't. 'And why didn't you call me?'

'I wasn't there,' Melinda said, maybe a little too quickly. Coward! 'Sorry,' she muttered to me. 'Can't help it.'

'I came by with Bryan Pascoe,' I said. 'We made them leave, but they sure weren't about to tell us why they were here.'

'What do you think they were looking for?' Arthur asked.

Suddenly, I realized that Arthur had just come in the house without either of us admitting him. But we'd locked the door behind us. Would the police get to keep a key? Surely not, after the house, had been re-opened to the family.

Arthur had a *key*. Though their affair was long over, he had a key, too.

For a brilliant red flash of a moment, I hated Poppy with all my heart. I looked at Arthur and wondered if I ought to fear him. Over the years, I had felt many things for Arthur: love, passion, anger, grief, annoyance, outrage, exasperation. But I had never thought I'd be frightened of him.

The tense silence stretched out unbearably.

'Roe – and you, too, Melinda – I did not kill Poppy. I was crazy about her, and she was about me, but it didn't last. I never said anything to the chief, because I want to catch whoever killed her. I want to catch him myself. This is the last thing I can do for Poppy. I want to do it right.'

I looked at him doubtfully, but Melinda was convinced. She turned to me. 'I think we should,' she said quietly.

'*No*,' I told her emphatically. The news would spread everywhere. John would be hurt by this knowledge; John David would be even more wounded. Sooner or later, the little bit of mortality that was Chase would know about it.

'We have to,' Melinda said, just to me.

I gave her a very dark look and eased off the bed. She took up the letter and handed it to Arthur. He put on a pair of reading glasses that he'd pulled from his breast pocket. As he read, we both watched him carefully. While he was busy, I slipped the two pictures into my pocket. Melinda watched me and gave a tiny nod. Arthur would probably burst a blood vessel if he saw them. As it was, disgust twisted his lips as he read the words scrawled on the paper.

'Even her father,' he muttered.

'That wasn't her fault,' Melinda said, instantly indignant. 'For God's sake, she was thirteen!'

Arthur gathered himself, glancing up at us, then back to the sprawling handwriting. I couldn't read him, had no idea what he was thinking. He folded the paper and put it in his pocket.

'There was something about her,' he said.

Melinda looked at me in consternation. Though she'd known about Arthur and Poppy, this sudden wistful admission from the cop in charge of the investigation threw her completely.

'Listen, Arthur,' I said as gently as I could. 'Maybe someone else should be in charge of this case. What about that Cathy Trumble? She seemed real able.'

'She didn't know Poppy like I did,' Arthur said. 'I know the chief would take me off the case if he knew I'd been involved with Poppy, but I'm the best investigator on the force, and I have to find out who did this to her. She was the most exciting, the most wonderful . . . I never dreamed anyone could be as wonderful as you were, Roe, but Poppy was something extraordinary.'

Melinda gave me a horrified stare, I could feel my cheeks flame red, and I turned my hands palm up. What could I say? For years after he'd dumped me (to marry Lynn, and then divorce her), Arthur had thought he loved me. For years he'd turned up at odd moments in my life, his eyes begging me to take him back. He'd never shown that level of devotion when we were dating, when it would have been appropriate and welcome.

Maybe that was the way it had worked with Poppy, too. He'd gotten hooked on her when she'd moved on to someone else.

'We were together when she shopped for that rug downstairs, the one that had all her blood on it,' he said, almost conversationally. 'She told me that every time she looked at it, she thought of me. We had sex on it.'

That definitely fell into the category of 'More than I want to know'. 'But she switched to someone after you, Arthur,' I said. 'Who was it?'

'She told me,' Arthur said, 'long ago . . . She told me that when she was inducted into the Uppity Women, she was going to make sure I got a promotion. Chief of detectives is coming up. Jeb Green's gotten a better job in Savannah. Poppy told me my career would take off. She promised me so much, and gave me so little.'

She'd told Cartland she'd help him progress in state government. He'd been so besotted with her, he'd been willing to leave his wife and children. Poppy had been trying to be a total package: illicit lover, career advancer, wife, mother, suburban queen. I wondered if I'd ever known the real woman. What had she been like when she was alone?

'We never really knew her,' Melinda said to me. She sounded as sad as I felt. She hooked her dark hair behind her ears and gave Arthur a determined look. 'Listen, Detective Smith. We don't want to hear any more about you and Poppy. What we want is to know what to do about the letter. And we want to know what you're going to do about her mother.'

Arthur seemed to jerk himself out of the pool of reminiscence he'd fallen into. 'What about her mother?' he asked. 'Does this have something to do with the messages Bryan Pascoe has been leaving at the station?'

'If you returned your phone calls, you could have picked her up already,' I said, angry and somehow hurt by all Arthur's unwelcome revelations. I explained about the gas station receipt, about the attendant's memory of the day Poppy had been murdered.

'I'll go find out.'

Arthur left in a hurry, determined to track down the Wynns and interrogate them. After he'd gone, Melinda and I had to gather ourselves back together for a few minutes. We were quite shaken by Arthur and his odd behavior.

'Even if it was Sandy Wynn who killed Poppy, and that part of it gets wrapped up,' Melinda said, 'we still have to finish this job.' She waved her hand at the bedroom, still considerably out of order.

'You're right. John David shouldn't find this stuff.' I stuck the plastic ID tag into my pocket to dispose of later with heavy scissors. I ripped the fellatio picture and the frank snap of Cartland Sewell into tiny bits and flushed them down the toilet. Neither of us wanted to give those to Arthur. I didn't know how I was ever going to look Bubba in the face again, as it was. 'That wasn't the same person,' I told Melinda as the picture bits disappeared. 'In both those pictures. Different guys.'

'Oh? I guess I didn't compare.' She gave me a lopsided smile.

'Well, the one in the close-up picture was a lot, ah, bigger in diameter than Cartland's.'

'Think of knowing that about someone,' Melinda said, and, amazingly, she giggled. 'You know, Avery is my one and only. Pretty rare in this day and age, huh?'

I nodded respectfully. My own list was quite short, but it did have more than one name on it. 'I can't understand anyone letting Poppy take pictures,' I said. 'I'm feeling pretty much on the naive side, too. It seems like common sense would tell the man that such a thing could only lead to trouble. You can deny and deny – but if the other person has a picture, denials are pretty useless.'

'Avery and I sure wouldn't do that,' Melinda said. 'And I can't see the point. I know what he looks like. He knows what I look like. What's the point of taking pictures? Just something for the kids to find and bring out in the middle of a dinner party, right?'

'That's my opinion, too. I just don't get it.'

'Maybe we're just too middle-class?'

I laughed. 'Maybe so, Melinda. Maybe so.'

I called my house to see if Phillip had returned. When he didn't answer, I called the Finstermeyers and got Josh's mom, Beth.

'We were just trying to call you,' she said. 'Listen, would it be all right if I took the boys Christmas shopping with me? The Bodine mall is having all kinds of after-Thanksgiving sales, and with these two guys for bodyguards, I thought I might come out of it alive. I'd have them back by seven or eight tonight.'

'Sure, that's fine with me.' Phillip seemed to be really clicking with Josh. I felt quite pleased about that. 'Um, could I speak to Phillip for a minute?'

'Sure.'

'Hey, Sis.' Phillip's voice was deeper and more relaxed than I remembered it.

'Listen, Phillip, do you have enough money for a trip to the mall?'

'Well, I am sort of broke.'

'On your way out of town, why don't you swing by Poppy's house – Mrs Finstermeyer will know where that is – and I'll spot you some cash.'

'Thanks!' Phillip sounded quite enthusiastic. 'Oh, and Roe? When I went to your house to get my coat, I saw you had a few messages on the answering machine. I didn't listen to them, because I was in a big hurry.'

'Thanks back at you,' I told him. 'I'll check them before too long.'

In a few minutes, I'd handed Phillip the entire contents of my billfold, and Melinda and I went back to work.

Two hours later, we were tired and rumpled. Melinda had started sneezing from breathing so much dust. And we had found only one more memento, a stained male bikini. When I held it up, Melinda said, 'I don't even want to think about that.' I could not have agreed more. I dropped the shiny black thing right into the garbage bag – the third one we'd filled with the odd trash that everyone accumulates. Melinda and I were just not capable of returning 1998 sales slips, old tissues, and outdated catalogs to their original places, especially since we had no idea where those places had been.

We lifted the bare mattress and the box spring, we checked under the bed, and we shifted all the furniture slightly. We looked over, under, and inside everything.

After a vacuuming and a final look around, Melinda and I agreed that the bedroom was cleaner and more orderly than it had been before someone came into the house on Tuesday. For our grand finale, we remade the bed. The police had taken the linens to the lab.

We trailed wearily downstairs and sat at the table beside the glass doors. With the stained rug gone and all trace of the blood removed, it was a lot easier to forget what had happened on this spot. Since John David had never seen Poppy's body, I hoped he might be able to tolerate staying in the house.

'I wish we could tell some of the other Uppity Women what we're looking for. They'd help us,' Melinda said.

'Yeah, it's too bad we can't tap into that energy,' I said, leaning my head on my folded arms. I could not remember ever having felt so tired in my life. I must be getting old, I thought, to let some housecleaning exhaust me to such an extent. 'But it would defeat the purpose of us searching if we let everyone in on why we needed to do it.'

'Listen. Cara Embler's out swimming. In this weather!' Melinda shivered. It had turned into a raw day, and Cara was either dedicated or an utter fool to be out swimming in the cold, wet air.

'Better her than me,' I muttered. 'You know she's going to be the next Uppity Woman?'

'Oh?'

'Yes, she was next on the list after Poppy.'

'And she's so energetic.'

'All that exercise. She has to do something to keep busy, since she doesn't work, I guess.'

'I'm glad Avery isn't a doctor. They're gone so much. Swimming is lots better than eating when you're lonely, like I do.'

Melinda cast a disparaging eye down at her own somewhat-rounded stomach.

'You look great to me.'

'Well, I can hardly fit into the size I was wearing before I had Charles,' Melinda said frankly. She was punching buttons on the phone. 'I have to check in at home.'

I was left staring at a wedding picture of John David and Poppy. I tried to imagine maintaining a marriage so screwed up that the partners would not be interested in each other's infidelity. My mother had certainly cared when my father had been unfaithful. Boy, had she cared! Though they would never have fought in front of me, I'd been a teen, and I'd been aware of the thick tension in our house.

I recalled John David crying that morning in the motel room, and I tried to grasp what people could do to each other short of killing each other. In the background, I heard Melinda's voice as she talked to her babysitter, her laughter as the girl probably passed along something cute Marcy had said.

My mind wandered back to the previous Monday, the day of Poppy's death. My phone call from her, our conversation. How irritated Melinda and I had been with our sister-in-law. Our drive over to Swanson Lane, my march into the house. The unlocked front door.

I wondered if Poppy usually kept it locked, or if her mother had surprised her by just walking in. My eyes opened wide as I considered this new idea. Why had Sandy picked that particular time to try to retrieve the letter? It had been dated a year and a half ago. That meant that when Poppy had been pregnant, she had demanded that letter from her father in exchange for – what? Marvin's never seeing his grandchild? Poppy wouldn't have known then that she'd have a boy.

Okay, back to the basic memory, I told myself. The front door had been open. I had walked in. I had called up the stairs. I had walked up the stairs. The shower had been dry, so I'd known Poppy had been out of it for a while. The room had been neat; the bed had been made. The closet door had been shut. I could even picture my feet moving downstairs in those shoes, my favorites. Then I'd seen Moosie, right? (Who was still missing, incidentally. I made a mental note to check on that.)

The cat had stropped my ankles, then run ahead of me into the kitchen. I'd felt the cold air keenly, the closer I got to the back of the house. When I'd come into the kitchen and looked over the breakfast bar to my left, I'd seen the glass door open.

I hadn't been able to see Poppy's body until I'd come around the end of the breakfast bar with its high stools. There was Poppy's body, sprawled on the floor. She lay half in and half out the door, partially on the rug under the dining table, partially on the linoleum. I'd heard Cara splashing in the pool. I'd looked out into the backyard, over Poppy's body, and seen the concrete around Poppy's own pool dotted with darker water stains. Looked down again at Poppy, horribly dead, her hands . . . I had to gulp back my nausea.

Could Sandy Wynn have done that to her own daughter?

The older I got, the less I seemed able to understand or predict the behavior of those around me. Instead of gaining wisdom, so that people seemed simpler, I learned more about the complexity of human nature.

'So, what do you think?' Melinda's voice made me jump.

'I think that we've probably found everything there is to find,' I said. 'I may be wrong, and if I am, there'll be hell to pay. We didn't find anything of Arthur's, for example, and we know he was one of Poppy's lovers. Maybe that means he was already here, searching. Maybe he's the one who trashed the bedroom. Maybe he just wouldn't let her photograph him, or he was too alert for her to risk taking some little memento. Or maybe that black underwear was his.' Melinda and I wore matching expressions of disgust as we considered that.

'You sure he wasn't the one in the, you know, the picture with Poppy?' She carefully found something else to look at while I tried to remember. It wasn't that Arthur had looked awful naked – quite the contrary – but I just couldn't remember. There hadn't been anything outstanding in the pertinent department.

'I just don't know,' I said finally, and Melinda nodded. 'To return to our original subject, I just don't think Poppy would have risked hiding anything really awful down here in the more or less public rooms. Not only might John David have found it but also she'd have realized Chase would be walking very soon. And there were other people in and out. Babysitters and friends, and other lovers even. I think we've found it all, or very close to all.'

'But are we comfortable with stopping now? Just letting the chips fall where they may?'

Melinda was sitting opposite me, her thin hands folded together. I tried to pretend I had some energy. I sat up straight.

'Yes, I think so,' I said, not sounding sure at all.

'You're right,' Melinda said more decisively. She was sure enough for the two of us. 'I think she put everything, um, naughty up in their room, where she could keep a close eye on it, and I think we've found everything. I can't imagine another hiding place in that room. We looked everywhere.'

'No, we didn't.'

'What?'

'We didn't look in the needlepoint cushion of that chair.'

Melinda knew instantly what I meant. She was out of the kitchen and up the stairs in that smooth, unhurried stride that made her look so efficient. She was back in a moment, cushion in hand.

She handed it to me, and I looked it over. Poppy had done the needlepoint for the top of the flat cushion herself. I have no craft ability whatsoever, so I couldn't have told you what kind of pattern it was, but the design was thistles on a cream background. The top was shaped like a large pancake to match the round seat of the chair. The bottom of the cushion was covered in a sage green silky material. It had turned out real pretty. Now we were about to deface it.

'I feel bad about this,' I said, hesitating over the pretty thing. A dead woman's hands had crafted this, and I was reluctant to begin. I wriggled the padding in a sort of wave motion, and I felt something rustle inside the cushion.

'Oh hell, there's something in there,' I told Melinda.

We looked at each other with a kind of despair. I felt dirty outside because of all the dust we'd stirred up in the corners of the bedroom – though that had been easy enough to clean up – and I felt dirty inside because of all the dirt we'd discovered in Poppy's life – which wasn't easy to dispose of at all. It was a neat parallel, and it made me sick. I never wanted to know this much about another human being, I decided. People needed their secrets. My mother had always told me that ignorance is dangerous, but the way I felt now, ignorance would be true bliss.

Melinda said, 'I can sew it shut if we just cut a thin slit.'

The sharpest knife we could find glided easily into the sage green material. Melinda held the cushion absolutely flat and still while I enlarged the opening. Melinda's fingers were far longer than mine, so she assumed the task of extraction: Tweezed between her long forefinger and middle finger, the piece of paper hissed like a snake against the silk as she drew it out.

I unfolded the paper with as much terror as if it had been an actual reptile.

It was the results of a DNA test. 'A paternity test,' I told Melinda. 'It looks like Poppy took two samples in to be tested against Chase's DNA. She paid for it up front, cash. Get this – it was ordered by Dr Stuart Embler.' I looked at Melinda significantly, then returned my attention to the letter. 'She told them – well, I can't figure out exactly what she told them, but subject A was not the father, and Subject B was.'

Melinda opened and closed her mouth several times, as if she thought she knew what to say, then decided that she didn't. I knew exactly how she felt.

'What are we going to do?' she asked finally.

'What a good question,' I said. 'And I don't have the slightest idea what the answer is. Should we make an appointment with Aubrey?'

'But he'd know then. We can't have anyone knowing if we can prevent it. On the other hand, this seems like too much for us. This is really huge.'

'Yes.'

'Chase may be John David's son, and he may not. My God, what will happen to Chase if he isn't John David's?'

'He'll still be Poppy's son, so that means . . .'

'Her parents will get him? Absolutely not.'

'But we don't have the right to lie about it!'

'No! But we can't take Chase away from John David!'

'But he has another father! A real father!'

'Maybe John David is the real father. Maybe John David is subject B.'

We both took a deep breath. 'I say we burn this piece of paper,' I said. I looked at my sister-in-law steadily.

'I say we should sleep on it and talk to Aubrey tomorrow,' Melinda countered, neatly reversing her trend of a few moments before.

I was sorely tempted to grab it from her hand and rip it to shreds, as I had the repulsive pictures. Why the hell had I remembered the cushion on the chair? John David would never in a million years have messed with that cushion. If it had crinkled when he sat on it, he still wouldn't have opened it up, an opinion I based simply on John David's being a man.

Well, the deed had been done, and we were the possessors of yet another piece of unpleasant knowledge.

Chapter Eleven

When I got home that evening, cooking was the bottom thing on my list of desirable activities. The day after Thanksgiving is just not a day to slave over the stove. That's pretty much been done. So I was delighted to discover, among the messages on my answering machine, one from Robin inviting Phillip and me out to dinner. I almost dropped the phone in my haste to punch in his number so I could accept.

Phillip, back from a day out with another teenager, was less excited. The company of three adults seemed less appealing to him after a long afternoon with Josh, eyeing girls at the mall. I suspected my brother was lapsing back into his normal self, becoming more relaxed around me, rather than being so anxious to mind his manners and be helpful. He'd absorbed the fact that I wasn't going to throw him out.

'Can't I just stay here and eat leftovers?' he said in a voice suspiciously close to a whine.

'No, you can not,' I said in a voice suspiciously close to a direct order. I wondered again why my father hadn't called to set up the return of Phillip.

Robin's message was the third I'd listened to. The first two had been from, respectively, Cara Embler (who said she had found Moosie and would keep him at her house until we decided what to do with the cat), and the Clean Scene guy, Zachary Lee (who hoped we had found his service satisfactory and would recommend him to our friends). I looked at my watch and decided not to listen to my remaining messages. I was dusty, dirty, and badly in need of a general cleanup. I was thrilled Moosie had been found, and I made a mental note to call John David the next day and tell him the whereabouts of the little cat.

I told Phillip he looked fine. He hadn't any more clothes anyway, and I hoped Robin would take that into consideration when he picked out a restaurant. I threw my clothes into the hamper, reflected that laundry day would have to be really soon, and tossed the small Wal-Mart bag I'd brought home with me onto the bathroom counter. Maybe tomorrow morning, I thought. Now was the worst time in the world.

The shower was blissful. I was clean all over, and relaxed, and much more optimistic when I emerged. I looked at myself in the mirror carefully. My bosom looked a little different, the aureoles darker, and when I put on my bra, I noticed that I was very sore indeed.

It took all I had to walk past the small bag, leaving it unopened.

Corinne was really fond of Italian food, and there was a new Italian restaurant about halfway between Lawrenceton and the interstate, an area that was beginning to run together in a big blur of commerce. Actually, the restaurant was not too far from the Grabbit Kwik, the filling station where Sandy Wynn had filled her car's tank with gas on Monday.

I pushed the death of Poppy out of my mind. I tried not to think of all the unpleasant things Melinda and I had learned today. I forced myself not to think of the bag on the counter of my bathroom.

All that not thinking left my mind pretty empty. I'm afraid I wasn't a very good conversationalist that night. I made an attempt to be a good listener, to encourage Corinne to talk, so I wouldn't seem stupid by my silences. And I asked Robin a lot of questions. Phillip decided to talk about drug use in his school in California, to impress us unworldly southerners, I suppose. Robin reminded him in a few well-chosen anecdotes that he had spent the past two years living in Los Angeles among the movie crowd, and any stories Phillip chose to tell, Robin could easily top.

Corinne, as it transpired, had left her Chihuahua and her toy Manchester in the care of one of her daughters, and she had called to check on their well-being that very afternoon. Corinne was one of those women who had to have something to mother; for all I knew, that made her like most women. Now that her children were very much grown and gone, and her grandchildren visited from time to time but not for days in a row, the dogs had filled that gap for her. Though she was intelligent enough to realize not everyone wants to listen to detailed animal stories, she was besotted enough not to care, and we heard many anecdotes about Punky's little trick with the bouncy ball, and Percy's little wake-up routine.

That reminded me that I hadn't laid eyes on Madeleine in a couple of days, and during a lull in the dog worship, I asked Phillip if he'd seen the massive old cat.

'No,' he said. 'Maybe she didn't like me and so she's staying away until I leave.'

'Nothing would make Madeleine miss a meal,' I said.

'Was your cat named for the little girl in the books?' Corinne asked brightly.

'No, for the poisoner,' I answered, abstracted. 'Madeleine Smith, Glasgow, 1857.'

'Oh,' Corinne said.

We didn't hear any more dog stories for a while.

When Robin dropped us off, Phillip loped ahead to get in the house to watch some television show he was dying to see. Robin came in the foyer with me and shut the door behind him. He had a big, long, smoochy kiss on his mind, but when he pulled me to him, my sore chest protested.

'Not so tight,' I said, trying to smile.

'What's wrong?' Not too surprisingly, he was bewildered. I'd been Passionate Woman the night before, and now I was practically pushing him away. But I was so averse to the idea of sex that I would have kicked him in the shins if he'd suggested it. I answered him by bursting into tears.

'What?' Terrified, Robin gripped my elbows. 'What's wrong? Are you upset about Poppy? Madeleine? I'll look for her tomorrow, I swear, baby.'

'No, not that.' I wanted to tell him about my long, unpleasant day, and I wanted to tell him what I was beginning to suspect might be the truth. But this wasn't the place, and his mother was waiting out in the cold in the car for him to return.

'Your mom leaves Monday?' I sobbed.

'No, I forgot to tell you. Before she left home, she changed her reservation, because the airline called her with a last-minute cancellation,' Robin said. 'She leaves tomorrow afternoon. One of her best friends lost his son in an accident overseas, and the memorial service is scheduled for Sunday afternoon. Mom wants to be back for it. It's just amazing she was able to get a seat on the plane. She was on the phone for hours, she told me, but she got it done.' He sounded admiring. 'But tell me what's wrong.'

'I can't tell you right now,' I said. I wasn't actively crying anymore, just kind of giving the occasional sob or gasp. This was crazy. I had no control over it whatsoever. I was just along for the ride. 'Lots of stuff happened today. We need to talk tomorrow, after you take your mom to the airport. Call me.'

'Sure,' he said. Hesitantly, he leaned over and gave me a peck on the forehead. That was easier for him to reach anyway.

I was almost too tired to take off my clothes. I wished my brother good night, asked him to check the doors before he went to bed, cast a disconsolate look at Madeleine's food bowl – still full – and tucked myself into bed. I thought I might lie awake a little and rehash the day, but the minute my head came into contact with my pillow, I was out.

Someone was shaking me.

Someone had hold of my shoulder and was saying, 'Roe, wake up!' in a terrified voice.

I opened my eyes to sunlight. I had not slept two hours or so, as I'd assumed – I'd slept the night through, and then some. Phillip was standing by the bed, his face full of horror.

'What?' I asked, sitting up. My heart was racing and my mouth felt like a herd of something dirty – maybe mud-covered water buffalo – had wallowed in it. 'What?' I asked again, more sharply this time. I was fully awake.

'My mom has gone and your cat is dead.'

I started to say something, closed my mouth, and opened it again. 'Say that again,' I demanded.

'Those messages you didn't listen to last night?' This was definitely said with an accusatory edge. 'One of those messages was from our dad. He says my mom left and he doesn't know where she's gone. He says she's gone off with some guy.'

For a wild moment, I wondered if Betty Jo, too, would hitch-hike over to Lawrenceton. Then I came to my senses.

'That's really awful,' I said. 'But he doesn't think she's in any danger? I mean, there's no question but that she left voluntarily?' Phillip looked blank. 'She arranged to run off with this man,' I said, trying to clarify. 'He didn't abduct her.'

'Right,' Phillip said, calming down a bit. 'She definitely left because she wanted to. She told Dad she'd get in touch with him soon. She told him to call me. She said she knew I was safe with you.'

That was rich, coming from the woman who'd whisked Phillip off all the way to California to keep him from my contaminating companionship.

'I'm glad she feels that way,' I managed to say, wanting a cup of coffee more than I had ever wanted any beverage in my life. 'Now, I want to talk more about that later, because I know that's definitely the more important thing, but did you say Madeleine was dead?'

Personally, I considered Madeleine much more important, but I was trying to be sensitive to Phillip's pain.

'Oh, yeah, I went out in the backyard this morning, since the weather is good, and I was like kicking around this pinecone, and when it landed on something in the bushes around the wall—' my backyard, like Poppy's, was enclosed by a solid wood privacy fence, though mine was definitely shorter '—I went to see why it sounded so funny, and your big old cat was lying there on the ground, and she was all wet and everything, and she's dead.' Phillip looked at me pathetically. He had had a tough morning, and it was only . . .

'What time is it?' I asked.

'Nine-thirty,' Phillip said. 'See? There's a clock right by the bed, Sis.' He may have been a tad sarcastic.

'Okay, so I didn't look.' I groped for my glasses on the night table and put them on. I took a deep breath, then went into the bathroom to wash my face, trying to prepare to content this day.

I'd slept until 9:30 a.m. maybe four times in my life, and one of those had been after my senior prom, when I'd stayed out all night, as was the local tradition. I was dazed by so much sleep, and wondered what had prompted it. Then, glancing at the Wal-Mart bag, I suspected I knew, but I thrust the knowledge away from me forcefully. I had enough to deal with just at the moment, thanks very much. Pulling on the heaviest bathrobe in my closet, I slid my feet into my Birkenstock clogs and ventured out into the backyard. The day was clear and cold, and my ankles stung in the chilly breeze.

Madeleine was lying under a bush. She was nearly invisible, and I wasn't surprised we hadn't seen her from the house. She looked as peaceful as any dead thing can look. Apparently, the old cat had just lain down and died.

I believed that Madeleine was now in heaven with her original mistress, my friend Jane Engle. This conviction came to me so simply and naturally that I knew I would never question it.

'Phillip, I need you to go get a shovel from the garage,' I said. 'You can bury her right where she is; maybe move the hole away from the bush a little so you won't hit too many roots.'

'Me?' Phillip sounded absolutely amazed. 'She was your cat!'

'Point noted,' I snapped. 'But the one who loves the animal least gets the hole-digging duty. I loved this old cat, and I'm really upset, and you're twenty years younger than I am, and you get to dig the damn hole!'

I spun on my heel, as much as you can do that in clogs, and stomped back into the house to listen to my phone messages.

I sniveled and wiped my eyes and nose on a napkin before I poked the play button on my answering machine. The first message (after the three I'd listened to the night before) was from my father, and it went as Phillip had said. What Phillip hadn't said, of course, was that my dad sounded both stunned and indignant, as if he'd never expected his straying from fidelity could have such dire consequences. And, apparently, Dad had never considered the fact that his wife might have followed his example. I noticed right away – and Phillip hadn't mentioned this, either – that my dad said nothing about Phillip coming home.

Hmm. Dad and I needed to talk.

The next message was from my mother, confirming that Poppy's body would be back in Lawrenceton on Saturday, today, and would be ready for burial on Monday. John David had set the service for ten o'clock at St Stephen's, and the interment would follow immediately.

I'd have to check the work schedule and see if I needed to arrange for the morning off. At this rate, Sam would cut me from the payroll. The library budget was always tight. I'd been picked to take a course in Atlanta about computer usage for librarians, and I was very excited about it. I'd been on the verge of asking Sam if I could come back on the staff full-time. Maybe now I'd better not make that call, I thought.

Melinda had left a message to say Aubrey could see us at ten-thirty this morning.

'Oh my God,' I muttered, glancing at the clock. I washed my face again and put on some makeup, though my eyes looked red and swollen behind the rims of my glasses. I wore black ones today, with gold decorations on the earpieces. These made me look serious but fun-loving, I thought. I pulled on a pair of cerise pants and a cerise-and-white-checked sweater, so I wouldn't look funereal. Then I thought I looked too cheerful, but there was nothing I could do about it. I had to go so I wouldn't be late. I hate being late.

Besides, I thought as I backed out of my driveway, the day would probably take care of obliterating any cheerfulness.

Melinda got out of her car as I pulled into the lot by the church. She was wearing sweats today, jolly red-and-green sweats that had a huge reindeer head on the front of the shirt. With this outfit, she wore cute little red sneakers with green laces, and her red coat. The Christmas buildup had begun.

'Avery's got the kids,' she said. 'He's pretty miffed at me because I wouldn't tell him why we needed to talk to Aubrey. He's very obviously trying to be brave about hiding it. I can't think of the last time I had a secret from Avery.' She sounded mildly amused.

'Have you seen John David?'

'Yeah, he's over at our place, too. He's asking questions about baby care and what to do when. I feel like a big fat traitor, coming here to ask Aubrey if we should tell.'

'It seems to me this was your idea,' I said somewhat indignantly. I sure had better ways I could spend my morning, what was left of it.

'I know, I just . . . I guess I didn't foresee how complicated this would be. Emotionally.'

'Well, we're here now,' I said, acting ungracious and grumpy. I started down the sidewalk to the outside entrance to Aubrey's office, which was at the back of the church.

Aubrey seemed maybe a little less than delighted to be seeing us on a Saturday morning, since Saturday and Monday were his days off. Well, tough. We had a major moral dilemma.

Realizing I was definitely in a truculent mood, I advised myself to put the brakes on.

Catch more flies with honey, I reminded myself, glancing around to make sure that reminder had been given mentally rather than out loud. Since Aubrey and Melinda were discussing the Altar Guild rotation, I was pretty sure I was in the clear.

'Aubrey,' I said rather sharply. 'Melinda and I have run into a problem.'

We began to explain.

Thirty minutes later, Melinda and I were leaving Aubrey's office, none the wiser. I had considered Aubrey pretty much unflappable, but I found I'd been wrong. Aubrey seemed to be as confounded as we were, and his parting words had been that he planned to pray about the problem and hope God would give him guidance. He had raised more questions than we already had. How could we be sure *either* of the samples had come from John David? (That one floored us.)

'This is extremely serious,' Aubrey said. 'We should not do anything in a hurry. I tend to think you should turn this piece of paper over to the police. If Poppy was putting pressure on the father of her son, he might have reacted with violence. But let me think another day.'

Waiting for God to give us guidance seemed as good a course as any.

The only resolution I'd formed was that it would not be me who told John David what we'd discovered. No sir.

I dropped by to see my mom and John. They certainly seemed in better spirits now that the plans for the funeral were definite. Mother was just buzzed at the idea of finally having something to do, at some conclusion having been reached. True, Poppy's murderer had not been named, but at least the family could go through the ritual of burying her. John, she said, had just returned from the funeral home, where he'd gone with John David to select a casket and make all the arrangements with the funeral director.

'I offered to go with them, and so did Avery,' Mother said. She was wearing a blouse and skirt featuring a lot of dark blue, and she looked as neat and elegant as always, but the sun coming through the window hit her squarely in the face and I noticed, as if for the first time, that my mother was getting an enlarged network of tiny wrinkles at the corners of her mouth and eyes. She was still impressively attractive, and I was sure she always would be, but there was no denying that age had laid its hand on her.

'I was glad to go with my son,' said John very quietly. 'John David was with me when I ordered his mother's casket. Avery was too upset that day. Of course, I never thought I'd have to return the favor. Poppy was so young, so full of life.'

She had been. She had looked forward to every day of her existence, at least over the past few years. I was willing to bet on that.

No matter what her faults, she had been robbed. So had John David and Chase.

I said good-bye without telling Mother about my father's phone message. I'd have to tell her sooner or later, but right now, until I knew what I was supposed to do with Phillip, I thought I'd just keep Dad's marital problems to myself.

'I guess it would look bad if I went out to the club for a round of golf,' John said longingly as I paused in the doorway. My mother patted his hand.

'I don't think there would be anything wrong with that,' she said, and I wondered again at my mother's late-in-life love affair. 'You need to get out of the house, and the funeral is two days away. The exercise will do you good, if you bundle up.'

'You're nagging,' John said fondly.

I smiled but tried to hide it. 'I have to be going,' I said. 'I left Phillip at home, busy doing a job for me.'

'I'll talk to you soon,' Mother said automatically.

'I'm sure you will.' I smiled openly.

I was thinking of Madeleine on the way home. Though I felt temporarily wept out, I was grieving about the old orange cat. I had spent a lot of years with Madeleine, as many years as Jane Engle had had with her. I remembered how cute Madeleine's kittens had been, and I wondered how many grandchildren she had. Probably great- and great- great grandchildren, come to think of it.

That reminded me of Cara's call about Moosie. It wasn't right that Poppy's cat should be in the care of a neighbor, not when I could take the cat in until John David could get back on his feet. After all, I had a fenced-in backyard and cat food, though possibly my fence was low enough for Moosie to leap over, claws or not.

To get to Cara's house, which faced onto the street parallel to Swanson, I had to drive past Poppy's house once again. To my extreme irritation (I didn't seem to be able to be moderate about anything these days), Arthur's car was parked in front of the house.

This was tacky, to say the least. After all, the house had been released to John David, and he and Chase might arrive at any moment to resume living in it again. John David couldn't stay in a motel forever, and now that the initial shock of Poppy's death had passed, he might be ready to return to his very clean home.

I parked behind Arthur's car in the driveway and marched up to the front door. I still had the key I'd borrowed from John David, and I opened the door and went in.

'Arthur!' I bellowed.

He appeared at the head of the stairs, looking considerably startled.

'What the hell are you doing here?' I asked, surprising even myself.

'I'm the detective in charge of the investigation into the death of the home owner,' he said evenly. 'I have a right to be here.'

'Now that you've given John David the green light to move back in? I don't think so,' I said with more confidence than I felt.

'Are you jealous because I came to love Poppy rather than you?' Arthur asked as he came down the stairs. I remembered that yesterday I had wondered if I should be afraid of this man, and I'd had a friend with me then.

'No, I'm not jealous of Poppy, especially over your affections. I think Poppy loved life, but I think she lived it badly. I don't think she ever appreciated what she had, or what she could do with it.'

Arthur stood right in front of me, looking down at me, and he was maybe a little puzzled. 'What could Poppy have wanted that she didn't have?' he asked.

Smarter lovers, for one thing.

'Poppy could have wanted stability, but instead she created instability. She could have wanted to heal from the badness in her past, but instead she clung to the . . . the emotional problems that caused her to live so . . . dangerously.' Maybe I sounded a tad pompous.

'She was wonderful,' Arthur said, unbelievingly. 'She was smart, and she was funny, and she was pretty. Like you.'

'But unlike me, she liked to sneak,' I said bluntly. 'Unlike me, she liked multiple partners. This isn't about how great I am in contrast to Poppy. This is about you letting go of a dream of Poppy, a Poppy who never really existed. You can't afford to pin her down this tightly, Arthur. Let her go, so you can look for who killed her.'

I wondered how much sleep Arthur had been getting. He was definitely on the smelly side, and he certainly needed a shave. That curly pale hair was dirty, and his shirt was rumpled.

'Was it you who searched the house after she died, Arthur? The one who searched her bedroom?'

'I think it was Bubba Sewell,' Arthur said. 'He seemed awfully concerned with how long the house would be off-limits to the family. I don't know what he was looking for.'

I did. 'She didn't take pictures of you?' I said, unwisely.

'Pictures? What the hell are you talking about?'

'When were you with her? It's been almost two years, right?' I'd just had the worst idea in the world. I was wondering if you added Chase's age, plus nine months . . .

'Less than that,' he said, and my heart sank. Arthur was a candidate for Chase's father.

'Oh, well, doesn't make any difference,' I said bracingly. 'What were you actually doing here today, Arthur? Were you just mooning around, or were you working on the investigation?' Poppy must have had a higher regard for Arthur than for the others, but I wasn't up to explaining to Arthur why that was so.

'A little of both,' Arthur said. His voice was mild, which was a relief. 'I've been talking to Sandy Wynn. She called Poppy that day, said she was coming to talk to her. She admits she was here the morning Poppy was murdered.'

'Did she do it?'

'She says that when she got here, Poppy was already dead.'

'Where did she park her car? Did anyone see her car?'

'The woman across the street. Almost everyone on this street goes to work in the morning, but this woman, the one who also described the Sewells' van, incidentally, was home with the runs that morning. In between trips to the bathroom, she sat in her living room and watched television, with the front curtains open.

She didn't get a good look at Lizanne, but a better one at Sandy. She picked her picture out of a photo array. Sandy parked down the street, in the driveway of a house for sale, and walked up to Poppy's.'

'Why would she do that if she didn't plan on doing something bad?'

'She planned on talking Poppy into giving her something, something that belonged to Marvin Wynn. Of course, thanks to you and Melinda, we know what that thing is – the letter. Sandy broke down when I showed it to her. She said Poppy forced Marvin to write that letter by threatening to tell John David and the rest of the world what Marvin had done when Poppy was a teenager. Poppy swore that if Marvin would write such a letter, she'd never tell. He did what she demanded, but as time went on, Marvin regretted it more and more. He began to lose sleep, and slide into depression. Sandy got scared for him.'

'Why would Poppy do such a thing, stay silent? Why wouldn't she tell? Why make any bargain? He was in the wrong, and she was so young.'

'Her word against his. No evidence. Poppy was in her thirties, way beyond her teens. Nothing would have come of it.'

'Nothing but the ruin of his reputation,' I pointed out. 'No matter if it came to court or not, Poppy would have ruined him forever. Plenty of people would have believed her.'

'But it would have ruined her, too, in the process. At the very least, it would have made her life, and John David's and the baby's, very painful for a few months.'

I mulled that over. 'So this way, with her demanding he write the letter, he could believe she'd never tell, and she could believe he'd never make passes at young girls again?'

'I guess that was Poppy's thinking.'

'Do you believe Sandy? Do you believe she didn't kill Poppy?'

'Yes. She was too stricken to think about stepping over Poppy's body to search for the letter that morning. I believed her when she said it just didn't occur to her. She did her best to get the letter back once Poppy was dead, but I don't believe she killed Poppy for it. I think she did walk to the gate in the front of the fence when Poppy wouldn't come to the door, which Sandy says was then locked.'

But it hadn't been locked when I tried it. I was getting more and more confused.

'So she walked over to the fence at the side of the house, came in the gate, and walked around to the sliding glass doors,' I said. 'And there she saw Poppy's body?'

'Yes. She says she cried for a while, then left the way she'd come, and drove back home. By the time she got there, she was hearing from us here that Poppy was dead. She and Marvin packed up and returned to Lawrenceton. She never told Marvin where she'd been.'

'Okay,' I said slowly, trying not to get sidetracked by my rush of disgust at having put them up in my house. 'So, Sandy leaves, the front door is locked, and she doesn't have the letter. Then Lizanne comes?'

'No, Lizanne came first. She, too, knocked on the front door, got no answer, went to the fence and heard a quarrel, heard Poppy's radio, decided she couldn't ream Poppy out, not with someone else here. She threw something onto the ground.' Here Arthur gave me a very sharp look. 'Something that later vanished. And then she left. Then Sandy walked up, left within five minutes. Then you and Melinda came, and you found the front door open.'

I had a sudden idea, and I walked down the little hall to the kitchen. It was in better shape than it had been when we arrived yesterday. Melinda and I hadn't searched it, but we had straightened it and cleaned the counters and stovetop. Poppy's little radio still sat on the counter, though now it was dustless. I pressed a button to turn it on, and when the music came on, I looked at Arthur expectantly.

'What?' he said. His voice sounded quite businesslike, brisk. He's back to being himself, I thought.

'When Lizanne described her experience here that day, the day Poppy died, she said she'd walked to the fence.' I gestured to my left, which was where the gate in the fence was at the front. 'She said the music was so loud, she couldn't hear what the voices were saying, but she said the music was classical, that the radio was broadcasting NPR. This radio isn't on a classical station. I checked it the other day. So if we assume that the person Poppy was talking to was the person who killed her, and Poppy therefore didn't survive after that visit to change radio stations, then it wasn't Poppy's radio that was on.'

I walked around the breakfast bar and looked out the sliding glass door. Arthur came to stand beside me. We exchanged glances.

'It was Mrs Embler's radio,' he said.

'I'm guessing it was. What did she tell you about that morning?'

'Just that she swam as usual. Didn't hear or see anything out of the ordinary. Not too surprising, considering the fact that she was wearing a swimming cap and the radio was on, and there's a privacy fence in between the houses.'

'But the gate in the privacy fence had to be open at some point,' I said. 'She's got Moosie.'

'The cat? You saw Moosie in the house after Poppy was dead?'

'Yes, I did.' I stared at the boards of the high privacy fence, the fence the declawed Moosie couldn't climb. 'You know, Arthur, I could swear that when I was standing here, looking out, the day Poppy died, Cara was swimming then. She had the radio on.'

'So?'

'Still swimming? In this temperature? From the time Lizanne got here, waited, left; then Sandy came, found Poppy dead, and left; until the time I came in and found her body?'

'That could be,' Arthur said, but he sounded doubtful.

'And Moosie – who can't climb the fence because he hasn't got claws – vanished, between the time I came in the house and the time the police arrived.'

Arthur stared at the back gate.

'What the woman across the street *didn't* see was anyone leaving,' he said very quietly. 'Anyone except Sandy and Lizanne, that is. Yet I'm fairly certain neither of them killed Poppy. So where did this talking person, the one Lizanne heard, go?' He turned to stare down at me. 'I should have been taken off this investigation,' he said expressionlessly. 'I should have gone to the chief, I should have told him the whole story of my involvement with Poppy, and he should have put someone else on it. I thought I'd been away from her long enough, but I hadn't.'

'Maybe someone did sneak out between the time Sandy took off and Melinda and I got here. Maybe Moosie got out the front door. Maybe I left it ajar while we were waiting for the police and ambulance after I'd found the body. But I don't think so. I think I shut Moosie in the house when I came out to tell Melinda. I think someone came in to check the backyard, maybe for something they'd left there, while Melinda and I were sitting out front. I think that person came through the gate in the fence, from the Embler's yard. I could hear Cara splashing while I stood here, with this door open, by Poppy's body. I remember that clearly. But Cara usually swims at ten in the morning and at three in the afternoon. Everyone knows that. When I was here, it was about one. And I know what I think I saw on the concrete of the pool area.'

'What?'

'Wet marks. I think they were wet footprints.'

'You didn't remember until now?'

'I didn't realize what they were. I was so upset at seeing the body, I didn't think too much about the splotches on the concrete. But when I think of them in terms of what we just figured out, I realize that what I saw were footprints.'

'That's hardly conclusive evidence.'

'I know. Did you see any when you came?'

'I was so overwhelmed by the sight of Poppy dead – I owe your family my sincerest apology. I didn't notice half of what I should have noticed, didn't ask half the questions I should have asked.'

'Arthur, just get the right person now. I'm glad you cared for Poppy. I'm glad someone who cared for her was there with her.' I wasn't altogether sincere, but I didn't want Arthur to spend any more time bashing himself. I wanted action. 'I'll bet she came back through the fence to dry up the water,' I said absently. 'That's why you didn't see it. And that's when Moosie escaped.'

'Maybe, if I get a search warrant, we can find the knife.'

'I'll bet she threw it away. It's in the garbage right now, and today is pickup for our part of town.' At every house but Poppy's, garbage cans were sitting at the curb, waiting to be emptied.

'Then I'll have to hurry to get a search warrant.' Arthur turned on his heel, ready to run out the front way, but I put my hand on his arm. I could hear the garbage truck coming down Poppy's street, and next it would turn onto the Emblers'. There wasn't time. I had to do something.

'Just wait a *minute,*' I said.

'What are you doing?'

'Come with me, and wait on this side,' I said. I'd had a sudden idea, and I was determined to carry it through. I remembered Poppy done to death on her own floor, in her own kitchen. I owed her this.

I walked around Poppy's pool, knocked on the gate, turned the knob, and walked through.

Chapter Twelve

Cara Embler was drying her short hair with a huge fluffy white towel. A little puddle of water had trickled down her legs and lay pooled at her feet. By her back door, there was a table piled high with identical towels, all snowy white and neatly folded. Organized, not prone to impulse, that was Cara.

She was surprised at my appearance in her yard, but not shocked. After all, she'd called me about Moosie. He was sunning himself on the patio, and when I came in, he jumped up and ran to me, stropping himself around my legs as he'd done on the day I'd found Poppy. I saw her two dogs looking through her set of sliding glass doors. They barked energetically when I walked through the gate and pulled it to behind me. I didn't close it all the way.

'Hi, Roe,' Cara said, turning down the radio, which was sitting on a table by a matching chair. 'I would have gotten all Moosie's stuff together and put him in a carrier if I'd known you were coming. I'd gotten him some cat food and some litter, and a toy.'

She did love animals. 'I just came over on impulse,' I said, which was the truth. 'Are you ready to come home with me, boy?' I lifted him up into my arms and scratched his head.

'I've enjoyed having him, but the dogs go nuts when he teases them,' Cara said. The schnauzers were peering anxiously out of the glass door, yipping from time to time. They were beautiful animals, obviously well cared for. 'Why'd you come in from Poppy's side?' Cara asked. She combed her short hair.

'I had to get some things out of the house for John David. Things for Chase,' I replied, lying. I was feeling my way, and I was suddenly cold down to my heart. What had I done? But having come through the gate in the fence, seeing Cara's assurance, I could not stand the thought that she might walk free. I could not imagine why, out of all the women Poppy had cuckolded, this one would strike back, but I knew in my gut that Cara Embler had killed my sister-in-law.

'Want to come in? It's a little brisk out here.' But Cara seemed to be used to it. She wrapped a white terry robe around her. She started to put on a pair of yellow plastic clogs, then seemed to reconsider. I wondered why. She swept a hand toward the house invitingly.

If we went inside, Arthur couldn't hear.

'How many times did you go through the fence that day?' I asked.

Cara looked stunned for a second. 'What day?'

'The day Poppy died. When you killed her.'

The words hung between us, enormous and terrifying.

Cara's eyes changed then. The veil she'd held between the world and herself dropped, and the real Cara looked out at me.

'You don't know anything,' she said contemptuously.

'I found your husband's ID tag, the one from the hospital.'

'You did, huh? That was where Stuart lost it?'

'Isn't that why?'

'Why I killed her? Over my husband poking his thing in her? If I killed everyone he fucked, there'd be a lot of dead women around Atlanta. That hospital is like Peyton Place. Granted, one in my own backyard is over the top. But consider the woman.' Cara's face shone with malice. 'She gets pregnant so easy, she doesn't even know who the father is. She thinks I don't even know my husband's had her, that that'll scare me! But at least I can be sure it's not him, because his sperm count is so pathetic, we had to adopt. You know how hard it is to get a healthy white male infant? Not as hard for a prominent cardiologist and his wife as it would be for a garbageman and his wife, but still . . . difficult, expensive, and time-consuming. And then he doesn't even love us! We brought him up as ours, we gave him everything, and he doesn't even love us!'

'How'd you know Poppy didn't know the father of her kid?' I

was very uneasy at Arthur hearing this, but I had cast the die and couldn't retreat.

'She had the gall to come over here – while I was here, mind you – and ask my husband how to get samples for DNA testing! I was out of the room, of course, but I made sure I could hear every word they said. She asked Stuart to order the test through the lab his practice uses, so she could push it through without questions asked. He told me all about it. That's what he thought of your precious Poppy. He told her to get a swab from someone's mouth, or their hair with the roots on, not cut hair. Easy enough. It wasn't a court-ordered procedure. She just wanted to know.'

'But if you didn't care if your husband slept with her, why'd you kill her?'

'I wanted her to die for me,' Cara said. 'You know, a member of Uppity Women has to die for the next person on the waiting list to get in. And I wanted in. So Poppy Queensland died for me.'

I couldn't believe I'd understood her correctly. I must have been squeezing Moosie, because he protested and began to struggle. Absently, I began stroking him again, and he relaxed, bless his feline heart.

'You wanted to be in Uppity Women so much, you killed Poppy to get in?'

'You know what I gave up when I married Stuart? I was through with college – I graduated with honors – and I'd decided to go to vet school. I've loved animals all my life, and I wanted to be a veterinarian. But my husband said it would lower his status as a cardiologist if he had a wife who was an animal doctor, so I thought, Well, that's enough, being Stuart's wife. I can run the house. I can entertain. I can do charitable work. I can raise his kids. I can contribute.'

'Wasn't enough?' I said in a low voice with a big quaver. Cara's face was ugly with loathing.

'It was never enough,' she answered, her voice almost a growl. 'We couldn't have our own children. We adopted the one baby, and Stuart decided after that, that one was enough, because he felt Henry was a lot of trouble. As if he did anything for the boy. So I took up swimming again, and I got really good, and I began winning medals, I got so good. But Stuart didn't like that, either, because he said swimming meets for seniors were silly, that I should just swim for my own pleasure and have done with it.'

'I hear he went with you, though, to a lot of them, right?' I was backing toward the fence. I sincerely hoped Arthur was right behind it.

'He decided it was a good advertisement – for a cardiologist to have a wife who did such a heart-healthy thing, at her age!'

I didn't have an idea in the world what to do next.

'So you really did kill her so you could get into Uppity Women?'

'I really did.' Cara was almost proud.

I didn't believe her for a second. Maybe that was what Cara chose to believe, but I thought it went maybe a few miles deeper than that.

'You came back in your yard with the knife and put it back in the house, didn't you? And got back in the pool?'

'I dove into the water after I killed her, and I washed all that blood off me and the knife. I figured the chlorine would take care of it, and it did,' she said. 'And then I couldn't think of what to do with the knife. I didn't exactly want to put it back in the kitchen drawer.' She looked at me and rolled her eyes, as though she were confessing a charming foible. 'And I didn't want to stick it in the garbage, because what if my garbage got searched somehow?' I began to have a real bad feeling. She strolled over to the raised flower bed by the fence and scratched her fingers through the pine bark that the gardener had put in as mulch. 'So I buried the knife in here. And here it is!'

She smiled at me.

It was at least a foot long, and wicked-looking. I was so creeped out by Cara that a toothpick would have frightened me, but at the sight of this knife, I was almost paralyzed.

I had time to think, Where the hell is Arthur? when he came flying through the gate, which crashed back against the fence and rebounded, knocking the drawn gun from his hand quite neatly.

Cara disregarded Arthur completely and leaped at me. She gave me a powerful shove.

I threw Moosie at her.

Moosie screeched and bit and drew blood on Cara's chest, and the barking of the dogs in the house reached a frantic crescendo as Cara staggered backward, ending up near the lawn furniture again. Her wet feet slipped in the puddle of water where she'd been standing, and she fell heavily. As her head hit the concrete, I landed in the pool with enough force to send me right down. My glasses were knocked off by the force of the impact, and as I plummeted deeper, I looked up and saw them drifting lazily after me to the bottom.

The water was cold, cold, cold. The shock to my system was severe, and for a long moment I seemed unable to move my limbs, unable to save myself. It was fortunate that I wasn't wearing a heavy coat or boots. I shook off the paralysis and began to force water down with my hands so I could rise. My face broke the surface and I gasped for air. The first thing I saw was Moosie's face peering out from under the table by the back door, the one that held the towels. Moosie's sense of self-preservation was far superior to mine.

Arthur was scrambling to his feet, going for the gun that had skittered to the very edge of the pool. Cara was twitching, but silent. The fall had knocked the air out of her.

I made it to the side of the pool and shoved the gun toward Arthur. I was not about to pick it up. I don't know a thing about guns, and they make me very nervous. I began to pull myself up to sit on the side of the pool. I expected Arthur would throw me a towel, or give me a hand. I *didn't* expect that he'd walk over to Cara and kick her in the ribs as hard as he could.

'Stop,' I said. 'Arthur! Stop!' I sat and shivered, my feet still in the water. I had never trembled so violently in my life. The moderate day seemed frigid now. I simply could not get up to interfere.

I was scared of Arthur, too, scared to get close enough to grab his arm. He was almost as frightening as Cara. Cara deserved every kind of punishment for killing Poppy, but I hated watching her being beaten.

He drew back his leg again, and I screamed, 'No!'

My voice penetrated the fog of rage that hung around him almost palpably.

Arthur's foot touched the ground again. He shook himself, then said in a thick voice, 'Cara Embler, you are under arrest for the murder of Poppy Queensland. Anything you say . . .'

Chapter Thirteen

I came out of my own warm bathroom, toweling my wet hair, just as Cara had dried hers. Only Phillip's presence in the house was keeping Robin from waiting in here in my bedroom, and oddly, I was glad of that. I needed a few more seconds to myself, more than my quick shower had afforded. I was warm now, and with the heat turned up in the house, my hair would dry fairly quickly. Short of sticking me in the oven, Phillip and Robin had done everything they possibly could to warm me up. This had been tremendously important to them.

I couldn't suppress a snigger as I thought of how they'd competed with each other to be the most solicitous. That wouldn't last long, of course, and they'd be back to their more normal selves shortly, but I would enjoy it while it lasted.

At the moment, I'd just discovered I had a whole new set of worries.

I should have gotten dressed again. I wasn't an invalid. But I felt like putting on a nightgown and bathrobe, so I did. I hadn't been hurt, but I was exhausted and achy. I'd actually thrown up after I'd come out of the pool. I'd found this acutely embarrassing, but none of the law-enforcement personnel had seemed to think much of it. They were quite busy dealing with their own embarrassment, Arthur Smith. No matter how we glossed over it, Arthur had been mooning around Poppy's house when he shouldn't have been, and Arthur had kicked a suspect. Oh, he said Cara had tried to get up and attack me again, and I'd nodded weakly when they asked me if that was so, but I could tell they didn't believe us, especially Cathy Trumble. Besides, Arthur was in a peculiar mental state, and there was no disguising that, either.

Cathy Trumble had questioned me intently for about thirty

minutes, until it became obvious that I had to get into dry clothes. She sent me home in a patrol car, with the warning that she was going to come by within a couple of hours to take a full statement from me.

Cara had gone off to the hospital under guard. I pitied the officer who had to call her husband. Dr Stuart Embler was going to be pretty unhappy with anyone who'd arrested his wife. He could afford the best lawyers, too. Bringing Cara to trial might be a struggle; I'd have to testify in court, if it came to a trial. I figured I wouldn't count on that until it happened. If there's one thing television has taught Americans, it's that justice doesn't always move at the pace, or in the direction, that it should.

My black glasses were somewhere at the bottom of the Emblers' pool. I got my tortoiseshell ones and pushed them up the bridge of my nose. With a brush in my hand, wrapped in my favorite golden brown gown and robe, I wandered out into the den. To my surprise, Robin was there by himself.

'Where's Phillip?'

'I sent him to the store for some Epsom salts.'

'Epsom salts? Why?'

'It was the only thing I could think of that you didn't already have.'

'Why the need to get Phillip out of the way? Don't you like him?' I was pretty anxious about this, since I wasn't sure at all that my dad meant to get Phillip back right away.

'Yes, I do. I just wanted to be alone with you for a little while.'

'It's not going to take him very long to get Epsom salts.'

'I did also mention that if he wanted to stop by the Finstermeyers' house to tell Josh why he couldn't come over for supper tonight, I was sure that would be better than calling him.'

'Okay,' I said cautiously. 'So, here we are, by ourselves.'

Robin was beginning to wilt around the edges. 'Don't you want to have some alone time? So I can just sit and hold you?'

'Probably Phillip is old enough to understand that you might want to hug me or cuddle me from time to time.' I said this with an absolutely straight face.

Now Robin was looking really downcast.

'But what I'd like for you to do is come get on the bed with me and hold me,' I said.

He brightened considerably. 'Sure. I understand you're tired and upset. I just want to be next to you.'

Within five minutes, we were snuggled up in my big bed, Robin in his T-shirt and jeans, and I in my gown. I pulled a quilt up over us. I would have been utterly content if I hadn't had one long bridge to cross.

I was lying with my head on his chest, listening to his heartbeat. I was hoping that heart was feeling extra large today. I might be taxing it.

I took a deep breath, started to speak, let it out. I was just a big chicken.

'Robin,' I began. Then I stopped dead.

'What, baby?'

'Exactly,' I said, and didn't get any further. It was the second time today I'd been terrified. My eyes were focused on the pattern of the quilt – oddly enough, it was the Wedding Ring. I didn't dare look up.

'Are you trying to tell me about the kit on the bathroom counter?'

'Yes.'

'I saw it when I started your bathwater. Did you use it?'

'Yes.'

His big hand reached over and rested lightly on my pelvis. 'Are you . . .' his voice broke. 'Are you carrying our child?'

'Yes.'

I stole a look up at his face. It was radiant. If he had smiled, any wider, his face would have cracked. My own heart gave a leap, and I felt my whole body relax against him.

'You're not going to be an unwed mother,' he said firmly.

Another fear discarded. I was far too traditional to face single parenthood with equanimity. All at once, I felt lighter than air.

So, naturally, being so happy, I started crying. 'Not just because of the baby,' I said, 'don't marry me just for that.'

'You know it's not just because of the baby.' He scrambled out of the bed and rummaged around in the pockets of his jacket. He dove back under the covers and pressed a little velvet box into my hand. 'Proof,' he said triumphantly. 'I've been carrying this with me for two weeks, trying to find the right moment to ask you if you'll wear it.'

I hesitated before opening the box. I thought of the past few days. 'It's hard to believe anything can end this well,' I said. I didn't want to ruin the moment, but I was plagued by the deceptions of my sister-in-law. She had lied to everyone, offering each of us in her life just a little glimpse of one facet of her true character. In the end, she had become so splintered, she could not present a coherent whole to anyone. Maybe Poppy had lost her core.

'I love you,' I said to Robin. 'And I'm proud that you're the father of my baby.' It was an incredible feeling, hearing myself saying the words I'd never believed I'd get to say to anyone. I opened the box, to see a lovely yellow diamond with clear tiny ones set around it. The ring was small and delicate, and I thought it was beautiful.

'Hey, Sis! What's for supper?' Phillip yelled from the living room.

I groaned, then rested my head against Robin's.

'Lest the moment get too tender and mushy,' Robin said, but he didn't sound angry. He sounded tolerant.

'We'll be fine,' I said bravely, and tried to call up a mental list of what was in the refrigerator.

Acknowledgments

Dead Over Heels

I'd like to acknowledge the fact that Joan Hess gave me exactly one suggestion for this book when I was in a bind; and give thanks for a most informative morning spent with Jackie Cranford. But most of all, I'd like to give credit or blame to Dean James, who thought of the title for this book over a margarita in Austin, Texas.

A Fool and His Honey

I thank the cybercitizens of DorothyL for their support, encouragement, and just being themselves, so that day by day I can 'talk' to other people who love the mysterious world as much as I do. In the writing of this book, I prticularly laud the Ohio contingent, who answered all my questions so patiently, and often at great trouble to themselves.

Last Scene Alive

Many people gave me information I used or mis-used in this book. First and foremost was Tom Smith, who knows more about the movie industry than I could ever include in one book. Also of great help were William Peschel, who gave me a great account of his time spent as an extra; Dr John Alexander, who never minds answering odd questions; and Donna Moore, one of my cyber-friends on DorothyL, who gave me the titIe for this book.

Poppy Done to Death

My thanks for the advice of wonderful people like John Ertl, Kate Buker, the Reverend Gary Nowlin, and Michael Silverling. I may not have always used their information and advice correctly, but that fault is only mine. Special thinks to Ann Hilgeman and all the other real Uppity Women.